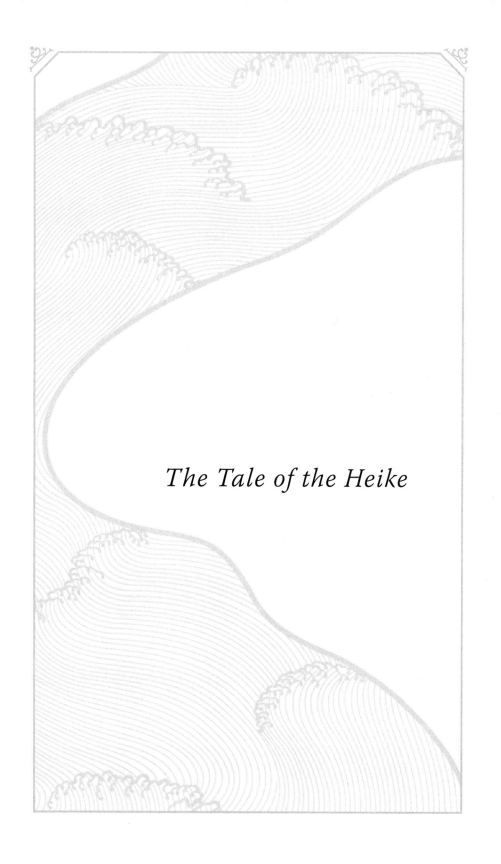

The Tale of the Heike

Also translated by Royall Tyler

The Tale of Genji

The TALE

of the HEIKE

Translated by

ROYALL TYLER

VIKING

Tale

VIKING

Published by the Penguin Group

Penguin Group (USA) Inc., 375 Hudson Street, New York, New York 10014, U.S.A. • Penguin Group (Canada), 90 Eglinton Avenue East, Suite 700, Toronto, Ontario, Canada M4P 2Y3 (a division of Pearson Penguin Canada Inc.) • Penguin Books Ltd, 80 Strand, London WC2R 0RL, England • Penguin Ireland, 25 St. Stephen's Green, Dublin 2, Ireland (a division of Penguin Books Ltd) • Penguin Books Australia Ltd, 250 Camberwell Road, Camberwell, Victoria 3124, Australia (a division of Pearson Australia Group Pty Ltd) • Penguin Books India Pvt Ltd, 11 Community Centre, Panchsheel Park, New Delhi–110 017, India • Penguin Group (NZ), 67 Apollo Drive, Rosedale, Auckland 0632, New Zealand (a division of Pearson New Zealand Ltd) • Penguin Books (South Africa) (Pty) Ltd, 24 Sturdee Avenue, Rosebank, Johannesburg 2196, South Africa

Penguin Books Ltd, Registered Offices: 80 Strand, London WC2R 0RL, England

First published in 2012 by Viking Penguin, a member of Penguin Group (USA) Inc.

10 9 8 7 6 5 4 3 2 1

Illustrations by Teisai Hokuba from *Heike monogatari zue,* text by Takai Ranzan, published in Japan in two parts, in 1829 and 1849

LIBRARY OF CONGRESS CATALOGING-IN-PUBLICATION DATA
Heike monogatari. English.
    The tale of the Heike / translated by Royall Tyler.
    p.   cm.
    ISBN 978-0-670-02513-8
    1. Taira family—Fiction. 2. Japan—History—Gempei Wars, 1180–1185—Fiction. I. Tyler, Royall. II. Title.
    PL790.H4E5 2012
    895.6'32—dc23
    2012000598

Printed in the United States of America
Designed by Carla Bolte • Set in Adobe Warnock Pro with Adobe Charlemagne display
Genealogies and maps by Jeffrey L. Ward

ALWAYS LEARNING   PEARSON

 CONTENTS

THE TALE OF THE HEIKE

....

BOOK TEN

....

BOOK TWELVE

....

THE INITIATES' BOOK

GENEALOGIES

MAPS

❧ ACKNOWLEDGMENTS ❧

I am grateful first to Michael Watson, who suggested the format for the translation, showed me where to find the required performance information, and helped me to obtain the source work for the illustrations. Tom Conlan, whose love of *Heike monogatari* provided enduring moral support, advised me on many matters from a historian's perspective. Alison Tokita, Hugh de Ferranti, and Komoda Haruko provided information on music and performance. Susan Tyler proofread and edited successive drafts, meanwhile making valuable comments from her own knowledge of medieval Japan. I am grateful to them all.

Wendy Wolf, my editor, is by now an old friend to whom I owe more than I can say. It is a pleasure also to thank, for their skill and enthusiasm, the whole Viking Penguin team: Bruce Giffords, the production editor; Carla Bolte, the designer; Maureen Sugden, the copy editor; Paul Buckley, the jacket designer; and others whose names and functions I do not know but who also played their part in making this book what it is.

✥ INTRODUCTION ✥

Richly varied in incident and mood, *The Tale of the Heike* (*Heike monogatari*) tells of a tyrant's cruelty and overweening pride, his death, and the ultimate destruction of his house. No work of Japan's classical literature influenced more pervasively the art, literature, and drama of later centuries. *Heike* is a seminal masterpiece of Japanese culture.

The tyrant was Taira no Kiyomori (1118–81). "Heike," pronounced *hay-keh*, means "Taira house," especially (although not exclusively) Kiyomori's extended family. In his time the Heike lorded it over their great rivals, the Genji ("Minamoto house"), and it is the Genji who rose up in the end to destroy them. The Genji leader Minamoto no Yoritomo (1147–99), another major figure in Japanese history, looms from a distance over the later sections of the work.

The events related in the tale, with some dramatic license, convulsed late-twelfth-century Japan and left indelible cultural memories. Formal records confirm them in outline and often in detail, and knowledge of the historical background (see "Hōgen and Heiji," below) helps to explain the story's force. *Heike* could be said to dramatize history as collectively experienced by the tale's original audience and their recent forebears. It also answers a deep urge to pacify, by telling their story, the threatening spirits of the bitter, defeated Heike dead.

An earlier masterpiece, *The Tale of Genji* (early eleventh century), left Japan an atmosphere of beauty and elegance that still enthralls countless readers. The legacy of *The Tale of the Heike* consists especially of dramatic episodes, touching or tragic. The most famous of these is perhaps the encounter of Kumagai and Atsumori (9:16). Others relate the trials of the dancers Giō (1:6) and Kogō (6:4), the exiled Shunkan's despair (3:2), the extravagant austerities of the monk Mongaku (5:7), the burning of the great temples of Nara (5:14), the deaths of Kiso no Yoshinaka and Kanehira (9:4), Yoshitsune's dazzling victory at Ichi-no-tani (9:12), and Nasu no Yoichi's exploit at Yashima (11:4). These and many others inspired centuries of theater (Noh, Bunraku, Kabuki) and visual art (painting, prints), followed more recently by film, television, modern retellings, manga, and warrior fantasies of all kinds. Awareness of transience, often cited as a governing theme in Japanese literature, received its most famous statement in the tale's opening lines.

AUTHORSHIP AND TEXTS

Who wrote *The Tale of the Heike*? *Essays in Idleness* (*Tsurezure-gusa,* circa 1330, by Yoshida Kenkō) identifies the author as one Yukinaga. This Yukinaga taught a blind man named Shōbutsu to perform what he had written; then Shōbutsu expanded the work on his own and had Yukinaga write his additions down. Nothing else confirms this account, and the development of the tale as we have it clearly followed a longer and more complicated path than that, but the passage is suggestive. For one thing, this reported give-and-take between an educated writer and a blind performer indicates an interplay between written and oral origins that is visible both in the character of surviving *Heike* texts and in the relationship between the work and its audience.

Many versions of *Heike* survive. Some are shorter, some longer. They fall under two headings: those to be read (*yomihon*) and those to be performed (*kataribon*). The most important "reading" text is probably the *Enkyō-bon* ("the Enkyō [also read Engyō] manuscript"), a copy made in 1419–20 from a manuscript dated 1309–10. The best-known performance text is the *Kakuichi-bon,* the one translated in this book. Akashi no Kakuichi, the head of his line of blind *Heike* performers, dictated it to a disciple in 1371, three months before his death.

Historians value the expansively discursive *Enkyō-bon* because it contains a wealth of material not present in the performance versions. In contrast, the relative economy of performance texts like the *Kakuichi-bon* seems meant to hold the interest of an audience—or eventually of a silent reader, since even Kakuichi's version came in time to be more read than heard. Most readers in modern Japan know no other.

In comparison with the *Enkyō-bon,* the Kakuichi text therefore suggests sustained and effective editing. The story of Kumagai and Atsumori provides an example. In the *Enkyō-bon,* Kumagai tells Atsumori, "Yoritomo has decreed that any man who beheads a worthy enemy shall have in reward a thousand *chō* of land." The beheading of a ranking opponent was formally recorded on the battlefield, and the victor was indeed rewarded in land. However, these words ill suit the more elevated tone of the Kakuichi account, which therefore omits them. It also drops both a *chōka* ("long poem") by Atsumori on the beauties of nature and his certainty of dying this day in battle, and an extended passage about Kumagai's returning Atsumori's head, with a letter, to Atsumori's father. Finally, Kakuichi's Atsumori carries a flute, the discovery of which moves Kumagai deeply. In the *Enkyō-bon,* however, he carries a *hichiriki.* This reed instrument was equally necessary to a musical ensemble of the time, but far less generally appealing.

Perhaps editorial discernment also shaped the Kakuichi account of the death of the warrior Seno-o Kaneyasu (8:8). In the *Enkyō-bon,* Kaneyasu first slits his belly, and then a follower of his takes the point of his sword in his mouth and throws himself onto it. The follower's dramatic suicide not only robs Kaneyasu's of some of its dignity but also undermines the brilliance and horror of Imai Kanehira's death in the next book. Some motifs are too strong to use effectively more than once in the same work. The Kakuichi *Heike* has Kaneyasu die fighting and his wounded follower survive until the next day.

Above all, however, it is the thirteenth and concluding "Initiates' Book" (*Kanjō no maki*) that makes the Kakuichi *Heike* unique. Other versions scatter the content of this book, chapter by chapter in roughly chronological order, through the material covered by Kakuichi's Book Twelve. They therefore end with the execution of Rokudai, the last scion of the Heike. So does the *Enkyō-bon,* apart from two concluding chapters on the death of Cloistered Emperor Go-Shirakawa and on the good fortune of Minamoto no Yoritomo. Only Kakuichi gathered this material into a separate, continuous story that ends his version and so became its trademark, as it were. The Initiates' Book was a "secret piece" performed only by the most accomplished members of his guild. The "initiates" of its title were presumably those who had received *kanjō* ("initiation," properly a religious term) as masters in his line.

LANGUAGE, WRITING, PERFORMANCE, TRANSLATION

The *Heike* text can be set down in different ways. One manuscript is written exclusively in Chinese characters (*kanji*), another almost entirely in phonetic script (*kana*). Most are somewhere in between. In any case, the language remains the same. It is a little closer to modern Japanese than that of earlier literature. Japanese readers today can follow *Heike* in the original more easily than they can *Genji*.

The mood and style vary widely. There are intensely lyrical passages that exploit the vocabulary and imagery of Japanese poetry, while others have a strongly Chinese flavor. There are battle narratives and formal documents. There are also poems in the classic, thirty-one-syllable form (*waka*, "Japanese poem"), together with occasional song (*imayō*) lyrics. Tacitly or explicitly, however, authorities agree that apart from the poems and songs, *Heike* is in prose. In Japanese the text looks like prose, all translations into foreign languages have been in unbroken prose, and discussions of the work in English describe the work as prose. So why does this translation look the way it does?

The answer appeals to two distinctions: the one between prose and verse, and the one between reading and performance.

Only the text of the *Odyssey* remains. Anyone good at ancient Greek can read it, and over the centuries many have done so. Although no one knows what the *Odyssey* sounded like when performed, the text is in verse, and verse suggests song. Homer undoubtedly sang it somehow, accompanying himself on a stringed instrument.

That is how Kakuichi and his fellows performed *Heike.* They accompanied themselves on the biwa, an instrument of the lute family, and were called *biwa hōshi* ("biwa monks"). All were blind and wore Buddhist robes. They traveled widely and performed for audiences high and low.

Did they really perform all of so lengthy a work? Records mention complete performances (*ichibu Heike*), but it is unclear how long these might have taken and how common they might have been. The earliest written evidence, consisting of entries in three early-fifteenth-century diaries, suggests that by then a noble patron could seldom hear even a major consecutive sequence, let alone the entire work. Two whole books, in sessions a month apart, seem to have been a rarity. Most performances covered one or two, less often up to five or six chapters (performers call them *ku*, scholars *shōdan*), of a complete book. The patron could not necessarily choose the program, and in any case audiences must often have demanded favorite pieces, thus encouraging relative neglect of the rest. Even in the heyday of the *biwa hōshi,* someone wishing to know the whole tale may have had to read it, too, if possible.

But what would a performance have been like, if *Heike* is in prose? The answer begins with the proposition that the text is not really prose at all.

That is not to call it verse instead. Rather, the issue is that in English and other such languages, "prose" implies the possibility of verse. In past centuries an author could expound all sorts of subjects in verse. To call the *Heike* text prose is to imply that it *could* have been written in verse, like the *Odyssey.* But that is not so. Sustained verse narrative, in a form corresponding to verse in English or in ancient Greek, is impossible in the language of the tale. The classical Japanese definition of verse is too restricted.

Poetic convention banned from poetry most of the vocabulary and most of the subjects needed for a continuous story. It also assumed only one brief form: the thirty-one-syllable *waka*. The rare, longer *chōka* (like Atsumori's in the *Enkyō-bon*) only extends the *waka* mood a little and could serve no better to narrate events. In short, *Heike* is not in prose because no counterpart possibility of verse, or even any remotely adequate conception of verse, existed then. It is really neither verse nor prose.

This opens the possibility of translating it into something other than prose, providing that a reason and adequate authority can be found for doing so. The reason here is a wish to modulate silent reading by conveying after all a hint of the varied voicing heard in performance. The authority is the eighteenth-century *Heike* performance score (*Heike monogatari fushitsuki*) selected by Yamashita Hiroaki for his edition of the tale (*Heike monogatari,* 2 vols., Meiji Shoin, 1975 and

1979). This score prescribes the voicing pattern for each passage. For the text itself, however, the translation relies on Kajihara Masaaki and Yamashita Hiroaki, eds., *Heike monogatari,* 2 vols., Iwanami, 1991 and 1993; and Ichiko Teiji, ed., *Heike monogatari,* 2 vols., Shogakukan, 1994. Credit is also due the superbly accurate translation by Helen McCullough (*The Tale of the Heike,* Stanford University Press, 1988).

Guided by *Heike monogatari fushitsuki,* this translation divides the text into three major formats: "speech" (*shirakoe*), "recitative" (*kudoki*), and "song." These can be imagined as analogous to spoken dialogue, recitative, and aria in oratorio or opera.

"Speech," which the performer declaimed without ornament, is here laid out as justified prose set against the right margin of the page. Documents such as petitions, official communications, and formal prayers are presented in the same way, in italics. "Recitative," the most common voicing pattern in the tale, was sung within a relatively restricted musical range. These passages are laid out in highly irregular lines that start at the left margin and occasionally overflow the full width of the page. "Song" covers a dozen named styles of elaborately ornamented voicing, the distinctions between which are beyond the reach of the printed word. These passages are presented as verse. *Waka* poems and *imayō* lyrics, a special class of "song," are indented a little more deeply than the verse, in lines (*waka* are italicized) that match the syllabic meter of the original.

To a reader in another land and language, all these centuries later, "speech," "recitative," and "song" may often seem to overlap in mood and content. Between the first two especially, it may not be obvious why a passage is in one rather than the other, apart from the need to vary delivery in order to retain audience interest. Some "recitative" passages invite spirited treatment in English, but others, despite goodwill, do not. Moreover, the content of some "song" passages may seem remote from anything likely to be sung in English. Still, there are in general clear differences among the three. Treatment of a subject in "song," especially, often suggests a hierarchy of value.

"Song" naturally serves to convey intense emotion or stirring conflict. However, it is also prominent when the subject is an emperor or when the narration dwells on a classical Chinese analogy—in effect, a hallowed precedent—for the Japanese situation at hand. Such treatment affirms the all-but-transcendent standing of emperors and their role as gentle models of tolerance and cultivation. It also conveys the enormous prestige, for Japan, of Chinese antiquity and historical experience, and it confers a corresponding dignity on the Japanese parallel. Another kind of "song" passage (for example, 4:3) simply lists warrior names and titles, thus highlighting the noble names and honorable offices that give these passages narrative dignity and rhetorical weight.

"HŌGEN AND HEIJI": HISTORY AND ANGRY SPIRITS

A major preoccupation in *The Tale of the Heike* is defense of the throne against insubordination and rebellion. A roster of historical rebels appears at once (1:1), followed by others, more or less complete, later on. Prominent among the culprits mentioned are Taira no Masakado (died 940), whose insurrection in the east of the country was put down by Kiyomori's ancestor Sadamori; Fujiwara no Sumitomo (died 941), who rebelled in the west; and the brothers Abe no Sadatō (1019–62) and Munetō, who rose up in the north.

By the twelfth century, two complex warrior houses stood ready to quell such disorder: the Heike (Taira) and the Genji (Minamoto). While a few of their members belonged to the court hierarchy in the capital, most were based in the provinces. For centuries they had supported the central government militarily, as needed, against external, provincial challenges. However, in 1156 (the Hōgen Conflict) and 1159 (the Heiji Conflict), rivalry among court factions drew Heike and Genji warriors into clashes within the capital itself.

The Hōgen and Heiji conflicts unleashed brutality unknown in Japan for hundreds of years and left lasting scars. The relatively short *Tale of Hōgen* (*Hōgen monogatari*) and *Tale of Heiji* (*Heiji monogatari*) make the gravity of these events clear, and *The Tale of the Heike*, in which the words "Hōgen and Heiji" recur like a refrain, confirms it at length. The Hōgen and Heiji conflicts so embittered the losers that their angry spirits seemed to threaten the victorious Heike or even to explain their eventual downfall.

It had all started forty years earlier, in 1141, when Emperor Sutoku (born 1119, reigned 1123–41) suffered a great humiliation. His father, Retired Emperor Toba (born 1103, reigned 1107–23), forced him to abdicate in favor of a little boy born to Toba's beloved Bifukumon-in (Fujiwara no Nariko, 1117–60). This child then became Emperor Konoe (born 1139, reigned 1141–55).

When Konoe died young, Sutoku hoped to succeed him or at least to see his own son do so. Instead Toba arbitrarily appointed one of Sutoku's half brothers, Emperor Go-Shirakawa (born 1127, reigned 1155–58). Meanwhile Bifukumon-in, Toba's favorite, was accusing Sutoku of having cursed Konoe to death, in collusion with the powerful Fujiwara no Yorinaga (1120–56). Yorinaga, the "Haughty Left Minister" or "Uji Left Minister" of the tale, had prevailed in a power struggle within his own house and become the de facto regent. In 1155 Toba dismissed him and elevated his Fujiwara rival. Then, in mid-1156, Toba died. The Hōgen Conflict broke out immediately.

The Hōgen era began a few months before Toba's death and continued until the early summer of 1159. The short Heiji era, which followed, ended in early 1160. The Genji warriors in *The Tale of the Heike* look back bitterly and repeatedly to "Hōgen and Heiji," and they burn to erase the shame of their forebears' defeat.

This is what happened: With Toba gone, Sutoku and Yorinaga moved to depose Go-Shirakawa and return Sutoku to the throne. For armed support they called on Tameyoshi (1096–1156), Minamoto no Yoritomo's father, and on Taira no Tadamasa (died 1156), an uncle of Kiyomori's. To counter them Go-Shirakawa recruited Yoshitomo (1123–60), Tameyoshi's eldest son, and Kiyomori himself.

Yoshitomo prevailed in the Hōgen Conflict, on Go-Shirakawa's behalf. He was then forced to oversee the execution of his own father and of five of his younger brothers. Kiyomori executed Tadamasa. These were the first executions in Japan in more than three centuries. Yorinaga was killed in flight. Sutoku was banished to the province of Sanuki on Shikoku, where (according to *The Tale of Hōgen* and other sources) he cursed the victors. Widespread opinion attributed the Heiji Conflict and other troubles to his wrath. In the nineteenth century, the outspoken thinker Hirata Atsutane still traced to Sutoku's baleful influence the late-twelfth-century shift of power from the imperial court to the warriors. Atsutane, a champion of return to direct imperial rule, urged placating him by reestablishing in Kyoto the shrine originally built there by Go-Shirakawa in 1184 (10:13).

After the Hōgen Conflict, Kiyomori allied himself with Go-Shirakawa's closest adviser, Shinzei (Fujiwara no Michinori, 1106–59), while Yoshitomo cultivated Shinzei's bitter enemy, Fujiwara no Nobuyori (1133–59). In early 1160, Kiyomori was away on a pilgrimage when Yoshitomo and Nobuyori moved against him, thus initiating the Heiji Conflict. They captured Go-Shirakawa and his son, Emperor Nijō (born 1143, reigned 1158–65), and they killed Shinzei. Kiyomori raced back to the capital. His eldest son, Shigemori (1138–79), and others attacked the palace, crushed the rebels, and killed Nobuyori.

Yoshitomo was killed while fleeing eastward. His son Yoritomo, then a boy, faced execution, but Kiyomori's stepmother, Lady Ike (Ike no Zenni), persuaded Shigemori to intercede on his behalf. Kiyomori responded by merely banishing him to the province of Izu. From there Yoritomo eventually launched the campaign that destroyed Kiyomori's house. Meanwhile Go-Shirakawa had abdicated in 1158 and nominally renounced the world in 1169. These steps left him free to play his active, influential, and highly ambiguous role in the events of the tale.

The Yukinaga credited in *Essays in Idleness* with writing an early *Tale of the Heike* was a literary-minded provincial governor whose father, Fujiwara no Yukitaka, figures in the tale itself. On the fifth of the first month of Juei 3 (1184), holding the office awarded to him earlier by Kiyomori (3:17), Yukitaka called on the regent, Kujō Kanezane (1149–1207). The tale does not mention the meeting, but Kanezane recorded it in his extensive diary (*Gyokuyō*), a major historical source on the period. The Genji army was driving toward the capital at the time.

Kanezane asked about the recasting of the Great Buddha of Tōdaiji, since Yukitaka was charged with overseeing the work (end 6:9). His question touched on the Heike crime that the tale treats as heinous above all: the burning of Nara and the

destruction of the Great Buddha (5:14) in the twelfth month of Jishō 4 (1180). Yuki-
taka assured Kanezane that it was going well. He then passed to what was for him
a closely related subject. He said:

> My son and daughter are subject to spirit possession. It always happens in a
> time of crisis. The possessing spirits are those of Retired Emperor Sutoku and
> the Uji Left Minister [Yorinaga]. Their oracles are unfailingly accurate. It is
> very strange. Please tell no one.

He also mentioned spirit demands, delivered through his children, for a shrine at
Sutoku's grave in Sanuki and Buddhist services there for his repose.

It is not hard to imagine Yukinaga, an eyewitness to his time, feeling called on
to write the initial version of a story that repeatedly conveys anxiety about the very
spirits who (according to his father) sometimes possessed him. When Kiyomori's
daughter, Emperor Takakura's empress, approaches the term of her pregnancy
(3:1), angry spirits invade her body. Chief among them are Sutoku's and Yorinaga's,
followed by those of the recently executed Narichika and Saikō. Kiyomori at once
placates Sutoku and Yorinaga by awarding them a laudatory posthumous title
(Sutoku) and higher court rank (Yorinaga). Once his daughter has borne an impe-
rial heir, however, he forces the boy's father to abdicate in favor of this grandson
(4:1), the child emperor Antoku. The obvious parallel with Sutoku's humiliation
frightens people, despite the Heike lords' voluble rationalizations and justifica-
tions. "Yes," the text observes, "the angry dead inspire fear" (3:1).

AUTHORITY IN THE WORLD OF THE TALE

The tyrant Kiyomori, whose arbitrary power rested on force, nonetheless had
other key figures to contend with. The *Heike* reader may wonder sometimes where
in the world of the tale decisive authority really lies.

Kiyomori headed the Heike, as Yoritomo did the Genji. Both secured the coop-
eration of local warriors linked to them by lineage or by long-established ties of
service and reward. However, Yoritomo campaigned against the Heike from his
base at Kamakura (near modern Tokyo), far from any corrupting or competing
influence from the capital. In contrast, Kiyomori had seized power in the capital
itself, from within the world of the old civil and imperial aristocracy. He some-
times rode roughshod over this aristocracy, but he never swept it away. This made
the question of authority in his heyday particularly complex.

In the distant past, the emperors really had (sometimes) ruled the relatively
small part of Japan under central control, but direct imperial rule remained a
recurrent ideal down to modern times precisely because it was rare. Powerful fig-
ures around the sovereign sought his effective power, leaving him only intangible

prestige. Many centuries earlier the nonimperial Fujiwara house had successfully imposed its senior representative as "regent" upon almost every emperor—so much so that the relationship between the regent and the emperor had become enshrined in sacred legend. As Taira no Shigemori puts it in an impassioned speech to his father, Kiyomori (2:6),

> Yes, this land of ours is remote, a few scattered millet grains,
> yet here rule the descendants of the Great Sun Goddess,
> for whom Ame-no-koyane's lineage governs the realm.

The Sun Goddess, the origin of the imperial line, had concluded a solemn pact to this effect with Ame-no-koyane, the Fujiwara ancestral deity. Shigemori's words therefore uphold an unassailable ideal. However, despite the rhetoric that treated the emperor as an inspiring monarch, a twelfth-century emperor ruled little. The regent's "governing" role, too, had dwindled, and at times Kiyomori displayed contempt for the incumbent (1:11).

A regent typically imposed himself by marrying his daughter to the reigning emperor and becoming the maternal (commoner) grandfather of the next one. Things might not go that smoothly in practice, but the pattern was established, and Kiyomori insisted on following it. He married a daughter to Emperor Takakura, whom he then swept aside in order to put his grandson on the throne. This shockingly presumptuous success (seen from the tale's perspective) replicated a regent's. However, he left the nominal regent in place. Being in theory merely the emperor's servant and defender, he did not disturb the formal hierarchy of the court.

A very young emperor was easier to control than a mature one, but the duties of the imperial office, although purely ceremonial, were still burdensome. Both the emperor and the real power holders therefore had something to gain from early abdication. An abdicated emperor became an *in.*

Since English offers no equivalent for the word *in,* this translation resorts to the established approximation of "retired emperor." If a retired emperor wanted further freedom and aspired to piety, he could become a nominal monk. He then went on living at home, wearing clerical robes, and could among other things travel on pilgrimage. In translation he then becomes "the cloistered emperor." The Go-Shirakawa of the tale is an outstanding example. He spent only two or three years as emperor, then abdicated and a few years later donned clerical robes. That left him free to pursue many interests. Indeed, any gentleman could become the same sort of monk, living at home and free to do more or less as he pleased. He was then called a *nyūdō* ("novice"). Some of the warriors in the tale are *nyūdō*. Kiyomori became one at the height of his power, in order to ward off an illness. Being a *nyūdō* did nothing to curb his tyranny.

After the late eleventh century, retired emperors came to assert authority of their own. For this reason most of the twelfth century has been called "the period of government by retired emperors" (*insei jidai*), and because the retired (or "cloistered") emperor could make real decisions in certain areas, as the reigning emperor could not, he was sometimes referred to as "the lord sovereign over the realm" (*chiten no kimi*). The expression does not occur in *Heike*, but it applies to Go-Shirakawa. That is why this translation often refers to him, as occasionally also to the reigning emperor, as "the sovereign." It is not always clear which of the two is meant.

Go-Shirakawa's shifting fortunes under Kiyomori limit any notion of the "government" he could actually wield, but some meaningful decisions remained within his reach. The most significant involved defining who was an "enemy of the court" (*chōteki*): that is to say, who was a defender of the emperor and who was a rebel against him.

The role proper to both Genji and Heike was to quell any "enemy of the court," the assumption being that such an enemy would appear out in the provinces. The Hōgen and Heiji conflicts arose because of issues that split the court (the imperial line, extended by the house of the Fujiwara regents) against itself. Each side then regarded the other as an enemy of the court. In the tale Kiyomori repeatedly stresses the selflessness with which he defended the court (his winning side) against those bent on its destruction. Nonetheless Go-Shirakawa (assisted by the monk Mongaku) manages under desperate circumstances to tip the balance against the Heike by defining *them* as enemies of the court. He sends the exiled Yoritomo a "retired emperor's decree" (*inzen*) requiring him, out of loyalty to the court, to suppress the Heike (5:10). This decree is almost certainly a dramatic fiction. (Go-Shirakawa's more plausibly historical decree, appointing Yoritomo to command the imperial forces, appears in 8:5.) For just that reason, however, it highlights the authority widely attributed to a retired (or "cloistered") emperor.

THE HIERARCHY OF THE COURT

Just as warlords pursued their own interests behind a veil of service to the throne, loyal service was the ideal associated with ambitious participation in the government over which the emperor nominally presided, with the regent's assistance. The top post in this government was that of chancellor (*daijōdaijin*), an office that Kiyomori came to hold. Next came three ministers: the left minister (*sadaijin*), the right minister (*udaijin*), and the palace minister (*naidaijin*). The government's highest-level advisers constituted the body of "senior nobles" (*kugyō*). Below them came the "privy gentlemen" (*tenjōbito*), so named because they enjoyed the privilege of entering the "privy chamber" adjoining the emperor's living quarters. Acquisition of this privilege by Kiyomori's forebears is a critical issue early in Book One.

Three guard units secured the palace compound: the Palace Guards (*konoefu*), the Watch (*hyōefu*), and the Gate Watch (*emonfu*). Each had a left and right division. Command of a division of the Palace Guards was a special honor. Government bureaus oversaw such areas as ceremonial, civil affairs, justice, war, and treasury. There were counselors, controllers, secretaries, chamberlains, and, of course, governors appointed to the provinces. A successful noble was likely to hold dual appointment in the civil and guards hierarchies. Each office had its place in an order of precedence. An incumbent also held a numbered rank, from one down to nine, and each rank was subdivided into two or more grades (for example, junior and senior). Finally, a high-level office mentioned repeatedly in the tale is that of "Dazaifu deputy" (*Dazai no sochi*), the government representative to its outpost in Kyushu.

The same government hierarchy figures in *The Tale of Genji*, written some two centuries earlier. In the Penguin *Genji*, every office and title mentioned is translated, for reasons explained in the introduction to the book, but not so in the Penguin *Heike*. There are just too many of them. Moreover, the *Genji* narrator speaks from within the world to which this hierarchy gave vital form, while the *Heike* narrator does not. *Heike* is broader in scope, the focus of interest is elsewhere, and after two hundred years the hierarchy has lost much of its substance. However, where titles and offices are translated, they follow as much as possible the practice adopted in the Penguin *Genji*.

What really matters is the significance, both to the character concerned and to the tale's intended audience, of belonging to this hallowed hierarchy at all. This is poignantly clear from the way the narrative still refers to a Heike lord, even after the Heike have fled from the capital, solely by his now-empty formal title. The title is still the man. In 9:7 the fugitive Heike even proceed with a round of promotions and appointments that one of their number, in a poem, calls a "dream." The translation identifies these lords by name rather than by title, since the reader would soon lose track of them otherwise, but it is indeed the titles that support the Heike dream of recovering all that they have lost. When Taira no Munemori (Kiyomori's son and successor) is beheaded at last (11:18), his son Kiyomune faces the same fate, but before the sword falls, he longs to know that his father died well. The passage reads in English, "'How was my father when he died?' Kiyomune pathetically inquired." The original, however, identifies Kiyomune not by name but as "the intendant of the Right Gate Watch," and it has him ask not after his father but after "His Excellency the minister." Such is the pride that sustains a man to the last.

RELIGION IN THE TALE

Differing modes of religious faith and practice pervade *The Tale of the Heike,* and religious institutions play a major role in its story. These institutions include great temples or temple complexes devoted to the study and practice of Buddhism and major shrines established to honor deities more or less native to Japan. Although utterly dissimilar in most ways, both doctrinally and architecturally, these temples and shrines were closely linked in medieval times. Buddhist temples had their associated shrines, and shrines their temples, and the deities on either side merged into one another in shifting, idiosyncratic ways. Broadly speaking, native deities were honored as local, tangible manifestations of the universal, transcendent Buddhist divinities, while these divinities were revered as the eternal essences of native deities manifest in particular ways and at particular places in Japan.

The chief Buddhist institutions in *The Tale of the Heike* are still there and remain famous today, however reduced they may be from what they once were. The most prominent is Mount Hiei, an immensely powerful temple complex on the mountain of that name, just northeast of the capital. The main temple there is Enryakuji, but the tale also mentions three major centers of the extended monastic complex: the Central Hall, the East Pagoda, and the West Pagoda. Mount Hiei loomed so large in the life of the capital that it was usually enough just to call it "the Mountain." It upheld the Tendai Buddhism brought to Japan from China in the early ninth century, and it stressed faith in the Lotus Sutra and the Buddha Amida. The abbot of Mount Hiei was a major figure, and the vast community below him included thousands of monks, in a hierarchy that extended from scholars down to workers and fighters. Below the Mountain stood Miidera, another powerful Tendai temple. As the tale makes all too clear, Enryakuji and Miidera were bitter, sometimes violent rivals.

The Buddhism taught on Mount Hiei was "exoteric" (*kengyō*) because in principle it required no secret, initiatory transmission. By the twelfth century, however, it was strongly influenced by the "esoteric," or tantric, Buddhism (*mikkyō*) most closely identified with Mount Kōya. The Tendai abbot Meiun, for example, had mastered both (2:1). Mount Kōya dates from the same time as Mount Hiei, but, being far from the capital, it was less entangled than Mount Hiei in the capital's affairs. The great monk and culture hero Kōbō Daishi, traditionally credited with inventing Japanese phonetic writing, founded it when he brought Shingon Buddhism (as the esoteric teaching is more particularly known in Japan) back from China. Taira no Kiyomori received a divine gift on Mount Kōya (3:5), and his grandson Koremori went there to renounce the world (10:9, 10).

Two older temples of great importance, Kōfukuji and Tōdaiji, were located in the old capital of Nara. Both were large, powerful monastic communities with a strong population of warrior monks. Kōfukuji, the Fujiwara ancestral temple, dated from the early eighth century and championed Hossō Buddhism, which was then new to Japan. Tōdaiji, where, in 752, Emperor Shōmu dedicated a bronze Great Buddha that for Japan was the wonder of the age, upheld a school of Buddhism known as Sanron. Both temples burned when Taira no Shigehira set fire to the town in his campaign against the Nara monks, and the Great Buddha melted. The horror of this crime haunted him thereafter, until at last the Nara monks had him executed (11:19).

The shrines most prominent in the tale are Ise, Iwashimizu, Itsukushima, Kasuga, Kumano, and the shrine complex on Mount Hiei. Ise, south of modern Nagoya, enshrines the Sun Goddess (Amaterasu), the source of the imperial line. Kiyomori's widow has little Emperor Antoku, her grandson, salute Ise before she plunges with him into the sea (11:9). The Sun Goddess and Ise figure in many passages of the tale.

Iwashimizu, on a hill named Otokoyama, southwest of the capital, enshrines Hachiman, an important divinity everywhere in Japan and, more particularly, the patron deity of the Genji. Iwashimizu (also called Yawata in the tale because the characters used to write "Hachiman" can be read that way, too) played an enduring role in the religious life of the city. In the provinces, Kiso no Yoshinaka addresses a formal prayer to a local Hachiman shrine before his devastating triumph at Kurikara Ravine (7:5, 6).

The patron deity of the Heike was enshrined on Itsukushima, an island (now better known as Miyajima) just off the coast near Hiroshima. The beautiful shrine buildings, which seem to float over the water, are still the ones that Kiyomori built long ago in obedience to a divine command (3:5). As for the deity's name, it involves a kind of complexity normal at such shrines: The "Itsukushima Deity" is actually triple. In this case all three divinities, each with a distinct identity and history, are female. The name "Hachiman," too, sums up a triple divinity, while the divine presence at Sumiyoshi and Kasuga is quadruple. With the exception of Hachiman, the name of a deity as it appears both in the tale (Itsukushima, Sumiyoshi, Kasuga, and so on) and in common usage over the centuries is the name of the place where the shrine sanctuaries stand, not of any particular divinity enshrined there.

This issue is worth mentioning especially because of the role played in the tale by the various shrines on Mount Hiei, and also by the shrines summed up under the place-name "Kumano." The Hiei shrines are many and their names (Hiyoshi, Jūzenji, Marōto, Hachiōji, etc.) are confusing, but they mean a great deal to the monks (for example, 1:15). Confusing, too, is the deity name "Sannō" ("Mountain King"), which corresponds to none of these shrines individually. In 1:14, Sannō, the divine presence of the entire Mountain, speaks through a medium.

Kumano, a region at the southern tip of the Kii Peninsula, figures repeatedly and dramatically in the tale. In the twelfth century, it was a major pilgrimage center.

Kiyomori was at Kumano when the Heiji Conflict broke out, and his son Shigemori made a portentous pilgrimage there shortly before his death (3:11). Since a Kumano pilgrimage took in three major (as well as dozens of minor) shrines, the place was sometimes called "Triple Kumano" (Mi-Kumano). Kumano Hongū ("Main Shrine"), first in order of precedence, stood beside a river, inland from the sea; then came Shingū ("New Shrine"), on the coast at the river mouth; and finally the Nachi waterfall, some way back from the sea. Mongaku performs his startling and picturesque austerities at Nachi (5:7), and it is to Nachi that Koremori comes on his final journey (10:11), after renouncing the world on Mount Kōya. He first salutes the sacred waterfall, associated as it is with the merciful bodhisattva Kannon, then continues to the shore and sets out at last in a boat to seek rebirth in paradise (10:12).

This paradise, or Pure Land, is that of Amida, the buddha of infinite light and life. The Buddhist scriptures place it at an incalculable distance toward the west, the direction of the setting sun. At Kumano, Amida was associated particularly with the divinity of Kumano Hongū, but access to him was universal. Faith in his salvation pervades the tale. Like a few others in medieval Japan, the despairing Koremori seeks rebirth in paradise by drowning himself, but such examples were rare. Amida faith requires nothing like that. It is very simple.

Time and again the tale mentions someone calling, or being urged to call, "the Name": that of Amida in the ultimately Sanskrit-derived invocation *Namu Amida Butsu* ("Hail Amida Buddha"). The Name had to be voiced, although the final syllable was partially dropped. One called it not as a prayer for admission to paradise but rather as an expression of the conviction that welcome into Amida's paradise was certain, in accordance with Amida's Original Vow (*hongan*) to save any sentient being who calls sincerely upon him. The faithful debated over the centuries how many callings were needed, and a widely accepted answer was ten, but no one could deny the efficacy of a single calling made in full faith. The devout called the Name continually.

Calling the Name became urgent as death approached. The defeated Taira no Tadanori asks to be allowed to do so on the battlefield, before his opponent beheads him (9:14). A dying person might wish to face an image of Amida and hold a five-colored cord attached to the image's hands, so that Amida should be able to draw the departing soul straight to paradise. Shigehira does this before his execution (11:19), and so, too, Kenreimon-in at her death (13:5). The practice assumes the visualization of Amida's welcome to the soul that the illustration for 13:5 shows in ethereal outline: Amida comes forward to greet the soul, accompanied by the bodhisattvas Kannon and Seishi and by a host of saints and celestial musicians. Witnesses knew that the soul had gone to paradise because an unearthly perfume lingered in the air after the heavenly host's departure and the purple cloud on which it rode still floated in the sky.

THE CAPITAL, THE PROVINCES, AND THE TŌKAIDŌ

In the time of *The Tale of the Heike*, there was only one city in Japan: the capital (*kyō* or *miyako*, often in this translation just "the city"), founded in 794 when Emperor Kanmu moved away from Nara. It is now the city of Kyoto. The capital was the imperial seat (roughly the meaning of the word *miyako*) and the center of civilization. Anyone from elsewhere was more or less a rustic, which is how the Heike lords viewed the Genji warriors from the wilds of the east. In those days the Kanto area, the site of modern Tokyo, was distant, rough, and uncouth, and the regions beyond it even more remote. The provinces to the west were perhaps slightly less so, thanks to traffic along the Inland Sea, but Kyushu (known then as Chinzei or Tsukushi) was still very distant.

The streets and avenues of the capital were laid out in a grid pattern adapted from the capital of Tang China. The north-south thoroughfares were named, while the east-west avenues (*jō*) were numbered. This translation identifies the east-west *jō* by their Japanese names: Ichijō (First Avenue), Nijō (Second), Sanjō (Third), Shijō (Fourth), Gojō (Fifth), Rokujō (Sixth), Shichijō (Seventh), Hachijō (Eighth), Kujō (Ninth), and Jūjō (Tenth). The tale identifies the location of a dwelling by naming the nearest street intersection. Examples are "Naka-no-mikado and Higashi-no-tōin" and "Hachijō-Karasumaru." The Kamo River ran north-south along the east side of the city, between wide gravel banks. Mention of the Kamo riverbank at Rokujō becomes increasingly menacing as the tale progresses, because so many executions took place there.

Nara (the "old capital" or "southern capital") had been the imperial seat during most of the eighth century, but before then the capital had moved from place to place, often with each new reign. Taira no Kiyomori's decision to move the capital to Fukuhara (5:1), on the site of modern Kobe, was shocking because it violated centuries of proud stability. Fukuhara was then a port that figured in the Heike-controlled trade with Song China. The tale evokes the site as unsuitable for a proper capital, but it concedes that moving the capital was not without precedent in the longer perspective of history, and it then lists these moves. Fukuhara soon proved a failure, and Kiyomori had to give it up (5:13).

The events in the tale range over almost all of Japan, but one long stretch of land deserves special mention: the Tōkaidō (Eastern Sea Road) route from the capital to the east, especially Kamakura. Travelers who followed it came first to the Ōsaka barrier, an ancient checkpoint long honored in *waka* poetry, on the low pass between the city and the shore of Lake Biwa. There Semimaru, in legend a banished son of Emperor Daigo (reigned 897–930), had played his biwa beside the Shinomiya brook. The traveler then descended to Lake Biwa and beyond, passing more spots famous in poetry. Several *Heike* passages acknowledge their fame, but none as fully as 10:6, which evokes Shigehira's journey to Kamakura in the form of a full-fledged *michiyuki* (travel song), the only one in the tale.

HEIKE PERFORMANCE AFTER THE FIFTEENTH CENTURY

Japan remained relatively stable for a hundred years after Kakuichi's death, and *biwa hōshi* then enjoyed perhaps their greatest popularity at all levels of society. The century and more of internecine warfare that followed naturally challenged them, but warrior lords continued to value *Heike* for its evocation of a stirring past. *Heike* performers were called to artistic gatherings, and no doubt they remained active at the village level as well. In time some seem to have broadened their repertoire into other areas of popular music and begun to cultivate also the three-stringed samisen, then recently introduced to Japan.

During the Edo period (1600–1868), the Tokugawa shoguns patronized *Heike* performance and adopted it as a form of ceremonial music. Under such patronage the Japan-wide guild of *Heike* performers flourished and new schools of *Heike* performance appeared. During the seventeenth century, cultural pursuits of all kinds diffused through the population at large, especially in the cities, and printing flourished. Printed editions of *Heike* (not necessarily the Kakuichi version) became readily available, and amateurs began to study *Heike* recitation. The development of a music-notation system for the work yielded the score already mentioned and culminated in the widely disseminated *Heike mabushi* (1776), which supports one line of *Heike* performers even today.

The performers' guild collapsed soon after the Meiji Restoration (1868). With new ideas and practices flooding into Japan from abroad and intense competition from other arts, most members had to turn to other kinds of music, or even to such traditional occupations for the blind as massage or acupuncture. Nonetheless a thread of traditional *Heike* performance survived.

In Kyushu, in the south, Yamashika Yoshiyuki, the last blind biwa singer, died in 1996. He had received no formal *Heike* transmission, but his diverse repertoire, like that of his fellows, included *Heike*-derived material. Like the *biwa hōshi* long before him, he performed these narratives for patrons under secular circumstances and also sang sacred texts in festival and ritual settings.

In Nagoya, central Japan, Imai Tsutomu (born 1958) is the last recognized successor to the blind Edo-period *Heike* performers. His formally acquired repertoire includes eight selections: "The Sea Bass" (1:3) and a portion of "One Man's Glory" (1:5), "Stupas Cast into the Sea" (2:16), "Autumn Leaves" (6:2), "The Pilgrimage to Chikubushima" (7:3), "Ikezuki" (9:1), "First Across the Uji River" (9.2), "Yokobue" (10:8), and "Nasu no Yoichi" (11:4). He has recorded these on CD.

In the north the Tsugaru lineage arose in the late eighteenth century and remains active today. These performers, who are sighted, descend artistically from sighted amateurs rather than blind professionals. Their ultimate authority is a book rather than a teacher: the complete, performable *Heike mabushi*. It is therefore possible for them, at least in principle, to perform the whole tale. In 1998 the Tsugaru performer Hashimoto Toshie (a woman) undertook to do so over the course of ten years.

Performance of famous *Heike* passages, or of *Heike*-derived material, continues, especially in the modern (late-nineteenth-century and after) biwa schools known as Satsuma-biwa and Chikuzen-biwa. Examples of these new interpretations, often moving and dramatic, are available on CD. In addition, YouTube offers glimpses of biwa performance in a variety of styles. Most consist of the tale's exceedingly famous opening lines (the beginning of 1.1, known in Japanese as "Gion Shōja"). Imai Tsutomu, who did not receive this passage through orthodox transmission because his lineage considered it too weighty for any but the most advanced disciple, has recorded a reconstruction done by a specialized musicologist (Komoda Haruko). However, anyone is now free to perform it on the Internet, in any style, before the whole world.

TIME IN THE TALE

Years. Japan counts years not from a point of origin like the birth of Christ but within an "era" or "year period" (*nengō*) that belongs in a succession of similar eras. In modern times these eras coincide with an imperial reign (Meiji, Taishō, Shōwa, Heisei), but earlier they did not. A new era could be proclaimed at any time. Thus Kiyomori moved the capital to Fukuhara in Jishō 4 (1180) and died in Yōwa 1 (1181). These Japanese years correspond only approximately to 1180 and 1181, because the Japanese calendar was then lunar, not solar. A lunar month (like a lunar year) began roughly six weeks later than its numbered solar counterpart. For this reason the burning of Nara (5:14), conventionally dated to the end of 1180, properly occurred in the first days of 1181.

The counterpart Common Era date for each year or imperial reign mentioned in the text appears in small type to the right of a "song" or "recitative" line and where appropriate within a passage of "speech." In this way the reader has ready access to the historical framework shared by the tale's characters and original audience.

Hours. The day was divided into twelve "hours," six for the daytime and six for the night, each named for one of the twelve beasts of the zodiac. These "hours" shortened or lengthened as the relative length of day and night changed from season to season. At the equinox an "hour" therefore corresponded to two clock hours. Approximate counterpart clock times are indicated in the same way as dates. Each corresponds to the midpoint of the named "hour."

NAMES AND CAPITALIZATION

The names of the ranking Taira, Minamoto, and Fujiwara figures in the tale are relatively simple. Examples are Taira no Kiyomori, Minamoto no Yoritomo, and Fujiwara no Motomichi. In these the last element is the "given name," which the *no* ("of") links to the surname. In other cases, however, what looks like a surname may refer instead to the man's home locality. For example, Imai no Shirō Kanehira and Higuchi no Jirō Kanemitsu are brothers. The Shirō ("fourth son") and Jirō ("second son") indicate order of birth and serve also as personal names under informal circumstances. Other such possibilities are Tarō ("first son"), Saburō (third), Gorō (fifth), and so on. The hero Minamoto no Yoshitsune appears often in the original text simply as Kurō ("ninth son"). For the sake of simplicity and consistency, the translation usually includes (or substitutes) the more formal given name.

Women's names are more elusive. Formal genealogies record a personal name only for a woman of very high birth; otherwise they simply mention a "daughter." In any case, a woman's personal name was rarely used in public. A lady mentioned in 12:5 is an example. Her personal name was probably read "Noriko," but her name in actual use was Kyō-no-tsubone, an appellation that alluded to where she lived or had once lived. Other women in the tale are referred to by appellations that associate them with male, office-bearing relatives. An example is Dainagon-no-suke, Taira no Shigehira's wife and a nurse of Emperor Antoku. A woman of the loftiest rank—the mother of an emperor, an empress, or a senior princess—would acquire an exalted "*in* title" (*ingō*), which would then be her name. Kiyomori's daughter, the mother of Emperor Antoku, became Kenreimon-in; other examples are Bifukumon-in and Jōtōmon-in. Dancers like Giō (1:6) used their professional names.

Buddhist monks and priests took two-character religious names, read in Chinese style. These alluded to Buddhist scriptures, virtues, or ideals.

Buddhist writings and practices originated in India but reached Japan via China. Japan received the names of deities and so on in Chinese translation or transliteration, then absorbed them according to its own conventions of pronunciation. In theory such names should be restored in English to their Sanskrit original, if it exists. In practice, however, the confusion is so great that consistency is all but impossible. This translation does not attempt it. Some names appear in their Sanskrit form, others—the more common ones—as they were pronounced in Japan.

The readings given in the translation for most of the names in the tale follow those indicated in the source editions cited. However, a few are unfamiliar to a modern reader acquainted with Japanese history. In these cases, the better-known reading has been adopted:

Reading adopted	Original reading
Betsugi	Hetsugi
Daigensui	Taigensui
Dakini	Dagini
Doi	Toi
Genjō	Kenjō
Kazan	(Emperor) Kasan
Kinpusen	Kinbuzen
Kizu, Kizu River	Kotsu, Kotsu River
Kumagai	Kumagae
Shinzei	Shinsei (Fujiwara no Michinori)
Susano-o	Sosano-o
Takeda	Taketa
Teshigahara	Tesshigahara

In names romanized with a double *o*, the two *o*'s have been separated by a hyphen in order to avoid confusion over how to pronounce them: Susano-o, Seno-o.

Finally, an effort has been made in this translation to reduce capitalization to a minimum, in order to lighten the text as much as possible.

THE NOTES

Not every reader needs notes. Richard Henry Dana wrote in the introduction to *Two Years Before the Mast:*

> There may be in some parts a good deal that is unintelligible to the general reader; but I have found from my own experience, and what I have heard from others, that plain matters of fact in relation to customs and habits of life new to us, and descriptions of life under new aspects, act upon the inexperienced through the imagination, so that we are hardly aware of our want of technical knowledge. Thousands read the escape of the American frigate through the British channel . . . with breathless interest, who do not know the name of a rope in the ship; and perhaps with none the less admiration and enthusiasm for their want of acquaintance with the professional detail.

Some will wish to read *The Tale of the Heike* in that spirit, unaided. Others will welcome the notes or even require them. Perhaps the latter will find them helpful and the former tolerable after all.

THE ILLUSTRATIONS

The illustrations are from *Heike monogatari zue*, a popular retelling of the tale (text by Takai Ranzan, 1762–1838) published in Edo in two parts, in 1829 and 1849. They are by Teisai Hokuba (1770–1844), a star pupil of the great print artist Hokusai (1771–1844), and they are reproduced here from a copy in the translator's collection. *Heike monogatari zue* provided both text and three illustrations (redrawn) for the first *Heike* passages published in any European language. François Turrettini's French translation of a few early chapters appeared in Geneva in 1871.

⁖ PRINCIPAL FIGURES IN THE TALE ⁘

Antoku, Emperor (1178–85, r. 1180–85). Eldest son of Emperor Takakura by Kiyo-mori's daughter, Kenreimon-in. Drowned at the battle of Dan-no-ura. A rumor current at the time had it that Antoku was really a transformation of the Dragon King's daughter (the Itsukushima deity) and that he had merely returned home to the sea. A later one held that he had been a girl all along and had survived the battle as a fisherman's daughter. The ambiguous signs described at the beginning of 3:4 presumably encouraged this story. (7:13, 20; 8:1, 3–4; 9:1, 18; 11:2, 9)

Atsumori, Taira no (1169–84). Son of Taira no Tsunemori and nephew of Kiyo-mori. Beheaded by Kumagai Naozane at Ichi-no-tani. (7:19; 9:16, 18)

Awa-no-naishi. According to different texts, daughter or granddaughter of Shinzei (Fujiwara no Michinori). Accompanied Kenreimon-in to Ōhara. (13:1–5)

Benkei, Musashibō (?–1189). A warrior-monk under Yoshitsune. Not especially prominent in the tale, but looms very large in the later legend of Yoshitsune. (9:7, 9; 11:3, 7; 12:4)

Dainagon-no-suke. Wife of Shigehira and a nurse of Emperor Antoku. Captured at Dan-no-ura, she accompanied Kenreimon-in to Ōhara. (10:2, 4, 6; 11:10–11, 19; 13:2–3, 5)

Doi. See Sanehira.

Go-Shirakawa, Emperor (1127–92, r. 1155–58). Father of Emperor Takakura and Prince Mochihito, grandfather of Emperors Antoku and Go-Toba. A major factor in the Hōgen Conflict and, after his abdication, a powerful and active retired emperor. (1:5–7, 9, 11–14; 2:1, 3, 6–7, 10, 12, 16; 3:1, 3, 15, 19; 4:1–4, 6, 8; 5:1, 10–11; 6:1, 4–5, 7, 10, 12; 7:13, 16, 20; 8:1–2, 5, 10–11; 9:1, 5, 17; 10:1, 5, 13; 11:13; 12:1; 13:3–4)

Go-Toba, Emperor (1180–1239, r. 1183–98). Chosen by Go-Shirakawa to replace Antoku after the Heike flight from the capital. In his maturity Go-Toba became a major poet. In 1221 he raised rebellion against the Kamakura sho-gunate and ended his days in exile on the island of Oki. (8:1, 10; 10:14; 11:13–14; 12:9)

Higuchi. See Kanemitsu.

Ichijō. See Tadayori.

Ike, Lady (Ike no Zenni [Fujiwara no Muneko], ?–?). Taira no Kiyomori's step-mother and the mother of Yorimori. After the Heiji Conflict, she persuaded Kiyomori, through Shigemori, to exile rather than execute the young Yoritomo. (5:10; 7:19; 10:3; 11:18)

Imai. See Kanehira.

Inomata. See Noritsuna.

Kagekiyo, Akushichibyōe (Fujiwara no Kagekiyo, ?–1195?). This fierce Heike warrior from the east survived Dan-no-ura. Some eastern warriors favored the prefix *aku-* ("bad"), which turns Kagekiyo's name into something like "Badass Shichibyōe." (4:11; 7:2; 8:9; 9:10; 10:14; 11:5, 7, 11; 12:9)

Kagesue, Kajiwara Genda (1162–1200). Eldest son of Kajiwara Kagetoki. (9:1–3, 7, 11, 15; 11:7)

Kagetoki, Kajiwara (d. 1200). A major Genji commander. His bitter dislike of Yoshitsune led to Yoshitsune's downfall. (7:1; 9:7, 11, 16; 10:6, 7; 11:1, 6, 7, 17; 12:9)

Kajiwara. See Kagesue and Kagetoki.

Kakumei (?–1241?). Kiso no Yoshinaka's learned warrior-scribe. Once a monk on Mount Hiei, Kakumei had studied also in Nara. He served Yoshinaka after falling out with Taira no Kiyomori. (7:5, 10; 8:11)

Kanehira, Imai no Shirō (?–1184). Foster brother of Kiso no Yoshinaka and one of his chief men, younger brother of Kanemitsu. Defended Yoshinaka to the last and died a dramatic death. (7:1, 4, 6–7; 8:6, 8, 10; 9:1, 4)

Kanemitsu, Higuchi no Jirō (?–1184). Elder brother of Kanehira and one of Kiso no Yoshinaka's chief men. (7:4, 7–8; 8:8–9; 9:5)

Kaneyasu, Seno-o (?–1183). A warrior in Kiyomori's service, he fought in Hōgen and Heiji. (1:11; 2:4; 3:12; 5:14; 7:6; 8:8)

Kanezane, Kujō (Fujiwara, 1149–1207). Minister, regent, and a dominant court figure of his time. Author of *Gyokuyō,* a voluminous diary that is a major source of historical information on the period. (1:5; 3:4; 4:2; 5:1)

Kawano. See Michinobu.

Kenreimon-in (Taira no Noriko, 1155–?). Daughter of Taira no Kiyomori. Adopted by Go-Shirakawa, she became a consort of Emperor Takakura in 1171, then his empress. Gave birth to the future Emperor Antoku in 1178 and to the future Emperor Go-Toba in 1180. Received the title Kenreimon-in in 1181. After the Heike collapse, retired as a nun to Ōhara. (1:5; 3:1–3; 4:2; 5:1, 14; 6:2, 12; 7:13, 19; 11:1–2, 9–11; 12:3; 13:1–5)

Kiso. See Yoshinaka.

Kiyomori, Taira no (1118–81). Eldest son of Taira no Tadamori—unless it is true that (as a rumor reported in 6:10 has it) he was really a son of Emperor Shirakawa, adopted by Tadamori. He became head of the Heike in 1153.

(1:1–6; 2:1, 3–7, 9–12, 16; 3:1–5, 11, 15–19; 4:1–9, 13, 16; 5:1, 3–4, 12–14; 6:4–10; 7:5, 20; 8:4, 11; 9:7; 10:2, 5, 12, 14; 12:19; 13:1–5)

Kiyomune, Taira no (1171–85). Eldest son of Taira no Munemori, hence a grandson of Kiyomori. Captured with his father at Dan-no-ura and later executed with him. (7:19; 11:2, 10–11, 13, 16–18)

Kiyotsune, Taira no (d. 1183). Third son of Shigemori. Drowned himself in despair after the Heike had fled the capital. (6:10; 7:14, 19; 8:4; 13:4)

Kogō. Granddaughter of Shinzei, lover of Takafusa, and beloved also of Emperor Takakura. (6:4)

Koremori, Taira no (1158–84). Eldest son of Taira no Shigemori, hence Kiyomori's grandson. A failure as the commander of the Heike northern campaign, he fled the capital with the rest of his house, leaving his immediate family behind, then left the Heike camp at Yashima to renounce the world on Mount Kōya and drown himself off Nachi. (1:5, 16; 2:4, 11; 3:3, 11–12; 5:11–12; 7:2–4, 6, 12, 14, 19–20; 9:7; 10:1, 8–10, 12–14; 12:7–9)

Kozaishō (d. 1184). Wife of Taira no Michimori. She drowned herself after Michimori's death at Ichi-no-tani. (9:9, 19)

Kumagai. See Naozane.

Meiun (1115–83). Son of Koga no Akimichi. Abbot of Mount Hiei. Dismissed from his post and banished, then reinstated; then killed by Kiso no Yoshinaka's men. (2:1, 2; 3:19; 8:10)

Michichika, Minamoto no (1149–1202). A ranking court noble who accompanied Emperor Takakura to Itsukushima (his record of the pilgrimage survives) and Go-Shirakawa to Ōhara. (3:4; 5:1; 13:3)

Michimori, Taira no (d. 1184). A Heike commander, nephew of Kiyomori, and husband of Kozaishō. Killed at Ichi-no-tani. (5:14; 7:2–3, 6, 12–13, 19; 9:6, 9, 18–19; 10:4; 11:3)

Michinobu, Kawano (also Kōno, also Ochi) no Shirō (1156–1223). A Genji sympathizer from the province of Iyo, Kawano struggled against the Heike in the period preceding the battle of Dan-no-ura. (9:6; 11:2, 6, 7)

Mochihito, Prince (1151–80). Second son of Go-Shirakawa. Killed after a failed anti-Heike revolt incited by Yorimasa. (4:3, 5–8, 11–14; 5:1, 14; 6:4)

Mongaku (1139–1203). A monk, formerly a warrior named Endō Moritō. Played a critical role in inciting Yoritomo to rebel against the Heike and later saved Rokudai from execution. (5:8–10; 12:2, 7–9)

Morikuni, Taira no (1113?–86). An adviser to Kiyomori and Shigemori, and the father of Moritoshi. (2:3, 6–7; 5:12; 6:10)

Moritoshi, Taira no (d. 1184). A Heike warrior killed at Ichi-no-tani. (7:2, 4; 9:9, 12–13)

Motofusa, Fujiwara no (1145–1230). A senior Fujiwara noble, dismissed as regent by Kiyomori, 1179. (8:1, 11)

Motomichi, Fujiwara no (1160–1233). A senior Fujiwara noble, regent most of the time between 1179 and 1186, and then again in 1196. A son-in-law of Kiyomori and close to Go-Shirakawa. (1:5; 3:15–17, 19; 5:1, 11, 13–14; 7:13; 8:1–2, 11; 9:5)

Munemori, Taira no (1147–85). Kiyomori's third son (called "second" in the tale because Motomori, Kiyomori's original second son, was dead by this time) and the lackluster head of the Heike after his father's death. (1:5, 12, 15; 2:3, 6, 11; 3:4, 11, 18–19; 4:1, 4–6, 13–14; 5:12; 6:7–8, 10, 12; 7:4, 7–8, 12–13, 15, 19–20; 8:1, 3–4, 6, 11; 9:6–7, 9, 17; 10:2–4, 6–7, 9, 11, 13, 15; 11:2, 6–8, 10–11, 13, 16–18)

Nakatsuna, Minamoto no (1126–80). Eldest son of Yorimasa. (4:6, 10–11; 5:9)

Naoie, Kumagai Kojirō (1169–1221). Genji warrior, the son of Naozane. Wounded at Ichi-no-tani. (9:7, 10, 16)

Naozane, Kumagai (1141–1208). The Genji warrior who with regret took the head of Atsumori, in one of the most famous episodes of the tale. (9:2, 7, 10, 16)

Narichika, Fujiwara no (1137–77). A ranking Fujiwara noble, brother-in-law of Shigemori, father-in-law of Koremori, close associate of Go-Shirakawa, and chief member of the Shishi-no-tani plot against the Heike, for which he was executed. (1:12–13; 2:3–6, 8–11; 3:1, 7, 15, 18; 4:3; 7:14)

Naritsune, Fujiwara no (d. 1202). Son of Narichika, exiled in connection with the Shishi-no-tani plot but eventually pardoned to appease the angry spirit of his late father. (2:4–5, 9–10, 15; 3:1–3, 7–9)

Nii, Lady (d. 1185). Tokiko, known as Nii-dono ("lady of the second rank"), then Nii-no-ama ("nun of the second rank"). Kiyomori's wife; mother of Munemori, Tomomori, Shigehira, and Kenreimon-in; sister of Tokitada; and sister-in-law of Emperor Takakura. Became a nun when Kiyomori became a "novice" monk. Drowned at Dan-no-ura with Emperor Antoku in her arms. (3:3; 4:3; 6:7; 7:19; 8:1; 10:4, 6, 9, 13; 11:1–2, 9)

Norimori, Taira no (1128–87). Younger bother of Kiyomori, father of Michimori and Noritsune, father-in-law of Naritsune. Despite the tale's account, he survived Dan-no-ura. (1:15; 2:5, 9, 15; 3:1, 3–4, 7; 7:12, 19; 9:6–7, 19; 11:10)

Noritsuna, Inomata no Kobeiroku (?–?). A warrior from the province of Musashi. Craftily managed to kill Taira no Moritoshi during the battle of Ichi-no-tani. (9:2, 12, 13)

Noritsune, Taira no (1160–85?). Nephew of Kiyomori, younger brother of Michimori, and a valiant warrior. Despite the tale's account, he was killed at Ichi-no-tani. (7:13, 19; 8:7; 9:6, 9–10, 12, 18–19; 11:3, 5–6, 10)

Noriyori, Minamoto no. Half brother of Yoritomo and Yoshitsune and overall commander of the Genji campaign. His achievement fell far short of Yoshitsune's. Eventually executed by Yoritomo. (8:11; 9:1–3, 5, 7, 11; 10:1, 14–15; 11:1, 7, 17; 12:5)

Rokudai (1173–?). Son of Taira no Koremori and the last scion of the Heike. Spared at the plea of Mongaku, he was executed at some time during the first decade of the thirteenth century. (7:14, 19; 10:1, 10, 12; 12:7–9)

Sadayoshi, Taira no. A warrior and provincial governor in the close service of Kiyomori. On behalf of the Heike he conducted a successful military campaign in Kyushu. (2:3–4, 6–7; 3:11–12; 6:11; 7:13, 19; 10:13)

Sanehira, Doi no Jirō. A major commander under Minamoto no Yoritomo. (5:4; 7:1; 9:4, 7–11, 16; 10:2, 5, 14; 11:7, 13, 17)

Sanemori, Saitō (1126–83). Active first on the Genji side, then served the Heike, joining the Heike northern campaign as an old man. His poignant death is particularly famous. His two sons, Saitōgo and Saitōroku, served Koremori. (5:11; 6:7; 7:7–8, 14)

Sanesada, Fujiwara no (1139–91). Known as the Tokudaiji left minister, this successful courtier was particularly close to Go-Shirakawa. (1:12; 2:11; 3:4; 5:1–2; 8:1, 11; 10:1, 15; 13:3, 5)

Sasaki. See Takatsuna.

Seno-o. See Kaneyasu.

Shigehira, Taira no (1157?–85). Fifth son of Taira no Kiyomori (called "fourth" in the tale because Motomori, Kiyomori's original second son, was dead by this time). Responsible for burning the great temples of Nara, he was eventually beheaded by the Nara monks. (1:15; 2:3; 3:3; 4:11, 16; 5:12, 14; 6:10, 12; 7:12–13, 19; 8:9; 10:1–8, 11, 13, 15; 11:17, 19)

Shigemori, Taira no (1138–79). Eldest son of Kiyomori. His early death removed the last restraint from Kiyomori's tyranny. (1:5, 9, 11–13, 15–16; 2:4–8, 10–11, 16; 3:1, 3–4, 6, 11–15, 18; 4:6; 5:10; 6:10; 10:10–12, 14)

Shigenori, Fujiwara no (1135–87). Fourth son of Shinzei and father of Kogō. Known as Sakuramachi because of his love of cherry blossoms. (1:5; 4:1; 6:4)

Shigetada, Hatakeyama no Jirō (1164–1205). A young Musashi warrior and a commander under Yoshitsune. Played a prominent role in the crossing of the Uji River. (9:2, 3, 7, 18)

Shigeyoshi, Taira no. Awa no Minbu Shigeyoshi. A Heike vassal in the province of Awa (Shikoku). First assisted the Heike but then, at Dan-no-ura, betrayed one of their crucial secrets to the Genji. (6:8; 9:17; 10:14; 11:2, 6–8, 11)

Shinzei (d. 1159). Religious name of Fujiwara no Michinori, an exceptionally learned scholar whose ambition led to his involvement and death in the Heiji Conflict. (1:12–13; 2:4; 3:15; 8:2, 11; 13:3)

Shunkan (1143–79). A prominent member of the Shishi-no-tani plot against the Heike. Kiyomori banished him to Kikai-ga-shima, where he died. (1:12–13; 2:3, 10, 15; 3:1–3, 6, 8–9, 18)

Sotsu-no-suke. Wife of Tokitada and Emperor Antoku's first wet nurse. (3:4; 4:1; 5:1; 11:11; 12:3)

Sukemori, Taira no (1158–85). Shigemori's second son, drowned at Dan-no-ura. Known especially for his youthful clash with the regent. (1:11; 4:2; 7:12, 14, 19; 8:4; 9:8; 10:1, 13–14; 11:10)

Tadamori, Taira no (1096–1153). Father of Kiyomori, Tsunemori, Norimori, Yorimori, and Tadanori. (1:1–3, 5; 2:3; 4:8; 6:10; 9:16)

Tadanobu, Satō Saburōbyōe (1161–86). A warrior from the north, younger brother of Tsuginobu, and a close retainer of Yoshitsune. (9:7; 11:3, 5, 7)

Tadanori, Taira no (1144–84). Younger brother of Kiyomori, distinguished both as a warrior and as a poet. (1:3; 4:11, 16; 5:11, 13; 7:2, 4, 13, 16, 19; 8:3; 9:14, 18)

Tadayori, Ichijō no Jirō (?–1184). Genji warrior from the province of Kai, challenged by Yoshinaka just before Yoshinaka's death. (4:3; 5:12; 9:4)

Takafusa, Fujiwara no (1148–1209). Ranking Fujiwara noble, son-in-law of Kiyomori and lover of Kogō. (1:5; 4:1–2; 6:3–4; 13:2, 4)

Takatsuna, Sasaki Shirō (?–?). An Ōmi Genji warrior. Received the horse Ikezuki from Yoritomo and rode it first across the Uji River. (9:1, 2, 3, 7)

Tokimasa, Hōjō (1138–1215). Father-in-law of Yoritomo and, like his daughter Masako, a major figure in the Kamakura *bakufu* government that Yoritomo founded. (12:5, 7–8)

Tokitada, Taira no (1128–89). Brother-in-law and distant relative of Kiyomori. Exiled after being captured at Dan-no-ura. (1:4, 10, 16; 3:4; 4:1; 5:1; 7:13, 19; 8:2, 4, 11; 10:3–4; 11:10–11, 13, 15; 12:3)

Tomoe (?–?). In the tale a great warrior under Kiso no Yoshinaka and presumably his mistress. No historical document confirms her existence. (9:4)

Tomomori, Taira no (1152–85). Fourth son of Kiyomori (called "third" in the tale because Motomori, Kiyomori's original second son, was dead by this time) and an outstanding leader in war. Died at Dan-no-ura. (1:5, 15; 2:3; 4:11–12; 5:13; 6:10; 7:4, 12–13, 15; 8:4, 7, 11; 9:11, 17; 10:11, 15; 11:1, 7–9, 10–11, 18; 12:9)

Tsuginobu, Satō Saburōbyōe (1158–85). A warrior from the north, elder brother of Tadanobu, and a close retainer of Yoshitsune. (9:7; 11:1, 3)

Tsunemasa, Taira no (d. 1184). Son of Tsunemori and brother of Atsumori, known for his skill on the biwa. (7:2–3, 17–19; 8:3; 11:10)

Tsunemori, Taira no (1124–85). Younger brother of Kiyomori, father of Tsunemasa and Atsumori. (7:12, 19; 8:3; 9:16–17; 11:10)

Yasuyori, Taira no (?–?). A member of the Shishi-no-tani conspiracy, exiled to Kikai-ga-shima with Naritsune and Shunkan. (1:12; 2:3, 10, 15; 3:2)

Yorimasa, Minamoto no (1104–80). After fighting in the Hōgen and Heiji conflicts, Yorimasa was already old when he drew Prince Mochihito into a failed rebellion against the Heike. (1:11, 15; 4:3–6, 10–12, 14–15; 5:9; 7:10; 11:19)

Yorimori, Taira no (1131–86). Son of Tadamori and a half brother of Kiyomori. Yoritomo promised him protection because his mother was Lady Ike, who saved Yoritomo's life. He therefore stayed in the capital when the Heike fled (1183). The only senior Heike noble to be neither exiled nor executed. (1:15; 3:4, 6; 4:2, 13; 5:1; 7:12, 19; 10:9, 13; 13:5)

Yoritomo, Minamoto no (1147–99). Third son of Minamoto no Yoshitomo, half brother of Noriyori and Yoshitsune, cousin of Yoshinaka. Exiled to Izu after the Heiji Conflict, thanks to the intercession of Lady Ike, he eventually raised rebellion against the Heike and prevailed. Founded the Kamakura *bakufu.* (3:17; 4:3; 5:3–4, 6–7, 10–12; 6:5–7, 12; 7:1–2, 7, 12, 19; 8:4–6, 10–11; 9:1, 3–5, 9–10, 12; 10:3–7, 13–14; 11:1, 7, 10, 14–15, 17–18; 12:2–9)

Yoshinaka, Kiso (Minamoto) no (1154–84). Cousin of Yoritomo and Yoshitsune, usually referred to in the tale, somewhat pejoratively, simply as "Kiso" after his home region or sometimes as "Lord Kiso." Although first into the capital after the Heike flight, he was later killed by Yoritomo's men. (4:3, 14; 6:5–6, 11–12; 7:1–19; 8:1–2, 4–11; 9:1–5; 10:13, 15; 11:1, 17; 12:4; 13:4)

Yoshitomo, Minamoto no (1123–60). Father of Yoritomo, Yoshitsune, and others. Killed in the aftermath of the Heiji Conflict. Yoritomo longed to avenge his death (1:7; 2:6; 4:3, 10; 5:7, 10; 10:1, 4; 11:18; 12:2)

Yoshitsune, Minamoto no (1159–89). Half brother of Yoritomo and one of the most celebrated heroes in Japanese history. Despite his daring successes on Yoritomo's behalf, Yoritomo eventually (beyond the end of the tale) had him pursued into northern Japan and killed. (4:3; 8:11; 9:1, 3, 5, 7–9, 12; 10:1, 5, 14–15; 11:1–8, 10–13, 15–18; 12:3–5, 8)

Yukiie, Minamoto no (?–1186). Yoritomo's uncle and one of his commanders. Originally Yoshimori, he changed his name to Yukiie in 1180. Yoritomo eventually had him killed. (4:3; 7:4, 6, 13; 8:1–2, 9; 9:5; 12:5, 8)

Yukitaka, Fujiwara (Nakayama) no (1130–87). Father of Yukinaga, named in *Essays in Idleness* as the original *Heike* author. Favored by Kiyomori, oversaw rebuilding of the Great Buddha Hall and building of the new capital at Fukuhara. (3:17; 5:1; 6:9)

Yukitsuna, Tada no. The Shishi-no-tani conspirator who revealed the plot to Kiyomori. (1:12–13; 2:3; 3:1; 4:3)

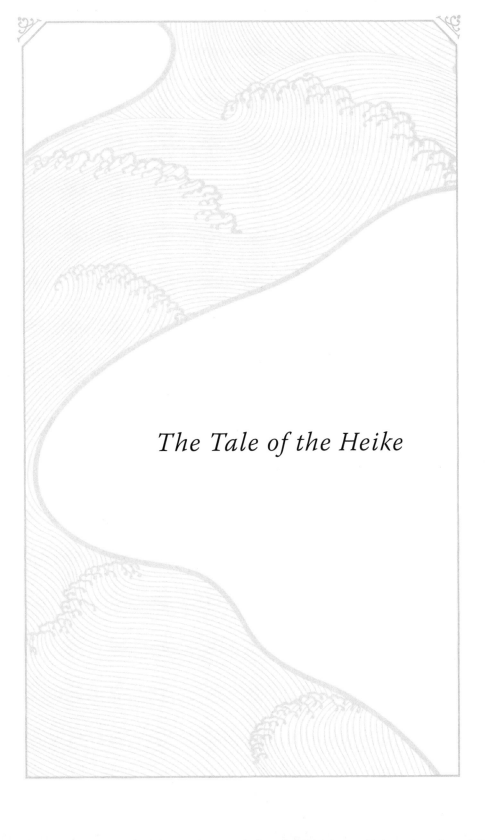

The Tale of the Heike

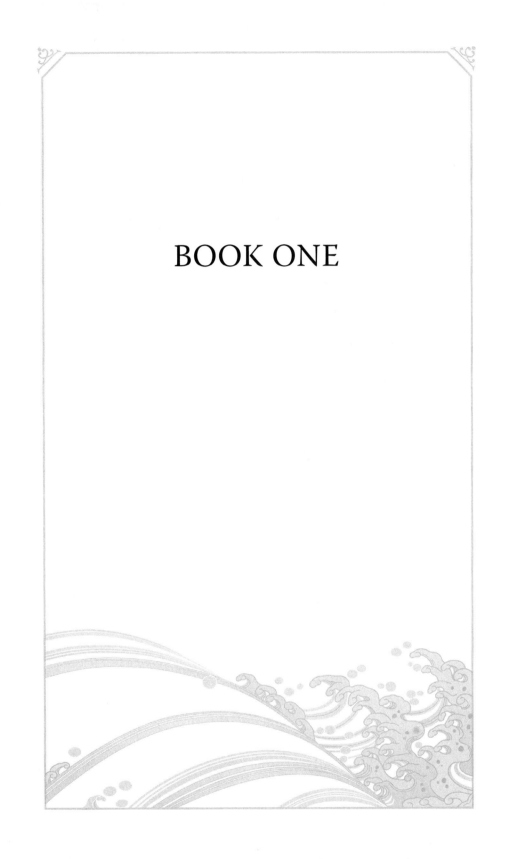

BOOK ONE

1. The Jetavana Temple

(song)

The Jetavana Temple bells
ring the passing of all things.
Twinned sal trees, white in full flower,
declare the great man's certain fall.[1]
The arrogant do not long endure:
They are like a dream one night in spring.
The bold and brave perish in the end:
They are as dust before the wind.
Far away in the Other Realm,[2]
Zhao Gao of Qin, Wang Mang of Han,
Zhu Yi of Liang, Lushan of Tang
spurned the governance established
by their lords of old, by sovereigns past,
sought pleasure and ignored all warnings,
blind to ruin threatening the realm,
deaf to the suffering people's cries.
So it was that they did not last:
Their lot was annihilation.
Closer to us here, in our own land,
Masakado in the Shōhei years, [931–38]
in the Tengyō era Sumitomo, [938–47]
during Kōwa, Yoshichika, [1099–1104]
during Heiji, Nobuyori, [1159–60]
each stood out in pride and valor,
yet all still pale beside that man
among us in the recent past:
the novice monk of Rokuhara,
former chancellor, his lordship

....

1. The Japanese reader must always have heard in the opening lines the familiar boom of a bronze temple bell, but scripturally these bells were silver and glass. At the Jetavana Vihāra (Japanese: Gion Shōja, built for the Buddha by a wealthy patron) they hung at the four corners of the temple infirmary and were rung when a disciple died. At the Buddha's passing the twin-trunked sal trees that stood around where he lay, including their yellow flowers, turned pure white.

2. China. Chinese historical examples, like those that follow, will be annotated only when their general significance is not immediately obvious.

Taira no Kiyomori.

Taira no Kiyomori,
tales of whose deeds and ways
surpass the imagination,
exceed all that the tongue can tell.
What ancestry could this lord claim?
He was the firstborn of Tadamori,
lord of Justice; his grandfather
Masamori, governor of Sanuki,
looked nine generations back
to a prince of the first rank:
Kazurahara, lord of Ceremonial,
the fifth son of Emperor Kanmu. [r. 781–806]
That prince's offspring, Takami,
died without holding rank or office.
His son, known as Takamochi,
first received the surname Taira
with appointment as deputy
to the governor of Kazusa.
Imperial no more, he was a subject.
Next, his son, Yoshimochi,
the guardian of the Northern Marches,[3]
assumed a new name: Kunika.
Six generations followed him,
Kunika down to Masamori,
living as provincial governors.
None of them was ever granted
listing as a privy gentleman.

2. *The Night Attack in the Palace*

(recitative)

So it was until Tadamori, then the governor of Bizen,
put up for Retired Emperor Toba [r. 1107–23]
Tokujōju-in, the temple that His Eminence[4] had vowed to build.
Tadamori made it thirty-three bays long, and within,
he enshrined a thousand and one buddhas.
The dedication took place in Tenshō 1, third month, thirteenth day. [1131]

....

3. The northern provinces of Echizen, Etchū, and Echigo, along the Japan Sea.

4. "His Eminence" will always refer, below, to a retired emperor, just as "His Majesty" refers to a reigning one. A cloistered emperor will be "His Cloistered Eminence."

His Eminence decreed in return
that any governor post then vacant should go to Tadamori.
Tajima, which chanced to be open, became his.
By way of thanks, he also granted Tadamori admission to the palace.
Thus in his thirty-sixth year Tadamori gained this privilege at last.
The jealous cloud dwellers[5] then plotted together:
On the night of the Gosechi Warmth of Wine banquet,[6]
in the twelfth month and on the twenty-third day,
they would arrange to assassinate him.

> Their plot reached Tadamori's ears.
> "I have never been a scribe," he said.
> "No, I was born a warrior,
> and to my house, just as to me,
> sudden shame would be a bitter blow.
> There is, after all, that saying
> that a man's duty is to live
> so as always to serve his lord."
> In this spirit, he prepared to act.

Tadamori went to the palace, a large dagger thrust loosely beneath his robes,
faced the room's shadowy depths,
softly drew it, and held it to his sidelocks.
It gleamed like ice.
Every gentleman present stared, wide-eyed.

> *(speech)*
>
> Among Tadamori's men was one Iesada, a junior officer of the Left
> Watch, a grandson of Sadamitsu (himself once a Taira) of the Bureau
> of Carpentry, and a son of Suefusa, an officer of the Right Ward of the
> city. Under a pale green hunting cloak Iesada wore green-laced armor,
> and he clasped beneath his arm a sword with a bowstring bag at-
> tached. He settled, ready and waiting, into the small court next to the
> hall. The head chamberlain became suspicious of him, and so, too, did
> everyone who saw him.[7]

"You, this side of the rain tank, next to the bell rope,
in the plain hunting cloak: Who are you?
You are out of order! Remove yourself!"
A sixth-rank chamberlain spoke their command.
Iesada replied,

....

5. The nobles who frequent the emperor's "cloud palace" (*kumoi*).

6. Toyo-no-akari, an annual event associated with the Niinamesai (First Fruits Festival) or, in an accession
year, the Daijōsai (Enthronement Festival).

7. Iesada's unmarked hunting cloak betrays him as lacking authorization to enter the palace.

"My lord from generations past,
the governor of Bizen province,
has heard that there may be tonight
an attempt made against his life.
I am here in case he should need me.
I cannot possibly leave now." He would not move.
     The conspirators must have seen
that their plot had come to nothing.
That night there was no attack.
     Called by His Eminence to dance,
Tadamori responded promptly,
at which the company sang a new song:
          "This Taira from Ise:
          Look at his squinty eyes!"—
words fraught with a double meaning:
          "This wine jug from Ise:
          It's just a vinegar jar!"
And it is true enough: The Taira—
be this said with all due respect—
while descended from Emperor Kanmu,
had come to live far from the city,
as local squires in Ise province.
There was nothing that Tadamori could do.
He slipped from the hall before the music ended.
Behind the emperor's residence, in plain view of some privy gentlemen,
he called over a lady palace official and had her take his dagger.
Only then did he leave. Iesada was waiting for him.
     "What happened, my lord?" Iesada asked.
     Tadamori wanted to tell him the story,
but he knew that if he did, a man like Iesada would charge into the hall,
brandishing his murderous sword.
"Nothing," he answered.
     Gosechi merriment as a rule
     involves singing light, amusing songs:
          "Paper white and fine,
          paper purple-dyed,
          gaily thread-wound brushes,
          brushes lacquer-handled,
          painted with swirl-patterns . . ."
and other ditties in that vein.
But there lived not that long ago

a gentleman named Lord Suenaka,
a provisional Dazaifu viceroy,
so dark-complected that his familiars
knew him only as Viceroy Black.
In his early, head-chamberlain days,
Suenaka, too, danced his Gosechi dance;
at which the company, in the same way,
struck up a new song, all their own:

> "Black, black is the color,
> black the color of the Head:
> What manner of man, pray,
> lacquered him so black?"

Then there was Lord Tadamasa, a former chancellor.
Tadamasa was in only his tenth year when he lost his father, the counselor
   Tadamune.
Lord Fujiwara no Ienari, still the governor of Harima,
took him as a son-in-law and made much of him.
When *he* did his Gosechi dance, all sang,

> "This Harima rice
> must be pure scouring rush,
> pure *muku*-leaf brush,
> the way it brings up a youngster's shine!"

"Yes," people conceded, "things like that did go on in those days.
Nothing actually happened, though.
In this latter age, you never know what to expect.
There could be trouble."

> Sure enough, once the Gosechi festivities were over, the privy gen-
> tlemen protested with one voice, "To appear at an imperial banquet
> equipped with a dagger or to frequent the palace with an armed
> attendant—such things are permitted only in conformity with rules
> and regulations. They require the emperor's express authorization.
> Lord Tadamori, however, joined the Gosechi company with a warrior
> in a plain hunting cloak, supposedly a hereditary retainer of his, posted
> in the small court beside the hall and with a dagger at his side. Both of-
> fenses are unprecedented, and each compounds the other. Leniency is
> out of the question.

He must be struck from the roster at once and dismissed from his duties."
The astonished retired emperor called Tadamori in for questioning.
Tadamori respectfully replied,

> "As far as that man of mine is concerned,
> stationed to serve me in the small court,

I never knew that he was there.
But there have been rumors, lately,
concerning a plot against my life;
and he, being an old retainer,
in all likelihood heard them, too,
so that he acted to spare me shame
without breathing a word to *me*.
I could do nothing to stop him.
Shall I summon and deliver him to you, if he has erred?
Then there is the dagger. I entrusted it to a palace lady.
You might call for it and weigh the matter by considering whether or
    not it is real."
His Eminence agreed. He called for the dagger and examined it:
Scabbard and handle were no doubt black lacquer,
but the blade was only silver foil over wood.

"Keen to avoid threatened dishonor,
he showed himself armed with a dagger,
yet knew doing so might lead to charges,
so prudently gave it a wooden blade.
This was a stroke of genius!
All those who in life wield bow and arrow
should show equal sense in what they do.
As for that man of his in the small court,
that is what a warrior's man does.
Tadamori has committed no offense."
The retired emperor was so impressed
that all talk of punishment ceased.

3. *The Sea Bass*

Tadamori's sons all became second-in-command of a corps of guards,
and now that they had admission to the palace,
no one could object to their being there.
Tadamori came up to the capital again from Bizen.
"How did the Akashi coast strike you?" Retired Emperor Toba asked.

Aloft in the dawn
the moon shone down Akashi
coast, while the sea wind
dashed upon the brightening shore
waves dark with the last of night,

Tadamori answered, to his patron's delight.

The poem went into *A Collection of Golden Leaves*.[8]

Tadamori was visiting at his patron's palace a gentlewoman whom he adored.

Once he forgot in her room a fan that bore on its edge a painted moon.

"Where is this moon from?" the others asked, laughing.

"We were wondering where you got it."

She answered,

> *This moon you mention*
> *happened to steal in to me*
> *from above the clouds,*[9]
> *sealing at a stroke my lips*
> *to further revelations.*

For that poem he loved her even more.

The son she gave him was Tadanori,

the future governor of Satsuma.

Birds of a feather flock together,

so they say, and Tadamori

had an eye for the very best:

For that is exactly what she was.

So it was that Tadamori became the lord of Justice. He died in his fifty-eighth year, on the fifteenth of the first month of Ninpei 3. [1153] Kiyomori, his eldest son, succeeded him. In the seventh month of Hōgen 1, [1156] the Uji Left Minister provoked unrest, and Kiyomori, who then governed Aki, so distinguished himself in His Majesty's service that he moved as governor to Harima. Appointment as the Dazaifu deputy followed in Hōgen 3. [1158]

Then in the first year of Heiji, Lord Nobuyori raised rebellion, [1159]

and in the twelfth month Kiyomori led imperial forces to quell the rebels.

Many a deed of signal valor, and his consequent claim to weighty reward,

won him the following year senior third rank.

Next, in succession he rose from consultant

to intendant of the Gate Watch,

police superintendent, counselor,

grand counselor, and then minister.

Not for him either left or right:

No, he rose straight to palace minister,

then to chancellor at junior first rank.

....

8. *Kin'yōshū* (1127), an imperially commissioned anthology of *waka* poetry. The syllables of the place-name Akashi also form the word that means "bright," hence a wordplay of a kind fundamental to the practice of classical verse.

9. From the palace.

Never granted the post of commander,[10]
he was nonetheless given leave
to travel as he pleased with armed guards.
An imperial decree granted him, too,
use of an ox carriage and a hand carriage;[11]
and in and out the palace gate,
borne in his carriage, he went, like a regent.
The statute reads, "In the chancellor
the emperor finds his proper teacher
and the four seas[12] their paragon.
He governs the realm, expounds the way,
and attunes the yin and the yang.
Should no one suitable be at hand,
the office is to be left vacant."
Hence the office's jocular name:
People call it the "Left Vacancy."
This was certainly no position
for the wrong appointee to sully;
but Kiyomori held in his hands
at once the realm and the four seas,
and nobody could gainsay him.
They say that the Heike owed their success to the god of Kumano.
The story goes that, while still governor of Aki,
Kiyomori was sailing down the Ise coast to call at the Kumano shrines
when a huge sea bass jumped straight into his boat.
The ascetic guiding his pilgrimage cried,
    "This fish is a boon from the gods!
    You must partake of it at once!"
    Kiyomori replied, "Of old, they say,
    a white fish leaped into the boat
    carrying King Wu of Zhou.
    Yes, this is an excellent omen."
    On the way he had taken care
    to keep the ten precepts,[13] eschewing flesh,
    yet now he prepared the fish to eat
    and shared it out with all his men.

....

10. Commander of the Left or Right Palace Guards, an intensely coveted post.
11. A two-wheeled palanquin used within the palace grounds by personages of the highest dignity.
12. The whole world.
13. The fundamental Buddhist rules of virtuous conduct.

Perhaps that is why unblemished fortune
lifted him even to chancellor.
His children, too, rose faster in office
than a dragon can mount the clouds.
Outstripping nine generations this way
made him a model of shining success.

4. *The Rokuhara Boys*

In time Lord Kiyomori fell ill. To lengthen his days,
he renounced the world in his fifty-first year, Nin'an 3, [1168]
on the eleventh month and day.
He became a novice monk with the religious name Jōkai.
Perhaps this step took effect, for his prolonged discomfort ceased
and his allotted span of years remained unbroken.
Men bowed to his will as grass to the wind.
The world looked up to him as the land looks up to the blessings of rain.
As for his sons, no scion of a great house,
no stellar talent could look them in the eye or stand equal beside them.
Indeed Tokitada, the Taira grand counselor and Kiyomori's son-in-law, said,
"No one else really counts as human at all."
No wonder everyone sought, by hook or by crook, alliance with the Heike.
All alive within the four seas mimicked the ways of Rokuhara,[14]
down to the mere cut of a robe or crease of a hat.

     Now the sway of the sage king,
     the reign of the wise sovereign,
     the steady guidance of the regent
     still fail to reach degenerates
     who, where nobody can hear them,
     mouth foul slander and rebellion,
     for some people are just like that;
     not, though, under Kiyomori.
     In his day there was no loose talk.
And this is why.
Lord Kiyomori chose three hundred youths
in their mid-teens, with a boy's short-trimmed hair,
and dressed them in red. They were everywhere in the city.
If anyone spoke ill of the Heike and no such youth overheard him,
well and good. Otherwise the report went out.

....

14. Kiyomori's residence compound in the capital.

They would burst into the offender's house, seize goods and chattels,
arrest him, and drag him off to Rokuhara.
People saw what they saw and thought their thoughts, but no one spoke.
"The Rokuhara Boys," everyone called them.
Riders and carriages gave them wide berth.
They might march straight in through the gate of the palace,
    and still no one dared even ask their names.
    The city elders seemed to avert their gaze.

5. One Man's Glory

One man had scaled the heights of glory,
and with him prospered his whole house.
Shigemori, the first of his sons,
was palace minister and left commander;
his second, Munemori, counselor
and at the same time right commander;
while his third son, Tomomori,
held the third rank and the post of captain.
His eldest grandson, Koremori,
held the fourth rank as a lieutenant.
Sixteen senior nobles were Taira,
and of the privy gentlemen, thirty;
while sixty more served as governors,
guards officers, or diverse officials.
No other house seemed to exist.
There was established in Jinki 5, during the reign of Emperor Shōmu, [729] [r. 724–49]
a Central Guard for the sovereign, with a commander.
In Daidō 4 this corps was renamed Palace Guard, and since those days [806]
brothers have only three or four times led both its left and right divisions.
In the reign of Emperor Montoku, [r. 850–58]
the right minister, Yoshifusa,
commanded the left, and Yoshiō,
a grand counselor then, the right:
both men were sons of Fuyutsugi,
the Kan'in minister of the left.
In the reign of Emperor Suzaku, [r. 930–46]
Saneyori, Lord Ononomiya,
commanded the left division
and Morosuke, Lord Kujō, the right;
these men were sons of Tadahira.

In the days of Emperor Go-Reizei [r. 1045–68]
Norimichi, Lord Ōnijō, took the left
and Yorimune, Lord Horikawa, the right;
both men were sons of Michinaga.
In the reign of Emperor Nijō, [r. 1158–65]
the left followed Motofusa, Lord Matsu,
the right Kanezane, Lord Tsukinowa.
Tadamichi was the father of both.
All belonged to the line of regents.
No lesser house could boast the same.
Now a grandson of Tadamori—
once, for his access to the palace,
fiercely resented—sported at will
finery in the forbidden colors,
damask, brocade, and embroidered silks,
and held dual office, minister and commander,
while the other commander was his brother.
Even in these latter, degenerate days,
all this remained exceedingly strange.
Kiyomori had eight daughters, too, and fortune smiled on them all.
One was betrothed in her eighth year to the Sakuramachi counselor,
Lord Shigenori, but the Heiji Conflict ended that.
Instead she went as senior wife
to the left minister, Kanemasa, and bore many children.
Now people dubbed Shigenori "Sakuramachi" because,
fastidious as he was in his tastes, he loved the Yoshino cherry blossoms,
planted rows of Yoshino cherry trees in his grounds,
built a retreat among them, and took up residence there.
Those who saw his blossoms each spring spoke of Sakuramachi, the Cherry Grove.

 Blossoms fall after seven days.
 Saddened to lose them, Shigenori
 prayed so hard to the Bright Sun Goddess
 that *his* endured three times longer.
 Our emperor, too, being a sage king,
 the goddess let divine virtue shine,
 and the blossoms understood her:
 They lasted all of twenty days.
  A second daughter became empress
 and gave His Majesty a son,
 first heir apparent, then enthroned;
 so she was called Kenreimon-in.

Beyond being Kiyomori's daughter,
she was the mother of the realm.
Of her, one need hardly say more.

> The third daughter of Lord Kiyomori became senior wife to the regent
> Motozane. She acted during the reign of Emperor Takakura as his fos-
> ter mother, and she received an edict appointing her honorary em-
> press. A grand figure, she was called Lady Shirakawa. The fourth
> daughter likewise married the regent Motomichi and the fifth the
> grand counselor Takafusa. The sixth married the director of upkeep,
> Lord Nobutaka.

Another daughter, from an Itsukushima Shrine maiden in Aki,
went to Cloistered Emperor Go-Shirakawa and lived like an imperial consort.
The last one, from Tokiwa, a maid at the residence of Lady Kujō,
oversaw for Lord Kanemasa his staff of gentlewomen.
"The Mistress of the Gallery," people called her.

> This, our island land of Japan,
> has only sixty-six provinces,
> and the Heike ruled over thirty.
> Half the realm and more was theirs,
> quite apart from all their estates,
> their countless fields, paddy and dry.
> Precious silk, damask, and gauze
> like flowers overflowed their halls.
> Horses and carriages thronged their gates,
> as though gathered there for market day.
> Yangzhou gold, pearls from Jingzhou,
> Wujun damasks and Shujiang brocades—
> the treasures of the world were theirs.
> Pavilions for singing, halls for dancing,
> magic shows and circus amusements—
> no emperor, reigning or retired,
> could have enjoyed more varied pleasures.

6. Giō

Lord Kiyomori, who held in his hands the world within the four seas,
dismissed censure, ignored mockery, and indulged every odd whim.
For instance, two *shirabyōshi* dancers were then the talk of the town:
Giō and Ginyo, daughters of the dancer Toji.
Giō, the elder, was Kiyomori's favorite, so people prized Ginyo as well.
He built Giō's mother a fine house and provided her monthly

with rice in the amount of one hundred bushels and one hundred strings of cash.
The household prospered and lived very comfortably.

> In our land *shirabyōshi* dancing
> began in Emperor Toba's reign,
> long ago, when a pair of women,
> Shima no Senzai and Waka no Mai,
> first devised it. They wore in those days
> *suikan* robes; tall, black-lacquered hats;
> daggers silver-trimmed, hilt and scabbard;
> and called this dance of theirs "Manly Grace."
> But hat and dagger dropped out in time,
> leaving only the *suikan* robe;
> hence the current name: *shirabyōshi*.[15]

Every *shirabyōshi* dancer in the capital learned of Giō's success.
Some envied her, others were jealous.
"Oh, she's a lucky girl, that Giō Gozen!" the envious cried.
"Who wouldn't want to be just like her?
I know: The only reason she's done so well is that *gi* in her name.
I'll use it, too!"
One dubbed herself Giichi, another Gini, others Gifuku, Gitoku, and so on.
"How could anyone succeed on the mere strength of a name?"
the jealous objected. "It all depends on the karma you bring from past lives."
So many also ignored the *gi*.

> This had been going on for three years when another famous *shirabyōshi* dancer appeared in the capital. She was from Kaga province, and her name was Hotoke. This was her sixteenth year. Everyone in the city, high or low, praised her to the skies. "There have always been plenty of *shirabyōshi* around," they kept saying, "but never one who could dance like this!"
>
> Hotoke Gozen remarked, "Everyone everywhere has heard of me, but it is disappointing that Lord Kiyomori, who stands so high in the world these days, has not yet called me to his residence. I shall go there on my own, as entertainers do. I see no reason not to."
>
> So off she went to Nishi-Hachijō.[16]

"Your Excellency," they told him, "Hotoke Gozen is here. Everyone in the city
knows her."
"Here?" exclaimed Kiyomori. "She's an entertainer—she comes when called.

....

15. *Shirabyōshi* entertainers were certainly popular in Kiyomori's time, but the meaning of the word remains unclear. Alas, this passage does *not* explain it.

16. A second residence of Kiyomori's, located north of Hachijō and west of Ōmiya.

The nerve of her, to turn up uninvited! *Kami* or *hotoke*, god or buddha,
she has no business appearing in Giō's presence. Send her away!"
Hotoke, bluntly dismissed, was leaving when Giō addressed her lord and
     master:

> "It is normal for any dancer
>   to present herself uninvited.
> Besides, they say she is only a girl.
> Now that she has come so bravely,
>   you are too harsh to order her gone.
> I would feel sorrow and shame for her!
> Her profession is mine. I understand.
> You need not have her dance or sing,
>   but it would simply be a kindness
> at least to see her before she goes.
> Do please, this once, call her back."

"Fine, fine," Kiyomori replied. "I'll get her back and ask her in,
if you feel that strongly about it." He sent someone after her.
Hotoke Gozen was in her carriage, leaving after that sharp rebuff,
when his summons reached her. She turned back and entered.
He came forward to greet her.
"I didn't mean to see you today," he said,
"but for some reason Giō insisted, so in the end I humored her.
Now that you're here, I might as well hear your voice. Sing me an *imayō*."[17]
"As you wish, my lord," she said. And she did.

> "Seeing you, my lord, this way,
>   as never before,
> a maiden pine feels the gift
>   of a thousand years.
> On the Tortoise Island rock
>   rising from your lake,
> cranes gather in flocks, it seems,
>   for their own delight."[18]

> She sang the song through three times,
>   amazing everyone who heard her.

Lord Kiyomori seemed captivated.
"You can certainly sing *imayō*! You must be quite a dancer, too.
Dance for me, then! Get us a drummer!"
She did him a dance to the beat of a drum.

....

17. A kind of popular song especially current at the time of the tale, the late twelfth century.
18. Pines, tortoises, and cranes all stand for happy longevity.

Hotoke Gozen dancing. At lower left: Giō. Behind her: Ginyo. At upper right: Munemori (left) and Shigemori (right). Below them: Norimori. Kiyomori is too grand to be shown.

Hotoke Gozen was a true beauty:
her hair, her face, her lovely figure,
her deliciously lilting voice.
Her dancing could not have failed to please.
By the time she had finished her dance—
most unwillingly—Lord Kiyomori,
entranced, could think only of *her*.
"I hardly know what to say, my lord," Hotoke protested.
"When I came, I did so unasked and was ordered to leave.
Only Giō Gozen's intercession moved you to call me back.
I blush to imagine her feelings if you keep me. Please allow me to withdraw."
    "Certainly not," answered Lord Kiyomori.
"Does Giō being here bother you? Then Giō will have to go."
"But, my lord," said Hotoke, "how *could* you?
It would be painful enough if you were to keep me here with her,
but I hate to imagine her opinion of me if you keep me alone.
If you do not forget me, my lord,
        then I will come again when you call.
        But today," she pleaded, "I beg to go."
He answered, "You will do no such thing.

Giō, leave immediately!"
He had her brought this order three times.
She had long known it might end this way
but never thought "yesterday or today."[19]
Repeated commands to "get out now!"
decided her, but, she told herself,
"not until I tidy my room
and remove anything unsightly."
It is never easy to part,
even for two who have only met
briefly, sheltering under a tree
or sharing the water from a stream,
and harder still after three years
spent sharing all of life together.
Giō, heartsick, shed tears in vain.
She could not stay. No, it was time;
but first (perhaps thinking to leave

Giō writes her poem on the sliding door.

19. From Ariwara no Narihira's "death poem" in episode 125 of *Ise monogatari* (tenth century): "That this path is ours, / every one of us, to take, / I heard long ago, / yet never imagined then, / yesterday, or today." Translation from Joshua S. Mostow and Royall Tyler, *The Ise Stories: Ise monogatari* (Honolulu: University of Hawaii Press, 2010), p. 247.

something of hers, after all, behind)
she wrote, weeping, on a sliding door,
> New shoots emerging,
> wilting fronds are equally
> grasses of the field,
> destined, every one, to feel
> the withering touch of fall.

She rode home again in her carriage
and collapsed, sobbing, within her doors.
"What is the matter?" her mother and sister
begged to know, but she could not answer.
Only the maid who had been with her
was able to tell them the story.
Soon the monthly rice and strings of cash stopped coming.
Now it was Hotoke Gozen's relations who tasted at last the good life.
"They say his lordship's sent Giō packing":
This word went around the city.
"Good!" people said. "Let's go and see her. Let's have some fun!"
Some sent her letters, others approached her through messengers,
but Giō had no wish as things stood to see or entertain anyone.
She accepted none of the letters and of course turned every messenger back.
All this only made her feel worse, and she spent more and more time in tears.

So that year came to an end. The following spring Lord Kiyomori sent a man to Giō with this message: "How have you been getting on? Hotoke Gozen seems very bored. Come and cheer her up. Sing her some *imayō* songs and dance for her."

Giō did not even reply.

"Why don't you answer me, Giō?" Lord Kiyomori demanded to know. "So you won't come? Just say so, then. I have an idea how to deal with you."

This upset Toji, Giō's mother. In fear of what might come next,
she begged her daughter, in tears, "Oh, Giō, do *please* answer him,
instead of provoking him this way!" To which Giō:

"Had I the slightest wish to go,
I would send him word to expect me,
but since I most certainly do not,
I cannot think how to reply.
He knows just what to do, he says,
if I refuse. I suppose he means
he will expel me from the city
or claim my life—one or the other.

Expulsion would not trouble me;
as for my life, he is welcome to it.
Now that he is finished with me,
I want never to see him again."
No, she would not send him an answer.
Her mother pleaded with her once more. "As everyone knows," she said,
"you simply cannot live in this land and safely ignore Lord Kiyomori's wishes.
The troubles that crop up between men and women are nothing new.

Some promise each other endless love
only in the next moment to part;
for others, what seemed a passing affair
unites them for the rest of their lives.
Nothing is so unfathomable
as the ways of men and women.

Besides, he was very fond of you for three years, and you should be grateful for that. Ignoring his summons could not possibly cost you your life. No, he will only expel you from the capital. You are young, you and your sister, and you will get on well enough out there among the rocks and trees. Your poor old mother will be expelled, too, though, and for *her* it is misery just to imagine life out in the wilds. Oh, please allow my life to end in the city! Then I will know you are filial in this life and the next!"

To Giō the thought was unbearable, but she could not bring herself to disappoint her mother. She set out in tears of pathetic distress. Going alone would have been too painful, so Ginyo went with her. Their party of four, including two other dancers, reached Nishi-Hachijō in one carriage.

She was led not to her usual seat but to one far down from the place of honor.
"I don't understand," she said to herself. "I have done nothing wrong,
yet I find myself not merely rejected but seated ignominiously low.
This is too cruel! What am I to do?"
She pressed a sleeve to her eyes to hide her tears, but they still trickled through.
Hotoke saw, and she felt very sorry.
"This is not right!" she said. "It is not as though you had never summoned her
    before.
Please bring her up here, or else let me go to her myself."
"Certainly not," Kiyomori replied.
Hotoke could do no more. She left it at that.
Kiyomori then spoke to Giō, in utter disregard of her feelings.
"How are you getting on these days?" he said.
"Hotoke seems very bored. I want you to sing her an *imayō*."

In his presence Giō knew that she could not refuse.
Fighting back tears, she sang this song:

> "The Buddha himself, long ago
>   was like anyone,
> and we ourselves, in time to come,
>   will be buddhas, too.
> What misery it is to share,
>   as we do, the buddha nature
> yet to be so far removed
>   from that happy state!"

Weeping, she sang the song through twice,
and the assembled Taira lords—
senior nobles, privy gentlemen,
ranking officials, retainers, too—
all of them wept with emotion.

Lord Kiyomori looked pleased. "You got the feeling just right," he said.
"I'd gladly see you dance, too, but I'm busy today. Something has come up.
Don't wait for another invitation. I want you here often,
to cheer Hotoke up with your dancing and singing."
Giō could not manage an answer. She left, pressing her sleeves to her eyes.
"I shrank from disobeying my mother and set out on a painful errand,
only to suffer a new blow. It is too much! More blows will follow if I go on.
No, my mind is made up: I will throw myself into the water and drown."
So she spoke. Ginyo replied, "If you drown yourself, my sister, I will, too."
Their horrified mother wondered what was to become of them all.
She wept as she strove again to talk sense into Giō.
"You have every reason to blame him," she said.
"I never imagined such a thing, and I deeply regret having convinced you to go.
But Ginyo says that she will drown herself, too, if you do.
Then your poor old mother will have lost both her daughters,
and her life will mean nothing anymore. So she will join you.
To drive your mother to drown herself before her appointed time—
that *must* be one of the five deadly sins.[20]
We lodge in this life only briefly.
Whether or not we suffer humiliation hardly matters,
beside the darkness of lives to come. Whatever trials this one may bring,
consider the horror of passing from it into the evil realms!"[21]

....

20. Patricide, matricide, killing a saint, injuring a buddha, or sowing discord among the community of monks.
21. Those of hell, hungry ghosts, and beasts.

She argued her case with passionate tears.
Giō replied, trying not to cry, "When you put it like that, yes,
I would indeed commit one of those crimes. So I will not take my life.
But more miseries will follow if I stay in the capital. I will leave at once."
      Giō became a nun in her twenty-first year.
      In the hills beyond Sagano,[22]
      she put together a brushwood hut
      and made her home there, calling the Name.
      In only her nineteenth year, Ginyo,
      her younger sister, did the same,
      saying, "I promised to drown myself
      with you, if ever you took that step.
      Now I am just as glad as you
      to reject the world and its ways."
      In retreat with her sister, Giō,
      she prayed for bliss in the hereafter:
      a moving sight that touched their mother.
      Toji, now that her girls were nuns,
      knew her white hair was no excuse.
      In her forty-fifth year, she shaved it
      and, in company with her daughters,
      gave herself to calling the Name,
      longing for birth in paradise.
      So spring fled, summer blazed,
      and autumn winds began to blow—
      when, our eyes lifted heavenward
      toward the meeting of the Stars,
      we write down our fondest wish
      on a mulberry-paper slip
      slender as that lover's oar,
      rowing across the celestial stream.[23]
      The sun sank westward down the sky,
      toward the ridgeline of the hills,
      bringing to mind what they say:
      that it drops straight from our sight
      into the Western Paradise.
      Ah, we, too, the sisters sighed,

....

22. "Saga moor." Saga is a broad area west of the city.

23. These lines evoke the Tanabata festival on the seventh night of the seventh lunar month. The Herd Boy star then rows across the River of Heaven (the Milky Way) to spend that one night of the year with his love, the Weaver Maid.

shall be born there in good time,
to life beyond the weight of care!
But all too often in their thoughts
they dwelled on sorrow from the past,
and their tears flowed on and on.
Now twilight faded into dark.
They barred at last their wattled door,
lit the flame of their dim lamp,
and were all three calling the Name
when suddenly they heard a knock.
Terrified, they cried together,
"How awful! Some demon thing
has come—no, no, there is no doubt!—
to frustrate our humble prayers!
By daylight, even, no one comes
to visit such a brushwood hut,
tucked away in this far village.
Who, then, would call by dark of night?
It is so light, our bamboo door!
Why, anyone could break it down!
No, we had better open it.
If, a stranger to all mercy,
that thing has come to claim our lives,
then our only hope is trust
in Amida's Original Vow,
so long our refuge anyway,
and in ceaseless calling of his Name.
They say that with his host of saints
he comes to where he hears that cry
and welcomes the believing soul.
Then shall that welcome not be ours?
Now call the Name and never pause!"
Each urging the others to be brave,
they did indeed open the door.
No demon stood there before them:
It was Hotoke Gozen.

    "What? Hotoke Gozen? Am I dreaming? Is this real?"

    Hotoke fought back her tears. "It may shock you to hear all this," she answered, "but it would be wrong of me not to tell you. So here is the whole story. It was entirely my idea to present myself at Lord Kiyo-mori's residence, and when I did, I was ordered to leave. Only your intervention convinced him to call me back. We women can so seldom follow our wishes! I wanted to leave, but he made me stay. I hated it. And then one day he got you back, and you sang an *imayō*. That brought it all home to me: One day the same would happen to *me*. I did not like that at all. And then there was the poem you left on the sliding door, the one that said 'destined, every one, to feel the withering touch of fall.' I knew you were right.

I did not know where you had gone,
but I envied you, once I heard that you had all become nuns together.
I kept asking for leave to go, but he always refused.

    Reflection reveals worldly glory
for what it is: a dream in a dream.
Pleasure and riches are vanity.
Human birth is a rare privilege;
so, too, hearing the Buddha's Teaching.
Should I now fall to the pit of hell,
no aeons of lives might raise me again;
nor can youth save me, for many die young,
and breathing out never assures
that the breath will pass in again.
Summer heat shimmer, a flash of lightning:
Life vanishes still more swiftly.

    I could not bear to ignore the life to come just for the sake of a moment's pleasure; so this morning I stole away, to come to you as you see me now." She slipped the robe from over her head, and there she was: already a nun. "Please forgive me my past misdeeds now that I am with you in this new guise. Say that you will, and I will call the Name with you, until we are reborn together on the same lotus throne. If you prefer not to, then I will wander wherever my steps lead me, until I collapse on the moss beneath some pine, there to call the Name while I still have breath and achieve that priceless rebirth in paradise." She spoke in tears.

    Giō pressed her sleeves to her eyes.
"Why, I never imagined you feeling that way! I had no idea!
Life is hard for us all, and I should have accepted what happened to me
solely as my own misfortune; but there have been times
when the thought of *you* made me so bitter
I knew I would never get where I longed to go.
I felt like a failure in this life and the next. But now here you are, so changed
that that stubborn weakness of mine is gone.
I *will* be reborn in paradise.

Hotoke Gozen comes to Giō's hut.

What a joy it is, to be certain that I will reach my goal!
When we became nuns people said, and I agreed,
that no one like us had ever done such a thing before.
The decision made sense enough—I was angry with life and with myself—
but it was nothing compared to *your* renouncing the world.
You nursed no grudge or sorrow. In only your seventeenth year,
you have mastered aversion to this polluted world and longing for the Pure Land.
That, to me, is powerful aspiration indeed.
Welcome, then, friend and guide in the Teaching!

> Come, let us all pray together!"
> The four of them, confined in retreat,
> decked the altar morning and evening
> with offerings of incense and flowers,
> praying with single-minded devotion
> until each in her time reached her goal,
> or so they say. And, sure enough,
> at the Chōgō-dō, the chapel
> of Cloistered Emperor Go-Shirakawa,
> the death register lists the four,
> all together, as departed:
> Giō, Ginyo, Hotoke, Toji.
> Their story is profoundly moving.

7. Empress to Two Sovereigns

From ancient times to this day, the Heike and Genji
have jointly chastised in His Majesty's service anyone who flouted his will.
Thus the realm long remained undisturbed.
But after Tameyoshi was slain during the Hōgen years [1156-59]
and during Heiji Yoshitomo, too, came to grief, [1159-60]
their Genji successors were all exiled or killed.
The Heike alone flourished. No one stood against them.
Their triumph seemed assured for all time.

> However, a succession of armed skirmishes followed Retired Emperor
> Toba's passing. There were repeated executions, banishments, and dis-
> missals from office. The world within the seas was not at peace. Inse-
> curity still reigned. During the Eiryaku and Ōhō years [1160-63] especially,
> imperial reprimands began reaching the circle around Retired Em-
> peror Go-Shirakawa, while those around the reigning emperor [Nijō]
> began receiving expressions of Go-Shirakawa's displeasure. Each man
> addressed, high or low, trembled with fear, like one poised on the brink

of an abyss or treading on thin ice. The two emperors, reigning and re-
tired, should have been of one mind in all things, since they were father
and son, but strange incidents occurred. This was because the world
had entered a degenerate age, and men gave pride of place to evil ways.
The reigning emperor rejected time and again what his father had to say,
and one among the issues between them caused widespread shock and scandal.

> Her Grand Imperial Majesty,
> empress to the late Konoe, [24] [r.1141–55]
> was a daughter of Lord Kin'yoshi,
> the Ōi-no-mikado right minister.
> Once bereaved, she left the palace
> for her home at Konoe-kawara.

Empress no longer, she lived quietly, out of the light.
By the Eiryaku years she was somewhat past her prime, [1160–61]
being then perhaps in her twenty-second or -third year,
but people still called her the greatest beauty in the land,
and the emperor, who, with his single-minded passion for women,
secretly had his own Gao Lishi scouting for prospects beyond the palace,
wrote her love letters. When she ignored them, he made himself perfectly clear:
He issued her father a decree demanding her for palace service.[25]
For the realm this was a grave matter.
The senior nobles met in council, each to state his view.
"Consider first a precedent from the Other Realm:

> In China there was Zetian,
> empress to Taizong of Tang
> and stepmother to Gaozong,
> who became, after Taizong died,
> empress to Gaozong, too.
> This is a foreign precedent
> and constitutes a special case.

In our realm, however, in the more than seventy reigns after Emperor Jinmu,
there is no such example of anyone being empress twice."
So with one voice the lords declared.
The retired emperor disapproved, too, and sought to dissuade his successor.
His Majesty declared, "The Son of Heaven has no mother or father.
I owe the priceless office of supreme command
to merit gained from upholding the ten excellent precepts.

....

24. Fujiwara no Tashi (1136?–1201) was appointed empress by Konoe in 1150.

25. Gao Lishi, a Tang court official, discovered the beautiful Yang Guifei for Emperor Xuanzong. In
Heian Japan an eligible young woman who "entered the palace" or "entered palace service" became an
imperial wife.

On so inconsequential a matter,
why should your emperor not have his wish?"
Forthwith he decreed the very day [in 1160]
when she was to enter the palace.
The retired emperor could do no more.
From the lady this news drew many tears.
"That autumn of Kyūju, when I lost him— [1154-56]
if only I, too," she lamented, "had vanished
like dew from the moors or left the world!
Then I would hear no such hateful talk!"
Her father, the minister, sought to reconcile her to her plight.
He began, "I have read that those who refuse to bend to the world are mad.
The edict has been issued. There is no room for representations.
You must go at once to the palace. You have no other choice.
Perhaps this is a happy sign that you will be called the mother of the realm,
if only you bear him a prince,
and that I, old and foolish as I am, may still be revered as an emperor's grandfather.
You could render your father no more filial service."
So he addressed her, but she never replied.
In those days, during casual writing practice, her brush formed these words:

> That gulf of sorrow
> failed to swallow me, and now
> must the stream of life
> sweep me on to spread abroad
> a name never heard before?

People got wind of her poem somehow,
and all agreed that her touching fate
cried out for sympathy.
The day came: She was to enter the palace and serve the emperor.
Her father attended with care to her escort of senior nobles
and to all the display carriages[26] in her train.
She had too little heart for the journey to board hers promptly.
Midnight had passed when at last they helped her into her carriage.
Thereafter she resided in the Reikeiden.
She regularly urged His Majesty not to neglect the morning council.[27]

> Sliding panels in the Shishinden
> or in other such palace pavilions

....

26. The women riding in a "display carriage" arrange to flaunt as much as possible their beautiful trailing sleeves and skirts.

27. A stock trait of the good empress, who loyally recalls the emperor to sterner duties after a night of tender pleasures.

pictured the great sages of China:
Yi Tin, Diwu Lun, Yu Shinan, Li Ji,
Taigong Wang, Sima, the learned Luli.
Other paintings, elsewhere, depicted
long-armed, long-legged men and horses.
In the Demon Room, a painted hero
slew a demon, and the guards' office
displayed a likeness of General Li.
Ono no Michikaze, who governed Owari,
wrote that he redid seven times,
and no wonder, the sages' inscriptions.[28]
On one door of the Seiryōden,
long ago, Kanaoka apparently painted
far-off hills and the moon at dawn,
but Emperor Konoe, as a child,
had for his mischievous amusement
daubed ink all over the moon;
and there it was, just as it had been.
The sight must have recalled to her
a flood of fond memories.

> *Little did I think,*
> *caught up in my misfortune*
> *ever to return*
> *and in the cloud dwelling see*
> *the same moon as long ago.*

The love that those two had shared
was touching beyond all words.

8. The Clash over the Name Plaques

Then came the spring of Eiman 1, [1165]
when the news went out that His Majesty was unwell.
By early summer his condition was grave
and there was talk that his eldest son, now in his second year
and born to the daughter of Iki no Kanemori, of the Treasury Bureau,
was to be named heir apparent.
Suddenly, in the sixth month, on the twenty-fifth day,
his father appointed him a prince[29] and abdicated that night in his favor.

....

28. Michikaze (894–966) was one of the three great calligraphers of his day.

29. A prince must be granted this title by his father, the emperor. Not all imperial sons received it.

The realm felt thoroughly ill at ease.

Those versed in the ways of the past offered this advice on the matter:

> "In Japan there have been child emperors.
> They include Seiwa, in his ninth year [858]
> when Emperor Montoku abdicated.
> As the Duke of Zhou ruled for King Cheng,
> facing south and daily making countless decisions,
> this young emperor's commoner grandfather,
> Fujiwara no Yoshifusa,
> assisted him. He was the first regent.
> Toba's accession came in his fifth year, [1107]
> Konoe's in his third, but of them both, [1141]
> people complained that they were too young.
> The child now at issue is in his second.
> No precedent supports his accession,
> which would be rash to say the least."

But it came to pass on the twenty-seventh,
in the seventh month, that Emperor Nijō
breathed his last in his twenty-third year,
as though a bud had dropped from the bough.
Behind jeweled blinds and brocade curtains,
all his ladies shed tears of grief.
His remains were carried that night
through Rendaino to Mount Funaoka
some way northeast of Kōryūji,
and it was there that a quarrel broke out
between the massed Enryakuji monks
and the counterpart host from Kōfukuji.
The issue was when and where each temple
would place the plaque bearing its name.
The custom, after an emperor's passing,
is that the monks from both capitals,
northern and southern, escort the body
to its last resting place and around it
fix commemorative name plaques.
Tōdaiji, founded by Emperor Shōmu, [745]
goes first, by inviolable privilege.
Kōfukuji, founded by Lord Tankai,30 [early 8th c.]
follows. Next, opposite Kōfukuji,

....

30. Fujiwara no Fuhito (659–720), the founder of Fujiwara power.

Enryakuji, of the northern capital,
claims its turn to put up its plaque.
These are followed by Miidera,
built to honor the vow Emperor Tenmu made [r. 673–86]
in times long gone by, then founded [mid-9th c.]
by Abbot Kyōdai and Chishō Daishi.[31]

For reasons best known to themselves, however, the Enryakuji monks
ignored precedent and put up their plaque right after Tōdaiji, hence before
Kōfukuji.
The Kōfukuji monks were considering what course to take when a pair of them,
Kannonbō and Seishibō from the temple's West Golden Hall,
both famous monk-warriors, took the matter into their own hands.
Kannonbō, in black-laced armor, gripped his plain wooden spear short;
Seishibō, his armor green-laced, wielded a great sword with a black-lacquered
scabbard.
They charged together and dashed the Enryakuji name plaque to the ground.
Then they rejoined the monks from the southern capital, singing,

> "Ah, the lovely waters,
> roaring: the great waterfall
> scorns the burning sun,
> flowing on and on and on,
> tra-la, tra-la, tra-la!"[32]

9. The Burning of Kiyomizudera

Enryakuji, so violently challenged, would normally have responded,
but perhaps the monks had a deeper plan, for they said not a word.
A sovereign's passing should move the very plants and trees,
insentient though they may be, to visible grief, but this fracas was too dismal.
High and low fled, terrified, in every direction.
Noon on the twenty-ninth of the month brought news
that a horde of monks was pouring down Mount Hiei toward the capital.
Warriors and the police raced to Nishi-Sakamoto[33] to stop them,
but they broke through easily and surged on into the city.
Somehow a rumor went around that on the retired sovereign's order
the Enryakuji monks from Mount Hiei meant to suppress the Heike.
An armed force went to the palace and secured all its guard posts,

....

31. The great monk Enchin (814–91).
32. From an *ennen* dance song of the time, performed as entertainment after a major temple ceremony.
33. Below Mount Hiei toward the southwest, hence just northeast of the city.

while the Heike themselves rushed to gather at Rokuhara.
Retired Emperor Go-Shirakawa, too, made a hurried progress there.
Lord Kiyomori, at the time still a grand counselor, was greatly alarmed.
Lord Shigemori urged calm, objecting that the rumor was nonsense,
but the Heike of every rank remained in a state verging on panic.

> The Enryakuji monks ignored Rokuhara.
> They fell instead on an innocent temple,
> Kiyomizudera, and burned every hall,
> every last monks' lodge to the ground.
> Their aim, some said, was to cancel the shame
> suffered that night of the funeral;
> for Kiyomizudera, you see,
> is a dependency of Kōfukuji.
> A sign stood, the morning after the fire,
> before the main gate. On it was written
> "Hey, you! *Now* what do you have to say
> about that line from the Lotus Sutra:
> 'Kannon will turn that pit of fire into a refreshing pool'?"
> The following day brought this retort:
> "His aeons of wonders confound understanding."
> The Hiei monks went back up their mountain;
> His Eminence left Rokuhara for home.
> Only Lord Shigemori escorted him.
> His father, Lord Kiyomori, did not go.
> Talk had it that he was being cautious.

When Lord Shigemori returned from escorting His Eminence,
his father remarked, "His visit was a great honor, I suppose,
but things he has thought and said in the past are what started that rumor.
Do not become too friendly with him."
Lord Shigemori replied,

> "Never betray these suspicions of yours
> in look or word. You will rue the day
> if anyone notes evidence of them.
> Avoid crossing him, and be kind to all.
> Do that and the gods and buddhas
> will keep you and grant you protection,
> so that you have nothing to fear."
> He moved to leave. "Shigemori,"
> his father said, "you are bighearted to a fault."

Once back among his close familiars, His Eminence observed,
"Well, he certainly said some strange things. That is *not* my thinking."

A monk named Saikōbō, a key man of his, chanced to be present.
"As they say," he remarked, "'Heaven has no mouth and must speak through
    men.'
The Heike lord it beyond their station. Perhaps heaven has a plan."
        Everyone murmured, "You can't say *that*!
        The walls have ears! Frightening,
        that's what it is, just frightening!"

10. *The Heir Apparent Named*

The Purification and the Enthronement Festival were canceled that
year because the new emperor [Rokujō] was mourning his father. On the
twenty-fourth of the twelfth month,[1165] a decree appointed Re-
tired Emperor Go-Shirakawa's son by Kenshunmon-in a prince. The
next year the era name changed to Nin'an. [1166–69] On the eighth of the
tenth month, the boy earlier appointed a prince was elevated to heir
apparent at the Tōsanjō residence. He was in his sixth year and the em-
peror's uncle, while the emperor, his nephew, was in his third. The
order of seniority was backward. However, in Kanwa 2, [986] Ichijō be-
came emperor in his seventh year and his successor, Sanjō, [r. 1011–16] then
in his eleventh, was appointed heir apparent. The situation therefore
was not unprecedented. His Majesty had acceded to the throne in his
second year, when his predecessor abdicated, and he was only in
his fifth when, on the nineteenth of the second month, [1168] he with-
drew in favor of the heir apparent. He was then called the new retired
emperor.
Before even coming of age,
he became an august retired emperor.
China can never have known the like,
nor our land either. In Nin'an 3, [1168]
on the twentieth of the third month,
the new sovereign assumed his dignity
in the Great Hall of State. For the Heike
this meant a brighter blaze of glory.
His mother, Kenshunmon-in, was a Taira,
a younger sister of Lady Nii,
the senior wife of Lord Kiyomori.
Indeed the Taira grand counselor, Lord Tokitada,
was Kenshunmon-in's elder brother, hence His Majesty's commoner relative.
Within and without the palace, he wielded great power.
Every appointment to rank or office conformed to his will.

So it was, too, in the time of Yang Guifei:[34]
Her brother, Yang Guozhong, flourished greatly,
enjoying widespread esteem and influence.
On every matter, however great or small,
Kiyomori sought Tokitada's advice.
People dubbed him the "Heike Regent."

11. *The Collision with the Regent*

Then came the sixteenth of the seventh month in the first year of Kaō. [1169]
Retired Emperor Go-Shirakawa renounced the world, but even then
he still governed so actively that he and the emperor were effectively one.
The senior nobles and privy gentlemen in his intimate entourage
and even the men, high or low, who belonged to his corps of guards
all enjoyed office, rank, and emoluments beyond their station.
And yet, as is the way with the hearts of men, they were not content.
"Ah, if the old fellow would just croak, that province of his would open up,"
they would whisper to each other, among friends.
"His office would be mine, if only he'd have the good grace to die."

> The now-cloistered emperor, too, made some remarks strictly in private. "Many men down the generations have suppressed the enemies of the court," he said, "but there has never been a case like this. Sadamori and Hidesato struck down Masakado, Yoriyoshi destroyed Sadatō and Munetō, Yoshiie crushed Takehira and Iehira; but the reward for their efforts never went beyond a posting as provincial governor. It is not right that Kiyomori should behave exactly as he pleases. He gets away with it because the latter days are upon us and the Sovereign's Way[35] is at an end." So he spoke, but he never found an occasion to issue a reprimand. The Heike, meanwhile, had no particular feeling against the court.

The disorder that was to engulf the world sprang from a root
struck in the tenth month of Kaō 2, on the sixteenth day. [1170]
Lord Shigemori's second son, Captain Sukemori,
then in his thirteenth year, was still the governor of Echizen at the time.

> The wintry fields were so pretty
> after a light fall of snow

....

34. The Chinese emperor Xuanzong (685–762) was so smitten by her beauty that he neglected matters of state to the point of provoking rebellion.

35. A phrase that recurs often in the tale, usually paired with "the Buddha's Way." The full expression (*buppō ōbō*) summed up the ideal complementarity between the "way" (or "law," or "teaching") of the Sovereign (government) and that of the Buddha (the ideals and protection of religion).

that he led thirty young housemen
on a ride around Rendaino,
Murasakino, Ukon-no-baba,
and had them bring many hawks,
to start and take quail and lark.
All day long they hunted,
until, as the light began to fail,
they headed home to Rokuhara.

Fujiwara no Motofusa, the current regent, was then on his way to the palace
from his residence at the Naka-no-mikado and Higashi-no-tōin crossing.
Intending to enter through the Yūhō Gate,[36]
he traveled south down Higashi-no-tōin and west along Ōi-no-mikado.
Where Ōi-no-mikado and Inokuma cross, Sukemori ran straight into his train.
"Identify yourself!" the regent's escort cried. "You are out of order!
You are in the presence of the regent! Dismount! Dismount!"

Alas, the fiercely arrogant Sukemori
cared nothing for what people thought;
nor had a single one of his housemen
reached even the age of twenty.
None of them had learned etiquette
or had any idea how to behave.
The regent? He meant nothing to them.
Dismount? Most certainly not!
Break through, rather, at a gallop.
By now it was dark. The regent's escort
did not know Kiyomori's grandson,
or perhaps they pretended not to.
They pulled Sukemori and the others
down from their mounts, covered with shame.

Sukemori dragged himself back to Rokuhara and told his grandfather,
Lord Kiyomori, the story of what had happened.
Kiyomori was furious. "It's all very well for this man to be regent," he declared,
"but he owes anyone of mine consideration. Instead, without a qualm,
he humiliates a mere boy. No, I will *not* forgive him for this!
This is the sort of thing that loses you people's respect. I'll teach him a lesson.
Oh, yes, I'll take care of this regent!"
To all this, Lord Shigemori replied,
"I see no reason to feel offended.
An insult from Yorimasa or Motomitsu

....

36. A gate (*mon*) into the outer palace compound.

would certainly humiliate our house,
but for a son of mine not to dismount
when he meets the regent on the road—
that is where the outrage lies."
He summoned the housemen involved and reprimanded them sternly.
"Hereafter," he told them, "you will do well to remember what I say.

For the folly of your offense,
I will apologize to the regent."
So he spoke, then withdrew.

> This is what happened next. Without a word to his son, Lord Kiyomori
> gathered ruffians from the depths of the countryside, together with
> others who feared only his orders—sixty and more of them, under
> Nanba and Seno-o. "On the twenty-first of next month," he said, "the
> regent is to go to the palace, to arrange His Majesty's coming-of-age.
> Ambush him wherever you please, cut off his outriders' and atten-
> dants' hair, and cleanse the shame suffered by Sukemori."

The regent never dreamed what awaited him.
His Majesty was to come of age in the following year, don a man's headdress,
and offer a banquet and new appointments to his assembled officials.
To plan all this, the regent needed time in his palace quarters.
He therefore made his train more elegant than for any commonplace
   outing.
He set off westward along Naka-no-mikado, planning to enter by the Taiken
   Gate.

The Rokuhara force lay in wait
near where Inokuma crossed Ōi-no-mikado:
three hundred helmeted riders in full armor.
They surrounded him front and rear
and with one voice raised their battle cry.
His outriders and attendants,
dressed up for today's grand occasion,
they chased and chivied in all directions,
dragged them down from their mounts,
trampled them into the dust,
and cut off every last man's hair.
One who lost his was Takemoto,
a member of the Right Palace Guards
and one of the regent's ten attendants.
There was also Takanori,
a Fujiwara and former chamberlain.
"This isn't *your* hair, you realize,"

the man who took it informed him.
"No indeed, it's your master's."
Next they ran the tips of their bows into the regent's carriage,
tore down his blinds, cut the chest and rump straps of his ox,
and raced back to Rokuhara, whooping with glee.
"Well done!" said Kiyomori.
One of the regent's grooms was an Inaba herald, Toba no Kunihisamaru by name.
He was junior, yes, but still a man of fine feeling.
He stayed with the carriage and brought it back to the regent's residence.
The rite of the master's return ensued, inexpressibly bitter.
To dry his tears, the regent pressed his court-dress sleeves to his eyes.

> Lords Kamatari and Fuhito
> naturally need no mention here;
> never once, though, since the days
> of Lords Yoshifusa and Mototsune
> had a regent been treated this way.
> This was when the Heike began to go bad.

In great agitation Lord Shigemori dismissed all the housemen involved.
"Whatever outlandish order my father may have issued," he declared,
"you could at least have given me some inkling of it.
And you, Sukemori, are a disgrace.

> They say that sandalwood smells sweet
> the moment it puts forth its first two leaves.
> By his eleventh or twelfth year,
> a boy should understand right conduct
> and uphold it on every occasion.
> That you have committed this outrage
> reflects badly on Lord Kiyomori.
> Your behavior is grossly unfilial."
> For a time he banished his son
> to the distant province of Ise.
> For this, both sovereign and ministers
> were, it seems, grateful to him.

12. Shishi-no-tani

Discussion of His Majesty's coming-of-age was called off that day.
The meeting took place instead on the twenty-fifth,
in the cloistered emperor's own privy chamber.
Under the circumstances the regent could hardly attend,
and on the ninth of the twelfth month he therefore received advance notice

of the decree that on the fourteenth elevated him to the office of chancellor.
On the seventeenth he formally expressed his thanks.
However, people at large seemed by no means pleased.
Meanwhile the year drew to a close.

> Early in the next year, Kaō 3, [1171] on the fifth of the first month, the
> emperor's coming-of-age was held at last. On the thirteenth he set out
> on the customary round of imperial visits. Cloistered Emperor Go-
> Shirakawa received him, as did Kenshunmon-in, and both must have
> found him enchanting in a man's headdress. A daughter of Lord Kiyo-
> mori entered his service as a consort in her fifteenth year. She did so
> as the cloistered sovereign's adopted daughter. It was then that the
> chancellor Moronaga, still only palace minister and left commander,
> resigned his commander's post.

The Tokudaiji grand counselor, Sanesada, was rumored to be his successor.
The Kasan-no-in counselor Kanemasa had hopes of his own.
Then there was the newly appointed grand counselor Narichika,
third son of the late Naka-no-mikado counselor Fujiwara no Ienari.
He openly coveted the post, and he enjoyed the cloistered emperor's favor.
He therefore commissioned all sorts of prayers.
First, at the shrine of Hachiman,[37] he assigned one hundred monks, on retreat,
to read the Great Wisdom Sutra in full, continuously, for seven days.

> While they were so engaged,
> three turtledoves flew in
> from toward Otokoyama,
> landed on the mandarin orange tree
> before the Kōra sanctuary,
> and pecked one another to death.
> "The dove is Hachiman's messenger.
> At this temple, here by his shrine,
> no such wonder has ever been seen."
> So Kyōsei, the temple abbot,
> testified to His Majesty.
> At the Bureau of Shrines meanwhile,
> divination disclosed this meaning:
> "Disorder throughout the realm:
> a threat less to the emperor
> than to officials and ministers."

....

37. Iwashimizu Hachiman, the great Hachiman shrine on Otokoyama, southwest of the capital.
Elsewhere, the tale sometimes calls this shrine Yawata, another reading for the characters used to write
"Hachiman."

Lord Narichika felt no alarm. By day there were too many people about,
so he walked nightly, for seven nights, from his home,
near the Naka-no-mikado and Karasumaru crossing,
all the way to the Upper Kamo Shrine.[38]
On the seventh and last night, he came home exhausted,
lay down at once, and dropped off to sleep.
In a dream he then found himself again at Upper Kamo.
The doors of the sanctuary opened wide, and a voice of eerie power intoned:

> *Ah, cherry blossom,*
> *never blame the wind that blows*
> *down the Kamo River:*
> *There is nothing it can do*
> *to spare you your coming fall.*

Lord Narichika, undaunted,
confined an ascetic at Upper Kamo,
built for him a ritual dais
within the cryptomeria cave
behind the sanctuary hall,
and launched him on one hundred days of performing the rite of Dakini.[39]
During this time a lightning bolt struck the mighty cryptomeria tree,
sending up great flames that also threatened the sanctuary.
The people of the shrine raced en masse to put them out.
Then they sought to banish the holy man and his most unholy rite,
but he would not move. "I have made a great vow," he insisted,
"to spend a hundred days on retreat at this shrine, and this is the seventy-fifth.
No, I shall stay." The shrine priests reported this to the palace.
"Banish him as your laws require," came the decree in reply.
With their staffs of white wood, the shrine men battered his head,
then hounded him southward from their land, beyond Ichijō.

The gods reject the unrighteous,
they say, and this Narichika,
with his prayers for appointment
above himself, to commander,
may well have provoked the blaze.
In matters of rank and office,
neither the cloistered emperor
nor the regent had his will;

....

38. The Upper and Lower Kamo shrines, north of the city, especially protect the emperor and the capital. The name "Karasumaru," just above, is familiar to many now as "Karasuma." The reading has changed.

39. An esoteric, magic rite to invite prosperity and good fortune.

only Heike desires counted.
So it was that both Sanesada
and Kanemasa lost out.
Lord Kiyomori's eldest son,
Shigemori, from right commander
moved to left, and Munemori,
his second, a counselor,
over the heads of several seniors
rose to command the right.
For this there are simply no words.
Sanesada especially—
ranking grand counselor that he was,
scion of the highest nobility,
gifted scholar, firstborn of his house—
passing *him* over was dreadful.
People whispered among themselves,
"He's certain now to renounce the world."
But no, he decided to watch and wait.
He resigned his grand-counselor post
and, they say, retired to his home.

Lord Narichika declared, "I could not really have objected
if Sanesada or Kanemasa had been appointed rather than me.
But Kiyomori's second son! That, I cannot stomach.
This comes from their always getting what they want.
I will find a way to bring down the Heike and get what *I* want."
These were terrible words.
While his father had risen to counselor,
he, the youngest son, was a grand counselor at senior second rank.
He had been granted several large provinces, and his sons and retainers
prided themselves on the high esteem they enjoyed at court.
What can have possessed him, then, when he already had everything?
Some devil or other, surely.
In the Heiji years, too, as the governor of Echigo and a Guards captain,
he had sided with Nobuyori and was nearly executed,
but Lord Shigemori interceded for him, and his head remained on his shoulders.

A stranger, however, to gratitude,
he amassed arms in a secret location,
recruited a force of warriors,
and bent every effort to his designs.

Shishi-no-tani, a ravine below the Eastern Hills, runs at the back into
Miidera land. It makes a perfect fortress. The prelate Shunkan had a villa

there, and there the conspirators met regularly, to plot the downfall of the Heike. Once Cloistered Emperor Go-Shirakawa himself made a progress to the villa, accompanied by the monk Jōken, a son of the late minor counselor Shinzei.

His Cloistered Eminence mentioned the subject to Jōken that night at the drinking party.

Jōken was horrified. "How appalling!" he cried. "A lot of people know about it already, and there will be very big trouble if it gets out."

Narichika paled and rose abruptly to his feet. The sleeve of his hunting cloak caught the wine jar that stood before the sovereign and knocked it over.

"What does *that* mean?" Go-Shirakawa asked.

Narichika shot back, "Down go the Heike!"

His Eminence laughed aloud. "Come up here, each one of you," he called. "Come up and entertain us!"

The police lieutenant Yasuyori responded first. "Ah, these wine jars!" he complained.[40] "There are too many, and I'm so drunk!"

"What are we going to do about it?" asked Shunkan.

"There's nothing like taking heads!" the monk Saikō answered. He knocked the head off a wine jar and vanished into an inner room.

Jōken remained speechless with shock. The whole thing was terrifying.

Who were they, then, these conspirators?

The Ōmi captain and novice monk Renjō,

in lay life known as Narimasa;

Shunkan, the superintendent of Hosshōji;

Motokane, the governor of Yamashiro;

Masatsuna, from the Bureau of Ceremonial;

police lieutenants Yasuyori, Nobufusa, Sukeyuki;

the chamberlain Yukitsuna, of the Settsu Genji;

and many others beside them,

all members of the cloistered emperor's guard.

13. *The Fight over Ugawa*

This Hosshōji superintendent, Shunkan, was a grandson of Lord Masatoshi, the Kyōgoku Genji grand counselor:

a gentleman from no very warlike line, but excessively evil-tempered.

....

40. As in the mocking song sung by the courtiers to Tadamori in 1:2, the syllables *heiji* mean both "house of Taira" and "wine jar."

Resenting that anyone should pass his residence, near the crossing of Kyōgoku
   and Sanjōbōmon,
he constantly posted himself at his gate, teeth clenched in visible rage.
Perhaps descent from this man made Shunkan,
monk though he was, testy and haughty enough to join this absurd conspiracy.

> Lord Narichika summoned the chamberlain Yukitsuna. "I look to you
> as my battle commander," he said. "Whatever provinces and estates
> you desire will be yours if our enterprise succeeds. In the meantime
> here is material to make bags for the bows." He gave Yukitsuna fifty
> bolts of white cloth.
>
> On the fifth of the third month of Angen 3, [1177] when Lord Mo-
> ronaga became chancellor, Shigemori rose to palace minister in his
> stead, over the head of Grand Counselor Sadafusa. It was a fine thing
> indeed to be both minister and Palace Guards commander. A con-
> gratulatory banquet was held at once. The guest of honor was appar-
> ently Lord Tsunemune, the Ōi-no-mikado right minister.

Moronaga's birth would normally have forbidden so high an appointment,
but there was his father, Yorinaga, the Haughty[41] Left Minister, to consider.
The cloistered emperor's North Guard did not exist of old.
It was established in the time of Retired Emperor Shirakawa,
and many of its members had served in the Palace Guards.
Tametoshi and Morishige, in their youth Senjumaru and Imainumaru, were the
   stalwarts among them.
In Retired Emperor Toba's day, Suenori and Sueyori, father and son,
served their sovereign and sometimes apparently conveyed petitions to him.
All these acted strictly within the limits imposed by their station.
Under Cloistered Emperor Go-Shirakawa, however,
the men of the North Guard overreached themselves egregiously,
scorned senior nobles and privy gentlemen alike,
and broke every rule of right conduct. Juniors rose to command rank,
and some ranking guardsmen were even granted access to the privy chamber.
The more this sort of thing went on, the more arrogant they became.
No doubt that explains why they supported this ill-conceived plot.

> Two among them had once served
> the late Shinzei, a minor counselor first,
> then a novice in religion:
> Moromitsu and Narikage.
> One began as a local official

41. Literally, "evil" (*aku*). However, *The Tale of Hōgen* describes him at length not as cruel or corrupt
but rather as so overwhelmingly (hence discouragingly) accomplished that he became arrogant,
overreached himself, and courted ruin.

active in the province of Awa;
the other was from the capital.
Being, both of them, of low birth,
they had tasted mean employment,
but quick wits had lifted them up:
Moromitsu to junior officer
in the Left Palace Guards and Narikage
to the very same rank in the Right.
In unison, then, both at once
moved to posts in the Gate Watch.
When the Shinzei affair arose,
the two together renounced the world.
Now both novices, Saikō and Saikei,
still served His Cloistered Eminence
by overseeing his storehouses.

Saikō had a son, Morotaka by name. Being a lively fellow, too,
he steadily rose to the fifth rank and a junior officer post in the police.
On the twenty-ninth of the twelfth month of Angen 1, [1175]
the year-end appointments list named him to govern the province of Kaga.

In the way of running his province,
he violated law and decorum,
confiscated land and estates
equally from shrines and temples,
from the wealthy and the mighty,
with disconcerting abandon.
Certainly, long ages have passed
since the wise Duke Zhao ruled Zhou,
but government with a light hand—
that, at least, one could have asked.
While he pursued his arrogant ways,
in the summer of Angen 2
his younger brother, Morotsune,
went to Kaga as deputy governor.

The monks of Ugawa, a mountain temple near the provincial seat,
had heated water and were taking their bath
when Morotsune, just arrived in the province,
burst in on them, threw them out of the bathhouse,
got into the bath himself, and had his underlings dismount to wash their horses.
The monks were furious.
"Never before," they cried, "has a provincial official violated these precincts.
Respect precedent at once and desist from this outrage!"

"Past deputies were incompetent,
and the people looked down on them.
This one you will find to be different.
Obey the law!" Morotsune ordered,
but the monks moved resolutely to repel these officious intruders.
The government men seized every chance to break into the temple again.
Blow after blow, the skirmish raged,
until Morotsune's favorite horse ended up with a broken leg.

There ensued, with bows and arrows,
swords, and weapons of every kind,
a fierce clash that lasted for hours.
Morotsune must have foreseen defeat,
because that night he made himself scarce.
Next the provincial authorities
assembled a thousand horsemen.
These rode off to attack Ugawa
and burned every hall to the ground.
Now Ugawa comes under Hakusan,[42]
to which its senior monks appealed.
And who were they, then, these monks?
Chishaku, Gakumyō, Hōdaibō,
Shōchi, Gakuon, the Tosa adept.
The warrior-monks of all three shrines,
all eight subtemples of Hakusan,
rose in a body, two thousand men,
and on the ninth of the seventh month,
late in the afternoon, closed in
on Deputy Morotsune's house.
Sunset decided them to wait
and launch their attack the next day.
For now they stayed where they were.
The autumn wind, laden with dew,
fluttered the sleeves of their bow arms;
lightning bolts, bright in the heavens,
flashed and gleamed from their helmet stars.[43]
No doubt despairing of victory,
the deputy fled that night to the city.

....

42. A major sacred mountain, associated with a large and powerful religious community, on the Japan Sea side of Honshu.

43. *Hoshi,* small metal bosses on a warrior's helmet.

Dawn came, and the attack.
The monks roared out their battle cry.
From the compound arose no sound.
A scout sent to investigate
reported that every last man was gone.
That was that, then. The monks withdrew.
Instead they appealed to Enryakuji.
Adorning the sacred palanquin
belonging to Hakusan's central shrine,
they bore it all the way to Mount Hiei.
On the twelfth of the eighth month, at noon,
it reached Higashi-Sakamoto.
The news spread; at which, from the north,
mighty claps of thunder boomed
and moved on to the capital.
White clouds lowered over the earth,
and mountain and city alike,
even to the pines on the slopes,
turned a brilliant white.

14. *The Vows*

Into the Marōto Shrine grounds
went the Hakusan palanquin,
for Marōto is none other
than Hakusan Myōri Gongen;[44]
plainly said, they are father and son.
What would come of the appeal
naturally remained to be seen.
The meeting, though, gave the gods joy
such as they had known in life:
more joy than when Urashima's son
came at last on his descendants
seven generations past his own,
and also surpassing that unborn son's
when he saw his father on Vulture Peak.[45]

. . . .

44. The divinity of Hakusan.

45. An ancient legend tells how the fisherman Urashima traveled to the sea god's palace and married his daughter but then became homesick and returned to his native village seven generations after he had left. The Buddha's son, Rāhula, remained in the womb for six years and emerged on the night when his father, who preached the Lotus Sutra on Vulture Peak, attained enlightenment.

> The three thousand monks of Mount Hiei
> in serried ranks, all the holy priests
> from the Seven Shrines, sleeve to sleeve,
> chanting together sutras and prayers,
> made a spectacle beyond words.

The assembled host of the Mountain let it be known to the cloistered emperor
that for Morotaka, the governor of Kaga, they demanded exile
and for his deputy, Morotsune, prison.
The answer was slow to come.
Those senior nobles and privy gentlemen who mattered exclaimed,
"Dear me, he *must* issue prompt judgment!
Petitions lodged by Mount Hiei have always received special attention.
Tamefusa, the lord of the Treasury, and Suenaka, deputy viceroy of Kyushu,
were both pillars of the court, yet complaints from Hiei got them exiled.
How could these men, Morotaka and what's-his-name,
deserve a moment's thought? There are no doubts to weigh.

> The minister holds his tongue,
> preferring to keep his wages;
> the lesser official chooses silence,
> fearing reprisal," they say.
> Every one of them kept his mouth shut.

"The flow of the Kamo River, dice at backgammon, and the monks of Mount
    Hiei—
these are things beyond my control,"
Retired Emperor Shirakawa is said once to have declared.
In Retired Emperor Toba's time,
Enryakuji received Heisenji in Echizen as a dependency.
"I have righted a wrong," Toba declared when he issued his decree,
for Mount Hiei commanded his deep allegiance.
Lord Masafusa, then the deputy viceroy of Kyushu, put this question to
    Shirakawa:
"Were they to advance against you with the palanquins of their gods,
Your Majesty, to press a complaint, what would you do?"
"Indeed," Shirakawa replied, "a complaint from the Mountain is difficult to
    ignore."
Long ago, on the second of the third month of Kahō 2, the governor of
    Mino, [1096]
Minamoto no Yoshitsuna, was busy abolishing a newly created estate
when he killed En'ō, a monk sworn to permanent retreat on Mount Hiei.
The Hiyoshi Shrine priests and the senior Enryakuji monks, over thirty in all,
therefore advanced, petition in hand, on the retired emperor's guards office.

The regent, Moromichi, ordered Yoriharu of the Yamato Genji to stop them.
Yoriharu's men shot arrows, killing eight and wounding more than ten.
The others fled. Next came news that the senior Enryakuji prelates
were on their way down to the capital, to address the retired emperor.
Warriors and police rushed to Nishi-Sakamoto and turned them back.
Judgment on Yoriharu was slow to come. Up on the Mountain,
they bore the gods of the Seven Shrines, in their palanquins, to the temple's
    Central Hall
and chanted in their presence, for seven days, the Great Wisdom Sutra.
Then they called down curses on the regent. The great monk Chūin,
presiding on the last, seventh day, mounted the high seat, rang his bell,
and pronounced these solemn words to the assembly and to the gods:
    "You who, since we first drew breath,
    have tenderly nurtured us, O gods!
    Strike, we pray, with a humming arrow[46]
    the regent Moromichi!
    O Great Hachiōji Gongen, strike!"
    He spoke this prayer in a mighty voice.
    That night a wonder occurred.
    Dreamers heard a humming arrow
    fly from the Hachiōji Shrine
    off toward the imperial palace.
    The next morning, at the regent's,
    they found when they opened his shutters
    planted there a branch of star anise,[47]
    dew-laden as though fresh from the Mountain.
    This was a terrifying sign.

> At once the regent fell gravely ill, apparently stricken by Sannō, the divinity of the Mountain. In intense distress, his mother, a very great lady, disguised herself as a woman of the people and confined herself on retreat at the Hiyoshi Shrine.
>
> She prayed there for seven days and nights and announced the following vows. She offered one hundred open-air *dengaku* dances; one

....

46. A humming arrow (*kaburaya*) ended in two elements. The first was a hollow wooden bulb pierced with holes that made the arrow hum loudly in flight. The second was a forked iron arrowhead (*karimata*) with two points. The *kaburaya* was not a battle arrow, although the forked arrowhead could certainly injure its target. The sound was meant to frighten and impress. *Kaburaya* were often exchanged at the start of hostilities between two sides, and they also served to repel evil influences (in this passage Moromichi himself, seen from the perspective of the Hiei monks). A related arrow type, the *hikime*, served even more clearly to inspire fear and awe by means of sound, since it lacked the *karimata* head.

47. *Shikimi*, customarily offered on a Buddhist altar.

hundred devotional procession costumes; one hundred horse races, wrestling bouts, and mounted archery matches; one hundred discourses on the Sutra of the Benevolent King; one hundred discourses on the Sutra of the Medicine King; one hundred Medicine King images one and a half handbreadths tall; and life-size images of the Medicine King, Shakyamuni, and Amida.

Deep in her heart, she also made three further vows.
No one else could have known of them, since they were secret,
but, strange to relate, on the night of the last, seventh day,
one of the many pilgrims then at the Hachiōji Shrine,
a shrine maiden and medium newly arrived from the far north,
suddenly fainted. When they carried her off to a place apart,
she quickly revived and began to dance.
People looked on in wonder. She danced for an hour,
until the Sannō divinity came down into her and she spoke a frightening
    prophecy:
        "Hear my voice, sentient beings!
        The regent's mother has been on retreat,
        here at my shrine, for seven days.
        She has undertaken three vows,
        begging me for the regent's life.
        Should he live, she will, first,
        mingle here with the crippled and sick
        and for a full thousand days,
        morning and evening, serve my shrine.
        This lady had not earlier known
        life's sorrows, but now she is lost,
        all because of love for her son.
        Wholly indifferent to revulsion,
        she will, as she herself declares,
        mingle with the unsightly maimed
        and for a thousand days, day and night,
        devote herself solely to my service.
        I am profoundly touched.
Second, she will build a gallery all the way here, to Hachiōji,
from the Bridge Hall at the Ōmiya Shrine.
I feel for the three-thousand-strong host of Hiei monks
who come here on pilgrimage, rain or shine.
This gallery will benefit them greatly.
Third, should the regent be granted life, she will sponsor at this shrine,
each and every day, a formal Lotus Sutra debate.

All three vows are admirable, but while the first two could be dispensed with,
the daily debates on the Lotus Sutra strike me as especially worthy.
Nonetheless, although this complaint should have been easily resolved,
the court withheld judgment. Instead my shrine servants were wounded or
    killed
and returned to me to report, weeping, the outrage they had suffered.
I will never forget this, not through all ages to come.
Moreover, the arrows that struck them lodged equally in me,
a visible manifestation of higher divinity.

      See, then, with your own eyes,
      whether or not I speak the truth!"
      She bared one shoulder, and there,
      beneath her left arm, a wound
      gaped like the mouth of a large wine cup.
      "No, it is simply too much.
      Whatever her prayers and promises,
      her son cannot live out his full life.
      Provided she sponsors the Lotus debates,
      I will give him another three years.
      If that is not enough for her,
      the matter is out of my hands."
      With these words Sannō ascended.[48]

          The regent's mother had never mentioned these vows to anyone, so she
          could not suspect anyone of having passed on knowledge of them.
          Awestruck that the oracle had known them so precisely, she replied, in
          tears, "I would be grateful enough for a day or even an hour, and three
          years is a very great boon." She made her way down the Mountain, still
          weeping.
In haste she returned to the city and donated the regent's Tanaka estate,
located in the province of Kii, in perpetuity to the Hachiōji Shrine, ·
where, they say, a Lotus debate has been held daily ever since.

      Meanwhile the regent Moromichi
      felt better and better, until soon
      his health was as good as ever.
      People high and low were relieved.
      Three years then sped past like a dream,
      until, in the second year of Eichō, [1097]
      the sixth month and twenty-second day,
      an evil boil broke out at the hairline

....

48. The expression used when a possessing spirit leaves the medium.

on Lord Moromichi's forehead,
and he had to take to his bed.
On the twenty-seventh he died,
in only his thirty-eighth year.
Daring in spirit, strong in mind,
he made a most impressive figure,
but with the end fast approaching,
he clung to life, and no wonder.
Not even yet in his fortieth year,
alas, he went before his father.
Not every man dies after his father,
but death comes to all: The very Buddha,
complete in all virtues, the bodhisattvas
approaching final emancipation,
can do nothing to resist it.
The deeply compassionate Sannō
exists to benefit sentient beings;
therefore his censure is just.

15. *The Palanquins of the Gods*

The monks of Mount Hiei petitioned repeatedly to have Morotaka,
the governor of Kaga, exiled and Mototsune, his deputy, jailed.
When they got no response, they canceled the Hiyoshi Shrine festival.
Early in the hour of the dragon, on the thirteenth of the fourth month of
    Angen 3, [1177, ca. 8 A.M.]
they adorned the palanquins of the gods of Jūzenji, Marōto, and Hachiōji
and marched on the guard posts of the palace compound.
At Sagarimatsu, Kirezutsumi, the Kamo riverbank, Tadasu, Umetada,
    Yanagihara,
and around Tōboku-in, countless junior monks, shrine servants, and temple
    menials
thronged to watch the palanquins surge westward along Ichijō.
The sacred treasures glittered on high, as though sun and moon had fallen to
    earth.
Senior Genji and Heike commanders secured the posts
on all four sides of the compound and ordered their men to stop the monks.
For the Heike, Lord Shigemori, palace minister and left commander,
led three thousand horse to secure the Yōmei, Taiken, and Yūhō gates to the
    east.
His younger brothers Munemori, Tomomori, and Shigehira

Minamoto no Yorimasa.

and his uncles Yorimori, Norimori, and Tsunemori did the same to the west and
    south.
For the Genji, Yorimasa, the palace warden, secured the Nuidono post
at the North Gate, with just three hundred horse under Watanabe no Habuku
    and Sazuku.
This was a vast area, and his small force was spread all too visibly thin.

> The monks noted this weak spot and moved to bring their palanquins
> in past the Nuidono guard post, at the North Gate. Being the man he
> was, Yorimasa dismounted, removed his helmet, and saluted the pa-
> lanquins. His men did so, too. Then he sent the monks a message
> through an envoy, one Watanabe no Chōjitsu Tonō.

Tonō wore that day, over a gray-green *hitatare*,[49] leather-laced armor
embellished with tiny yellow-dyed cherry blossoms;
at his waist, a sword with gold-alloyed copper fittings;

....

49. A warrior's standard garment in the tale, worn over wide trousers (*hakama*).

The sacred palanquins at the Taiken Gate entrance to the palace grounds.

and on his back a quiver filled with white-fletched arrows.
A rattan-wrapped bow rode clasped under his arm.
He doffed his helmet, which he slung on a cord over his back,
respectfully saluted the palanquins of the gods, and began,
"I have a message from Lord Yorimasa to the monks of the Mountain:

> The Mount Hiei complaint is just;
> that of course goes without saying.

That judgment has been delayed so long is to be deplored.
Obviously, you can bring the palanquins in through here if you wish.
However, Yorimasa's men are few. If you seize that advantage,
break past this post, and carry the palanquins in this way,
the youth of the city will bandy it about that the Hiei monks
did so with sheepish looks on their faces, to your discredit in years to come.

> To allow the palanquins passage
> would mean, for Lord Yorimasa,
> to breach His Majesty's decree,
> while to stop them would, equally,
> mean for a man long devoted
> to Sannō and the Medicine King
> giving up the calling of arms.
> The dilemma is insoluble.

Lord Shigemori has secured the guard post to the east with a large force.
On the whole you would do better to enter through there."
So he spoke, then withdrew. His words gave the shrine servants pause.

> "Why in the world should we do that?"
> many among the younger monks cried.
> "Take them straight in here, past *this* post!"

But there advanced from among the elders the greatest speaker on the
    Mountain,
the preacher Gōun, from Settsu province, who expressed himself as follows:

> "Lord Yorimasa is quite right.
> Those who march to press a complaint
> with the palanquins of their gods
> should pit themselves against real force
> if they are to win lasting praise.

In any case Lord Yorimasa descends in direct Genji line from the Sixth Prince,
and in war he has never been known to err.
Indeed, he excels not only at arms but also at skill as a poet.
At an impromptu poetry gathering in Emperor Konoe's reign,
the assigned topic was 'Blossoms Deep in the Mountains.'
No one but Yorimasa knew what to write:

> *With so many trees*
> *crowded on the mountainside,*
> *which the one may be*
> *no one knows, until those boughs*
> *reveal their wealth of blossoms.*

That is the splendid poem he made.
How could anyone cruelly shame,
over one tense moment, a man
delicate enough in feeling
to elicit an emperor's praise?
Turn the sacred palanquins back!"
Such was his judgment, and the monks
far and near, a host of thousands,
all agreed: He is right, quite right!
So off they went, palanquins first,
eastward to the Taiken Gate guard post,
intending to enter from there.
Mayhem ensued. The warriors
loosed upon them a rain of arrows.
Many lodged in the palanquin
bearing Jūzenji. Shrine servants died,
monks in large numbers sustained wounds.
The groans and screams of agony
must have risen to Brahma's heaven,
struck with fright the God of the Earth.
The great host of indignant monks
there at the guard post abandoned their gods
and wept their way back up the Mountain.

16. The Burning of the Palace

By imperial command, the chamberlain and minor controller Kanemitsu
convened an emergency council of senior nobles in the privy chamber.
When the sacred palanquins entered the city in Hōan 4, [1123]
in the seventh month, His Majesty sent them on to the Sekisan Shrine;[50]
and when the same happened in the fourth month of Hōen 4, [1138]
the Gion Shrine superintendent was told to receive them there.
The council chose to follow the Hōen example.

....

50. Below Mount Hiei, just northeast of the capital. It enshrined, as it still does, a protector deity brought
from China to guard the mountain.

Chōken, the Gion superintendent, admitted them to the shrine at dusk.
Shrine servants went to work removing the arrows still planted in them.
Between the Eikyū and Jishō years, the monks of Mount Hiei [1113–18; 1177–81]
carried their palanquins to the palace guard posts on six occasions.
Warriors were summoned to stop them each time,
but never before had their arrows struck a palanquin of the gods.

"When spirits and gods are angry,
disasters visit every street.
Terrifying! Terrifying!"
So people said among themselves.

In the middle of the same night, that of the fourteenth,
the rumor spread that the monks of the Mountain would soon be back.
The emperor therefore summoned at once a hand carriage,
in which he made a progress to the cloistered emperor's Hōjūji residence.
The empress boarded a carriage and left as well.
Lord Shigemori accompanied her in service dress, a quiver on his back.
His eldest son, Koremori, a Guards lieutenant and deputy of Her Majesty's
household,
in full civil dress and flat, formal quiver, attended her as well.
Regent, chancellor, senior nobles, privy gentlemen rushed to do the same.
High and low in the city, palace staff of every degree were near panic.

On Mount Hiei the council of monks,
three thousand strong, agreed as one.
Palanquins bristling with arrows,
shrine servants killed, many monks wounded,
all compelled a single course:
Ōmiya and Ninomiya,
every last shrine or sanctuary,
the Lecture Hall, the Central Hall,
temple buildings of every kind
they would reduce to ashes,
then melt away into the wilds.
At last the cloistered emperor agreed
soon to judge the Hiei complaint.
Therefore the Mountain's senior prelates
started up on their homeward way,
bearing the news, but the host of monks
stopped them at Nishi-Sakamoto
and drove them back to the city.

The Taira grand counselor Tokitada, then still intendant of the Left Gate Watch,
received the mission to calm them. Before the Great Lecture Hall,

the massed monks from the Three Pagodas seized and manhandled him,
    crying,
"Knock off that stupid court cap of his!"
"Grab him, dump him in the lake!"
They were about to do it, too, when he addressed them:
"Silence, a moment, please! I have a message for you all!"
From the fold of his robe, he drew paper and inkstone and wrote a few lines
that he passed to the monks. They spread out the paper and read:

> "That the assembled host of monks
> should permit themselves violence
> betrays the working of demon powers.
> That the sovereign in his wisdom
> should then marshal force to restrain them
> reveals the protection of the Buddha."
> So he had written. At the sight
> every man among them agreed
> that they would harry him no more.
> Each retreated down his valley,
> to the quiet of his own lodge.
> One sheet of paper and a few lines
> had soothed the wrath of three thousand monks
> and spared emperor and subject shame.
> Tokitada, for this achievement,
> merited astonished praise.

>> People were impressed that the monks of Mount Hiei, whom they had
>> thought good for nothing but making trouble, had actually under-
>> stood where right conduct lay. On the twentieth of that month, the
>> provisional counselor Tadachika was charged with executing further
>> orders. Morotaka, the governor of Kaga, was at last relieved of his post
>> and exiled to Idota in Owari. Morotsune, his deputy, was jailed. Sen-
>> tenced to prison, too, were the six warriors who, on the thirteenth, had
>> shot arrows into the sacred palanquins. They were Fujiwara no Masa-
>> zumi and Masasue, Ōe no Iekane and Iekuni, and Kiyowara no Yasuie
>> and Yasutomo, all junior officers in the left and right divisions of the
>> Gate Watch and the Watch.

On the twenty-eighth of the fourth month, during the hour of the boar, [ca. 10 P.M.]
fire broke out near the crossing of Higuchi and Tomi-no-kōji.
A strong wind was blowing from the southeast, and much of the capital burned.
Great cartwheels of flame leaped three to five blocks, diagonally, northwestward.
"Terrifying" is hardly the word.
    The Chigusa Mansion of Prince Tomohira,

the Red Plum Hall at the Kitano Shrine,
Hayanari's Haimatsu House,
the Demon Mansion, the Takamatsu,
the Kamoi, and Tōsanjō;
the Kan'in Mansion of Fuyutsugi,
Mototsune's Horikawa Mansion—
these and other famous landmarks,
more than thirty of them in all,
as well as the homes of senior nobles,
a full sixteen—every one burned;
not to mention, in addition,
the homes of privy gentlemen,
or those of mid-grade officials,
for there were too many to count.
At last wind-driven flames reached the palace.
The Suzaku Gate caught first,
then the Ōten Gate, the Kaishō Gate,
the Great Hall of State, the Buraku-in,
government offices, the Eight Bureaus,
the senior officials' morning room
in an instant burned to the ground.
Diaries kept in the great houses,
papers going back generations,
priceless treasures of every kind—
all were reduced to a heap of ash.
Imagine, then, the total damage!
Hundreds of people burned to death
and countless oxen and horses.
This was no common disaster.
Some dreamed that down from Mount Hiei
came several thousand large monkeys,
torches in hand, to burn the city.
It was in Emperor Seiwa's reign,
in Jōgan 18, that fire first claimed [876]
the Great Hall of State; in consequence
the accession of Emperor Yōzei,
on the third day of the following year,
had to be held in the Buraku-in.
Rebuilding started in Gangyō 1, [877]
the fourth month and the ninth day,
and was finished in the tenth month,

the eighth day, of Gangyō 2.
Then, in the reign of Go-Reizei,
Tenki 5, second month, the twenty-sixth, [1057]
the Great Hall of State burned again.
Rebuilding began in Jiryaku 4, [1068]
on the fourteenth of the eighth month,
but the work remained unfinished
when Go-Reizei passed away.
At its completion in Enkyū 4, [1072]
on the fifteenth of the fourth month,
men of letters made Chinese poems,
and, in welcome, musicians played
for His Majesty's formal visit.
These, though, are the latter days,
and the might of the realm runs low.
The Great Hall of State has not been rebuilt.

BOOK TWO

1. The Exile of the Abbot

(recitative)
In the first year of Jishō, the fifth month and day, [1177]
Meiun, abbot of Mount Hiei, was barred from religious services at the palace.
A chamberlain arrived to take back his Nyoirin Kannon,
and he was replaced as a palace chaplain.[51]
Next the police sent men to arrest him
for instigating his monks' descent on the palace with the palanquins of their
  gods.
Saikō and his sons denounced Meiun to Cloistered Emperor Go-Shirakawa.
"Morotaka, the Kaga governor," they said, "has confiscated an estate of his in that
  province.
This has made him so angry that, in concert with his monks,
he has instituted legal proceedings. For the court this is a crisis."
The cloistered emperor was furious.
"He's really in for it now," people murmured.
Such was Go-Shirakawa's wrath that Meiun returned his seal and keys and
  resigned.

> *(song)*
> On the eleventh of that month,
> the seventh son of Emperor Toba,
> Cloistered Prince Kakukai, instead
> became the abbot of Mount Hiei:
> He was a disciple of Gyōgen,
> the great prelate of Shōren-in.
> On the twelfth came a further blow:
> Two policemen arrived to seal
> Meiun's well and douse his fire,
> in formal denial of fire and water.
> Because of this the word went out
> that the monks would very soon
> be heading down, back to the city.
> The news started an uproar there.

....

51. Nyoirin is an esoteric form of the compassionate bodhisattva Kannon. A "palace chaplain" (*gojisō*) was one of a roster of distinguished clerics responsible especially for protecting the emperor, by their prayers, while he slept.

On the eighteenth the chancellor, Moronaga,
repaired to the palace with twelve other senior nobles.
They seated themselves in their usual conference chamber
and debated the subject of Meiun's crime.
Counselor Nagakata, then still a left grand controller,
spoke up from his station as the most junior among them.

    "It appears that those versed in the law
    advise reducing death by one step
    to distant exile. I wonder, though.
    Meiun, the former abbot, mastered
    both sides of the exalted Teaching,
    the exoteric and esoteric.
    Pure in conduct, he kept the precepts,
    so perfectly that under his guidance
    the emperor mastered the Lotus Sutra.
    From him the cloistered emperor
    received the bodhisattva vows.
    Strict punishment for such a teacher
    might offend the unseen powers.
Would sentencing him to distant exile and returning him to lay life really be
    wise?"
Nagakata expressed himself boldly, and the senior nobles present agreed.
The cloistered sovereign's profound displeasure settled the matter, however:
distant banishment after all.
When Lord Kiyomori called to announce the decision,
His Cloistered Eminence pleaded indisposition so as not to receive him.
Disappointed, Kiyomori withdrew.

    As established custom requires
    whenever punishment strikes a monk,
    Meiun was obliged to surrender
    his certificate of ordination;
    he became a layman once more,
    named Fujii no Matsueda.
    In descent he was six generations
    removed from Prince Tomohira,
    Emperor Murakami's seventh son,
    and his father was Lord Akimichi,
    the Koga grand counselor.
    He was a man of peerless worth,
    the greatest monk in all the realm.
    Sovereign and subject so revered him

that he headed Tennōji, too,
and six other major temples.
Nonetheless, Abe no Yasuchika, head of the Yin-Yang Office,
had been heard to question Meiun's name.
"I simply do not understand," he remarked,
"how a man as learned as he could call himself Meiun.
The first character, *mei*, sets next to each other the light of both 'moon' and 'sun,'
but the *un* that follows means 'cloud.'"
Appointed abbot in Nin'an 1, the second month and twentieth day, [1166]
Meiun first worshipped formally in the Central Hall on the fifteenth of the third.
He opened the treasury nearby and found a box a foot square, wrapped in white
    cloth.
Abbot that he was, a monk who had never sinned in his life,
he opened it and found inside a single scroll of yellow paper.

> Dengyō Daishi, the great founder,[52]
> had foreknown and written there
> the names of all future abbots.
> Customarily, each new one
> read as far as his own name,
> no further, then rerolled the scroll
> and restored it to its place.
> No doubt Meiun did the same.
> Although indeed a holy man,
> he did not in the end escape
> karma accrued from past lives.
> His is a sad and sobering tale.

> *(speech)*
> On the twenty-first of that month, Meiun's place of exile was fixed as
> the province of Izu, chosen over other locations suggested because of
> his denunciation by Saikō and his sons. The authorities sent police to
> his Shirakawa residence, with orders to expel him from the city that
> very day. Weeping, Meiun left Shirakawa and entered the Issaikyō as-
> cetic community at Awataguchi. On the Mountain the monks grasped
> that Saikō and his sons were in the end their chief foe. They wrote
> down their names and placed them under the raised left foot of Kon-
> pira, one of the Twelve Divine Generals in the Central Hall, so as to
> have Konpira trample them.
> "O Twelve Divine Generals!" they bawled.

....

52. Saichō (767–822), the great monk who brought Tendai Buddhism to Japan from China and founded
Mount Hiei.

"O seven thousand Yaksha minions![53]

Let not a day, not an hour go by

before you recall the lives of those three!"

Their curses were a terror to hear.

On the twenty-third, Meiun left the Issaikyō community for his place of exile.

It is all too easy, alas, to imagine so great a prelate's feelings

as he looked one last time on the city, hounded forward by the police,

and from the Ōsaka barrier started out toward the east.

     On reaching Uchide beach at Ōtsu,

     he caught sight of the Monju tower,[54]

     glimmering whitely in the distance,

     but one look was all he could bear.

     He then pressed a sleeve to his eyes

     and dissolved in a flood of tears.

Among the Mountain's many wise and learned monks,

Chōken, who rose later to supreme clerical rank,

was so saddened by Meiun's departure that he saw him off as far as Awazu.

Farther than that, however, he could not go,

so he bade Meiun farewell before turning back. Touched by Chōken's kindness,

Meiun gave him personal initiation into Triple Insight in One Mind,[55]

which for many years he had kept concealed in his heart.

     The Buddha himself, Shakyamuni,

     taught this practice, which passed down

     through Ashvaghosha of Varanasi

     and Nagarjuna of South India,

     until this day it repaid warm devotion.

     Truly, this realm of ours lies remote,

     like a few scattered grains of millet,

     and this is indeed the soiled, latter age.

     Nonetheless, Chōken, taught this practice,

     wrung tears of emotion from his sleeves

     while on his way back to the capital,

     lost in the loftiest of thoughts.

On the Mountain the monks rose up and gathered in council.

"Between Gishin, who began the line of our Tendai abbots,

and the present, when we have reached the fifty-fifth,

there is no record of any, ever, having been sentenced to exile.

....

53. All these, like the Konpira just mentioned, are protectors of the Buddhist faith.

54. Near the Central Hall on Mount Hiei, it enshrined the bodhisattva Monju (Sanskrit: Manjushri).

55. A key principle of Tendai Buddhism: simultaneous grasp of emptiness, transience, and the nonduality of the two.

Now let us further consider the matter.
It was during the Enryaku years that our sovereign built his imperial city [782-806]
and Dengyō Daishi ascended this Mountain to teach the Tendai doctrine.
No woman blighted by the five impediments has trodden these slopes since then;
they are now home to three thousand undefiled monks.
The peak has echoed long years to voices chanting the Lotus Sutra,
while, below, the Seven Shrines vouchsafe boons ever new.
In India, Vulture Peak, northeast of the Magadha royal city,
sheltered the Buddha in the depths of its cavern;
so, too, in our land, Mount Hiei, rising northeast of the capital,
offers the realm protection from baneful influences.
Here generations of sage emperors and wise subjects have built their altars.
These may indeed be the latter days of the Law,
but that excuses no one who injures our Mountain.
No, this is not to be endured."
So they spoke, amid cries and imprecations.
Then, to a man, they descended on Higashi-Sakamoto.

2. The Adept Yixing

The monks deliberated once more before the shrine of Jūzenji Gongen.
"Please hear us!" they prayed. "We simply must go down to Awazu,
recover our abbot, and ensure that he stays with us.
But he is closely guarded, and bringing him back safely will not be easy.
We have no choice but to trust in the might of our great divinity, Sannō.
If we really are to recover him successfully, without incident,
then, we implore you, show us now a miraculous sign!"
So the old monks begged their patron with fierce intensity.
Thereupon a young man, a servant of Jōen at Mudōji,
Tsurumaru by name, at the time in his eighteenth year,
betrayed great distress of body and mind.
Sweat poured from him, and all at once he began to rave.
     "Jūzenji has entered me!" he cried.
     "These are perhaps the latter days,
     but nonetheless I fail to grasp
     how they can simply march our abbot
     off to some other, distant province.
     The horror of this will last many lives.
     If this is how things are to be now,
     what is the good of remaining present
     here below the slopes of the Mountain?"

He pressed his sleeves to his eyes
and sobbed bitterly. Unconvinced,
the monks addressed him: "If in truth
you speak an oracle from Jūzenji,
then we must ask you to offer proof.
Return each of these, without mistake,
to the monk who actually owns it."
There were hundreds of elders present,
each with a rosary in his hand,
and they tossed all these rosaries
up onto the broad veranda
before the sanctuary of Jūzenji.
The possessed youth went rushing about,
collecting them and giving each back,
unerringly, to its rightful owner.
Deeply stirred by this miracle,
the monks, palms pressed together,
shed tears of joy. "All right!" they shouted.
"All right! Let's go and fetch our abbot!"
And off they went, like a moving cloud.
Some followed the lakeshore path
toward Shiga and Karasaki;
others sailed straight across the lake
from Yamada and Yabase.
The spectacle was too much for the guards,
although there were a good many of them.
They took to their heels in all directions.
The monks headed for the old provincial temple in Ōtsu.
Their arrival astonished the deposed abbot.
He protested, "But they say that a man under imperial ban
should never even see the sun or the moon.
When His Cloistered Eminence's decree orders me driven forthwith from the
    city,
I cannot possibly loiter a moment on my way.
Hurry back, you monks, hurry back up your Mountain."
Then he came out to the very edge of the room and spoke.
    "I was born," he went on, "into a house
    that furnishes ministers of state,
    and ever since I first gave myself
    to studying the Tendai doctrine
    in the peace of the Hiei valleys,

I aspired to master the full Teaching,
exoteric and esoteric,
and successfully grasped them both.
I only wanted our Mountain to flourish,
and I prayed ardently as well
for the prosperity of our realm.
Another cherished ambition of mine
was properly to nurture you monks.
Surely the gods who watch over us
know that I speak only the truth.
I have done nothing to merit blame.
Falsely accused, I have received
a harsh sentence of banishment—
one for which I would never presume
to reproach gods, buddhas, or men.
The warmth of feeling you have shown
in coming all the way here to find me
is something that I can never repay."
Tears of emotion soaked those sleeves,
dyed to a senior prelate's clove tan,
and every monk present wept with him.
They brought a palanquin forward.
"Please, Your Reverence," they urged him, "get in, quickly!"
"Once upon a time," he replied, "I stood at the head of three thousand monks.
Now that I am, as you see, a mere banished criminal,
how could I possibly let you monks, men of great learning and wisdom,
bear me on your shoulders? No, even if it were right for me to go with you,
I would put on straw sandals and walk, like the rest of you."
He would not board the palanquin.
Now, present in the throng was one Adept Yūkei, a fighting monk from the West
    Pagoda of Hiei.
Seven feet tall, he wore black leather-laced armor,
roughly plated with leather and steel and prolonged by sturdy skirts.
He had removed his helmet, which his monks now carried for him,
and he leaned, as on a staff, upon a long, plain-wood-handled halberd.
"Make way!" he cried, pushing ahead through the throng
until he came before the deposed abbot himself
and fixed on him, for a moment, a glittering gaze.
        "Your Reverence, this stance of yours
        is just what got you into this trouble,"
he said. "Now, get in." The frightened Meiun hastened to do so.

Overjoyed to have him at last,
the monks let no menial bear him;
no, it was the great ones among them
who, with whoops and shouts of triumph,
shouldered him onward up the slope
turn by turn—except for Yūkei,
whose fierce grip on the forward poles
all but broke both pole and halberd.
Up that long, steep climb he strode
as though walking on level ground.

They set the palanquin down before the Great Lecture Hall and deliberated
   further.
"We have now been down to Awazu," they said, "and recovered our abbot.
However, he is under imperial ban.
To keep here and recognize as our abbot a man condemned to exile
is to court reprisals. How are we to proceed?"
Yūkei stepped forward to speak his piece.

"Our Mountain," he declared, "is sacred
beyond any holy site in Japan.
Here we pronounce concerted prayers
for peace in the realm; here shines
the full dignity of mighty Sannō.
Here the Buddha's and the Sovereign's Ways
reign equally, like the horns of a bull.

Therefore the very monks of Mount Hiei are peerless in understanding;
nor does the world at large make light of the least of them.
And our abbot, then: He is lofty in wisdom, the chief of our three thousand.
He is weighty in virtue, the greatest monk of our Mountain.
Blameless, he has nonetheless been saddled with blame.

Does not the whole of Mount Hiei,
the whole capital rage at this?
Kōfukuji and Miidera—
do they not mock this spectacle?
Gone is the master of both schools,
the esoteric and exoteric,
and everywhere the scholar-monks
neglect what was once devoted study.
Nobody, surely, could fail to mourn.
To put the matter perfectly plainly,
they are welcome to call me, Yūkei,
the ringleader of the rebels,

welcome to jail me, to banish me,
welcome to cut off my head if they wish,
for I would take that in this life
as a very great honor and, in the next,
as a memory worth eternal pride!"
Tears poured in streams from his eyes
while the assembled monks murmured, "Yes!"
Everyone after that called Yūkei
"Reverend Thunderbolt"
and his distinguished student Ekei
"Little Thunderbolt."
The monks took their deposed abbot to the valley south of the East Pagoda,
where they accommodated him in the Myōkō lodge.
Perhaps not even divinity incarnate can escape when calamity strikes.
Of old, there was in the realm of Great Tang a learned adept named Yixing,
a chaplain to the emperor, Xuanzong.
It came to be noised about that Yixing was carrying on
with Xuanzong's great favorite, Yang Guifei.
In ancient times, as they do now, in states great or small,
people delight in malicious gossip. The rumor was quite untrue,
but the mere suspicion sufficed. Yixing was banished to Tokhara.[56]
Three roads lead to that land.
The Rinchi road is for the emperor, the Yūchi road for commoners.
Down the Anketsu road are sent those guilty of heinous crimes.
Yixing traveled this road, for he was a criminal.
On he went, seven days and nights, and never saw sun or moon.

All was darkness and desolation.
The path ahead vanished into gloom
among dense trees and plunging slopes.
No sound, until far down the ravine
a single bird called, and fresh tears
soaked his mossy, blameless sleeves.
False as that accusation was,
and the sentence that banished him,
heaven then had mercy on him,
showing him the Nine Luminaries,
so as thereafter to protect him.
On the instant he bit his finger

---

56. A vaguely conceived ancient kingdom, possibly in the northwest of India. The apparently Chinese names below ("Rinchi road," etc.) are given in Japanese form because the proper characters for them—if any—are unknown.

and drew in blood, on his left sleeve,
the Luminaries as he saw them.
This is the Mandala of the Nine,[57]
so revered in the Shingon school,
both in China and in Japan.

3. *The Execution of Saikō*

News that the monks had taken back their deposed abbot further enraged the
    cloistered emperor.
"The monks of Mount Hiei have made trouble often enough before," Saikō said,
"but if you ask me, they have gone too far this time.
I have never heard of such brazen impertinence.
It is time for decisive action."
So did Saikō, oblivious of his own coming demise
and heedless of the Sannō Deity's manifest will,
trouble the cloistered sovereign with his words.

> The subject who slanders others
> sows, they say, discord in the realm.
> And, indeed, it is perfectly true:
> "Orchids eagerly multiply,
> but the autumn winds lay them waste;
> a king aspires to greater glory,
> but the slanderer brings darkness."
> Perhaps this was just such a case.

The cloistered sovereign discussed the matter with Lord Narichika and those
    around him,
and word of a coming attack on the Mountain spread;
hence also a rumor that some of the monks there were saying,
"No one born and nurtured on imperial soil may defy an imperial command,"
and therefore secretly urging compliance with the cloistered sovereign's decree.
Meiun, at the Myōkō lodge, heard of these divided loyalties.
"Ah," he said sadly, "I wonder what trials await me next."
However, he heard no more about exile.
Because of the trouble on Mount Hiei,
Narichika had had to put aside the project that most deeply absorbed him.
Privately he went on preparing for it in various ways, but really only for show.
There was no sign that his rebellion could possibly succeed.

....

57. An esoteric mandala that depicts the Nine Luminaries (sun, moon, and seven other major celestial bodies) as deities.

His closest co-conspirator, Tada no Yukitsuna, therefore came to lose hope. The cloth that Narichika had given him, to make covers for his men's bows, he had sewn instead into *hitatare* and simple, unlined robes, and meanwhile he racked his brains over what to do. "No," he reflected, "considering the tremendous strength of the Heike, it is now all but impossible to overthrow them. I have lent myself to a pointless plot, and I am finished if word of it gets out." He decided to stay alive by shifting his loyalty to the Heike, before they should learn from someone else what was going on.

Late at night on the twenty-ninth of that same fifth month, Tada no Yukitsuna presented himself at Nishi-Hachijō and announced that he wished to speak to Lord Kiyomori.

"He never normally comes here," Kiyomori remarked. "What is this about? Go and hear what he has to say." He sent Morikuni, the heir apparent's chief equerry, to do so.

Yukitsuna insisted that he must speak to Lord Kiyomori in person, so Kiyomori resigned himself to meeting him in the gallery next to the middle gate. "It is very late, you know," he said. "Why must you see me now? What is all this about?"

"Too many people would be watching during the day. I preferred to come under cover of darkness," Yukitsuna replied. "Lately the cloistered emperor's men have been arming themselves and massing troops. Have you heard about that, my lord?"

Kiyomori seemed unimpressed. "I gather they mean to attack Mount Hiei," he said.

Yukitsuna moved closer to him and whispered, "No, my lord, that is not so. My understanding is that their object is the Taira house itself."

"Does the cloistered emperor know about this?"

"Of course he does.

In fact, Lord Narichika is raising forces on the strength of a decree from him."

Yukitsuna told Kiyomori the story, even embellishing it somewhat:

what Shunkan was doing, what Yasuyori and Saikō were saying, and so on.

Then he excused himself and left.

The astonished Kiyomori bellowed mightily to rouse his guards.

Terrified that his indiscretion might get him called in as a witness,

Yukitsuna hitched up his skirts and fled out the gate—not that anyone was after him—

feeling as though he had just set a great plain ablaze.

Kiyomori summoned Sadayoshi first.

"The capital," he said, "apparently teems with rebels aiming to overthrow the Heike.

Let all our people know, and muster our men."
Sadayoshi galloped off to do so.

     Right Commander Lord Munemori,
     Palace Guards Captain Tomomori,
     Secretary Captain Shigehira,
     Chief Left Equerry Yukimori,
     and the others, clad in armor
     and each bearing bow and arrows,
     assembled in the greatest haste,
     and so, too, a host of warriors
     swept in like gathering clouds or mists.
     At Nishi-Hachijō that night,
     there must have been easily
     six or seven thousand mounted men.[58]

Dawn brought the sixth of the month. Before it grew light,
Kiyomori summoned Abe no Sukenari, of the police.
"You will go as fast as you can to the cloistered emperor's residence,"
   he said.
"You will call out Nobunari, and you will tell him this:
'Those in the circle around His Cloistered Eminence
plan to destroy my house and sow chaos throughout the realm.
Each of them is to be arrested, interrogated, and punished.'
Inform His Cloistered Eminence that he is not to interfere."
Sukenari hastily complied.
He called out Nobunari, the master of the cloistered emperor's table,
and told him what was afoot. Nobunari paled.
Then he went before the sovereign and relayed all he had heard.
"Oh, no!" the cloistered emperor said to himself in dismay.
"My men's secret plans are out!" But to Nobunari he only muttered,
"What is he talking about?" He gave no real answer at all.
Sukenari raced back to Kiyomori with his report.
"I knew it!" Kiyomori exclaimed. "Yukitsuna was telling the truth.
Without his warning I would have been in danger."
He dispatched Kageie, the governor of Hida, and Sadayoshi, the governor of
   Chikugo,
with orders to seize the rebels. Parties of two or three hundred mounted men
accordingly bore down on the houses in question to do that.

....

58. On the basis of limited historical evidence, it is plausible to imagine the "real" figure in this case, as
in all others below in the tale, as very roughly 10 percent of the one cited.

Kiyomori next sent a messenger to the Naka-no-mikado and Karasumaru
　　crossing,
where Narichika lived. "I have a matter to discuss with you,"
the message said. "Please come immediately."
It never occurred to Narichika that he was in trouble himself.
"Oh, dear!" he thought. "He must have heard about His Cloistered Eminence
planning an attack on Mount Hiei and wants me to stop him.
His Cloistered Eminence is much too angry for that, though.
There isn't a thing I can do."
　　　　Graceful in a lovely, soft hunting cloak,
　　　　he rode in a gaily decked-out carriage,
　　　　accompanied by three or four housemen—
　　　　all of them, down to servants and groom,
　　　　outfitted with exceptional care.
　　　　Alas, it dawned on him only later
　　　　that this was his last such journey from home.
He noticed as he approached Nishi-Hachijō
that a wide area around it swarmed with warriors.
"There are so many!" he exclaimed to himself. "What in the world is going on?"
With a beating heart, he alighted from his carriage and entered the gate,
to find within a dense press of more warriors.
A cluster of especially terrifying ones awaited him at the middle gate.
They seized him by the arms and dragged him off.
"Maybe we'd better tie him up," they remarked.
Lord Kiyomori peered out from behind his blinds.
"No need for that," he said, so fourteen or fifteen surrounded him,
hoisted him onto the veranda, and shut him up in a tight little room.
Narichika thought he was dreaming. He had no idea what was happening.
While his men dispersed, swallowed into the crowd,
his servants and groom, deathly pale, abandoned his carriage and fled.
　　　　Meanwhile they captured and brought in
　　　　the novice Renjō; the prelate Shunkan;
　　　　Motokane, who governed Yamashiro;
　　　　Masatsuna, from Ceremonial;
　　　　and the three police lieutenants,
　　　　Yasuyori, Nobufusa, Sukeyuki.
　　　　The monk Saikō heard of all this
　　　　and, no doubt eager to save himself,
　　　　raced with his whip brandished high
　　　　to the cloistered emperor's residence.
　　　　Heike men intercepted him.

"You're wanted at Nishi-Hachijō,"
they announced. "Go there now."
"But I have a report for His Cloistered Eminence. I am just on my way to him,"
Saikō protested. "I will go there straight afterward."
"You miserable monk!" they retorted. "What report would *that* be?
Oh, no, no more nonsense from *you*!"
They pulled him down from his horse, suspended him in midair,
and kept him dangling all the way to Nishi-Hachijō.
Since he had been a ringleader from the beginning,
they bound him with special care and dragged him into the small court.
Lord Kiyomori stood above him on the wide veranda.
"This," he said, "is what happens to anyone who would overthrow me.

> Drag the miserable cur over here!"
> They moved him to the veranda edge,
> and there Kiyomori, fully shod,
> furiously trampled Saikō's face.

"Oh, yes," he raged, "I watched the cloistered emperor pick up the likes of you
  from among the dregs of men,
appoint you to offices you had no right to hold, and give the lot of you,
fathers and sons, treatment beyond anything you ever deserved.
Then you went and provoked a crisis by banishing the blameless abbot of Mount
  Hiei.
And now, to top it off, it turns out that you've been plotting rebellion
to destroy my house. So tell me all about it!"
Saikō, always a man of exceptional courage, neither blanched nor flinched.
Instead he sat up straight and laughed derisively.

> "You have it backward," he said. "It is *you*, Lord Kiyomori, who talk
> bigger than you are. Others may feel different, but as for myself, I will
> not have you speak to me that way. Being in His Cloistered Eminence's
> employ, I was in no position not to subscribe to what the master of his
> household, Narichika, presented to me as an imperial decree. So I did.
> But what *you* say sticks in my craw. Your father was Tadamori, the late
> head of the Bureau of Justice, but you never even entered court service
> until your fourteenth or fifteenth year. Then, when you began fre-
> quenting the household of the late counselor Fujiwara no Ienari, the
> youth of the city nicknamed you 'Stuck-up Heida.' In the Hōen years,
> on your commander's orders, you captured thirty pirate chieftains,
> and for that you were awarded the fourth rank and made a lieutenant
> of the Watch, but at the time people criticized even that as too good
> for you. The very idea that a man dismissed as unworthy to enter the
> privy chamber should rise to hold the office of chancellor—now, *that*

Kiyomori interrogates Saikō.

I would call exceeding *your* station! On the other hand, it is hardly un-
precedented for a houseman to become a provincial governor or an
officer in the police. In what way, then, have I exceeded mine?"

He addressed Kiyomori so boldly that for a moment Kiyomori was
too angry to speak. At last he said, "Don't just behead this fellow. No,
tie him up good and tight."

Matsura no Tarō Shigeyoshi obeyed his lord's command.

He crushed Saikō's arms and legs and tortured him variously.

Since Saikō had never contested the charge, the torture was severe,

and he told everything. They filled four or five sheets of paper with his confession.

Then Kiyomori ordered his jaw split, which they did.

Next he was beheaded at the Gojō-Suzaku crossing.

His elder son, Morotaka, formerly governor of Kaga, was in exile to Idota in
    Owari.

A local official there, Oguma no Koresue, carried out the order to execute him.

Saikō's younger son, Morotsune, was in prison.

They took him out and executed him on the riverbank at Rokujō.

Morohira, his younger brother and a junior officer in the Left Gate Watch,

together with three of his men, was likewise beheaded.

These nobodies got above themselves,

meddled in what never concerned them,

had an innocent abbot banished,
and so, it seems, reaped their reward:
For the godly wrath of great Sannō
struck them and instantly laid them low.
So it is that they met their fate.

4. The Lesser Remonstrance

Dripping with sweat, shut up in that tiny room, Narichika said to himself,
"Oh, no! That business we've been planning must have leaked out!
But who leaked it? It must be one of His Cloistered Eminence's guards!"
His mind was turning over every conceivable possibility
when he heard loud footsteps approaching from behind.
"This is it, then," he thought. "I'm finished. They're coming for me."
It was Lord Kiyomori himself, loudly tramping the board floor,
slapping open the sliding door into where Narichika sat.
He wore a short, plain, white silk robe and wide trousers that hid his feet;
the unadorned dagger at his side lolled casually in its scabbard.

> Seething with rage, Kiyomori
> glared at the figure before him.
> "I should have taken care of you
> already back in Heiji," he said,
> "but Shigemori offered his life
> for yours until I relented.
> That is why you still have your head.
> What do you have to say about *that*?

> And what do you have against us, then, that you should scheme to de-
> stroy our house? They say it takes a man to feel gratitude, since a beast
> feels none. However, our time is not yet over, no indeed. So here I am,
> at your service and eager for a full account of your plans."

> "But this is all wrong!" Narichika answered. "Someone must have
> slandered me. Please inquire further!"

> Kiyomori did not even let him finish. Instead he called loudly for an
> attendant. Sadayoshi appeared. "Give me that Saikō's confession," he
> ordered. Sadayoshi brought it to him. Kiyomori took it and read it out
> to Narichika several times. "Absolutely disgusting!" he exclaimed.
> "And *now* what do you have to say for yourself?" He threw the docu-
> ment in Narichika's face, slammed the sliding door shut again, and
> stormed off. Still in a rage, he called for Tsunetō and Kaneyasu. Seno-
> ono Tarō Kaneyasu and Nanba no Jirō Tsunetō arrived.

"Take that man and drag him down into the court!" he commanded.
Neither leaped to obey.
"There are Lord Shigemori's feelings to consider, my lord," they said.
Kiyomori's fury only grew.
"I see," he said. "For you the palace minister's orders outweigh mine.
You hardly care what I say. So I have no choice."
The two men must have seen trouble coming.

> Both stood up immediately
> and forced Narichika to the ground.
> Lord Kiyomori brightened up.
> "Flatten him! Make him howl!" he said.
> Each put his mouth next to an ear.
> "You're going to have to scream, my lord,
> somehow or other," they whispered,
> then went ahead and stretched him out.
> Narichika screamed several times
> as horribly as any sinner
> guilty of crimes among the living
> and captive now in the afterworld,
> when weighed against his own karma,
> faced with the Great Mirror of Truth,[59]
> and judged by the gravity of his sins
> to suffer commensurate torment
> at the hands of the fiends of hell.
> Xiao and Fan were thrown into jail,
> Han and Peng were killed and pickled,
> Chao Cuo ended up executed,
> Zhou and Wei were sentenced for crimes.
> Xiao He, Fan Kuai, Han Xin, Peng Yue—
> all ministers loyal to Han Gaozu—
> suffered ignominy and defeat
> from the slander of little men.
> Was Narichika's case like theirs?
>   Caught up now in this painful plight,
> Narichika shuddered to think
> what might become of Naritsune,
> his first son, and the rest of his children.

....

59. The mirror held up to the soul newly arrived before Enma, the king of the underworld and judge of the dead.

It was the sixth month and very hot,
but he could not loosen his clothes,
and in the unbearable heat
he felt sure he would suffocate.
Sweat and tears streamed from him.

"But Lord Shigemori—at least *he* won't abandon me," Narichika assured himself. He could not imagine, however, who might take Shigemori his message.

Lord Shigemori arrived only much later, with his eldest son, Koremori, riding in the back of his carriage and accompanied by four or five men from the Palace Guards and two or three attendants. He had not a single warrior with him. So utterly relaxed was his manner that Kiyomori, his father, could hardly believe his eyes; nor could anyone else. Sadayoshi went straight up to him while he alighted. "How can you possibly go without even one armed guard," he said, "in a crisis like this?"

"Crisis?" Shigemori replied. "A crisis is a calamity that threatens the realm. How could anyone call a private incident like this a crisis?" The armed men present fidgeted nervously.

"And where have you put Grand Counselor Narichika?" Shigemori inquired.
He slid doors open here and there for a look.
One had crossed timbers lashed over it: in there, presumably.
He opened it.
There lay Narichika, facedown, dissolved in tears, and avoiding his visitor's eyes.
"What have they done to you?" Shigemori asked.
Only then did Narichika look up, poor man, relief written all over his face,
much as a sinner in hell might gaze on the bodhisattva Jizō.[60]
"How can this possibly have happened to me?" he said.
"Now that you are here, though, I can at least entertain some hope.
I nearly faced execution back in the Heiji years,
and only your kindness kept my head on my shoulders.
I rose to senior second rank and the post of grand counselor,
and already I have passed my fortieth year.
I could never repay what you have done for me, not over countless lives of trying.
And now, just as you did before, you are offering me my worthless life back.
If I survive this, I will renounce the world,
confine myself on retreat on Mount Kōya or at Kokawa,
and devote myself to praying for your enlightenment in the life to come."

....

60. Jizō visits sinners in hell, to offer them hope and relief.

"Very well, but there is no question of anyone taking your life," Shigemori
answered.

"And even if there were, here I am, ready to give mine for yours."

With this he left to go before his father, Kiyomori.

"You should think carefully," he said, "before you do away with Narichika.

> Akisue, his ancestor,
> served Retired Emperor Shirakawa.
> None in this line, before Narichika,
> achieved the senior second rank
> or the office of grand counselor.
> In the cloistered sovereign's eyes,
> he enjoys favor beyond compare.
> I venture to doubt that it would be wise
> impulsively to take his head.
> Banishment from the capital
> surely will do quite well enough.
> Sugawara no Michizane,
> enshrined as Tenjin at Kitano,
> suffered from Tokihira's slander,
> which sullied his name and exiled him
> over the western sea to Kyushu;[61]
> so, too, Takaakira, who,
> slandered by Tada no Mitsunaka,
> could only confide his bitterness
> to the clouds over the westward road.[62]
> The slander in both cases was false,
> but neither man escaped banishment:
> a fate ascribed ever since to error
> on Emperors Daigo's and Reizei's part.
> Such things did happen in the past—
> imagine, then, in these latter days!
> Now that you have him in custody,
> what harm could it possibly do
> to wait before executing him?
> For, as we read in the classics,

....

61. The scholar and statesman Sugawara no Michizane (845–903) died in unjust exile at Dazaifu, in Kyushu. When his angry spirit began causing vengeful havoc in the capital, the court appeased him by declaring him a deity under the name Tenjin and enshrining him in the city (Kitano Tenmangū). As Tenman Tenjin he was enshrined also in Dazaifu. The tale alludes to him repeatedly.

62. The brilliant Minamoto no Takaakira (914–82), another victim of unjust exile to Kyushu, has been cited for centuries as a possible model for the hero of The Tale of Genji.

'When in doubt, lighten punishment
and increase the weight of reward.'
As you know, Narichika's younger sister is my wife and Koremori his son-in-law.
You may imagine that I address you in this vein
because he is a close relative, but that is not so.
No, I do so only for the sake of the world at large, for our sovereign, and for our
 house.
Some years ago, during the Hōgen era,
the late Shinzei stood at the height of his power when the death penalty,
lapsed since the execution of Fujiwara no Nakanari under Emperor Saga, [r. 809–23]
was imposed once more for the first time in twenty-five reigns,
and Haughty Left Minister Yorinaga was dug up again, to be verified.
In the way of government actions, these things struck me then as serious excesses.
This is why the men of old, too, used to say, 'Executions multiply rebels.'
And so it was. Two years later, in Heiji, chaos resumed.
They dug Shinzei up from underground, cut off his head, and put it on public show.
What he had done in Hōgen soon rebounded on him.
Now, *that* is a terrifying thought.
Narichika, on the other hand, poses no great threat as an enemy of the court.
On either side there is reason for fear.
For yourself, glory cannot last much longer, and you probably need not worry;
but undoubtedly you still wish your children and grandchildren good fortune.
> The deeds of the fathers, good or bad,
> clearly touch their descendants' lives.
> The house with a rich store of good
> will thrive far into times to come;
> the one long given to evil ways
> faces only calamity—
> so I have heard. No, believe me,
> to execute Narichika tonight
> would be a very grave mistake."
> Lord Kiyomori must have agreed,
> for he renounced beheading him.

>> Next, Lord Shigemori went out to the middle gate, where he addressed
>> the Taira housemen. "Do not under any circumstances let an order
>> from Lord Kiyomori persuade you to put Lord Narichika to death," he
>> said. "He will regret it later if he lets rage get the better of him. Do not
>> blame me if you err and then suffer for it." The warriors shook with
>> fear. "And another thing," he went on. "Tsunetō and Kaneyasu, I vigor-
>> ously deplore your harshness toward Lord Narichika this morning.
>> Why were you not afraid that I might hear of it? Ignorant louts, that is

all you are." The two men displayed intense contrition. Having spoken,
Shigemori returned to his residence.
Meanwhile Narichika's attendants had raced with the news
back to the Naka-no-mikado and Karasumaru crossing, where he lived.
His wife and their gentlewomen wailed loud and long.
"Warriors are on their way here at this moment," they reported.
"Apparently they are to take Lord Naritsune and all the other children away.
Flee as fast as you can, please, never mind where."
        "What good could it possibly do me,
        as I am now, to linger behind,"
        Lord Narichika's wife replied,
        "clinging in safety to further life?
        All I want is to vanish with him,
        two dewdrops gone after one night.
        Oh, but it is such agony
        never to have for a moment guessed
        that this morning would be my last!"
        She collapsed in a storm of weeping.
        Word arrived that the warriors
        were already approaching fast.
        No: After all, she could not bear it—
        so to be taken, covered with shame.
        She put her daughter, in her tenth year,
        and her little son, in his eighth,
        into her carriage and started off,
        without a thought at first for where.
        She did have to choose *somewhere*, though.
        So she followed Ōmiya northward
        into the hills, to Unrin-in.
        Her attendants allowed her to alight
        at a nearby monks' lodge; then one and all,
        anxious to look after themselves,
        said good-bye and returned to their homes.
        Now she was alone with her children.
        Nobody came to see how they were.
        Poor thing, her mood is easily guessed.
        She watched the sun course down the sky
        and pictured her husband's fleeting life
        extinguished that very evening.
        She all but died herself at the thought.
        Behind her, at the house she had left,

the many servants and gentlewomen
had done nothing to tidy things up.
They had not even secured the gate.
There stood the horses in their stable,
but no one saw to bringing them feed.
By dawn on those earlier mornings,
horses and carriages thronged the gate,
ranks of visitors sported and danced,
oblivious to all notion of tact,
and the neighbors, ever fearful,
dared not even raise their voices.
So it had been, until yesterday,
but in one night everything had changed.
There it was, all too plain to see:
the truth that the mighty must fall.
"Joy, once over, yields to sorrow"—
so wrote Ōe no Asatsuna,
and indeed, how right he was!

5. *The Plea for Naritsune*

The Tanba lieutenant Naritsune had spent that night
at the cloistered emperor's residence, in waiting on the sovereign.
He had not yet left when some of his father's men arrived in great haste,
asked to speak to him, and reported what had happened.
"Why has no word of this yet come from Norimori?" he asked,
but the words were hardly out of his mouth when Norimori's messenger arrived.
This Norimori, a consultant, was Lord Kiyomori's younger brother.
Known as the "Gateside Consultant" because he lived just inside the Rokuhara
    main gate,
he was Naritsune's father-in-law.
"For some reason," his message said,
"Lord Kiyomori wants me to bring you straight to Nishi-Hachijō."
Naritsune understood what the matter was.
He called out the gentlewomen attending the cloistered sovereign.

    "Last night there seems to have been
    a commotion in the city," he said.
    "At first I thought the monks of Mount Hiei
    must be on their way down again,
    and it had nothing to do with me.
    But no: My own life was at stake.

I gather that this very night
my father is to be executed,
and as for me, I have little doubt
that very soon I shall be, too.
I should like to go in to see His Cloistered Eminence one last time,
yet I fear that it would be wrong for an all-but-condemned man to do so."
The women went before their lord and told him everything.
Thunderstruck, he saw that he had been right about Kiyomori's messenger that
   morning.
Alas, he reflected, knowledge of their secret plot had leaked out!
The thought was extremely distressing.
However, he let it be known that they were to admit Naritsune.
Naritsune entered. The cloistered emperor wept with him, in silence.
Too choked with tears to speak, Naritsune said nothing for some time.
At last, though, he knew that the moment had come.
Pressing his sleeves to his streaming eyes, he withdrew from the presence.
The cloistered emperor watched him go.
"How I hate this latter age!" he said to himself, shedding gracious tears.
"I suppose that I will never see this young man again."

     Everyone on his household staff
     tugged at Naritsune's sleeves,
     clung in anguish to trailing folds,
     and not one of them failed to weep.
     Naritsune then made his way
     to the house of his father-in-law,
     where his wife, soon to give birth,
     felt close to dying already
     at this morning's dreadful news.
     Naritsune, his tears still flowing,
     wept afresh at the sight of her.

          He had a nurse named Rokujō. "The first time I came to give you suck,"
          she said, weeping, "I took you up in my arms straight from the blood
          of birth, and after that I never minded aging with the passing years,
          because my only joy was seeing you grow. It all seems such a little
          while ago, and yet twenty-one years have gone by, and in that whole
          time I have never been far from your side. I worried whenever you
          were slow to come home from the palace or from His Cloistered Emi-
          nence's residence, wondering what could have happened to you."
          "Do not grieve," Naritsune replied. "There is Lord Norimori: I am
          sure that he will plead successfully for my life."
          His nurse, however, wept and wailed without shame.

Messenger after messenger came,
sent out from Nishi-Hachijō.
"The only thing to do is to go,"
Norimori declared. "Only then
can we know how this will turn out."
So he set forth, with Naritsune
riding in the rear of his carriage.
Ever since Hōgen and Heiji days,
the Heike had known only success;
no grief, no distress had touched them.
Alone, the unhappy Norimori,
thanks to his hopeless son-in-law,
had at last to deal with sorrow.
On approaching Nishi-Hachijō, Norimori halted his carriage
and sent word ahead to request admission.
"Tanba Lieutenant Naritsune is not to be allowed in," Kiyomori insisted,
so Naritsune was made to alight at the nearby house of a Taira houseman.
Norimori proceeded alone through the gate,
leaving his son-in-law surrounded by warrior guards.
Parted this way from his sole support, Naritsune felt forlorn indeed.

Norimori waited respectfully at the middle gate, but Kiyomori declined to come out to meet him. By Gendayū Suesada, Norimori then sent in this message to him: "I bitterly regret my close relationship with this very foolish man, but I can do nothing now to change it. My daughter, whom I allowed him to marry, has lately been indisposed, and her distress at this morning's news has brought her close to death. There is surely no compelling reason now not to entrust her husband for some time to my care. Being who I am, I can guarantee that he would commit no further folly."

Suesada took his words to Kiyomori, who replied,
"There you go again, Norimori. You never quite understand, do you?"
For some time that was all. Then Kiyomori answered more fully:
"The grand counselor Narichika has been planning to destroy the Taira house
and sow chaos throughout the realm. And Naritsune is his son and heir.
Your relationship to him, close or distant, can do nothing to sway me.
If their conspiracy had succeeded, tell me:
Do you suppose that you yourself would have come through it safely?"
Suesada returned to Norimori with this answer.
Bitterly disappointed, Norimori renewed his plea:

"Ever since Hōgen and Heiji,
I have fought in repeated battles,

always ready to die for you,
and I would gladly shield you, too,
should some future storm threaten.
Yes, it is true, I am old now,
but I still have many young sons
who merit your full confidence.
If, nonetheless, you will not allow me to take Naritsune under my care,
then you must be convinced that I, Norimori, am a traitor.

Having so incurred your suspicion,
I have lost my place in the world.
I shall therefore bid you farewell,
enter upon the Buddha's Way,
retire to some far mountain hamlet,
and devote myself solely to prayer
for release in the life to come.
There is nothing to gain from this one.
To live, after all, means to hope.
From lost hope springs bitterness.
Better, then, to renounce the world
and tread instead the true path."
Suesada came again before Lord Kiyomori.
"Lord Norimori has made up his mind to take the great step," he said.
"Please act for the best."
"This is all very well," the astonished Kiyomori answered,
"but for him to be thinking of leaving the world is just too much.
Tell him, then, that for the time being I leave Naritsune in his care."
Suesada returned to Norimori and reported what he had heard.

"Alas!" Norimori exclaimed,
"how much better to have no children!
If no tie to my daughter bound me,
I would not suffer such agony!"
And with these words he took his leave.
Naritsune was waiting for him. "Well? How did it go?" he asked.
"Kiyomori was so angry that he refused to see me at all.
He kept rejecting my appeal, until I threatened to renounce the world.
That seemed to work. He said that he would let you stay at home with me.
I hardly expect this to end well, though."
"I see," Naritsune replied. "Your great kindness has won me at least a reprieve.
But what did he say about my father?"
"That is not a subject I could have raised."
Naritsune burst into tears.

"It is a wonderful thing," he said,
"that thanks to your intercession
I should live on a little longer,
but life itself is precious to me
only so that I can, one last time,
be together with my father.
If his fate is to be beheaded,
then what good could my living do?
I would rather have you instead
beg that we should die together."
Norimori looked deeply distressed. "I did do my best for you, you know,
but I simply could not mention your father.
This morning Shigemori spoke at length to Kiyomori about him,
and I gather that for now he is out of danger."
Naritsune pressed his palms together, weeping for joy.
    "Who but a son could so quickly
    set his own difficulties aside
    and rejoice as does this young man?"—
    so Norimori reflected.
    "Yes, the true tie binds parent to child.
    Why, people are right to have children!"
    The two shared the same carriage home,
    just as when they had come that morning.
    For the women there, Naritsune
    might as well have returned from the dead.
    They clustered around him and wept for joy.

6. The Remonstrance

Lord Kiyomori had arrested a great many men,
but perhaps, in his estimation, not yet enough;
for now, in black-laced armor and silver-inlaid breastplate over red brocade,
clasping under his arm the lance with a silver-wound shaft
that the Itsukushima Deity gave him long ago in a sacred dream
when he went on pilgrimage there as the governor of Aki—
the lance that he kept every night by his pillow—
he strode to the gallery of the middle gate with a face like thunder.

There he summoned Sadayoshi. Wearing scarlet-laced armor over a tan *hitatare*, Sadayoshi, the governor of Chikugo, respectfully presented himself before his lord. After a moment of silence, Kiyomori asked, "What do you think of this, Sadayoshi? During Hōgen, Tadamasa and

more than half the Heike supported Retired Emperor Sutoku, and Tada-
mori, my father, looked after his eldest son. That made it very difficult
to choose otherwise, but I nonetheless respected the testament of Re-
tired Emperor Toba, and I fought at the head of his troops. That was my
first great service to Cloistered Emperor Go-Shirakawa.
Then, in the first year of Heiji, in the twelfth month,
when Nobuyori and Yoshitomo seized both emperors, reigning and retired,
barricaded themselves in the palace, and shrouded the realm in darkness,
it was I who crushed the evildoers at the risk of my life,
who in due course arrested Tsunemune and Korekata,[63]
and who, in short, repeatedly faced death for the cloistered sovereign.
Whatever arguments anyone may have put to him,
I fail to understand how he could have turned against us
before seven generations were out. But he did.
That dismal troublemaker Narichika, that contemptible ruffian Saikō—
he lent an ear to their blandishments and plotted our destruction.
I hold that bitterly against him.

> Any more slander from anyone,
> and I just know what he will do:
> He will hand down a formal decree
> demanding suppression of the Heike.

Once we are enemies of court, it will be far too late for regret.
So I am wondering, while I go about restoring calm,
whether to have His Cloistered Eminence move to the Toba Mansion
or even to move him here, to Nishi-Hachijō.
If I do that, his guards may well loose an arrow or two.
I shall have to warn my men about that.
Anyway, no more loyal service to this cloistered emperor!
Saddle me my horse! Bring me full-length armor!"

Morikuni rushed to Lord Shigemori and started to describe the turn
that things were taking.

"Oh, no!" Shigemori cried. "Lord Narichika's head must already
be off!"

"No, my lord," Morikuni answered, "but Lord Kiyomori has on full-
length armor, and his men are all ready to bear down on the cloistered
emperor's Hōjūji residence. He claims that he means to keep the clois-
tered emperor confined in the Toba Mansion, but secretly he intends
to banish him to Kyushu."

....

63. These somewhat complicated developments are discussed in the introduction under "'Hōgen and
Heiji': History and Angry Spirits."

The idea struck Shigemori as preposterous, but his father, in his mood of that morning, seemed quite capable of such insanity. He raced to Nishi-Hachijō as fast as his carriage would go. At the gate he alighted and entered.

There was his father, in long armor,
amid dozens of Taira nobles
dressed in robes of every color
and armor to suit each man's taste,
in two seated rows, in the gallery
adjacent to the middle gate.
Provincial governors, Guards officers,
and such spilled from the veranda
into the court in serried ranks.
Banner poles clustered in order,
girths tightly cinched on the horses,
helmet cords securely fastened;
they seemed ready to leave that instant.
Shigemori's court hat and dress,
his expansively patterned trousers
swishing and rustling into view,
made a most unusual sight.

Lord Kiyomori lowered his gaze. "Oh, no, not again!" he must have groaned to himself. "Here he comes, looking so high and mighty, as though he were better than anyone else! How I'd like to give him a piece of my mind!"

But Shigemori, son of his father though he might be, within himself honored the five precepts and valued compassion and, without, honored the five virtues[64] and upheld propriety. Presumably for that reason, Kiyomori felt ashamed to speak to him in armor, because he partially closed a sliding door and, behind it, hastily threw over his armor a plain silk cassock. The metal of his breastplate still showed, however. He tugged that part of the garment every which way to hide it.

Lord Shigemori seated himself above Munemori, his younger brother.
Kiyomori said not a word. Shigemori said nothing either.
Eventually Kiyomori found his voice.
"Narichika's rebellion hardly deserves notice," he said.
"The cloistered emperor is the one who planned it all.

....

64. The five precepts prohibit killing, stealing, licentiousness, lying, and drinking alcohol. Shigemori names the five virtues in his speech, below.

While I go about quieting things down again,
I am considering moving him, either to the Toba Mansion or, even, here.
What would you have to say to that?"
He had hardly finished speaking when Shigemori burst into tears.
"What is the matter with you?" his exasperated father asked.
Struggling to control himself, Shigemori began:

"What I hear in your words, my lord, is the end of your glory.
A man will always turn to evil when fortune no longer smiles.
Seeing you now in this guise, I scarcely credit my senses.
Yes, this land of ours is remote, a few scattered millet grains,
yet here rule the descendants of the Great Sun Goddess,
for whom Ame-no-koyane's lineage governs the realm.
Never, since the beginning, can it have been right and proper
for a man risen to chancellor to don the trappings of war.
Is that not so, especially for you who have renounced the world?
That a man should put off the robes favored by all the buddhas,
abruptly don helmet and armor, and take up bow and arrows,
amounts, within, to his brazenly breaking the precepts
and, without, to his violating benevolence, righteousness,
fitting conduct, wisdom, good faith: the five cardinal virtues.
It is not for me, I know, to accuse you of doing either,
but I cannot hold back the deep conviction of my heart.
There are in this world, you see, four great obligations:
to heaven and earth, to sovereign, to father and mother,
to sentient beings. That to the sovereign is greatest:
'Under heaven there is no land that is not the king's.'
Even the sage who washed his ears in Ying River water
or the one who harvested bracken on Mount Shouyang
knew, they say, that it was wrong to disobey the king.
Still better should you yourself know it, Father, who have
    achieved
what none of your forebears ever did: the summit of chancellor.
And I, too—talentless and benighted, as everyone knows—
even I have reached the lofty height of minister of state.
Besides, more than half the counties and provinces in the land belong to our
    house;
every estate is ours to dispose of as we please.
Do we not owe all this to our sovereign's exceptional favor?
Were you to ignore such great and repeated kindness
in a lawless attempt to bring His Cloistered Eminence low,
you would also offend the Great Sun Goddess and Hachiman.

Japan is the land of the gods,
and the gods do not accept violence against what is right.
Therefore, what His Cloistered Eminence planned did not lack its half share of
    justice.
In quelling the enemies of the court and calming the waves on the four seas,
our house has certainly rendered the throne peerless service,
but our pride in the rewards that followed can fairly be called arrogance.
Prince Shōtoku wrote in his Seventeen-Article Constitution:[65]
'Every man has his mind and his predilections.
I may judge another right and myself wrong,
I may judge myself right and another wrong,
but who can truly define where right and wrong lie?
Each is the other's wisdom or folly.
They go round and round in an endless circle.
        Should a man wax wroth against you,
        look therefore to your own failings.'
Your great good fortune is not yet over, however, for the plot stands revealed.
Moreover, you have in custody Narichika, one of the conspirators.
Whatever eccentricities His Cloistered Eminence may ponder, you have nothing
    to fear.
Administer punishment to fit the crime, then modestly report what you have done.
        With ever-increasing diligence,
        render your sovereign loyal service
        and grow in compassion for the people:
        Then you will have the gods' protection
        and never offend the Buddha's will.
        Once the gods and buddhas are with you,
        the sovereign, too, will see the light.
        Sovereign and subject, now at one,
        will acknowledge no distance between them.
        With justice and error ranged side by side,
        how could one not cleave to justice?"

7. The Signal Fires

"To that extent His Cloistered Eminence has right on his side," Shigemori
    went on,
"and I must protect his Hōjūji residence even at the risk of failure.

....

65. Prince Shōtoku (574–622) exerted a seminal influence on Japanese culture, both politically and
religiously. His Seventeen-Article Constitution (604) defines the principles of good government.

After all, I owe him everything, from my entry onto the ladder of rank
to my appointment as palace minister.
That obligation weighs more heavily than a thousand or ten thousand jewels;
it is deeper in hue than any scarlet dipped once or even twice in the dye.
That is why I should go to his residence to mount patient guard.
A modest number of warriors have given me their word
that they are prepared to die for me should the need arise.
Were I to summon them, however, and guard the residence with them,
dire consequences might easily follow.

>Alas! Should I, for my sovereign's sake,
>bend every effort to loyal service,
>I would in that same instant forget
>the gratitude I owe my father:
>gratitude higher than Mount Sumeru.
>O sorrow! Should I exert myself
>to escape being unfilial,
>at that moment I would become
>a treacherous, disloyal subject.
>I can move neither forward nor back;
>right and wrong confound my judgment.

So I have only one request, and it is this: Please, cut off my head.
I cannot possibly go to guard His Cloistered Eminence's residence,
nor can I accompany you, my father, when you go there yourself.
Of old, Xiao He accrued greater merit than any other
and therefore rose to the highest office in the land,
with permission to enter the palace wearing shoes, with a sword at his side,
but then he incurred the emperor's displeasure.
Gaozu reproved him severely and imposed harsh punishment on him.
Such examples as his suggest that a man
may reach the pinnacle of wealth, glory, favor, and lofty office
yet still, when he has risen as high as he possibly can,
discover that the greatest good fortune may after all come to an end.

>'Where wealth resides, there prosper privilege and rank;
>the tree that fruits twice a year suffers at its root.'[66]
>So I have read. I wish it were not so.

How long am I to go on living amid these endless troubles?
With what dismal karma must I have been born in this latter age,
that these miseries should now face me?

....

66. Lines from the Chinese *History of the Later Han Dynasty*.

Order one of your men, then, this instant,
to drag me down into the court and there behead me!
There is nothing to it!
Hear me, all of you! That is my wish!"

Weeping such tears as to drench his sleeves,
Shigemori spoke passionately,
and every man of the Taira house,
possessed or not of fine sympathies,
from his own sleeves wrung many a tear.

The chancellor himself, Lord Kiyomori, found himself undone by this speech from a palace minister, his son, whose judgment meant so much to him. "No, no," he protested, "I would never go that far! I am only concerned that the cloistered emperor might, on evil advice, attempt something unfortunate."

Shigemori replied, "But even if he did, by what right would you take any measure against him?" He rose, went out to the middle gate, and from there addressed the men. "You heard me just now, did you not?" he said. "My idea this morning was to stay here precisely in order to maintain calm, but the hue and cry was so great that I returned home. If you do accompany Lord Kiyomori to the cloistered emperor's residence, make sure that you see my head fall first. You who came with me, it is time to leave." With these words he returned to his residence.

There he summoned Morikuni.
"I have just received word of a disaster that threatens the realm," he said.
"Tell every man loyal to me to race here, fully armed." Morikuni did so.
"Cool and collected as he always is," the men reflected,
"he must have good reason to issue this call."
All armed themselves and galloped there at top speed.

Warriors gathered, hordes of them,
from Yodo, from Hazukashi,
from Uji, Okaya, Hino, Kanjuji,
from Daigo, Ogurusu, Umezu,
from Katsura, Ōhara, Shizuhara,
and from the village of Seryō.
Some, in armor, wore no helmet;
others, with their quiver of arrows,
turned out not to have brought a bow.
One foot or none in the stirrups,
they assembled in frantic haste.
"Lord Shigemori has raised an alarm":
So the rumor ran through them all.

At Shigemori's call, warriors rush to his residence (upper right).

The several thousand warriors
stationed at Nishi-Hachijō,
without a word to Kiyomori,
rushed to Shigemori's residence
in one babbling mass of men.
There remained behind not a single man even slightly practiced at arms.
Kiyomori, dumbfounded, summoned Sadayoshi.
"What can Lord Shigemori be up to," he wondered aloud,
"calling all these men together this way?
Does he mean to send a force against me, as he spoke right here of doing?"
Sadayoshi shed bitter tears. "Every man is what he is," he said.
"Lord Shigemori would never do that.
He surely regrets everything that he said."

Kiyomori must have hesitated to quarrel with his son, for then and there
he gave up the idea of going after the cloistered emperor. He removed
his armor, donned a monk's stole over his cassock, and—a rare thing
indeed for him—sat there fingering his beads and calling the Name.

At Shigemori's residence Morikuni, by his lord's order, registered
every arrival. He took down the names of more than ten thousand
warriors who had rushed to answer the call.

Shigemori looked the list over, then went out to his middle gate and
from there addressed them. "It is a wonderful thing," he said, "that you
should have been true to your promise and come.
Allow me to cite you such an example from the Other Realm.
King You of Zhou had a favorite, named Baosi, whom he loved best of all.
She was the greatest beauty in the land.
One thing about her displeased him, though:
She was so solemn that she never smiled.
Now, it was the practice in that realm, whenever war threatened,
to light fires hither and yon, to beat drums, and so to muster the troops.
These fires were called 'signal fires.'
Once, when an armed rebellion broke out, they indeed lit them.
At the sight the king's favorite exclaimed,
'Why, look at all those fires!' And, for the first time, she smiled.
That single smile sparked a hundred charms.
The king was so pleased that he had signal fires lit often,
even in the absence of any threat.

> The local lords assembled their men
> but found no enemy to fight.
> Lacking an enemy, they left.
> The same happened time and again,
> until nobody came at all.

Then, in the neighboring state, an evil horde arose
and attacked the capital of King You.

> The signal fires were lit, of course,
> but—so everybody assumed—
> only to amuse the favorite.
> Not a single warrior came.
> The capital fell, and King You died.
> And then that favorite, Baosi,
> turned into a fox, scampered off,
> and vanished. A frightening tale!
> When in the future I have reason
> to call all of you together again,
> please assemble as you have done.
> A disturbing report did reach me,
> but when I looked into the matter,
> the report turned out to be wrong.
> Go now, go home immediately."

So it was that he dismissed them.

In point of fact, no such report had ever reached him.
In the spirit of his remonstrance to his father,
it was instead an invention designed to reveal
whether or not the men would follow him, and how many,
and, while he had no real intention of fighting his father,
to dissuade his father from pursuing rebellion against the throne.

"That a lord is no true lord
excuses no subject from being a subject;
a father's being no true father
excuses no son from being a son.
To your lord be loyal, to your father filial."
So Confucius wrote; so Shigemori was.
His Cloistered Eminence heard the news.
"I knew this well enough already,"
he said, "but before Shigemori,
the man, one can only feel awe.
He has met anger with kindness."
The people, too, were impressed, saying,
"No doubt it was fortunate karma
that raised him to minister and commander,
but it is hard to believe that a man
could so excel in conduct and bearing
and, even in wisdom and learning,
tower so over all other men!"
"When a state has a minister
able to remonstrate with the ruler,
that state is settled and secure;
when a household has a son
willing to remonstrate with his father,
that household is properly ordered."
So it is said. Not in ancient times
or in these latter days of ours
has there ever been any like him.

8. The Exile of Narichika

On the second day of that same sixth month,
they led the grand counselor Narichika to the senior nobles' hall,
where he was offered a farewell meal,
but despair choked him, and he could not even manage his chopsticks.

They brought the carriage forward and urged him quickly to board it.
He did so with a sinking heart.
Front and rear, left and right, warriors rode all around him.
Not one of his own people was with him.
"I would gladly bid farewell to Lord Shigemori," he said.
But no, they would not allow it.
He complained from within the carriage, "It is unheard of,
even for a man banished for a grave crime, to be denied a single companion."
The warriors guarding him wet the sleeves of their armor with tears.

>Westward to Suzaku they went,
>then turned south. The palace, behind them,
>dwindled slowly into the distance.
>The servants tending the carriage, the groom
>so long familiar—each one of them
>weeping, wringing tears from his sleeves;
>and his wife, then, and his children at home—
>just imagine their misery!
>The Toba Mansion now: As they passed,
>he thought of His Cloistered Eminence
>and the many progresses he had made there,
>always with Narichika beside him.
>There was the Suhama Villa, his own—
>but he could only watch it go by.
>The carriage rolled on, out the south gate.
>"Boatman, you're late!" impatiently
>the warriors called, while Narichika
>asked only, "Where are you taking me?
>If I am to die, oh, please, let it be
>here where we are now, near the city!"
>That, at least, he felt he could expect.

"Who are you?" he inquired of a warrior near him.
"Nanba no Jirō Tsunetō," the man replied.
"Could there be, by chance, anyone of mine close by?
I have a message to leave him, before I board the boat. Please ask."
The man went running about to look but found not a soul
who would admit to any connection with Narichika.

>"All those men I had, in the good times—
>one or two thousand of them, surely!
>And to think that now not a single one
>has come, even at a safe distance,

to watch me go! Oh, it is too hard!"
So thought Narichika, weeping,
and the sturdy warriors beside him,
as before, moistened their sleeves.
In the way of trusty companions,
he now had only unending tears.
On his pilgrimages to Kumano
or to Tennōji, he had then sailed
in double-keeled ships, with triple cabins,
followed by twenty or thirty more;
now here he was in this miserable boat—
one flimsy cabin, closed by a curtain—
in alien, warrior company,
leaving the city for the last time
to venture far, far over the waves.
Anyone can imagine his grief.
That day the boat reached Daimotsu,
a harbor in the province of Settsu.

Death was the sentence that Narichika almost certainly faced. Only Lord Shigemori's intercession had successfully reduced it to exile.

When still a counselor, Narichika had enjoyed title to revenue raised from the province of Mino. In the winter of Kaō 1, [1169] Masatomo, the deputy who governed for him, had visitors: shrine servants from the Hirano estate, which belonged to Mount Hiei. They had come to sell their kudzu-fiber cloth. Masatomo, drunk at the time, spilled ink on the cloth. When they protested loudly, he barked at them to shut their mouths and trampled them in contempt. Soon enough several hundred shrine servants burst into his house. Masatomo defended himself as the law allowed and killed a dozen of them.

On the third day of the eleventh month of that year, the infuriated monks of Mount Hiei therefore formally demanded exile for Narichika, the titular governor, and jail for Masatomo. Ordered accordingly into exile in the province of Bitchū, Narichika was duly escorted along Shichijō as far as the western part of the city, but five days later the cloistered emperor, for his own reasons, commanded his return. Despite the Hiei monks' rumored curses, on the fifth of the first month in the new year Narichika was named concurrently intendant of the Right Gate Watch and chief of the police.

These appointments came to him over the heads of Lords Sukekata and Kanemasa. Sukekata was an old man. Kanemasa was then riding high, and it galled him, as the heir to his house, to be passed over that way. The truth was that Narichika had received his reward for building the Sanjō Palace. On the thirteenth of the fourth month of Kaō 3, he was promoted to the senior second rank, this time over the head of the Naka-no-mikado counselor Muneie.

In Angen 1, [1175] on the twenty-seventh of the tenth month, he rose to supernumerary grand counselor. People laughed. "The monks of the Mountain were supposed to have laid a curse on him!" they said. But that curse may well explain, after all, what happened to him in due course. The punishment of the gods and the curses of men may strike sooner or strike later; there is no knowing when.

On the third of the sixth month, a messenger from the capital reached the harbor of Daimotsu. A great commotion greeted him. "Have you brought the order to execute me?" Narichika asked. No, the messenger had not. He had come to announce the place of Narichika's exile: the island of Kojima, off the coast of Bizen.[67]

There was also a letter from Lord Shigemori.

"I did all I could," Shigemori had written,

"to have you sent somewhere isolated, near the capital, but my appeal failed.
I am thoroughly ashamed of myself.
However, he did at least honor my plea for your life."

And, to Tsunetō, "See to it that you serve him well. Do not disappoint him."

He added detailed instructions on how to prepare for the voyage.

So Narichika was torn away
from the sovereign whom he revered,
from the wife and children he so loved
that each moment without them hurt.
"But where, oh, where am I going?"
he wondered. "Never, never again
shall I see my dear family.
A few years ago, the Hiei monks
had me exiled, but my sovereign,
in his regret at losing me,
called me back from west Shichijō.
No, this rebuke is not from *him*.
But how can any of this have happened?"
He looked to the heavens, fell prostrate,
wept, but nothing brought him solace.

....

67. The island of Kojima, mentioned several times in the tale and especially prominent in 10:14, no longer exists, because the sea between it and the mainland has been filled in. It is now the Kojima Peninsula in present Okayama Prefecture.

At dawn the boat sailed, distances lengthened,
and choking tears never ceased to flow.
For him life was already over,
and yet, though a dewdrop, he lingered on.
The boat's white wake stretched out astern,
the city slipped farther and farther away,
day after day after day went by,
and at last that far destination
loomed ahead. They rowed the boat in
to Kojima Island in Bizen
and left him in a dismal hovel
good only for the local peasants.
Behind it, as on many an island,
rose a hill; the sea spread before it.
Wind through the pines on the rocky shore,
the clamor of waves: All was misery.

9. The Akoya Pine

Narichika was not the only one to be banished. Many were:
Renjō to the province of Sado, Motokane to Hōki, Masatsuna to Harima,
Nobufusa to Awa, Sukeyuki to Mimasaka.
Lord Kiyomori was on his Fukuhara estate at the time.
On the twentieth he had Settsu no Saemon Morizumi take Norimori this message:
"I have a plan. Send Naritsune here at once."
"It would be one thing if this command had come that very day," Norimori
    reflected,
"but it is too bad of him to stir up new worries now."
He let Naritsune know that he was ordered down to Fukuhara.
Naritsune set off in tears.
"Oh please, put in another plea for him," the women begged,
"even if it is unlikely to do any good."
"I have already tried every argument possible," Norimori replied.
"There is not a word more I can say, short of actually leaving the world.
But whatever desolate coast he ends up on,
I will go there and assist him while I still have life and breath."
Naritsune had a little son, now in his third year.
Being young, Naritsune usually showed no great interest in children,
but this moment of parting must have brought his son vividly to mind.
"I would gladly see him a last time," he said. The nurse brought him in.
Naritsune took him on his lap, stroked his hair, and wept.

"Ah," he sighed, "in your seventh year,
I was going to have you come of age
and serve His Cloistered Eminence,
but now all hope of that is gone.
If you live and in due course grow up,
become a monk and pray for me,
pray for me in my lives to come."
The little boy was much too young
to understand what all this meant,
but he nodded sagely nonetheless,
and at this his father and mother,
the women, and all the others present,
whether or not tender of heart,
moistened their sleeves with tears.

    The Fukuhara messenger informed Naritsune that he was to lodge at Toba that night. "I should much prefer to spend tonight, just tonight, in the capital," Naritsune replied. "The delay would hardly matter." But the messenger made it clear that that was impossible.

    That night Naritsune therefore reached Toba. This time Norimori was so angry that he did not ride in the carriage with him.

    On the twenty-second, Naritsune arrived at Fukuhara. Lord Kiyomori ordered Kaneyasu to escort him into exile in the province of Bitchū. Nervous that talk of the journey might reach Norimori, Kaneyasu treated him with great consideration all the way. However, Naritsune was not to be comforted. He spent day and night calling the Name and sighing for his father.

There on Kojima Island in Bizen,
Tsunetō, Narichika's warden, felt that the harbor was too near to be safe;
so he moved Narichika to the mainland and installed him at Ariki,
a monastic community at Niwase on the Bizen-Bitchū border.
From Ariki in Bizen to Seno-o in Bitchū, Naritsune's location,
the distance was barely three and a half miles,
and perhaps Naritsune felt some tenderness in the breeze from that direction,
for one day he summoned Kaneyasu to ask,
"How far is it from here to Ariki, where I gather my father is?"
Kaneyasu apparently hesitated to tell him the truth, for he answered,
"About twelve or thirteen days, one way."
Naritsune wept bitterly.

    "Japan," he said, "in times gone by,
had just thirty-three provinces;
but these were split more recently

into sixty-six. And what this means
is that Bizen, Bitchū, and Bingo
were in those days all one province.
They say that in the east as well
both Dewa and Michinoku,
with all their sixty-six counties,
constituted a single province—
one then partitioned, so that twelve
stood alone as a new one: Dewa.
That is what confused Captain Sanekata.
When banished to Michinoku, he roamed the whole province,
hoping to see the Akoya Pine, one of its famous sights; but he never found it.
On his way back, he met an old man.
'I beg your pardon,' he said, 'but you must have lived here a long time.
Do you know the Akoya Pine, which is one of the sights of Michinoku?'
'There is no Akoya Pine in Michinoku,' the old man replied.
'Perhaps there is one in Dewa.'
'So even you do not know where it is!' Sanekata cried.
'What is the world coming to,
that everyone here should have forgotten something that is the pride of the
    province?'
He was about to pass by, disappointed, when the old man caught his sleeve.
'Dear me, sir, it must be this old poem—
> *In Michinoku,*
> *the mighty Akoya Pine*
> *so blots out the sky*
> *that the moon, which should be out,*
> *never seems to rise at all.*
—this poem that you have in mind.
The Akoya Pine in *Michinoku:*
is *that* the one you are thinking of?
That poem was composed, you see,
when the two provinces were one.
They split off twelve counties, I believe,
to make the province now called Dewa.'
Very well, then: Sanekata
crossed the border into Dewa,
and there he saw the Akoya Pine.
From Dazaifu, down in Kyushu,
all the way to the capital,
it officially takes the envoy

charged with bringing the new-year trout
fifteen days, so twelve or thirteen
should bring a man almost to Kyushu!
Travel between Bizen and Bitchū
could never take more than two or three.
You claim that somewhere so near is far
only in order to keep from me
knowledge of where my father is!"
Despite missing his father intensely,
he never asked that question again.

10. The Death of Narichika

Soon Shunkan of Hosshōji, Yasuyori, and Naritsune
were banished to Kikai-ga-shima, off the Satsuma coast.[68]
To reach this island, the traveler from the capital must make a long sea journey.
Ships seldom call there, and the inhabitants are few.
Of course, there *are* people on the island, but they are not like us.
They are dark, oxlike, and very hairy, and they do not understand human
    speech.
The men wear no *eboshi* hat; the women do not let their hair hang loose.
Going unclothed as they do, they little resemble people.
Having no food, they think only of slaughtering living beings.

The peasants till no hillside paddies,
and so it is that they have no rice;
since they lack mulberry trees and leaves,
they have nothing resembling silk.
A peak at the center of the island
smolders with everlasting fire,
and stuff called "sulfur" lies everywhere;
some even call this "Sulfur Island."
Thunder constantly crashes and booms.
Lower down, it just rains and rains.
No, not for one miserable moment
does human life seem possible here.

Narichika had been looking forward to some peace at last
when he learned that Naritsune, his son, had been banished to Kikai-ga-shima.
That was that, then. He lost all hope and resolved to renounce the world,
as he let Lord Shigemori know in a letter.

....

68. Probably Iōshima, about thirty-five miles south of Kagoshima.

Shigemori in turn informed the cloistered emperor, who gave his approval.
Narichika became a monk at once.
Putting off the bright sleeves he had worn in his glory days,
he clothed himself instead in the black of one who has left the world.

> Narichika's wife was in hiding
> at Unrin-in, north of the city.
> Life is hard at the best of times
> somewhere wholly new; and for her,
> assailed by a flood of memories,
> each day was a trial, each night misery.
> Once she had had in her service
> many gentlewomen and housemen,
> but some now feared worldly censure,
> and others strove to keep out of sight.
> Not a soul came to call on her.

Just one houseman, though, a man of exceptional kindness,
did after all visit regularly. His name was Genzaemon-no-Jō Nobutoshi.
One day she asked him to come to her.
"Is it true?" she inquired. "I had heard that he was at Kojima in Bizen,
but the news lately mentions instead somewhere named, I believe, Ariki.
How I wish I could send him one more little note, to ask how he is!"
Nobutoshi fought back his tears.
"I have enjoyed his kindness ever since my boyhood," he said,
"and I have never been far from him.

> When Lord Narichika went down,
> I told him I would do anything
> to go there with him, but Rokuhara
> said no, and I had to give up.

I can still hear his voice when he called me to him.
His words of reproof are graven in my heart. I cannot forget them.
Never mind what may happen to me.
I shall take him your letter as fast as I can."
The lady was very happy. She wrote the letter at once and gave it to him.
Each of the children wrote one, too.
Nobutoshi took them with him all the way to Ariki in Bizen.
He first announced his arrival to Tsunetō, the warden.
Impressed by Nobutoshi's devotion, Tsunetō admitted him to see his lord.

> Narichika's only talk was still of the capital, and his spirits were very
> low. Then word reached him: "Nobutoshi is here from the city."
>   "Am I dreaming?" he wondered, straightening himself in haste.
> "Have him enter," he said.

Nobutoshi came in and forgot at a glance the sadness of this poor
dwelling, for the figure before him was in a monk's black robes. His
eyes darkened, and he felt his heart fail.

He carefully conveyed all that his lord's wife had said.

Then he took out the letters. Narichika examined them.

The wandering traces of the brush
melted before his blinding tears
until he could make nothing of them.
"The children miss you so terribly
that my grief is unbearable, too."
So she had written. And now he knew
that these past days of longing for her,
to his sorrow, had been nothing yet.

So four or five days passed. "I should like to stay on here, to witness his
end," Nobutoshi said to Tsunetō, but time and again Tsunetō refused.
Nobutoshi could do no more.

"Very well," Narichika told him, "go home now to the city." He
added, "I will be dead soon. When I am gone, please, make sure that
you pray for me." He wrote his answering letter.

Nobutoshi received it and promised to come again. Then he said
good-bye. Narichika replied, "I doubt that you will find me here when
you return.

It is too painful to see you go.
Stay just a little longer, please!"
Over and over he called him back.

But no, Nobutoshi could not stay. Swallowing his tears, he returned to the city
and gave the lady her husband's letter.

She saw as soon as she opened it that he had renounced the world,
for in it she found a lock of his hair.

She took no second look, for that keepsake now was her enemy.[69]

Weeping, she fell to the floor. The children, too, gave voice to full-throated grief.

The nineteenth of the eighth month
it was, when at Kibi-no-Nakayama
in Niwase, between Bizen and Bitchū,
they finally killed Narichika.
Various rumors told how he died.
They poisoned his wine, but that did not work.

....

69. From an often-quoted poem found in *Kokinshū* and in *Ise monogatari* (episode 119): "These keep-
sakes of his / now are enemies of mine: / if they were elsewhere, / I might have at least some hope / one
day of forgetting him." Translation from Mostow and Tyler, *The Ise Stories*, pp. 239–40.

Nobutoshi delivers the letter to Narichika's wife.

So, under a twenty-foot-high cliff,
they planted sharp stakes and pushed him over.
He met death impaled on the spikes.
This was so exceedingly cruel,
the like of it has seldom been known.
Narichika's wife learned that her husband was gone from this world.
"I so wanted to see him again, and he to see me, as we both had always been,"
she reflected, "and that is why I am not yet a nun.
But now that time has come."
She went to a temple, Bodai-in, and took the great step.
Thereafter she occupied herself as well as she could with her devotions
and prayed for her husband's happiness in future lives.

Her father had been Atsukata,
the governor of Yamashiro.
Exceptional beauty that she was,
His Cloistered Eminence had loved her
beyond all others, but Narichika,
too, was so great a favorite of his
that one day he gave her to him.
Now her children gathered flowers,

drew water, poor things, for the altar,
and prayed for their father's future rebirth.
So it was that, with passing time
and with cruelly shifting fortune,
she changed, just as the angels do
when blighted by the five signs of decline.

11. Tokudaiji Sanesada's Pilgrimage to Itsukushima

Now, the Tokudaiji grand counselor Sanesada
had been passed over for appointment as Palace Guards commander
in favor of Kiyomori's second son, Lord Munemori.
Thereafter he went for some time into seclusion.
In fact, he spoke of wishing to renounce the world.
His despairing housemen had no idea what to do.
One of them, a chamberlain named Fujiwara no Shigekane, had his wits about him.
One moonlit night Lord Sanesada had his southern lattice shutters raised
and was sitting, alone, chanting poems to the moon,
when Shigekane arrived, perhaps hoping to lift his spirits.
"Who is it?" Sanesada inquired.
"Shigekane, my lord."
"What brings you here?"
"The moon, so beautiful tonight and shining so peacefully."
"Your visit is very welcome. I have been feeling, somehow, very gloomy and bored."
Shigekane chatted with him about this and that and managed to cheer him up.
Sanesada then spoke his mind:

> "All I see in the world around me
> suggests that Heike might is growing.
> Kiyomori's first and second sons
> are the left and right commanders.
> Next come his third son, Tomomori,
> and Koremori, his first grandson.
> Once these two rise in their turn,
> no one from any other house—
> no, not as far as I can see—
> has any chance at commander.
> For me there is just one last resort:
> I might as well renounce the world."

>> Shigekane wept. "If you do that, my lord," he said, "all of us who belong
>> to your household, high or low, will be cast adrift. But I have thought of
>> a novel way out. Here is my idea: The Taira are intensely devoted to

Itsukushima in the province of Aki. Why should you, too, not make a pilgrimage there and pray at the shrine? You might do a seven-day retreat. The shrine's pretty dancing maidens— 'priestesses,' they are called, and there are many of them—will be impressed. They will be attentive to you. They will also want to know what you are praying for. Tell them the truth. When you start back to the capital, they will be sorry to see you go. So take the chief ones among them back to the city with you. When you get there, they will want to pay their respects at Nishi-Hachijō. Lord Kiyomori will ask, 'What prayer can have drawn Lord Sanesada all the way to Itsukushima?' So they will tell him. Now, Lord Kiyomori is very susceptible. He will be pleased that you went to pray at a shrine so important to him, too, and he will find a way to favor you after all."

Lord Sanesada heard him out. "Brilliant!" he said. "What a marvelous idea! I shall go there at once." He began his preparatory abstinence on the spot. Then off he went to Itsukushima.

He really did find at the shrine
beautiful "priestesses" aplenty.
During his seven-day retreat,
they looked after him constantly
and showered attentions on him.
Over those seven days and nights,
they danced their shrine's *kagura* dances
no fewer than three times and played
the biwa and koto. They sang sacred songs.
Lord Sanesada had such a good time
that, for the gods, he sang *imayō*,
rōei, fūzoku, saibara—
all the most delightful songs.
The priestesses said, "Most pilgrims to this shrine are gentlemen of the Taira.
Your pilgrimage is exceptional. What prayer has inspired this retreat?"
Sanesada replied, "I was passed over for appointment as Palace Guards
commander.
My prayer is for redress."
Soon the seven days were over.
He bade farewell to the deity
and started back to the capital,
at which a dozen young priestesses,
the shrine's finest, sorry to lose him,
readied a boat and sailed with him
a day's journey, to see him off.
He said good-bye to them then. But no:

It really was more than he could bear.
One more day's journey, then! Two days!
he kept saying until, in the end,
he took them all the way back to the city.
He lodged them in his own residence,
entertained them in countless ways,
and showered them with many gifts
before he let them start home again.
Now that they had come so far, the priestesses understood
that they could not leave without greeting Kiyomori, their great lord and
    patron.
They therefore called at Nishi-Hachijō.
Kiyomori hastened to meet them.
"What are all of *you* doing here?" he wanted to know.
"Lord Sanesada came on pilgrimage to the shrine," they explained,
"and he spent seven days there on retreat.
We saw him off a day's journey on his return,
but when the time came to say good-bye, he was so sad to let us go
that he kept begging for a day or two more,
and so we stayed with him all the way."
"And what prayer then took him all the way to Itsukushima?" Kiyomori inquired.
"He said he was praying for appointment to the post of commander."
Kiyomori nodded.
    "Poor fellow!" he said. "He turned aside
    from all the mighty temples and shrines
    open to him here in the city
    to pray instead at the one *I* revere!
    What a wonderful thing to do!
    Well, if he feels *that* strongly about it . . ."
    He had his eldest son, Shigemori,
    resign the post of left commander
    and gave it instead to Sanesada
    over his second son, Munemori,
    who at the time commanded the right.
    How beautifully the ploy had worked!
    And what a shame that Narichika
    had never planned anything so clever
    but had instead raised futile rebellion,
    destroyed himself and his family—
    indeed, his whole house—and on them all
    brought down final disaster.

12. The Battle with the Rank-and-File Monks

Now, His Cloistered Eminence had been receiving from Kōken,
a great prelate of Miidera, instruction in the Shingon mysteries.
Kōken had taught him the essence of the three major esoteric sutras—
the Dainichi-kyō, the Kongōchō-kyō, and the Soshitsuji-kyō—
and on the fourth of the ninth month
the sovereign's formal initiation was to take place at Miidera.
The monks of Mount Hiei were furious.
"From the very beginning," they said,
"initiations and ordinations have always been the prerogative of our
  Mountain.
Such has been the established rule.
After all, that is the very purpose of our Sannō Deity's teaching.
If this initiation takes place at Miidera nonetheless,
we will burn Miidera to the ground!"
His Cloistered Eminence understood the need for discretion.
After finishing his preparations, he gave up the idea.
So it was that he took Kōken with him to Tennōji,
where he built a subtemple named Chikō-in.
Having elevated the Tennōji[70] well water to "wisdom water of the five sacral jars,"
he accomplished at this hallowed spot, where the Buddha's word first sounded in
  Japan,
the initiation of the Consecrated Teacher.[71]

The cloistered sovereign had, after all, forgone initiation at Miidera in order to calm the uproar on the Mountain. Nonetheless, the scholar-monks and the temple rank and file remained at odds with one another and fought repeatedly. The scholar-monks lost every time. Doom seemed to threaten Mount Hiei, and crisis the court. Properly, the rank and file were either youths who had served the scholars and then become the simplest kind of monk, or worker-monks half clerical and half lay. Since the time of Kakujin, the Kongōju-in abbot, such men of the Three Pagodas of the Mountain had turn by turn provided flowers for the altars, under the rubric of "summer retreat support." Known in more recent years as "practitioners," they had come to despise the full-fledged monks and had defeated them in recurring skirmishes. They ignored their masters' orders and plotted war. The monks proper appealed to the

70. Tennōji, built circa 623 by Prince Shōtoku, is in Osaka. Destroyed during World War II, then rebuilt, it preserves an important tradition of early music and dance (bugaku). Tennōji musicians figure in 12:8, in connection with the execution of Yukiie.
71. The highest initiation in esoteric Buddhism.

senior nobles to suppress the practitioners immediately, and the senior
nobles reported their appeal to the warrior hierarchy.
So it came to pass that Kiyomori,
armed with a decree from the cloistered sovereign,
dispatched one Muneshige from the province of Kii,
at the head of two thousand men from the inner provinces,
to join forces with the monks proper against the practitioners.
The practitioners' established base was the Tōyō lodge,
but now they went down to the Sanga estate in Ōmi,
raised a large force, climbed back up the Mountain,
and entrenched themselves in a fortress on Sōizaka.

> That same ninth month, on the twentieth day,
> early in the hour of the dragon, [ca. 8 A.M.]
> monks to the number of three thousand
> and two thousand imperial horsemen—
> in all a force of a full five thousand—
> bore down upon Sōizaka.
> Certain that victory was theirs
> this time at last, the monks preferred
> to have the imperial troops go before them,
> while the latter deferred to the monks.
> Being so much at cross-purposes,
> neither could put up much of a fight.
> Stones catapulted from the fort
> killed nearly all of them, on both sides.
> The practitioners had recruited
> ne'er-do-wells of every description:
> thieves from provinces hither and yon,
> armed robbers and mountain bandits,
> even pirates, inflamed with greed
> and with only contempt for their lives.
> Every one fought like a man possessed,
> and this time, too, the scholars lost.

13. *The Ruin of Mount Hiei*

> Thereafter Mount Hiei simply fell to pieces.
> Apart from the Twelve Perpetual Chanters,[72]

72. Twelve monks dedicated to chanting the sutras day and night in the Sanmai-dō, a hall in the West
Pagoda area of Mount Hiei.

only rare monks continued to live there.
In valley after valley, the preaching lapsed;
in lodge after lodge, devoted practice died.
The windows of sacred learning closed;
meditation seats remained unclaimed.
Nothing the Buddha taught throughout his life
now gave forth its fragrance of spring flowers.
Clouds veiled the autumn moon of the Three Truths.[73]
Nobody upheld the lamp of the Teaching,
lit three hundred years ago and more,
and smoke that once rose from incense
burning through the hours seemed gone for good.
Imposing temple halls towered aloft,
three-tiered, into the blue empyrean;
roof- and crossbeams pierced the sky
until the rafters vanished into mist.
But now only winds from off the peaks
tended gilded images spattered with rain.
The moon's soaring light shone through cracked eaves.
Dawn bejeweled with dewdrops lotus thrones.
Such are the evils of this latter age
that, in all Three Lands,[74] the Buddha's Teaching
by slow degrees has fallen very low.
A journey to far-off India,
to see where the Buddha lived and died
and where he began to teach the Law,
reveals both the Bamboo Grove Temple
and the Jetavana Temple now to be
lairs only to foxes and to wolves.
Their foundation stones alone remain.
No water fills the White Heron Pond;
its only depths are a tall growth of weeds.
The stupas that the king erected there,
to warn off the unworthy and urge all to dismount,
now lean, moss-covered, at mad angles.
And so it is in China, too. Tientai-shan,
Wutai-shan, Bomasi, Yuquansi—

....

73. Emptiness, transience, and the nonduality of the two.
74. India, China, Japan.

the last monk is gone from every one,
and each of them is falling to ruin.
Both great bodies of the holy Teaching,
the Mahāyana and the Hinayana,
lie moldering in abandoned chests.
Likewise, in our realm, the Seven Great Temples
there in Nara languish pitifully.
The Eight, the Nine Schools are gone forever.
Atago and Takao, where once
halls and pagodas rose, eave to eave,
in a single night turned to wasteland.
Tengu[75] live there now, and nothing else.
That may explain why the Tendai doctrine,
noble beyond price as it has been
(so lamented every thoughtful witness)
now, in Jishō, seemed at last extinct.
One monk, before quitting the Mountain,
had written on a pillar of his lodge:

> *Has it come to this?*
> *That these well-forested slopes*
> *whence such prayers once rose*
> *must now become a mountain*
> *devoid of human presence?*

His words hark back, or so it seems,
to what Saichō prayed for long ago,
when founding the temple on this Mountain:
blessing from all enlightened buddhas.
The poem's conception is very fine.
The eighth of the month is Yakushi's day,[76]
but no voices rose to call his name.
In the fourth month, Sannō descended,
but nobody presented offerings.[77]
The sacred fence, once a bright, fresh red,
had dulled with age, and old *shimenawa*[78]
alone remained to deck the sanctuaries.

....

75. *Tengu* are supernatural mischief makers and shape changers who haunt deserted areas, especially around Buddhist temples.

76. "Yakushi" is translated elsewhere as "Medicine King." He is the buddha of healing.

77. The Sannō Deity's main festival took place in the fourth month.

78. A rice-straw rope that demarcates a shrine or a plot of ground as sacred space.

14. *Zenkōji Destroyed by Fire*

There came the news that Zenkōji[79] had burned down.
The story of the temple's sacred image is this:
Of old, a plague of the five diseases swept the Indian land of Shravastī.
So many people died that the wealthy Somachatta
managed to get Jambudvīpa gold dust from the Dragon Palace
and, with the Buddha Shakyamuni and Maudgalyāyana,
cast it into an Amida triad a foot and a quarter tall.
It was the holiest image in all of Jambudvīpa.[80]

> After the Buddha passed away,
> the image stayed on in India
> five hundred years, until at last
> the eastward movement of the Teaching
> carried it to the land of Paekche.
> After a further thousand years,
> when King Sŏngmyŏng reigned in Paekche
> and, in Japan, Emperor Kinmei, [r. 539-71]
> the image came from across the sea
> to the harbor of Naniwa
> in Settsu province, where it remained
> through many rounds of stars and frosts.
> Because it gave off golden light,
> the new era was named Konkō.
> In the third of the Konkō years,
> the third month had just begun
> when Ōmi no Honda Yoshimitsu
> came from the province of Shinano,
> stood before the golden image,
> and invited Amida home with him.
> By day it was Yoshimitsu
> who bore the image on his back,
> but by night it was Amida
> who carried Yoshimitsu.
> So they arrived in Shinano,
> where, in the county of Minochi,

....

79. A major Tendai temple in the province of Shinano, now Nagano-ken.

80. In Japanese, Enbudai, the southern continent of the Buddhist world that surrounds Mount Sumeru and the one inhabited by humans. The Dragon Palace is the undersea palace of the sea god. Maudgalyāyana (Japanese: Mokuren Sonja) was a major disciple of the Buddha Shakyamuni.

Yoshimitsu enshrined Amida.
Not once in the ensuing years—
five hundred and eighty of them—
did fire ever destroy the temple.
"When ruin threatens the Sovereign's Way,
the Buddha's Way collapses first,"
or so they say, which may explain
why so many hallowed temples
were destroyed. Their loss announces,
people claimed, the end of the Sovereign's Way.

15. *Yasuyori's Prayer*

On Kikai-ga-shima, each exile's life hung in the balance,
as a dewdrop hangs from the tip of a leaf,
and none clung that desperately to it; nevertheless
food and clothing reached the island from the Kase estate in Hizen,
which belonged to Noriyori, Naritsune's father-in-law;
and these supplies sustained Shunkan and Yasuyori, too.
Yasuyori had become a monk at Murozumi in Suō, on his way into exile,
adopting Shōshō as his name in religion.
Having wanted so long to take that step, he made this poem:

> *And so, at long last,*
> *I have given up for good*
>   *a world of sorrows*
>   *that I desperately regret*
>   *not having renounced before.*

Naritsune and Yasuyori, who had long been devoted to Kumano,
wanted at all costs to enshrine the three Kumano deities on the island,
so as to pray that they might return to the capital. Shunkan, however,
ignored them, never having been a man of any kind of faith. The pair
therefore went off on their own around the island to look for a setting
that might resemble Kumano.

They came to a sweeping embankment,
beautifully forested and bright
with leafy scarlet and gold brocade.
The slopes of nobly cloud-topped peaks
offered to their wondering gaze
a gauzy expanse of shifting green.
The mountain prospect, the lovely woods—
this was a setting beyond compare.

Southward the eye took in the sea,
a fuming abyss of rolling billows;
northward towered colossal crags
whence spilled a majestic waterfall,
a hundred feet high, loud as thunder,
and flanked by ancient, sighing pines.
The view so very closely resembled
Nachi, the seat of Hiryū Gongen,[81]
that they named this waterfall Nachi.
They called the two peaks Hongū and Shingū
and named the other places nearby
after all the lesser Kumano shrines.
Then Yasuyori led Naritsune
every day on their island route
around the Kumano pilgrimage,
praying that they should soon return:
"All hail, Gongen Kongō Dōji![82]
Grant us your compassion, we beg!
Return us soon to our proper home!
Bring us again to our wives and children!"
The days went by. They could not change to new pilgrim robes,
since they had none. They dressed in hemp
and for their ablutions drew from a swale
water that in their minds they drew
from the pristine Iwada River.[83]
Whatever height they chanced to climb
in their minds was the Hosshin Gate,[84]
and on each of their pilgrimages
Yasuyori pronounced a prayer.
Lacking the paper for sacred streamers,
he spoke instead while offering flowers:

> *The current year, the first of Jishō, consists of twelve months and over*
> *three hundred and fifty days. On this fortunate day, at this fortunate*
> *hour, in the presence of the Triple Kumano Deity, whose wonders are*

....

81. "Hiryū" means "flying dragon," while "Gongen" ("provisional manifestation") is a sacred title. Hiryū Gongen (also, below, Hiryū Daisatta [Sanskrit: *mahāsattva*, "great being"]) is associated with waterfalls. By staring for a time at the high, narrow waterfall, any visitor to Nachi can witness the optical illusion of a vigorous *rising* movement—one easily taken for a visible manifestation of Hiryū Gongen.

82. The protector deity of Kumano. At Dan-no-ura (11:7), Tanzō's ship flies the banner of Kongō Dōji.

83. A river on the route between the capital and Kumano. Koremori crosses it in 10:11.

84. The main gate (now gone) to Kumano Hongū, the senior Kumano shrine.

unparalleled in Japan, and of Hiryū Daisatta, his manifestation of righteous wrath, we, the devout donors Fujiwara no Naritsune, of the Palace Guards, and the monk Shōshō, in full sincerity of heart and in perfect unity of body, speech, and mind, with profound respect make this declaration.

Shōjō Daibosatsu[85] instructs those who cross the ocean of suffering; he is the king of triply accomplished enlightenment. To the east the Jōruri Medicine King heals every disease. To the south resides the sublime teacher from Fudaraku, the master of supremely beneficent realization. Nyakuōji, who rules the sahā *world and banishes all fear, manifests buddha countenances on his head, and grants the prayers of sentient beings.[86] From the emperor down to the least of his people, all therefore address to him appeals for peace in this world or for happy rebirth in the next, each morning drawing water to wash away the defilement of the passions and turning each evening toward the mightiest mountains to call the holy names.*

Likening in our minds soaring peaks to the loftiest heights of divine virtue and the depths of plunging valleys to the profound reach of the Universal Vow, we struggle upward through cloud and descend slopes through heavy dews. What but faith in your mercy could move us to tread so steep a path? What but trust in your divine virtue could draw us into this wilderness? Accordingly, O Shōjō Daigongen, O Hiryū Daisatta, open wide your eyes of compassion, listen with all the acuity of your hearing, discern the matchless ardor of our entreaty, and vouchsafe the boon for which we pray.

So it is that to guide sentient beings, each according to that being's faith and capacity, and to save all beings who lack faith, the divinities of Hongū and Shingū leave dwellings made of the seven treasures, temper their manifold radiance, and mingle with the dust of the six realms and the three worlds.

Sleeve to sleeve we therefore pray, despite settled karma, for the happier fortune that you have in your gift, and in that spirit we bring before you ceaseless offerings. Clad in the liturgical stole, bearing blossom offerings of enlightenment, we shake with the ardor of our entreaty the very floor of your shrine and in perfect purity of faith throw ourselves upon your mercy. If you, the gods, accept our prayer, how could you not

---

85. The divinity of the first sanctuary of Kumano Hongū and a manifestation of Amida.

86. The *jōruri* (lapis lazuli blue) paradise of the Medicine King (Iō, Yakushi) lies in the east. Fudaraku, in the south, is the paradise of Kannon. The *"sahā* world" is the profane world ruled by desire. The Kumano deity Nyakuōji manifests buddha countenances on his head because his Buddhist counterpart is Eleven-Headed Kannon.

answer it? Eyes lifted in awe, we beseech you: O divinities of the twelve
sanctuaries, soar, wing to beneficent wing, across the ocean of sorrows,
relieve for us the pain of exile, and fulfill our profound desire for return
to the capital! We bow twice before you.
Such were the words of Yasuyori's prayer.

16. Stupas Cast into the Sea

Naritsune and Yasuyori came regularly before the triple Kumano Deity,
and sometimes they spent the whole night there on retreat.
They had passed one such night singing *imayō* songs
when, toward dawn, Yasuyori dozed off and had a dream.
A small boat with a white sail came in from the open sea.
Twenty or thirty women in scarlet trouser-skirts disembarked
and sang three times, to the beat of a drum:

> Beyond the vows made by all other buddhas,
> Thousand-Armed Kannon's deserves fullest trust.
> Even dead trees, even withered grasses
> suddenly, so they say, bloom and yield fruit.

Then, in an instant, they were gone.

> Yasuyori woke up amazed,
> and to Naritsune he said:
> "Those women I saw—why, I believe
> they must have been provisional forms
> assumed by the Dragon God himself.
> Of the three Kumano deities,
> the one to the west makes manifest
> Thousand-Armed Kannon,
> among whose twenty-eight followers
> the Dragon God himself belongs.
> This intimates plainly enough
> that the gods have accepted our prayer."

Another time both dropped off after a night of vigil and dreamed
that two leaves blew in from the sea and lodged, one in each man's sleeve.
They turned out to be leaves of the *nagi* tree common at Kumano,
and together they bore a poem apparently gnawed into them by insects:

> *Your prayers reach the gods*
> *swift and forever mighty*
> *in such profusion*
> *that you may well, after all,*
> *see the capital once more.*

*Yasuyori (seated) making stupas while Shunkan
(not mentioned in the text as present) looks on.*

So greatly did he long for home,
that the desperate Yasuyori
also made one thousand stupas,[87]
each marked with the Siddham *A,*
the date, his true and common names,
and two poems he had written:
          Here, alas, am I,
      marooned on a tiny isle
          far off Satsuma:
      Take the news to my father,
      winds that blow across the sea!

....

87. Japanese: *sotoba.* In principle a monument of any size enshrining a relic of the Buddha. These *sotoba,* as the illustration shows, are simply flat strips of wood inscribed with sacred letters (Siddham is an ancient Indian script) and the messages mentioned.

> *Spare a thought for me,*
> *when, abroad on a journey*
> *sure not to be long,*
> *I still find my heart aching*
> *only to go home again.*

He took them out to the seashore.
"Hail and obeisance to the Refuge!"
he intoned. "O Brahma and Indra,
O Four Great Heavenly Kings,[88]
O gods who compact the earth,
O guardian powers of the city,
and, above all, O mighty gods
Kumano, Itsukushima:
Carry one of these, at least,
all the way to the capital!"
As each wave broke on the shore
and then slid back, he tossed one in—
one he had that moment made;
and so day after day passed by,
while the count of stupas grew.
Perhaps it was his ardent yearning
that turned into the perfect wind,
or perhaps the gods and buddhas
guided the stupa on its way,
for just one among the thousand
washed up on the beach in Aki,
before the Itsukushima Shrine.
Now, a certain monk related to Yasuyori
had set out to travel through the western provinces,
and he meant, should he only find a way to do so,
to cross to Kikai-ga-shima and learn Yasuyori's fate.
He visited Itsukushima first of all
and met there a man in a hunting cloak, presumably from the shrine.
In conversation with him, he asked,
  "Now, 'tempering the light and mingling with the dust

....

88. Brahma (Japanese: Bonten) and Indra (Japanese: Taishakuten), Indian gods absorbed into the Buddhist pantheon, appear frequently in medieval Japanese writing. Each has his own heaven, Indra's being the Tushita (Japanese: Tosotsu) Heaven at the summit of Mount Sumeru. From the slopes of Mount Sumeru, the Four Heavenly Kings (Jikoku-ten, Zōchō-ten, Kōmoku-ten, Tamon-ten) protect the four directions.

in order to benefit all sentient beings'[89]
takes many forms. What affinity, then,
led the divinity of this island
to form a bond with the fish of the deep?"
"You see," the man replied, "Dragon King Sagara's
third noble daughter reveals to the senses
the Dainichi of the Womb Mandala."[90]
He went on to tell of the countless wonders
worked here since first the divinity came
and now, too, when her boons save so many.
If eight sanctuaries stand here, eave to eave,
and, in fact, if the shrine is on the sea,
no doubt that is why; and why, too, the moon
shines down on the rising and ebbing tides.
At flood, torii and red shrine fence
gleam as though made of some precious stone;
at ebb, the white sand before the shrine
seems even in summer an expanse of frost.

> Struck with awe, the visiting monk chanted sutra passages for the deity. Meanwhile the sun set, the moon rose, and the tide came in, carrying here and there bits of rocking flotsam. Among them he noticed a stupa-shaped object and picked it up for a closer look. "Marooned on a tiny isle," he read. The waves had not washed away the words. They were graven into the wood and stood out quite clearly.

"How extraordinary!" he exclaimed to himself.
He slipped the stupa into his backpack chest and started out for the capital.
There he secretly traveled to Murasakino, north of Ichijō,
to call on Yasuyori's old mother, now a nun, and on his wife and children.
He showed them the stupa.

> "What business did this stupa have,
> to fail to drift off toward China
> yet to reach *us*, all the way here?
> It does nothing," they lamented,
> "except now to make us feel worse!"

....

89. The basic expression of the principle that the eternal, universal buddhas manifest themselves in the sensible, local forms of the Japanese divinities.

90. This daughter of Sagara, known as Tagori-hime, is one of the Eight Dragon Kings of Buddhist mythology and one of the three female deities (or triple female deity) of the Itsukushima Shrine. Her buddha counterpart is the Dainichi (Sanskrit: Mahāvairochana) of the Womb (Taizōkai) Mandala—with the Diamond (Kongōkai) Mandala, one of the two fundamental mandalas of esoteric Buddhism.

The cloistered emperor, from his distance, heard the news and examined the
    stupa.
"How dreadful!" he cried, shedding gracious tears.
"So in fact these men are still alive!"
He forwarded the stupa to Shigemori,
and Shigemori in turn showed it to his father.

> Kakinomoto no Hitomaru mourned
> a boat vanishing round an island,
> while Yamanobe no Akahito
> sang of cranes crying in the reeds.[91]
> The deity of Sumiyoshi
> grieved over a fallen crossbeam,
> and the divinity of Miwa
> talked of the cedars at his gate.
> Since Susano-o-no-mikoto
> first strung thirty-one syllables
> together into a Japanese poem,[92]
> the gods and the buddhas alike
> have voiced in the words of poetry
> every emotion under the sun.
> Neither stock nor stone, Kiyomori—
> even he—seemed to respond with pity.

17. Su Wu

Since Lord Kiyomori had been moved to compassion, everyone in the capital,
    young or old,
went about humming the Kikai-ga-shima exile's poem.
He had made a thousand of those stupas, though, so they must have been very
    small.
How extraordinary that one should have reached the capital all the way from
    Satsuma!
Perhaps that is what truly passionate fervor can achieve.

> Of old, the Han sovereign attacked the land of the Xiongnu. He first
> dispatched three hundred thousand mounted men under the command
> of Li Xiaoqing. The Han force was weak, however, and the Xiongnu
> were strong. Not only did they destroy the Han army, they also took Li

91. Two widely known poems by two major *Man'yōshū* (eighth-century) poets. The Sumiyoshi and Miwa
deities, below, expressed themselves in poems included in early, imperially commissioned anthologies.
92. This poem by Susano-o (*-no-mikoto* is an honorific title), the brother of the Sun Goddess Amaterasu,
is translated in 11:12.

Xiaoqing prisoner. The next Han force, under Su Wu, numbered five hundred thousand men. It was still too weak, and the stronger Xiongnu destroyed it as well. They also took more than six thousand Han prisoners, from whom they separated out the general, Su Wu, and six hundred and thirty senior officers. They cut a leg off each and sent them away. Some died at once, some later on. Su Wu, however, did not die. With his single leg, he climbed hills to gather nuts, picked *seri* parsley from the swales in spring, and in autumn collected fallen ears from the rice paddies; and so he managed to sustain his dewdrop life.

The geese on the paddies were too used to him to fear him.
All of these, Su Wu reflected, return in the end to their home!
The thought stirred such longing in him that he wrote down what he had to say,
added the note "See that this reaches the emperor of Han,"
and tied it to the wing of a goose that he then released.

> Sure enough, those geese in autumn
> flew back from the northern marches
> to the capital city of Han.
> One day at dusk, Emperor Zhao,
> relaxing in the Shanglin Garden
> under a lightly overcast sky,
> was feeling somehow melancholy
> when a line of geese passed above him.
> One of the geese flew down to him,
> bit off the letter tied to its wing,
> and dropped it at the ruler's feet.
> An official picked up the letter
> and gave it to his sovereign lord.
> The emperor opened it and read:
> "At first, confined to a rock cave,
> I spent three springs in misery;
> now, cast out in desolate fields,
> I am a barbarian with one leg.

Even if my bones are to lie scattered in this alien land,
my spirit will return to serve my emperor once more."

> That was when people started calling
> letters "goose notes" or "goose missives."

"How terrible!" the emperor said. "This is the much-praised writing of Su Wu!
He is still there, among the barbarians!"
This time he dispatched a force a million strong, under Li Guang,
and this time the stronger Han army crushed the Xiongnu.

News of the victory brought Su Wu forth from the wasteland.
"Behold me!" he cried. "I am the Su Wu of old!"
So it was that after nineteen years of stars and frosts,
a palanquin carried home the man with one leg.

> Su Wu was sent in his sixteenth year to the land of the Xiongnu, and thereafter he always managed somehow to hide the banner that the emperor had given him. He had kept it with him the whole time. Now he took it out at last for a deeply moving audience with his sovereign. His peerless service won him many large provinces, as well as oversight of all vassal states. As for Li Xiaoqing, he remained in the barbarian land and never returned. Not that he did not long desperately to do so, but the Xiongnu king would not let him go. The Han emperor, who did not know this, condemned him as disloyal. He exhumed the bones of Li Xiaoqing's dead parents and had them flogged. He also punished his close family.

This news reached Li Xiaoqing, who was outraged.
Nevertheless he still longed to go home,
and he therefore addressed to the emperor
an account to prove that he remained loyal.
"What a terrible thing!" the emperor sighed.
He regretted after all having had the bones of the man's parents dug up and
    flogged.

> Su Wu, of old in Han China,
> tied to the wing of a goose a letter
> that he wished to reach his old home,
> while in our own realm Yasuyori
> sent poems home on the ocean waves.
> One wrote as the brush moved,
> one put together poems.
> One lived long, long ago,
> and one in our latter age.
> One wrote among the Xiongnu,
> one on Kikai-ga-shima.
> So far apart in setting and time,
> they still shared the same inspiration.
> Their stories are a wonder to tell.

BOOK THREE

1. *The Pardon*

(recitative)

On the first day of Jishō 2, at the cloistered emperor's residence, [1178]
the new year received its formal welcome, and on the fourth
the emperor made his prescribed progress to visit his father.
All this went forward in much the same manner as usual,
but His Cloistered Eminence was still indignant over the death, that summer,
of Narichika and everyone in his close circle.
The duties of government weighed upon him, and his mood was black.
For his part, Lord Kiyomori had suspected the cloistered emperor
the moment the chamberlain Yukitsuna informed him of the plot.
Outwardly the same, he remained on alert within, and bitterness showed in his
smile.
On the seventh of the first month, a comet appeared in the east,
the kind called "Chi You Banner," or "Red Essence." It brightened on the
eighteenth.
Meanwhile Lord Kiyomori's daughter Kenreimon-in, then still empress,
felt unwell, to the distress of every courtier and of the realm at large.
Sutra reading began in the great temples, and imperial envoys
set off with offerings to the great shrines.
Physicians tried every remedy, yin-yang masters all their skill.
No major or secret temple rite went unperformed.

(speech)

But Kenreimon-in's was no ordinary indisposition. Apparently she
was pregnant. The emperor was in his eighteenth year. She, in her
twenty-second, had not yet given him a child. Now the exulting Heike
imagined how wonderful it would be if she had a boy.

"The Heike have really struck it rich this time," people of other fam-
ilies kept saying among themselves. "It will be a prince, I know it will."

Once pregnancy was confirmed, great healers and holy monks were
set to performing the most powerful and secret rituals, while impas-
sioned prayers for the birth of a prince went up to the stars, the con-
stellations, the buddhas, and the bodhisattvas.

On the first day of the sixth month, the empress donned the pregnancy band.
Cloistered Prince Shukaku, the abbot of Ninnaji, came to the palace,
where he performed the Peacock Sutra Rite and prayed for divine protection.

Cloistered Prince Kakukai, the abbot of Mount Hiei, came as well.
He performed the rite to change a girl in the womb into a boy.

(song)
>Meanwhile month followed upon month,
>and the empress's indisposition grew.
>Just so, surely, Lady Li of Han,
>whose smile flashed a hundred charms,
>suffered, ill in the Zhaoyang Palace.
>Her Majesty's plight inspired pity
>beyond that given Yang Guifei of Tang,
>who, dissolved in tears, called to mind
>rain-drenched pear blossoms on the bough,
>lotus flowers wilting in the wind,
>maiden flowers weighed down by dew.
>Alert to her weakness, stubborn spirits
>seized upon this chance to invade her.
>Once Fudō's rope had bound the medium,
>these spirits then revealed themselves.[93]

Chief among them were the powers who declared their names:
the soul of that emperor banished to Sanuki,[94]
the undying wrath of the Haughty Left Minister from Uji,
the wraith of Grand Counselor Narichika,
the baleful phantom of the monk Saikō,
the living spirits of the men banished to Kikai-ga-shima.
So Lord Kiyomori acted to mollify the living and the dead.
The banished sovereign swiftly received a laudatory posthumous title.
The Haughty Left Minister rose to chancellor at the first rank, top grade.
The imperial envoy to him was, they say, the clerk Koremoto.

>The grave of the Haughty Left Minister
>lay in the province of Yamato,
>by the Hannya-no burning ground
>in the village of Kawakami,
>in Sōnokami county.
>That autumn in the Hōgen years,
>they had exhumed his remains
>and scattered them by the roadside,

93. Fudō Myōō ("The Unmoving, the Mantra King") was the chief deity invoked by an exorcist. Fudō carries a sword (to cut attachment to objects of desire) and a rope (to bind demons).
94. Sutoku.

where they mingled with the soil,
amid the new growth each spring.
When the envoy appeared at last,
to read out the imperial decree,
how glad the departed must have been!
Yes, the angry dead inspire fear.
Therefore Prince Sawara, dismissed
as heir apparent, came in time
to be known as Emperor Sudō,
and the Igami Princess, too,
stripped of her station, in due course
reclaimed her old title of empress.[95]

    The madness of Retired Emperor Reizei, [r. 967-69] Cloistered Emperor
    Kazan's [r. 984-86] renunciation of sovereign authority over the realm—
    they say that the spirit of Motokata, lord of Civil Affairs, was respon-
    sible for both. They also say that the spirit of Palace Chaplain Kanzan
    caused Emperor Sanjō to go blind.

When Norimori learned of all this, he said to Lord Shigemori,
"I gather that prayers of every kind are being offered for the empress's
    confinement.
Say what you like, though, I know of nothing more effective than a special
    amnesty.
The Kikai-ga-shima exiles, especially—what could yield greater merit than
    recalling them?"
Lord Shigemori went to his father.
"Poor Norimori," he said, "seems extremely anxious about Naritsune.
If the empress's indisposition is as serious as report has it,
then the late Narichika's spirit must indeed be involved.
If your wish is to pacify the dead, then you *must* recall the living Naritsune.

    Allay the concerns of others
    and you will have your desire;
    grant other people what they wish
    and your own prayers will be fulfilled.
    The empress will, without delay,

....

95. Prince Sawara, a younger brother of Emperor Kanmu (reigned 781–806), starved himself to death on
his way into exile on the island of Awaji. In 800, to counter the threat his spirit posed, he was
posthumously elevated to emperor. The Igami princess, a daughter of Emperor Shōmu (reigned 724–49)
and empress to Kōnin (reigned 770–81), was dismissed over an affair involving her son. She cursed the
emperor, her husband, and died in prison. In 800 both were enshrined in a Goryōsha ("angry spirit
shrine").

bear the emperor a son,
and our house will prosper greatly."
So he admonished his father.
Lord Kiyomori was in an unusually accommodating mood.
"Very well," he said, "but what about those monks, Shunkan and Yasuyori?"
"Recall them, too. It would only mean bad karma to leave a single one there."
"Yasuyori is all very well," Shigemori's father replied, "but Shunkan—
I was forever putting in a word for him. He owes me everything.
But no, he had to go and turn that Shishi-no-tani villa of his, of all places,
    into a fort
and indulge his whims with the strange things that apparently went on there.
No, I cannot imagine pardoning Shunkan." So spoke Lord Kiyomori.
Shigemori returned home and called in Lord Norimori, his uncle.
"Naritsune is to be pardoned," he said. "You may set your mind at rest."
Norimori pressed his palms together in gratitude and delight.

    "When Naritsune was leaving,"
    he said, "he seemed to me perplexed
    that I had not taken charge of him,
    and every time he looked at me,
    I saw tears in his eyes.
    I feel very sorry for him."
    To this, Shigemori replied,
    "Far be it from me to blame you.
    Anyone would feel for a child.
    I will have a good talk with my father."
    With these words he withdrew.
So the decision was to call the Kikai-ga-shima exiles home.
Lord Kiyomori issued the writ of pardon.

    His envoy left the capital.
    Norimori was so happy
    he sent likewise a man of his own.
    "Keep going, hurry, day and night":
    So the messengers were ordered.
    They were to travel by sea, though,
    and that way is not always smooth.
    Lashed by wind and wave, they journeyed,
    from late in the seventh month
    to the twentieth of the ninth,
    when they reached Kikai-ga-shima.

2. *Stamping in Frenzy*

Lord Kiyomori's envoy was one Motoyasu, a junior officer in the Left Gate
    Watch.
He disembarked and shouted over and over again, "Exiles from the capital,
Tanba Lieutenant Naritsune, Hosshōji Superintendent Shunkan,
Taira Police Lieutenant and Novice Yasuyori: Are you here?"
Naritsune and Yasuyori were off on their regular Kumano pilgrimage.
Only Shunkan was nearby to hear him.
"I'm so desperate, I must be dreaming," he said to himself.
"Either that or the demons from the realm of desire have driven me mad.
No, this can't be real!" In blind haste, half running, half falling,
he raced to present himself before the envoy.
"What do you want?" he cried. "Yes, I am Shunkan, in exile here from the
    capital!"
An assistant, who carried Lord Kiyomori's writ of pardon in a purse around his
    neck,
took the document out and gave it to him. Shunkan unfolded it. He read:

    "Exile has redeemed your great crime.
    Hasten now, dispose yourselves
    to return to the capital.
    In connection with solemn prayers
    for the empress's coming birth,
    a special amnesty is proclaimed.
    The Kikai-ga-shima exiles,
    Naritsune and Yasuyori,
    are therefore pardoned." That was all.
    The document said nothing else:
    Of the name Shunkan not a trace.
    It must be on the wrapper, then!
    He looked: But no, it was not there.
    He read backward, from the end,
    he read forward, from the beginning,
    but the writ bore only two names.
    It said nothing about a third.
    Soon Naritsune and Yasuyori arrived.
    Naritsune went over the writ himself,
    then Yasuyori did the same;
    and still it listed just two names,
    with never a sign of the third.

In dream, yes, this might happen,
but this was no dream. It was real.
In the way of reality, though,
it made a more convincing dream.
Not only that, but many letters
had arrived from the capital
addressed to the two gentlemen named;
for Shunkan, though, nary a one
to inquire how he was getting on.
So, he reflected, everyone
I might have counted as family
has left the capital for good!
The thought was utter agony.
"Why, all three of us," he cried,
"share guilt for a single crime! All three
suffered banishment together.
Why is it, then, that amnesty
calls back only two of us
and leaves one behind, alone?
Have the Heike forgotten me?
Was it a mere slip of the brush?
What can possibly have happened?"
He cast his gaze to the heavens,
lay prostrate on the earth,
weeping, wailing, all in vain.
Seizing Naritsune's sleeve, he cried,
"This fate has overtaken me
because the late grand counselor,
your father, raised futile rebellion!
You cannot disown me now!
If there is no pardon for me,
oh, take me aboard your ship—
if not to the capital itself,
then at least as far as Kyushu!

While you two were here, yes, news from home still came as naturally as swallows in spring or as geese to the fields in autumn. But now how will I ever have news again?" Shunkan was contorted with anguish.

"I understand your feelings," Naritsune replied. "Our joy at being recalled is one thing, but seeing you like this makes it painful to leave. I would like nothing better than to take you with us, but the envoy from the capital says that that is impossible. It would only mean disaster if all three of us were to leave the island without authorization and came to be found out. No, I will go on ahead, talk things over with people, gauge Lord Kiyomori's mood, and then send someone back for you. In the meantime please go on waiting as patiently as you have done so far. What matters above all is to stay alive. You have missed your pardon this time, but I see no reason you should not have it in the end." He did his best to sound encouraging, but Shunkan, oblivious to watching eyes, only wept in misery.

The ship's crew clattered about in preparation for sailing.
Shunkan clambered up the side and fell, fell and clambered back up again,
all too plainly desperate not to be abandoned.

> The two left him, as parting gifts,
> Naritsune a sleeping quilt,
> Yasuyori a Lotus Sutra.
> They loosed the moorings and cast off.
> Frantically clutching the rope,
> Shunkan followed into the water,
> waist-deep, then to his armpits,
> till he could only barely stand,
> hands clenched on the gunwale,
> crying, "Is this really it, then?
> You really mean to leave me here?
> I never believed you would do this!
> Why, I always thought we were friends!
> Oh, please, please, let me aboard!
> At least take me as far as Kyushu!"
> But his pleading was in vain.
> "No, we may not," the envoy said.
> They broke his grip. The boat rowed off.
> Stripped of hope, Shunkan waded back,
> there to collapse at the water's edge,
> stamping his feet like a little boy
> bellowing for nurse or mother.
> "Take me aboard! Take me with you!"
> he howled, but the receding boat
> left, as they say, only white waves.
> Even now it was not far away,
> but blinding tears veiled it from him.
> Up onto a high place he ran,
> waving, waving toward the sea.
> Not even storied Sayo-hime,

あまりにきえづ
俊寛僧都
ゆるし
赦免の涙に
いえ
づ
悲歎の圖

Shunkan watches the ship leave. Despite the sail shown, the text mentions only rowing.

bidding farewell at Matsura
to that ship bound for Cathay,
waved her scarf more passionately.[96]
The boat rowed on; then it was gone.
The sun went down, and yet Shunkan
never returned to his rough bed.
Feet still washed by the breaking waves,
drenched with all the dews of night,
he lay there through to the new day.
"He's a kind man, though, Naritsune"—
so Shunkan reassured himself;
"he'll speak eloquently for me."
Poor fellow! Even in his plight,
he could not bring himself to drown.
Now he knew how they despaired,
the brothers Sōri and Sokuri,
when abandoned on their rocky isle.[97]

3. The Imperial Birth

So the party left Kikai-ga-shima to reach Hizen province and Lord Norimori's
    Kase estate.
From the city, Norimori sent a messenger to tell them:
"Wind and sea will be rough the rest of this year and the journey dangerous.
Stay there, take good care of yourselves, and come up to the capital in spring."
Naritsune therefore saw the year out at Kase.

Meanwhile, in the eleventh month,
the twelfth day, in the small hours,
Her Majesty's labor began:
news that aroused great excitement
citywide and at Rokuhara,
where, in the Ikedono pavilion,
the empress was to give birth.
The cloistered emperor was soon there,
and the regent, and the chancellor,
and every one of the senior nobles

96. The legendary Sayo-hime waved her scarf in farewell when her lover sailed for China from the harbor of Matsura, in northern Kyushu.
97. An originally Indian story of two brothers cruelly abandoned by their stepmother on a desert island. It appears in *Hōbutsushū* (A Precious Treasury), a collection of pious stories correctly attributed in 3:7 to Yasuyori. The preface speaks of the author's exile on Kikai-ga-shima.

and privy gentlemen.
  Everyone who was anyone,
  figures of rank and property,
  eager to rise in grade or office,
  turned up to the last man.
Precedent permitted a general amnesty to honor such an occasion.
One had been declared in Daiji 2, the ninth month and eleventh day, [1127]
when Taikenmon-in gave birth.
On that authority many guilty of grievous crimes were pardoned:
all except the prelate Shunkan, whom alone the amnesty excluded.
Her Majesty vowed solemnly to pay homage in person, if only the birth went
    well,
at Yawata, Hirano, Ōharano, and so on. The great monk Sengen announced her
    resolve.
The shrines mentioned included Ise and many others—over twenty in all.
There were sixteen temples, too, Tōdaiji and Kōfukuji among them.
At all there were to be sutra readings, ordered by men from her household.
Wearing swords and hunting cloaks patterned in three colors,
they proceeded from the east wing, through the southern garden,
and out the middle gate to the west, bearing for the sutra readings
offerings of many hues, and swords and robes, too, as sacred gifts.
They made a brilliant spectacle.
        Never one to get excited about anything, good or bad, Lord Shigemori
        started out a good while later, leading a train of carriages. His eldest
        son, Koremori, followed, with the others behind him. He brought with
        him on presentation trays forty robes of various colors and seven
        silver-fitted swords, while grooms led twelve horses. Apparently all
        this followed the precedent set by Lord Michinaga in the Kankō
        era, [1004-13] when Jōtōmon-in gave birth.
Lord Shigemori was quite right to offer the horses,
since he was not only the empress's elder brother but also her acting father.[98]
The Gojō grand counselor Kunitsuna likewise presented two.
People wondered, concerning this gift, whether it demonstrated pure devotion
or simply an excess of wealth.
    From Ise to Itsukushima in Aki,
    seventy shrines and more received
    horses decked out to please the gods.
    The imperial stables for their part
    offered horses with sacred streamers

....

98. Because Kiyomori has severed formal ties with his children by becoming a "novice" monk.

to the number of several dozen.
The abbot of Ninnaji performed
the rite of the Peacock Sutra;
the Tendai abbot Kakukai
that of the Seven Medicine Kings;
Cloistered Prince Enkei of Miidera
undertook the rite of Kongō Dōji;
in fact, every ritual one could imagine—
the Five Great Kokūzō, the Six Kannon,
Ichiji Kinrin, the Five-Altar Rite,
the Six-Letter Purification,
the Eight-Letter Rite of Monju,
yes, and the Life-Giving Fugen—
every one of these was performed.
Smoke from the *goma* ritual fire filled the whole pavilion;
the ringing of liturgical bells echoed among the clouds aloft;
awesome scripture-chanting voices set the hair bristling on every head.
No spirit bent on evil could possibly have faced them down.
The order went out to the resident sculptors of holy images
to prepare life-size ones of the Medicine King and the Five Mantra Kings.
Nonetheless Her Majesty's labor went on and on, with no sign of imminent
　birth.

　　　　　　Lord Kiyomori and his wife, Lady Nii, hands pressed to their chests,
　　　　　　sat aghast and confused. To anyone who sought his orders, Kiyomori
　　　　　　replied, "Oh, anything, anything, whatever might conceivably work."
　　　　　　Later on he remarked, "I would have been less terrified in the thick of
　　　　　　battle."
　　Five great healers, ranking prelates,
　　Bōkaku, Shōun and Shungyō,
　　Gōzen and Jissen—each flung out
　　his own appeal to the deities,
　　demanding aid from his temple's divinity,
　　forcefully requiring his own,[99]
　　after all his years of devotion
　　to help him in this extremity.
　　Surely, one felt, they would prevail.
　　Among them the cloistered emperor,
　　purified for a pilgrimage

....

99. The deity who was the object of his daily personal devotion.

he soon planned to Imagumano,
and seated very close indeed
to Her Majesty's brocade curtains,
gave vigorous voice to reciting
the Sutra of Thousand-Armed Kannon,
at which came a sudden change.
The spirits driven into the mediums,
in whom they had raised a colossal uproar,
now for a little while fell silent.
His Cloistered Eminence addressed them. "Spirits, whoever you may be,
as long as this old monk is here, you will never get anywhere near her.
All of you raging phantoms especially, who have shown yourselves here today,
owe everything you were in life to the favor of your sovereign.
Gratitude may mean nothing to you,
but how *dare* you obstruct what must be!
Be gone now, this instant, be gone!"
And he went on in the words of the sutra:
"If a woman cannot give birth
and demon powers work against her,
however great her pain may be,
let her, in truly heartfelt faith,
chant the Spell of Great Compassion,
and those demons will melt away,
to be reborn at last in peace."
While he sharply rubbed together
the crystal beads of his rosary,
the birth went forward quite easily,
and, what is more, the child was a boy.

Lord Shigehira (at the time still deputy master of the empress's household) emerged from behind the curtains to announce in a loud voice, "The delivery went well, and the new arrival is a prince!" The cloistered emperor, the regent, the ministers, the senior nobles and privy gentlemen, the monks' assistants, the healers, the head of the Yin-Yang Office, the chief physician, everyone present, of every degree, gave a great shout of joy heard even beyond the gate, and the jubilation took some time to abate.

Lord Kiyomori was so happy that he wept aloud.
This must be what people mean when they speak of "tears of joy."
Lord Shigemori went to the empress and placed ninety-nine gold coins by the
    prince's pillow.

"Understand," he said, "that heaven is your father and earth your mother.
Live as long as the wizard Dongfang Shuo; make yours the heart of the Sun
 Goddess."
Then, with a mulberry bow, he shot mugwort arrows in the four directions.

4. The Roster of Great Lords

Lord Munemori's wife had been meant to nurse the new prince,
but she had died in childbirth that seventh month past,
so the child was given suck by the wife of Lord Tokitada, the Taira grand
 counselor;
she was known later on as Lady Sotsu-no-suke.
The cloistered emperor's carriage appeared immediately at the gate.
Bursting with joy, Lord Kiyomori presented him with a thousand taels of
 gold dust
and two thousand of raw Fuji cotton. There were some whispers of disapproval.
Certain irregularities had occurred in connection with the birth.
First, the cloistered emperor had functioned as one of the healers.
Second, when an empress gives birth,
the custom is to roll a rice-cooking pot down the roof from the ridgepole:
toward the south for a boy, toward the north for a girl.
This time, though, they had rolled it northward, which caused a puzzled
 commotion.
The pot had to be retrieved and sent rolling down again.
People muttered among themselves that this was a bad sign.

> The funniest thing was Lord Kiyomori's expression of blank amaze-
> ment, and the most admirable the behavior of Lord Shigemori. The sad-
> dest was that after losing his beloved wife, Munemori had resigned as
> grand counselor and commander and had gone into seclusion at home.
> How wonderful it would have been if *both* brothers had been there! And
> then there were the seven yin-yang masters summoned to perform a
> thousandfold purification. One was an old man named Tokihare, the
> head of the palace Housekeeping Office. He had only a few attendants
> with him, and the press of people was like a dense growth of bamboo
> shoots, rice, hemp, or reeds. "I am an official!" he cried, struggling to
> make way through the crowd. "Let me through!" His right shoe came off
> in the process, and he got his headdress knocked off when he stopped
> for a moment. The sight of a formally dressed old gentleman solemnly
> moving along with his topknot exposed, on so grand an occasion, was
> too much for the younger courtiers. They burst into laughter.

Yin-yang masters apparently adopt a special gait to keep themselves safe, and yet this mishap occurred. No one at the time thought much about it, yet in the light of later events it came to seem clearly portentous.

These gentlemen came to Rokuhara
on the occasion of the birth:
the regent, Lord Motofusa;
the chancellor, Moronaga;
the left minister, Tsunemune;
the right minister, Kanezane;
the palace minister, Shigemori;
the left commander, Sanesada;
Sadafusa, the Minamoto grand counselor;
Sanefusa, the Sanjō grand counselor;
Kunitsuna, the Gojō grand counselor;
Sanekuni, the Fujiwara grand counselor;
the inspector Sukekata;
the Naka-no-mikado counselor Muneie;
the Kasan-no-in counselor Kanemasa;
the Minamoto counselor Masayori;
the provisional counselor Sanetsuna;
the Fujiwara counselor Sukenaga;
the Ike counselor Yorimori;
the Left Gate Watch intendant Tokitada;
the police superintendent Tadachika;
Saneie, a left captain and consultant;
Sanemune, a right captain and consultant;
the consultant and captain Michichika;
the Taira consultant Norimori;
the Rokkaku consultant Iemichi;
the Horikawa consultant Yorisada;
the left grand controller Nagakata;
the right grand controller Toshitsune;
the Left Watch intendant Shigenori;
the Right Watch intendant Mitsuyoshi;
the master of the grand empress's household Tomokata;
the Left City commissioner Naganori;
the Dazaifu deputy Chikanobu;
Sanekiyo, newly of the third rank.
All these thirty-three gentlemen,
apart from the right grand controller,

were arrayed in formal court dress.
Absent were Lord Tadamasa,
the Kasan-no-in former chancellor,
the Ōmiya grand counselor Takasue,
and eight more. All of them, they say,
went later to Nishi-Hachijō
and called there on Lord Kiyomori,
dressed in plain hunting cloaks.

5. The Rebuilding of the Great Pagoda

On the last day of prayers for the empress came the distribution of rewards.
The decree provided that the prince-abbot of Ninnaji should see to repairing
    Tōji,[100]
as well as to performing the Latter Seven-Day Rite, the Daigensui Rite,
and the esoteric initiations. His ranking disciple Kakusei received further
    promotion.
The prince-abbot of Mount Hiei petitioned for promotion to the second
    princely rank
and for the privilege of entering and leaving the palace grounds in an ox-drawn
    carriage.
The Ninnaji abbot declared himself opposed,
and for this reason the prelate Enryō was promoted instead to higher rank.
There seem to have been too many other rewards to allow listing them all.
Her Majesty, having been long away, now returned to the palace from Rokuhara.
Lord Kiyomori and his wife had both prayed, once their daughter was empress:
"Oh, may she give birth to a prince!
And may that prince then ascend the throne, so that we stand above all others
as an emperor's commoner grandfather and grandmother!"
They began monthly pilgrimages to Itsukushima in Aki,
the shrine that inspired their personal devotion, in order to make this prayer.
Their daughter conceived immediately, and the child was indeed a boy.
Theirs was the height of good fortune.

> But how did this Taira faith in Itsukushima begin? When Lord Kiyo-
> mori governed Aki, under Retired Emperor Toba, his province was
> charged with rebuilding the great pagoda on Mount Kōya. Kiyomori
> assigned Endō Rokurō Yorikata of Watanabe to the project. It took six

....

100. A major temple founded in 794 and still prominent in Kyoto. Great power was attributed to the rites mentioned below. The Japanese name for the first of them is Goshichinichi Mishiho. The esoteric (tantric) deity Daigensui is covered with writhing snakes.

The old monk disappears (left). At lower right: Kiyomori and his party.

        years. Kiyomori visited Mount Kōya when it was finished. He first
        worshipped at the pagoda and then went on to the Oku-no-in.[101]
There an old monk appeared, as though from nowhere,
eyebrows frost-white and forehead wrinkled like waves on the sea,
leaning on a forked staff. He addressed Lord Kiyomori at length.
    "Here the esoteric teachings live
    undiminished since the days of old,"
    he said, "as nowhere else in the land.
    The Great Pagoda is at last rebuilt.
Now, Itsukushima in Aki and, in Echizen, the Kehi Shrine[102]
are the very presence of Dainichi, lord of the Twin Mandalas.
Kehi, though, prospers greatly, while Itsukushima languishes as though ignored.
Report this to His Majesty and restore it. Do that and, be assured,
rank and office will be yours beyond all other men. You will have no rival."
So he spoke, then rose and went away.
    Where the old monk had been,
    an unearthly fragrance filled the air.
    Lord Kiyomori had him watched:

....

101. The Inner Sanctum of Mount Kōya, the holiest spot on the mountain. Kōbō Daishi (Kūkai), the founder, resides here within his mausoleum in a state of eternal meditation (10:9).
102. Kehi Jingū, in present Fukui-ken, was believed to manifest the Dainichi of the Womb Mandala.

Still in sight for three hundred yards,
he then simply disappeared.
That was no ordinary man—
so the awestruck lord understood—
but the great teacher Kōbō Daishi!
Moved to a new surge of faith,
he resolved not to let this pass:
In the Mount Kōya Golden Hall,
he would paint the Twin Mandalas.
The western he assigned to Jōmyō,
a master holy-image painter;
the eastern he would paint himself,
and did so. For some reason
he drew blood from his own head,
they say, to paint upon Dainichi,
central amid eight lotus petals,
the tall crown that he wears.

Lord Kiyomori made his way up to the capital and called there on the retired
emperor.
His report deeply moved the sovereign, who extended his appointment.
So it was that Kiyomori restored Itsukushima. He replaced the torii,
rebuilt the sanctuaries, and constructed several hundred yards of galleries.
The work once done, he went there himself and spent the night in vigil.
He dreamed that a divine youth, his hair in side loops, came forth from the
sanctuary.
"I bring you a message from the Triple Goddess," he said.[103]
"Take this blade and with it pacify the four seas. You shall be the emperor's
protector."
He gave the dreamer a lance with the shaft spiral-wrapped in silver.
Lord Kiyomori found it there beside his pillow when he awoke.
The Triple Goddess gave him this oracle:

"Did you heed me, or have you forgotten
what I told you through the holy man?
If you conduct yourself ill, however,
you will do your descendants no good."
With these words the goddess ascended.
What a marvelous thing to happen!

103. The chief member of this triad is Ichikishima-hime, the third daughter of the Sun Goddess. Note
90 describes the second, Tagori-hime. The third is Tagitsu-hime, a daughter of Susano-o. These are also
the deities of the ancient Munakata Shrine in northen Kyushu.

6. Raigō

In Emperor Shirakawa's reign, Lord Morozane's daughter became
    empress. [1072-86]
Kenshi was her name. His Majesty loved her and longed for a son by her.
Now, there lived at Miidera an adept known as Raigō, a monk of great power.
His Majesty summoned him. "You will offer such prayers," he informed him,
"as to ensure that the empress bears a prince.
If she does, your reward will be anything you desire."
"Very well, Your Majesty," Raigō replied.
He returned to Miidera and there for one hundred days
devoted every particle of his being to offering up the prayers required.
During those hundred days, the empress conceived readily,
and in Jōhō 1, the twelfth month and sixteenth day, she gave easy birth. [1074]
The child was a boy.

> The delighted emperor summoned Raigō. "What is your wish?" he
> asked. Raigō requested an ordination platform for Miidera.[104]
>
> "That wish is not one that I had foreseen," His Majesty replied. "I
> assumed that you would ask for promotion. A prince's birth is wel-
> come because it assures the succession and secures peace in the realm.
> What you ask would enrage Mount Hiei and provoke turmoil. There
> would be war between Enryakuji and Miidera, and the Tendai teach-
> ing would be lost."
>
> The emperor rejected Raigō's request.

Raigō returned to Miidera bitterly disappointed and prepared to starve to death.
Alarmed, His Majesty summoned Ōe no Masafusa, then still the governor of
    Mimasaka.
"I gather that you are one of Raigō's patrons," he said.
"Go to him and try to make him see sense."
Masafusa obediently set off for Raigō's lodge, to speak to him for the emperor.
He found Raigō shut up in a smoke-blackened personal chapel,
whence there issued, in fearsome tones, these words:

> "The Son of Heaven does not jest;
>   his word is said to be like sweat.[105]

If my modest wish is to go unmet, then, since my prayers gave the prince life,
I will take him with me into the demon realm."

....

104. Possession of a formally consecrated site for the ordination of monks, hence authorization to
conduct such ordinations, was a supreme honor for a temple. Raigō's incendiary request reflects the
intense rivalry between Mount Hiei and Miidera.

105. Because neither can be taken back.

He refused to see Masafusa, who returned to the emperor and reported his
　　words.
Soon, to His Majesty's astonishment and dismay, Raigō died of starvation.
　　　Shortly thereafter the prince fell ill.
　　　Many prayers were offered for him,
　　　but they seemed to do him no good.
　　　Some dreamed that an old, white-haired monk
　　　stood by his pillow, ringed staff in hand;[106]
　　　some saw this monk with their waking eyes.
　　　"Frightening" is hardly the word.
　　　So it was that on the sixth day,
　　　in the eighth month of Shōryaku 1, [1077]
　　　the prince, in his fourth year, passed away.
　　　He had been named Atsufun.
　　　　　The grief-stricken emperor summoned Ryōshin, the abbot of Mount
　　　　Hiei, a prelate of imposing rank and a monk of impressive power.
　　　　"What am I to do?" he asked.
　　　　　Ryōshin replied, "My Mountain alone, Your Majesty, brings to fru-
　　　　ition such desires as yours. The future Emperor Reizei came into the
　　　　world because the minister of the right, Lord Morosuke, entrusted
　　　　Ryōgen, my great predecessor, with prayers to that end. This will pre-
　　　　sent no difficulty." He returned to Mount Hiei, and there, for one hun-
　　　　dred days, he prayed with fierce intensity to Sannō, the god of the
　　　　mountain. During those hundred days, the empress conceived, and in
　　　　Shōryaku 3, [1079] on the ninth of the seventh month, she gave easy
　　　　birth to a prince, the future Emperor Horikawa.
Yes, angry spirits were to be feared in earlier times as well.
Now, despite the general amnesty declared most exceptionally for this august
　　birth,
the monk Shunkan alone received no pardon. This was unfortunate.
　　　That same year, in the twelfth month,
　　　on the eighth day, it was decreed
　　　that the prince should be heir apparent.
　　　His tutor was Lord Shigemori,
　　　and the master of his household
　　　the counselor Yorimori.

....

106. A staff topped by nine jangling metal rings. The old monk is an adept of the esoteric mysteries.

7. Naritsune's Return

In the new year, Jishō 3, late in the first month, [1179]
Lieutenant Naritsune left the Kase estate in Hizen and hurried on up to the
    capital.
The weather was still very cold, though, and with the sea so rough
the ship crept from harbor to harbor and island to island,
not reaching Kojima in Bizen until about the tenth of the second month.
From there Naritsune sought out where his father had lived.
He discovered, on bamboo pillars and battered sliding doors,
traces of the brush made by his father to pass the time.
"Nothing brings a man back like writing in his own hand,"
he and Yasuyori reflected, reading and weeping, weeping and reading.
They also noted this: "Angen 3, seventh month, twentieth day: entered
    religion. [1177]
Twenty-sixth of that month: Nobutoshi came down."
So Naritsune learned that Minamoto no Nobutoshi, of the Left Gate Watch,
had come on a visit to his father.

      Written on the wall nearby, they found:
      "Amida's welcome will not fail;
      rebirth in paradise is sure."
      "So," Naritsune concluded
      when his eye fell on these words,
      "he did aspire to the Pure Land";
      and he felt, amid boundless grief,
      a slight touch of comfort.

He found his father's grave in a grove of pines. No mound announced its
    presence.
On a slight, sandy rise, he brought his sleeves together and, in tears,
spoke as though to one living:

      "That you now watch us from beyond,
      I heard on my island, from afar,
      but life fails to follow my wishes,
      and I could not then hurry to you.

Yes, I survived exile on that island, and after two years I have been called
    back.
That is no doubt a joy, but only seeing you again, alive,
could have made my life worth living. I came as soon as I could,
      but there is no need now for further haste."
      He spoke with great fervor, weeping.

And Naritsune's father, for his part,
had he really been still alive,
would certainly have asked his son
how he was these days, but, alas,
the gulf between one life and the next
inflicts only sorrow and pain.
Who could reply, from beneath the moss?
There came to Naritsune's ears
only wind rushing through the pines.
Naritsune and Yasuyori spent the night circumambulating the grave, calling the
Name.
The next morning they rebuilt the mound, surrounded it with a railing,
and before it put together a provisional shelter,
where for seven days and seven nights they called the Name and copied sutras.
On the last day, they erected a tall, funerary stupa, on which Naritsune wrote:
"Holy spirit of the departed,
put behind you birth and death;
seek only enlightenment."
And beneath the date, he added:
"His filial son, Naritsune."
The local peasants, though uncouth,
knew that a son is a great treasure,
and from each the sight drew tears.
The years may come, the years may go,
but a parent's loving-kindness
is never to be forgotten,
though it passes like a dream
or like a fleeting vision.
Tears of yearning always flow.
How the buddhas of the three worlds
and the ten directions, the blessed host,
must have pitied Naritsune!
How his father's shade surely rejoiced!
Naritsune bade the dead farewell.
"I should stay with you awhile," he said,
"to build you greater merit still
by calling upon Amida,
but there are in the capital
those who await me anxiously.
Be assured that I will come again."
In tears he then started on his way.

Perhaps the departed, in the earth,
was equally sad that he should go.
On the sixteenth of the third month, with light still in the sky, Naritsune reached
Toba.
There his late father had had a mountain villa, Suhama Hall.
For years now it had been deserted. The compound wall had lost its covering
tiles,
and the gate, though still standing, had no doors. Naritsune went into the garden.
There was no sign of human presence, and the moss grew deep.

He gazed across the lake. The spring breeze
from Autumn Hill raised on its waters
an endless procession of white ripples
cloven by sporting mandarin ducks,
purple, and by the white of gulls.
Longing for him who had enjoyed them,
he shed tears in an endless stream.

The house, yes, was still there, but the latticework above the transoms was gone;
so, too, were the shutters and the sliding doors.
"Here my father did such and such. . . .
This is how he passed through this door. . . .
That tree he planted himself."
Voicing such reminiscences, he fondly recalled his father's presence.

On this sixteenth of the third month,
a few cherry blossoms still lingered,
while willow, plum, peach, and damson
each flaunted its seasonal glory.
He who had owned all this was gone,
but even so, no flower forgets spring.
Naritsune stood beneath the blossoms.

"Peach and damson never reveal how many springs have come and gone;
vaporous mists retain no tracks: Who can have lived here long ago?"[107]

This was once my home,
and if, in this world of ours,
such blossoms could speak,
ah, what questions I would ask
about those days long ago!

To himself he hummed these old poems,
and Yasuyori, too, was moved,

....

107. A Chinese couplet by Sugawara no Michizane, included in *Wakan rōeishū* (1012), a collection of Chinese and Japanese poems for singing aloud. The Japanese poem that follows is also old (from *Goshūishū*, 1086).

moistening his ink-black sleeves.
Having meant to leave at sundown,
he could not bear after all to go
and stayed well on into the night.
Through the advancing hours, the moon,
as ever in a ruined house,
shone light of mounting brilliance
through cracks in the ancient eaves.
Day would soon rise above the hills,
yet still he had no wish to leave.
But Naritsune could not stay forever. A carriage had come for him,
and he did not want to keep waiting those who expected him.
In tears he set out from Suhama Hall.
As the two entered the capital, their hearts must have felt both joy and sorrow.
A carriage had come for Yasuyori, too, but he did not board it.
"I cannot bear to leave you yet," he said, and rode instead in the rear of
    Naritsune's,
as far as the Kamo riverbed at Shichijō. There, their ways were at last to part,
but they still could not face the moment of farewell.

Two who spend just half a day
happily beneath the blossoms,
companions for a single night
passed contemplating the full moon,
travelers caught by a shower,
who shelter under the same tree:
All these grieve when they say good-bye.
How much truer, then, this must be
of two who have suffered together
island exile, shared sea voyages,
braved as one the waves, and in life
both experienced the same karma.
Surely they understood full well
the strength of a bond from lives gone by.
Naritsune went to the residence of his father-in-law, Norimori.
His mother, until then living on Mount Ryōzen, had come there the day before,
to await him. She cried when she saw him come in:
"I, who live on . . . !"—and that was all.[108]
There she lay, her head under a robe.

....

108. From a lament by Nōin Hōshi, included in the early-thirteenth-century anthology *Shinkokinshū:*
"I, who live on, saw the autumn moon again this year, but I shall not see again the friend I have lost."

The gentlewomen and staff of Norimori's household crowded around, all weeping with joy. Imagine, then, how happy Naritsune's wife was, and his nurse, Rokujō! The burden of endless grief had turned Rokujō's black hair white, and his wife, once so vivacious and pretty, had wasted away almost beyond recognition. The child in his third year when Naritsune went into exile was now old enough to wear his hair bound in loops. And there beside him was another, perhaps now in his third year.

"And who is *this*?" Naritsune asked.

"Why, this, you see . . ." Rokujō began, then pressed her sleeves to her eyes and wept.

Oh! Naritsune cried to himself, remembering that his wife had been pregnant when he left and how worried he had been. And the child had grown up so nicely!

Naritsune once more served the cloistered emperor,
and he rose to consultant and captain.
Yasuyori, who had a villa at Sōrinji in the Eastern Hills,
settled there to think long and hard about the past.

> *Here at my old home,*
> *moss in so thick a carpet*
> *overgrows the eaves;*
> *far less moonlight than I thought*
> *comes shining in through the cracks.*

Naritsune's reunion with his family.

Soon he retired there for good
to ponder all those past sorrows
and, they say, wrote a book of stories
entitled *A Precious Treasury*.

8. Ariō

So it was that of the three Kikai-ga-shima exiles, two were recalled to the capital.
The monk Shunkan, poor man, remained behind alone on that dreadful island.
Now, there was a youth whom Shunkan had favored and kept in his service since
    boyhood.
Ariō was his name. When Ariō learned that the exiles would be back that day,
he went to meet them at Toba, but his master was not with them.
He asked what had happened. They told him that Shunkan's crime was so grave,
he had been left on the island. Ariō was upset, to say the least.
He regularly roamed around Rokuhara, keeping his ears open,
but never heard a word to suggest the likelihood of a pardon.
He went to where his master's daughter was living in hiding.
"Fortune has not favored your father," he said. "He is not coming back.
I have made up my mind to go to the island myself, at all costs,
and find out what has happened to him. Please give me a letter for him."
She wrote it in tears. Ariō wanted to say good-bye to his parents
but said nothing to either, knowing that they would not let him go.
A trading ship bound for China was to sail in the fourth or fifth month,
but that meant a summer departure, and he could not wait.
He set out late in the third and after a long voyage reached the Satsuma
    coast.

At the port that offered passage
onward to the island, people stared.
They stole his clothes, but Ariō
never felt a breath of regret.
To keep the young lady's letter
from prying eyes, he secured it,
safely hidden, in his topknot.
So, aboard a merchant vessel,
he successfully reached the island.
The little he had heard in the city
did not begin to describe it.
There were no paddies, no dry fields.
There were no villages, no hamlets.

People there were, yes, but to him
   their speech made no sense at all.
He wondered whether one of them might know the fate of his master.
"Pardon me," he said. The answer came, "Whaddaya want?"
"The superintendent of Hosshōji was exiled here from the capital.
Do you know what has become of him?"
But "Hosshōji" and "superintendent" clearly meant nothing to the man,
who shook his head. "Nope," he said.
Another one, though, did a little better. "Yes," he replied,
"there were three of those people here. Two were called back to the capital,
and off they went. That left the third—he just wanders around.
I have no idea where he is."
   Perhaps he is in the mountains, then,
   the anxious Ariō surmised.
   Far into their depths he made his way,
   scaling peaks, descending ravines,
   but white clouds obscured every sign,
   and where the path led was never clear.
   Not even dreams showed his master's form:
   Wind gusting through the trees shattered them.
   Failing to find him in the mountains,
   Ariō went down to search by the sea.
   Gulls printing bird tracks in the sand,
   plovers clustering on offshore bars—
   no other living thing met his gaze.
   Then one morning, from the stony beach,
   a figure came lurching into view,
   gaunt and as thin as a dragonfly.
   He might perhaps have once been a monk,
   but the hair grew skyward from his head,
   tangled with myriad scraps of seaweed,
   as though he wore a wreath of thorns.
   Bony joints stuck out, skin hung loose,
   and the clothes—there was no way to tell
   whether they were silk or common cloth.
   In one hand he held a strip of kelp;
   from the other hand dangled a fish.
   Visibly his will was to walk,
   but actually he only staggered.
   In the capital, Ariō thought,

I have seen beggars by the score,
but never one in the least like this!
"The ashuras dwell beside the ocean,"
the Buddha says. Indeed, the three,
the four evil realms that they inhabit
lie high in the mountain wilderness
and along the margin of the sea.
Could it then be, this place I have reached,
the realm haunted by Hungry Ghosts?
Perhaps this creature knows what has become of my master.
"Beg your pardon," Ariō said, and got the reply, "What do you want?"
"Have you any idea what became of someone in exile here from the capital—
a man known as the superintendent of Hosshōji?"
Ariō did not know his master, but how could his master not have known him?
"I am he," Shunkan answered, dropped his burden, collapsed on the sand.
Now Ariō knew his master's fate!

        Shunkan had fainted. Ariō rested his master's head on his lap. "I am
here," he said. "Oh, how can you do this to me, after all I went through
for so long at sea? How can you make me feel as though I have come all
this way for nothing?" He was weeping.

        Soon Shunkan recovered his senses somewhat, and Ariō helped
him to his feet. "I can hardly believe," Shunkan said, "that you cared
enough to come all the way here to find me.
Day and night my every thought goes to the capital,
and the faces of those I love
appear to me sometimes in dreams, sometimes in waking vision.
Now I am so terribly weak and wasted
I can no longer tell what is a dream and what is real.
So, you see, to me your coming
can be nothing but a dream.
But if it is, then what will I do
once I am awake again?"
"I am real," answered Ariō.
"That I find you still alive,
in this terrible condition,
strikes me as a miracle."
"Yes, and me, too. Just imagine
how I felt when those two others,
last year, left me alone and helpless.
I would have chosen drowning,
were it not that Naritsune

did what he could to console me,
telling me that I should await
more news from the capital.
So I decided to stay alive, foolishly believing that that news might really come.
But there is nothing to eat on this island. While I was strong enough,
I went into the mountains to collect this stuff they call sulfur,
which I traded for food with merchants from Kyushu,
but I grew weaker daily, and now I have given that up.

So it is that in fine weather
I make my way out to the shore,
where they fish with nets and lines,
there to beg on bended knee
for whatever fish they give me.
At low tide I gather shellfish,
collect kelp, or, from the rocks,
seaweed that keeps me alive
one dewdrop moment longer:
That is how I have survived.
What other choice did I have?

I would like to tell you everything, right here—but no, first come to my house."
"Even now," thought Ariō, "looking that way, he still has a house? I cannot
believe it!"
They went on until they came to a grove of pines. Within it stood a hut.
Shunkan had built it from bamboo pillars and beams of bundled reeds
and had covered it thickly, above and below, with pine needles.
It could not possibly keep out either wind or rain.
Once the superintendent of Hosshōji had controlled more than eighty estates
and had lived within his gates amid servants, family, and retainers
a full four or five hundred strong.
He now made a strange sight, so disastrously reduced.

There are several kinds of karma:
One has consequences in this life,
one in the next, and one thereafter.
Everything that Shunkan had turned
in his life to personal use
had been the Buddha's property
or else that of his own great temple.
His habit of appropriating
offerings made with true devotion
seems therefore to have provoked,
in this very life, disaster.

9. *The Death of Shunkan*

Shunkan now grasped that Ariō was real. "When they came last year for Naritsune and Yasuyori," he said, "even then there was no letter from anyone of mine, and you have brought none either. Did you not tell them you were coming?"

Sobbing, Ariō collapsed on the ground and for a time remained silent. Then he rose again and, fighting back tears, began: "After you left for Nishi-Hachijō, officers came and arrested the whole household. They questioned them about the rebellion and then put them all to death. Your wife, who was desperate somehow to hide the children, moved them to a remote spot on Mount Kurama. I am the only one who went there sometimes to help them. They were all in a state of despair, but your son, who missed you terribly, used to beg me whenever I went there to take him to Kikai-ga-shima. But then, this second month past, he caught smallpox and died. This, after everything else, was too much for his mother, who fell into a decline and weakened daily, until on the second of the third month she passed away.

Now only your daughter is left; she lives with her aunt in Nara.
And here is a letter from her." He took out the letter and gave it to Shunkan.
Shunkan unfolded and read it. It said exactly what he had just heard from Ariō.

"Why is it," his daughter had written,
"that the two others have been recalled
but you have not come up here yet?
It is so hard, being a girl!
If I were a boy, nothing at all
could stop me from going to find you
on the island where you are now.

Please, please come straight back up to the capital with Ariō."
Her father pressed the letter to his face and for a moment said nothing.
"Look at that, Ariō!" he then cried. "Look what foolishness she has written!
She wants me to go back up with you! I cannot bear it!
Would I have spent three years here if I were my own master?

This is her twelfth year, I believe.
How, if she must be this silly,
can she possibly get married,
go out into decent service,
or look after herself in life?"
His tears revealed all too plainly
how, even if not in darkness,
a father's heart may yet wander,

lost, on the path of parental love.
"During banishment on this island,
for lack of any calendar
I have lost track of months and days.
I merely see the flowers open
or the leaves fall and thereby know
the season to be spring or autumn.
When cicada voices bid farewell
to the last of the barley harvest,
then I know that summer has come;
and winter I judge by falling snow.
By keeping an eye on the moon
waxing fifteen nights, waning the same,
I follow the month's thirty days;
by crooking my fingers to keep count,
I know that this is his sixth year—
the little boy who, I now learn,
has already gone on before me.

> When I started for Nishi-Hachijō, he desperately wanted to come with me, and I put him off by promising that I would be back soon. The memory is so clear it could be yesterday. How could I not have stayed to watch him longer, if only I had known that I would never see him again? The tie from parent to child or child to parent, the bond between husband and wife—no, these are not for one life only. But if so, why did no dream or vision ever tell me that they were gone? I resolved to stay alive by any means, whatever others might think of me, only because I longed to see my family again. I feel for my daughter, but she *is* alive, after all, and she will survive the hardships that come her way. For me to go on living now, at the cost of much trouble to you, would only be selfish." He stopped taking even the rare food that came his way, devoted himself to calling the Name, and prayed for right thoughts at the last. On the twenty-third day after Ariō's coming, he passed away in his hut. This was his thirty-seventh year.

Ariō clung to the lifeless remains, rolled his eyes to the heavens,
writhed on the ground, wept and mourned, but nothing changed.
And after he had wept his fill,
"I should really accompany you into the next life," he said,
"but in this one only your daughter survives, no one else, to pray for you.
So I will live on a while in this one, to offer prayers for you in the next."

> Without ever touching his master,
> he broke up the hut and laid its parts

over the body, added pine boughs
and that thick blanket of pine needles,
and of the pyre made salt-fire smoke.
When at last the cremation was done,
he gathered the white bones together,
hung them in a pouch around his neck,
and boarded a merchant vessel
that took him at last to Kyushu.

Ariō went on from there to visit Shunkan's daughter,
to whom he related in full all he had seen.
"I fear that your letter only made him feel worse," he explained.
"Having no paper or inkstone, he could not write you an answer.
The despair he felt lasted until he died.
No, never again, not through aeons of future births and lives,
will you hear your father's voice or see his form."

The girl, in her twelfth year, very soon
became a nun and gave herself up
to devout practice at Hokkeji[109]
in Nara, where her every prayer
went to securing happiness
for her parents in their next life.
Ariō hung around his neck
his master's bones, climbed Mount Kōya,
and laid them in the Oku-no-in.
Then he repaired to Rengedani,
became a monk there, and set out
on holy pilgrimage through the land,
praying likewise for his master.
Having heaped such grief on so many,
the Heike faced a frightening end.

10. *The Whirlwind*

It was the fifth month of that year, on the twelfth, at midday, [1179]
when a great whirlwind swept through the city.
Many houses collapsed.
It started where Naka-no-mikado and Kyōgoku cross,
thence to travel southwestward,
demolishing gates great and small,

....

109. A nunnery founded circa 741 by Kōmyō, Emperor Shōmu's empress.

sending them flying four or five hundred yards and more,
filling the air with rafters, sill beams, pillars, and other debris.
Roofing bark and shingles raced through the air
like leaves in a winter gale, and the deafening roar
matched the roar of the winds of karma in hell.
Not only buildings were lost, but many lives, too.
Oxen and horses died in vast numbers.
No, this was no common event. It called for divination
performed by the Bureau of Shrines:
"Within the next hundred days,
a richly rewarded minister
will need to exercise caution.
Further, perils will threaten the realm.
The Buddha's and the Sovereign's Ways
will both lapse into decline,
and armed clashes will follow."
So divined the Bureau of Shrines,
and likewise the Yin-Yang Office.

11. *To Consult or Not the Chinese Physician*

Lord Shigemori must have felt profoundly downcast when he learned what had
    happened,
for he went in those days on pilgrimage to Kumano.
Before the Shōjōden of the main shrine,
he spent the night addressing the divine presence in these terms:
"I observe that my father, the novice and chief minister,
conducts himself evilly and unjustly, persecuting at times the sovereign
    himself.
As his eldest son, I remonstrate with him often, but I lack the wit to change his
    ways.
Such is his behavior that I fear even for his own glory,
and I cannot imagine his successors adding luster to either his name or theirs.
Unworthy as I am, these, then, are my thoughts:
Should I, like any mediocrity, merely follow the prevailing tide,
I would stray from the ways proper to a good official and a filial son.
Far better, then, to forsake thoughts of greatness, to withdraw,
abandoning glory for this life, and instead to seek enlightenment.
Being a man as weak and benighted as any other, and as confused about right
    and wrong,
I have never done what I truly aspire to do.

Hail, O Mighty Divinity!
Hail, O Guardian Kongō Dōji!
If the descendants of our house
are long to enjoy prosperity,
mingling with the great at court
and serving His Majesty,
cause my father to restrain
the evil leanings of his heart!
Assure the realm enduring peace!
But if our glory cannot outlast him
and shame awaits those who follow,
O then put an end to my life,
and save me from pain in lives to come!
Between these, my two entreaties,
grant me, I beg you, divine aid!"
So he prayed in bitter earnest,
and what seemed a lantern flame
then flew from his body and went out.
Many saw it, but fear silenced them.

On his way back, his party was crossing the Iwada River
when Lieutenant Koremori, his firstborn, in the company of his other sons,
all of them wearing pale gray-violet under pilgrim white,
began sporting merrily in the water, for it was summer,
and through the white, once wet, the color showed precisely as mourning gray.
Sadayoshi, the governor of Chikugo, noticed.
"You know," he remarked, "your pilgrim garb now looks extremely ill-omened.
Perhaps you should consider changing it"; whereupon Lord Shigemori:
"My prayer is answered. No, you are not to change your clothes."
From the Iwada River, he sent a special offering of thanks to Kumano.

This puzzled the people with him.
They failed to understand his meaning.

Strangely enough, however, Lord Shigemori's sons would soon be wearing true mourning. Only a few days after his return to the capital, he fell ill. He commissioned no healing rites, being certain that the god of Kumano had accepted his prayer.

A great physician from Song China was then visiting Japan. Lord Kiyomori, who happened to be at his Fukuhara villa, sent Moritoshi, the governor of Etchū, to Shigemori with this message: "I gather that you are ill and getting worse. By chance a first-class physician from Song is present among us. That is great good luck. I want you to summon him and have him treat you."

Shigemori listened. Then, with help, he sat up and called Moritoshi before him.

"Tell my father," he said, "that I have respectfully heeded his words regarding medical intervention. Now I ask you to hear mine.

Wise sovereign though he surely was,
he who reigned in the Engi years [Daigo, r. 897–930]
admitted to our imperial city
a physiognomist from overseas;
ever since, this has been considered
a lapse of judgment on his part
and an embarrassment to our realm.
How, then, could I, who am nothing,
bring to the seat of our sovereign
a physician from a foreign land?
Would this not shame our realm?

Han Gaozu, the dynasty founder, conquered his realm with a three-foot sword, but when he attacked Qing Bu of Huainan, a stray arrow wounded him. Empress Lu had a fine physician examine him. The man said, 'Yes, I can heal this wound, but not for less than fifty catties of gold.' Gaozu replied, 'While my protection was strong, I suffered no harm from wounds in many battles. Now my good fortune is over. My life is at heaven's disposal. Not even Pian Que could help me. But I do not wish to seem miserly.' He gave the physician his fifty catties but rejected all treatment. His words linger in my ears. They mean a great deal to me.

Yes, I joined the senior nobles awhile
and rose in office to minister.
Reflecting more on this destiny,
I understand it was heaven's will.
How could I disregard that will
and irresponsibly trouble others
to provide a physician's care?
If this is what my karma requires,
such care would do me little good,
and if my time has not yet come,
then I will recover on my own.
No, Jivaka's[110] art was not enough:
The World-Honored Shakyamuni
crossed into final extinction

....

110. The great physician of the Buddha's time in India.

there by the Niranjana River.
He did so to teach us a lesson:
No one can heal a fated sickness.
If it were possible to do so,
how could he have passed beyond?
Such an illness defies healing:
That much is transparently clear.
And that sick man was Shakyamuni,
that physician Jivaka himself.
I am no Buddha, and that man,
learned in medicine, from Song,
is certainly no Jivaka either.
Say he has learned the four treatises
and mastered the hundred modes of healing:
Even so, he could hardly save
polluted flesh so mired in this world.
He may know the five medical classics by heart and a remedy for every disease,
but what power could he possibly have over a karmic ill from lives gone by?
If thanks to his skill I were to survive after all,
that would effectively set at naught the medicine of our own land,
and if he could do nothing for me, then seeing him would have been pointless.
And more than anything else, for a minister of the realm
casually to consult a visitor by chance present here from abroad—
that would, first, bring shame on our country and, second, degrade our ways.
Not even at the cost of my life would I wish to embarrass our land.
Tell my father that."

Moritoshi returned to Fukuhara and, in tears, conveyed Shigemori's words.

Kiyomori said, "I have never heard of a minister, even in ancient times, so concerned with the honor of our land. In fact, it is hard to believe that such a man exists in this latter age. This minister is too good for Japan. I know that he is going to die."

Weeping, he hurried up to the capital. On the twenty-eighth of the seventh month of that year, Lord Shigemori took Buddhist vows. His name in religion was Jōren. On the first of the eighth month, he passed away, in a state of right thoughts at the last. He was in his forty-third year and plainly at the height of his powers. His death was a great loss.

Violent as Lord Kiyomori was in his ways,
only Shigemori's calming influence and good judgment had maintained peace.
Every denizen of the capital, high or low,
lamented that there was no telling now what might befall the realm.

Partisans of the former right commander, Lord Munemori,
rejoiced that all the world would now look to their own lord.

> A father, for love of his child,
> grieves even when one little favored
> departs early from this life.
> And imagine, then, Lord Shigemori:
> He was a pillar of the Heike
> and in all ways the sage of his time.
> The agony of losing a son,
> the imminent decline of his house—
> these surpassed every notion of grief.
> So it was that the world at large
> mourned a great minister's passing
> while, for its part, the house of Taira
> bewailed the waning of its armed might.
> Ever distinguished in his person,
> Shigemori was loyal at heart,
> a model of every accomplishment,
> and virtuous in every word.

12. *The Sword of Mourning*

Lord Shigemori had an unusual nature.
Perhaps he could even see into the future, because in the fourth month past,
on the seventh day, he dreamed an extraordinary dream.
He was walking along an endless beach; where it was, he could not tell.
Beside the path stood a great torii. "What torii is this?" he asked.
"This is the torii of the Kasuga Deity," he was told.[111]
Many people were gathered there, and one held up a monk's head.
"Whose head is that?" the dreamer inquired.
"This is the head of the chancellor and novice Kiyomori, of the Taira," the
    answer came.
"The god of this shrine has taken it, so excessively evil are his deeds."
Shigemori then woke up.

> "Since the Hōgen and Heiji years,
> we Taira have repeatedly
> quelled the enemies of the court,
> gaining honor beyond our due:
> our leader now—an awesome thought—
> soon to become, through his daughter,

111. The Kasuga Shrine, in Nara, is the tutelary shrine of the Fujiwara.

Shigemori's dream. At right: The dreamer.

    the grandfather of an emperor
    and of our number over sixty
    occupying exalted office.
    Our wealth, for twenty years and more,
    has simply defied description,
    but now my father's past abuses
    threaten all of us with ruin."
    Thoughts like these, of what had been
    and what might be, rolled through his head
    until he could do nothing but weep.
    Someone knocked at the double doors.
"Who is that?" Shigemori asked. "Go and find out."
"Seno-o Tarō Kaneyasu is here, my lord," came the reply.
"What is it? What is the matter?"
"A strange occurrence, my lord. Something happened just now.
I have come to tell you because I felt that I could not wait for dawn.
Please ask your people to withdraw." Shigemori did so and received
    Seno-o.
Seno-o related to him in full what he had just dreamed.
The dream was exactly the same as his lord's.
    Why then, Seno-o Kaneyasu, too,

is in direct touch with the gods!

Lord Shigemori was impressed.

Koremori, his eldest son and heir, was preparing that morning to set off for the palace when his father called him in. "This is hardly the way for a father to speak, but you are to my mind the best of my sons. I do not like at all, though, how our world is going. Sadayoshi? Serve the lieutenant wine."

Sadayoshi brought wine and prepared to pour.

"I should prefer the lieutenant to take the cup first," Shigemori went on, "but I know that he would never drink before his father. So I will take it and then give it to him." He accepted the cup three times, then offered it to Koremori.

Once Koremori, too, had accepted the cup three times, Shigemori spoke again: "Now, Sadayoshi, the gift!"

Sadayoshi obediently brought out a sword in a brocade bag.

"Oh!" said Koremori to himself as he watched. "This must be Koga-rasu, the heirloom sword of our house!" But no, it was plain and un-adorned, the kind worn for a minister's funeral.

Koremori paled and considered it with evident distaste. His father shed bitter tears.

"Listen to me, Koremori," he said. "Sadayoshi has made no mistake.

You may wonder how this can be.

The sword before you is a plain one, for the funeral of a minister.

I have kept it with me in case anything should happen to Lord Kiyomori,

but I will soon precede him, so it is yours."

His words struck Koremori dumb;

the least answer was beyond him.

Choked with tears, he collapsed, facedown,

and that day never went to court;

instead he lay still beneath a robe.

Later on, returning from Kumano,

Shigemori sickened and died.

All these things then at last made sense.

13. The Lanterns

In all things Lord Shigemori aspired to abolish sin and cultivate good karma.

Lamenting the heights and depths of rebirth in lives to come,

he therefore built at the foot of the Eastern Hills a temple forty-eight bays long,

inspired by the six-times-eight great vows of the Buddha Amida,

and in each bay he hung a lantern: forty-eight, for forty-eight bays.

The ninefold lotus throne glittered before the viewer's eyes;

the phoenix mirror shone as though one gazed on paradise itself.
Each month, on the fourteenth and fifteenth days, the Heike and other houses
sent pretty gentlewomen in the flower of their youth to gather there, six to a bay:
    for the forty-eight, two hundred eighty-eight gentlewomen in all.
They were assigned by turns to call the Name through the six hours of day and
    night,
and during those two days their devout invocations never ceased.

> Amida's compassionate vow,
> to greet all who call his Name
> and welcome them to paradise,
> here was truly plain to see,
> and the radiance of his promise
> to gather all who call on him
> to himself and abandon none
> shone down, it seemed, on Shigemori.
> When at noon on the fifteenth day
> the great invocation ended,
> he himself joined the procession,
> turned toward the west, and chanted,
> "Hail, O Well-Gone, Lord Amida,
> you who reign over paradise,
> save, I pray, all sentient beings
> in the three worlds and the six realms."
> Thus he turned his every merit
> to vow rebirth in the Pure Land,
> moving to mercy all who saw him,
> all who heard him to heartfelt tears.
> So it came to pass that people
> called him the "Lantern Minister."

14. Gold to China

Lord Shigemori also reflected that whatever root of good karma
he might strike in our own land, his descendants could hardly pray for him
    forever.
Wishing also to put down good karmic roots somehow in the Other Realm,
so that such prayers might be offered on his behalf throughout all future time,
in the Angen years [1175-77] he summoned from Kyushu a ship captain named
    Miao Dian.
He had his entourage withdraw far off and met the man in private.
Calling for three thousand five hundred taels of gold, he said,

"You are by reputation a thoroughly honest man.
Five hundred taels of this gold are therefore yours.
Three thousand are to go to Song: one thousand for the monks of Mount
    Yuwang
and two thousand for the emperor, to buy paddy fields for the monastery,
so that the monks may offer prayers for me in my lives to come."

      Miao Dian received the gold,
      braved ten thousand leagues of waves,
      and crossed over to the land of Song.
      On Mount Yuwang he met Deguang
      in the abbot's temple residence
      and explained the matter to him.
      Abbot Deguang wept tears of joy.
      His monks received a thousand taels,
      and he sent the emperor two thousand,
      with Shigemori's humble request.
      The emperor, profoundly moved,
      made over in gift to Mount Yuwang
      five hundred *chō* of paddy fields.[112]
      Thus for a Japanese minister,
      Lord Taira no Shigemori,
      prayers to assure a good rebirth
      even now go up there, they say.

15. *The Confrontation with Jōken*

      This loss of his beloved son
      surely plunged Lord Kiyomori
      far into the depths of despair,
      for he hurried to Fukuhara
      and there shut himself away.
In the eleventh month of that year,
on the night of the seventh and at the hour of the dog, [1179, ca. 8 P.M.]
a powerful earthquake struck. It lasted a good while.
Abe no Yasuchika, the head of the Yin-Yang Office, rushed to the palace.
"This earthquake, as divination shows, urges the most scrupulous conduct.
Konkikyō, one of our three divination classics, puts it this way:
'In terms of years, within the year; of months, within the month; of days, within
    the day.'

....

112. In theory about twelve hundred fifty acres.

This is a desperate emergency." Tears were pouring down his cheeks.

The official charged with transmitting his words paled, and His Majesty was
   alarmed.

The young nobles present laughed.

"He's quite a sight, Yasuchika," they said, "bawling away like that!
Nothing is going to happen."

> Nevertheless Yasuchika,
> only five generations removed
> from Abe no Seimei himself,[113]
> knew all the secrets of the stars
> and divined the truth of things
> as though it lay there in his palm.
> He who never made a mistake
> was rated a divine master.
> A bolt of lightning struck him once
> and burned the sleeve of his hunting cloak,
> but he himself remained unscathed.
> Neither ancient times nor latter days
> can have known another like him.

On the fourteenth, word went out that Kiyomori, hitherto at Fukuhara,
was now, for reasons best known to himself, on his way into the capital,
at the head of several thousand mounted men.

No one in the city knew exactly what to expect, but all, high or low, shook with
   fear.

Parties unknown spread it about that Kiyomori had it in for the imperial house
and meant now to settle old scores. The regent, Lord Motofusa,
who may have had his own sources of information, rushed to the palace.

"The senior minister's present arrival in the capital," he told His Majesty,
"surely involves a plan to do away with *me*! Oh, what is to become of me?"

The sovereign was shocked. Weeping in gracious sympathy, he replied,
"Whatever may happen to *you* will be as though it had happened to me."

> Governance of the realm, in truth,
> lies with emperor and regent.
> What to make, then, of these events?
> What the Sun Goddess can have thought,
> what the great god of Kasuga—
> that was a cause for grave concern.

>> On the fifteenth, speculation became certainty: Lord Kiyomori was
>> out to settle scores with the imperial house. In dismay the cloistered

---

113. This celebrated master of yin-yang divination and magic lived from 921 to 1005.

emperor appointed the great monk Jōken, a son of the late minor counselor Shinzei, to speak for him to Kiyomori. This was his message: "In recent years the court has been troubled, anxiety has disturbed the hearts of the people, and the world at large has become less and less secure. These things are a source of deep concern, but your presence has always been reassuring. However, rather than bring peace to the land, you have now, I gather, disposed yourself assertively to act on resentment against the imperial house. What does this mean?"

Jōken loyally set off for Nishi-Hachijō and waited there from morning to night.
In all that time, no one said a word to him.
He therefore decided that it was pointless to stay.
Entrusting Gendayū Suesada with the gist of his message,
he excused himself and was on his way out when—with "Get Jōken in here!"—
    Kiyomori finally appeared. They called Jōken back.
        "Now, reverend sir, pray tell:
        Do you take my words for nonsense?
First, considering merely the future of my house,
the palace minister's death has been a bitter blow.
I daresay that is not beyond your comprehension.
Ever since the Hōgen era, one treachery has followed another,
leaving the emperor not one moment of peace.
I myself have provided only general oversight in these matters.
It is the palace minister who did all the work, at the cost of great effort,
and who on repeated occasions soothed the imperial wrath.
His expert handling of other exceptional events, too, made him a rare treasure.
        This brings an old example to mind.
        When Taizong of Tang lost Wei Zheng,
        excessive grief moved him to write,
        in his own hand, on the stele
        he had erected at the tomb:
        'Long ago Yinzong, in a dream,
        learned of a perfect adviser;
        now I, as I am, wide awake,
        have lost a prudent minister.'
        This was, they say, his gesture of sorrow.
        And another such example,
        recent, comes from our own land.
        When Akiyori passed away, [1148]
        after heading Civil Affairs,
        Retired Emperor Toba mourned him.

He put off his progress to Yawata

and gave up the pleasures of music.

A ranking subject's death has always affected the emperor, reign after reign.

After all, the bond of emperor to subject is surely closer than parent to child,

more loving than child to parent. Yet while the palace minister still roamed the

bardo,[114]

His Cloistered Eminence made a progress to Yawata and indulged in music.

There was no sign that he cared at all.

Very well. Perhaps *my* sorrow meant nothing to him,

but why should the palace minister's loyal service have so slipped his mind?

And even if it did, how could he not have felt some sympathy for me?

So in the end His Cloistered Eminence cared nothing for either of us,

which for me, now, means a grave loss of face. That is my first complaint.

> Then another thing: Whereas the palace minister received the prov-
> ince of Echizen with the assurance that it would remain in his line
> forever, he was no sooner gone than His Cloistered Eminence took it
> back again. What kind of oversight is that? That is my second com-
> plaint. In addition, when a counselor post came vacant and Fujiwara
> no Motomichi spoke up for it, I lent him vigorous support; but no, His
> Cloistered Eminence ignored me and appointed instead the regent's
> son. I can make no sense of this. No doubt I sometimes get things
> wrong, but he could have listened to me at least this once! Motomichi
> is his father's heir, after all, and he certainly has the rank. His appoint-
> ment would have made perfect sense. His Cloistered Eminence's fail-
> ure to agree was extremely disappointing. That is my third complaint.

Furthermore, the rebellion that Narichika and those others cooked up at

Shishi-no-tani—

this was no little whim of theirs. Oh, no, they had the cloistered emperor's

backing.

I might perhaps refrain from saying so, but given everything that my house has

done for his,

I do not see how he could drop us for seven generations at least.

Besides which, I am going on seventy and probably have few enough years

before me,

and he wants any trivial excuse to get rid of me even before I am dead.

No, I cannot imagine my descendants being called henceforth to serve the

imperial house.

> Lose a son at my advanced age

....

114. In Japanese *chūu*, but probably better known in English by this Tibetan term. The intermediate state, lasting forty-nine days after death, during which the soul wanders before entering a new incarnation.

and you are a tree dead, stripped of branches.
Now that I have so little time left,
the most earnest effort of mine
could never achieve anything;
and so, as far as I am concerned,
the world can do as it pleases."
At times he raged, at times he wept,
moving Jōken to fear and pity,
even as sweat poured from his body.
No man alive could have spoken a word in answer.
Moreover, Jōken belonged to the cloistered emperor's intimate circle.
He had witnessed everything plotted at Shishi-no-tani
and, having conspired himself, knew all too well that he might at any moment be
  jailed.
He felt as though stroking a dragon's beard or treading on a tiger's tail.
But he, too, was a man of strong character, and he never lost his nerve.
He said, "You have indeed rendered signal service, time after time.
Your current irritation is easy to understand.
However, such office, rank, and recompense as have come your way should
  satisfy anyone.
They prove that His Cloistered Eminence appreciates the magnitude of your
  merit.
That some close to him nonetheless foment disorder
and that he personally supports their designs—
that is a notion encouraged only by subjects of evil intent.
People all too often wrongly believe their ears and doubt their eyes.
To give weight to the careless talk of small men
and, despite unique imperial favor, to set yourself against your sovereign—
that is frightening in both worlds, the seen and the unseen.
    The mind of heaven, boundless blue,
    remains wholly inscrutable,
    and so, too, the imperial will.
    For the low to challenge the high
    is hardly a subject's proper way.
    You would do well to ponder this.
    At any rate, I will now report
    the substance of what you have said."
    Jōken withdrew, and all present
    murmured, "That was really something!
    Lord Kiyomori was just furious,
    and even so Jōken never flinched!

No, before excusing himself
he took care to answer right back!"
Everyone was deeply impressed.

16. The Ministers Banished

Jōken returned to the cloistered emperor's residence and told him the story.
The sovereign saw that Kiyomori had right on his side. He found no reply.
On the sixteenth, Lord Kiyomori set in motion the plan he had formed.
He dismissed from office regent, chancellor, senior nobles, and privy gentlemen,
to the number of forty-three, and banished them.[115]
The regent he exiled to Kyushu as viceroy of Dazaifu.
"The way the world is these days," the regent remarked, "better just to lie low."
At Furukawa, within the bounds of Toba, he entered religion, in his thirty-fifth
    year.
A master of manners and protocol, he resembled, so people felt, a spotless
    mirror,
and for that reason he was greatly missed.
When a man condemned to distant exile then leaves the world,
he need not proceed to his assigned destination—in this case the province of
    Hyūga.
Instead he went no farther than Ibasama, near the provincial capital of Bizen.
        Ministers had been exiled before:
        Soga no Akae of the left;
        Toyonari of the right;
        Uona of the left; of the right,
        Sugawara no Michizane;
        of the left, Lord Takaakira;
        of the right, Korechika—
        already six precedents in all.
        As to the banishment of a regent,
        this, it seems, was the first time.
        The son of the late Lord Motozane,
        the second-rank captain Motomichi—
        Lord Kiyomori's son-in-law—
        was named regent and minister.
The Ichijō regent Koretada died in Emperor En'yū's reign, in Tenroku 3, [972]
on the first of the eleventh month. His younger brother,
the Horikawa regent Kanemichi, was then still a counselor at junior second rank,

....

115. The regent at the time was Fujiwara no Motofusa; the chancellor, Fujiwara no Moronaga.

hence below the next brother, Kaneie, a grand counselor and right commander.
Outstripped at first, Kanemichi then leaped, past his brother,
to palace minister at full second rank and to appointment as private assessor.[116]
Startling though this promotion was, it paled beside Motomichi's.
From second-rank captain, Motomichi passed straight over grand counselor
to regent. No one had ever heard the like before.
This Motomichi is the gentleman later known as Lord Fugenji.
The senior noble charged with arranging the announcement,
the presiding secretary, and even the clerk were plainly flabbergasted.

> Chancellor Moronaga, now dismissed,
> was sent off in exile to the east.
> Caught up earlier, during Hōgen,
> by family guilt in his father's fall—
> the Haughty Left Minister, Yorinaga—
> he had already been banished once,
> he and three brothers; nor did his elder—
> the right commander Kanenaga—
> or the two younger—Takanaga,
> a right captain, and Hanchō, a monk—
> ever again see the capital.
> No, they died at their place of exile.
> Nine springs and falls Moronaga spent
> at Hata in the province of Tosa,
> until, in the eighth month of Chōkan 2, [1164]
> he was called back and regained his rank.
> In the first month of the following year,
> he rose to second rank, senior grade,
> and in Nin'an 1, the tenth month, [1167]
> from the counselor he had once been
> to supernumerary grand counselor.
> No grand counselor post then being open,
> an extra one was added for him.
> Never before had there been six.
> In fact, precisely that promotion,
> from what he had been to what he became,
> was unheard of, except in two cases:
> Fujiwara no Mimori
> and Minamoto no Takakuni.[117]

....

116. The office of *nairan*.
117. The former was promoted in 827, the latter in 1067.

Moronaga, so skilled at music,
learned, and gifted at all the arts,
rose swiftly even to chancellor,
whereupon for some karmic misdeed
he was banished a second time:
of old, during Hōgen, to Tosa
on the shores of the southern ocean
and now, in Jishō, to the far east [1177-81]
and the province of Owari.
Any man who knows poignant beauty
longs to gaze, in all innocence,
on the moon of exile: Moronaga
never once contested his fate.
Bo Juyi of Tang, long ago,
although tutor to the crown prince,
tarried by the Xinyang River.
Moronaga recalled those days
while from the coast at Narumi
he surveyed ocean distances
illumined by a brilliant moon.
To the shore winds' sighing, he sang,
plucked the biwa, gave voice to poems,
sagely passing the months and days.
Once he set off on pilgrimage
to Atsuta, the province's third shrine.
That night, to entertain the god,
he played the biwa and sang verses,
but so benighted was the place
that no one there grasped the beauty of it.
The old men, the village women,
fishermen, farmers bowed their heads,
cocked their ears, but, low notes or high,
this scale or that meant nothing to them.
Even so, when Hu Ba played the *kin*,
the finny tribe leaped in joyous sport,
and the dust, when Yu Gong sang,
danced on the rafters. So it is
that wondrously perfected art
appeals to feeling beyond thought.
The hair rose upon every head,
and all present were enthralled.

By and by the night hour grew late.
The piece known as *Fragrant Breeze*
evoked the sweet smell of blossoms,
and in radiance *Running Stream*
vied with the moon high in the sky.
"I pray that profane letters practiced in this life
and the fault of frivolous words and fancy talk . . ."[118]
He sang these famous words and played
on the biwa such secret pieces
that emotion mastered the gods;
the sanctuary trembled and shook.
"But for these evil Heike deeds,
I could not have witnessed this wonder,"
he told himself, shedding heartfelt tears.
Minamoto no Suketoki, son of the inspector grand counselor Sukekata,
had been at once a captain in the Right Palace Guards and the governor of
     Sanuki;
he lost both posts. Fujiwara no Mitsuyoshi, consultant, intendant of the Left
     Watch,
and provisional master of the empress mother's household, lost three.
So did Takashina no Yasutsune, until then lord of the Treasury,
Right City commissioner, and governor of the province of Iyo.
Likewise Fujiwara no Motochika, chamberlain, left minor controller,
and an officer of the empress's household, lost all three posts.
The inspector grand counselor Sukekata, his son Suketoki,
and his grandson the left lieutenant Masakata, the three of them,
were ordered expelled forthwith from the capital.
Fujiwara no Sanekuni, a senior noble, and Nakahara no Norisada,
an officer in the police, were directed to execute the order.
They did so that very day.
     "The three worlds are vast," Sukekata said,
     "but for the five feet of my body
     they provide no space at all.
     Life is indeed short, as they say,
     but one day can seem very long."
     He stole from the palace by night
     and started out for distant regions

....

118. The first in a set of lines written by the Tang poet Bo Juyi (772–846), to pray that his sin (as a poet) of "frivolous words and fancy talk" should turn in the end into praise of the Buddha. Summing up as they do the dilemma of art and religious aspiration, Bo Juyi's lines were quoted countless times by writers in medieval Japan.

beyond the many-layered clouds:
first toward Ōeyama and Ikuno,
then on to pause at Murakumo,
in Tanba. But they found him at last
and drove him on, so the story goes,
to the distant province of Shinano.

17. Yukitaka

Among the housemen of Lord Motofusa, the former regent,
there was one Ōe no Tōnari, an officer in the police.
He was no favorite of the Heike either, and the news reached his ears
that a Rokuhara force was already on its way to seize him.
With his son Ienari, a junior officer in the Left Gate Watch,
he therefore fled with all possible speed, never mind where.
Up Mount Inari the two went and, at the summit, dismounted.
Father and son discussed what to do next.
"One possibility," Tōnari said, "would be to head for the east
and throw ourselves on the protection of Yoritomo,
that former officer of the Watch now exiled to Izu province.
Yoritomo, too, though, is under imperial ban,
and I doubt that by himself he could really do that much for us.
Is there after all in Japan a single estate that does not belong to the Heike?
No, there is no escape, and besides, it would be too embarrassing
to have strangers invade the home where we have lived so long.
Let us just go back again, then, and if the Rokuhara men are there,
we will slit our bellies and die. That is what we must do."
They turned back and headed home to Kawarazaka.
Sure enough, three hundred Rokuhara riders in full armor,
led by Gendayū no Hangan Suesada and Settsu no Hangan Morizumi,
launched their attack with a mighty battle yell.
Tōnari emerged on the veranda.
     "Watch this, now, gentlemen!" he cried.
     "Take the tale back to Rokuhara!"
     He set fire to his mansion.
     Father and son then slit their bellies
     and burned to death in the flames.
So it was that many, high and low, came to grief. And why?
Because, they say, Lord Motomichi, the new regent,
and the third-rank captain Motoie, the former regent's son,
had been locked in rivalry for the appointment.

Tōnari and Ienari kill themselves in their burning house.

If so, then never mind the fate of a single regent, whatever it might be:
Did more than forty men really have to be done in just for that?
Despite Emperor Sutoku's posthumous title the previous year,
despite the posthumous promotion of the Haughty Left Minister from Uji,
the world was still ill at ease, and more trouble seemed likely.
Talk spread that some demon had got into Lord Kiyomori.
He simply could not control his temper. For this reason
the whole capital trembled to think what affliction might yet strike the realm.
Now, there lived in those days a former minor controller, Yukitaka by name:
the eldest son of the late Nakayama counselor Lord Akitoki.

> During the reign of Emperor Nijō,
> Yukitaka did quite well in office,
> but now, dismissed ten years ago,
> he wore perforce, summer and winter,
> the same clothes; nor did his meals
> resemble at all what he wished.

>> There he was, hovering on the brink of final ruin, when a messenger
>> from Lord Kiyomori delivered this: "I wish to speak to you. Come at
>> once."

>> Yukitaka was terrified. "I haven't seen anyone who matters for over
>> ten years!" he said. "Someone must have denounced me!" His wife and

sons wept and wailed that some awful fate awaited him. However, messengers kept coming from Nishi-Hachijō, and he could not refuse to go. He borrowed a carriage and set out.

To his amazement Lord Kiyomori came forward to greet him, and they talked. "Your father," Kiyomori said, "was someone I consulted on matters great and small, and for that reason I hold you, too, in high regard. It has pained me that for years now you have been living in seclusion, but I had no control over His Cloistered Eminence's policies. Enter my service, then. I will find you a suitable position. Very well, you may leave." With this, Lord Kiyomori retired into an inner room.

When Yukitaka came home, his gentlewomen felt as though he had returned from the dead. They clustered around him and wept with joy.
Lord Kiyomori sent Gendayū no Hangan Suesada to him,
with titles to many estates that were now to be his.
Divining Yukitaka's likely plight, Kiyomori presented him with one hundred rolls
    of silk,
one hundred taels of gold, and copious rice.
For the purposes of Yukitaka's official service,
he also provided him with menservants, an ox driver, an ox, and a carriage.
Yukitaka, overjoyed, hardly knew what to do with himself.
"Am I dreaming, though?" he kept wondering. "Is this just a dream?"
On the seventeenth of the month, he was named a chamberlain with the fifth
    rank,
and he also regained his post of left minor controller.
This year was his fifty-first, and for once he grew visibly younger.
His prosperity seemed unlikely to last.

18. The Exile of the Cloistered Emperor

On the twentieth, an armed force surrounded the cloistered emperor's Hōjūji
    residence on all four sides.
Rumor had it that they meant to set fire to the building and burn everyone in it
    to death,
as Nobuyori had done during the Heiji years.
Gentlewomen and maids rushed out in panic, their heads still uncovered.
His Cloistered Eminence was dismayed.
The former right commander, Lord Munemori, advanced his carriage.
"Your Eminence will oblige me by boarding immediately," he said.
"But what is this about?" the sovereign demanded to know.
"I am guilty of nothing, as far as I am aware.
Presumably I am to be banished to some far province, some remote island,

like Narichika and Shunkan. Our emperor reigns, after all.
I only make suggestions to him on policy matters.
If it is wrong of me to do that, then henceforth I shall refrain."
"That is not the issue," Munemori replied.
"My father wishes you to move to the Toba Mansion
while he goes about restoring peace in the land."
"Very well, then, Munemori, accompany me there."
Munemori declined to do so, however, for fear of displeasing his father.
"Ah," the cloistered emperor reflected, "this fellow is no match for his brother,
the late palace minister. Some time ago I faced the same threat,
but Shigemori, at the risk of his life, put a stop to it, and all has been well since
    then.
Kiyomori behaves this way because he has no one to warn him against it.
I do not like at all the look of what lies ahead." He shed august tears.
Then he boarded his carriage. Not one senior noble went with him,
only Kongyō, a man-of-all-work, and some junior members of his guard.
A single nun rode in the rear of the carriage.

    This honorable nun had once been
    wet nurse to the cloistered sovereign:
    Second-Rank Lady Kii, she was called.
    Westward along Shichijō,
    then south down Suzaku they went.
    Men and women of the lowest degree cried,
    "Oh, dear, there goes His Cloistered Eminence,
    off into exile, I just know it!"
    All of them shed copious tears.
    "The earthquake that night, on the seventh,"
    people remarked—"yes, it was a portent."

        The carriage reached the Toba Mansion. Nobunari, the master of the
        imperial table, had managed somehow to slip in and was present in
        close attendance. His Cloistered Eminence summoned him. "As far as
        I can see," he said, "they will execute me tonight. I would like a bath. Is
        that possible?" Nobunari, already unmanned by the events of the
        morning, received this request with terror and awe. Tying back the
        sleeves of his hunting cloak, he got to work breaking up the brush-
        wood fence and splitting a support post for firewood. Then he drew
        water, poured it, and prepared a proper bath for his lord.
Elsewhere the monk Jōken went to speak to Lord Kiyomori at Nishi-Hachijō.
"I understand that the cloistered emperor has moved to the Toba Mansion," he
    said,
"and that he has nobody with him. I find that very painful.

Surely no harm could come of your allowing me to go to him, alone. I would
    gladly do so."
"Very well, I know I can trust you not to overstep yourself."
So Jōken went to the Toba Mansion.
He alighted from his carriage at the gate and entered.

> He found the cloistered emperor
> reading the scriptures in a loud voice,
> eerily imposing in tone.
> Softly, Jōken came up to him
> and saw tears falling from his eyes
> onto the open scripture page.
> The sight was simply too much:
> Jōken pressed his face
> in sorrow into his clerical sleeves
> and in the very presence wept.
> There before the cloistered sovereign
> sat one single figure: the nun.
> "Ah, there you are, Jōken," she said.
> "Our lord took refreshment at Hōjūji,
> yesterday morning, but nothing since,
> either last evening or this morning;
> nor did he sleep a wink last night.
> By this time I fear for his life."
> Jōken swallowed any further tears.
> "All things have their end," he began.
> "For twenty years now, and more,
> the Heike have prospered greatly,
> but their evil ways pass all bounds,
> and destruction looms before them.
> Will the Goddess of the Sun,
> will the most noble Hachiman
> forsake now His Cloistered Eminence?
> If the Seven Shrines of Hie Sannō,
> objects of our sovereign's devotion,
> uphold still their vow to protect
> the teachings of the One Vehicle,
> then to the Lotus Sutra scrolls
> now before him they will fly
> and protect him from further harm.
> Then he will reign in his wisdom,
> and the evildoers will vanish

as foam vanishes from the water."
So he spoke, bringing a touch of comfort.

> Emperor Takakura was already lamenting the exile of the regent and
> the ruin of so many officials when, far beyond that, he learned of the
> cloistered sovereign's confinement in the Toba Mansion. Thereafter he
> refused all nourishment. Pleading illness, he remained permanently in
> his sleeping chamber. Kenreimon-in, his empress, and her gentle-
> women were at their wits' end with worry about what would become
> of him.

With the cloistered emperor confined to the Toba Mansion,
a sacred rite began at the palace. Every night in the Seiryōden,
his private residence, before the Whitewashed Altar,[119]
Emperor Takakura prayed to the divinities of the Ise Shrines,[120]
and every prayer was solely for his father, the cloistered emperor.
Emperor Nijō had no doubt been a wise ruler,
but on the grounds that an emperor has neither father nor mother,
he had repeatedly contradicted the cloistered emperor's stated opinion.
Perhaps that is why he had no successor and why Emperor Rokujō, who followed
   him, [r. 1165–68]
passed away on the fourteenth of the seventh month of Angen 2. [1176]
This makes a very distressing story.

19. *The Seinan Detached Palace*

> "Every principle of conduct
> yields before filial piety.
> By filial piety a wise king
> governs all within his realm."
> So they say, and that is why
> Tang Yao held in high regard
> a mother aged and infirm,
> why Yu Shun revered a father
> utterly stubborn in his ways.
> That His Majesty wished to follow
> this sage king and this wise lord
> is worthy of the highest praise!

A letter reached the Toba Mansion in secret from the palace.

....

119. The altar before which the emperor performed rites addressed to the native Japanese deities.
120. There are two Ise Shrines: the Inner (*naikū*, dedicated to the Sun Goddess) and the Outer (*gegū*, dedicated to the god of increase). The tale's references to "Ise" or the "Ise Shrine" generally assume both, with emphasis on the former.

"The way the world is now," His Majesty had written,
"what good could it do me to stay on here in this august abode?
Better to follow the examples of Uda and Kazan: to leave home,
flee the world, and become an ascetic wandering mountains and
    forests."
The cloistered emperor replied,
      "Please give up any such notion.
      Simply knowing that you are there
      is to me a source of comfort.
      Who else would be left to me,
      were you so to vanish from sight?
      Be patient, rather: Watch and wait
      until this old man's fate is sealed."
      So His Cloistered Eminence wrote.
      Pressing the letter to his eyes,
      the emperor dissolved in tears.
      The sovereign is a ship, his people water.
      Water keeps the ship afloat;
      water can capsize it as well.
      Subjects sustain their sovereign;
      subjects also overthrow him.
      In Hōgen and Heiji, certainly,
      Lord Kiyomori sustained his,
      but now, during Angen and Jishō,
      he set his sovereign at naught.
      The Book of History gives such cases.
      Koremichi, the Ōmiya chancellor;
      the Sanjō Palace minister, Kinnori;
      Mitsuyori, the Hamuro grand counselor;
      the Nakayama counselor, Akitoki—
      all were gone by this time, every one.
      From earlier days Seirai and Shinpan
      were the only gentlemen left alive,
      and they—convinced that as things stood
      no good could ever come of court service
      even, perhaps one day, as counselors—
      had in the prime of their manhood
      turned their backs upon the world.
      Shinpan, who once had overseen
      the Bureau of Civil Affairs,
      now befriended the Ōhara frosts,

while Seirai, in his time a consultant,
mingled only with the mists of Kōya,
and each, they say, worked toward one goal:
enlightenment in the life to come.
There were men, once upon a time,
who hid among the clouds of Mount Shang
or who beside the river Ying
cleansed their hearts under the moon.
Could anyone, then, say of these two
that learning and purity of heart
were not what moved them to give up the world?
Seirai, for one, there on Mount Kōya,
said when he learned of these events,
"Ah, how right I was to renounce it!
Such news as this is bad enough,
but what a blow it would have been
to see it all with my own eyes!
The disorders in Hōgen and Heiji
filled me with horror at the time,
but such things are certain to happen
now that the world enters its last days.
And what disasters, then, may follow?
Oh, rather, to climb into the clouds,
to vanish deep into the mountains!"

It was the twenty-third of the month. Kakukai, the abbot of Mount Hiei, had repeatedly tendered his resignation, and Meiun, the previous abbot, had come to replace him. Lord Kiyomori meanwhile did as he pleased, but his daughter was the empress, after all, and the regent his son-in-law. No doubt he took it for granted that he could get away with anything. "I leave matters of government entirely in His Majesty's hands," he declared, and went down to Fukuhara.

Lord Munemori hastened to the palace to report. "Things would be different if this cession of authority had come from the cloistered emperor," His Majesty said, "but as they are, go, talk to the regent, and do whatever you think best." He refused to hear anything further on the subject.

There in the Seinan Detached Palace,
as it were,[121] the cloistered emperor

....

121. Calling the Toba Mansion "the Seinan Detached Palace" assimilates it to the palace in a well-known Chinese exemplary story.

had spent more than half the winter.
Loud moaned the gales over moor and mountain;
bright shone the moon on the frozen garden,
where no human footsteps ever marred
the broad expanse of fallen snow.
Layered ice choked the garden lake;
the flocks of water birds were gone.
The bells of the great temples boomed,
startling the hearer as at Yiaisi;
the shadowed snows on the Western Hills
called to mind Incense Burner Peak.[122]
The fulling block beat, cold, nightlong,
haunting the cloistered sovereign's pillow;
wheel tracks traced through frosts of dawn
stretched away past the distant gate.
People, horses passing on the road
conveyed to the sovereign within
sad lessons on the labors of men.
Sturdy guards posted at the gate,
vigilantly watching, day and night,
moved him to ask, "What bond from past lives
can have brought them and me together?"
The tiniest detail of his days
injured his heart in some new way,
and memory kept him in its thrall:
happy excursions here or there,
pilgrimages to holy places,
that great day of his jubilee—
he could not stem the welling tears.
So the new year came, the fourth of Jishō. [1180]

....

122. Yiaisi, a temple, and Incense Burner Peak are from a poem by Bo Juyi.

BOOK FOUR

1. The Pilgrimage to Itsukushima

(recitative)

The first day of Jishō 4, indeed the first three days, [1180]
brought the Toba Mansion no callers. Lord Kiyomori forbade them,
and the cloistered emperor, intimidated, encouraged none.
Only the Sakuramachi counselor Shigenori,
son of the late minor counselor and novice Shinzei,
and his younger brother, the Left City commissioner Naganori,
had authorization to make their visit after all.
On the twenty-first of that first month, the heir apparent donned the trousers[123]
and also had his solemn first taste of fish.
All this was felicitous indeed, but at the Toba Mansion
talk of it reached His Cloistered Eminence only from afar.
On the twentieth of the second month, the emperor, in no way indisposed,
was forced nonetheless to abdicate, and the imperial dignity passed to the heir
    apparent.
This happened because Lord Kiyomori had his way in all things.
"The age is ours!" the Heike assured one another in great excitement.
The new emperor received the mirror, the jewel, and the sword.[124]
The senior nobles gathered in their council chamber,
following ancient usage resting on precedent.
The palace dame Ben came forth bearing the sword,
which Captain Yasumichi received at the Seiryōden west front.
Dame Bitchū likewise brought forward the jewel in its case,
which Lieutenant Takafusa accepted.
And then the mirror: Dame Shōnagon, first called on to bear it,
heard that if this night she so much as touched it or the jewel,
she would never in all her life serve the new emperor as a dame of the palace,
and she therefore refused to do so.
She was no longer young, and people remarked with disdain
that she could hardly expect a second spell of imperial favor.
Dame Bitchū, however, in the youth of her sixteenth year,

....

123. *Hakamagi:* a boy's coming-of-age ceremony.
124. The regalia that confirm the sovereignty of the emperor. They are a major issue in Books Ten and Eleven. "Jewel" probably means the kind of curved bead (*magatama*) well known from Japanese antiquity, but whether this item of the regalia is one large one or a string of small ones remains unknown.

came to the rescue and volunteered. It was a fine gesture.
One by one, officials took charge of each imperial treasure
and conveyed it to the new emperor's Gojō residence.
At Emperor Takakura's Kan'in Mansion, the lamps burned low,
the crier of the hours fell silent, and no guards declared themselves on duty.
Those long close to him, desolate, wept with sorrow amid the rejoicing.
The left minister appeared in the senior nobles' council chamber
to announce the abdication, and men of heart shed tears that wet their sleeves.

> (song)
> The mere prospect of years to come
> spent in quiet retirement,
> for an emperor who, on his own,
> cedes the throne to his heir apparent,
> surely stirs melancholy thoughts.
> Then imagine his growing despair
> when in truth he has been deposed!
> No words can convey such feelings.

The new emperor was in his third year.
"Dear me, this abdication came awfully early," people muttered at the time.
The Taira grand counselor Tokitada was the husband of Sotsu-no-suke, His
    Majesty's nurse.
"How," he demanded to know, "could anyone call this abdication premature?

> In the Other Realm, King Cheng of Zhou
> acceded in his third year; Emperor Mu
> of the land of Jin in his second.
> In our own, Emperor Konoe
> did so in his third and Rokujō
> in his second year. In baby clothes
> it was, not in ceremonial dress,
> that each presided over the court,
> borne on the regent's back when enthroned,
> in council cradled in his mother's arms.
> So we learn from records of the past.
> Emperor Xiao Shang of Later Han
> acceded on only his one-hundredth day.
> Such enthronement precedents as these
> appear in both China and Japan."
> Those well versed in established ways
> whispered nonetheless among themselves,
> "It's frightening! Keep your lips sealed!
> So he really thinks those examples valid?"

Thanks to the heir apparent's accession, Lord Kiyomori and his wife
became an emperor's maternal grandfather and grandmother.
Accordingly they received a decree raising their rank to match that of an empress,
income from diverse annual appointments, and service from those on duty at
 the palace.
Housemen in robes bearing painted scenes or embroidered with flowers
frequented their home as they might have a retired emperor's residence.
Even after renouncing the world as a novice monk,
Lord Kiyomori seemed to enjoy unending glory.
Only one decree had in the past granted empress rank to such a figure:
that accorded long ago to the Hoko-in novice Lord Kaneie.
It transpired early in the third month of the year
that the new retired emperor planned a progress to the Itsukushima Shrine
 in Aki.
A recently retired sovereign might certainly make a first pilgrimage
to Yawata, for example, or to Kamo or Kasuga—but a progress all the way to Aki?
People hardly knew what to make of it. Someone remarked,
 "Retired Emperor Shirakawa
 made his progress to Kumano,
 Go-Shirakawa to the Hiyoshi Shrine.
 Plainly the choice is up to him.
 He has a solemn vow in mind.
 And Itsukushima, you know,
 receives intense Heike devotion.
 On the surface he is with them,
 but underneath he means to pray,
 so I gather, that the deity
 soothe Kiyomori's rebel spirit,
 which keeps His Cloistered Eminence
 shut up in the Toba Mansion,
 as it seems, forever and a day."
The monks of Mount Hiei waxed wroth.
"If he's not going to Iwashimizu, or to Kamo or Kasuga either,
he should make his progress to Sannō, on our own Mountain.
What custom, pray tell, sanctions a pilgrimage to Aki?
Very well then, down we go with our shrine palanquins,
to put a stop to this progress of his!"
Such was their decision.

> *(speech)*
>
> The progress was therefore postponed. Lord Kiyomori eventually
> persuaded the monks to calm down. On the eighteenth, before setting

out for Itsukushima, Retired Emperor Takakura called at Kiyomori's Nishi-Hachijō residence to say good-bye. Toward evening on that day, he summoned Lord Munemori. "On my way out of the city tomorrow, I should like to stop at the Toba Mansion and call on His Cloistered Eminence. Would that be possible, do you think? It might be best not to do so without informing Lord Kiyomori."

His words drew tears from Lord Munemori, who replied, "How could he possibly object?"

"Very well then, Munemori," His Eminence answered, "please inform the Toba Mansion tonight." Lord Munemori hurried there with the news. The cloistered emperor had so longed to hear it that he said, "I must be dreaming."

On the nineteenth, well before dawn, Takasue, the Ōmiya grand counselor, went to rouse Takakura for his journey.

So it was that this long-anticipated progress began from Nishi-Hachijō.

With the third month more than half over,
a misty moon yet hung, pale, in the dawn sky.
Geese, homeward bound for northern lands,
passed high aloft among the clouds,
their cries touching him with melancholy.
The night was still dark when he set out
on his journey to the Toba Mansion.
At the gate he stepped down from his carriage,
entered, and found nobody about.
Shadows gathered under the great trees.
"Ah, what a sad, sad place to live!"—
the words sprang unbidden to his mind.
These days were the very last of spring,
and summer had come to the tall groves.
Blossoms on the bough were fading fast,
and time had cracked the warbler's song.
On the sixth of the first month last year,
at his father's Hōjūji residence
when he arrived for his new-year greeting,
music had rung out in brilliant welcome;
all the lords had stood in reverent line,
every corps of guards in serried ranks.
The senior nobles who administered
His Cloistered Eminence's household
came forward when his carriage drew up
and threw open the curtained gate,

while household staff spread his path with mats,
and no detail of protocol was missed.
Now he felt that he must be dreaming.
Shigenori announced his arrival,
and the cloistered emperor, to await him,
moved to the inner room behind the steps.
This year was Takakura's twentieth,
and with dawn moonlight full upon him
he looked very beautiful indeed.
He so resembled his late mother, Kenshunmon-in,
that memories of her overwhelmed the cloistered sovereign, and he wept.
Seats had been prepared nearby for both retired emperors,
and no one heard a word of what they said to each other;
the only other person with them was the nun. They talked for a good
      while,
and the sun was high in the sky when the visitor took his leave.
He went on to the harbor of Kusazu, in Toba, where he boarded his boat.
      Retired Emperor Takakura
      looked his last with a heavy heart
      on the decrepit old residence,
      now his father's desolate home,
      while His Cloistered Eminence
      pictured in mind his son at sea,
      aboard a ship tossed by the waves,
      and felt profound anxiety.
      In truth, now that the pilgrim
      had set aside his ancestral shrine,
      the great Ise sanctuary,
      as well as Yawata and Kamo,
      to journey all the way to Aki,
      how could the divine presence there
      fail to respond to his petition?
      It seemed impossible to doubt
      the fulfillment of all his prayers.

2. *The Return*

That same month, on the twenty-sixth, Takakura reached Itsukushima,
where he lodged with Lord Kiyomori's beloved shrine maiden.
During his two-day stay, he dedicated sacred texts and commissioned *bugaku*
      dances.

The officiant, they say, was Kōken, the great prelate of Miidera,
who mounted the high seat, rang the bell, and in a great voice addressed the
    sacred presence,
extolling His Eminence's magnificently humble devotion
in quitting the ninefold glories of his palace to brave the eightfold tide roads of
    the sea,
at which sovereign and subject alike shed tears of deep emotion.
    His pilgrimage took him first of all
    to the main shrine, then to Marōto[125]
    as well as the many others on his way.
    Five hundred yards or so from the main shrine,
    on the other side of the mountain,
    he reached the Shrine of the Cascade.
    Kōken composed a poem there,
    which he fixed to a pillar of the hall:
        From celestial heights
        streams in supple strands of white,
            the noble cascade
        pouring down before my eyes,
        yielding me unending joy.
The chief priest, Saiki Kagehiro, was promoted to upper fifth rank, junior grade,
while the provincial governor, Fujiwara no Aritsuna, rose to lower fourth, junior,
with authorization to frequent the retired emperor's privy chamber.
Son'ei, the abbot of the temple linked to the shrine, likewise gained a higher title.
The divinity was clearly pleased, and no doubt Lord Kiyomori, too.
On the twenty-ninth, the retired emperor boarded his waiting ship and set out
    for home,
but the wind was too strong. The ship had to row back
and put in once more to the Itsukushima harbor of Ari-no-ura.
His Eminence said, "The deity does not wish us to leave. Present a poem."
Lieutenant Takafusa therefore:
        Nor is our own wish
        to go away: We would stay on
            at Ari-no-ura,
        to receive from the white waves
        the blessings of the divine.
    In the middle of the night, the sea calmed and the wind dropped. The
    ship rowed out again, and that same day the retired emperor reached

<hr>

125. As on Mount Hiei, the Marōto Shrine of Itsukushima enshrines "guest" deities—five of them in this case.

the harbor of Shikina in the province of Bingo. In the Ōhō years, [1161–63] his father, too, had made a progress here, and the governor, Fujiwara no Tamenari, had built him a residence. Lord Kiyomori had had it refurbished to accommodate the imperial pilgrim, but the retired emperor dispensed with its comforts.

"Why, it's the first of the fourth month," his people were saying, "the day of the costume change!" They were roaming about here and there, their thoughts on the capital, when their sovereign lord spied wisteria near the shore, blooming in intense color and twined around a pine.

He summoned the grand counselor Takasue. "Send a man to fetch me some of those flowers," he said.

Takasue called over the clerk Nakahara no Yasusada, who happened to be rowing past in a small boat, and sent him for them. Yasusada picked some and delivered them with the stem still wound round a pine branch. His Eminence expressed pleasure in Yasusada's wit. He was impressed.

"They should have a poem with them," he continued, whereupon Takasue:

> *Eager to embrace*
> *a sovereign lord sure to live*
> *a thousand long years,*
> *these billowing blossoms cling*
> *to the branches of a pine.*

Then many of the company gathered around him.
Amid the friendly banter, His Eminence remarked with a smile,
"That shrine maiden in white seems to have fallen for Lord Kunitsuna."
Kunitsuna was vigorously disputing this
when a messenger girl turned up with a letter for him.
Sure enough! They gleefully nodded to one another.
Kunitsuna accepted the letter and read:

> *White the fading wake,*
> *the robe white, and wringing wet*
> *these sleeves with my tears:*
> *All because of you, my lord,*
> *I have lost the heart to dance.*

"I like that one. You'll have to answer her," His Eminence said,
giving Kunitsuna his inkstone. The grand counselor replied,

> *Just imagine, then,*
> *with visions of you rising*
> *from the ocean waves,*
> *how each oncoming billow*
> *drenches my sleeves with salt drops.*

Yasusada presents the wisteria.

From there the retired emperor
arrived in the province of Bizen,
at the harbor of Kojima.
On the fifth the weather was fine,
the breeze mild, the sea so calm
that the imperial ship set forth
with those of his gentlemen,
cleaving the cloudy, vaporous waves
to reach that day, at the hour of the cock, [ca. 6 P.M.]
the Yamata coast in Harima.
Thereafter he boarded a palanquin
and went on to Fukuhara.

On the sixth, with his whole entourage desperate to hurry on to the city,
he nonetheless lingered to see every sight of Fukuhara.
He even viewed Lord Yorimori's country villa at Arata.
On the seventh, upon his departure from Fukuhara,
the grand counselor Takasue conferred by his order
promotions on two of Lord Kiyomori's family members:
his adopted son Kiyokuni, the governor of Tanba, to senior fifth rank, lower,
and his grandson the lieutenant Sukemori, governor of Echizen, to junior fourth,
    upper.
That day Takakura reached Terai, and on the eighth he entered the capital.
Senior nobles and privy gentlemen came to welcome him at Kusazu in Toba.

When at last he was back again,
he did not call at the Toba Mansion
but rather at Nishi-Hachijō,
and there he saw Lord Kiyomori.

In the fourth month, on the twenty-second day,
the new emperor formally assumed the dignity of his office.
The ceremony should properly have been held in the Great Hall of State,
but that had burned down a year earlier and had not yet been rebuilt.
The decision was to hold it in the hall of the Council of State,
but Lord Kujō Kanezane objected. "That location," he said,
"corresponds to a common nobleman's household office.
Without a Great Hall of State, the correct venue for the accession is the
    Shishinden."
In the Shishinden, therefore, it was done.
"Back in Kōhō 4," people complained, "on the first day of the eleventh month, [967]
Emperor Reizei's accession occurred in the Shishinden
because an indisposition prevented him from repairing to the Great Hall of
    State.

This precedent is dubious at best.
A far better one is that of Emperor Go-Sanjō, in the Enkyū era: [1069-74]
It sanctions accession in the quarters of the Council of State."
Lord Kanezane had spoken, however, and his word was final.

> From the Kōkiden the empress
> had moved to the Ninjuden.
> As she approached the tiered dais,[126]
> she made a lovely sight indeed.
> The gentlemen of the Taira house
> were all in attendance on that day,
> except for the sons of Shigemori,
> deceased just the year before.
> Mourning confined each to his home.

3. The Roster of Genji

The chamberlain Sadanaga recorded on ten sheets of sturdy paper
the flawless and felicitous accomplishment of the accession rite
and presented them to Lady Nii, the wife of Lord Kiyomori. She smiled with
    pleasure.
The world was still restless, however, despite this happy brilliance.
Prince Mochihito, the cloistered emperor's second son
and a maternal grandson of the grand counselor Suenari,
lived then near the Takakura-Sanjō crossing; people called him the Takakura
    Prince.
Back in Eiman 1, on the sixteenth of the twelfth month, [1165]
he had secretly come of age at the Kawara residence of Emperor Konoe's empress.
He was then in his fifteenth year.
So beautifully did he write and such scholarly talent did he display
that by rights he should have assumed the throne,
but the late Kenshunmon-in's jealousy kept him confined at home.

> At spring parties beneath the blossoms,
> he wielded the brush to set down his poems;
> at moonlit autumn gatherings,
> he drew lovely music from his flute.
> Such was the style in which he lived.
> Meanwhile Jishō 4 came round. [1180]
> It was his thirtieth year.

....

126. The *takamikura:* the broad, circular, curtained dais on which the emperor stood during an essential phase of the accession ritual.

The third-rank novice Minamoto no Yorimasa, then living at Konoe-kawara, turned up clandestinely one night at the prince's with a frightening proposal. "Your Highness," he said, "you stand in the forty-eighth generation from the Great Sun Goddess and in the seventy-eighth reign from Emperor Jinmu. You should have been elevated to heir apparent and then reigned in turn, but here you are, in your thirtieth year and still only a prince. Does this not distress you? The way the world is now, everyone feigns meek obedience, but is there really out there a single soul who does not secretly envy the Heike?

This is what you should do. You should raise rebellion and destroy the Heike,
save His Cloistered Eminence from the sorrow of endless confinement in the
    Toba Mansion,
and yourself succeed to the dignity of the sovereign.
You would uphold in doing so the highest filial piety.
Should you decide to proceed, Your Highness, should you issue your august
    command,
there are many Genji who would gladly hasten to your side."
And he continued:
    "First of all, in the **Capital**
        there are the sons of Mitsunobu,
        lately the governor of Dewa;
        Mitsumoto, the Iga governor;
        Mitsunaga, a magistrate;
        Mitsushige, a chamberlain;
        and the gallant Mitsuyoshi.
    In hiding in **Kumano**
        there is Jūrō Yoshimori,
        the last son of the late Tameyoshi.
    In **Settsu** there is one man
        who might figure on the list,
        except that when Narichika
        plotted revolt, this Yukitsuna
        joined with him, all the while
        reporting back to the Heike.
        No, he cannot be trusted,
        but he does have younger brothers:
        first Jirō Tomozane,
        then the gallant Takayori,
        and, last, Tarō Yorimoto.
    Kawachi will offer you
        Yoshimoto, for the present

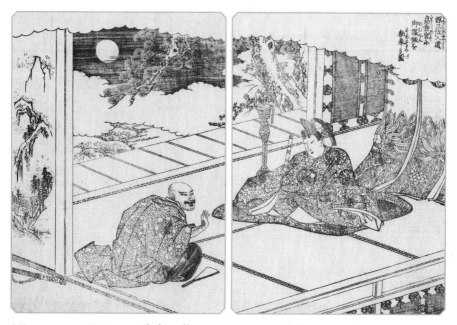

Minamoto no Yorimasa (left) talking to Prince Mochihito.

　　the acting governor of Musashi,
　　and his son Yoshikane.
The **Yamato** roster includes
　　the sons of Uno Chikaharu:
　　Ariharu, Kiyoharu,
　　Nakaharu, and Yoshiharu.
Then there is **Ōmi** province
　　and the men of Yamamoto,
　　Kashiwagi, and Nishigori.
Mino and **Owari** boast
　　Yamada no Shigehiro;
　　Kawabe no Shigenao;
　　Kawabe no Shigemitsu;
　　Izumi no Shigemitsu;
　　Urano no Shigetō;
　　Ajiki no Shigeyori
　　and his eldest, Shigesuke;
　　Kida no Shigenaga;
　　Kaiden no Shigekuni;
　　Yashima no Shigetaka
　　of the heir apparent's guard

and his eldest, Shigeyuki.
In **Kai** you may wish to call
   on the great gallant Yoshikiyo
   and his eldest, Kiyomitsu;
   on Takeda no Nobuyoshi;
   Kagami no Tōmitsu;
   Kagami no Nagakiyo;
   Ichijō no Tadayori;
   Itagaki no Kanenobu;
   Henmi no Ariyoshi;
   Takeda no Nobumitsu;
   Yasuda no Yoshisada.
And likewise in **Shinano**,
   on Ōuchi no Koreyoshi;
   Okada no Chikayoshi;
   Hiraka no Moriyoshi
   and his fourth son, Yoshinobu;
   Kiso no Yoshinaka,
   son of the late Yoshikata,
   once head of the corps of guards
   assigned to the heir apparent.
In **Izu** you will not neglect
   the great exile, Yoritomo,
   who once served in the Right Watch.
Farther still, **Hitachi** offers
   Shida no Yoshinori,
   guardsman to the heir apparent;
   Satake no Masayoshi
   and, among his sons, the first,
   Tadayoshi, then the third,
   Yoshimune, and the fourth,
   Takayoshi, then at last
   his fifth-born, Yoshisue.
Finally, **Mutsu** can boast
   the last son of Yoshitomo,
   lately chief left equerry,
   Kurō Hōgan Yoshitsune.
All these descend in direct line
from Minamoto no Tsunetomo,
famous as Rokusonnō,

and from the novice Mitsunaka.
Once, neither Heike nor Genji
could lay claim to greater success
at chastising an enemy
bent on challenging the court
or at rising to new glory.
Now, though, we of the Genji
languish more abjectly below them
than mud under the clouds above,
than servant under master.
In a province we do the governor's bidding;
on an estate we are at the manager's beck and call.
Harried by office duties and constant errands, we have never a moment's
    peace.
Imagine, then, the low state of our spirits!
Were you to decide to act, Your Highness, and to issue your call to these men,
they would race day and night to join you,
and they would destroy the Heike in no time at all.
Yes, I am old, but I would place myself at your service with my sons."
So he spoke. The prince, who doubted the wisdom of such a venture,
refused for some time to lend it his support.
But there was an outstanding physiognomist, the minor counselor Korenaga,
grandson of the Akomaru grand counselor Munemichi
and son of Suemichi, a former governor of the province of Bingo.
People called him in those days "Counselor Physiognomy."
This Korenaga came to call on Prince Mochihito.
"You have the marks of one destined to be emperor," he said.
"You must not renounce your concern for the realm."
His words, added to Yorimasa's, tipped the balance.
"So be it, then," the prince declared.
"It appears that the Great Sun Goddess calls me to do my duty."
The resolve to proceed now burned within him.

From Kumano he summoned Jūrō Yoshimori and appointed him chamberlain. Yoshimori changed his name to Yukiie and started down to the east as the prince's designated envoy. He left the capital on the twenty-eighth of the fourth month. After Ōmi he went on to Mino and Owari, announcing His Highness's call to the Genji along the way. On the tenth of the fifth month, he reached Hōjō in Izu, where he conveyed the call to the exiled Yoritomo. He continued on to Shida no Ukishima in Hitachi, to bring the message to his elder brother, Shida

no Saburō Yoshinori. Then he trod mountain trails to do the same for
another: his nephew, Kiso no Yoshinaka.
Tanzō, then the superintendent of Kumano and deeply loyal to the Heike,
somehow received a report that Jūrō Yoshimori of Shingū, on Prince Mochihito's
   order,
was rousing the Genji of Mino and Owari and fomenting rebellion.
"The men of Nachi and Shingū," he said, "are certain to side with the Genji.
I myself, though, owe the Heike everything, and I could never turn against them.
No, I shall treat them to an arrow or two and inform the Heike."
In this spirit he marched on the port of Shingū with a thousand armed men.

>   Shingū had its fighting clerics,
>   the Torii and Takabō monks,
>   and, in the way of warriors,
>   Ui, Suzuki, Mizuya, Kamenokō,
>   while Nachi boasted a cleric
>   high in rank and high in valor
>   at the head of two thousand men.
>   Both sides raised their battle cry
>   and exchanged initial arrows.
>   Then came the shouts—"That's how we shoot,
>   we Genji!" and, in the same spirit,
>   "Take *that* from a Heike bow!"—
>   constant cries from successful archers,
>   ceaseless whine of humming arrows.
>   The battle lasted all of three days.
>   Tanzō, the Kumano superintendent,
>   his relatives and housemen struck down
>   in large numbers and himself wounded,
>   fled as fast as he could to Hongū.

4. The Weasels

Once the cloistered emperor had said,
"I imagine they mean to pack me off in exile to some distant island."
But no, this was now his second year in the Toba Mansion.
On the twelfth of the fifth month, weasels ran riot there in his quarters.
Astonished, he personally recorded the divination pattern,
summoned the Ōmi governor Nakakane, and gave him this order:
"Take this pattern to Yasuchika, have him consider it carefully,
and report to me what he has to say."
Nakakane took it straight to Abe no Yasuchika, the head of the Yin-Yang Office,

but the man was out. "He's off in Shirakawa," they told him.
He went there, found him, and conveyed the cloistered sovereign's message.
Yasuchika issued his judgment on the spot.
Nakakane returned to the Toba Mansion and was headed in through the gate
when the guards stopped him. Never mind, he knew his way.
He climbed over the compound wall, crawled under the veranda,
and thrust Yasuchika's judgment up between two boards.
His Cloistered Eminence opened the document and examined it.
"Joy and sorrow within three days," it read.
"The joy is all well and good," he remarked,
"but considering my situation, I wonder what the sorrow will be."
Meanwhile, Lord Munemori had been pleading on the cloistered emperor's behalf,
and Lord Kiyomori had had a change of heart.
On the thirteenth he released Go-Shirakawa from the Toba Mansion
and allowed him to move to the residence of Bifukumon-in,
at the Hachijō-Karasumaru crossing.
Yasuchika was quite right about good news within three days.

    All the while this was happening,
    Kumano superintendent Tanzō
    sent to the capital, by runner,
    word of the prince's rebellion.
    Munemori, in great agitation,
    forwarded it to Lord Kiyomori,
    just then away at Fukuhara.
    The very instant he heard the news,
    Kiyomori raced to the city.
    "This is no time for scruples,"
    he said. "Arrest Prince Mochihito
    and banish him to Hata in Tosa."
    The grand counselor Sanefusa,
    representing the senior nobles,
    oversaw enforcing the sentence;
    the secretary controller Mitsumasa
    undertook, they say, to carry it out.
    He had Gendayū Kanetsuna
    and Mitsunaga of Dewa
    proceed straight to the prince's house.
    Actually, Gendayū Kanetsuna
    was Yorimasa's second son.
    He got this duty nevertheless
    because the Heike did not yet know

that in fact it was Yorimasa
who had moved the prince to rebel.

5. *Nobutsura*

That same fifth month, on the fifteenth night,
Prince Mochihito was contemplating the full moon in a carefree mood,
when a hurried messenger came, so he said, from Lord Yorimasa,
bearing a letter. His Highness's foster brother Munenobu, of the Left Gate
    Watch, took it,
presented himself before His Highness, and opened it. It read:
"Your Highness's rebellion has been discovered;
the police are on their way now to your house, to banish you to Hata in Tosa.
Leave immediately and proceed to Miidera. I shall join you there."
"But how am I to do *that*?" the prince cried in great agitation.
Now, among his housemen there was one Nagatsura, an officer of the Watch.
"There is only one way, Your Highness," Nagatsura said.
"You will have to go dressed as a woman."
"Very well." The prince let down his hair, and, over layered robes,
donned the broad, conical hat of a woman walking abroad.
Munenobu accompanied him, holding a long-handled parasol,
while a page, Tsurumaru, carried a few things in a bag on his head.
They might have been an imperial noble's junior housemen taking a lady
    somewhere.
Fleeing north up Takakura Street, they came to a wide ditch.
The prince leaped it lightly.
"What a way for a lady to hop over a ditch!"
a passerby stopped to exclaim, staring suspiciously.
The prince hurried on as fast as he could.

> Nobutsura remained behind,
> to mind the prince's residence.
> The few gentlewomen were sent off
> wherever they could go to hide.
> Searching for anything unsightly
> that might need tidying, Nobutsura
> discovered the prince's treasure,
> a flute given the name Koeda,
> lying forgotten by his pillow.
> The prince, too, had noticed the loss
> and that instant was sorely tempted
> to risk going back to retrieve it.

"Oh, no!" Nobutsura exclaimed when he found it.
"This flute is His Highness's most treasured possession!"
Within five hundred yards, he had caught up with the prince and restored it
  to him.
His Highness was overjoyed. "If I die," he said,
"I want you to put this flute with me in my coffin.
And now," he continued, "come with me." Nobutsura, however, replied,
"The police are on their way to your house to arrest you,
and it will look very bad if no one at all is there.
Everyone, of every degree, knows I belong to your household.
They will all say that I, too, fled if I am not there tonight.
Any breath of such a suspicion would taint a warrior's name.
I will go back now, take them on, get rid of them, and rejoin you."
He raced off toward His Highness's residence.
            Nobutsura had on that day,
            under a pale green hunting cloak,
            green-laced armor, and the sword
            proper to his post hung at his side.
            He opened the gates on both sides—
            the great one onto the avenue, Sanjō,
            the small onto Takakura—
            and waited for them to arrive.
            Kanetsuna and Nagamitsu,
            leading three hundred mounted men
            that night, at the hour of the rat, [midnight]
            pressed forward toward the mansion.

Gendayū Kanetsuna seemed to have something in mind. He stopped
well short of the gate, while Mitsunaga rode straight in through it,
stopped, and announced in a loud voice, "It has come to the attention
of the authorities, Your Highness, that you are plotting rebellion. By
official order the police are therefore here to detain you. Come out
immediately!"

Nobutsura stood just inside the veranda. "His Highness is not at
home at present," he answered. "He is away on a pilgrimage. What is
going on? What is this all about?"

"Not at home?" came the reply. "Where's he supposed to be, then, if
not here? No more of your nonsense! Men, get in there and look
around!"

Nobutsura retorted, "You understand nothing, do you, you men from the police!
You even barge straight in through a gate on horseback! What a way to behave!
And then you send your underlings to search the premises? How *can* you?

210 • THE TALE OF THE HEIKE

Here I am: Hasebe Nobutsura of the Left Watch.
Get anywhere near me and you'll be sorry!"
    Among those underlings there was one,
    Kanetake by name, a mighty man,
    who fixed his gaze on Nobutsura,
    then leaped onto the veranda.
    Fourteen or fifteen of his fellows,
    at the sight, came right after him.
    Nobutsura cut the sash and cord
    of his hunting cloak, tossed it away,
    drew his sword—ceremonial,
    true enough, but carefully forged
    under his personal supervision—
    and laid fiercely about him.
    With long blades and halberds the foe
    came at him, but, cutting and slashing,
    this sword of an officer of the Watch
    dashed them back down to the ground
    as gales strip leaves from the trees.
The full moon of the fifth month burst brilliant from the clouds,
but the attackers, unlike Nobutsura, were strangers to the house.
He harried one down a long gallery and scored a deep thrust,
cornered another in a tight spot and fetched him a lethal whack.
"What do you mean," a voice demanded to know,
"by resisting men bearing an official command?"
"Command? *What* command?" Nobutsura retorted. His sword bent,
he jumped back to right it and straighten it under his foot,
then in a flash laid low fourteen or fifteen good men.
Three inches snapped off the tip;
his hands went to his waist to slit his belly, but the dagger was gone.
He could only spread his arms wide and lunge for the small gate onto Takakura,
but a fellow with a great halberd came after him.
Nobutsura moved to leap it but missed, and the point pierced his thigh like
    a needle.
Despite his bravery, they now had him surrounded, a horde of them,
and they took him captive, alive.
Then they searched the house, but there was no prince.
Nobutsura was all they got. They took him to Rokuhara,
where Lord Kiyomori awaited him, seated behind his blinds.
Standing on the veranda, Lord Munemori had them sit Nobutsura down on the
    ground.

"'*What* command?' You really said that, then attacked?" Munemori asked.
"Next you apparently wounded and killed rank-and-file members of the police.
Very well: Interrogate him, get the truth out of him,
then drag him out to the riverbank and cut off his head!"
Nobutsura, quite unfazed, burst into laughter.
"People have been prowling around His Highness's residence lately," he replied,
"but we had no idea what might be wrong, and we took no precautions.
Then, just like that, in they come, in full armor. 'Who are you?' I say.
'We bear an official command,' they reply.
Now, bandits, pirates, robbers, and the like often, or so I hear,
claim, 'Your son will be here in a moment,' or 'We bear an official order.'
So I said, 'Command? *What* command?' and lit into them.
Oh, yes, given full armor and a sword of true steel,
I'd not have let one of those men escape unscathed!
Where is His Highness now? I have no idea! And if I did,
interrogation would get you nowhere with a warrior resolved to say nothing."
The many Heike warriors present murmured among themselves.
"What a man!" they said. "Oh, it would be too bad to behead a man like that!"
"Last year, you know," someone put in, "when on duty at the cloistered emperor's,
he went off alone after six robbers that the other guards hadn't been able to stop,
cut down four, and took two prisoner.
That's how he got his officer's post in the Left Watch.
Yes, he's a man to face a thousand, you can certainly say that."
They all told one another how sorry they would be to see him executed,
whereupon Lord Kiyomori, for reasons best known to himself,
banished him to Hino in the province of Hōki.
When the Genji came into their own, Nobutsura went down to the east,
joined Kajiwara Kagetoki, and reported in full how it had all happened.
Deeply impressed, Lord Yoritomo generously appointed him to govern Noto.

6. Kiō

Prince Mochihito headed north up Takakura Street, then east along Konoe,
crossed the Kamo River, and climbed the slopes of Mount Nyoi.
Of old when Tenmu, the Kiyomibara Emperor, was still heir apparent,
he came under attack by bandits and, so the story goes,
fled into the Yoshino mountains disguised as a woman.
The prince on his present journey did the same.

> All night long he made his way
> up mountain paths unknown to him,
> as he had never done before,

and on the sand his bleeding feet
left stains as red as safflower dye.
Dense thickets of summer grass,
dew-drenched, tried his patience sorely.
And so, as dawn touched the sky,
he came at last to Miidera.
"Worthless this life of mine may be,
but I have no wish to give it up.
Therefore, monks, I come before you
to throw myself on your protection."
So he spoke, and the monks rejoiced.
They decked out Hōrin-in to lodge him,
and there served him a simple meal.
Dawn brought the sixteenth day, and word spread like wildfire
that Prince Mochihito had rebelled and was gone. The city was in an uproar.
The talk reached His Cloistered Eminence.
"Ah, yes," he said, "the good news was my release from the Toba Mansion,
but Yasuchika mentioned bad news as well, and this is it."
Now, Minamoto no Yorimasa had long kept his peace
and might have done so still, and yet this year he incited rebellion.
Why? Because Lord Munemori, Kiyomori's second son,
had done what he never should have done.
Yes, it behooves the great in this world to think long and hard
before doing or saying, on impulse, things better left unsaid and undone.
Witness the case of a fine horse, renowned throughout the imperial city,
that belonged to Nakatsuna, Yorimasa's eldest son.
This bay was incomparable: so easy to ride, so swift, so manageable
that there could be none like him. His name was Konoshita.
Word of the horse reached Munemori, who sent Nakatsuna a message:
"I would gladly see for myself this famous steed of yours."
Nakatsuna replied, "The horse to which you refer is indeed mine,
but recently I rode him too hard and have sent him to the country to recover."
"So be it, then." Munemori said no more.
Alas, he brought the matter up before a gathering of Taira housemen.
"Why," said one, "that horse was around just the day before yesterday!"
"Yesterday, too," said another; and a third,
"*And* this morning there was Nakatsuna, putting that horse through his paces!"
"I see. Nakatsuna refuses to part with him. I cannot accept that.
Go and tell Nakatsuna that I want him."
Munemori packed the man off at a gallop, and notes demanding the horse
continued to fly—

five or six, seven or eight in the space of a single day.
Yorimasa heard what was going on and summoned Nakatsuna.
"The horse might be solid gold," he declared,
"and still you could not hold out against such pressure to let him go.
Send him to Rokuhara immediately."
Nakatsuna had no choice. He did so, with this accompanying poem:

> If you are that keen,
> then come here and look at him.
> He is to me, this
> bay all you like, my shadow:
> Nothing can part me from him.[127]

Lord Munemori never replied.
"What a horse!" he cried. "Look at that!
Yes indeed, this is quite a horse,
but not so fine his tightfisted owner.
No, I do not like that man at all.
Brand this horse of his with his name."
So they did. Branded "Nakatsuna,"
the horse went straight to the stables.
"Saddle that confounded Nakatsuna," Munemori would order
when a visitor turned up, asking to view the famous steed.
"Mount the nag! Give him a taste of the whip!"
And so on. Nakatsuna himself heard about this.
"Here I'd give my life for that horse," he raged,
"and it's bad enough having sheer power rob me of him.
Now, because of him, the whole land will be laughing at me!"
The story reached Yorimasa's ears. He said to Nakatsuna,
"Those Heike seem always to be spouting such nonsense,
and they haughtily assume that they can get away with it.
Very well then, a long life would mean nothing to me.
I shall look out for a chance to act."
The word later on, though, was that he did nothing on his own
but recruited Prince Mochihito instead.
In this connection people thought back to the ways of Lord Shigemori.

> Lord Shigemori was at the palace once when he went to call on the
> empress. While he was there, an eight-foot snake coiled itself around
> the left leg of his trousers. He realized that the gentlewomen would
> panic and frighten Her Majesty if he said anything, so he pinned the

....

127. The wordplay on "bay"—"bay horse" and "howl," hence (here) "threaten"—replaces the original's play on *kage* ("bay horse" and "shadow"): "Threaten me all you like, this bay horse is my shadow [insepar-able from me]."

snake's tail with his left hand, caught its head with his right, and slipped the creature into the sleeve of his formal robe. As calm and collected as can be, he then rose to his feet and called for a chamberlain. Nakatsuna, who was still a chamberlain, came forward and identified himself. Shigemori passed him the snake. Nakatsuna took it via the archery pavilion to the small court next to the privy chamber, where he summoned a clerk from the chamberlains' office. "Take this," he said, but the clerk shook his head vigorously and fled. In the end he had to call his retainer Kiō, from the Palace Guards. Kiō took the snake and disposed of it.

The next morning Lord Shigemori saddled a good horse and sent it to
    Nakatsuna.
"Your comportment yesterday greatly impressed me," he said.
"This horse is a pleasure to ride. He will serve you well
when you sally forth by night to visit some lovely lady."
Mindful of whom he was addressing, Nakatsuna replied,
"With humble gratitude I acknowledge receipt of the horse.
But *your* comportment yesterday, my lord, was worthy of *Genjōraku*."[128]
    How, though, when Lord Shigemori
    always showed such marvelous tact,
    could Munemori be so unlike him,
    even to taking a man's cherished horse
    and imperiling the whole realm?
    Oh, he was a terrible man.
        On the sixteenth of the month, by night,
    Minamoto no Yorimasa;
    his eldest son, Nakatsuna;
    his second son, Kanetsuna;
    with the chamberlain Nakaie
    and *his* eldest, Nakamitsu,
    leading three hundred mounted men,
    each set fire to his own house
    and started for Miidera.
Among Yorimasa's housemen was that man from the Palace Guards,
    Watanabe Kiō.
He had ridden too late to join the others, and they had left him behind.
Lord Munemori summoned him. "Well, well," he said,
"you did not after all go with Yorimasa but stayed here instead."
With every mark of respect, Kiō replied,

....
128. A *bugaku* dance in which the solo dancer mimes capturing a snake.

"I had long resolved that should anything happen,
I would race forward and give up my life for my lord.
For reasons best known to himself, however, he kept his plan from me."
"I see. Then are you still in sympathy with this enemy of the court?
Or do you lean also my way? Do thoughts of future wealth and glory
inspire you to wish to serve the Taira house? Tell me the truth."
Kiō wept as he replied,

> "Greatly as I value the bond,
> generations old, with my lord,
> I cannot act in sympathy
> with an enemy of the court."
> So he spoke, and Munemori:
> "Very well, then come and serve *me*.
> No doubt Yorimasa was generous,
> but you will find me no less so."
> Munemori then left the room.
> From that moment on, it was, "Kiō—
> is he present just now for duty?"
> "Yes, my lord!" Or it was, "Kiō,
> I want you here!" "Coming, my lord!"
> He was on call the whole day long.

The sun was low when Lord Munemori came forth.
Kiō addressed him with every mark of respect:
"I gather, my lord, that Lord Yorimasa has gone off to Miidera.
No doubt you will wish to send a force to attack him.
You need not fear much of a fight.
You will find there the monks of Miidera and the men of the Watanabe League.
I know them well. I would gladly be able to choose my opponent,
and a horse I once had would have served me perfectly,
but a close friend of mine made off with him.
Would it be possible for you, my lord, to let me have one?"
Lord Munemori saw no reason not to.
He put a fine saddle on a favored steed of his own, a pale gray named Silver.
Kiō returned home. "The sun can't set soon enough," he said.
"Then I'll gallop this horse to Miidera, lead Lord Yorimasa's charge, and die."

> At long last the sun went down.
> Kiō sent his family off to hide.
> The journey that now lay before him
> filled his heart with grim foreboding.
> Over a hunting cloak that bore
> patterns picked out in three colors,

with bold chrysanthemums on the seams,
he donned red-laced, heirloom armor.
Next he secured with a stout cord
a helmet studded with silver stars,
slung at his waist an imposing sword
and, over his back, a quiver
with twenty-four arrows fletched black and white.
To these he added—perhaps he wished
to uphold a Palace Guard custom—
a pair of hawk-fletched target arrows.
Black-lacquered, rattan-wrapped bow in hand,
he mounted Silver and, with a fresh horse
and a shield-bearer groom beside him,
set fire to his house. Once it was burning,
he galloped away toward Miidera.
At Rokuhara news of the fire
started uproar and pandemonium.
Lord Munemori came rushing out.
"Is Kiō here?" he demanded to know.
"No, my lord," they said, "he is gone."
"Confound it! I was lenient with him,
and now he has gone and done me in!
Get after him, seize him, and kill him!"

Kiō, who drew a mighty bow and whose arrows sank deep, also shot one arrow after another with blazing speed. He was a formidable warrior.

"He'd get twenty-four men with those twenty-four arrows of his," the housemen murmured. "Lie low!" Not one dared face him.

At Miidera, meanwhile, they were talking about Kiō. "We should have brought him with us," the Watanabe men said. "There's no telling what may have happened to him, caught that way at Rokuhara."

Yorimasa knew his man, though. He said, "Oh, no, he would never let himself fall into their hands—not without good reason. He is deeply devoted to me. He will be here at any moment."

He had hardly finished speaking when Kiō arrived. "I knew it!" said Yorimasa. Respectfully, Kiō addressed Nakatsuna:

"I have brought Silver from Rokuhara, in place of your Konoshita.
Please accept him."
Nakatsuna was extremely pleased.
Then and there he cut off tail and mane,
branded the animal, and the next night

sent him back to Rokuhara.
In through the gate went Silver, at midnight.
He headed straight to his stable,
where the horses nipped at one another.
All the stable hands were astonished.
"Silver is back, my lord!" they announced.
Munemori rushed out for a look.
"Once," the brand read, "I was Silver.
Now, a shaven-pate novice,
I am Taira no Munemori."
"That miserable Kiō!" Munemori cried. "I gave him a second chance,
and look what he has done to me! Well, I've learned my lesson.
When you attack Miidera, do whatever you must to take the scoundrel alive.
        I'll cut off his head with a saw!"
Munemori was hopping with rage.
Alas, Silver's mane and tail
never grew back, and the brand stayed.

7. The Appeal to Mount Hiei

At Miidera the monks blew conchs and rang the bell to convene their council.
They adopted unanimously the following position:
"Recent developments invite the conclusion that in our time
the Buddha's Way is in decline and the Way of the Sovereign suppressed.
If we do not now chastise Kiyomori's violence, when will we ever do so?
His Highness's arrival to join us demonstrates beyond doubt
that Hachiman and the great Shinra Deity[129] grant us their protection.
Why, then, should not all powers of heaven and earth descend to aid us,
why should not buddhas and gods lend us their might to quell the foe?
Now, the Mountain to our north is the home of Tendai learning,
and Nara offers ordination after the summer retreat.
If we appeal to each, will they not join forces with us?"
With one voice they therefore appealed to Mount Hiei and Nara.
The letter to Mount Hiei read as follows:

> FROM: *Miidera*
> TO: *Enryakuji Administration*
> SUBJECT: *Assistance to avert destruction of this temple*
> ARGUMENT: *The novice Jōkai flouts at will the Way of the Sovereign and seeks to destroy the Way of the Buddha. To compound the gravity of the*

....

129. The protector deity of Miidera, said actually to be Susano-o.

situation, on the night of the fifteenth past, the second prince born to the cloistered emperor secretly took refuge at this temple. A so-called retired emperor's decree then commanded us to surrender him, but it is not possible for us to comply.

We gather that a government force is therefore to be dispatched against us. Our temple faces annihilation. Could monks anywhere not deplore our plight? Of special significance is the fact that Enryakuji and Miidera, although separate institutions, share the same Tendai teaching. They resemble, as it were, the left and right wings of a bird or the two wheels of a cart. Neither can do without the other. Under these circumstances, should Enryakuji join forces with us to save our temple from annihilation, then all enmity between us will be forgotten and we shall see again the days when both bodies of monks inhabited the same mountain.

This appeal sent in conformity with the will of the council of monks.
Jishō 4, fifth month, eighteenth day
The monks of Miidera

So read the appeal to the monks of Mount Hiei.

8. The Appeal to Nara

The monks of Mount Hiei read this appeal.
"Who do they think they are?" they exclaimed.
"Why, Miidera is a branch temple of ours,
and they talk about the two wings of a bird or the wheels of a cart?
The very idea!" They did not even reply.
Moreover, Lord Kiyomori commanded Meiun, the Enryakuji abbot,
to see to keeping his monks quiet. Meiun hurried up the Mountain and did so.
Therefore Enryakuji notified the partisans of Prince Mochihito
that it had not yet taken a position on the appeal.
Meanwhile Lord Kiyomori sent off to Mount Hiei
twenty thousand bushels of Ōmi rice and three thousand extra-long bolts of silk
    from the north.
These gifts went out to monks scattered over the Mountain's spurs and ravines,
but so suddenly that some got double or more and some got none.
Parties unknown posted this lampoon:

> *Monks of the Mountain,*
> *clad in your silks from the north,*
> *   those robes are too sheer*
> *to conceal what you would hide:*
> *the shame of your secret ways.*

And another, apparently by one who never got any at all:

> *And we, too, alas,*
> *who have never laid our hands*
>   *on one scrap of silk,*
> *end up in the company*
> *of those who can only blush.*

In the meantime the appeal to Nara read as follows:

FROM: Miidera

TO: Kōfukuji Administration

SUBJECT: Assistance to avert the destruction of this temple

ARGUMENT: The supreme virtue of the Buddha's Way is to safeguard the Way of the Sovereign, and that way owes its everlasting vigor to the Way of the Buddha. At present Lord Taira no Kiyomori, known in religion as Jōkai, arbitrarily arrogates to himself authority over the realm, lays waste to His Majesty's government, and within and without provokes bitterness and lamentation.

Therefore this month, on the night of the fifteenth day, the second prince born to the cloistered emperor abruptly arrived at this temple in order to escape unforeseen disaster. Next came a so-called retired emperor's decree, demanding that we surrender him. However, the temple monks refused categorically to do so. For that reason we now expect Kiyomori's forces to attack.

The Buddha's and the Sovereign's Ways both face extinction. Of old, the Tang emperor Wuzong moved to suppress the Buddha's Way by force of arms; whereupon the monks of Qingliang-shan joined battle and stopped him. Thus a legitimate sovereign failed in the attempt. How much more dismally, then, must fail a subject guilty of eightfold treachery! Prominent for Kōfukuji among these crimes must be the exile of a blameless head of the Fujiwara house.[130] If that shame is not to be expunged now, then when? Monks of Kōfukuji, if in our common cause you save the Buddha's Way from destruction, and if for the sake of the wider world you ward off the evildoers, then you will have achieved all we or anyone could ask.

This appeal sent in conformity with the will of the council of monks.

Jishō 4, fifth month, eighteenth day

The monks of Miidera

So read the appeal to the monks of Kōfukuji.

The monks of Kōfukuji examined this letter and sent an immediate reply. It read:

....

130. The regent, Fujiwara no Motofusa.

FROM: *Kōfukuji*

TO: *Miidera Administration*

SUBJECT: *Your communication regarding imminent destruction of Miidera by Taira no Kiyomori*

RESPONSE: *The Tendai and Hossō schools uphold each its own doctrine, yet both issue from the same golden utterances of the Great Teacher. The northern and southern capitals are at one in following the Buddha. It is this temple's duty, as it is that of others, to quell the evil of any Devadatta.*[131] *And, indeed, Kiyomori is the dregs of the Taira house, the dust and sweepings of those who bear arms.*

His grandfather, Masamori, served in the household of a chamberlain of the fifth rank and ran errands for provincial governors. He became a country police inspector in the days when Tamefusa, lord of the Treasury, was governor of Kaga. When Akisue, the director of palace upkeep, was governor of Harima, Masamori oversaw the governor's stables. Nevertheless his father, Tadamori, gained access to the privy chamber.

Young and old, city dwellers and country folk lamented the flaw that had marred Retired Emperor Toba's judgment, while Buddhist and Confucian sages alike mourned that the predictions of disaster made for Japan in the Yamato Prophecy[132] *had proven correct. No doubt Tadamori had taken wing into the empyrean, but the world still despised his all-too-earthly origins. No ambitious manservant aspired to service in his house.*

In the twelfth month of Heiji 1, however, impressed by Kiyomori's valor in battle, Retired Emperor Go-Shirakawa vouchsafed him extraordinary recognition. Thereafter he rose to chief minister, with authorization to keep an armed escort. His sons became ministers or ranking officers in the Palace Guards. Daughters of his are now empresses: one in her own right and another honorary, by decree.[133] *His younger brothers and lesser sons are all senior nobles, his grandsons and nephews provincial governors. Moreover, he lords it over the land, appoints and dismisses functionaries at will, and suborns to his purpose every minion and maid in official employ. Anyone, even imperial, who crosses him in some small matter, he arrests; anyone,*

---

131. A cousin who turned against the Buddha Shakyamuni and attempted to destroy him. In Buddhist discourse the type of any evil influence seeking to harm the Buddha's teaching.

132. A poem by a sixth-century Chinese monk, predicting the future of Japan.

133. One daughter (Kenreimon-in) was the mother of Emperor Antoku, while another was the honorary mother of Emperor Takakura.

even a senior noble, who offends his ear with a word or two, he appre-
hends.

Therefore the sovereign himself receives him, flatters him, and culti-
vates his goodwill in the hope of living longer and being spared humili-
ation, while the scion of an ancient line greets him on his knees. Robbed
of property held by his house for generations, the regent nonetheless
bites his tongue in fear; deprived of their hereditary estates, cowed
princes say not a word. Intoxicated by success, last year in the eleventh
month Kiyomori confiscated the residence of the cloistered emperor
and banished the regent. Brazen treachery of this order has never been
seen in past or present.

It was our duty even then to march against the brigand and hold
him to account for his crimes. In awe of the gods' will, however, and
obedient to decrees said to emanate from His Majesty, we kept our
peace while the months and days went by. Then he sent again armed
men to encircle the second prince born to His Cloistered Eminence,
whereupon Triple Hachiman and the Kasuga Deity secretly bore His
Highness's conveyance to your temple, where they entrusted him to the
Shinra Deity's care.

The Way of the Sovereign is clearly destined not to fail. Consequently
your temple's protection of him, at the risk of its very existence, can only
inspire rejoicing in the hearts of men of goodwill. Sensitive as we are to
your kindness, here in our distant province we have already caught
wind of Kiyomori's plan to have murderous warriors invade you, and
we are therefore prepared. Early on the morning of the eighteenth, we
roused the monks, announced our intentions to the other Nara temples,
issued orders to our branch temples, and assembled our warriors. Then
your messenger arrived in great haste to deliver your appeal.

At that moment the gloom of the past few days lifted. Yes, under
the Tang the united monks of Qingliang-shan repelled a government
army. Shall not we, then, monks of the northern and southern capitals
in Japan, repel the perverse hordes of a traitorous subject? Secure your
position to the right and left of His Highness and await news of our depar-
ture. Mark the above well, and never doubt us. Such is our message
to you.

    Jishō 4, fifth month, twenty-fifth day

    The monks of Kōfukuji

So read the reply to the monks of Miidera.

9. The Interminable Debate

At Miidera the body of monks assembled to reach a decision.
"Mount Hiei has had a change of heart," they reasoned, "and Kōfukuji is not
     here yet.
We cannot afford delay. Let us attack Rokuhara by night.
Say that we do: The older and younger monks then will split into two divisions.
The older ones will descend Mount Nyoi and engage the attackers from the rear.
Four or five hundred foot soldiers will advance into Shirakawa, burning houses
     there,
provoking local and Rokuhara warriors to raise the alarm and rush to the scene.
Then they will fall on Iwasaka and Sakuramoto, delaying the enemy's progress.
Meanwhile our main force of armed monks, under Nobutsuna's command,
will drive toward Rokuhara, set fires upwind, and strike a decisive blow.
That way we can hardly fail to burn Kiyomori out and kill him."
The adept Shinkai, who had prayed in the past on behalf of the Heike,
then joined the council with the several dozen disciples who shared his lodge.
"You may attribute my views to sympathy for the Heike," he began,
"but even so you will grant, I trust, that I would not violate solidarity with you
or do anything to sully our temple's name. Once upon a time,
the Genji and the Heike were rivals in zeal to protect the imperial house,
but since then the fortunes of the Genji have waned,
and for twenty years now the world has belonged to the Heike.
Not a blade of grass in the land fails to bow before them.
Such is the layout of their compound that no limited force could expect to
     take it.
I suggest devising some other plan, recruiting more men, and attacking later."
He went on and on, in order to buy more time.

> Now, there was at Miidera an aged monk known as the adept Keishū.
> With armor under his robe and a great battle sword slung before him,
> with his head cloth-wrapped as a warrior-monk and leaning on the
> plain shaft of a long halberd, he advanced to say his piece.
>   "The proof that we *can* succeed is ready at hand," he declared.
> "When our founder, Emperor Tenmu, was still heir apparent, he re-
> treated far into the Yoshino mountains in deference to Prince Ōtomo,
> then emerged once more and passed through Uda county, in the prov-
> ince of Yamato. Despite having with him a band of only seventeen
> mounted men, he got across Iga and Ise and with forces from Mino
> and Owari destroyed Prince Ōtomo and succeeded at last to the
> throne. As it says in the classics, a man naturally pities the desperate
> bird that seeks refuge in his bosom. What others may wish to do, I

know not, but to my own followers I say, Come, die tonight in an attack on Rokuhara!"

Such was his contribution to the debate, whereupon Genkaku of Enman-in stepped forward. "We have discussed this too long already," he said. "The night is passing. Hurry! Let us be on our way!"

10. The Roster of Fighting Monks

To engage the attackers' rear,
the elders under their commander,
Minamoto no Yorimasa,
set off, among them such mighty men
as adepts Keishū and Nichiin,
the Dazaifu deputy's brother Zenchi,
and a pair of Zenchi's disciples,
Gihō and Zen'ei. A thousand men,
each brandishing a burning torch,
set out for the slopes of Mount Nyoi.
The main force had for its commander
Yorimasa's firstborn son,
Nakatsuna, governor of Izu.
Kanetsuna, his second, was there, too,
and the chamberlain Nakaie
with Nakamitsu, his firstborn.
Among the corps of fighting monks
were Genkaku of Enman-in,
Aradosa of Jōki-in,
Iga-no-kimi, and Onisado,
each one of them so powerful
that with a grip on his weapon
he feared neither devil nor god
and stood fast against a thousand.
From Miidera's Byōdō-in
came Aradayū; Rokurōbō,
the Shima adept; the Tsutsui monks;
the Kyō adept; and Akushōnagon.
From Kita-in the Six Tengu:
Shikibu, Taifu, Noto, Kaga,
Sado, Bingo—a sturdy lot.
Matsui-no-Higo, Shōnan'in-no-Chikugo,
Gaya-no-Chikuzen, Shunchō,

Tajima, and of the sixty men
who shared a lodge with adept Keishū,
two above all: Kōjō from Kaga
and Gyōbu Shunshū. The rank and file
boasted Ichirai, second to none,
and temple servants like Jōmyō Meishū,
Ogura no Songatsu, Son'ei,
Gikei, Rakujū, Gen'yō Steelfist.
Then there were the warriors proper:
Watanabe no Habuku;
Harima no Jirō; Sazuku;
Satsuma no Hyōe; Chōjitsu Tonō;
Kiō, the guardsman from the palace;
Atō no Uma-no-jō;
Tsuzuku no Genda; Kiyoshi;
and Susumu: These led the way
as one thousand five hundred men
strode forth from Miidera.
When Prince Mochihito joined them,
the monks had cut the Ōsaka barrier and Shinomiya roads with deep trenches,
dug a dry moat, and laid down abatis.[134]
Now they had to clear the abatis and bridge the moat,
which took time. All too soon cocks were crowing on the barrier road.
"We will get nowhere near Rokuhara until broad day. What are we to do?"
said Nakatsuna. Genkaku spoke up, as he had before in council:
"Of old, in the days of King Zhao of Qin, the king imprisoned Lord Mengcheng,
but thanks to the queen, Mengcheng escaped with three thousand men.
They came to the Han Ravine barrier, where the gate was not to be opened until
     cockcrow.
Now, one among Mengcheng's three thousand, Tenkatsu by name,
mimicked a cock so well that they called him Cock-a-Doodle.
Mengcheng had him run to a high place and crow,
at which every cock nearby did the same.
Deceived, the barrier warden opened the gate and let them through.
Now, too, I assume that the enemy started those cocks crowing.
Get on with it! Attack!"
     Meanwhile, in this fifth month, the short night
     began ever so slowly to dawn.

....

134. An abatis (pronounced *abatee*) is an obstacle made of felled tree branches or entire trees laid side by side, with the branch tips toward the enemy. The word is still a current military term.

Nakatsuna said, "A night attack, yes—I felt confident of success, but an attack in broad daylight would certainly fail. Call them back!"

So they called the men back from Mount Nyoi, and the main force returned from Matsuzaka. "This is all because adept Shinkai kept the debate going till daybreak!" the younger monks cried. "Let's get over to his place and wreck it!" Which they did. Several dozen of the disciples and others who shared Shinkai's lodge were killed. Shinkai dragged himself to Rokuhara, where he told the story with tears streaming from his old eyes. Alas, tens of thousands of mounted warriors were just then assembling there, and no one paid him much attention.

At dawn on the twenty-third, Prince Mochihito reflected,
"Miidera cannot do it alone, Mount Hiei has turned its back,
and Kōfukuji is still not here. The next few days bode ill."
He therefore abandoned Miidera and started off to Nara.
Now, His Highness owned two flutes made of bamboo from China.
Semiore and Koeda were their names.
Semiore—"Broken Cicada"—had come to him in this way:
Of old, Emperor Toba sent the emperor of Song China a thousand taels of gold

and got in return, so it appeared,
a joint of bamboo right for a flute,
bearing along its length a growth
just like a living cicada.
Merely to open finger holes,
then and there, in such a treasure—
why, that would have been unthinkable!
First, by His Majesty's order
Kakusō, abbot of Miidera,
built himself a special altar
and before it worked a great rite
seven whole days; once that was done,
and not before, came the finger holes.
Then one day the counselor
Sanehira went to the palace
and there played this flute, Semiore.
Absentmindedly he assumed
that it was like any other flute
and set it down below his knees.
The flute apparently felt the slight,
for at that the cicada broke off.
That is how the flute got its name.
Expert that he was on the flute,

Prince Mochihito inherited it.
Now, though, he saw the end coming.
He made a gift of Semiore
to Miroku in the Golden Hall.[135]
Perhaps he did so to be there
when Miroku, in that great dawn,
preaches beneath the dragon-flower tree.
All this makes such a sad story!

> The prince gave the older monks leave to stay behind. The more suit-
> ably able youths and the hardened temple warriors went with him.
> Yorimasa brought all his men. They say the band numbered a thou-
> sand in all. Adept Keishū presented himself before His Highness, lean-
> ing on a staff with its head carved in the shape of a dove. Tears poured
> from his old eyes as he spoke:

"I should by rights follow you to the ends of the earth,
but I have lived eight decades by now and have trouble walking.
My disciple Shunshū is at your disposal.
His father was Sudō Toshimichi, who back in the time of the Heiji wars
fought under Yoshitomo and died in battle on the Rokujō riverbed.
He is a distant relation, and I took it upon myself to bring him up.
I know him as I know myself. He will go with you wherever you go."
Keishū fell silent and sought to stem his tears.

> Deeply touched, Prince Mochihito
> wondered what he had done for this man
> to deserve such steadfast devotion,
> and in his turn he wept freely.

11. The Battle on the Bridge

Between Miidera and Uji, Prince Mochihito fell six times from his horse,
and no wonder, since he had not slept the night before.
His men pried the planks off a three-span stretch of the Uji Bridge
and took him to the Byōdō-in,[136] where he rested.
At Rokuhara the order went out:
"Aha! His Highness is apparently fleeing to Kōfukuji. After him! Kill him!"

---

135. The "Golden Hall" (*kondō*, the central hall of a typical temple complex) of Miidera. Miroku (San-
skrit: Maitreya), the buddha of the future, waits in the Tosotsu (Sanskrit: Trāyastrimsa) Heaven to de-
scend to earth countless aeons from now. He will then preach beneath a "dragon-flower tree" (*ryūgeju*).
136. A temple dedicated in 1052 by the regent Fujiwara no Yorimichi, on the site of his villa beside the
Uji River. Its Phoenix Hall (Hōō-dō), one of Japan's most famous architectural monuments, was built
the following year.

These were the chiefs of the Heike army:
Left Watch Intendant Tomomori;
Shigehira, a secretary captain;
Chief Left Equerry Yukimori;
and Satsuma governor Tadanori.
Under them served these corps commanders:
Kazusa governor Tadakiyo;
his first son, Tadatsuna;
the Hida governor Kageie;
his first son, Kagetaka;
the magistrate Nagatsuna;
Kawachi magistrate Hidekuni;
Musashi no Saburōzaemon Arikuni;
Etchū no Jirō Moritsugi;
Kazusa no Gorō Tadamitsu;
Akushichibyōe Kagekiyo.
These men led a force, in all,
of over twenty-eight thousand horse.
After crossing the Kohata hills,
they pushed on to the Uji Bridge
and saw that the enemy occupied
the Byōdō-in. They shouted thrice,
and those off on the prince's side
answered with their own battle cry.
The advance guard uttered loud warnings:
"Look out! They've stripped the planks from the bridge!"
But those coming up behind them ignored them and raced ahead,
shoving two hundred into the river, to drown and be swept away.
From either end of the bridge, the sides exchanged opening arrows.
For the prince, shafts from Ōya no Shunchō, Gochi-in no Tajima,
Watanabe no Habuku, Sazuku, and Tsuzuku no Genda
sped straight through armor and shields.
Minamoto no Yorimasa wore a long white silk *hitatare*
under leather armor with indigo-dyed, white-fern-patterned lacing.
He must have known that this day was his last, for he had left off his helmet.
His son, Nakatsuna, wore red brocade under black-laced armor.
The better to draw a powerful bow, he, too, wore no helmet.
    Now Tajima slipped his halberd
    from its scabbard and strode alone
    out onto the bridge. At the sight
    the Heike side raised a great shout:

"Get this fellow, men, shoot him down!"
Their finest archers lined up their bows,
fitted arrow to string, and let fly
again and again, but he, unfazed,
ducked the high ones, jumped the low,
and those coming straight at him
he knocked down with his halberd and broke.
Friend and foe alike watched in awe.
So it was that forever after
they called him "Tajima Snapshaft."
There was among the practitioner-monks one Tsutsui no Jōmyō Meishū,
wearing darkest indigo under black-laced leather armor,
a helmet complete with five-plated neckpiece, and a black-lacquered sword.
He bore on his back twenty-four arrows fletched with black feathers,
carried a bow black-lacquered over closely wrapped rattan,
and grasped a mighty halberd with the plain shaft that he favored.
So equipped, he marched onto the bridge and called out in a great voice,

"You will have long heard tell of me.
Here I am now, before your eyes!
At Miidera everyone knows me: me, the practitioner-monk Tsutsui no
Jōmyō Meishū, a man stalwart against a thousand!
Any of you with the stomach for it, come, come and fight me! See how you do!"
Those arrows of his in rapid succession he set to the string and let fly.

Twelve men within bowshot died;
eleven were wounded. In his quiver
only one last arrow remained.
With a clatter he dropped the bow,
untied the quiver, let it fall,
kicked off his fur boots, and, barefoot,
darted across the bridge on a beam.
Nobody else dared to follow
down this, to him, broad avenue.
Six men came at him from the far end.
Five he mowed down with his halberd,
but the fierce clash with the sixth
broke the shaft; he tossed it away,
drew his sword, and went on fighting:
the "spider strike," the "twisted rope,"
the "four-arm cross," the "dragonfly,"
the "waterwheel"—that sword of his
slashed through all the eight directions

until eight men lay dead before him.
On the helmet of the ninth,
down it came then with such force
that the blade broke at the hilt,
flew off, splashed into the river.
A dagger now his only weapon,
in battle frenzy he faced death.
Came up behind him then Ichirai, a monk-servant of the adept Keishū,
a wizard at swift swordplay, to join the fray,
but the beam was too narrow, and he could not pass.
Leaning his hand on Jōmyō's helmet, with "Pardon me!" Ichirai leaped over him
and lit into the foe. In that battle he died.
Meanwhile Jōmyō crawled back again. On the grass at the Byōdō-in gate,
he took off his armor and counted sixty-three arrow hits.
Five had gone through but done little damage. He burned moxa over the
    wounds,
swathed his head in a length of cloth, donned the white raiment of a pilgrim,
cut down his bow to make a staff, and with simple clogs on his feet
started for Nara, calling the Name.

> Jōmyō's exploit inspired the Miidera men and the Watanabe League to
> pour eagerly across along the bare beams. Some returned with tro-
> phies; others, wounded, slit their bellies and jumped into the river. The
> battle on the bridge raged like fire.

The spectacle moved the corps commander Tadakiyo to appeal to his chiefs.
"Just look at that!" he said. "Look at the fierce fight on the bridge!
We really should cross, but what with the fifth-month rains, the river is rising.
Any attempt to ford it and we will lose many men and horses.
We might instead go around by Yodo or Imoarai, or by the Kawachi road."
At these words a man from the province of Shimotsuke,
Ashikaga no Matatarō Tadatsuna, stepped forward to reply,

> "Yodo, Imoarai, you say?
> The Kawachi road? Are we to go
> hunting first for reinforcements
> off in India or China?
> No, it is up to us to fight *now*!

> There is the enemy, right there in front of us. If we do not strike now
> and he gets into Nara, the Yoshino and Totsugawa men[137] will rush to
> join him. Then we will be in real trouble.

....

137. Mountain ascetics (*yamabushi*) from the Yoshino mountains south of Nara and famously fierce
fighters.

The Heike cross the Uji River.

A big river, the Tone, runs between Musashi and Kōzuke. The Chichibu clan and the Ashikaga were feuding and forever at war when the main Ashikaga force once moved to attack across the Nagai ford, while the rear guard was to cross at Koga and Sugi. The Nitta Novice, a Kōzuke man, had thrown in his lot with the Ashikaga and positioned boats at the Sugi crossing, but the Chichibu had destroyed them all. 'We warriors will never live it down if we don't get across right here, right now!' That is how everyone felt. 'If we all drown, so be it! Here we go!' And we did get across, by making horse rafts.[138] That is the way we are, we fighting men of the east. With the enemy in sight on the far side of a river, no deeps or rapids can stop us.

And the river that we see here—
is it really deeper or faster
than the Tone River I spoke of?
I doubt that very much indeed.
Follow me, then, gentlemen!"
He rode straight into the water,
and after him Ōgo, Ōmura,
Fukazu and Yamagami,
Naha no Tarō,
Sanuki no Hirotsuna,
Onodera no Zenji Tarō,
Heyako no Shirō, and, besides,
a host of their trusted men:
Ubukata no Jirō, Kiriu no Rokurō,
Tanaka no Sōda, and so on—
in all, three hundred riders.
Ashikaga shouted in a great voice, "Keep the stronger horses upstream,
the weaker ones below them! As long as their hooves touch bottom, keep a slack
   rein.
Tighten the reins to make them swim once they lose footing.
Give anyone in danger of being swept away a bow tip to hang on to.
Link arms and cross shoulder to shoulder.
Get a firm seat in your saddle and press your feet onto the stirrups.
If your horse's head goes under, pull it back up, but not too far.
If water threatens to overwhelm you, slip back onto the rump.
Relieve your horse of your weight as much as you can—let the water bear it.
Do not shoot arrows from the river. Ignore any from the enemy.
Keep your neck plate toward them. Never bend too far forward,

....

138. Tight formations of horses and riders all linked together.

lest you expose the crown of your helmet and take an arrow there.
Head directly across the current, at a right angle.
Do not let it carry you off, but also do not fight it.
Now, get on over there! Just go!" So instructed,
the three hundred crossed swiftly to the far bank and lost not one man.

12. *The Death of the Prince*

Over a figured ocher robe, Ashikaga wore armor laced with red leather.
Deer antlers sprang from his helmet; gilt fittings gleamed on the sword at his side.
His arrows were fletched black and white, and his bow was close-wound with
    rattan.
He rode a dappled roan with a saddle gilt-edged at the pommel
and inlaid with a picture of a horned owl perched in an oak tree.
Rising in his stirrups, he announced his presence in a great voice:
    "You in the distance, hear my voice!
    Closer, behold me with your eyes!
    Matatarō Tadatsuna is my name.
    I am the son of Ashikaga
    Tarō Toshitsuna, and I look
    back over ten generations
    to Tawara no Tōda Hidesato,
    who slew the rebel Masakado
    and was granted a rich reward.
    This year is my seventeenth.

        For such as me, without office or rank, to challenge a prince, to draw
        the bow and let arrows fly, is to invite the wrath of heaven; yet might
        of arms and divine favor all lie with the Heike. Let any ally of Yorimasa
        who wishes to test me come forward. I will oblige!" With this he
        charged through the Byōdō-in gate, and a melee ensued.

        Taira no Tomomori, the chief commander, was watching. "Cross,
        cross over *now*!" he ordered, and twenty-eight thousand men plunged
        in. Dammed by so many horses and men, the waters of the swift Uji
        River rose on the upstream side.
What water did break through swept off all in its path.
Underlings hugging the downstream edge of the mob of horses
got across, many of them, dry from the knees up,
but somehow the government's mounted troops from Iga and Ise provinces
lost control of their formation, and it broke up.
Six hundred of them washed down the river, drowned.
        Green, rose madder, red-laced armor

tumbled in the roiling current,
just as from Mount Kaminami
autumn winds blow flying leaves
down into the Tatsuta River,
where, as fall draws to a close,
they come to rest against some dam.
Three of these—three warriors
in armor with madder lacing—
rocked gently against the weir.
Nakatsuna spied them:

> *Ise warriors,*
> *madder-laced their armor, caught*
> *just like young sweetfish,*
> *press against the barrier*
> *of the famous Uji weir!*

From Ise province they were indeed.
Kuroda no Gohei Shirō,
Hino no Jūrō, Otobe
no Yashichi—these were their names.
Hino, rich in experience,
worked his bow tip between the rocks,
pulled himself up, righted the others,
and so, as they tell it, saved them all.
The whole of the main army got across and pressed the assault
in wave after wave through the gate of the Byōdō-in.
Amid the confusion Yorimasa dispatched Prince Mochihito toward Nara,
while he and his men stood fast, to stay the attackers with their arrows.
Aged over seventy in this battle, he took an arrow to the left knee: a grave
   wound.
Hoping to end his life in peace,
he was retreating toward the temple gate when the enemy came at him.
Kanetsuna, his second son, in armor laced with Chinese damask over blue
   brocade,
astride a pale roan, fell back fighting, time and again, to allow his father to flee.

> An arrow from Kazusa no Tarō penetrated Kanetsuna's helmet. He
> reeled, and meanwhile Jirōmaru, a powerful youth who served the
> governor of Kazusa, came up beside him and dragged him crashing
> down from his mount. Head wound or not, the famously powerful
> Kanetsuna seized the fellow, pinned his neck, and cut off his head. He
> was about to rise again when fourteen or fifteen Heike riders fell on
> him and killed him. Nakatsuna, with all his wounds, took his own life

in the Byōdō-in fishing pavilion.[139] Shimokōbe no Tōzaburō Kiyochika
made off with Nakatsuna's head and threw it under the veranda.
The Rokujō chamberlain Nakaie and his son, the chamberlain Nakamitsu,
fought fiercely and took trophies, but they ended up dying in battle.

> The Nakaie in question
> was the firstborn of Yoshikata,
> who commanded the corps of guards
> assigned to the heir apparent.
> When he was orphaned, Yorimasa
> adopted and so favored him
> that he swore, if need be, to die
> at his patron's side; and, alas,
> they did meet death together.
> Yorimasa called to attend him
> Watanabe no Chōjitsu Tonō.
> "Cut my head off," he ordered.

That was too much for Tonō, who wept freely.
"I could never do that, my lord," he replied. "Take your own life first,
then I will oblige." "I understand," Yorimasa replied.
He faced the west, called the Name ten times, and spoke his last, moving words:

> *This forgotten tree*
> *never through the fleeting years*
> *burst into flower,*
> *and now that the end has come,*
> *no thought but turns to sorrow.*

> Having uttered these final words,
> he pressed his sword point into his belly,
> collapsed forward, and died transfixed.
> This was no time, one might have thought,
> for anyone to make a poem,
> but ever since his youngest days
> Yorimasa had loved that art,
> and he kept faith with it to the last.
> Tonō, weeping, took his lord's head,
> secured it to a heavy stone,
> stole out beyond the enemy,
> and dropped it deep into the Uji River.

The Heike warriors hoped by hook or by crook to take Kiō alive,

....

139. A "fishing pavilion" (*tsuridono*) stood over the garden lake of a Heian mansion. This one presumably
remained from the villa that preceded the Byōdō-in.

but he was ready. He fought fiercely, sustained a grave wound, cut his belly, and
  died.
The monk Genkaku no doubt assumed that the prince had fled far enough.
He charged into the enemy, great sword in one hand, halberd in the other,
then leaped into the Uji River. Still fully armed, he sank to the bottom,
got across to the other side, scrambled up onto a height,
and in a great voice called out,

> "Come now, young Heike gentlemen,
> let's see *you* get yourselves over here!"
> And off he went, back to Miidera.
> Hida governor Kageie,
> seasoned warrior that he was,
> realized that Prince Mochihito
> in the turmoil had slipped away,
> no doubt for Nara. He dropped the fight
> and with his five hundred riders,
> whip and stirrup, pursued the prince.[140]
> Sure enough, His Highness had fled,
> accompanied by just thirty men.
> Kageie caught up with them
> before the Kōmyōzen torii
> and there showered them with arrows.
> One of these—whose, no one knew—
> pierced the prince's left side, and he fell.
> An instant later his head was off.

> > The men with him saw it all. Onisado, Aradosa, Aradayū, Iga-no-Kimi,
> > Gyōbu Shunshū, and the Six Tengu knew they now had nothing to live
> > for. With whoops and yells, they fought and were killed. Meanwhile,
> > with Heike men after him and his mount failing, Munenobu, His
> > Highness's foster brother, leaped into Niino Pond, ducked under the
> > pondweed, and, shaking, lay still. The enemy rode right past him. A
> > little later their force of several hundred returned, chattering excitedly.
> > Some bore, on a house shutter, a headless corpse dressed in white.
> > Munenobu peered at it, wondering who it could be. It was the prince.

"If I die," His Highness had said, "put this flute in my coffin with me"—
and there it was, his flute Koeda, stuck in his sash.
Munenobu longed to rush forward and embrace the body but dared not.
Once they were gone, he emerged from the pond, wrung out his clothes,
and, weeping, went up to the capital.

....

140. A rider beat his sturdy stirrups, rather than spurs, against his horse's flanks to urge it to greater speed.

Munenobu, from under the pondweed, watches the Heike men pass in triumph.

No one there had a good word for him.
>   While all this was going on,
>   the body of Kōfukuji monks,
>   seven thousand in full armor,
>   marched to meet Prince Mochihito.
>   The first of them had reached Kizu
>   when the last were still milling about
>   at the Kōfukuji south gate.
>   Then came the news that His Highness
>   had died in battle at Kōmyōzen,
>   before the torii. Helpless,
>   all they could do was dry their tears
>   and go no farther. One more league
>   and His Highness would have escaped
>   the cruelty of his bloody end.

13. *The Prince's Son Leaves the World*

Bearing aloft on the points of swords and halberds
five hundred heads and more taken from the prince's and Yorimasa's men,
as well as from the fighting monks of Miidera,

the Heike army returned as night came on to Rokuhara.
They raised a clamor too dreadful for words to describe.
Yorimasa's head itself, though, thanks to Chōjitsu Tonō,
had sunk to the depths of the Uji River. No one ever found it.
Those of his sons turned up here and there.
As for Prince Mochihito's, nobody knew what he looked like
because no one had been to see him for so many years.
Some years back he *had* called in Sadanari, from the Office of Medicine, to
    treat him,
so Sadanari might know. They summoned him, but he pleaded illness not to come.
Then there was a gentlewoman whom the prince had favored.
They found her and required her presence at Rokuhara.
His Highness had loved her greatly and even had a son by her.
She could hardly fail to know him. Sure enough, after a single glance,
    she pressed her sleeves to her face
    and burst into a flood of tears.
    Yes, she had recognized the prince.
Prince Mochihito had several children, by different mothers.
One was Sanmi-no-tsubone, as she was known,
a daughter of the Iyo governor Morinori and a gentlewoman to the Hachijō
    Princess.[141]
She had given him a boy, now in his seventh year, and girl in her fifth.
Lord Kiyomori sent the princess his younger brother Yorimori, with this message:
"It has come to my attention that Prince Mochihito has children.
The girl is not a concern, but you will oblige me by producing the boy at once."
The Hachijō Princess replied,
    "Early this morning, when word came
    that your order was on its way,
    his nurse foolishly fled with him,
    and where he is we do not know.
    He certainly is not here with us."
        Lord Yorimori could only convey this reply to his brother. "Not there?"
        Lord Kiyomori exclaimed. "Where else could he possibly be? Very well
        then, have warriors go and search the place."
Now, one Lady Saishō, to Her Highness a foster sister and gentlewoman,
was also Yorimori's wife. He kept this lady constant company there,
and Her Highness thought very well of him, until he arrived with this order
to surrender the prince's son. She treated him after that as though he did not
    exist.

....

141. A daughter of Emperor Toba.

The little boy addressed her in these words:
     "At so desperate a time,
     there can be no hope of escape.
     You *must* give me up right away."
     So he spoke, and she, shedding tears:
     "No boy in his seventh or eighth year
     is of an age to understand,
     and yet, faced with this disaster—
     one your mere existence has caused—
     you feel yourself responsible
     and so speak to me in these words.
     Oh, it is simply too pitiful!
     Here I have brought you up for years,
     only to have it end this way,
     with you under terrible threat!"
     She could not stop crying.

> Lord Yorimori repeated the order to surrender the prince's son, and in
> the end she could only comply. Sanmi-no-tsubone must have been
> heartbroken to know that she would never see him again. Weeping,
> she dressed him, smoothed his hair, and led him forth. It all seemed a
> dream.

The princess and her women, even to the little girls in her service,
wept until they wrung the tears from their sleeves.
Lord Yorimori took charge of the boy, boarded a carriage with him,
and delivered him to Rokuhara. Upon seeing him there,
Lord Munemori went to his father and said,
"Why I cannot exactly say, but the sight of this young prince fills me with pity
     for him.
Please make an exception, allow him to live. I will look after him."
"Very well," said Lord Kiyomori, "but see that he enters religion immediately."
Munemori reported his decision to the Hachijō Princess.
"I could not possibly object. Do so immediately," she replied.
Therefore they made a little monk of him and, once that was done,
gave him as a disciple to the abbot of Ninnaji.
In time he rose to head Tōji: Prince-Abbot Dōson was his title then.

14. *Tōjō*

Prince Mochihito had one more son, in Nara.
His guardian, Shigehide, the governor of Sanuki,
made a monk of him and took him down to the provinces of the north.

Kiso no Yoshinaka brought him along on his march to the capital,
thinking perhaps to put him on the throne, and there had him come of age.
Some knew him as the Kiso Prince, others as the Defrocked Prince,
still others as the Noyori Prince, because later on he lived in Saga, at Noyori.

Of old, a physiognomist
whom people knew as Tōjō foretold
that Fujiwara no Yorimichi
and Norimichi would both serve
as regent to three emperors
and live on into their eighties.
He was right. He also saw
in Korechika all the marks
of a man destined for exile.
In that, too, he was correct.
Prince Shōtoku was heard to say
that Emperor Sushun displayed, [r. 587–92]
to his eye, the traits of one
bound to suffer violent death.
And so it was: Sushun was killed
by Soga no Umako.
Indeed, this highly gifted man,
although no physiognomist,
could still show brilliant insight.
How sadly wrong he got it,
that minor counselor Korenaga!
Not all that many reigns ago,
two princes, Genmei and Guhei,
first one and then the other
lord of the Central Bureau
and both a sage sovereign's sons,
still failed to ascend the throne.
Did *they*, though, ever rebel?

And then there was Prince Sukehito, the third son of Emperor
Go-Sanjō. [r. 1068–72] He, too, excelled in talent and learning. Emperor
Shirakawa was still heir apparent when Emperor Go-Sanjō left a tes-
tament ordaining that Prince Sukehito should succeed him, but, for
reasons of his own, Emperor Shirakawa ignored it. He only awarded
Prince Sukehito's son the Minamoto surname and raised him in one
leap from having no rank to holding the third, with a captain's post
in the Palace Guards. They say that apart from the grand counselor

Sadamu, a son of Emperor Saga, no first-generation Genji had ever be-
fore risen from having no rank at all to the third.
This son of Prince Sukehito was Arihito, the Hanazono left minister.
The distinguished monks commissioned to subdue with their rites
Prince Mochihito's rebellion were all granted rewards.
Lord Munemori's son Kiyomune, an adviser, received the third rank,
and as the Third Rank Adviser he was known thereafter.
He was then only in his twelfth year,
at which age his father had been a mere junior officer of the Watch.
So sudden a leap to senior noble was unheard of, except for a regent's son.

> The occasion for this honor
> appeared thus in the formal record:
> "In recognition of the rout
> of Minamoto no Mochihito
> and a monk known as Yorimasa,
> together with all his sons."
> Minamoto no Mochihito—
> this referred to the prince himself.
> It was bad enough to have killed
> the son of a cloistered emperor,
> but to give him a commoner name—
> ah, that was a singularly low blow!

15. *The Nightbird*

Now, Minamoto no Yorimasa descended in the fifth generation from Yorimitsu,
the governor of Settsu. His grandfather was Yoritsuna, governor of Mikawa,
and his father Nakamasa, the head of the Armory.
During the Hōgen Conflict, he galloped before the imperial troops into battle,
but no great reward came his way.
During the Heiji Conflict, he abandoned all his relations to take that side again,
for only the slenderest recompense.
For years he served among the guards responsible for securing the palace
but was never granted access to the privy chamber.
Only after old age came upon him did a poem of his win him this privilege at last:

> *Utterly unknown,*
> *the watchman assigned to guard*
> *our sovereign's high hall*
> *catches glimpses of the moon*
> *only through obscuring trees.*

This poem gained Yorimasa
entry to the privy chamber
and for a good while the fourth rank,
but he still longed to reach the third.

> *Lacking any way*
> *to climb higher up the tree,*
> *here I stay, below,*
> *passing my days in this world*
> *gathering mere fallen fruit.*

So he got his third rank after all. Immediately after that he entered religion as a novice. This was his seventy-fifth year.

The greatest of all his exploits came in the Ninpei years, [1151-54] during the reign of Emperor Konoe. Night after night His Majesty was assailed by crushing fear. By his order, great monks and mighty healers worked the most powerful and most secret rites, but to no effect. His suffering came on him at the hour of the ox. [ca. 2 A.M.] From the direction of the Tōsanjō grove, a black cloud would rise, approach, and settle over His Majesty's dwelling. Then his agony always set in.

The senior nobles therefore met in council.
Yes, back in the Kanji years, when Emperor Horikawa reigned, [1087-95]
His Majesty night after night had suffered in just this way.
Commander of imperial forces Lord Yoshiie
then stationed himself on the veranda of the imperial residence.
When the time came, he twanged his bowstring three times
and in a great voice declared his name,
"Former governor of Mutsu,
Minamoto no Yoshiie!"
The hair rose on all who heard him,
and His Majesty's suffering ceased.

So it was that the council decided, following precedent, to have a warrior mount guard, and among those of the Genji and the Heike, the choice, so the story goes, fell on Yorimasa. He was still head of the Armory at the time.

"Warriors have always served the court to put down rebellion," he observed, "or to destroy those who flout the imperial will. Never have I heard of an order to suppress a specter that no eye can see." Still, the emperor had spoken, and he therefore repaired to the palace.

He took with him only one man—
a retainer, deeply trusted,
from the province of Tōtōmi:
I no Hayata, who carried,

by his lord's command, arrows
fletched from under the bird's wing.
Yorimasa mounted guard
on the emperor's veranda
in a hunting cloak of a single color,
holding two well-sharpened arrows
fletched with pheasant tail feathers
and a black, rattan-wrapped bow.
He grasped both arrows at once.
Lord Masayori, then left controller,
had loudly recommended him—
"If you wish to quell a specter,
Yorimasa is your man!"—
and his words settled the choice;
so if by chance that first arrow
missed, he would shoot the second
straight through the wretched fellow's neck.
At the hour foreseen for His Majesty's torment,
a black cloud moved, as those who knew said it would,
from toward the grove at Tōsanjō, then settled over where the emperor lay.
Yorimasa, glancing up sharply, saw in it a strange shape.
He knew he was finished if he missed.
Nonetheless he took an arrow,
fitted it carefully to the string,
called in the secret depths of his heart,
"Hail, Great Bodhisattva Hachiman!,"
drew to the full, and let fly.
He had a hit; his arm felt it.
"Got him!" He gave the archer's yell.
I no Hayata swiftly approached,
found where the thing had fallen,
and ran it through nine times with his sword.
Everyone there brought up light
for a good look at whatever it was:
a monkey's head, a badger's body,
a snake's tail, the limbs of a tiger,
and a cry like that of a thrush.
"Frightening" is hardly the word.
Deeply grateful, the emperor bestowed on Yorimasa a sword named Lion King.
The left minister from Uji received it from His Majesty's hands
and had come halfway down the steps to make the presentation

when—for this day was the tenth of the fourth month—
a cuckoo high in the sky called two or three times as it passed.
The minister exclaimed:

> How well, O cuckoo,
>   you lift your name to the skies
>   of the cloud dwelling!

At these words Yorimasa
dropped to his right knee,
spread his left sleeve wide,
glanced sidelong at the moon, and said,

> Thanks to a fine parting shot
>   from the crescent moon's drawn bow!

With this he accepted the sword.

> "Not only is he incomparable at arms, but as a poet, too, he is out-
> standing!" So sovereign and minister alike gave voice to their admira-
> tion. As for the creature, it was stuffed into a hollow log and sent down
> the river to the sea.

Then in the Ōhō years during Emperor Nijō's reign, [1161–63]
a werethrush calling in the palace compound
often troubled the imperial mood.
As precedent suggested, His Majesty called on Yorimasa.

The fifth month was nearly over,
and nighttime was coming on.
The thrush called a single time;
no second cry ever came.
In the dark he could not see
the target or make out its shape.
Where to shoot, he could not tell.
So to the string he fitted first
an outsize humming arrow,
which he shot into the air
above the emperor's palace
where, that once, the thrush had called.
Startled by the whizzing roar,
the thrush gave little high-pitched cries.
Yorimasa's second arrow,
still a humming one but smaller,
whistled upward, hit its mark.
Thrush and arrow fell to earth
there at Yorimasa's feet.

The palace rang with cries of amazement, and the emperor was deeply moved.

He commanded that Yorimasa should be awarded a robe.
The one who presented it this time was Kin'yoshi, the minister of the right.
As he laid it across the warrior's shoulders, he said in admiration,
　　"Of old, Yang You shot a goose through cloud;
　　Yorimasa has now shot a thrush through rain."
　　　　　Black the fifth-month night
　　　　　when, before our very eyes,
　　　　　　you made your name blaze!
So he spoke, and Yorimasa:
　　　　　And I who thought twilight past,
　　　　　and the night too dark to shine!
　　The robe now across his shoulders,
　　he withdrew. A little later
　　Izu province became his,
　　and his first son, Nakatsuna,
　　he named the new governor.
　　Risen now to the third rank,
　　he acquired great estates:
　　Goka-no-shō in Tanba,
　　Tōmiyagawa in Wakasa.
　　By rights he should have lived,
　　but no: Instead he raised
　　futile revolt and brought perdition
　　on his prince, himself, his sons.
　　His was a very bitter fate.

16. *The Burning of Miidera*

In the past, the monks of Mount Hiei had always been quick to outrageous
　　protest,
but this time they lay low and said not a word.
Kōfukuji and Miidera had sheltered the prince or come forward to welcome him,
and this made them enemies of the court. Both had invited attack.
On the twenty-seventh of that month, a corps of over ten thousand horse
commanded by Lord Kiyomori's fourth son, Shigehira,
and, under him, by Tadanori, governor of Satsuma,
set out toward Miidera.
　　At Miidera they dug a moat,
　　put up a defensive wall of shields,
　　assembled an abatis, and waited.
　　At the hour of the hare, the first arrows flew [ca. 6 A.M.]

to start the battle. It lasted all day.
On the defenders' side, three hundred
and more of the temple monks lay dead.
Then came the night clash, when, in the dark,
government forces burst into the grounds
and loosed fire. All these buildings burned:
Hongaku-in, Jōki-in, Shinnyo-in,
Keon-in, Fugen-dō, Daihō-in,
Shōryū-in, and the abbot's lodge
with its sacred statue of Abbot Kyōdai.
The temple's Miroku, among others,
went up in flames, and the Great Lecture Hall,
an equal eight bays in length and width;
the bell tower; the sutra repository;
the hall for holy initiations;
the shrine to the guardians of the teaching;
the sanctuary of Imagumano:
in all, six hundred and thirty-seven
halls, chapels, pagodas, mausoleums;
one thousand eight hundred fifty-three
laymen's houses in nearby Ōtsu;
the Tripitaka brought to Japan[142]
from distant China by Chishō Daishi.
Over two thousand buddha images
went up in smoke. One can only mourn.
Wondrous music would fill no more
the celestial realm of the devas,
and the three grievous afflictions
would torment still more the Dragon Gods.
Now, Miidera began as a private temple
whose owner hoped to rule Ōmi province.
When he gave it to Emperor Tenmu, it gained [r. 673–86]
imperial recognition and sponsorship.
Its central buddha was His Majesty's own:
Miroku. Abbot Kyōdai, whom all men called
a living Miroku, for a hundred and sixty years
pursued his practice there, till at last
he passed the temple on to Chishō Daishi.

. . . .

142. The Tripitaka is the complete collection of the Buddhist scriptures, in this case translated into Chinese.

On his jewel seat in the high Tosotsu Heaven,
Miroku awaits, so they say, the far-off dawn
when, descending to earth, he will be born
under the dragon-flower tree; but, if so,
how could this disaster have struck?
Chishō Daishi established this sacred spot
as a haven for study of the true teaching,
and since he drew holy water there each morning,
he called it Mi-i-dera, Temple of the Three Wells.
But although Miidera was once so holy,
nothing is left there now. In an instant
the exoteric and esoteric teachings
vanished utterly. The temple is gone:
nowhere now to practice the mysteries,
no ringing of the liturgical bell,
no flowers for the summer retreat,
no sound of ladling holy water.
Learned masters and famous teachers
allow their practice and study to lapse,
and the disciples who await their instruction
desert the sutras and the Buddha's word.

The temple's abbot, Cloistered Prince Enkei, was dropped as head monk of
Tennōji.
Thirteen other high-ranking clerics were dismissed and taken by the police.
Thirty men were banished, including the fighting monk Jōmyō.
No one mistook such chaos and turmoil for some minor incident.

"It just shows what lies ahead,"
people told one another.
"Soon enough now the Heike
will find that they have had their day."

BOOK FIVE

1. The Capital Moved to Fukuhara

(recitative)
The capital was abuzz: On the third of the sixth month of Jishō 4, [1180]
His Majesty was to proceed to Fukuhara.
It had been understood lately that the capital would move there,
but no one imagined that happening today or tomorrow.
People were in turmoil and hardly knew what to think.
And then, to top it off, they brought forward his progress, set for the third,
to the second. First thing that day, at the hour of the hare, [ca. 6 A.M.]
they advanced the palanquin. His Majesty, in his third year,
was so little that he entered it in all innocence.
When an emperor that young boards a palanquin, his mother joins him;
but not this time. No, it was his nurse Sotsu-no-suke,
Grand Counselor Taira no Tokitada's wife, who rode with him.
Her Majesty, His Cloistered Eminence, and His Eminence went, too.
The regent, chancellor, senior nobles, and privy gentlemen
all rushed to claim their places in the cortege.

> (speech)
> His Majesty reached Fukuhara on the third. Lord Yorimori's residence
> there was now the imperial palace. On the fourth, Yorimori received,
> in reward, promotion to the upper second rank over the right com-
> mander Yoshimichi, the son of Lord Kujō Kanezane. Never before had
> a commoner's second son vaulted this way past the son of a regent.

Lord Kiyomori had changed his attitude toward the cloistered emperor,
releasing him from the Toba Mansion and allowing him back to the capital,
but Prince Mochihito's rebellion infuriated him once more.
He moved His Cloistered Eminence to Fukuhara,
confined him there to a shingle-roofed house—
three bays on a side and surrounded by a high board fence with just one
    entrance—
and assigned a single man, Harada Tanenao, to guard him.
Gaining admission to see him was not easy.
The local youth called the house the "cage palace."

> (song)
> As for His Cloistered Eminence,
> "I have not the slightest desire,"

he said, "to run this world of ours.
My only wish is for liberty
to please myself and ease my mind
on pilgrimage hither and yon,
to temples and sacred mountains."
One might say that the Heike had now committed their greatest outrage yet.
"Ever since back in the Angen years," people kept saying, [1175-77]
"that man has banished or killed senior nobles and privy gentlemen,
exiled a regent, appointed his own son-in-law regent,
shifted the cloistered emperor to a Seinan Palace,
and murdered his second son, Prince Mochihito.
In short, moving the capital is probably just the last affront he could think of."
Moving the capital was not without precedent.
Emperor Jinmu, fifth of the earthly rulers
and fourth son of Fukiaezu-no-mikoto,
was born of Tamayori-hime, the sea god's daughter.
After twelve reigns in the age of gods,
he began the long line of human sovereigns.
In Miyazaki county of the province of Hyūga, he assumed the imperial dignity.
In the fifty-ninth year of his reign, he set out to conquer the east
and halted in his travels in the Central Land of Rich Reed Plains.[143]
Mount Unebi was the spot he chose,
in Yamato, as we call it now;
at Kashihara he cleared a site
and built his Kashihara Fane:[144]
for so it is named.
Thereafter generations of sovereigns moved the imperial seat
thirty times and more—indeed, forty in all—elsewhere, even to other provinces.
The twelve emperors from Jinmu to Keikō[145]
established their seats in Yamato
and never went farther afield.
But Seimu, in his very first year,
moved all the way to the province of Ōmi
and built his new seat there in Shiga county.
In his second year, Emperor Chūai

....

143. An ancient, noble name for Japan.

144. The chronicles that cover these times call the residences of these early emperors *miya*, which in medieval Japanese meant either "shrine" or "prince" (or "princess"). As the word for an emperor's residence it is thoroughly archaic, hence the translation "fane."

145. Their reign dates, being more mythical than historical, are omitted.

moved to the province of Nagato
and erected his own there, in Toyora.
And there it was that this sovereign died;
whereupon his empress, Jingū Kōgō,
who replaced him, subjugated
Kikai, Koguryŏ, and the Khitans.[146]
After defeating these foreign lands,
she returned home and, in Chikuzen,
in Mikasa county, bore a male heir;
wherefore we call that dwelling of hers
the Birth Fane. Awesome to tell,
it was none other than Yawata
whom she had borne to the world.

Upon succeeding to the throne, her son came to be known as Emperor Ōjin.[147]
In due course she moved to the province of Yamato,
to inhabit the fane of Iwane-wakazakura.
Emperor Ōjin dwelled in that province, too, in the fane of Karushima-Akari.

Emperor Nintoku, in the first year of his reign,
moved to the Takatsu Fane at Naniwa,
in the province of Settsu. Emperor Richū,
in his second, removed to Yamato,
where he established his seat in Tōchi county.
In his initial year, Emperor Hanzei moved
to Kawachi and his fane of Shibagaki.
Emperor Ingyō, forty-two years into his reign,
returned to Yamato and the Tobutori Asuka Fane.
In his twenty-first year, Emperor Yūryaku
moved to reside in the fane of Asakura
at Hatsuse, likewise in Yamato.

In his fifth year, Emperor Keitai moved his seat to Tsuzuki in
    Yamashiro; [early 6th c.]
then, in the twelfth year of his reign, to Otoguni.
Emperor Senka, in his first year, returned to Yamato province,
to spend his life at his fane of Hinokuma-no-Iruno.
In Taika 1, Emperor Kōtoku moved to Nagara in Settsu, [645]

....

146. Respectively, the Ryukyu Islands, an ancient Korean kingdom, and the vaguely conceived kingdom of a Mongolic people in far northern China. All this is myth.

147. The fifteenth emperor, largely mythical despite his enormous Konda tomb, which still rises near Osaka. Deified after his death, he is the central figure in the triad known collectively as Hachiman (Great Bodhisattva Hachiman), the tutelary deity of the Genji.

there to inhabit the Toyozaki Fane. Empress Saimei, in her second year,
moved again back to Yamato and lived in the fane of Okamoto.
In his sixth year, Emperor Tenchi removed to Ōmi and the fane of Ōtsu. [r. 668–71]
In his inaugural year, Emperor Tenmu moved back to Yamato, [r. 673–86]
to inhabit thereafter the fane of South Okamoto.
He is known to all as the Kiyomibara Emperor.
Empress Jitō and Emperor Monmu passed their two sage reigns [r. 690–97; 697–707]
in the Fujihara Fane, also in Yamato.

> Empress Genmei to Emperor Kōnin: [r. 707–15; 770–81]
> These seven sovereigns lived out their reigns
> in one capital, Nara.

Then in Enryaku 3, the tenth month and second day, [784]
Emperor Kanmu moved his seat from Kasuga, in the imperial city of Nara,
to Nagaoka in the province of Yamashiro. In the first month of his tenth year,
he sent the grand counselor Fujiwara no Oguromaru,
the consultant and left grand controller Ki no Kosami,
the grand prelate Genkei, and others to inspect Uda in Kadono county,
also in Yamashiro. The two officials reported as follows:

> "The lay of the land, Your Majesty,
> offers at your left the Blue Dragon,
> the White Tiger at your right,
> the Red Bird before you,
> and behind you the Dark Warrior: [148]
> each of the four gods in his place.
> For your capital it is perfect."

> > Emperor Kanmu therefore conveyed his desire to the Kamo Deity
> > present in Otagi county and on the twenty-first of the twelfth month
> > of Enryaku 13 [794] moved from his Nagaoka capital to the new one.
> > Since then, through three hundred and eighty years or more of stars
> > and frosts, thirty-two sovereigns have reigned there and watched the
> > seasons turn.

Yes, sovereigns had from the earliest times moved the capital hither and thither,
but Emperor Kanmu, who knew that this site had no rival, could not let it go.
He consulted ministers, senior nobles, men of talent in every line,
to ensure that this new imperial seat should last forever.
To this end he had fashioned a man's clay likeness, eight feet tall,
wearing iron armor and an iron helmet, bearing an iron bow and iron arrows,
and on a peak of the Eastern Hills he had this figure buried, facing west.

....

148. Ancient Chinese directional deities seen painted on the walls of some *kofun* tumulus tombs. The
emperor and the gate of his palace faced south.

Should there be in ages to come talk of moving the capital,
this warrior was to discharge his duty and shield the established one.

> So it is that whenever trouble
> comes to pose a threat to the realm,
> the barrow over this figure rumbles.
> Known as the General's Barrow,
> it is still there.[149]

Now, it is from Emperor Kanmu that every Taira descends.
And Heian, the name of his capital, is written with characters that mean,
for *hei,* "peace" and, for *an,* "ease." The city merited Taira respect.
Their own imperial ancestor had held it in the highest regard,
and it was appalling of them to move the imperial seat for no reason at all.
It is true that during his reign Emperor Saga had considered doing just
      that, [r. 809-23]
when Retired Emperor Heizei made such trouble, goaded by his mistress of staff;
but his ministers, his nobles, and the people of every province objected,
until in the end he desisted.
Not even the lord who stands sovereign over the realm could accomplish that
      move.
How terrifying that Lord Kiyomori, a mere commoner, should have done so!
And the old capital had been so beautiful!

> All around the sovereign's citadel,
> divine protectors shed tempered light.[150]
> Miracle-working temples, aloft
> on hilltops or in the cleft of valleys,
> lifted their expansive tiled roofs,
> and the people all lived free of care.
> From there the five inner provinces,
> the far-flung seven circuits of the realm
> lay open to unimpeded access.
> But now each and every crossroads
> lay dug up, barring carriage traffic.
> Those who nonetheless had to travel
> went in little carts, took long detours.
> Houses that once up and down the streets
> jostled eave to eave in their pride
> day by day crumbled into ruin.
> Others, disassembled, went straight

....

149. The Shōgun-zuka is at the summit of Mount Kachō east of Kyoto (Yamashina-ku).
150. Local divinities who represent the "tempered light" of the eternal, universal buddhas.

into the rivers, Katsura or Kamo,
where their timbers, re-formed into rafts
and loaded with building materials,
furniture, and various odds and ends,
were hauled on down to Fukuhara.
Anyone could watch, before his eyes,
a brilliant city once in full flower
dull, alas, to vacant wasteland.
On a pillar of the abandoned palace,
somebody left these poems:

> *No fewer, by now,*
> *than four times one hundred years*
> *have passed since the days*
> *that saw this city's founding:*
> *Must it now fall to ruin?*

> *Farewell to flowers*
> *blossoming in Miyako,*
> *and off on the wind*
> *we blow to Fukuhara,*
> *eyes out for peril ahead.*

Construction of the new capital was to begin in the sixth month of that year,
on the ninth day. To preside, Lord Tokudaiji Sanesada, the left commander,
received appointment from among the senior nobles,
together with the consultant captain Lord Tsuchimikado Michichika.
Their executive aide was the chamberlain and left minor controller Yukitaka,
and with them they brought a group of officials.
The party's task was to survey the open ground west of Wada-no-matsubara
and portion it into the proper nine sectors, divided by east-west avenues.
They found room for five sectors, but no more,
so back they went again to report the difficulty.
The council of senior nobles met to discuss it,
some suggesting Inamino in Harima, others Koyano in Settsu,
but there was no sign that the matter would go further.

> The old capital was breaking up;
> the new one was going nowhere.
> Everyone felt adrift, like clouds.
> Those who had long occupied the land
> bewailed its loss, and the new arrivals
> grumbled on among themselves
> how hard it was to get anything built.

It all made better sense as a dream.
Lord Michichika had this to say:
"Apparently in the Other Realm
they put through three broad avenues
and build twelve gates.
Well then, what is the matter with building a palace
on land broad enough to accommodate up to five avenues?
For the moment the thing to do is to build a provisional one."
His proposal passed. The grand counselor Kunitsuna received for this purpose
the province of Suō and from Lord Kiyomori the order
to proceed and cover the cost from the resulting income.
This Kunitsuna was so rich already
he could have built a palace easily from his own resources.
As it was, how could this venture not burden the realm and distress the people?
Performing the rite of imperial enthronement, as needed, is one thing,
but with all the disorder then plaguing the land,
this was no time to move the capital or build a new palace.

> Wise sovereigns in ages past
> thatched their palaces with sedge
> and did not even square the eaves.
> When they saw too little smoke
> rising from hearths near and far,
> they renounced their modest taxes,
> for their hearts went to the people
> and they cared about their realm.
> In Chu, building the Zhanghua Palace
> drove the common people to flee;
> in Qin, raising the Afang Palace
> plunged the realm into confusion,
> they say. Ah, thatch left untrimmed,
> rafters uneven at the eaves,
> boats and carriages soberly plain,
> clothing innocent of woven pattern:
> so did men live, once upon a time!
> And thus it is that Taizong of Tang,
> having built his Lishan Palace,
> considered its great cost to the people—
> for such may well have been his reason—
> and never went there in the end
> but let ferns grow from between the tiles

and thick vines swallow every fence.
"What a difference!" people exclaimed.

2. Moon Viewing

This was the schedule reached:
Ninth of the sixth month, begin work on the new capital.
Tenth of the eighth month, raise the ridgepole of the new palace.
Thirteenth of the eleventh month, His Majesty to make his progress there.
The old capital lapsed into ruin; the new one prospered.
That dreadful summer passed, and soon it was autumn.
Then half of autumn, too, was gone, and those living at Fukuhara
set out for famous places to watch the moon.

> Some, recalling storied spots
> Commander Genji once frequented,
> roamed the coast from Suma to Akashi,
> crossed over to the isle of Awaji,
> watched the moon from the Eshima rocks.
> Others sought Shirara, Fukiage,
> Waka-no-ura or chose instead
> Sumiyoshi, Naniwa, Takasago
> and brought home poems inspired
> by Onoe under the moon at dawn.
> Those detained in the old city
> gazed at the moon from Fushimi
> or from Hirosawa Pond.
> Lord Sanesada's longing thoughts
> went to the moon of the old capital,
> and past the tenth of the eighth month
> he journeyed there from Fukuhara.
> He found the city wholly changed.
> Only rare houses were still standing,
> rank weeds clustered before their gates,
> dews heavy on neglected gardens.
> Wormwood groves, wastes of scrubby weeds
> offered shelter only to birds
> or to crickets, plaintively singing
> where wildflowers dotted the field:
> gold, tiny chrysanthemums;
> mauve, nodding thoroughwort.
> One remaining spark from bygone days,

the empress mother, lived even now[151]
by the Kamo River, at Konoe.
Lord Sanesada went to see her.
He had a man knock at the main gate.
At this, from within, a woman cried,
"Who is it, requesting admittance
where now no caller ever comes
to brush dew from the wormwood fronds?"
    "Commander Sanesada is here from Fukuhara," the man answered.
    "The main gate is locked," she replied. "Come in through the small one
    to the east." Sanesada assented and did so.
Having little to occupy her time, the empress mother,
perhaps from a wish to recapture old memories,
had had her southern shutters thrown open and, when Sanesada arrived,
was playing the biwa. "Is this a dream," she exclaimed, "or are you real?
Come in! Come in!"
    In the Uji chapters of *Genji*,
    one of the Eighth Prince's daughters,
    sorry to bid autumn farewell,
    tunes her biwa and all night long
    plays to ease her unhappiness.
    At dawn, then, with the moon in the sky,
    perhaps in the end overcome,
    she beckons to it with the plectrum:
    a mood now easy to understand.[152]
    One of this lady's gentlewomen,
    Kojijū, had gained the nickname
    "Wait-All-Evening," because she replied
    to her mistress once, when asked,
    "Waiting all evening, and in the morning
    watching him go—which of the two
    do you find more intensely moving?":

      Waiting all evening,
      while interminable hours
        pass, to booming bells:
      How could cockcrow in the morning
      when he leaves compare with that?

....

151. Emperor Konoe's empress and the sister of Sanesada.
152. A scene from chapter 45 ("The Maiden of the Bridge") of *The Tale of Genji*.

This was the poem that earned her her nickname.

Lord Sanesada called the gentlewomen in to chat about past and present, and late that night he made this *imayō* song on the decline of the old city:

> To the ancient capital
>> I return, to see
> a spreading wasteland of weeds,
>> and desolation.
> The moon, shining in the sky,
>> reveals all below,
> and only the autumn wind
>> blows piercingly chill.

Three times he sang the song over,
very beautifully, and the ladies,
empress and gentlewomen alike,
moistened their sleeves with tears.
Meanwhile night was turning to day.
He bade them farewell and once more
set off to Fukuhara.

Summoning one of the chamberlains in his entourage, he said,
"Kojijū looked utterly heartbroken. Go back to her, then,
and give her from me whatever message comes to mind."
The man ran back to the residence and, with every mark of respect,
announced that his lord wished him to say:

> *How could it compare?*
> *you apparently once asked,*
>> *speaking of cockcrow.*
> *What about it this morning*
> *makes you then so specially sad?*

Kojijū replied, struggling not to weep,

> *Waiting certainly*
> *weighs when long hours go by,*
>> *marked by booming bells,*
> *but cockcrow can break your heart*
> *when it hurts to let him go.*

The chamberlain returned to his lord
and reported his exchange with her.
"Yes," his lord said, "that's why I sent *you*."
Sanesada was deeply impressed.
After that the man came to be called
"Chamberlain Can't Compare."

3. Spirit Mischief

The move to Fukuhara over, the Heike began having nightmares
that regularly set their hearts pounding. They often witnessed apparitions.
One night an enormous face, a full bay wide,
peered into the room where Lord Kiyomori lay.
Untroubled, Kiyomori glared hard at it until it melted away.
The Oka Palace, as it was called, having been only recently built,
had no trees worth mentioning anywhere near it,
but one night there came a crash, as of a great tree falling,
and a roar of laughter that if human could well have come from two dozen people.
This was obviously some *tengu* prank, and they posted a "whistler guard":
one hundred men by night, fifty by day, to shoot whistling arrows.[153]
But when the archers shot toward the *tengu,* they got back dead silence,
whereas arrows shot (so they thought) elsewhere provoked loud laughter.
There was also the morning when Lord Kiyomori
stepped from his curtained bed and threw open the double doors
only to see, heaped in the inner court garden,
dead men's skulls beyond counting, rolling and churning,
up and down, in and out, rattling against one another with a huge clatter.
"Attendant! Attendant!" he called, but, as it happened, no one came.
Meanwhile the skulls clumped into a great mound,
bursting the bounds of the garden, some hundred and fifty feet high—
a mountain of skulls, now suddenly crammed with living eyes,
all of them training on Lord Kiyomori an unblinking glare.
Kiyomori glared back, unperturbed, and under his gaze

      they disappeared without a trace,
      like frost or dew in burning sun.

Another incident involved one of Lord Kiyomori's horses.
He kept it in his stable, assigned many grooms to its care,
and lavished attention on it day in and day out,
but one night a mouse chewed a nest into its tail and bore her young there.
This was so strange that he had seven yin-yang masters divine its meaning.
Their verdict enjoined extreme caution.
Ōba no Saburō Kagechika of Sagami, the horse's first owner,

....

153. A "whistling arrow" (*hikime*) ended in a hollow wooden bulb pierced with holes that made it emit a sharp whistle in flight. The sole purpose of the *hikime,* which had no metal head, was to inspire fear and awe by means of sound—especially in noxious supernatural powers like these mischievous *tengu.* A *hikime*'s whistle seems to have been pitched higher than the hum of the *kaburaya,* described in note 46.

Kiyomori's nightmare visions.

had given it to Kiyomori as the best in all the eight provinces of the east.
Named Mochizuki, "Full Moon," it was black with a white blaze.
Lord Kiyomori gave it to Abe no Yasuchika, the head of the Yin-Yang Office.

> Of old, in Emperor Tenchi's reign,
> a mouse one night chewed her nest
> into the tail of one of the steeds
> sheltered in the imperial stables
> and there gave birth to a litter of young,
> whereupon evil foreign insurgents
> rose like a swarm of angry bees:
> *The Chronicles of Japan* tell the tale.

Another time one of Lord Minamoto no Masayori's young housemen
had a frightening dream. He found himself in what he took to be the
Bureau of Shrines. A large gathering of senior officials, formally
dressed, was engaged in some sort of debate, at the end of which they
expelled from their company one whose seat had been the most junior
among them. This figure appeared to be a Heike ally. "Who is this gen-
tleman?" the dreamer asked an old man.

"The divinity of Itsukushima," the old man replied.

Next an imposing elder, seated in the place of honor, announced,

"The Sword of Command, bestowed some time ago on the Taira house, we now award to Yoritomo, in exile in the province of Izu."

Another, similarly imposing elder seated next to him interjected, "But please let it pass thereafter to my descendants."

The dreamer asked further what all this meant. The speaker replied, "The one who gave the Sword of Command to Yoritomo is the Great Bodhisattva Hachiman, and the one who wanted it to pass to his descendants is the Kasuga Deity. As for myself, I am the Takeuchi Deity."[154]

The dreamer then awoke and told his dream to others. In time the story reached Lord Kiyomori. He sent Gendayū Suesada to demand that Lord Masayori surrender the young man, who promptly fled.
Masayori hastened to call on Lord Kiyomori.
"There is absolutely no truth to this rumor," he declared,
so the matter went no further. Strangely enough, however,
back when Kiyomori was still governor of Aki,
he went on pilgrimage to Itsukushima, and there, in a sacred dream,
the divinity conferred upon him a perfectly real lance,
with a silver-wound handle, that Kiyomori kept by his pillow forever after,
and one night this lance suddenly disappeared.

> Until now the mainstay of the court
> and the protector of the realm,
> the Heike, so people sadly said,
> had flouted the imperial will
> and so found the Sword of Command
> withdrawn from their possession.

Among those who shared such thoughts, when this news reached him,
was the monk and former consultant Seirai, on Mount Kōya.
"So," he said, "the Heike have had their time.
There has been reason enough for the Itsukushima Deity to favor them.
That divinity is female, though, or so I gather,
being Dragon King Sagara's third daughter.
Naturally Hachiman awarded the Sword of Command to Yoritomo,
but I do not see why Kasuga should have ordered it passed to his descendants.
Did he mean that once the Heike are finished, and then in their turn the Genji,
Lord Kamatari's successors, the sons of the regental house,[155]
should assume military command of the realm?"
A monk who was there with him remarked,

....

154. Takeuchi no Sukune, the deity of a subsidiary sanctuary at Iwashimizu.
155. Fujiwara no Kamatari (616–69), the founder of the Fujiwara line.

"The gods reveal themselves in all sorts of tactful forms,
now a layman, now a woman. They certainly call the Itsukushima Deity female,
but a divine being possessed of the three wisdoms and the six superpowers
can appear as a layman without any trouble at all."

These two had turned their backs on the world
and set out to follow the true path,
so that there should have stirred in them
no further thought of the world and its ways;
only the yearning for paradise.
But we humans all so easily praise
good government, when we learn of it,
and lament, when told of them, sorrows.

4. *The Courier*

On the second of the ninth month,
Ōba no Saburō Kagechika,
a man from Sagami province,
sent a courier to Fukuhara
with this message: "This past eighth month,
on the seventeenth, Yoritomo,
the Izu exile, once of the Right Watch,
sent his father-in-law, Hōjō Tokimasa,
to strike under cover of darkness
the province's deputy governor,
Izumi Kanetaka, at Yamaki,
his home. Kanetaka was killed.
Next, Doi, Tsuchiya, and Okazaki,
with more than three hundred riders
holed up at Mount Ishibashi.
I myself led a force of a thousand—
all, as I knew, Heike loyalists—
to attack them there, and soon enough
we reduced them to half a dozen
around Yoritomo himself,
who, after putting up fierce resistance,
fled for refuge to Sugiyama.
Then Hatakeyama joined us,
with over five hundred men of his own,
while Miura Yoshiaki's sons
added three hundred mounted men

to the strength mustered by the Genji.
The two sides clashed along the shore,
there between Yui and Kotsubo.
Hatakeyama, defeated in battle,
fell back to Musashi province.
His next move was, with his whole clan—
the Kawagoe, Inage, Edo, Kasai, Oyamada,
and seven more warrior leagues,
in all over three thousand men—
to attack the Miura fortress of Kinugasa.
Miura Yoshiaki was killed.
All of his sons fled from Kurihama,
by sea, to Awa and Kazusa."
So read Kagechika's report.

For the men of the Heike, the novelty of the move to Fukuhara had worn off.
Young senior nobles and privy gentlemen, poor fools, would often sigh and say,
"Damn it, I want to see some action! Let's get out there and after them!"
Hatakeyama Shigeyoshi, Oyamada Arishige, and Utsunomiya Tomotsuna
happened just then to be in the capital on guard duty.
Hatakeyama remarked, "This report must be in error.
I can hardly vouch for the Hōjō, close as they are to Yoritomo,
but for the rest, I cannot imagine them supporting an enemy of the court.
No doubt a corrected version will come soon."
Some agreed that that made sense, but others demurred.
"Far from it," many whispered. "The realm faces disaster."

> Lord Kiyomori was furious. "How I wish I had executed Yoritomo
> when I had the chance!" he exclaimed. "I reduced his punishment to
> exile, at the late Lady Ike's tearful insistence, but does he honor what
> he owes me for that? No! Instead he shoots arrows at us!

Not even the gods and buddhas could pardon him that!
That Yoritomo—oh, yes, heaven's wrath will soon be upon him!"

5. The Roster of Imperial Foes

> Who, then, in this realm of ours,
> first opposed the imperial will?
> In Emperor Jinmu's fourth year,[156]
> there appeared in the province of Kii,
> in Nagusa county, Takao village,

....

156. Jinmu, the first emperor of Japan, is said to have come to the throne in 660 B.C.

a spider, thick-bodied and long-legged,
stronger than any powerful man.
It took so many people's lives
that imperial troops marched against it.
They read out His Majesty's decree,
knotted together a net of vines,
threw it over the spider, and killed it.
Since that time there have been others
who, driven by fierce ambition,
sought to end imperial rule:

Ōishi no Yamamaru;

Prince Ōyama;

the minister Moriya;

Yamada no Ishikawa;

Soga no Iruka;

Ōtomo no Matori;

Fun'ya no Miyada;

Tachibana no Hayanari;

Hikami no Kawatsugi;

Prince Iyo;

the assistant Dazaifu viceroy
Fujiwara no Hirotsugi;

Emi no Oshikatsu;

Heir Apparent Sawara;

Empress Igami;

Fujiwara no Nakanari;

Taira no Masakado;

Fujiwara no Sumitomo;

Abe no Sadatō

and Abe no Munetō;

Minamoto no Yoshichika,
the governor of Tsushima;

the Haughty Left Minister Yorinaga;

the ruthless Gate Watch intendant Nobuyori—
all in all, there were twenty of them,
none of whom ever achieved success.
Their bodies lay in the wilderness;
their heads hung at the gates of prisons.
In this present world of ours, the throne inspires no awe.
In ancient times an imperial edict, read aloud to a dead tree,
drew from it blossoms and ripening fruit

and commanded obedience from the very birds of the air.
In fact, it was in somewhat more recent times
that Emperor Daigo visited his Shinsen-en garden [r. 897–930]
and spied there, beside the pond, a white heron.
He summoned a chamberlain. "Catch me that heron," he said, "and bring it here."
How to go about catching it, the chamberlain had no idea,
but His Majesty had spoken. The man started toward it.
The heron spread its wings, preparing for flight.
"I bring you His Majesty's command," the chamberlain announced,
at which the bird folded its wings and bowed low.
The chamberlain picked it up and took it to the emperor.
"It is wonderful, indeed," His Majesty said to the heron,
"that you have actually come in answer to your sovereign's call."
Then he turned to the chamberlain.
"Have this heron awarded at once the fifth rank," he ordered. And so it was done.
"Henceforth," His Majesty proclaimed, "you are the Heron King,"
and, before releasing the bird, he hung a tablet with that title around its neck.

> His Majesty had no need,
> none at all, for the heron.
> He had simply wanted known
> the weight of an emperor's word.

6. The Xianyang Palace

Examples of failed resistance to the sovereign occur in China as well.
Prince Dan, heir apparent to the state of Yan,
captured by the First Emperor of Qin,[157] spent twelve years in captivity.
Weeping, he then uttered this appeal:
"In the land of my birth, I have an aged mother. I beg for leave to go and see her."
The First Emperor laughed derisively.
"There will be no leave for you, my friend," he answered,
"until horses sprout horns and crows have white heads."
Prince Dan lifted his eyes to the heavens and prostrated himself in agony on the
    earth.
"Oh, please," he prayed, "make horses grow horns and turn the crows' heads
    white!
I so long to go home again and see my mother once more!"

....

157. The First Emperor of Qin (Qin Shi Huangdi, 259–210 B.C.), mentioned repeatedly hereafter, is a
towering figure in Chinese history. After unifying China in 221 B.C., he built a huge palace, undertook
other vast projects, and left a colossal mausoleum, including the famous Terra-Cotta Army. He also
burned all existing books.

The Bodhisattva Wondrous Sound,
in the Pure Land of Vulture Peak,
warned against unfilial conduct.
So, too, Confucius and Yan Hui,
once born into the world in China,
first taught filial piety there.
And because the Three Treasures[158]
in both realms, seen and unseen,
take pity on the burning wish
to show an aged parent love,
a horned horse did after all
turn up one day at the palace,
and a crow with a white head
perched there in a garden tree.
Witness to these prodigies,
the First Emperor kept faith
with that noble principle
that a sovereign, having spoken,
cannot go back on his word.
He issued Prince Dan a pardon
and granted him leave to go home.
Nonetheless the First Emperor rued his indulgence.
There lay between Qin and Yan a land known as Chu.
A great river ran there, spanned by a bridge called the Bridge of Chu.
The First Emperor sent troops to make sure that when Prince Dan
crossed it and reached the middle, he should fall.
Once they let him onto the bridge, he was therefore certain to do so,
and he did, right down into the river.
He did not drown, however. No indeed.
Instead he walked on to the opposite bank as though on solid ground.
He then looked back, wondering how he had done it.
Innumerable turtles had surfaced, their backs affording him passage dry-shod.
    This they had done because once more
    the sacred powers seen and unseen,
    touched by his filial devotion,
    had made sure that he came to no harm.
This incident embittered Prince Dan against the First Emperor, and he refused to
    give up.
When the First Emperor sent more troops to kill him, the terrified prince

....

158. The Buddha, his teaching, and the community of monks.

enlisted the help of a warrior named Jing Ke, whom he appointed minister.
Jing Ke then turned to a second warrior known as Master Tian Guang.
Tian Guang said,

> "Is your wish to rely on me
> due to what you already know
> of what I was when in my prime?
> The finest steed may swiftly fly
> a thousand leagues, but when at last
> the passing years bring on old age,
> he serves less well than any nag.
> I myself cannot help you,
> but I will find you fighting men."

Jing Ke replied,

> "All this is a deep, dark secret. Tell it to no one."

> Master Tian Guang answered, "To incur suspicion is to suffer the greatest shame. I know that you will suspect me if the secret ever gets out." With these words he bashed his head into the plum tree at the gate and died.

There was yet another warrior named Fan Yuqi, from the land of Qin.
The First Emperor wiped out his father, uncles, and brothers,
and he fled for refuge to Yan.
The First Emperor then issued a proclamation, addressed to all within the four seas:
"Whoever takes the head of Fan Yuqi and brings it to me,
he will have from me five hundred catties of gold."
Jing Ke heard about this and went to find the man.
"I gather," he said, "that you have a bounty of five hundred catties of gold on your
   head.
Give me your head, then. I will take it to him. While he is gloating over it,
I will easily draw my sword and run him through." So he spoke.
Fan Yuqi leaped to his feet, breathing hard.

> "The First Emperor killed them all,"
> he said. "Father, uncles, and brothers.
> Night and day my thoughts go to them.
> The pain burns in my very marrow.
> Oh, yes, if you mean to kill him,
> then giving you my head is easy,
> easy as giving a grain of sand."

He cut off his head himself and died.
Another warrior still was Qin Wuyang, also from Qin.
After slaying an enemy in his thirteenth year, he fled to Yan.
No man-at-arms could compare with him.

Mighty heroes fainted when he raged;
when he smiled, babies snuggled into his arms.

> Jing Ke engaged Wuyang to guide him to the capital. On the way they
> were lodging below a remote mountain when they heard music from
> a village nearby. Divining by tone and modulation the outcome of
> their enterprise, they discovered that their foe was water and that they
> were fire. In time the sun rose. A white rainbow pierced it but did not
> go through. They gathered that their mission would fail.

But they could hardly turn around and just go back.
So they announced their arrival at the First Emperor's Xianyang Palace,
bearing a map of Yan and the head of Fan Yuqi.
The First Emperor sent an official to receive these gifts, but Jing Ke answered,
"Your Majesty, I can present them to you only in person, not through a third."
    The First Emperor gave his consent.
He ordered a banquet for the envoys from Yan.

> The First Emperor's Xianyang Palace,
> itself his whole capital city,
> measured eighteen thousand leagues,
> then three hundred and eighty more,
> around its walls. The palace proper
> stood on an artificial hill
> three leagues high. A Long-Life Hall,
> a Gate of Immortality
> towered there, beside a sun
> wrought of gold and a silver moon.
> Pearls, lapis lazuli, and gold
> blanketed the ground like sand.
> On all four sides, an iron screen
> soared aloft four hundred feet,
> while over the palace buildings
> spread a net, also of iron.
> Screen and net were to keep out
> the agents of the underworld,
> and since they blocked the airy paths
> geese take to land on autumn fields
> or to fly, when spring returns,
> home to the northern marches,
> an iron Goose Gate pierced the screen
> to let the geese freely through.

The First Emperor went regularly to the Afang Palace, where he governed.
Three hundred and sixty feet high, it was a thousand yards long

east to west and, north to south, five hundred yards wide.
Fifty-foot spears topped with banners stood beneath the portico yet never
    touched it.
The roof was tiled with lapis lazuli; the floor shone with silver and gold.
Up jade steps Jing Ke carried the map, Qin Wuyang the head.
Such awe did the palace inspire that Wuyang trembled.
The courtiers noted this with suspicion.
    "Wuyang plans some treacherous act,"
    they said. "None who poses a threat
    can be allowed near the sovereign,
    nor does any true gentleman
    countenance a clear threat nearby;
for to approach a present menace is to make light of death."
Jing Ke turned back and faced them.
    "Wuyang has no such thought in mind,
    but he has led a rustic life,
    and this palace is new to him;
    he is just troubled and confused."
    His words silenced the courtiers.
They came at last before the sovereign.
But when they presented him with the map and the head,
the sword at the bottom of the map chest threw off an icy gleam.
Instantly the First Emperor moved to flee.
    Jing Ke got a hard grip on his sleeve
    and pressed the sword point to his chest.
    Victory seemed already his.
    Warriors by the tens of thousands,
    side by side in the palace court,
    were powerless to intervene.
    They could only mourn that their lord
    should now fall to an assassin.
        The First Emperor spoke. "Allow me a moment more," he said. "Let me
        hear my favorite consort play the *kin*[159] for me one last time." Jing Ke
        granted him this brief reprieve. None of the First Emperor's three
        thousand consorts played the *kin* as beautifully as Lady Huayang. Her
        music soothed the fiercest warrior's heart, brought birds down from
        the sky, and set trees and grasses swaying.
And now, as she knew, the First Emperor would never hear her again.
Her tearful touch on the strings must have been lovely beyond all words.

. . . .

159. A fretless Chinese relative of the koto. Its use in Japan lapsed in the late tenth century.

Jing Ke himself lowered his gaze to listen
and allowed his thoughts to wander from his treacherous plan.
Then Lady Huayang began a new piece. She sang,

> "Tall a seven-foot screen may be,
> but a leap will surely clear it.
> Strong, thin silk certainly is,
> but a sharp tug will tear it."

Jing Ke had no idea what this was about, but the First Emperor did.
A mighty tug parted the sleeve that Jing Ke held,

> and over the screen the First Emperor leaped,
> to hide behind a copper pillar.
> Jing Ke, enraged, hurled the sword at him.
> A physician just then in attendance
> blocked it with his medicine pouch,
> but the blade still ran that pillar
> halfway through. Having no other,
> Jing Ke threw no more. The emperor returned,
> called for his sword, and cut Jing Ke
> into countless pieces; Wuyang, too.
> Then the First Emperor sent an army
> that put an end to the state of Yan.
> "Ah, yes," the Heike toadies muttered,
> "Yoritomo has that coming, too."

7. Mongaku's Mighty Austerities

Now, to speak of Minamoto no Yoritomo:
In the twelfth month of Heiji 1, his father, Yoshitomo, then chief left equerry,
    rebelled, [1159]
so that in his fourteenth year, on the twentieth of the third month of
    Eiryaku 1, [1160]
Yoritomo found himself banished to Hiru-ga-shima in the province of Izu.
He spent more than twenty years there and no doubt lay safely low all that time,
but in the year we have reached, he, too, raised rebellion. Why?
Because, they say, the holy man Mongaku of Takao urged him to do so.
This Mongaku's father was Endō Mochitō,
a Watanabe man and a junior officer in the Left Palace Guards.
As a warrior named Endō Moritō, Mongaku had served Shōseimon-in.[160]
Then, in his nineteenth year, he aspired to enlightenment, left the world,

....

160. The second daughter of Emperor Toba.

and set out to follow the path of stern practice.
"Let's just see how hard ascetic practice really is," he said to himself.
Under the blazing sixth-month sun, without a breath of air stirring,
he entered a hillside thicket and lay down on his back.
Noxious insects—horseflies, mosquitoes, wasps, ants, and so on—bit and stung
    him,
but he never moved, nor rose again for seven days.

       On the eighth day, he got up. "So," he said, "is that about what ascetic
       practice amounts to?"
          Came the answer, "If *that's* what it took, no one would even sur-
       vive it!"
          "Fine," Mongaku concluded, "no problem, then." And off he went to
       practice in earnest.
He headed for Kumano, meaning to undertake a retreat at the Nachi waterfall.
First, though, he decided to see what standing under the famous waterfall was
    like.
He went straight there.

       The tenth of the twelfth month was past.
       Snow lay deep on the ground, and ice
       silenced every valley stream.
       Wind off the peaks blew freezing cold,
       and the waterfall's silvery threads
       hung in a fringe of white icicles.
       All that the eye could see was white;
       the very trees had disappeared.
       Nonetheless down Mongaku went
       into the pool beneath the falls,
       where, immersed up to his neck,
       he chanted toward the promised count
       the *darani* of Lord Fudō.[161]
       He kept this up two or three days,
       but by the fourth or fifth no more:
       Overwhelmed, he lost his footing
       and drifted about there, on the water.
       From several thousand feet above[162]

....

161. A *darani* is a formula or spell transliterated through Chinese from Sanskrit, hence unintelligible as language. Fudō (note 93), a deity ubiquitous in the Japanese mountains, is blue-black in color and surrounded by flames. Around his sword coils the black dragon Kurikara (the Hiryū Gongen of 2:15), the deity of flowing water, for which Kurikara Ravine (7:6) is named. His two canonical followers, Kongara and Seitaka, appear below.

162. The waterfall is about four hundred feet high.

Mongaku under the Nachi waterfall. On cloud at top right: Kongara and Seitaka.

the cataract poured down on him.
Who could have withstood its force?
The rushing flood swept him on
through rocks as sharp as dagger blades,
now surfacing, now submerged,
a full five or six hundred yards.
It was then that a beautiful youth came to him, took both his hands,
and lifted him up. Those who saw this were amazed and lit a fire to warm him.
No, it was not yet his time to die. He soon began breathing again.
When he somewhat regained his senses, his eyes glittered with wrath.
        "I have made a most solemn vow,"
he said, "to stand thrice seven days
beneath the Nachi waterfall,
chanting three hundred thousand times
the *darani* of Lord Fudō.

This is only the fifth day. Who, I want to know, has had the gall to carry me here before the first seven days are over?"

The hair rose on the heads of all present, and they said not a word. Mongaku went back under the waterfall. The next day eight divine youths came and tried to lift him up again, but he fought them off tooth and nail. The day after that, his breath finally failed.

Perhaps wishing not to sully the waterfall pool with death,
two celestial youths with their hair in side loops came down from the lip of
    the fall
and with warm, fragrant hands caressed his whole body,
from his head to the nails on his hands and feet, and even to the palms of his
    hands.
Mongaku then began breathing again, feeling as though he were dreaming.
"Who are you," he asked, "that you should show me such compassion?"
    "Kongara and Seitaka are our names,"
    they answered. "We are the minions
    dispatched by Mantra King Fudō.
    So mighty was the vow you made
    and so bravely have you followed through
    that by the Mantra King's decree
    we have come to assist your practice."
"And where is he, then, this Mantra King?" Mongaku loudly inquired.
    "In the Tosotsu Heaven," they said,
    and soared away into the clouds.
    Mongaku pressed his palms together
    in farewell homage. "So!" he thought.
    "Even the Holy Mantra King,
    Fudō himself, knows of my practice!"
    Bursting once more with confidence,
    he stood again under the waterfall.
    Thereafter wonders never ceased.
    The icy winds left him untouched;
    the waters thundering down felt warm.
    So in the end he did endure
    thrice seven days, as he had vowed.
    Then he undertook at Nachi
    a mighty thousand-day retreat,
    after which his pilgrimages
    took him three times to Ōmine;
    to Kazuraki twice; and to Kōya,
    Kokawa, Kinpusen, Hakusan,
    Tateyama; the summit of Fuji;
    the sacred shrines of Izu, Hakone,
    Togakushi in Shinano;
    and Mount Haguro in Dewa:
    in short, every sacred mountain
    in the whole land of Japan.

Perhaps longing after all for home,
he then went up to the capital,
famed as an ascetic so fierce
that he could pray birds down from the sky.

8. The Subscription List

Thereafter Mongaku pursued his practice in peace,
in the inner fastnesses of the mountain called Takao.
And there, on Takao, is to be found the temple known as Jingoji.
Wake no Kiyomaru founded it long ago, in the reign of Empress Shōtoku. [r. 764–70]

Left for ages unrepaired,
it merged in spring into the mist,
loomed in autumn from thick fog.
The doors, blown flat by the wind,
lay rotting under fallen leaves.
Cracked roof tiles let in rain and dew,
and nothing sheltered the altar.
The temple had no priest at all,
nor any casual visitors,
save the light of sun and moon.

Mongaku made another great vow, this time to rebuild Jingoji, and to this end he promoted a subscription list, which he advertised to patrons far and wide. In the process he arrived one day at the Hōjūji residence of Cloistered Emperor Go-Shirakawa.

He sent in to the sovereign an urgent appeal to contribute,
but the gentleman was engaged in music making at the time and refused to hear it.
Now, fierce ascetic that he was, Mongaku feared no man in the world.
Manners and protocol meant nothing to him.
On the assumption that his appeal had not actually reached the sovereign,
he took direct action. He burst into the small court and roared,

"You are the sovereign, are you not,
lord of mercy and compassion?
How can you close your ears against me?"
Then he unrolled his subscription list
and read out in a great voice,

I, Mongaku, a disciple of the Buddha, humbly declare the following purpose: with assistance from the greatest lords and the least of the people, from both clerics and laymen, to build a temple on the sacred ground of Mount Takao and to conduct services there for the benefit of this life and the life to come.

Hear, then, my appeal for this assistance.

Reflection reveals True Reality to be vast. Sentient beings and the Buddha go by different, provisional names, yet dark clouds of delusion mass to obscure the dharma nature, swathing the peaks of the Twelve-fold Chain of Causation, dimming the radiance of the moon that shines for all time in the lotus blossom of the heart, and preventing the Three Virtues and the Four Mandalas from appearing in the lofty heavens. This is deplorable. The sun of the Buddha has set, and the realm of transmigration from birth to birth and death to death is shrouded in darkness. We lose ourselves in lust and wine. Who can put away from himself the folly of the mad elephant or of the leaping ape? We foolishly speak ill of others and of the Teaching. How, then, are we to escape attack by vengeful fiends from the King of Hell? Though I have cleansed myself of the dust of the profane world and clothed myself in monastic robes, evil leanings still mount within me day and night; morning and evening my ears remain deaf to better promptings. It is suffering to return to the fiery pit of the Three Realms and forever to turn in agony on the wheel of the Four Births. Therefore each scroll of the Buddha's peerless Teaching, vast as these scrolls are in number, expounds the path toward buddhahood; not one, whether teaching tactful means or, directly, highest truth, fails as a guide toward the far shore. So it is that I weep before the spectacle of transience and that I urge all, high or low, clerics or laymen, to bend their steps toward the supreme lotus throne and to build a sanctuary for the King of Boundless Awakening.

On lofty Takao the trees are as those on Vulture Peak, and the mosses that carpet the plunging ravines are as those of the cave on Mount Shang. Babbling brooks stretch their cloth through the rocks, while on the heights monkeys call and sport among the branches. The nearest house is far away: no tiresome voices, no dust. At hand are only peace and untroubled faith. The lay of the land perfectly inspires adoration of the Buddha. The contribution I ask is small. Who would then refuse me? They say that the stupa a child makes from sand turns straight into the seed of future buddhahood. How much more truly must this be so of a sheet of paper or a half coin donated in a pious cause! I pray that this temple be built, that our emperor's reign satisfy every one of his wishes, and that all people near and far, city and country, sing the praises of a new reign of Yao or Shun and smile amid the contentment of everlasting peace. May the spirits of all the dead, great and small, swiftly pass through the gate of the One True Vehicle and mount their waiting throne; may they forever take pleasure in the moon of the Buddha's threefold infinitely living reality!

Such is the spirit that animates the work of raising these contributions.
I have spoken.
Jishō 3, the third month
Mongaku

So went Mongaku's peroration to the cloistered emperor.

9. Mongaku's Exile

There happened then to be present in His Cloistered Eminence's company
Chancellor Moronaga, playing the biwa and giving admirable voice to Chinese
   poems;
Grand Counselor Sukekata, beating the rhythm for his own rendition of folk
   songs and *saibara;*
and Suketoki, the chief right equerry; and Morisada, an adviser, playing the
   wagon and singing *imayō.*[163]
They were having a fine time
there behind their jeweled blinds and brocade curtains,
and His Cloistered Eminence was singing along with them
when Mongaku's bawling cut in, ruining the tuning and breaking the beat.
"Who's that?" the sovereign asked. "Box his ears!"
The shocked younger gentlemen all rushed to oblige. One, Sukeyuki, raced
   ahead.
"What's this gobbledygook?" he shouted. "Get out of here!"
"Not until His Cloistered Eminence donates an estate to Jingoji on Mount
   Takao,"
Mongaku snapped, and stayed put. Sukeyuki moved to slap him.
Mongaku gripped his subscription list and whacked off Sukeyuki's court hat,
then clenched his fist and flattened him backward with a punch to the chest.
   Topknot flapping in the breeze,
   Sukeyuki made himself scarce, fast,
   right back up onto the veranda.
   Mongaku, from the fold of his robe,
   drew an icily gleaming dagger,
   horsetail-hair-wrapped handle and all,
   and made it plain he would run through
   anyone bold enough to approach him.
   Charging about hither and yon,
   subscription list in his left hand,

....

163. *Saibara,* a kind of song popular at the Heian court, is often mentioned in *The Tale of Genji,* as is the *wagon,* or "Japanese koto." The gentlemen are playing very elegant music.

brandished dagger in his right,
he looked—so sudden was the sight—
as though each hand wielded a blade.
Senior nobles, privy gentlemen
cried out in loud astonishment,
and the concert disintegrated.
The residence was sheer bedlam.
One Andō Migimune, a warrior from Shinano province
then serving in the cloistered emperor's corps of guards,
ran up, sword drawn, demanding to know what was happening.
Mongaku went after him with evident gusto, whereupon Migimune,
perhaps reluctant to cut down a monk, readjusted his grip
and dealt Mongaku's dagger arm a great blow with the flat of his sword.
That slowed Mongaku down somewhat.
Migimune dropped his weapon, shouted "Gotcha!," and grappled with him.
While they wrestled, Mongaku managed to stab Migimune's right arm.
Migimune kept the pressure on him nevertheless.
Powerful men equal in strength, they thrashed about on the ground
each sometimes on top, sometimes underneath.
Onlookers of every degree, with virtuously disapproving looks,
crowded forward to wallop Mongaku themselves wherever they could,
but he ignored them, except to spout further invective.
They dragged him out the gate and turned him over to the police,
who tied him up. Standing there, restrained, he glared at the sovereign's
    residence
and bellowed, hopping with rage,

> "So you refuse to contribute. Fine!
> But just you wait! For what you have done
> to Mongaku, that same Mongaku
> will see to it that you rue the day!

The three worlds are a burning house,
and an emperor's palace burns just as hot as anything else.
Pride yourself all you like on the excellence of your throne:
Once you're off to the Yellow Springs,[164] the demons there,
ox- and horse-headed, will get you, oh, yes—you can count on *that*!"
They decided that this monk was too utterly weird and marched him off to jail.
Sukeyuki stayed away from court service awhile;
he was so ashamed of having had his hat knocked off.
As a reward for having grappled with Mongaku,

....

164. The Chinese name for the underworld.

Migimune received direct promotion to right equerry aide.
Meanwhile Bifukumon-in passed away and a general amnesty was declared.
Mongaku was soon released.

>He might have gone somewhere else for a while, but no, he started in
>again fund-raising with his subscription list—and not just fund-
>raising either, because he also went about prophesying ruin. "Chaos
>awaits us!" he would bawl. "Sovereign and subject alike are doomed!"
>The authorities saw that they could not allow him to remain in the
>capital. They exiled him to Izu. Now, Nakatsuna, Lord Yorimasa's el-
>dest son, was then the governor of the province. By his order

Mongaku was to be sent down via the Tōkaidō and then by sea.
He therefore proceeded to the province of Ise
with a guard detail of two or three released prisoners in police service.
They said to him,

>"It's a custom we have, you see,
>we and the other police flunkies,
>when we go on this kind of job,
>to do what we can for our man.
>Now that you're up against it this way,
>reverend sir, and heading out
>in exile to a distant province,
>do you perhaps have any friends?
>You might consider asking them
>to provide you with a few gifts—
>eatables and so on, you know."
>Mongaku answered, "Actually,
>I just can't think of anyone
>to approach for a favor like that.
>No, there *is* someone after all—
>somebody in the Eastern Hills."
>They found him a bit of scruffy paper.

"I can't write on paper like this!" he exclaimed, and threw it back at them.
"Righto," they said, and found him something thicker.
Mongaku grinned. "To tell the truth, I can't write at all. You, do it for me."
He had one write this:
"I, Mongaku, was collecting contributions to rebuild Jingoji on Mount Takao,
when I collided with the present reign and fell short of my goal.
First I was jailed; then I was banished to the province of Izu.
It is a long way there. I need supplies, provisions, and so on.
Please give these to my messenger."

The man wrote it all down. "And to whom should I address it, reverend sir?"

"To Reverend Kannon at Kiyomizu," Mongaku replied.

"You're joking!" they cried.

"Nonetheless I place all my faith and trust in Kannon.

Who else do you expect me to write to?"

They sailed from the harbor of Ano in Ise province.

Off the Tenryū coast of Tōtōmi, a sudden storm blew up great waves

that threatened to capsize them. The crew and helmsman fought to save the ship,

but the storm redoubled in fury, until some could only call Kannon's name

while others invoked Amida a last ten times, as do the dying.

Mongaku, however, just lay there snoring, dead to the world.

Then suddenly, somehow, he awoke to the crisis. Leaping to his feet,

he stationed himself at the prow, glared out to sea, and roared,

> "Are you out there, you Dragon Kings?
>
> Hey, Dragon Kings! I'm talking to you!

What's the matter with you, going after a ship like this—

one carrying a holy man with vows as great as mine?

Watch out, you Dragon Kings! The wrath of heaven will be upon you!"

Perhaps that is why the wind and waves soon subsided, and they reached Izu at last.

> Since the day he left the city,
> Mongaku had had one constant prayer:
> "If I am to return to the capital,
> to rebuild and dedicate Jingoji,
> then on this journey I will not die.
> If my vow is to be all in vain,
> then I will fall somewhere on the way."
> Between the capital and Izu,
> not once did the winds favor him.
> A full thirty-one days the ship
> hugged the coast, island to island,
> while Mongaku ate nothing at all
> yet still lost none of his vigor
> and pursued his usual practice.
> Nothing that that man did or said
> ever seemed ordinary.

10. The Fukuhara Decree

They gave Mongaku into the care of Kondō Kunitaka,

who lived in the hills behind Nagoya, in the province of Izu.

From there Mongaku called often on Yoritomo,
to pass the time discussing affairs old and new.
One day Mongaku remarked, "Among all the Heike lords,
it was Shigemori who had genuine courage and wisdom.
Now their day will soon be over—he died last year, in the eighth month.
To my eye no Heike or Genji currently has *your* promise
as a leader of men. Lose no more time, then:
Raise rebellion and take command of this land of Japan."
Yoritomo replied, "That, reverend, is not a thought I have ever entertained.
Now that I owe my trivial life to the late Lady Ike's words on my behalf,
I pray for her daily by chanting the essence of the Lotus Sutra.
That is my sole occupation."
Mongaku insisted.
> "There is a book where it is written:
> 'Who refuses what heaven offers,
> the same shall incur heaven's blame;
> failure to act when the time comes
> invites nothing but disaster.'
Do you suppose that in speaking this way I mean only to test you?
Look, then, into the depths of my devotion."
From the fold of his robe, he produced a skull wrapped in white cloth.
"What is *that*?" Yoritomo asked.
"This is the skull of your father, the late chief left equerry.
> After the events of Heiji,
> his skull moldered beneath the moss,
> there before the prison gate.
> No one ever said prayers for him.
> Mongaku, though, had his own idea.
> Yes, I begged the skull from the guards,
> and by now, for ten years and more,
> I have worn it around my neck,
> roaming the land on pilgrimage
> to great temples and sacred mountains,
> praying everywhere for his soul.
> Surely by now he has been spared
> a whole kalpa of suffering.
So you see, I, too, have given your father faithful service."
> Although not entirely convinced,
> Yoritomo, upon being told
> that this was his own father's skull,
> soon enough shed many tears.

Then he got down to serious talk. "How can I possibly start an uprising," he asked, "when I am still under imperial ban?"

"That will present no difficulty," Mongaku answered. "I shall go up to the capital immediately and secure you a pardon."

"But that is impossible! You are under the same ban! Your talk of obtaining a pardon for somebody else makes no sense!"

"No doubt it would be mad of me to ask a pardon for myself, but I see nothing wrong with asking one for *you*. It will not take more than three days to reach the new capital, Fukuhara. Add a fourth there, while I request an imperial decree, and the whole trip should take seven or eight days at most."

Back he then went to Nagoya, where he told his disciples he was off for a quiet seven-day retreat at the Oyama Shrine in Izu. In reality he reached Fukuhara three days later. He had a slight connection there with Fujiwara no Mitsuyoshi, a former Right Watch intendant, on whom he now called.

"I am speaking of the Izu exile Minamoto no Yoritomo," he informed the gentleman. "If only he could obtain a decree from the cloistered emperor, lifting the imperial ban against him, he would mobilize his men throughout the eight provinces of the east, destroy the Heike, and restore peace to the realm."

Mitsuyoshi replied, "I hardly know what to say. I have been relieved of all three of my offices, and these days things are not easy for me. Besides, His Cloistered Eminence is a prisoner. I can promise nothing. Still, I will put the idea to him." Mitsuyoshi secretly reported the conversation to the cloistered emperor, who issued the decree immediately.

Mongaku hung the decree around his neck,
and three days later there he was again, back down in Izu.
"Confound it!" Yoritomo had meanwhile been worrying.
"There's no telling what nonsense this holy man may be spouting
or what awful trouble he's going to get me into."
But no, at noon on the eighth day, Mongaku turned up.
"Your imperial decree, sir, as requested," he said, and produced it.
The words "imperial decree" so awed Yoritomo
that he washed his hands, rinsed his mouth, put on a new hat,
donned a pure white robe, and bowed three times before reading it:

> *In recent years the Taira have displayed contempt for imperial rule and utter lack of respect for the way of good government. They propose to destroy the Buddha's Teaching and to extinguish the authority of the court. Now, this realm of ours is the land of the gods, where the paired shrines of the great imperial ancestors work many wonders. Ever since*

*the dynasty was founded, several thousand years ago, every attempt to
overthrow it or to imperil the state has therefore failed. For this reason
go forth now and, with the gods' help and in conformity with this decree,
chastise the Heike and disperse the enemies of the imperial line. The
time has come: Exercise now the martial prowess to which you are heir,
surpass the loyal service rendered by your forebears, distinguish your-
self, and exalt the honor of your house. Such is the burden of this decree,
which is hereby given into your hands.*

Jishō 4, seventh month, fourteenth day

*Received by former intendant of the Right Watch Mitsuyoshi for
transmission to former Right Watch officer Minamoto no Yoritomo*

Yoritomo, so they say,
put into a brocade bag
this most precious of decrees
and even during the battle
fought at Mount Ishibashi
kept it hung around his neck.

11. *The Fuji River*

Meanwhile at Fukuhara a council of senior nobles ordered a punitive force
dispatched in haste, before Yoritomo could gather an army.
Overall command lay in the hands of the Palace Guards lieutenant Koremori.
Tadanori, the governor of Satsuma, served as his deputy.
The force, thirty thousand strong, left Fukuhara on the eighteenth of the ninth
    month,
reached the old capital on the nineteenth,
and on the twentieth set off at once on its eastward mission.

In his twenty-third year, Koremori,
with his fine looks and his martial air,
made a picture no brush could convey.
With him he had borne, in a chest,
Karakawa, for so it was named:[165]
the heirloom armor of his house.
On the road he wore red brocade
under armor with green lacing,
mounted the while on a dappled gray
and seated on a gold-edged saddle.
His deputy, Lord Tadanori,

....

165. Karakawa ("Chinese Leather") because it was laced with tiger-skin leather.

wore, over brocade of dark blue,
black-laced armor, and he rode
a sturdy, powerful black steed
bearing a black-lacquered saddle
sprinkled with flecks of silver and gold.
Horses, saddles, armor, helmets,
bows and arrows, daggers and swords—
all of them so glittered and shone
as to give pleasure to every eye.
Lord Tadanori had long frequented a certain gentlewoman, a princess's daughter.
Once when he went there, she had a visitor with her,
another gentlewoman of the highest rank.
The two ladies went on talking rather a long time,
and the evening slipped by, yet the guest still made no move to leave.
For some time Tadanori paced about under the eaves,
fanning himself somewhat assertively.
The lady he had come to see murmured this, with elegant grace:

> *Dear me, how the crickets sing,*
> *out there on the moor!*

Tadanori gave up fanning himself and went home.
The next time he went to see her, she said,
"Do tell me why the other day you stopped your fanning."
"Well," he answered, "because I gathered that I was annoying you."
Now that Tadanori was leaving, she sent him a short-sleeved underrobe
with this expression of regret that he was bound far away:

> *Down the eastward road,*
> *brushing endless leafy fronds*
> *in passing, your sleeves*
> *still will gather no such dews*
> *as mine, languishing behind.*

Tadanori replied,

> *That I leave you now*
> *need not move you to lament,*
> *for before me lies*
> *that barrier crossed of old*
> *toward immortal glory.*

"That barrier crossed of old":
Tadanori had in mind,
surely, memories of the day
when Taira no Sadamori
led imperial forces east

to subdue Masakado.
What an elegant way to say it!
    When in years gone by a commander
started out for some distant region
to suppress an enemy of the court,
he went first of all to the palace,
to receive the Sword of Command.
His Majesty by then had repaired
to the Shishinden, to await him,
while the Palace Guards stood, rank on rank,
below the great hall's steps. Two ministers,
inner and outer, manned their posts,
and a banquet welcomed all nobles.
The commander and his deputy
received their swords as custom required.
Those precedents, however, were set
too long ago to be followed now.
The one invoked looked back instead
to the day when Taira no Masamori
marched off to Izumo, to crush
Minamoto no Yoshichika;
for this time the commander received
merely a traveling official's bell,
to be carried in a leather bag
around the neck of some underling
on the way to execute his orders.
In the old days, such a commander,
charged with suppressing rebellion,
bore in mind on leaving the capital
three indispensable principles:
from the day he received the sword,
to forget his house; when on the road,
to forget his wife and children;
and, when engaged with the enemy,
to forget his very life.
This Heike commander, Koremori,
and his deputy, Tadanori, too,
must therefore have felt that way.
Theirs makes a rousing story.
On the twenty-first day of the same month, the retired emperor, Takakura,
set off on a pilgrimage to Itsukushima in the province of Aki.

He had been there already once before, in the third month.
Perhaps that is why the world was quiet for a month or two thereafter
and no misfortune afflicted the people. But then Prince Mochihito's rebellion
again disturbed the realm and threw society into chaos.
His Eminence seems therefore to have gone
in order to pray that peace be restored, and with it his own health.
This time he left from Fukuhara, which greatly lightened his journey.
He personally drafted his formal prayer to the deity,
and the regent, Lord Motomichi, wrote out the fair copy.

> *The dharma nature is said to be unclouded. The mid-month moon shines high in a clear sky. With profound wisdom, sensible manifestations of the divine blend the opposing currents of yin and yang. At far-famed Itsukushima, wonders surpass comparison. Distant peaks enfold the sanctuaries, rendering visible lofty compassion; ocean waters lap the halls, conveying the depth of the Salvific Vow.*
>
> *As to myself, I first assumed the undeserved dignity of the sovereign; now, in the spirit of Laozi,[166] I enjoy a retired emperor's peace and ease. Yet I nonetheless summoned all my resolve, in private, to come on pilgrimage to this secluded isle. Here below the sacred fence, I begged for divine favor, with strenuous earnestness I offered up my prayers, and within the sanctuary I hearkened to an oracle that remains even now graven upon my heart. Divination revealed when peril most threatened me: late summer and early autumn. All at once sickness invaded my body, defeating the best that physic could do. Days and months passed. More and more clearly, I saw how right the divine response had been. No prayers I commissioned ever dispersed the miasma. Only one course of action remained. Rousing my courage, I prepared to repeat that arduous journey. Endless cold winds on the way broke my dreams, and by the light of comfortless suns my gaze descried only distant horizons.*
>
> *Now at last I have reached the sacred grove and spread in reverent awe a pilgrim's mat. I present my offerings: on colored paper and in black ink, a full copy of the Lotus Sutra accompanied, in single scrolls, by the sutra's opening and concluding scriptures, by the Amida Sutra, and by the Heart Sutra; and, written out by me in gold, the "Devadatta" chapter of the Lotus.*
>
> *The mighty pines and oaks here sow beneath their spreading boughs the seeds of beneficence, and voices chanting the scriptures merge in subtle harmony with the murmur of rising and falling tides. A mere*

---

166. The legendary Chinese sage perhaps more familiar to many readers as Lao-tzu (an older romanized spelling).

*eight days ago, this disciple of the Buddha bade farewell to the clouds
above the imperial dwelling, but thus braving a second time the waves
of the western ocean has taught him the strength of the bond that drew
him here, where every morning pilgrims come in no paltry numbers to
pray and where each evening a pilgrim host gives thanks for blessings
received. Many among the nobly born declare devotion to this shrine,
but one hears of no prince or retired sovereign making the journey, with
the exception of the current cloistered emperor. All unworthy, I have
devoutly followed his example.*

*Under the moon of Mount Songgao, Emperor Wu of Han failed to
behold the tempered radiance of the divine form, and the immortals of
the Penglai grotto remained concealed behind intervening clouds. Eyes
lifted to the heavens, I beg the divinity of Itsukushima; prostrate upon
the earth, I implore the Lotus Sutra: Consider once more my ardent
prayer and vouchsafe the boon that you only can bestow!*

Jishō 4, ninth month, twenty-eighth day

The Retired Emperor

Meanwhile off the brave warriors rode,
sallying forth from the capital
to march a thousand leagues to the east.
Whether they would return safe and sound,
no one knew, such danger they faced.
They would be lodging on dewy moors,
sleeping on the moss of high peaks,
crossing endless mountains and rivers.
So it was, after many days,
that on the sixteenth of the tenth month
they came to Kiyomi-ga-seki
in the province of Suruga.
Their force when they left the capital
had numbered thirty thousand men,
but they gathered more on the way,
to reach a full seventy thousand.
They established their advance camp
on the Fuji River, at Kanbara,
while the rear still lingered far back
at Tegoshi and Utsunoya.

Commander Koremori summoned his field commander, Tadakiyo, the governor
of Kazusa.

"The way I see it," he said, "we should cross over Ashigara and fight in the Kanto."
Tadakiyo sought to discourage this rash idea. "When you left Fukuhara, my lord,

Lord Kiyomori enjoined you to leave military decisions to me.
The warriors of the eight eastern provinces have all flocked to Yoritomo,
who by now must have several hundred thousand of them.
You indeed command seventy thousand mounted men,
but they come from provinces widely scattered. They and their horses are
    worn out.
As yet there is no sign of the forces due to join us from Izu and Suruga.
I suggest that we stay where we are, with the Fuji River before us,
to await the arrival of reinforcements."
Koremori had no choice. They went no farther.

> In the meantime Yoritomo
> crossed the Ashigara mountains
> and came, in Suruga province,
> to the banks of the Kise River.
> There, from Kai and Shinano,
> Genji men galloped to join him.
> A muster of all forces present,
> held on Ukishima-ga-hara,
> registered two hundred thousand men.

A man in the service of Satake no Tarō, of the Hitachi Genji, was on his way to the capital with a letter from his master when Tadakiyo stopped him, seized the letter, and read it. It was for a gentlewoman and apparently harmless. Tadakiyo returned it. "How many men does Yoritomo have?" he asked.

"I have been on the road eight or nine days," the fellow replied, "and the whole time I have seen armed men everywhere. Moor and mountain, rivers and seas swarm with them. I can count up to a few hundred, or perhaps to a thousand, but beyond that I am lost. Whether there are many or few, I have no idea. But yesterday at the Kise River, I heard someone say that the Genji have two hundred thousand mounted men."

"Ah!" Tadakiyo exclaimed. "How I wish our supreme commander, Lord Munemori, had taken less time to act. Had he sent off the punitive force just one day earlier, we would have been over Ashigara by now and into the eight provinces, where the Hatakeyama men and the Ōba brothers would undoubtedly have joined us. With them on our side, not a leaf nor a blade of grass in the Kanto would have failed to bow before us." But his bitter regret did nothing to remedy the situation.

Commander Koremori summoned Saitō Sanemori, from Nagai in Musashi, to receive advice from him on the men of the east.

"Tell me, Sanemori," he said, "how many of their bowmen can match your
   strength?"
Sanemori smiled ruefully. "So, my lord," he replied, "you think I shoot a long
   arrow?
Mine are only thirteen handbreadths long. Any number of them can do that.
No one known as a powerful archer shoots an arrow less than fifteen hands long.
And the bow, too—a strong man shoots one that it takes five or six to string.
An arrow from such a bowman can pierce a double or triple suit of armor.
And the smallest of their local lords commands at least five hundred riders.
Once in the saddle, those men never fall,
nor do they let their horses fall, galloping through the roughest terrain.
Should a father or son be killed in battle,
they ride straight over the body to fight on.
The way war is fought in the provinces of the west,
when a warrior's father falls, he gives him a proper funeral and mourns him;
only then does he fight again.
Should the fallen be his son, his grief removes him from combat.
When the troops' rice stores give out, they till the fields in spring,
harvest the crop in autumn, and only then resume their campaign.
Summer is too hot for them, and winter too cold.
Things are not like that in the east.
The Genji of Kai and Shinano know the terrain well.
They will probably come up on our rear around the lower slopes of Mount Fuji.
You may imagine, my lord, that I speak this way only to alarm you, but not so.
As they say, what matters in war is less numbers than strategy.
For myself, I do not expect to survive this campaign and return to the capital."
The listening Heike warriors shook with fear.
     Then came the twenty-third of the tenth month.
     The initial exchange of arrows
     between the Heike and the Genji
     was to take place the very next morning,
     there beside the Fuji River.
Night fell. Looking out toward the Genji positions,
the Heike saw cooking fires lit by peasants from Izu and Suruga,
peasants who for fear of battle had fled either into the wilds
or onto boats now riding on the river or out at sea.
"Oh, no! Look at all those Genji fires!" the Heike warriors cried.
"Moor and mountain, rivers and seas, yes—the enemy is everywhere.
Oh, what are we to do?" They were terribly upset.
     In the middle of that same night,
     something startled the waterbirds

that in colossal flocks frequented
the Fuji marshes; suddenly
all rose with a beating of wings
like thunder or the roar of a storm.
"Heaven help us!" the Heike cried.
"Here come the Genji! He had it right,
Sanemori, when he told us
they'd be coming around at our rear.
We can't let ourselves be surrounded!
No, we have to escape from here
and dig in at the Owari River
and Sunomata!" With that they fled
pell-mell—too fast even to grab
their belongings. In the panic
one took his bow but forgot his arrows,
another his arrows but not the bow.
Some jumped onto others' horses;
some lost their own mounts the same way.

The disaster at the Fuji River.

Some leaped onto tethered steeds
and rode endlessly around in circles.
From nearby establishments they had called in, for their pleasure,
courtesans and singing girls, whose desperate screams now rent the air,
for some were having their heads kicked in, some their backs broken underfoot.
The next morning, the twenty-fourth,
at the hour of the hare, the Genji, [ca. 6 A.M.]
a full two hundred thousand strong,
bore down on the Fuji River
and thrice raised their great battle cry.
The heavens rang, and the earth shook.

12. *The Gosechi Dances*

From the Heike camp, dead silence. Yoritomo sent men to investigate. "They are all gone," he was told. Some brought back armor that the Heike had abandoned, others great curtains that had surrounded the enemy camp. "Not a fly buzzing in there," they reported.

Yoritomo dismounted. He removed his helmet, rinsed his mouth, and prostrated himself toward the capital. "I myself deserve no credit for what has happened," he declared. "All thanks are due Great Bodhisattva Hachiman." After so suddenly winning the day, he entrusted the province of Suruga to Ichijō no Jirō Tadayori and that of Tōtōmi to Yasuda no Saburō Yoshisada. He might well have pursued the Heike farther, but he remained anxious about his rear. He therefore withdrew from Ukishima-ga-hara and fell back to the province of Sagami.

The singing girls laughed and laughed in post stations all along the Tōkaidō.
"Talk about pathetic!" they cried. "The attacking commander
beats a retreat without shooting a single arrow? I can't believe it!
It's bad enough to flee an enemy you don't much like the look of,
but to run away just from a noise!" They could not get over it.
Lampoons appeared on every wall.
The supreme Heike commander in the capital was Lord Munemori,
and *mune* sounds like "ridgepole," *mori* like "warden";
moreover, Koremori held the "post" of Guards lieutenant.
So one lampoon played on these and also on *hiraya*, "one-floor house,"
since the same characters, read otherwise, mean "house of Taira."

Poor, low, one-floor house!
What despair must agitate
the ridgepole warden,

since the post he counted on
to prop him up has come down!

> *Frothing over rocks,*
> *the Fuji River waters*
> *   still run less nimbly*
> *than those Taira warriors*
> *running, running for their lives.*

Another lampoon alluded to Tadakiyo, governor of Kazusa,
abandoning his armor in the Fuji River.

> *In his armor went,*
> *into the Fuji River.*
> *   Yes, Tadakiyo,*
> *time to dress yourself in black*
> *and pray for the life to come.*

> *And so off he sped,*
> *hightailing it on his gray,*
> *   that Tadakiyo.*
> *A lot of good it did him,*
> *his crupper from Kazusa.*

On the eighth day of the eleventh month, the commander, Koremori,
arrived back up in the new capital of Fukuhara. Lord Kiyomori raged.
"Punitive-force commander and Guards lieutenant Koremori
shall be banished to Kikai-ga-shima," he announced.
"His field commander, Tadakiyo, the Kazusa governor, shall be executed."
On the ninth the Heike housemen, young and old, came together
to discuss whether Tadakiyo really deserved death.
One Taira no Morikuni, of the police, was among them.
"No one to my knowledge has ever called Tadakiyo fainthearted.
I believe he was in his eighteenth year
when two home-province desperadoes on the run holed up in the Toba
    Mansion's storehouse.
No one dared go in after them until Tadakiyo,
in broad daylight, leaped alone over the wall, burst in, killed one,
and captured the other. He will long be remembered for that.
I cannot imagine this lapse of his to be mere cowardice.
No, this rebellion is not something that we can afford to neglect."

> On the tenth, Koremori was promoted to captain in the Right Palace
> Guards. "He certainly didn't do much as the commander of the puni-
> tive force," people whispered among themselves. "What on earth are
> they rewarding him for?"

Long ago, when ordered to do so,
Taira no Sadamori and Tawara Tōda Hidesato marched to the Kanto
to suppress Masakado's rebellion, but success proved elusive,
and a council of senior nobles ordered the dispatch of a second force.
Fujiwara no Tadafun, lord of Civil Affairs, headed it with his deputy, Kiyowara
    no Shigefuji.
They camped one night at Kiyomi-ga-seki in Suruga.
There Shigefuji, looking out over the vast expanse of the sea,
    sang these lines from a Chinese poem:
      "Fires on the fishing boats, cold, burn the waves;
        bells on the post road sound through night mountains."
    Tadafun, impressed, shed admiring tears.
Meanwhile Sadamori and Hidesato disposed of Masakado at last.
They were on their way back up to the capital, their men bearing aloft
    Masakado's head,
when, there at Kiyomi-ga-seki, they met these two commanders.
Thereafter they all continued on toward the capital together.
When Sadamori and Hidesato received their rewards,
the senior nobles discussed the idea of rewarding Tadafun and Shigefuji as well.
The Kujō right minister Morosuke stated,
"The punitive force indeed went down to the Kanto,
but these two gentlemen followed by imperial order when Masakado put up stiff
    resistance.
They were almost there when the rebel was destroyed after all.
There is no reason not to reward them as well."
However, Fujiwara no Saneyori, the regent, observed,
"*The Book of Rites* advises, 'When in doubt, take no action.'" He forbade it.
    The outraged Tadafun swore this oath:
    "The descendants of Lord Saneyori
    shall be in my eyes as menials;
    the descendants of Lord Morosuke
    shall have my protection forever."
    So saying, he starved himself to death.
    Indeed, Morosuke's descendants
    went on to flourish exceedingly,
    while Saneyori's achieved nothing
    and no doubt have by now died out.
In the meantime Shigehira, Lord Kiyomori's fourth son,
became a captain in the Left Palace Guards.
On the thirteenth of the eleventh month, at Fukuhara,

the emperor moved into his newly built palace.
A Great Thanksgiving Rite should then have been held,
but His Majesty would then have had to proceed in the late tenth month
to the Kamo River for purification.

> For that they lay out a ritual space
> on open ground north of the palace,
> readying vestments and implements
> that priestly celebrants require.
> Next, beyond the Dragon-Tail Walk
> stretching before the Great Hall of State,
> they build a hall, the Kairyūden,
> in which His Majesty is to bathe.
> The Great Thanksgiving Sanctuary,
> built nearby, houses offerings
> made to the gods, and it is there
> His Majesty offers a sacred feast,
> followed by a pleasant concert.
> The heart of the rite then at last
> goes forward in the Great Hall of State.
> Afterward there is *kagura*
> in the Seishodō and a banquet,
> held for all in the Hōraku-in.
> At Fukuhara, unfortunately,
> there was no sign of a Great Hall of State,
> in fact nowhere to hold the key rite;
> no Seishodō, hence no way to perform
> *kagura*, and no Hōraku-in,
> so nowhere to offer the banquet.
> The senior nobles therefore decided
> this year to confine the observances
> to a Festival of First Fruits
> and to the Gosechi dances.
> Indeed, even this First Fruits Festival
> was held in the old capital,
> in the government's Bureau of Shrines.

> Now, the Gosechi dances began
> when the Kiyomibara Emperor,
> Tenmu, at his Yoshino Palace,
> one windy and brilliantly moonlit night,
> was taking pleasure in playing the *kin:*

An angel descended from heaven
and danced, turning her sleeves five times.
This was the first Gosechi dance of all.

13. *The Return to the Old Capital*

Emperor and subjects alike had deplored the move to Fukuhara.
Enryakuji on Mount Hiei and Kōfukuji in Nara, among many other temples and
    shrines,
had submitted on the issue formal expressions of dissent.
So it was that even Lord Kiyomori, who never honored any wish but his own,
gave in and ordered the return to the old capital.
Suddenly, on the second of the twelfth month, His Majesty was back.
        The new capital had sloped downward
        from the high hills that rose to the north
        to the sea that stretched south before it.
        The noise of the waves there was loud,
        and a strong wind constantly blew.
        No wonder His Eminence Takakura
        often felt very unwell there
        and left, when he could, in such haste.
                Regent, chancellor, senior nobles, privy gentlemen—all of them rushed
                to accompany him. Likewise all the ranking Heike nobles, Lord Kiyo-
                mori first among them, hastened up to the once-more-imperial city.
                Who would have stayed on a moment longer in dreary Fukuhara?
Earlier, in the sixth month of that year, they had demolished their houses
and transported to Fukuhara all the tools and materials needed
to put up new ones, of some sort or other,
but now this mad order to return told them all they needed to know.
They instantly dropped everything to start back up to the city.
        Not one of them had a place to live,
        so off they went to Yawata, Kamo,
        Saga, Uzumasa, and so on—
        any odd corner of the hills,
        western or eastern, where a temple
        might perhaps offer a gallery,
        a shrine, space in its pilgrim hall—
        and there great ladies and gentlemen
        sought refuge in what lodging they could.
What, then, explains that first decision to move the capital?
Nara and Mount Hiei were too close to the old one.

The slightest incident could provoke the Kasuga god tree[167]
or the sacred palanquins of Hiyoshi to pay a riotous visit.
Hills and sea, as well as distance, sheltered Fukuhara from such mishaps.
That, they say, must be what Lord Kiyomori had had in mind.

> On the twenty-third of the twelfth month,
> a Taira force of twenty thousand and more
> under Tomomori, the Left Watch intendant,
> and Tadanori, the Satsuma governor,
> set out to march into the province of Ōmi,
> to put down the Genji uprising there.
> One by one they crushed all local bands—
> Yamamoto, Kashiwagi, Nishigori—
> then crossed straight into Mino and Owari.

14. *The Burning of Nara*

As the authorities in the capital saw it,
the fact that the Nara temples had sided with Prince Mochihito
when he took refuge at Miidera, and had even come forward to welcome him,
made them enemies of the court.
In due course they proposed to attack both Miidera and Nara.
This threw the monks of the Nara temples into a violent uproar.
The regent solemnly assured them that should they have a grievance,
he would gladly apprise His Majesty of it as often as needed;
however, the monks ignored him.
Tadanari, among other things the director of the Kangaku-in,
was dispatched to them as an emissary.
"Drag him down from that conveyance of his!" they bellowed. "Cut off his
    topknot!"
He fled back to the city before they could get at him.
Next they sent Chikamasa, an officer of the Right Gate Watch.
"Cut off his topknot!" the monks bawled again.
He dropped everything and fled, too.
Two Kangaku-in servants lost their topknots that day.
Another of the monks' exploits was to make a big *mari* ball[168]
and call it Lord Kiyomori's head. "Hit it! Kick it!" they kept shouting.

167. Just as the Mount Hiei monks carried the sacred palanquins of their deities down into the capital in order to press a grievance (1:15), the monks of Kōfukuji invaded the city carrying the tree (*sakaki,* a broadleaf evergreen) sacred to the Kasuga Deity.
168. The ball used in the game of *kemari* ("kickball"). A circle of players kept the ball in the air as long as possible by kicking it high in the air.

"Loose talk brings trouble," people say.
"Watch your tongue or court perdition."
Lord Kiyomori was, after all—
awesome though the mere thought may be—
the reigning emperor's grandfather.
Carrying on like *that* about him,
the Nara monks sounded like devils.
Kiyomori got wind of all this. He could hardly approve.
Anxious to put an end immediately to the turmoil in Nara,
he appointed Seno-o no Tarō Kaneyasu, from Bitchū, to the Yamato provincial
    police.
Kaneyasu then set out for Nara with five hundred mounted men.
"Whatever mayhem the monks threaten," their orders said,
"do not for any reason respond in kind.
Wear no armor and carry no bows or arrows."
The monks, however, knew nothing of that.
They seized over sixty of Kaneyasu's men, one by one cut off their heads,
and exposed them all in a row beside Sarusawa Pond.
Kiyomori was furious. "Well then," he said, "attack Nara!"
The commander was Lord Shigehira, his deputy Lord Michimori.
The mounted force, over forty thousand strong, set out for the southern
    capital.

> Seven thousand monks, the old with the young,
> bound on their helmets and, at two places,
> Narazaka and Hannyaji,
> dug a deep trench across the road,
> built a wall of shields and an abatis,
> and lay in wait. Meanwhile the Taira
> split their forty thousand in two
> and rode down on these makeshift forts
> with deafening battle cries.
> The monks, all on foot, were armed with blades.
> The warriors galloped around and around them,
> harrying them one way, then another,
> showering them with volleys of arrows,
> killing countless defenders outright.
> The two sides traded opening arrows
> at the hour of the hare and fought all day. [ca. 6 A.M.]
> That night both fortified positions,
> Narazaka and Hannyaji, fell.
> One of the fleeing monks, a fierce fighter,

was Saka no Shirō Yōkaku.
In prowess with sword or bow, in strength,
no monk of the Seven Great Nara Temples
or Fifteen Great Temples compared with him.
Over close-fitting armor laced in green,
he wore outer armor with black lacing.
Five neck plates completed his helmet.
One hand gripped a plain halberd shaft,
the blade curved like a long grass frond,
the other a great sword, the hilt black-lacquered.
With a dozen or so men from his lodge,
he fought his way out the Tengai Gate,
to stand fast awhile, scything down
many enemies and their horses.
But the attackers just kept coming,
wave after wave, until the companions
once at Yōkaku's side were all dead.
Boundless courage he certainly had,
but with no one to cover his back,
he fled southward at great speed.

> They were fighting at night now. It was pitch dark. Shigehira, the Heike
> commander, stood at the gate of Hannyaji. "Start a fire," he ordered.
> One Tomokata, an estate official from Fukui in Harima, promptly split
> a shield to make a torch and set fire to a local's house.

This was the night of the twenty-eighth of the twelfth month.
A strong wind was blowing, and its erratic gusts soon carried the fire,
originally sprung from a single source, to many temples.
Those monks who felt shame and wished to be well remembered
had already met death at Narazaka or Hannyaji.
Others, who could still walk, had fled for Yoshino and Totsugawa.

> Ancient monks unable to walk,
> great scholars, cherished acolytes,
> women and children had fled pell-mell
> into the grounds of Kōfukuji.
> At Tōdaiji over a thousand people
> climbed to the second floor of the Great Buddha Hall
> and, lest the enemy follow them there,
> took up the ladders. Devouring fire
> swept straight into their huddled mass.
> Sinners burning in bottomless hell
> never uttered such hideous screams.

The burning of the Great Buddha of Tōdaiji.

Kōfukuji, founded by Lord Tankai,
is the Fujiwara ancestral temple.
The Shakyamuni in the East Golden Hall,
made in the earliest days of the Buddha's Teaching;
the Kanzeon in the West Golden Hall,
risen spontaneously from the earth;
the gallery, four-sided around its court,
gleaming as with rows of precious stones;
the imposingly lofty Two-Story Hall,
all brilliant vermilion and cinnabar;
the twin pagodas, topped by nine rings,
that rose, glittering, into the sky—
alas, every one went up in smoke.
For Tōdaiji, Emperor Shōmu conceived
an image of the everlasting,
indestructibly living Buddha
Roshana, made of gilt bronze,[169]
one hundred and sixty feet tall,
which he adorned with his own hands.
This Buddha's hair knot soared aloft,
disappearing into the clouds;
his noble full-moon countenance,
the white curl between his eyebrows,
inspired devotion ever renewed.
Now the head, melted, had fallen to earth;
the body had fused to a molten mound.
His eighty-four thousand perfections
were gone, as when the autumn moon
slides from sight behind fivefold clouds;
the ornaments of his enlightenment
now drifted on winds of the ten evils
like stars wandering the night sky.
Smoke filled the heavens. The sky was flame.
Eyewitnesses could not bear to look,
and those told the story fainted with horror.
The Hossō and Sanron holy scriptures,[170]

....

169. Roshana, the cosmic buddha associated with Kegon Buddhism and honored at Tōdaiji, corresponds to Mahāvairochana (Japanese: Dainichi), the cosmic buddha of Shingon (esoteric) Buddhism.

170. The Hossō and Sanron schools of Buddhism entered Japan from China in the eighth century, well before Shingon (Mount Kōya) and Tendai (Mount Hiei). The first was associated with Kōfukuji, the second with Tōdaiji.

down to the very last scroll, were gone.
In this land of ours, needless to say,
but equally in India or China,
no disaster approaching this one
can ever before have struck the Teaching.
Those statues made by King Udayana
from refined gold, by Vishvakarman
from red sandal were only life-size.
This Buddha, then, so unparalleled
in the whole realm of Jambudvīpa,
should clearly have lasted forever,
but he succumbed to the world's poisons,
leaving behind him eternal mourning.
Brahma, Indra, and the Four Kings,
the Dragon Gods, the Eight Guardian Tribes,
every denizen of the afterworld
could only experience shock and horror.
And how can the Kasuga God have felt,
who mounts guards over the Hossō doctrine?
The very dew on the Kasuga meadows
changed color, and bitter reproach
raged in the wind from Mount Mikasa.
      They recorded a careful count
of all those who had died in the flames:
on the Great Buddha Hall's upper floor,
one thousand seven hundred people;
eight hundred at Kōfukuji,
five hundred here, three hundred there:
three thousand five hundred in all.

> One thousand monks had died on the battlefield. The victors hung a
> few of their heads at the gate of Hannyaji and took a few more back to
> the city. On the twenty-ninth, having destroyed the southern capital,
> Shigehira returned northward. Lord Kiyomori alone indulged in
> vengeful rejoicing. The empress, Cloistered Emperor Go-Shirakawa,
> Retired Emperor Takakura, the regent and all below him lamented,
> saying, "Suppressing the warrior-monks was all very well, but did they
> really have to destroy the temples, too?"

The original plan had been to parade the monks' heads through the avenues,
then hang them on the trees in front of the prison, but that was unthinkable now.
The destruction of Tōdaiji and Kōfukuji was too great a disaster.
They just tossed the heads here and there into gutters and ditches.

"My mistress is a gentlewoman in the service of His Eminence," she
explained. "I was taking her a robe that was finally ready when, just a
moment ago, two or three men turned up, robbed me of it, and ran off.
My mistress cannot appear in His Eminence's residence without it,
and she has no one close to her to give her proper lodging. That is what
is making me cry."

They took the girl back with them and reported the matter.
His Majesty listened. "How awful!" he said.
"What kind of brutes could have done that?

People in the reign of Yao
were honest, for Yao at heart
put honesty before all else;
but such, in the present reign,
is my own heart, that warped men
roam abroad and commit crimes.
Am I not to blush with shame?"
So he spoke. Then he inquired,
"What color was the robe they took?"
The girl named the color.

This happened in the days when Kenreimon-in was still empress.
His Majesty asked her whether she had a robe of that color,
and she sent back one far more beautiful than the first.
He had it given to the girl.

"It is still the dead of night.
That might happen to you again,"
he said, and assigned a guard
to see her to her mistress's.
Such was his imperial kindness.
That is why his meanest subject,
man or woman, prayed for him
to live on ten thousand years.

3. Aoi

The most touching of all the stories about him
involved the maid of a gentlewoman in the empress's service.
This young woman became unusually intimate with her sovereign.
Theirs was no common, fleeting affair.
His Majesty called on her constantly to be with him.
So serious was his feeling for her that her mistress, the gentlewoman,
less employed her than honored her as though the maid were *she*.

"There used to be a song that ran,
'Do not lament the birth of a daughter;
do not applaud the birth of a son.
A son may never gain a fief;
a daughter may rise to be empress.'"
The subject of these lines, they say, did precisely that.

"Consort or even empress, yes,
she may be in time, that one;
and then, perhaps, revered—who knows?—
as dowager, mother of the realm!
What incredible good fortune!"
So people were fond of saying,
and, her name being Aoi-no-mae,
they secretly dubbed her "Empress Aoi."

The emperor gave up calling her to his side when he heard. Not that he no longer loved her; he only wished to avoid evil talk. Thereafter he spent all his time in his bedroom, lost in melancholy.

Lord Motofusa, the current regent, pitied him and hastened to the palace to lighten his mood. "If she means this much to you, Your Majesty, then there is a perfectly good solution," he said. "In my opinion you should summon her immediately. Never mind her rank. I undertake to adopt her without delay."

The emperor replied, "I wonder. That is a good idea, but as far as I can see, there is no precedent for it until I have retired from the throne. For me to summon her while I still reign would ruin my reputation for generations to come." He declined to summon her. The regent could only restrain his tears and withdraw.

This old poem then came to the emperor's mind. He set it down on thin, deep green paper.

Studiously concealed
passion will out after all:
I so long for you,
people are asking me now,
Could it be you are in love?

These words that had come to his brush,
he had Lieutenant Takafusa
take to the lady without delay.
She blushed and then, feeling unwell,
so she said, left to go home.
There she confined herself to bed
and, five or six days later, died.

he called out for an attendant,
but none was there to answer him.
That night there chanced to be on duty,
stationed at a distance from him,
a young official named Nakakuni.
"Nakakuni, at your service,"
this man called back. The emperor answered,
"Come here. I have a question for you."
Wondering what it could be,
Nakakuni approached the presence.
"Do you happen to know," the emperor asked, "where Kogō has gone?"
"How could I, Your Majesty?" Nakakuni replied.
"I cannot vouch for its being true, but I gather from what people say
that Kogō is now in Saga, behind a gate with just a single door.
Would you go and find her for me, without knowing whose house it is?"
"How could I, Your Majesty, unless I know who owns the house?"
"No, of course, you couldn't, could you?"
The imperial visage glistened with tears.

Nakakuni thought it over some more.
"Why, yes! Kogō plays the koto!
On such a beautifully moonlit night,
she cannot fail to be making music
in fond memory of her lord!
I myself have been called on sometimes
to accompany her on the flute—
I would know her touch anywhere!

There can't be *that* many houses in Saga. I'm bound to hear her music sooner or later, if I have a good look around." So he reflected.

"Very well, Your Majesty," he said, "I shall go and do my best to find her, even without knowing whose house she is in. If I do find her, though, she will probably not believe me unless I bring her a letter from you. I hope that I may take one with me."

The emperor saw that Nakakuni was right. He wrote the letter and gave it to him.

"Take a horse from the imperial stables," His Majesty said.
Nakakuni did so and set off, whip raised high under the bright moon,
to follow through on his meandering search.

"A village far into the hills,
where the stag bells." So the poet
once described Saga, and Nakakuni
felt its autumnal melancholy.

Whenever he came across a house
with such a gate, he stopped to listen
discreetly for some sign of her
but heard no one playing the koto.
"Perhaps," he thought, "she has devoutly
gone to visit the Shakadō,"[174]
so he went there, and he looked in
at many other temples, too,
but nowhere found any gentlewoman
resembling in the least Kogō.
"Rather than go back empty-handed,
better not to go back at all."
So Nakakuni said to himself.
"If I could, I would wander on
wherever the path I take might lead,
but everywhere is the sovereign's realm,
and no refuge could hide me for long.
Then what in the world am I to do?
Ah, yes! Hōrinji is not far off.
Perhaps the moonlight has drawn her there."
Nakakuni set off that way.

   He was approaching Kameyama
when, from near a grove of pines,
he made out faint koto music.
Wind on high, wind sighing through pines,
or perhaps that lady's koto?
He urged his mount on, and there it was:
the one-door gate and, from within,
the clear music of a koto.
From a safe distance, he lent an ear:
No, there was no mistaking now
Kogō's distinctive touch on the strings.
And what was it that she was playing?
"I Love Him So," a woman's song
of poignant longing for her lover.
"Sure enough," he said to himself, "she is thinking of our sovereign.
Of all the pieces she might have played, how sad that she should choose this
   one!"
Marveling at this stroke of fortune, he took out his flute, played a little,

....

174. A great temple in the Saga area, west of the capital.

Nakakuni hears Kogō's music.

and rapped smartly at the gate.

The music stopped. He called out,

"Nakakuni is my name.

I am here from His Majesty.

Please have someone open the gate!"

He knocked and knocked, to no effect.

Eventually, to his relief, he heard somebody emerge. He waited breathlessly.

The latch lifted, the gate cracked open, and a pretty little gentlewoman peeked out. "You must have the wrong house," she said. "No one here would be expecting a message from the palace."

Fearing that an inadequate answer might encourage her to close and lock the gate again, Nakakuni thrust it open, entered, and sat down on the veranda near the double doors.

"What can have possessed you, to move to such a place?" he began. "There may be reason to fear for His Majesty's life, the way he is pining for you. Perhaps you imagine that this is a fancy of mine, but I bring you a letter from him." He took it out and had the little gentlewoman give it to Kogō.

Kogō unfolded it and read it:

It really was from the emperor.

Immediately she wrote a reply
and sent it out with a set of robes
suitable for a gentlewoman.
With those robes over his shoulder,[175]
Nakakuni ventured to say,
"No other messenger, I am sure,
would wish to add anything more
after receiving your reply,
but can you really have forgotten
how, when you used to play in the palace,
I was called in for the flute part?
I would be sorry now to start back
without hearing a word in your voice."
Kogō must have understood how he felt, for she answered him in person.
"As you have probably heard, Lord Kiyomori made such frightening threats
that I fled the palace in terror when news of them reached me.
Living here lately has kept me from making music,
but I cannot remain here forever.
No, there is a step I mean to take tomorrow, out beyond Ōhara,
and the gentlewoman with whom I am staying begged me
to play for her once, tonight, before I go.
'It is late now,' she said. 'No one will be out there to stop and listen.'
        And yes, I so missed all I had left
        that I did play my dear old koto,
        and you knew my touch right away."
        She could not keep her tears from flowing,
        and Nakakuni, too, wet his sleeves.
In time Nakakuni swallowed his tears.
"A step that you plan to take tomorrow, beyond Ōhara—
you must mean that you will become a nun.
No, no, you cannot do that! Just imagine His Majesty's misery!"
And to the two grooms he had with him: "Do not allow her to leave!"
He left them there
        to mount guard over the house
        and rode off, back to the palace.
        He arrived under a lightening sky.
        "Surely His Majesty is asleep,"
he said to himself. "Whom can I ask to take him the news?"

....

175. The custom was to reward a messenger by draping a gift of clothing over his shoulder.

He had the horse he had ridden tethered—the one from the imperial stables—
tossed the gift set of woman's robes over the Prancing Horse partition,
and presented himself at the sovereign's residence.
The emperor was still in the same room as the evening before.

     He was murmuring these Chinese lines:
"'Southward they soar and northward fly,
yet autumn geese will bear for me no news of heat or cold.
Up from the east it rises and runs to the west,
but the dawn moon accepts only my gaze as my thoughts follow.'"

      Nakakuni came in upon him and told him about Kogō. His Majesty
      was deeply stirred. "Bring her to me tonight," he commanded.
Nakakuni feared the consequences if Lord Kiyomori ever found out,
but the emperor had spoken. He readied a handsome equipage—
attendants, ox driver, ox, and carriage—and set out for Saga. Kogō cited
many reasons not to obey, but in one way and another he persuaded her to
change her mind. She boarded the carriage and arrived at the palace,
where His Majesty lodged her well out of sight. He had her come to him
every night, and in time she bore him the princess known later on as
Bōmon-in.
Somehow Lord Kiyomori learned after all what was going on.
"They told me Kogō was gone," he said, "but that was a blatant lie."
He seized her, made her a nun, and banished her from the capital.
She had long wanted to leave the world, but not this way, under duress.
In her twenty-third year, in deep black robes, she came to live in Saga.
Her fate was cruel. This, they say, is the sort of thing
that destroyed the emperor's health and led at last to his death.

     Cloistered Emperor Go-Shirakawa
     had suffered a succession of blows,
     having lost Emperor Nijō,
     his eldest son, in the Eiman years [1165-66]
     and Emperor Rokujō, his grandson,
     in the seventh month of Angen 2. [1176]
     Next, his empress, Kenshunmon-in,
     to whom he had so solemnly sworn
     by the stars, above in the River of Heaven,
     that they would share one wing in flight
     and on earth their spreading branches—
     stricken as though by autumn vapors,
     she had vanished like morning dew.
     Since then years and months had passed,
     but these partings remained for him

as fresh as yesterday or today,
and his tears never ceased to flow.
Then, in the fifth month of Jishō 4, [1180]
his next son, Prince Mochihito, was slain,
and now Retired Emperor Takakura,
his last hope for this life and the next,
had gone before him into death.
Speechless with grief, he could only weep.
"'Bitter among all bitter blows
is losing a son in advanced age.
Painful among all miseries
is to die young, before mother and father.'"
These words of Lord Tomotsuna,
when his son, Sumiakira, died,
now spoke to His Cloistered Eminence
with the plain force of simple truth.
Even so, he never neglected
reading aloud the Lotus Sutra
and practicing the Three Mysteries,[176]
which gained him a vast store of merit.
Now that the whole realm was in mourning,
the court set aside its brilliant colors
to favor instead more somber hues.

5. *The Circular Letter*

Fearing after all the sheer cruelty of his conduct,
Lord Kiyomori sought to mollify His Cloistered Eminence
by giving him his daughter by the Itsukushima Shrine maiden in Aki:
a sweet and lovely girl now in her eighteenth year.
She went attended by many ranking gentlewomen, carefully chosen,
and accompanied by a throng of senior nobles and privy gentlemen,
just as a consort does when she enters the palace.
This was less than fourteen days after the retired emperor's passing,
and people whispered disapprovingly among themselves.
     Meanwhile talk began going around
     of one Kiso no Yoshinaka,
     a Minamoto in Shinano province.
          Yoshinaka's father was Yoshikata, a commander of the heir apparent's

....
176. The Shingon (esoteric) mysteries of body (mudra), speech (mantra), and mind (meditation).

corps of guards and the second son of Tameyoshi. He was in his
second year when, on the twenty-sixth of the eighth month of
Kyūju 2, [1155] Yoshikata died by the hand of Akugenda Yoshihira, of
Kamakura. His weeping mother took him to Shinano, where she
sought refuge with Kiso no Chūzō Kanetō. She begged Kanetō to
bring up her son and make a man of him. Kanetō agreed to do so, and
he fully upheld his promise for twenty years and more.

Young Yoshinaka, as he grew,
displayed quite remarkable strength
and bold courage beyond compare.
"What a bow he draws! What a fighter!"
people exclaimed among themselves.
"Whether on horseback or on foot,
he surely equals in every way
Tamuramaro in days of old
or Toshihito, Koremochi,
Tomoyori, Yasumasa,
or those forebears of his own,
Yorimitsu or Lord Yoshiie!"

One day Yoshinaka summoned his guardian, Kanetō, and said,
"Word has it that Yoritomo has raised rebellion
and subjugated the eight provinces of the Kanto
and that he is now moving on the capital by the Tōkaidō route,
aiming to overthrow the Heike.
Well, I have a mind to seize the Tōsen and Hokuroku provinces,
destroy the Heike just before he does,
and get myself known as one of Japan's two great commanders."
Such was the goal he suggested. Kanetō was pleased and impressed.
"That is just what I brought you up for!" he exclaimed.
"Now you are really talking like a descendant of Yoshiie!"
He set himself immediately to the task of planning rebellion.

In Kanetō's company, Yoshinaka had been up to the capital often,
to learn something of what the Heike were like and how they lived.
When he came of age in his thirteenth year, he went on pilgrimage to
    Iwashimizu
and declared there, before Great Bodhisattva Hachiman,
"My great-grandfather, Lord Yoshiie, became your son
and took the name Hachimantarō. Now I follow in his footsteps."
Before Hachiman's sanctuary he first tied his hair into a man's topknot
and assumed the name Kiso no Jirō Yoshinaka.

"The first thing to do," said Kanetō,

"is to send around a circular letter."
In Shinano he had a few words
with Nenoi no Koyata
and Unno no Yukichika,
neither of whom turned him away.
They were the first, and after them
every last warrior in Shinano
assented as leaves bow to the wind.
In Kōzuke the fighting men
of Tago county, glad to honor
their old bond with Yoshikata,
rallied, every one, to the call.
Yes, the Heike were finished.
Now was the time for the Genji
to achieve their long-cherished goal.

6. The Couriers

Kiso is a region in southern Shinano province,
on the Mino border and so quite close to the capital.
The Heike got wind of what was going on.
"The eastern provinces are rebelling!" they cried.
"And now the north, too? What are we to do?"
Lord Kiyomori declared, "Yoshinaka does not worry me.
He may have all the Shinano warriors behind him,
but for us, in Echigo, we have the descendants of Koremochi:
Jō no Tarō Sukenaga and Jō no Shirō Sukemochi.
These two brothers command a great many men.
They will soon dispose of him, at a word from His Majesty."
"I wonder, I just wonder," people murmured among themselves.
On the first day of the second month, Lord Kiyomori appointed Jō no
Tarō Sukenaga, from Echigo, to govern that province. Apparently this
measure had to do with his plan to kill Yoshinaka. On the seventh the
ministerial and lesser noble houses dedicated copies of the *Sonshō
darani* and pictures of Mantra King Fudō. They did so to dispel the
threat of war.
On the ninth came the news that Musashi Gon-no-kami Yoshimoto,
of Ishikawa county in Kawachi province, with his son Yoshikane,
had turned against the Heike and reached an understanding with Yoritomo
and that he was planning to flee toward the east.
Lord Kiyomori at once sent a punitive force against him

under Gendayū Suekata and Settsu no Hangan Morizumi.
They set out at the head of three thousand horse.

> In their fort Yoshimoto and his son
> had no more than a hundred men.
> The besiegers uttered their battle cry,
> started the opening arrow exchange,
> and for hours attacked in waves.
> Within, the defenders fought desperately.
> Most were killed, Yoshimoto among them.
> Yoshikane, badly wounded, was taken alive.

On the eleventh, Yoshimoto's head reached the capital,
where it was paraded along the great avenues.
There was a precedent for this in a time of imperial mourning:
The head of Minamoto no Yoshichika, once governor of Tsushima,
had been paraded likewise through the streets after Emperor Horikawa
    died.
On the twelfth a courier arrived from Kyushu:
Kinmichi, the chief priest of the Usa Shrine,
reported that Ogata no Saburō and everyone else in Kyushu,
even to the Usuki, the Betsugi, and the Matsura leagues,
had turned against the Heike and were now Genji allies.
"First the east and north and now this?" the Heike cried out in alarm.
"Oh, what are we going to do?"

> On the sixteenth, from Iyo province,
> another courier brought further news.
> The winter before, Kawano no Shirō Michikiyo
> and every man in Shikoku had spurned the Heike
> to make common cause with the Genji,
> whereupon the Nuka novice, Saijaku of Bingo,
> a dedicated Heike ally, charged over into Iyo
> and killed Michikiyo at the fortress of Takanō.
> Michikiyo's son, Michinobu, was away at the time
> in Aki, visiting his maternal uncle, Nuta no Jirō.
> Michinobu's loss fired him with hatred for Saijaku.
> "I'll get that man somehow or other," he resolved,
> and awaited a chance to do so. Meanwhile Saijaku,
> having dispatched Michikiyo and subdued Shikoku,
> this year on the fifteenth of the first month
> crossed to the harbor of Tomo in Bingo province,
> where he drank and caroused with a crowd of singing girls.
> While he lay there drunk, dead to the world,

Michinobu burst in with a hundred resolute men.
Saijaku had three hundred with him, but the sudden assault
threw them into confusion. Arrow and sword
quickly ended any resistance. Michinobu took him alive,
raced back to Iyo, marched to the Takanō fortress
where his father had met his death, and there,
with a saw, decapitated the man.
Others claim that he crucified him.

7. The Death of Kiyomori

After that, every man in Shikoku followed Kawano Michikiyo.
Word had it that even the Kumano superintendent Tanzō,
although deeply beholden to the Heike,
had turned against them and joined the Genji.
All the eastern and northern provinces were in a state of rebellion,
and so, too, those to the south and west.
News of barbarian uprisings beat upon the ears;
the emperor received constant reports of incidents announcing revolt.
The enemy menace rose up on every side.
To the intense distress of all—not the Heike alone, but anyone of feeling—
the world as people had known it seemed doomed.
   On the twenty-third, the senior nobles met in council.
Lord Munemori observed that the force dispatched to the Kanto had achieved
   little.
"I recommend sending another," he said, "this time under my command."
"That would be splendid!" the assembly flatteringly responded.
His Cloistered Eminence issued a decree:
All senior nobles and privy gentlemen holding military office
and with knowledge of arms were to join a force under Munemori,
in order to suppress the rebels in the provinces of east and north.
On the twenty-seventh, Lord Munemori was due to set forth
on his punitive campaign against the Genji in the east,
but he delayed his departure because Lord Kiyomori was unwell.
   The next day, the twenty-eighth, Kiyomori's condition was grave.
"This is it, then," people whispered at Rokuhara and throughout the city.

> From the very first day of Lord Kiyomori's illness, nothing passed his
> lips, not even water, and his body burned like fire. The heat within
> twenty-five or thirty feet of where he lay was unbearable. His only
> words were "Hot! Hot!" This was clearly no common affliction. When
> he stepped down into a stone basin filled with water from the Senju

spring on Mount Hiei, to cool himself, the water bubbled furiously
around him and soon boiled.

Water sprayed on him from a bamboo pipe, to give him relief,
recoiled as though from hot stone or iron and never reached him.
What water did touch him turned to fire.
Black smoke filled the room, and flames swirled high in the air.

> Perhaps Reverend Hōzō, long ago,
> saw something similar when he went,
> at the invitation of King Enma,
> to find where his mother had been reborn.
> King Enma, moved to compassion,
> gave him an escort of hell minions,
> who guided him to the hell of fierce heat.
> Once through the iron gate, Hōzō saw
> flames darting skyward like shooting stars,
> several hundred *yojanas*[177] high.
> The spectacle now was similar.

Lord Kiyomori's wife, Lady Nii, had a terrifying dream.
A fiercely burning carriage drove in through the gate,
escorted before and behind by beings with the heads of horses or oxen.
The front of the carriage displayed, on an iron tablet, the single character *mu*.
Lady Nii asked in the dream what to make of this.
"We have come from King Enma's court," she was told, "to receive Lord
   Kiyomori."
"What does that iron tablet mean?"
"For the crime of burning the sixteen-foot, gilt-bronze Roshana
on Jambudvīpa, the southern continent of men,
King Enma has sentenced Kiyomori to the depths of Muken,
the hell of unbroken agony. The *mu* is written, but not yet the *ken*."
Dripping with perspiration, the astonished Lady Nii related her dream,
and the hair rose on all those who heard her.

> To holy temples and holy shrines
> they offered with reckless abandon
> gold and silver, the seven treasures,
> even horses, saddles, and armor,
> bows and arrows, swords and daggers,
> together with their fervent prayers,
> but none of this made any difference.
> Lord Kiyomori's sons and daughters

---

177. A unit of distance, of uncertain length, often mentioned in the Buddhist scriptures.

gathered at their father's bedside,
bewildered and deeply distressed,
but no sign offered any hope.

On the second of the intercalary second month,[178] Lady Nii braved the terrible heat to approach her husband's pillow and address him, weeping. "My despair grows daily at the sight of you," she said. "If you still desire anything in this life, please, when your mind clears a little, tell me what it is."

Lord Kiyomori, once so forbidding, managed to whisper painfully under his breath, "In Hōgen, Heiji, and after, I subdued repeated uprisings against the court, received rewards beyond my station, and enjoyed the great good fortune of becoming chancellor and an emperor's grandfather. My children and grandchildren prosper, and in this life I have no further ambition. But there is one thing that I still desire. I cannot rest because I have not yet seen the head of the Izu exile, Yoritomo.

Never mind building me temples and pagodas,
never mind pious prayers for me once I am gone.
No, I want Yoritomo's head off and hung before my grave.
That is the only commemoration I wish."
What profoundly sinful words!
On the fourth his torment was such that, as a last resort,
he lay down on a board dripping with water. It did not help.
He writhed in agony, gasping for breath, and finally died in convulsions.

The din of horses and carriages
dashing madly hither and yon
rang through the heavens and shook the earth.
No sovereign's fate, no emperor's end
could have provoked a greater uproar.
This year had been his sixty-fourth—
not yet time to die of old age,
but all at once his destined span
was over. No sumptuous litanies,
no secret rites could help him now.
The glory of the gods and buddhas
vanished for him, the heavenly powers
withdrew all further protection.
What, then, could any mortal do?

....

178. Because the lunar calendar slowly fell behind the movement of the sun, it was necessary in some years to insert an intercalary (supplementary) month that repeated the number of the month preceding it.

Warriors by the tens of thousands,
each loyally ready to die for him,
surrounded him in ranks, high and low,
but not for one moment could they repel
the murderous demons of transience
invisible, irresistible.
To the great mountain at death's gate,
whence none return, to that river
the dead cross, over three fords;
to the Yellow Springs, to the bardo
he set off without doubt all alone.
Only his many crimes, new and old,
came forth to meet him as hell fiends.
There is good reason to pity him.
In any case, there was more to do.
On the seventh, at Otagi,
the funeral pyre turned him to smoke.
Reverend Enjitsu hung the bones
around his neck, went down to Settsu,
and buried them on Kyō-no-shima.
He whose fame had so resounded
the whole length and breadth of Japan,
who had wielded colossal power,
Kiyomori, in an instant
floated as smoke into the sky
over the city, while the remains
mingled soon with the sands of the shore,
and all he had been returned to earth.

8. Sutra Island

Strange things happened the night of the funeral.
The Nishi-Hachijō Mansion, lavishly adorned with gold, silver, and jade,
suddenly burned to the ground.
Houses burn often enough, it is true, but this was a great disaster.
Rumor spoke of arson, but who could have done it?
And that same night, south of Rokuhara,
twenty or thirty people—if indeed they were human at all—
were heard singing, "Ah, the lovely waters, roaring, the great waterfall . . ."
together with sounds of dancing and gusts of laughter.

Retired Emperor Takakura's passing in the first month of that year had

begun a time of national mourning, and only a month or two later
Lord Kiyomori, too, had died. How could the meanest peasant, man or
woman, not grieve? The Heike warriors judged that such hilarity must
issue from *tengu,* and a hundred of their hot-blooded youths went
after the laughing voices.

They came to His Cloistered Eminence's Hōjūji residence, deserted
these two or three years except for a caretaker, one Motomune, once a
Bizen provincial official. Twenty or thirty of Motomune's friends had
gathered to drink under cover of night. Given the circumstances, they
began by heeding a warning not to make any noise, but then they got
drunk and started dancing.

The young warriors burst in, seized every drunken reveler (thirty in all),
marched them to Rokuhara,
and lined them up in the court before Lord Munemori.
Munemori inquired into what had been going on and then declared,
"It would not be right to behead men as drunk as these."
He let them all go.

After a death the simplest people,
morning and evening, ring the bell,
performing the usual liturgies
to Amida and the Lotus Sutra,
but, Kiyomori's funeral over,
there were no alms or offerings.
The sole concern, morning or evening,
was battle tactics and strategy.
Lord Kiyomori had indeed suffered appallingly as he died,
but much about him showed that he was no ordinary man.
When he went on pilgrimage to the Hiyoshi Shrine,
Heike and other senior nobles accompanied him in such numbers
that—people said—not even a newly appointed regent
on his Kasuga pilgrimage or his first visit to Uji
could conceivably have gone with a more impressive train.

Marvelous, though, beyond all else
was the island of Kyō-no-shima,
which he built off Fukuhara
and which even in our own time
keeps the shipping there from harm.
Construction of this island began early in the second month of Ōhō 1, [1161]
but in the eighth month of that year typhoon-driven waves
swept away all the work done so far.
Late in the third month of Ōhō 3,

Kiyomori boiling. Top left: Lady Nii's dream of hell fiends.

Awa no Minbu Shigeyoshi
received the commission to start again.
In their council the senior nobles
proposed securing the foundations
by means of a living sacrifice,[179]
but that was judged too great a sin.
Instead they wrote the words of the sutras,
all of them, on the building stones—
hence the name Kyō-no-shima:
"Sutra Island."

9. Jishinbō

Old men claimed that Lord Kiyomori, however evil his reputation,
was really the great Buddhist master Jie[180] reborn. And this is why:
In the province of Settsu, there stands a mountain temple named Seichōji.
The head priest there, Jishinbō Son'e, once a scholar monk on Mount Hiei,
for many years had been an ardent devotee of the Lotus.
The spirit had moved him to leave the Mountain and come to this temple,
where over time he won all who knew him to faith.
At the hour of the ox on the night of the twenty-second, in the twelfth month of
    Shōan 2, [1172, ca. 2 A.M.]
he was leaning on his armrest, reading the Lotus Sutra,
when between dream and waking he saw a man of fifty or so,
in white pilgrim garb, tall lacquered hat, straw sandals, and gaiters,
approach him bearing a formal letter.
"Where do you come from?" Son'e asked.
"From the palace of King Enma. I bring you a message from him."
The figure gave Son'e the letter. Son'e opened it and read:

> SUMMONS
> To: Jinshinbō Son'e of Seichōji
> Settsu province, Japan
> Continent of Jambudvīpa
> From: Court of King Enma
> Date: Shōan 2, twelfth month, twenty-second day
> Notification: On the twenty-sixth next, in the Great Hall of State at
> the Citadel of King Enma, a hundred thousand gathered devotees of the

....

179. It seems to have been customary in Japanese antiquity to bury a person alive as a "human pillar" (*hitobashira*) in order to ensure success when constructing a bridge or harbor.

180. Ryōgen (912–85), the eighteenth abbot of Mount Hiei and a major figure in its history.

Lotus *are to chant the key passages of the sutra. Your presence is there-*
fore required. King Enma so decrees.
That is what Son'e saw written.
He could not decline the invitation.
Willy-nilly, he wrote a note of acceptance and then woke up.
Since as far as he knew he was dying, he told Kōyōbō, the temple abbot, the
  story.
Everyone who heard it marveled.
With his voice Son'e called Amida's Name
and in his heart prayed for Amida's welcome to paradise.
The night of the twenty-fifth soon came.
Son'e installed himself before his altar as usual,
leaning on his armrest while calling the Name and reciting the sutra.
At the hour of the rat, he felt so sleepy that he retired to his room and lay
  down. [midnight]
At the hour of the ox, two demon figures arrived, as before dressed in white.
"Hurry," they said, "you are to come with us."
    For him to ignore Enma's summons
    would be to risk dire consequences.
    Should he agree to go with them, though,
    he lacked the proper stole and bowl.
    While he was thinking all this over,
    the stole he required, of its own accord,
    settled lightly over his shoulders,
    and a golden bowl came down from the sky.
    Two sturdy attendants, two acolytes,
    ten junior monks, and a great carriage
    compounded of the seven treasures
    appeared before the gate of the temple.
    Son'e, transported with delight,
    boarded the carriage without delay.
    His equipage soared into the heavens,
    bound away toward the northwest,
    and swiftly reached King Enma's palace.
    Son'e saw walls stretching afar,
    a vast expanse of ground within them,
    and rising from it a Great Hall of State
    built wholly of precious substances.
The services for that day being over, the invited monks were leaving again
when Son'e stopped at the middle gate on the south side
and contemplated the prospect that the Great Hall offered.

He saw the officials of Enma's court bow low before their pious king.
"How extraordinary that I should be here!" he said to himself.
"I will go and inquire respectfully about my life to come."
So he approached the Great Hall of State.

> His two attendants meanwhile
> lifted umbrellas over his head,
> his two acolytes each bore a chest,
> and the ten others trailed behind him.
> So it was that in slow procession
> they approached the great edifice.
> King Enma descended the broad steps,
> amid a throng of his officials,
> to greet his guest. The two attendants
> now revealed themselves in truth
> as Tamon and Jikoku, the acolytes
> as the bodhisattvas Yakuō and Yuze,
> and the ten lesser monks as the ten
> demonesses who guard the Sutra.
> These followed and waited upon Son'e.

"All of the other monks have gone," King Enma began.
"Why, then, reverend sir, have you come?"
"I wish to know where I am next to be born."
"But rebirth in paradise, or not, depends solely on whether or not you believe."

> Enma gave an official this order:
> "A document box containing the record
> of this monk's numerous good deeds
> rests in the southern treasury.
> Go, bring it here, and let him see
> all that he has achieved in this life
> and all he has done to inspire others."
> Obediently the official addressed
> set off to the southern treasury,
> carried back the box described,
> opened it, and read out the contents.

Son'e groaned and wept, saying, "I beg you for only one thing:
Have pity on me and teach me the way to reach freedom from birth and death!
Show me the straight path to certain enlightenment!"
Compassionately King Enma then preached some lines of sacred verse.
The official dipped his brush and wrote them down:

> "Wife, children, throne, wealth, and followers—
> none of these stays by a man after death.

With him go only his karmic crimes,
which bind him in screaming pain forever."
King Enma delivered himself of this verse, then entrusted it to Son'e.
Overjoyed, Son'e remarked, "The chief minister who governs Japan
chose, on Cape Wada in Settsu province, a square twenty-five-acre plot
that he covered with lodges. Then, just as you have done today,
gathering here one hundred thousand Lotus devotees,
he filled each lodge with votaries of the sutra, had it expounded,
and saw to it that each litany was perfectly performed."
King Enma wept with joy and admiration.
"He is no ordinary man," he said.
"No, he is a manifestation of the great teacher Jie,
reborn in Japan to assure protection for the Tendai teaching.
Therefore I recite three times each day certain lines in his praise.
I want you to give them to him."

"I bow before the great teacher Jie,
protector of the Tendai teaching,
now manifest as a great general
so as by evil to lead all to good."
Son'e accepted the paper bearing these lines.

Ten warriors awaited him when he left again by the same middle gate.
They helped him into his carriage and escorted him, before and be-
hind. The carriage flew once more through the air and brought him
home. He began to breathe again, feeling as though he had dreamed.
He then repaired to Nishi-Hachijō, where he presented the paper to
Lord Kiyomori. Kiyomori, thoroughly pleased, entertained him, re-
warded him generously, and in token of his appreciation promoted
him to master of discipline.
And that is how people discovered
that Lord Kiyomori was a reincarnation of the great Jie.

10. The Gion Consort

There were those, too, for whom Lord Kiyomori was not Tadamori's son
but rather the son of Retired Emperor Shirakawa.
This is the story:
Back in the Eikyū years, there was a highly favored lady known as the Gion
Consort. [1113-18]
She was originally a gentlewoman,
and she lived in the Gion district, below the Eastern Hills.
Retired Emperor Shirakawa called on her frequently.

Once he was secretly on his way there,
escorted by one or two privy gentlemen and a few of his guards.
The twentieth day of the fifth month had passed, and night had fallen.
It was too dark to see anything much up ahead,
and besides, it was raining. The gloom was impenetrable.
Now, a chapel stood not far from this gentlewoman's house,
and there appeared next to this chapel some sort of creature, shining.

> The creature's head glittered and gleamed
> as though it sprouted silver needles.
> It had its two hands (if they *were* hands)
> lifted high; one, it seemed, held a mallet,
> the other something that gave off light.

> > Sovereign and escort together cried out in fear and surprise.
> > > "That's scary!"
> > > "I'd say it's a real demon!"
> > > "That must be the treasure mallet, that thing it's holding!"
> > > "Oh, what are we to do?"

From among the escort, His Eminence summoned Tadamori, who at the time was still a junior member of his guard. "I believe that you are the man I need," he said. "Will you shoot that creature for me or stop it with your sword?"

Tadamori dutifully started toward it, meanwhile reflecting, "It really doesn't look that powerful—it's probably just a fox or a badger. I'd hate to shoot it or run it through with my sword. No, I'll take it alive." So he kept going.

The light flared and dimmed, flared and dimmed two or three times.
Tadamori raced up and grasped the creature as hard as he could.
"What's going on?" an agitated voice cried. It was no monster, but a man.
The whole party then lit torches to get a good look at him.
They saw a monk of sixty or so—namely, the one in charge of the chapel.
He had been on his way to replenish the lamps on the altar,
with a jug of oil in one hand and, in the other, a lamp in an earthen dish.
It was pouring rain, so to avoid getting wet
he had tied wheat straw into a bundle to wear on his head as a hat.
The straw stalks gleamed like silver needles in the light of the flame.
Now they understood everything.

> "Why, it would have been just awful
> if he had shot or stabbed the fellow!
> Tadamori showed superb judgment—
> just what one wants in a warrior."
> Such were His Eminence's thoughts,

Tadamori and the mysterious creature.

> and he rewarded Tadamori
> by giving him, for his very own,
> the gentlewoman he loved so well,
> known to all as the Gion Consort.
> Now, at the time she was carrying
> the retired emperor's child.
> He said, "If she gives birth to a girl,
> then that girl will be my daughter;
> but if she happens to bear a boy,
> Tadamori, that boy will be yours,
> to bring up in the profession of arms."
> And she did indeed give birth to a son.

Tadamori meant to report the event, but he sought in vain an occasion to do so.

Then Retired Emperor Shirakawa set off on a pilgrimage to Kumano.

At a spot called Itogazaka, he had the bearers put his palanquin down and rested awhile.

A thicket nearby was full of wild yam sprouts.

Tadamori put one in his sleeve and came before His Eminence.

> *A sweet sprout I know*
> *will be crawling very soon:*
> *Yes, the time has come,*

he said, and His Eminence

caught his drift perfectly.

> *Keep that sprout, Tadamori,*
> *let it grow to nourish you,*

he added to complete the verse.
From that time on, Tadamori
brought the child up as his own.
The boy cried loud and long at night.
His Eminence, when he heard this,
vouchsafed a further thought in verse:

> *Cry at night he may,*
> *but heed me, Tadamori:*
> *look after him well.*
> *Through the years yet to come,*
> *pure wealth will accrue to him.*

And that is how Kiyomori got his name.[181]
In his twelfth year, he became second-in-command of the Watch.
In his eighteenth he was raised in that post to the fourth rank.
Those ignorant of the circumstances grumbled,
"Only sons of the very highest nobles get treatment like that!"
Retired Emperor Toba, however, knew the truth.
"As far as that goes," he said, "Kiyomori need not defer to anyone."

> Emperor Tenchi, in the old days,
> made a gift to Lord Kamatari:
> a consort of his, carrying his child.
> "If she gives birth to a girl," he said,
> "I will think of the child as mine,
> but a boy you may keep for yourself."
> The baby in the end was a son:
> none other than Abbot Jōe,
> who founded the temple on Tōnomine.
> Such things happened in ancient times,
> and so in this latter age Kiyomori
> may, sure enough, have been the son
> of Retired Emperor Shirakawa.
> Certainly that could nicely explain
> the momentous decisions he made—
> moving the capital and so on:
> decisions affecting the whole realm.

On the twentieth of the intercalary second month,

....

181. The poem reads the name Kiyomori to mean "pure wealth."

the grand counselor Lord Kunitsuna passed away.
His relationship with Kiyomori had been unusually close,
which is perhaps why he fell ill on the same day and died in the same month.
Descended in the eighth generation from the counselor Kanesuke,
Kunitsuna was a son of Morikuni, once the deputy right equerry.
Not yet even a chamberlain, he was only an aspirant scholar
in Emperor Konoe's reign, back in the Ninpei years, [1151-54]
when all of a sudden fire broke out in the palace.
The emperor escaped to the Shishinden,
but no one from the Palace Guards came to assist him,
leaving him stuck there, wondering what to do,
until Kunitsuna turned up with a light palanquin.
"Please, Your Majesty," he said, "under the circumstances
I beg you to avail yourself of this conveyance."
The emperor did so. "And who are *you*?" he asked.
"Fujiwara no Kunitsuna, an aspirant scholar serving in the chamberlains' office."
"Well, you certainly have your wits about you. I hope they appreciate you."
He praised Kunitsuna to Lord Tadamichi, the regent,
awarded him several estates, and took him into his service.
Again Emperor Konoe made during his reign a progress to Yawata.
The chief dancer for the occasion got drunk and fell in the water.
His costume was now soaking wet, and the *kagura* dancing was delayed.
Kunitsuna spoke up. "There is nothing remarkable in this," he said,
"but I did have my people bring along a similar costume."
He took it out, the dancer put it on, and the *kagura* was ready to start.
It began a little late, to be sure, but the singing was lovely
and the dancers' sleeves swayed ever so gracefully to the beat.
Gods and men alike respond to the delights of *kagura*,
as did the Sun Goddess long ago, in the age of the gods,
when such carryings-on tempted her out of the celestial rock cave.
That moment seemed almost to live again.

One of Kunitsuna's ancestors was the counselor Yamakage,
whose son, the distinguished prelate Jomu, excelled in wisdom and learning
as greatly as in virtuous conduct and in observance of priestly discipline.
In the Shōtai years, Cloistered Emperor Uda made a progress to the Ōi
    River, [898-901]
and at Mount Ogura, Sadakuni, a son of the palace minister Takafuji,
had his hat blown off into the stream.
He could only stand there, a sleeve over his head to hide his topknot,
until Jomu, they say, fished another hat from his vestment chest and passed it
    to him.

This Jomu was in his second year when his father, Yamakage,
went down to Kyushu as the Dazaifu deputy.
Jomu's stepmother, who hated him, put on a show of cuddling him in her arms
in order to drown him by dropping him into the sea.
Jomu's natural mother, however, while still alive,
had saved a turtle from a Katsura cormorant fisherman—
the man had caught it and meant to kill it for cormorant feed—
by removing her outer robe and trading it for the turtle, which she let go.
The grateful turtle surfaced under the little boy and bore him, safe and sound, on
    its back.
Perhaps this story is not entirely reliable, being so very old.
At any rate, in this latter age Lord Kunitsuna enjoyed a high reputation.
Under the regency of Lord Tadamichi, he became a counselor.
After Tadamichi's death Lord Kiyomori cultivated him for reasons of his own.
The enormously wealthy Kunitsuna had a new gift for him every day.
"He's my best friend in all the world," Kiyomori liked to say.
He adopted Kunitsuna's son as his own and named him Kiyokuni,
and Shigehira, Kiyomori's fourth son, became Kunitsuna's son-in-law.
    When the Gosechi festival of Jishō 4 was celebrated at Fukuhara, [1180]
the privy gentlemen took it upon themselves to call on the empress.
One of them sang the *rōei* poem "Speckled bamboo lines the Xiang lakeshore."[182]
Kunitsuna, who happened to be nearby, overheard him. He was appalled.
"Why," he reflected, "that song is said to be extremely ill-omened!
I refuse to listen to anything of the kind!" He stole away.
Now, this is what the song is about:
Of old, Emperor Yao had two daughters, Ehuang, the elder, and Nüying.
Both were consorts of Emperor Shun. After Shun died,
they took his body to the Cangwu burning ground, where he became smoke.
His two mourning consorts followed the cortege as far as the lakeshore at Xiang,
where their tears spattered the bamboos and left them speckled.
They remained at the spot, to seek comfort in playing the koto.
The bamboo growing there on the shore is speckled still,
and cloud broods over the place where they played.
Lord Tachibana no Hiromi composed a rhapsody on their sad story.
Although no genius at letters, Kunitsuna still had the sense to notice such things.
Appointment to grand counselor had never occurred to him.
However, his mother once made a pilgrimage to the Kamo Shrine
and prayed there fervently, for one hundred days,

....

182. A *rōei* is a passage of Chinese verse selected to be sung aloud, to the accompaniment of musical
instruments.

"I beg that Kunitsuna, my son, should serve at least a day as head chamberlain."
She then dreamed one night that a palm-leaf carriage drew up to her house.
Someone to whom she told the dream remarked,
"Why, you will be a senior noble's wife!"
"But I am already old!" she objected. "I cannot imagine that happening!"
Nonetheless her Kunitsuna became not merely head chamberlain
but, far more splendidly than that, grand counselor at senior second rank.

On the twenty-second, Cloistered Emperor Go-Shirakawa returned to his
    Hōjūji residence,
completed originally on the fifteenth day of the fourth month of Ōhō 3. [1163]
He had enshrined there at the time, close at hand,
the gods of Mount Hiei and Kumano,
and he had had the knolls, waters, and groves laid out precisely to his taste,
but for two or three years now the evil deeds of the Heike had kept him away.
Then Lord Munemori let him know that once the needed repairs were done,
the place was open to him again.
"Never mind that," His Cloistered Eminence answered, and moved in at once.
He first went to see where Kenshunmon-in, his empress, had lived.
The pines beside the lake and the willows at the water's edge
betrayed by their greater height the passage of years,
and he could not fail to recall how another emperor, once, had shed helpless
    tears
before the lotuses of Taiyi Lake and the willows of Weiyang Hall.
He then understood all too well that emperor's feelings long ago.

On the first of the third month, the order went out
that the ranking monks of Nara should resume their official functions
and administer branch temples and estates as before.
On the third, reconstruction began on the Great Buddha Hall at Tōdaiji.
The chamberlain and left minor controller Yukitaka was named to direct the
    project.
A year earlier this Yukitaka had been on a pilgrimage to Yawata,
and there, during a night on retreat, he dreamed that a celestial youth
with his hair in side loops emerged from the sanctuary.
"I am a messenger from Hachiman," the youth said.
"Keep this with you when you direct the rebuilding of the Great Buddha Hall."
He gave Yukitaka an official's ceremonial baton.
Yukitaka found the baton by his pillow when he awoke.
"How strange!" he thought. "What could possibly require such an appointment?"
He then put the baton in the front fold of his robe and made his way home,
where he left it out of sight and out of mind.
But the evil wreaked by the Heike caused the burning of Nara,

and Yukitaka was chosen after all, from among his peers,
to direct the work of rebuilding. What a marvelous instance of divine favor!

> On the tenth day of the third month,
> the acting governor of Mino
> sent a courier bearing this message:
> "The Genji of the eastern provinces
> have already pushed into Owari.
> They have barricaded the roads
> and are allowing no one to pass."
> A punitive force was dispatched at once,
> commanded by Taira no Tomomori,
> the intendant of the Left Watch;
> by the left commander Kiyotsune;
> and by the lieutenant Arimori.
> Thirty thousand riders set forth.
> Considering that Lord Kiyomori
> was not yet quite two months gone,
> out of joint though the times were indeed,
> this was a shocking thing to do.

> The Genji side, under Jūrō Yukiie
> and Yoritomo's half brother, Gien,
> was made up of six thousand mounted men.
> They camped across from the Heike force,
> on the other side of the Owari River.

> Very late on the night of the sixteenth,
> the Genji six thousand crossed the river
> and charged with fierce whoops and cries
> into the Heike thirty thousand.
> At daybreak on the seventeenth,
> at the hour of the tiger, the two sides [ca. 4 A.M.]
> exchanged arrows to open the battle
> and fought on until full daylight came.
> The Heike men remained unfazed.
> "The enemy has just crossed the river.
> His horses, arms, and armor are wet.
> You can't miss him! Cut him down!"
> A horde surrounded the Genji men,
> shouting, "Get them, every last one!"
> Nearly all the Genji were slaughtered.
> Their commander, Yukiie,
> barely saved himself and fled eastward,

but Gien, who had ventured too far
into the Heike camp, was killed.
The Heike next drove across the river
and chased the Genji like fleeing deer,
sending after them volleys of arrows.
Now and again the Genji shot back,
doing their best to defend themselves,
but they were few and the Heike many.
To all appearances they were doomed.
"As they say," observers remarked,
"'Never leave water at your back.'
The Genji strategy was just foolish."

Yukiie, the Genji commander, got over the border into the province of Mikawa,
where he removed the bridge across the Yahagi River,
put up a defensive wall of shields, and awaited the Heike.
They soon arrived, charged, and broke through. Once more he had to flee,
and the Heike followed in hot pursuit, to press their attack as before.
The Mikawa and Tōtōmi warriors would likely enough have joined them,
but Tomomori, the Heike commander, fell ill, and from Mikawa they had to turn
   back.
They had successfully destroyed the advance guard, yes,
but having failed to engage the rest of the Genji forces,
they had actually accomplished nothing at all.

The Heike had lost, the year before last,
palace minister Shigemori,
and this year Kiyomori had died.
Clearly their good fortune was over;
therefore none but their oldest allies
still remained at their disposal.
In the provinces of the east,
each blade of grass bowed to the Genji.

11. A Roar from the Sky

Meanwhile Jō no Tarō Sukenaga, of Echigo, was appointed to govern that
   province.
On the fifteenth of the sixth month, fired with gratitude toward the court,
he rode forth with some thirty thousand men to destroy Kiso no Yoshinaka.
He was preparing to move into position the next day, the sixteenth,
meaning to attack at the hour of the hare, when in the middle of the
   night

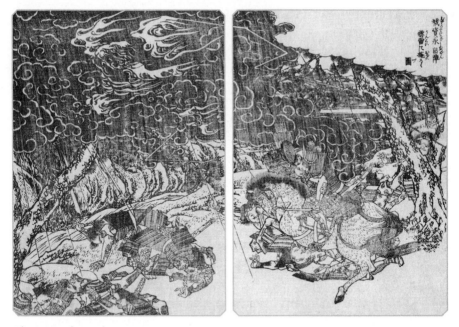

The voice from the storm.

a mighty wind blew up, rain poured down, and deafening thunder crashed.
When the sky cleared, an enormous, rasping voice resounded in the heavens:

"Behold here an ally of those Heike
who wantonly burned the Roshana Buddha,
gilt bronze, one hundred and sixty feet tall,
on the southern continent of Jambudvīpa."

The voice roared these words three times.
The hair rose on Sukenaga and all who heard it.
"Heaven's speech is too terrifying!" his men cried.
"Please, please see your way somehow to calling off this attack!"
But Sukenaga replied, "No such thing can sway a warrior."
At the hour of the hare on the sixteenth, he had marched a mere half mile
when a dense black cloud sailed in and dropped over him.
He cowered, fainted, and fell from his horse.
They put him in a palanquin and took him back to his residence,
where he lay for six hours. Then he died.
A courier brought the news to the capital, provoking Heike consternation.

On the fourteenth of that same seventh month, the era name was
changed to Yōwa. [1181] On that day Sadayoshi, the governor of Chi-
kugo, was appointed to govern Chikuzen and Higo as well. He then

marched on the western provinces to put down the Kyushu rebellion.
On that day, too, a special amnesty recalled the exiles of Jishō 3 [1179] to
the city. The former regent Motofusa, now a novice monk, came back
up to the capital from Bizen, and the former chancellor, Moronaga, did
so from Owari. The grand counselor Sukekata returned from Shinano.

    On the eighteenth, Lord Moronaga called on Cloistered Emperor
Go-Shirakawa.

Upon his return all those years ago
in the Chōkan era, he had played, [1163-65]
there on the emperor's veranda,
"Praise the King's Grace" and "Return to the Palace";
now, to mark his return in Yōwa,
he played for His Cloistered Eminence
"Autumn Wind." Each of these pieces
so acknowledged mood and season
that his art was a wonder to hear.
"Surely I am dreaming," the sovereign said.
"You must have forgotten your whole repertoire,
living out there among the peasants,
but I hope that you still have one *imayō* for me."
Sukekata struck up the rhythm and sang,
    "The Kiso River they tell of in Shinano,"
    but, having seen it with his own eyes,
    he changed it a little to sing instead,
    "The Kiso River I saw in Shinano"—
    an outstanding feat of ready wit!

12. *The Battle Beside the Yokota River*

On the seventh of the eighth month was held, in the hall of the Council of State,
the greater rite devoted to the Sutra of the Benevolent King,[183]
according to the precedent devised to destroy the rebel Masakado.
On the first of the ninth month, following one meant to quell the rebel
    Sumitomo,
a steel armor and helmet set was presented to the Grand Shrine of Ise.
The imperial envoy for the occasion was Ōnakatomi Sadataka,
the Bureau of Shrines priest responsible for oversight of the Ise rites.
He managed to start out from the city, but at the Kōga post station in Ōmi
he fell ill, and at the residence of the Ise Priestess he died.

....

183. This rite, the Daininnōe, was a last resort that could be performed only once in an imperial reign.

The esoteric adept charged with the Gōsanze altar,
during a Five-Altar Rite held to suppress those involved in the uprising,
died in his sleep at the Daigyōji Shrine.
Obviously neither gods nor buddhas were disposed to accept such prayers.
And when the adept Jitsugen of Anjōji, who conducted a Daigensui Rite,
reported the number of scrolls he had recited, it turned out, terrifyingly,
that he had prayed for suppression of the Heike.
"What on earth do you think you are doing?" the authorities demanded to know,
to which he answered, "You asked me to quell the enemies of the court,
and in our time, as far as I can see, that expression describes the Heike.
So I acted accordingly. Is something wrong?"
"This monk is insane," the Heike muttered. "Execution, then, or exile?"
But, caught up as they were in so many troubles great and small,
in the end they did nothing at all. After the Genji victory,
Lord Yoritomo in Kamakura marveled at what Jitsugen had done
and promoted him to the highest ecclesiastical rank.
On the twenty-fourth of the twelfth month,
the empress received the exalted title of Kenreimon-in.
Never before, it seems, had the mother of an infant emperor been so honored.
So that year ended, and Yōwa 2 came. [1182]

On the twenty-first of the second month, Venus encroached on the Pleiades. The Chinese *Astrological Digest* states, "When Venus encroaches on the Pleiades, the barbarians in the four directions rise up." It goes on, "By imperial order a commander of armies crosses the frontier of the realm."

On the tenth of the third month, the new appointments list was announced. Most Heike officials received a promotion. On the tenth of the fourth month, at the Hiyoshi Shrine, the ranking monk, Kenshin, undertook to chant, in due form, the essential passages of ten thousand copies of the Lotus Sutra. The cloistered emperor repaired to the shrine to receive the blessing of the event. When someone or other claimed that he was urging the monks of the Mountain to crush the Heike, warriors marched to the palace and secured the guard posts on all four sides. The Heike rushed to Fukuhara. Lord Shigehira led three thousand mounted men to the shrine to take the cloistered emperor in hand.

On the Mountain, word spread that the Heike, several hundred riders strong, were on their way up to attack.
The monks gathered in council down at Higashi-Sakamoto, to talk things over.
Mountain and city echoed with loud confusion.

The senior nobles and privy gentlemen in the sovereign's entourage paled,
and in fright many of his personal guards spat yellow gall.
Lord Shigehira met His Cloistered Eminence near Anō and escorted him home.

> "If this is how things are to be now,
> then no more pilgrimages for me;
> no, I am no longer my own master,"
> His Cloistered Eminence complained.

Actually, the monks of the Mountain had never meant to attack the Heike,
nor had the Heike ever intended to attack the Mountain.
Baseless rumor had fueled what occurred.
"It must have been demons getting up to their mischief," people said.
On the twentieth of that same fourth month,
the government made special offerings to the twenty-two great shrines,
considering that famine and pestilence were abroad in the land.
On the twenty-fourth of the fifth month, a new era name, Juei, was proclaimed.
And on that day Jō no Shirō Sukemochi, of Echigo, was named to govern this
    province.
He repeatedly declined the appointment as ill-omened,
his elder brother Sukenaga having so recently died,
but an imperial command cannot be refused.
He changed his name, Sukemochi, to Nagamochi.
On the second of the ninth month,
at the head of forty thousand men from Echigo, Dewa, and the four counties of
    Aizu,
he rode toward Shinano to destroy Kiso no Yoshinaka.
On the ninth he camped on the bank of the Yokota River.

> Yoshinaka, ensconced at the time
> in the fortress of Yoda, heard the news.
> He galloped forth to meet Nagamochi
> leading three thousand mounted men.
> Now, one of the Shinano Genji,
> Inoue no Kurō Mitsumori,
> had devised an ingenious plan.
> The Genji made up seven red banners,
> then split their force of three thousand
> into seven separate columns.
> These approached Nagamochi
> by ways high and low, red banners aloft.
> "Why, even here in this province,"
> Nagamochi cried when he saw them,

    "there are some who support the Heike!
    Look! We have reinforcements!"
    And on they came, until at a signal
    the seven columns merged into one
    and roared out a single battle cry.
    Up went the white banners they held ready.
    The Echigo men paled at the sight.
    "There must be tens of thousands of them!
    What on earth can we possibly do?"
    Some, in the panic and confusion,
    were driven at last into the river;
    others were chased over sheer drops.
    Few survived; far more were slain.
Nagamochi's most trusted lieutenants—
Yama no Tarō from Echigo, Jōtanbō from Aizu, far-famed warriors both—
were killed, while he, wounded, barely escaped with his life,
to fall back along the river to Echigo.

    On the sixteenth, in the capital, the Heike ignored such tidings.
Munemori, formerly left commander, was reappointed grand counselor
and then, on the third of the tenth month, elevated to palace minister.
On the seventh he presented his formal expression of thanks,
attended by twelve Heike senior nobles
and preceded by sixteen privy gentlemen, including the head chamberlains.
In the provinces of east and north, Genji forces swarmed like wasps,
preparing to fall on the capital. But no, to the Heike
these rising waves, these mighty storms brewing meant nothing.
Lavish as ever in their ways, they seemed rather to favor vanity.
Meanwhile the new year came: Juei 2. [1183]
Lord Munemori oversaw the banquet, which followed established practice.
On the sixth of the month, His Majesty, for his morning salutation,
went to call on the cloistered emperor at his Hōjūji residence.
Protocol followed Emperor Toba's counterpart call in his sixth year.
On the twentieth of the second month, Munemori rose to the junior first rank.
He resigned his palace-minister post that very day,
apparently to acknowledge responsibility for the uprisings.
    The monks of Nara and Mount Hiei,
      of Kumano and Kinpusen,
      the priests, high and low, of the Ise Shrines,
      every one, rejected the Heike,
      to share the fortunes of the Genji.
      Down came the imperial edicts,

in all directions, and every province
got its retired emperor's decree,
but everyone as a matter of course
assumed that these decrees and edicts
came in reality from the Heike.
They ignored every single one.

BOOK SEVEN

2. The Northern Campaign

Soon rumors spread that Yoshinaka,
who now dominated the eastern mountains and the north,
was already moving on the capital with an army of fifty thousand.
The Heike had been saying since the year before,
"Next year, when the spring grass comes in for the horses, there will be war."
Now hordes of warriors rushed to join them from the provinces to the south
on both sides of the mainland and from Shikoku, Kyushu, and elsewhere.
On the Tōkaidō side, no one came from anywhere east of Tōtōmi,
but the men from the west all arrived.
No one came either from Wakasa province northward.
The punitive force set out for the provinces of the north
to dispose first of all of Yoshinaka and then Yoritomo.

 The force followed these senior commanders:
  the Palace Guards captain Koremori,
  the Echizen governor Michimori,
  the Tajima governor Tsunemasa,
  the Satsuma governor Tadanori,
  the Mikawa governor Tomonori,
  the Awaji governor Kiyofusa,
 and such field commanders as these:
  Moritoshi, Tadatsuna,
  Kagetaka, Nagatsuna,
  Hidekuni, Arikuni,
  Jirōbyōe Moritsugi,
  Gorōbyōe Tadamitsu,
  Akushichibyōe Kagekiyo.
 Those six senior commanders
 and these able field commanders—
 in all over three hundred and forty—
 led the force of one hundred thousand,
 which, as the hour of the dragon began [ca. 8 A.M.]
 on the seventeenth day in the fourth month
 of Juei 2, set out for the north.
 Authorized to live off the land,
 once past the Ōsaka barrier
 they took to appropriating at will
 all goods saved to pay government taxes
 by prosperous houses along the way.
 From Shiga to Karasaki,

from Mitsukawajiri to Mano,
Takashima, Shiotsu, Kaizu,
they confiscated whatever they pleased.
For the locals this was too much.
They fled into the wilds.

3. The Pilgrimage to Chikubushima

The two commanders in chief, Koremori and Michimori, moved on ahead,
but their deputies, Tsunemasa, Tadanori, Tomonori, and Kiyofusa,
paused at Shiotsu and Kaizu in the province of Ōmi.
Among them Tsunemasa was especially skilled at poetry and music,
and even amid these troubles he sought peace and quiet beside the lake.[184]
Gazing out over the water, he saw in the distance an island.
He summoned his attendant, Tōbyōe Arinori, and asked its name.
"That is the famous Chikubushima," Arinori replied.
"Oh, yes, I have heard of it," Tsunemasa said. "I should like to go there."
Arinori, An'emon Morinori, and several others boarded a boat with him,
and off they sailed to Chikubushima.

It was the fourth month, the eighteenth day,
and the boughs were clothed in green
that harked back to the glories of spring,
while warblers in secluded dells
trilled their already halting song[185]
and cuckoos, soon to voice their first call,
sped past, heralding summer to come.
Blossoming wisteria billows
so prettily festooned the pines
that he hurriedly disembarked
to drink in indescribable beauty.
The mighty First Emperor of Qin
and Wudi, the emperor of Han,
sent, the first, comely youths and fair maidens,
the second, a far-seeing diviner,
to find the elixir of the immortals
on the ocean isle of Penglai,
warning that should they not succeed,
they were not to come back again,

....

184. Lake Biwa. Chikubushima, a small, steep-sided island at its north end, is still sacred.
185. The *uguisu* warbler sings best earlier in the spring.

so that in the end they grew old,
after wasted lives aboard their ships
searching in vain the boundless sea.
Surely, though—Tsunemasa felt—
the Penglai they sought must look like this.
It says somewhere in the scriptures,
"There is in Jambudvīpa a lake,
with, in its midst, a crystal mountain
that rises from the depths of the world,
and on it dwell heavenly maidens."
The passage describes this very island.
Tsunemasa knelt before the god
Daibenkudoku-ten. He said,
"Long ago you were Shakyamuni,
the very embodiment of the Law.
Both deities, Benzai and Myōon,[186]
separate in name, share nevertheless
in unison your higher nature
and offer salvation to all beings.
One pilgrimage to your shrine assures, they say, fulfillment of every prayer.
In you I therefore place my trust." So he spoke.
For a while then he offered the scriptures,
but in time the sun went down, and the moon of the eighteenth night rose,
illumining the lake's expanse and setting the sanctuary gleaming.
So lovely a scene emboldened the resident priests to say,
"Word of your skill has reached us, sir," and to place a biwa in his hands.

    Tsunemasa proceeded to play,
and when he reached those secret pieces
"High Mystery" and "On the Rock,"
the sanctuary filled with light
and the divinity, deeply moved,
appeared on Tsunemasa's sleeve
in the form of a white dragon.
Awed, overjoyed, Tsunemasa
in tears expressed his feelings thus:

      Could the mighty god,
      great in mercy, really mean
      to answer my prayers?

....

186. Daibenkudoku-ten, just mentioned, incorporates both. Of the two, the better known is Benzai-ten, the goddess of music, eloquence, and wisdom.

> *So plainly do I behold,*
> *revealed, the sacred presence.*
"You will subdue the raging foe
before my eyes and sternly crush
his evil hordes with your assault:
Of that I have no doubt at all."
Filled with joy, he boarded the boat
and sailed from Chikubushima.

4. The Battle at Hiuchi

Yoshinaka, then in Shinano, nonetheless built in Echizen the fort of Hiuchi.
Among the garrison were liturgical preceptor Saimei, abbot of Heisenji;
Inazu no Shinsuke; Saitōda; Hayashi Mitsuakira; novice monk Togashi Bussei;
Tsuchida; Takebe; Miyazaki; Ishiguro; Nyūzen; Sami; and others,
to the number of six thousand mounted men.
The site, surrounded by soaring crags and towering peaks, defied all comers.
Before it and behind it rose mountains.

> Past the fortress flowed two rivers,
> the Nōmi and the Shindō. Where they met,
> huge felled trees formed an abatis,
> and a mighty weir, running east-west
> below the mountains, made the fort
> seem to face a lake. As the poet wrote,[187]
> "Reflecting the mountains to the south,
> the water spreads wide, deep, and blue,
> its ripples red in the sinking sun.
> Beneath the Lake of Bitterest Cold
> lies a sandy floor, gold and silver;
> off the shore of the Kunming Lake
> ride the vessels of enlightened rule."
> This man-made lake at the fort of Hiuchi
> exploited dikes and turbid water
> to trick the gaze of any observer.
> One could cross, it seemed, only by boat.
> The Heike army therefore set up camp
> below the mountains on the other side
> and wasted there many motionless days.
One among the Hiuchi garrison, Saimei of Heisenji,

....

187. These seven lines are adapted from a poem by Bo Juyi.

profoundly sympathized with the Heike.
Skirting the foot of the mountains, he wrote a message,
inserted it into the bulb of a whistling arrow,
and stealthily shot the arrow into their camp.
    "The lake you see," he wrote, "is new.
    It is just a mountain torrent, dammed.
        Send foot soldiers tonight to dismantle the weir. The water will soon
        drain away. Your horses will have good footing. Cross without delay.
        From the enemy rear, I will support you with my arrows. This message
        is from Saimei, abbot of Heisenji."
Very pleased, the army commanders sent soldiers to do just that.
Being only a mountain stream, what had seemed a broad lake swiftly emptied.
    The Heike army crossed straight over.
    The garrison fought back awhile,
    but the enemy were too many
    and they themselves far too few.
    Obviously they could not prevail.
    Saimei had served the Heike well.
    Inazu no Shinsuke, Saitōda,
    Hayashi Mitsuakira,
    the novice Togashi Bussei—all fled,
    still intent on fighting the Heike,
    to the province of Kaga and to refuge
    at Kawachi under Hakusan.
    The Heike crossed right behind them
    into Kaga and put to the torch
    the forts of Hayashi and Togashi.
    Their onslaught seemed irresistible.
        From their lodgings nearby, the Heike sent the news by courier to the
        capital. Lord Munemori and the others who had remained behind
        went into transports of joy.
            On the eighth of the fifth month, the Heike forces gathered at
        Shinohara in Kaga. One hundred thousand men split into main and
        flanking forces. The former, seventy thousand men under Koremori
        and Michimori, assisted by Moritoshi and others, headed for Mount
        Tonami on the Kaga-Etchū border. The latter, thirty thousand under
        Tadanori and Tomonori, supported by Musashi no Saburōzaemon and
        others, started for Mount Shiho on the Etchū border with Noto.
Yoshinaka was in the Echigo provincial capital.
When he heard what had happened,
he quickly dispatched over fifty thousand horse in seven corps—

a tactic that he felt had already served him well in battle.

He first sent his uncle, Yukiie,
with ten thousand riders to Mount Shiho,
then Nishina, Takanashi, and Yamada no Jirō
with a rear assault force of seven thousand
to North Kurozaka.
Higuchi Kanemitsu and Ochiai Kaneyuki
he ordered with seven thousand men
to South Kurozaka.
Ten thousand and more he stationed, concealed,
at the main access point to Mount Tonami,
at a spot below Kurozaka,
at Matsunaga no Yanagihara,
and at Guminoki-bayashi.
Imai Kanehira, with six thousand,
crossed the shallows at Washi-no-se
and camped at Hinomiya-bayashi;
while Yoshinaka himself, with ten thousand,
forded the river at Oyabe and camped
at Haniū, north of Tonami.

5. A Prayer to Hachiman

"The Heike being so many," Yoshinaka declared,
"they are sure to cross Mount Tonami and pour onto the plain beyond,
there to challenge us head-on. But in a head-on confrontation,
numbers make the difference. We cannot afford to concede that advantage.
If instead we send standard-bearers ahead, bearing white banners,
they will assume with alarm that our vanguard is before them
and that we, too, must be many. 'If we end up having to fight on the flat,'
they will say, 'they know the terrain, and we do not.
They may surround us. We cannot let that happen.
This mountain is all cliffs and crags. They will never get around behind us.
We had better dismount awhile and rest the horses.'
That is what they will say, and that is what they will do.
And when they have done so, I will go through the motions of an engagement
to pass the time until sunset. Then I will drive them all down Kurikara Ravine."
He first had thirty white banners planted on Kurozaka.
Sure enough, the sight moved the Heike to exclaim,
"Look out! Here comes the Genji vanguard!
There must be a great many of them! If we are obliged to fight on the flat,

they know the terrain, and we do not.
They may surround us. We cannot allow that to happen.
This mountain is all cliffs and crags. They will never get around behind us.
The place seems to offer plenty of forage and water.
Better now to dismount awhile and rest the horses."
So right where they were on Mount Tonami, at a spot called Saru-no-baba,
they all slipped down from their mounts.

> Yoshinaka, camped at Haniū,
> surveyed the scene around him.
> From the summer mountains' green
> peeped a shrine's red, sacred fence
> and trim sanctuary crossbeams,
> with a torii before it.

He called for someone who knew the area.
"What is that shrine?" he asked. "What deity resides there?"
"That is Hachiman," the answer came. "All this land belongs to Hachiman."
Very pleased, Yoshinaka summoned his attendant secretary, Kakumei.
"It is great good fortune," he said, "that before engaging the enemy
I find myself in the presence of a shrine to Hachiman.
I believe that victory will be mine.
Therefore, for the sake of generations to come and to pray for aid in the present,
I wish to compose a formal prayer. Do you think that would be a good idea?"
"It would indeed," Kakumei replied. He dismounted and prepared to write.

> Kakumei on this occasion
> wore, over a dark blue *hitatare,*
> a suit of armor laced in black leather,
> with a black-lacquered sword at his side.

Twenty-four arrows, fletched with black hawk feathers, filled the quiver at his
  back,
and under his arm he clasped a rattan-wrapped, lacquered bow.
Removing his helmet, he hung it on a cord over his shoulders,
then drew from his quiver a small inkstone and folding paper.
He was a model of the man versed in both letters and war.

> This Kakumei had been born into the house of a Confucian scholar.
> He served in the Kangaku-in[188] as a chamberlain named Michihiro,
> then renounced the world, took the name Saijōbō Shingyū, and fre-
> quented the southern capital.
>   When Prince Mochihito sought refuge at Miidera and Miidera ap-
> pealed to Mount Hiei and Nara, the Nara monks commissioned

....

188. The academy, founded in the capital in 821, for the sons of the Fujiwara nobility.

Kakumei to write their reply. "Kiyomori is the dregs of the Taira house, the rubbish and sweepings of those who bear arms," he had written then.

Lord Kiyomori was enraged. "'The dregs of the Taira house'?" he roared. "'The rubbish and sweepings of those who bear arms'? What on earth does he mean by that? Arrest this Shingyū and put him to death!"

Kakumei, or Shingyū as he was then, therefore fled Nara and made for the north, where he became Yoshinaka's secretary and scribe.

This is the formal prayer that he wrote:

Prostrate obeisance to the Refuge.

Great Bodhisattva Hachiman laid the foundations of the Japanese imperium; from him issue the generations of our enlightened sovereigns. To guard their priceless throne and to benefit the multitude, he makes manifest three golden forms and throws open for each the portals of provisional presence. For many years now a certain Taira chancellor has lorded it over the four seas and visited suffering upon the people. He is an enemy equally of the Buddha's and of the Sovereign's Ways.

With respect to myself, Yoshinaka, undeserved good fortune gained me birth into a warrior house, and within the limits of my poor capacity I succeeded to my father's calling. The wickedness of the Taira chancellor defies reasoned thought. To heaven, therefore, I entrust my fate and offer my life to the nation. Having assembled a force of righteous warriors, I wish to repulse the vessels of evil. However, even as the opposing sides now face each other, my men still show no true unity of resolve, and some, I fear, may not see things as I do. I raised my banners on the field of battle and suddenly beheld the threefold sanctuary through which you temper your light for the good of all sentient beings.

That you will answer your servant's prayer is plain to see. That the evildoers will perish, one and all, there is no doubt. Tears of joy pour from my eyes; ardent faith fires my entrails. Note especially my great-grandfather, Lord Yoshiie, former governor of Michinokuni, who dedicated his life to serving your lineage and took the name Hachimantarō. Every member of the Minamoto line has always revered him. I myself, his descendant, have long bowed before his example. In aspiring now to so great a deed, I resemble a child hoping to measure the ocean with a shell or a praying mantis waving its forelegs to challenge a mighty chariot. If I nonetheless do so, it is for the sake of realm and sovereign, not for myself or for my house.

The celestial gods know the strength of my resolve. My faith is firm, my joy assured. Prostrate I implore divine aid, seen and unseen. Lend

Kakumei (left) and Yoshinaka at the Hachiman shrine.

me your subtle might and vouchsafe swift victory! Scatter the enemy to the four winds! And if my heartfelt prayer has your approval, if divine favor is to be mine, I beg you, show me a sign!

Juei 2, fifth month, eleventh day

Respectfully submitted: Minamoto no Yoshinaka

So read Yoshinaka's prayer. Then he and twelve of his men each took a humming arrow from his quiver and offered it, with the prayer, at the Great Bodhisattva's sanctuary.

Hachiman keeps faith with his faithful.
Surely the Great Bodhisattva descried
from afar his supplicant's keen resolve,
for three doves then flew from the clouds,
to flutter over the white Genji banners.

Long ago, while Empress Jingū
strove to press the attack in Silla,
her army, of the two, seemed the weaker
and her enemy's very strong.
When the outcome seemed all too clear,
she prayed to heaven. There and then
three spirit doves flew from the sky

and appeared before her army's shields.
The foreign army suffered defeat.
When Yoshinaka's great ancestor
Lord Yoriyoshi waged his campaign
to suppress Sadatō and Munetō,
his force likewise fell short of theirs.
Standing before their camp, he declared,
"This flame is from the gods, not me."
Then he loosed fire. Abruptly the wind
veered straight toward the evil horde.
Sadatō's Kuriyagawa fort,
his personal residence, burned.
The rebels went down to defeat,
and that was, after all, the end
of Sadatō and Munetō.
These examples Yoshinaka
kept in mind as he dismounted,
doffed his helmet, rinsed hands and mouth,
and bowed to the spirit doves,
certain of the deity's blessing.

6. The Rout Down Kurikara Ravine

Meanwhile the Genji and Heike took up opposing positions
a mere three hundred yards apart. No one on either side moved.
Then, from the Genji, fifteen sturdy warriors rode out beyond the line of shields
and shot fifteen humming arrows into the Heike camp.
The Heike, who did not grasp the maneuver behind this, answered in kind:
fifteen riders, fifteen arrows.
The Genji sent out thirty more men, who shot thirty more arrows.
Thirty more men of the Heike shot back their thirty.
Then came fifty, then a hundred, first from the Genji, then from the Heike,
until a hundred men on each side stood forward from their camp,
impatient to engage. The Genji, though, kept theirs under control,
killing time the whole day long; and the Heike,
suspecting no scheme to drive them down toward Kurikara Ravine,
played along with them, poor men, until the light began to fail.

As night descended, from north and south
the pair of flanking forces converged—
ten thousand mounted men in all—

to meet near the Kurikara chapel,
and there they raised a great battle cry.
The Heike saw flying behind them
what seemed a cloud of white banners.
"This mountain, though, on all sides
is nothing but boulders and escarpments!"
they protested among themselves.
"Who could possibly have imagined
a flanking force getting behind us?
How on earth can this have happened?"
Then, at Yoshinaka's command,
a battle cry rose from his main corps,
from the ten thousand riders hidden
at Matsunaga-no-yanagibara
and at Guminoki-bayashi,
and from Imai Kanehira's six thousand
lurking at Hinomiya-bayashi.
Behind the Heike and before them,
forty thousand full-throated shouts
all but shattered mountains and rivers.
As Yoshinaka had foreseen,
the Heike, with night now coming on
and the enemy threatening them
front and rear, faltered and broke.
"Shame! For shame! Turn back, turn back!"
many Heike cried, but most fled,
deaf to any reproach or appeal,
headlong down Kurikara Ravine.
No one could see his fellows ahead;
all simply clung to desperate faith
that the bottom would offer a road.
Down hurtled the father, down the son,
down the brothers, elder then younger,
down the lord, his retainer behind him:
men piling on horses, horses on men,
over and over, till, mounts and riders,
seventy thousand of the Heike
edge to edge choked the yawning ravine.
Springs ran blood; the dead lay in mounds.
To this day, so it is told,

arrow-strike nicks and sword cuts mark
the rocks up and down Kurikara.
Tadatsuna, Kagetaka, and Hidekuni, all trusted leaders of the Heike,
lay in the ravine beneath the dead.
Seno-o no Tarō Kaneyasu, of Bitchū, famed as a powerful fighter,
had fallen foul of Kuramitsu no Jirō Narizumi, of Kaga, who took him prisoner.
Captured, too, was Heisenji abbot Saimei, the traitor at Hiuchi.
"I really hate that monk," Yoshinaka declared. "Behead him first."
So Saimei's head fell. The Heike commanders Koremori and Michimori
barely escaped with their lives and made their way to Kaga.
Of their seventy thousand men, only two thousand survived.
The next day, the twentieth, Yoshinaka received two magnificent horses
from Hidehira in the north, one a roan, one a dappled gray.
At once he placed a gold-fitted saddle on each
and offered the pair as sacred steeds to the Hakusan Shrine.

      Yoshinaka declared himself satisfied. "Yukiie still worries me, though,"
      he said, "fighting at Shiho. I will go and see how he is getting on." From
      among his forty thousand men and horses, he picked the best twenty
      thousand and galloped off.

He reached the Himi river-mouth crossing at high tide.
Not knowing how deep the water might be, he drove in ten saddled horses.
They crossed safely, the tops of their pommels and cantles still dry.
      "The water is not deep!" he cried.
      "Cross now!" In plunged his army,
      twenty thousand strong, and got through.
      Sure enough, under fierce attack
      Yukiie had quit the fray.
      Yoshinaka, far from surprised
      to find him resting his horses,
      sent his twenty thousand fresh troops,
      yelling, straight into the Heike
      thirty thousand. In the melee
      sword sparks flew, and for a while
      the Heike managed to hold their own,
      but the assault undid them at last,
      and there, too, they met defeat.
      Their senior commander Tomonori,
      the governor of Mikawa, was killed;
      he was Kiyomori's youngest son.
      Many Heike men died as well.

Yoshinaka crossed Mount Shiho
to camp at Kodanaka in Noto,
before the Prince's Barrow.[189]

7. *The Battle at Shinohara*

Yoshinaka immediately donated estates to several shrines:
to the Hakusan Shrine, Yokoe and Miyamaru;
to the Sugō Shrine, the Nomi estate;
to the Tada Yawata Shrine, the estate of Chōya;
to the Kehi Shrine, that of Hanbara.
To Heisenji he donated the seven districts of Fujishima.
Those who aimed their arrows at Yoritomo
a few years before, at the battle of Ishibashiyama,
had fled to the capital and now served the Heike.
Chief among them were Matano no Gorō Kagehisa,
Nagai no Saitō Bettō Sanemori, Itō no Kurō Sukeuji,
Ukisu no Saburō Shigechika, and Mashimo no Shirō Shigenao.
While they bided their time until called again into battle,
these met daily to enjoy passing around cups of wine.
On his day to host the gathering, Sanemori declared,
> "Reflection on the state of our world
> suggests that strength lies with the Genji,
> while the Heike seem destined to fail.
> Come then: Let us join Yoshinaka."

"True enough," the company murmured.
When they met the next day at Shigechika's, Sanemori said,
"Well? How do all of you feel about what I said yesterday?"
Kagehisa stepped forward to reply:
> "But we are famous in the east.
> Everyone there knows who we are.
> Shifting allegiance to suit ourselves
> would only make us all look bad.

> How the rest of you feel, I do not know, but I myself will remain on the
> Heike side to the end, whatever that may be."

> Sanemori answered, with a bitter laugh, "Actually, I spoke as I did
> only to test you. Personally, I mean to die in our next battle. I have in-

189. The tomb of the heir apparent to Sujin, the semimythical tenth emperor.

formed those who matter, including Lord Munemori, that I will not
return to the capital."
All present shared his sentiments.

So it came to pass that each man
gathered together on that day—
loyal to their pact to the last—
died a cruel death in the north.

Meanwhile, to rest men and horses, the Heike camped at Shinohara in Kaga.
On the twenty-first of the fifth month of that year,
at the early-morning hour of the dragon, [ca. 8 A.M.]
Yoshinaka's army attacked them there with mighty battle cries.
Now, ever since Jishō, the Heike had retained in the capital two brothers,
Hatakeyama no Shōji Shigeyoshi and Oyamada no Bettō Arishige,
whom they had now sent out with their army to the north.
"You're seasoned warriors, you two," the brothers were told. "Direct the
fighting."
They now stood forward from the Heike camp, leading three hundred men.
On the Genji side, Imai Kanehira faced them, likewise with three hundred.
Each first sent out five, then ten men to try the other's mettle.
Then the two full contingents joined battle.

Noon, that day: Not a leaf stirred
while the men, under a blazing sun,
strove each to outshine all others,
bodies pouring rivers of sweat.
On Kanehira's side many died,
and of his housemen and retainers
Hatakeyama had so few left
that he was obliged to retreat.
Then there rode out from the Heike
five hundred men led by Nagatsuna.
From the Genji force, three hundred
under Kanemitsu and Kaneyuki
galloped forward to meet the challenge.
For a time both sides seemed to hold,
but Nagatsuna's men were recruits
picked up from this province and that,
and not one of them really fought;
rather they fled as fast as they could.
Nagatsuna himself was brave enough,
but, lacking anyone at his back,

he had no choice except to withdraw.
And while he was fleeing, all alone,
Nyūzen no Kotarō Yukishige, from Etchū, spotted a worthy opponent.
Whip and stirrup, he galloped up beside Nagatsuna and gripped him hard.
Nagatsuna seized him in turn and crushed him onto his pommel.
"Who are you?" he demanded to know. "I want to hear your name."
"I am Nyūzen no Kotarō Yukishige, from Etchū," came the reply.
"This is my eighteenth year."

> "Oh, no! The son I lost last year,
> if this year he were still alive,
> would now be in his eighteenth, too.
> I should properly take your head
> and let it lie here in the dust,
> but no, I spare your life." He let him go.

Nagatsuna dismounted and sat down to rest, until his allies should arrive.
"He did let me live," Yukishige reflected. "But what an opponent!
I simply must kill him, somehow."
Meanwhile Nagatsuna chatted on with him, quite relaxed.
The lightning-fast Yukishige drew his dagger, dove at him,
and twice plunged it in under his helmet.
Three of his men then galloped up to support his attack.
Nagatsuna by no means lacked courage, but his time must have come,
for the enemy were many and he had sustained grave wounds.
He fell at last on the spot.

> Charged forth then from the Heike side
> Musashi no Saburōzaemon Arikuni
> with three hundred, howling for war;
> and, from the Genji, Nishina, Takanashi,
> Yamada no Jirō with five hundred,
> eager for battle. The Heike men
> held out awhile, but many were killed.
> Far in among the enemy ranks,
> Arikuni shot the last of his arrows,
> lost his mount to a lethal shaft,
> yet still, now on foot, drew his sword
> to fight on, and slew many men
> until, bristling with arrows,
> he died at last, still on his feet.
> Seeing their commander's fate,
> his men fled, every one.

8. *Sanemori*

The Heike were all gone now, but a single rider,
Saitō Bettō Sanemori, from Nagai in Musashi,
turned back from the rout to carry on the fight.
For a special reason, he wore a red brocade *hitatare* robe, green-laced armor,
a helmet with spreading horns, and a gold-fitted sword.
On his back he bore arrows fletched with black-banded eagle feathers;
his hand gripped a lacquered, rattan-wrapped bow;
and he rode a dappled roan with a gold-trimmed saddle.
Tezuka no Tarō Mitsumori, one of Yoshinaka's men, noted a worthy opponent.
"Bravo!" he cried. "And who are *you*, then, when your whole side has fled,
to ride alone against us? I would gladly know you. Tell me your name!"
"And you—who are *you*?" Sanemori replied.

> "Tezuka no Tarō Mitsumori,
> a warrior from Shinano province."
> "Why, then," Sanemori answered,
> "you and I are worthy opponents.
> Believe me, I mean no disrespect,
> but for certain particular reasons
> I cannot now reveal my name.
> Come, Tezuka, let us close and fight!"
> He was moving up next to the foe
> when one of Tezuka's trusted men
> galloped up from behind the two,
> to ensure that his lord was not killed,
> got between them, and seized Sanemori.
> "So you have a mind, do you, to fight
> the greatest warrior in Japan?"
> Sanemori shouted, got his own grip,
> crushed the man onto his pommel,
> cut off his head, and tossed it away.
> At the sight Tezuka circled left,
> lifted the skirt of his enemy's armor,
> stabbed him twice, and as he weakened,
> seized him and fell with him to the ground.
> Sanemori had courage aplenty,
> but the fighting had worn him out,
> and besides, he was an old man.
> He ended up under Tezuka.

Tezuka entrusted the head to a man of his who had just galloped up and went in haste to report to Yoshinaka.

"I have just fought and killed a most unusual opponent," he said. "He might have been a rank-and-file warrior, except that he was wearing red brocade. But if he was a commander, his followers were nowhere in sight. I demanded his name repeatedly, but he never gave it to me. He spoke like a man from the east."

"Ah," Yoshinaka replied, "I expect that was Sanemori. If so, then I saw him once when I was a boy, on a visit to Kōzuke province. His hair was graying even then, though, and it must be snow white by now. I do not see how his hair and beard could be black. Higuchi no Jirō spent a lot of time with him and will certainly recognize him. Call Higuchi over here."

So Higuchi was summoned.

Higuchi took one look and exclaimed, "How awful! Yes, this is Sanemori." "But if it is," said Yoshinaka, "at over seventy his hair should be white. How can his hair and beard be black?"

Weeping copiously, Higuchi replied,

"I can explain this, and I will,
but the sight is too great a shock,
and weak tears have robbed me of speech.
It is fitting that a warrior,
on the slightest of occasions,
should speak words worth remembering.
I often heard Sanemori say,
'If I go again to war
after passing my sixtieth year,
I will dye my beard and hair black,
so as to look like a young man.
You see, it would be undignified
for an old man to seek to best
the young in battle, and besides,
it would hurt an old warrior so
to be ridiculed and despised.'
So that is what he must have done.
Have his head washed, then, and see."
It seemed likely that Higuchi was right.
Yoshinaka had the head washed,
and indeed the hair turned white.
This is how it happened that Sanemori wore red brocade.
He said when he came before Lord Munemori to bid him farewell,

"I know that I am far from alone in this, my lord,
but at any rate I feel acutely in my old age the shame
of having set out for the east a few years ago,
only to flee back to the capital from Kanbara in Suruga
without shooting a single arrow, at the mere whirring of waterbirds' wings.
Now duty calls me to the north, where I mean to die in battle.
Although originally from the province of Echizen,
more recently I settled, in your service, on your Nagai estate in Musashi.
Now, a saying urges a man to return home wearing brocade.[190]
Please grant me leave to wear a brocade *hitatare*."
"Well said!" Lord Munemori replied. He gave the permission requested.

    Once upon a time, Zhu Maichen
    waved brocade sleeves at Huiji-shan.
    Now, Saitō Bettō Sanemori
    had clearly won glory in the north,
    but only his empty name lived on;
    for his remains merged, alas,
    with the earth of the northern marches.

      It had been the fourth month past,
    the seventeenth day, when a great force
    numbering more than a hundred thousand
    and surely invincible set forth,
    but now, as the fifth month drew to a close,
    only twenty thousand or so returned.
    "Yes," people said, "you catch many fish
    when you completely fish out a stream,
    but the next year there are no fish at all.
    Burning the forest yields plenty of game,
    but there is no game the following year.
    They should have given thought to the future
    and kept a few more men in reserve."

9. Genbō

Tadakiyo and Kageie, the governors of Kazusa and Hida,
both renounced the world after Lord Kiyomori's death,
and the news that their sons had now perished in the north
seemed to crush them beneath too great a weight of grief,
for both in the end died of sorrow.

....

190. A Chinese saying, urging a man to display success when he returns home.

Parents lost their sons in provinces far and near, wives their husbands.
In the capital the gates to many homes remained closed.
Everywhere voices called the Name, amid loud cries of mourning.
    On the first of the sixth month,
the chamberlain Sadanaga summoned Ōnakatomi no Chikatoshi,
a midlevel functionary in the Bureau of Shrines,
to the southeast Seiryōden doorway and there informed him
that once these military troubles were over and peace was restored,
His Majesty would make a progress to the Grand Shrine of Ise.

> That divine presence, once descended
> earthward from the High Plain of Heaven,
> moved in the reign of Emperor Suinin,
> the third month of his twenty-fifth year,
> from Kasanui in Yamato province
> to Watarai in the province of Ise
> and to the banks of the Isuzu River,
> where mighty boulders underground
> bore up the deity's new, sturdy pillars
> and priests initiated the sacred rites.
> Since then none of the three thousand
> seven hundred and fifty shrines
> in Japan's sixty and more provinces,
> no god, no unseen power great or small,
> can compare with the Grand Shrine of Ise.

Nonetheless, for a long time no emperor made a progress there.
In the reign of Shōmu, however, there lived one Fujiwara no Hirotsugi,
an assistant Dazaifu deputy and provisional lieutenant in the Right Palace
    Guards.
A grandson of the left minister Fuhito, he was a son of the consultant Umakai.
In the tenth month of Tenpyō 15, in Matsura county of the province of
    Hizen, [743]
Hirotsugi rallied several tens of thousands of miscreants
to the cause of threatening the imperial sway.
A force under Ōno no Azumōdo, duly dispatched, therefore subdued him.
It was then that an emperor first went on pilgrimage to the Grand Shrine.
Emperor Antoku's announced pilgrimage apparently rested upon this precedent.
Now, this Hirotsugi had a horse that in one day
could travel all the way from Matsura to the capital and back.
After Hirotsugi's defeat, his allies all fled and came to grief,
while they say Hirotsugi himself charged on this horse into the depths of the sea.
His violent spirit then caused many frightening incidents.

On the eighteenth of the sixth month of Tenpyō 16, [744]
the great prelate Genbō was to conduct a solemn rite at Kanzeonji in Dazaifu.
When he mounted the high seat and rang the bell to begin,
the sky suddenly darkened, thunder roared,
and a lightning bolt struck him and whipped his head off into the clouds.

      This happened because Genbō had worked rites to quell Hirotsugi.

        Genbō had accompanied the minister Kibi no Makibi on his embassy to Tang China. It is he who had brought the Hossō doctrine to Japan. The men of Tang had laughed at his name. "Your 'Genbō' sounds like the characters that mean 'go home to destruction,'" they declared, or so the story goes. "You can expect trouble once you are home again in your country." And on the eighteenth of the sixth month of Tenpyō 19, [747] something dropped a skull inscribed "Genbō" into the grounds of Kōfukuji, while laughter as of a thousand voices resounded through the sky.

This was because Kōfukuji is a Hossō temple.

    Genbō's disciples took the skull
    and to contain it built a barrow
    known as Zuhaka, the Head Tomb.
    It is still there. And all this was due
    to the spirit of Hirotsugi.
    Hence that spirit received honor
    at Matsura, in the sanctuary
    formally named the Mirror Shrine.

During Emperor Saga's reign, Heizei, the previous emperor, [809-23]
urged on by his mistress of staff, Kusuko, provoked turmoil in the realm,
whereupon Princess Yūchi, Saga's third daughter,
was appointed high priestess of Kamo to pray that he should fail.
That is how the office of Kamo High Priestess began.

    In the reign of Emperor Suzaku,
    Masakado and Sumitomo
    raised rebellion, so inspiring
    the Yawata special festival.
    Under the current circumstances,
    these precedents gave rise in turn
    to prayers of many kinds.

10. Yoshinaka's Letter to Mount Hiei

Yoshinaka arrived at the Echizen provincial seat
and assembled his housemen and retainers in council.

"I plan to enter the capital via the province of Ōmi," he announced,
"but as usual there are the monks of Mount Hiei to consider;
they might well seek to block my way.
No doubt I could break through easily enough,
but these days it is the Heike who ignore the sanctity of the Buddha's Teaching,
burning temples, slaughtering monks, and perpetrating one outrage after
    another.
To go up to the capital as a protector and then to fight the Hiei monks
on the grounds that they had thrown in their lot with the Heike
would only be to repeat the ways of the Heike themselves.
So grave a mistake would be all too easy to make.
But then, what *should* I do?"
Kakumei, Yoshinaka's personal scribe, stepped forward to speak.
"There are three thousand monks on the Mountain," he said,
"and they cannot be all of one mind. Their views on the subject surely differ.
Some must favor joining the Genji while others support the Heike.
So you might try sending them a letter.
Their reply will reveal which way they lean."
"I like that idea," Yoshinaka replied. "Very well then, write!"
He had Kakumei write the letter and sent it to Mount Hiei.
The letter said:

> To the master of discipline resident in the Ekō lodge:[191]
>
> Due reflection on the evil deeds of the Heike suggests that ever since Hōgen and Heiji they have failed to uphold the conduct expected of His Majesty's subjects. Nonetheless, high and low bow before them with folded hands, while clerics and laymen alike prostrate themselves at their feet. They enthrone and dethrone emperors at will; they appropriate provinces and counties until gorged with their spoils. They confiscate the wealth of great houses, oblivious to justice or injustice. Heedless of guilt or innocence, they punish ministers and senior nobles; purloin their property, which they then pass to their followers; and assume possession of their estates, which they distribute as they please among their children and grandchildren. In the eleventh month of Jishō 3, they even confined the cloistered emperor to a Seinan Palace and exiled the regent to a remote region of the west. The people said nothing; they merely exchanged glances as they passed one another on the road.
>
> That is not all. In the fifth month of Jishō 4, the Heike surrounded the residence of Prince Mochihito, causing consternation throughout the city. To escape ignominious harm, the prince sought secret refuge at

----

191. Who this figure was is unclear.

Miidera. I had already received a command from him, and I was ready and eager to rush to his aid, but the streets swarmed with the enemy and there was no way through. No Genji from the nearby provinces could reach him, still less one from so much farther away. Alas, Miidera proved unable to safeguard him, and he therefore left for the southern capital. He was on his way there when a battle broke out at Uji Bridge. The escort commander, Minamoto no Yorimasa, and his sons ignored all danger to themselves in His Highness's righteous cause and performed wonders of martial valor, but the enemy overwhelmed them. Their bodies lay on the moss of those hallowed banks; the waves of the river washed their lives away. The prince's order remained graven on my heart, and I deeply mourned my kinsmen's deaths.

Consequently the Genji of the east and those of the north laid plans to march on the capital and destroy the Heike. In the autumn of last year, I raised my banners and took my sword in hand to achieve this immovable goal. On the very day I left Shinano, Jō no Shirō Nagamochi, of Echigo, was dispatched against me at the head of several tens of thousands of men. Our two sides met in battle on the Yokota riverbank in Shinano.

With a mere three thousand men, I bested those tens of thousands. The news drew a Heike army of one hundred thousand men toward the north. I met them repeatedly in Echizen, Etchū, and Kaga, at such forts as Tonami, Kurosaka, Shihosaka, and Shinohara. Each time I devised a new strategy, and each time I saw victory. I had but to strike for the Heike to fall, to attack for them to yield. Just so do autumn winds break plantain fronds and winter frosts wither every leaf. I owe this success not to my tactics but to divine aid. And now that the Heike army has been defeated, I mean to move on the capital.

My passage into the city will take me below Mount Hiei. One aspect of this route concerns me, however. Do the sympathies of the Tendai monks lie with the Heike or with the Genji? Should they support the traitors, I will be obliged to fight them, and destruction of Enryakuji will swiftly follow. When the Heike have so distressed our sovereign and so damaged the Buddha's Teaching, it is painful to imagine righteous warriors intent on chastising them having suddenly to do battle with three thousand monks. It is also troubling to foresee that, should I delay my progress in deference to Yakushi and Sannō, I might risk being known forever after, in a manner most injurious to a warrior's good name, for dilatory service to the court. I have therefore decided to inform you of my dilemma.

I beseech the three thousand monks of Mount Hiei, for the sake of the

gods and buddhas, of the realm, and of our sovereign, to join forces with
the Genji, punish the evildoers, and so receive His Majesty's grateful
blessing. Such is my heartfelt prayer.

> *With all respect,*
> *Minamoto no Yoshinaka*
> *Juei 2, sixth month, tenth day*

11. *The Reply*

Sure enough, after reading the letter,
the monks of Mount Hiei expressed divergent views in council.
Some advocated joining the Genji, others making common cause with the Heike.
All sorts of opinions received an airing.
The senior monks' deliberations yielded the following conclusion:

> "In the final analysis,
> our major role is to offer prayers
> that ensure our sovereign long life.
> The Heike are, in the current reign,
> His Majesty's commoner relatives,
> and they therefore command respect
> from all of us here on the Mountain.
> That is why we have always, so far,
> prayed that they, too, should flourish greatly.
> However, their evil passes all bounds,
> and the people have turned against them.
> The armies they have sent to quell
> rebellion in this province or that
> have all met, at the rebels' hands,
> ignominious destruction.

For some years now, the Genji have triumphed repeatedly in battle.
Their time is coming. Why should only our Mountain
ally itself with the Heike, whose time is past,
and oppose the Genji, whose future stretches before them?
The right course for us will be to distance ourselves from the Heike
and resolutely lend our strength to the Genji side." Such was their opinion.
With one mind the full council agreed and sent an answer to that effect.
Yoshinaka assembled his housemen and retainers,
then had Kakumei open and read the letter.

> *Your esteemed communication of the tenth reached us on the sixteenth.*
> *Perusing it cleared the gloom that has recently oppressed us. Yes, the*
> *Heike over the years have behaved deplorably, and turmoil has con-*

tinually troubled the court. Such talk is on everyone's lips, and endless material feeds it.

Now, the position of Mount Hiei, northeast of the imperial city, inspires at Enryakuji devout prayers for peace in the realm—a realm so long troubled by Heike crimes that it knows no peace at all. The exoteric and esoteric teachings are ignored, and again and again their divine protectors are spurned. But you, sir, born into an ancient warrior line, have achieved by blessed fortune unique distinction in our time. Following a sagacious plan, you swiftly raised a righteous force and, heedless of risk to yourself, established at one stroke exceptional merit. Less than two years have passed since then, and already your fame fills the four seas.

We monks of Mount Hiei rejoice. For the realm's sake and for that of your house, we delight in your prowess and in your brilliant success. Advance further on your present course and you will give us the joy of knowing that our prayers have not been in vain and reassure us that the land enjoys stalwart protection. The eternal buddhas of our temple and others and the gods honored in our Hiyoshi sanctuaries great and small will rejoice that their teaching is to flourish once more and that they are to enjoy again the reverence they knew of old. We beg you to discern our profound sincerity. Thus shall the Twelve Divine Generals, in the world unseen, add their might by order of the Medicine King to that of the champions who smite evil, while in the visible world we three thousand monks will for a time suspend study and practice in order to assist the imperial forces intent on chastising the wicked. The enlightened wind of Tenfold Cessation and Contemplation will blow the scoundrels far from our shores; the blessed rain of divine union in the Three Mysteries will restore our world to the ancient age of Yao. Such is our council's decision. Please mark it well.

Juei 2, seventh month, second day
The monks of Mount Hiei

12. The Heike Appeal to Mount Hiei

The Heike, who suspected no such correspondence,
understood that Kōfukuji and Miidera were now furious with them.
"No approach to them would achieve anything," they reflected.
"But we have done nothing to incur the wrath of Mount Hiei.
Enryakuji has no thought of turning against us.
Let us appeal solemnly to the great Sannō Deity
and convince the three thousand monks to make common cause with us."

Ten Heike senior nobles therefore signed a joint letter
and sent it to Mount Hiei. The letter said:

> *Reverend Sirs,*
>
> *Enryakuji counts for us as our tutelary temple and Hiyoshi as our
> tutelary shrine. Our wish is to revere none but the Tendai teaching.
> Therefore we of the Taira house address to you the special appeal set
> forth below.*
>
> *Founded in Emperor Kanmu's reign, when Dengyō Daishi returned
> from Tang China, Enryakuji disseminated thereafter the full and per-
> fect Tendai doctrine and transmitted on the Mountain itself the teach-
> ing of Vairochana. The fountainhead since then of the flourishing of the
> Teaching, your temple sustains the peace of the realm.*
>
> *Currently the Izu Exile, Minamoto no Yoritomo, shamelessly flouts
> the law of the land, and other Genji—Yoshinaka, Yukiie, and their ilk—
> fall in with his evil designs. They seize provinces near and far, appropri-
> ating local goods and tax revenue. Under these circumstances we
> humbly received, in recognition both of signal service past and of mili-
> tary prowess in the present, an imperial order to crush the rebels at
> once and to suppress their evil horde, and we set out repeatedly to do
> precisely that. Alas, our imperial army's every battle plan failed. De-
> spite our overwhelming numbers, the rebels appear to prevail. How can
> we quell their traitorous revolt unless the gods and buddhas assist us?*
>
> *So it is that we take sole refuge in the Tendai teachings and place our
> trust in the beneficence of Hiyoshi. Our line, too, can be said to spring
> from the imperial founder of Enryakuji. Rightly indeed do we accord
> your temple growing reverence and honor. Hereafter the joy of En-
> ryakuji shall be our joy and the wrath of Hiyoshi our own, and so shall
> we instruct our loyal descendants. For their tutelary shrine and temple,
> the Fujiwara have Kasuga and Kōfukuji; therefore the Hossō teachings
> have long been their refuge. We Taira, for ours, have Hiyoshi and En-
> ryakuji, and henceforth we shall prize the Tendai doctrine of full and
> swift enlightenment. For the Fujiwara, their association stems from the
> past and offers them their own prosperity and good fortune. Ours arises
> from our present prayer—to wit, that for our sovereign's sake the rebels
> shall be duly punished.*
>
> *O Seven Sannō Shrines, O Noble Scions of the Unseen Powers,
> O Protectors ranged far and wide around the Mountain, O Medicine
> King Buddha of the Twelve Lofty Vows, O Nikkō, O Gakkō! Consider
> this, our most earnest plea, and vouchsafe us your wondrous aid! Then
> shall these wickedly scheming traitors bow, vanquished, before their
> sovereign's gate; then shall the severed heads of the evildoers pour into*

the imperial city. We senior nobles of the Taira house therefore present
with one voice this most urgent appeal.
Taira no Michimori, governor of Echizen, junior third rank
Taira no Sukemori, Right Palace Guards captain, junior third rank
Taira no Koremori, acting Right Palace Guards captain and governor
of Iyo, senior third rank
Taira no Shigehira, Left Palace Guards captain and governor of
Harima, senior third rank
Taira no Kiyomune, Right Gate Watch commander, governor of Ōmi
and Tōtōmi, senior third rank
Taira no Tsunemori, master of the empress mother's household, direc-
tor of palace upkeep, governor of Kaga and Etchū, consultant at se-
nior third rank
Taira no Tomomori, counselor, Left Watch intendant, commander in
chief of the imperial forces, junior second rank
Taira no Norimori, acting counselor, governor of Hizen, junior second
rank
Taira no Yorimori, acting grand counselor, inspector general for Dewa
and Michinoku, senior second rank
Taira no Munemori, junior first rank
Juei 2, seventh month, fifth day
Deeply affected, the Tendai abbot
revealed for the moment none of this
but withdrew instead on retreat
to the shrine of Jūzenji Gongen,
where he prayed for three full days.
Only then did his monks, by his leave,
read the appeal that he had received.
A poem not seen at first now became visible on the outer cover:
> *Even to a house*
> *long and peacefully in bloom,*
> *the passage of years*
> *brings a month to join the moon*
> *sinking westward down the sky.*
"O Sannō Deity, have pity on us!
O three thousand monks, add your might to ours!"
Such was the gist of the Heike appeal,
but their conduct over the years
had too greatly offended the gods
and betrayed every hope of men.
Their prayers elicited no response;

their entreaties won over no one.
In truth the monks felt sorry for them,
understanding their situation,
but, as they reminded themselves,
"We have already told the Genji
that our strength is at their service.
We simply cannot capriciously
retract our announced decision."
None of the monks endorsed the appeal.

13. The Emperor's Flight from the Capital

On the fourteenth of that same seventh month, Sadayoshi, governor of Higo,
entered the capital with three thousand mounted men,
including the Kikuchi, Harada, and Matsura leagues,
after successfully quelling rebellion in Kyushu.
So Kyushu at least was quiet again,
but fighting still raged in the provinces of east and north.
  On the twenty-second, in the depths of the night,
a tremendous commotion arose around Rokuhara.
Men saddled horses, tightened girths, and galloped north, south, east, and west,
carrying things to hide. An attack clearly seemed imminent.
The next morning the story came out.
There was among the Mino Genji one Sado no Shigesada.
During the fighting back in the Hōgen years,
he had captured and delivered Chinzei no Hachirō Tametomo,
a fugitive after the defeat of the retired emperor's forces.
Appointed in reward a lieutenant in the Watch,
Shigesada eventually rose to lieutenant in the Right Gate Watch.
The Genji therefore shunned him, and he curried favor instead with the Heike.
In the depths of the night in question, he galloped to Rokuhara
to announce that Yoshinaka had come from the north with fifty thousand men,
who were swarming then through Higashi-Sakamoto, under Mount Hiei.
Two of Yoshinaka's men, Tate no Chikasada and the scribe Kakumei,
had charged with six thousand up Mount Hiei,
where the three thousand monks had joined them.
Now, Shigesada reported, they were on their way to attack the city.
Deeply alarmed, the Heike sent men off hither and yon to face them.
Their main force, three thousand under the counselor Tomomori
and the Palace Guards captain Shigehira, first stopped at Yamashina.
Michimori and Noritsune, the governors of Echizen and Noto,

led two thousand to hold the Uji Bridge, and with one thousand
the chief left equerry Yukimori and Satsuma governor Tadanori guarded the
Yodo road.
As to the movements of the Genji,
word spread that Yukiie was on his way up from the Uji Bridge
with several thousand men, and so, too, Yoshikiyo,
Yada no Yoshiyasu's son, from Ōeyama.
When told that the Settsu and Kawachi Genji,
hordes of them, were pouring into the city,
the Heike resolved to gather themselves in one place
to face what might follow. They recalled every man to the city.

> In the imperial city are won
> fortune and fame. After cockcrow
> no one there can afford sloth—
> no, not even in times of peace,
> let alone when disaster threatens!
> The Heike wanted only to vanish
> into a Yoshino wilderness
> remote beyond the farthest bourn,
> but every province in the land,
> every one of the seven circuits
> now had risen up against them.
> What haven would have welcomed them?
> "In the three worlds there is no peace,
> for they are like a burning house":
> The Buddha spoke these golden words
> when he taught the One Vehicle.
> How could they possibly be wrong?

On the twenty-fourth of the seventh month, in the small hours of the night,
Lord Munemori went to Rokuhara for a word with Kenreimon-in.
"I believed that the world would somehow always be as we knew it,"
he said, "but now, you see, everything has changed.
People are talking about meeting our fate, whatever it may be, in the city,
but I cannot bear to have you face so cruel a spectacle.
I have therefore decided to take you,
and with you the cloistered emperor and His Majesty as well,
on a journey to the provinces of the west."
"Whatever is to happen now," Kenreimon-in replied,

> "I leave, my brother, in your hands."
> The tears that overflowed her sleeves
> defied her efforts to contain them.

So, too, Munemori, from his sleeves
could well have wrung many a drop.

His Cloistered Eminence must have learned that the Heike were to flee
the capital that night and that they secretly planned to take him with
them, for he stole away from his residence and headed toward Kurama,
accompanied only by the chief right equerry Suketoki, Sukekata's son.
No one else knew.

Now, there was among the Heike housemen one Sueyasu, a sharp
fellow who served the cloistered emperor as well. Much agitation and
whispering could be heard in the sovereign's private part of the house,
and gentlewomen quietly crying. He strained his ears to catch what
was going on and heard a voice say, "His Cloistered Eminence has dis-
appeared! Oh, dear, where can he have got to?"

"This is bad!" Sueyasu thought. He galloped straight to Rokuhara
and reported the matter to Lord Munemori.

"There must be some mistake," Munemori answered, but he rushed
straight there nonetheless, to see for himself. His Cloistered Eminence
was indeed gone.

There was no sign either of Lady Tango or of his other intimate gentlewomen.
"What has become of him?" Munemori kept asking,
but no one confessed to knowing where he had gone.
All were in a state of shock.
Meanwhile news that the cloistered emperor was gone from the capital
spread pandemonium swiftly through the city.

Imagine, then, what panic struck
the Heike ladies and gentlemen!
The enemy might just as well
have broken straight into their homes—
the blow could hardly have been worse.
They had been making ready for days
to take possession of both sovereigns
and escort them toward the west—
and now to be abandoned this way!
They felt as though a mighty tree,
certain to shelter them from rain,
had let a downpour through.

"We still have His Majesty, though, so let us start him on his way."
It was only the hour of the hare when they advanced the imperial
palanquin. [ca. 6 A.M.]
Young as he was, in his sixth year, the emperor boarded it, unsuspecting.
Kenreimon-in, his mother, entered it with him.

They gave him the mirror, the jewel, and the sword.
"Take the seal and keys, too," the grand counselor Taira no Tokitada demanded,
"and the hour markers, and Genjō, and Suzuka!"[192]
But in the confusion many things were left out.
They even forgot the sword from the emperor's dayroom.
In haste Tokitada and his sons Nobumoto, the head of the palace storehouse,
and the Sanuki captain Tokizane—just the three of them—
set off in full court dress with His Majesty.
The bearers from the Palace Guards office and the officials to hold the palanquin
    cords
wore full armor, with bows and arrows.
The palanquin moved west along Shichijō, then south down Suzaku.
The next day, the twenty-fifth,
first light broke in a sky filled with the stars of the River of Heaven.
Clouds trailed about the Eastern Hills, and a bright moon lit the dawn.
Everywhere cocks were crowing.

    No one dreamed it would come to this.
    The turmoil, so few years ago,
    attending the move to Fukuhara
    now stood all too clearly revealed
    as a portent of what lay ahead.
    Lord Motomichi, too, the regent,
    had joined the imperial cortege,
    but where Shichijō crosses Ōmiya,
    a boy with his hair bound in side loops
    ran right in front of his carriage.
    Written on the boy's left sleeve,
    Motomichi saw the words "spring sun."
    He realized that, read "Kasuga,"
    these spell the name of the deity
    who watches over the Hossō teachings
    and protects the heirs of Kamatari.
    A voice, no doubt the boy's, reached him:
        And so there it is:
        These newest wisteria leaves[193]
            are truly dying;
        still, they might yet think to heed
        the counsel of spring and sun.

192. Genjō (a biwa) and Suzuka (a *wagon,* or "Japanese koto") were prized imperial treasures.
193. The current generation of Fujiwara nobles.

Lord Motomichi summoned his attendant, Takanao.
"I have been thinking," he said. "His Majesty, yes, is on his way,
but not the cloistered emperor. To me the Heike future seems bleak.
What is *your* opinion?"
Takanao traded glances with the groom who led the ox.
The groom understood. He turned the carriage around,

> and northward they went, up Ōmiya,
> oh, so fast they seemed to be flying,
> up to the city's Northern Hills,
> and in through the gate of Chisoku-in.[194]

14. *Koremori's Flight from the Capital*

A Heike houseman named Moritsugi demanded when he heard the news
that they should pursue the regent and stop him,
but the others restrained him, and he stayed where he was.

For some days now, Lord Koremori had been steeling himself
to face what he feared was coming, but it still hurt when it came.
He had married the daughter of Narichika, the Naka-no-mikado grand counselor.

> Face, peach blossoms laden with dew;
> eyes, all the graces of powder and rouge;
> hair, willow fronds in the wind, swaying—
> such beauty surely was hers alone.
> Rokudai, the son she had borne him,
> had now entered his tenth year,
> while their daughter was still in her eighth.
> All three pleaded not to be left behind.
> Koremori then spoke to his wife:

"As I have told you, the Heike are now fleeing toward the west.
I only wish that I could take you with me,
but they say that the enemy will be lying in wait for us on the way.
We cannot possibly pass unchallenged.
Please, if you hear that I have been killed, do not for that become a nun.
I want you instead to marry again, never mind whom,
to provide for yourself and properly bring up our children.
I cannot imagine that no one would wish to look after you."
So he addressed her consolingly, but she did not answer.
She only lay there in silence, a robe over her head.
He was about to leave when she clung to his sleeve.

....

194. A temple north of the city, in the present area of Murasakino.

"Here in the capital," she said,
"I have neither father nor mother.
Where will I ever find a husband
once you have gone off without me?
Marry, you say, anyone you please—
oh, I could almost hate you for that!
Past lives brought us together, you know.
You, yes, may feel affection for me,
but would just anyone do the same?
We promised always to stay together,
right to the end, to disappear
like dewdrops side by side in a meadow,
like flotsam sunk to the same ocean floor.
So did you just make them all up,
those sweet nothings of yours in the night?
If all this concerned no one but me,
I could manage life here alone,
nursing the pain of being forsaken.
But who, I ask, will look after the children?
What do you want me to do with *them*?
You are too cruel not to take us with you!"
So she spoke, now reproachful, now pleading.
Koremori answered her.
"Yes," he said, "it is perfectly true.
You were in your thirteenth year,
I in my fifteenth when we first met,
and I swore then that, fire or flood,
I would always remain beside you,
till we reached that last fork in the road.
But heartless, yes, I would be indeed,
now that in so dismal a manner
I am about to set off to war,
were I to subject you to bitter trials
on a journey to who-knows-where.
Besides, I am not ready to take you.
Once we settle on some far shore,
then I will send somebody for you."
With these words he left, resolutely.
In the gallery by the middle gate,
he donned his armor, then caught his horse
and was almost in the saddle

when his son and daughter came running,
took his sleeve, tugged at his armor skirts,
calling, "But, Father, where are you going?
Take me with you!" "I want to go, too!"
Both were crying. "Ah, such are the ties,"
Koremori lamented to himself,
"that bind us to this world of sorrow!"
He seemed less and less able to move.

> Meanwhile his five younger brothers rode through the gate and halted
> beside him: Sukemori, Kiyotsune, and Arimori of the Palace Guards,
> the consultant Tadafusa, and Moromori, the governor of Bitchū.
>
> "Still here?" they said. "What are you up to? The imperial palanquin
> must be long gone by now."

Koremori mounted and started off with them
but then turned back, rode up to the veranda,
and lifted the edge of a blind with the tip of his bow.
"Take a good look, all of you!
My children were desperate to come with me,
and while I gave them what comfort I could,
I forgot for a time how late I was leaving."
He burst into tears, and all those present
wept into their armor's moistened sleeves.

> Now, there were among his housemen two brothers: Saitōgo, in his
> nineteenth year, and Saitōroku, in his seventeenth. These two, on ei-
> ther side, gripped Koremori's bridle at the bit and declared themselves
> ready to follow him anywhere.
>
> Koremori replied, "When Sanemori, your father, went down to the
> north, you loudly insisted that you would go with him, but for his own
> reasons he left you here. Then he died on that northern campaign.
> Seasoned warrior that he was, he no doubt foresaw what has hap-
> pened. Now I am leaving Rokudai without anyone I trust to look after
> him. You will oblige me greatly by staying behind."

So he spoke. The brothers swallowed their tears and stayed.
"Never in all our life together
did I think you could be so callous!"
weeping, his wife cried where she lay.
His son, his daughter, the gentlewomen
tumbled, writhing, through the blinds,
heedless of any listening presence,
wailing in full-throated despair.
Their voices lodged deep in his ears.

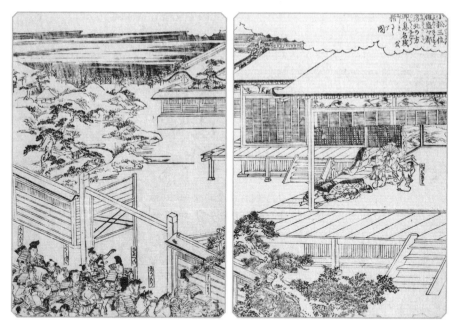

Koremori's farewell.

Even in the winds that blew
across the western ocean waves,
he must have felt he heard them still.
Before they fled the capital,
the Heike set fire to Rokuhara,
the Ike Mansion, the Komatsu Mansion,
Hachijō, Nishi-Hachijō, and so on—
many a senior noble's residence,
many a privy gentleman's house,
to the number of twenty and more,
and those, too, of their retainers,
as well as forty or fifty thousand
commoners' houses throughout the city
and Shirakawa. They burned them all.

15. The Honor of the Emperor's Presence

Some of these the imperial presence had honored.
Only foundation stones now marked those phoenix gates,
mere dents in the earth where his palanquin had stood.
In some an empress had once entertained her guests,

where now chill winds moaned over dewy garden wastes.
Mansions fragrant with incense, hung with green curtains,
whose woods offered game and whose waters fish—
mansions where lived the greatest lords of the land,
built with loving care at the cost of long labor—
were simply gone, reduced in an instant to ash.
Imagine, then, the retainers' modest houses,
their doors of woven wormwood, their light brushwood gates,
and the flimsy huts sheltering huddled servants!
The devouring flames burned out dozens of acres.
So must it have been, alas, when mighty Wu fell
and the Gusutai Palace turned to dewy brambles,
when ruin overtook once-tyrannical Qin
and smoke shrouded the Xianyang Palace parapet.
Once the Heike had held the steep Han Valley pass,
as it were, between the east and west Yao peaks,
but then the northern barbarians drove them out.
To the deep current of the Jing and Wei rivers
they next looked for aid, but the eastern barbarians
robbed them of that refuge. Could they have imagined
expulsion from the seat of all noble courtesy,
weeping, out into loutish, ignorant darkness?
One day they were godly dragons, above the clouds,
dispensing rain, the next dried fish in the market.
Fortune and misfortune both travel the same road;
glory and decline are the two sides of one hand.
What happened reveals that truth, plain for all to see.
Who could not grieve over the fall of the Heike?
In Hōgen, long ago, they bloomed like spring flowers;
in Juei, the present, they fell like autumn leaves.
In the seventh month of Jishō 4, three men had come up to the capital [1180]
to take up their tour of duty as guards at the palace.
Hatakeyama Shigeyoshi, Oyamada Arishige, and Utsunomiya Tomotsuna
were detained there until Juei. Events then commended their execution.
Lord Tomomori, however, demurred.
"Now that the good fortune of your house has run its course,"
he said to Lord Munemori, "beheading a hundred or a thousand men
would do nothing to make you again the master of the world.
They have wives and children at home, and their own followers.
Imagine, then, how all of these will mourn!
If by some miracle fate smiles on you again and you return to the capital,

then they will be grateful for your rare compassion.
Surely the better course for you, just this once,
will be to release these men and send them home."
"You are quite right," Munemori replied. He let them go.
They touched their heads to the ground before him and wept.
"You have sustained our worthless lives ever since Jishō," they insisted,
"and we ask only to follow His Majesty with you, wherever his progress may
    lead."
"But I have no doubt that your hearts are in the east," Munemori answered,
"and on this westward journey, I have no use for hollow shells of men.
Go now, as fast as you can."
They went down from the capital with tears in their eyes.
> Twenty years and more he had been to them
> lord and master. No wonder, then,
> that on leaving him they should have wept.

16. Tadanori's Flight from the Capital

Tadanori, governor of Satsuma, turned back from wherever he was
and, with five housemen and a page, rode up to Lord Shunzei's house on Gojō.[195]
He found the gate closed. It did not open for him.
He announced his name. "I am back from among the fleeing Heike," he added.
This provoked a commotion within.
Next he dismounted and declared in a loud voice,
"I have only one reason for returning: I wish to speak to Lord Shunzei.
If the gate is to remain shut, so be it,
but, Lord Shunzei, please come out so that I may talk to you!"
"I have an idea what this may be about," Shunzei said.
"There is nothing to fear from him. Let him in."
They opened the gate, and the two met.
It was in all ways a moving encounter.
> Tadanori said, "I have held you in high regard ever since you gave me
> my first lesson in poetry, long ago, but the turmoil in the capital these
> last two or three years and rebellion in province after province—all
> matters affecting the fortunes of my house—have prevented me from
> calling on you regularly, despite my continuing devotion to the art.
His Majesty has already left the city, and the days of Heike glory are over.
> There is to be, so I am told,

---

195. Fujiwara no Shunzei (1114–1204), the major poet of his time. He completed *Senzaishū*, the imperi-
ally commissioned anthology mentioned below, in 1187.

a new imperial anthology,
for which a selection must be made.
You would do me the greatest honor
ever to add luster to my life
if you were, in your great kindness,
to include just one poem of mine.
I long entertained that hope,
until disorder engulfed the world
and, to my bitter disappointment,
talk of this great project ceased.

Surely, though, once peace returns, your work on the anthology will resume.
Should you find anything suitable in the scroll I have brought you,
be it a single poem, and favor it with your kindness,
then the joy of it will reach me even beneath the moss,
and from afar you shall have my grateful protection."

From among his poems over the years,
he had picked the hundred he thought best
and written them all out on a scroll
that he kept with him at the last.
Now, from where his armor joined,
he took it and gave it to Lord Shunzei.

Shunzei opened the scroll and cast his eyes over it.
"Having received this precious token from you," he said,
"I shall not—you may be certain of that—treat it in any way lightly.
Have no doubt on that score. Why, the way you have come
shows so deep a devotion to poetry that it brings tears to my eyes."
Tadanori replied in great joy,
"Let the waves of the western ocean swallow me if they will,
let my corpse lie if it must in the wilderness,
in this vale of tears I will leave no regrets.
I bid you farewell."
He remounted his horse, tied his helmet cord,
and started out westward once more.

Watching him recede into the distance,
Shunzei heard what must have been his voice,
loudly singing these Chinese lines:
"The way that still lies before me stretches far;
my thoughts race to the evening clouds over Mount Yan."
Sorry indeed to see Tadanori go,
Shunzei all but wept as he went back in.

Later on, when peace came again,
he returned to his task of choosing
poems to go into the *Senzaishū*,
The Harvest of a Thousand Years.
Thinking back to Tadanori's visit—
his demeanor, the words he had spoken—
Shunzei felt still more deeply moved.
There were in that scroll deserving poems,
a good many of them, but Tadanori
was nonetheless under imperial ban
and Shunzei had to leave out his name.
The single poem he included,
on "Blossoms in the Old Capital,"
appeared only as "author unknown":

> By rippling waters
> the old Shiga capital
> vanished long ago,
> yet, as then, Mount Nagara
> blossoms with mountain cherries.

Tadanori was by that time
a banned enemy of the court,
so that Shunzei had no choice,
but the blow was very hard.

17. Tsunemasa's Flight from the Capital

Taira no Tsunemasa, the deputy master of the grand empress's household,
was the son of Tsunemori, the director of upkeep.
In his youth, as a temple page, he had served the prince-abbot of Ninnaji,
and despite the turmoil he must have looked back fondly on those days,
for with half a dozen housemen he rode to Ninnaji,
dismounted at the gate, and sent in these words:

> "The time of the Taira house is past,
> and I leave the capital today.
> Amid all the sorrows of this world,
> I have left only one regret,
> Your Reverence: that I must leave you.
> I first served you in my eighth year
> and remained until I came of age,
> in my thirteenth. During all that time

I never left you, except when ill,
and yet today I am bound a thousand leagues westward across the ocean
and do not know what day or hour will return me to you.
This so pains me that I have come to call on you a last time.
Having already donned my armor, however, and taken up bow and arrows,
I know that I am not in fit guise for you to receive me."
Such was his message. The prince-abbot was moved.

"Come in as you are," he said.
Tsunemasa had on that day
a *hitatare* robe of purple brocade
under armor with green, shaded lacing.
He wore at his waist a sword and scabbard
gold-trimmed and, on his back, arrows
fletched with black and white eagle feathers.
The bow that he clasped beneath his arm
was rattan-wrapped, lacquered in black.
He slung his helmet back over his shoulders
and there, before his old master's quarters,
knelt in a posture of deep respect.
The prince-abbot came out at once
and had his blinds raised. "Come in, come in!"
he said. Tsunemasa did so.

Tsunemasa then summoned Tōbyōe Arinori, one of the men with him.
Arinori carried a biwa, which he brought to his lord in its red brocade bag.
Tsunemasa took the instrument and placed it before the prince-abbot.

"Some years ago," he began,
"you kindly entrusted me with Seizan,
which I have had brought here today.
Parting with Seizan is painful indeed,
but the thought that so great a treasure
might come to grief out in the wilds
is one that I find I cannot bear.
Should fortune by some miraculous chance smile on my house again
and I return to the capital, then I would gladly borrow Seizan once more."
He wept as he spoke, and the prince-abbot was moved to make this verse:

> You who go your way
> with such lingering regret:
> In your memory
> you leave behind a token
> that I shall keep wrapped with care.

Whereupon Tsunemasa begged the use of his inkstone to write:

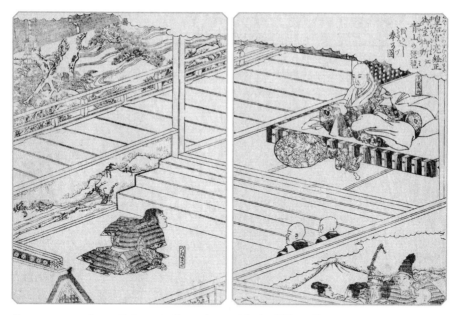

Tsunemasa returns Seizan to the prince-abbot of Ninnaji.

> The water that flows
> hither through the bamboo pipe
>   is never the same;
> but oh, how I wish that change
> would leave me always with you!

He bade the prince-abbot farewell
and was setting out when the others present—
acolytes, clerics, monk officials—
clung to his sleeves, mourned his departure,
and shed many tears. One among them,
a junior monk during his boyhood,
was now the distinguished prelate Gyōkei,
son of Mitsuyori, the grand counselor.
Grieving to see Tsunemasa go,
he went with him to the Katsura River
but unhappily could go no farther.
They parted in tears. Gyōkei gave him:

> So it is, alas:
> Ancient be they or still young,
>   mountain cherry trees
> when that time comes, soon or late,
> lose their blossoms, every one.

To which Tsunemasa replied,

> *For the journey dressed,*
> *I shall spread night after night*
> *solitary sleeves*
> *and travel, as I know full well,*
> *an interminable road.*

A man of his who carried for him
a rolled red banner swiftly unfurled it.
"There it is!" his housemen cried,
where they awaited him here and there,
and raced, a hundred strong, to join him.
Whips raised high, all galloped off
and soon overtook the imperial train.

18. Seizan

In his seventeenth year, Tsunemasa had gone down to Kyushu
as an imperial envoy to the great Usa Shrine.
Having been given Seizan, he took the instrument with him
and, before the main sanctuary, played the secret pieces.
The shrine priests, who knew little enough of music,
nonetheless moistened the sleeves of their green robes with tears of emotion.
Not even the servants, who had never heard music at all,
can have mistaken those wondrous notes for a shower of rain.
It was a marvelous moment.

> Now, to speak of the biwa Seizan:
> Of old, in Emperor Ninmyō's reign,
> in the spring of the year Kashō 3, [850]
> Fujiwara no Sadatoshi
> made the crossing to Tang China
> and there encountered Lian Chengwu,
> the great Tang master of the biwa,
> who taught him the Three Biwa Pieces.
> Sadatoshi returned to Japan
> with three biwas received from his master:
> Genjō, Shishimaru, and Seizan.
> Surely the Dragon God coveted them,
> for on the way so mighty a storm
> beset his ship that Sadatoshi
> dropped Shishimaru in offering
> into the sea but brought the two others

successfully home and to our emperor
gave them as treasures for his house.
During the reign of Murakami,
one fifteenth night in the Ōwa years, [961–64]
a new-risen moon shone in the sky
and a cool, refreshing breeze blew
while His Majesty played Genjō.
At that moment a shadowy form
appeared before him and a voice
light and marvelously distinguished
sang to the music he had begun.
The emperor put down the biwa and asked,
"What manner of man are you, and from where do you come?"
 "I am he," the shadow replied,
"who gave Sadatoshi the Three Biwa Pieces.
I am the great biwa master of Tang:
Lian Chengwu is my name.
I withheld from among those three
one especially secret movement
and sank for that to the demon realm.
Just now I heard the marvelous sound

The shadowy Lian Chengwu teaches the emperor a secret biwa piece.

that your plectrum draws from the strings
and therefore came into your presence.
I should like, if I may, to teach you
the movement I so unwisely omitted
and thus achieve enlightenment."
With these words he took up Seizan,
which stood there before His Majesty,
tightened the strings, and straightaway
taught the emperor the missing movement
in two parts: Shōgen and Sekishō.
No one thereafter, sovereign or subject,
dared to touch the strings of Seizan,
which then passed, an imperial gift,
to the prince-abbot of Ninnaji;
who gave it in loan, the story goes,
to Tsunemasa, then a young boy
and the abbot's favorite acolyte.
The back was of wisteria wood,
and on the front a painting showed
the moon rising into a dawn sky
from between green, summery peaks:
hence the name Seizan, or "Green Hills."
Genjō was a wonder equally rare.

19. The Heike Flight from the Capital

The grand counselor Yorimori, like the others,
started out after setting fire to his residence,
but at the Toba Mansion south gate he paused.
"I forgot something," he said.
He cut off his red insignia and, with three hundred men, rode back to the city.
The Heike houseman Moritsugi raced to come before Lord Munemori.
"Look, my lord!" he cried. "Lord Yorimori is staying behind,
and many of his men with him. I call this an outrage!
As to Lord Yorimori himself, I of course would not dare,
but I would gladly send an arrow after his men!"
"Scoundrels who forget all they have come to owe this house over the years
and who shy away from sharing our fate to the end," Munemori replied,
"are not worth the trouble." Moritsugi was obliged to desist.
"And Shigemori's sons, where are they?" Munemori continued.

"None has arrived," came the reply.

Tomomori wept. "Not a day has passed since we left the city," he said,

"and see already how cruelly men's hearts change!

This is exactly what I thought would happen,

and that is why I argued for making our last stand in the capital itself."

He glared angrily at Munemori.

> And what had decided Yorimori to stay? The thing is that Yorimori had always shown him goodwill. "I think very highly of you, you know," Yoritomo often assured him. "For me, as Great Bodhisattva Hachiman is my witness, Lady Ike still lives in you," and so on. Indeed, when Yoritomo sent a force up to the capital against the Heike, he carefully enjoined them never to direct their arrows against Yorimori's men.
>
> "The days of Heike glory are over, and already they have fled the city," Yorimori said. "For me salvation now lies with Yoritomo." That seems to be why he went back.

He sought refuge at Ninnaji, at the Tokiwa Mansion of the Hachijō Princess.

Saishō, his wife, was one of the princess's gentlewomen and her foster sister.

> "Should such a need ever arise,
>
> please," Yorimori begged Her Highness,
>
> "do what you can to keep me from harm."
>
> "If only my wishes mattered these days . . ."
>
> she answered him discouragingly.

He could count on Yoritomo's goodwill, that much he knew,

but what the other Genji might do, he had no idea.

He felt nagging anxiety at having so cut himself off from his fellows.

> Such was his mood that he felt caught
>
> between sharp rocks and the deep blue sea.

Meanwhile Lord Shigemori's sons, Koremori and his five brothers, with a thousand men,

caught up with the imperial cortege on the Mutsuda riverbank, at Yodo.

Munemori had been expecting them and greeted them with joy.

"What took you so long?" he asked.

"My children wanted desperately to come with me," Koremori replied,

"and trying to cheer them up delayed my departure."

"Why did you so unkindly leave Rokudai behind?"

"Because there is no knowing where our journey may take us."

Munemori's question drew tears from poor Koremori.

> And who were they, then, the Taira
>
> who fled the capital on this day?

These senior nobles:
    Munemori, once palace minister;
    Tokitada, grand counselor;
    Norimori, counselor;
    Tomomori, counselor;
    Tsunemori, director of upkeep;
    Kiyomune, Right Gate Watch commander;
    Shigehira, Palace Guards captain;
    Koremori, Palace Guards captain;
    Sukemori, Palace Guards captain;
    Michimori, Echizen governor.
And these privy gentlemen:
    Nobumoto, head of the Treasury;
    Tokizane, Palace Guards captain;
    Kiyotsune, Palace Guards captain;
    Arimori, Palace Guards lieutenant;
    Tadafusa, adviser;
    Tsunemasa, of the grand empress's household;
    Yukimori, chief left equerry;
    Tadanori, Satsuma governor;
    Noritsune, Noto governor;
    Tomoakira, Musashi governor;
    Moromori, Bitchū governor;
    Kiyofusa, Awaji governor;
    Kiyosada, Owari governor;
    Tsunetoshi, Wakasa governor;
    Masaakira, of the Bureau of War;
    Narimori, chamberlain;
    Atsumori, fifth rank without office.
And these monks:
    Senshin, the great prelate;
    Nōen, superintendent of Hosshōji;
    Chūkai, master of discipline;
    Yūen, adept.
And housemen, including
    provincial governors,
    police officials,
    guardsmen from the various corps,
    in all, one hundred and sixty.
Seven thousand Heike were there:

the small number whom death had spared
over the two or three years just spent
campaigning in east and north.
At the Yamazaki barrier chapel,
they set down His Majesty's palanquin
and prayed from there to Otokoyama.
This was Tokitada's poignant prayer:
"All hail, Hachiman, Great Bodhisattva,
return, in your mercy, His Majesty
and all of us here to the capital!"
They looked back the way they had come:
Mist seemed to fill the sky, and desolate plumes of rising smoke.
Lord Norimori made this verse:

> All so quickly gone!
> A man leaves his house behind,
>   there beyond the clouds,
> and where once he made his home,
> smoke rises into the sky.

To which Noritsune added:

> Behind us we see
> the city that was our home
>   now a burned-out waste
> and, before, an endless road
> over wastes of smoking waves.

And so it was: The capital,
once their home, was far away
across smoldering desolation,
while there lay ahead of them
ten thousand leagues of cloud and wave.
Imagine how they must have felt!

Sadayoshi, the governor of Higo, heard that there were Genji lying in wait at Kawajiri, and he rode there with five hundred men to dispose of them. However, the news turned out to be false, and he started back toward the capital. Near Udono he encountered the imperial cortege.

He dismounted and knelt respectfully before Munemori, his bow under his arm. "Where are you all bound, my lord, in your flight?" he asked. "If to the western provinces, then I fear that you will be harried as fugitives hither and yon, and suffer infamy. I beg you instead to face in the capital itself whatever must be."

Munemori replied, "But have you not heard? Yoshinaka is already attacking from the north with fifty thousand men. Higashi-Sakamoto, below Mount Hiei, is swarming with them. And the cloistered emperor vanished in the middle of last night. If only our fate were at stake, very well, but it would be too painful to expose His Majesty's mother and my own to cruel misfortune. For that reason I have preferred to have His Majesty undertake this journey after all, with a suitable escort."

"Very well," Sadayoshi answered, "then I request leave to meet my own fate in the capital." He portioned out his men among Shigemori's sons and with a small band of thirty riders returned to the city.

There the news reached Yorimori that Sadayoshi was back,
meaning to kill any Taira who had stayed behind.
"He must be thinking of *me*!" Yorimori reflected in panic.
Sadayoshi curtained off the burned-out Nishi-Hachijō Mansion and spent the
   night there,
but not a single Heike gentleman turned up.
Perhaps somewhat disheartened after all, he made up his mind
that at least no Genji horses should beat their hooves upon Shigemori's grave.
To this end he had the bones disinterred and, weeping, addressed them:
   "O misery and disaster!
   See, my lord, the fate of your house!
   It has been written since ages past:
   'To all the living shall come death;
   upon happiness follows sorrow';
   yet never have I, with my own eyes,
   witnessed such a catastrophe.
   Surely, my lord, you foresaw all this,
   prayed in that spirit to gods and buddhas,
   and so hastened the end of your life.
   I am lost in admiration.
   I should really have gone with you,
   still your companion at the last,
   but no, my worthless life dragged on,
   only to leave me facing this ruin,
   mourning everything we have lost.
   When I die, come forward, I beg,
   to welcome me into paradise."
   In tears he addressed his distant lord,
   sent the bones off to Mount Kōya,

dug up the earth surrounding the grave,
and let the Kamo River take it.
Perhaps by now he felt only despair,
for he then fled quite the other way,
eastward, to Utsunomiya—
a man he had once had in his care
and treated well. In that goodwill
he apparently placed his trust,
and Utsunomiya did indeed,
they say, show him great kindness.

20. *The Flight from Fukuhara*

All the senior Heike present—
Munemori first among them,
and excepting only Koremori—
were there with their wives and children,
but not so their juniors in rank,
who would have brought too many.
To flee, these had left their families
without the slightest indication
when they might be reunited.
Separation seems painfully long
even to those who know the day,
the hour of their assured return.
Imagine, then, the greater sorrow
when this day is the last together,
and good-bye is a final farewell.
Those leaving and those who stayed
could only wring tears from their sleeves.
Long-standing Heike retainers
remembered many and weighty favors
they could not dismiss; yet young and old
glanced back over and over again,
and made very slow progress forward.
Some slept by waves on rocky shores,
spending their days on the heaving sea;
some found their way to far distances,
braving precipitous slopes and crags.
Some whipped horses, some poled boats.

All of them fled as best they could.
When the Heike reached Fukuhara, their capital in times gone by,
Lord Munemori called together the best of his housemen, young or old,
several hundred in all, and addressed them in these words:
"This house, once rich in the stored benefit of good deeds, has none left;
accrued evil now casts its shadow over us and blights our lives.
Therefore the gods have abandoned us, and so, too, the cloistered emperor.
Now that we have left the imperial city to wander the world, where is our refuge?
And yet to seek shelter with a stranger under the same tree confirms a bond
    from past lives;
to drink with another from the same stream likewise reveals a tie from earlier
    births.
Consider, then, all of you, that yours is no passing deference to this house,
but that generation after generation you have been our retainers.
Some among you are close relatives, hence indissolubly bound to us;
others are beholden to us for liberal favor over the generations.
Then, when we prospered, you lived off our bounty.
Now, how could you fail to requite the debt you owe?
Besides, our most noble and sovereign lord is with us, bearing the three regalia.
Will you not follow him into any wilderness, be it ever so remote?"
So he spoke, and old and young wept.
"They say that the least bird or beast shows gratitude for kindness," they replied.
"How, then, could we as human beings not honor that principle?
For twenty years and more, we have owed all to our lord,
all that we have needed to care for our wives and children,
all that we have required in our own lives.
It is to our lord that we owe everything.

>To the man of bow and arrow,
>the man who fights astride his steed,
>divided loyalty means shame.
>Therefore we are resolved to go
>anywhere our sovereign leads,
>be it even beyond Japan,
>to Silla, Paekche, Koguryŏ,
>to the grasslands of the Khitans,
>to any region of the earth."

So all of them spoke, with one voice,
greatly reassuring their leaders.

>That night they spent in the Fukuhara of old,
>the early-autumn moon a waning crescent.

In the deep night silence, under an empty sky,
heads laid, as travelers' are, on grassy pillows,
they mingled a flood of tears with gathering dews
and gave themselves to growing melancholy.
Well knowing they would never come here again,
they gazed on all that Lord Kiyomori had built:
the hilltop retreat, looking out over spring blossoms;
the seaside retreat for watching the autumn moon;
the running spring, pine grove, and riding-ground pavilions;
the two-story viewing stand, the snow-view retreat;
the rustic thatched retreat; the great lords' houses;
the palace proper, erected for His Majesty
by Kunitsuna, on Kiyomori's orders,
with mandarin-duck tiles and smooth stone walkways.
Every one of these, after only three years,
betrayed invading ruin. Mosses choked the paths,
autumn weeds blocked gates, roof tiles sprouted ferns,
vines weighed fences down, while moss-grown lookouts leaned,
deserted but for wind through the pines. Their blinds gone,
sleeping chambers gaped, open only to moonlight.
    Dawn broke. They set the Fukuhara palace on fire;
then all, with the emperor, boarded their ships.
This, too, was a wrench, if one somewhat less painful
than when they abandoned the capital proper.
Smoke from seafolk fires at dusk, boiling down seaweed,
the stag on the hillside, belling into the dawn,
the noise of waves breaking, down long stretches of coast,
the moon gleaming back from teardrop-strewn sleeves,
cricket voices singing among wastes of grasses—
not a sight, not a sound that reached them did not hurt.
Yesterday they stood at the gates of the Kanto,
bridle to bridle, a full hundred thousand men;
today their seven thousand loosed hawsers to sail
the waves of western seas calm under distant cloud,
with the sun already sinking in a clear sky.
Beyond a mist-shrouded island, the moon rose.
Following the tides past ever-farther shores,
their ships seemed to mount to the clouded heavens.
"How far we have come!" they thought, shedding endless tears.
On the waves they saw gathered a flock of white birds.

"Why, there they are! That Ariwara, back then,
put a question to them by the Sumida River!
These must be"—they sighed—"his dear 'capital birds'!"[196]

In Juei 2, the seventh month and twenty-fifth day, [1183]
the Heike vanished from the capital for good.

....

196. In episode 9 of *Ise monogatari,* the homesick Ariwara no Narihira reaches the Sumida River, which now runs through Tokyo. He sees white birds playing on the water. When told they are *miyako-dori* (literally, "capital birds"), he says in a poem, "If your name be true, / then I will ask you something. / Say, capital birds, / of the one who has my heart: / does she live or has she died?" Translation from Mostow and Tyler, *The Ise Stories,* p. 36.

BOOK EIGHT

1. The Imperial Journey to Mount Hiei

(recitative)

In Juei 2, deep in the night of the twenty-fourth of the seventh month,
and in the company only of Suketoki, son of the grand counselor Sukekata,
the cloistered emperor slipped out of his residence and made for Kurama.
When the priests there objected that this was still too close to the city,
he braved the precipitous path to Yokawa, via Sasa-no-mine and Yakuōzaka,
and there he installed himself in the Jakujō lodge, in Gedatsudani.
When the Hiei monks rose up to demand that he go on to the East Pagoda,
he moved to the En'yū lodge in Minamidani,
where monks and warriors then mounted guard.

> *(song)*
> The cloistered emperor stole away
> to seek refuge on Mount Hiei,
> the emperor ventured from his palace
> to set out for the western sea,
> and the regent, so people said,
> made for the depths of Yoshino.
> Great ladies close to His Majesty,
> princes and princesses, fled
> to hide at Yawata, Kamo, Saga,
> Uzumasa, or in the hills
> to the east and west of the city.
> The Heike were undoubtedly gone,
> but the Genji had not yet entered.
> The capital had no master at all.
> Never since the city's founding,
> surely, had any such thing occurred.
> One would like very much to know
> what *The Record of Future Time*
> left to us by Prince Shōtoku[197]
> might have to say on the subject.
>> The news spread that His Cloistered Eminence
>> had gone to Mount Hiei. Everyone rushed there:

....

197. A prophetic text attributed to Prince Shōtoku and often mentioned in medieval writing.

the former regent, Motofusa;
the current regent, Motomichi;
the chancellor; both the ministers,
left and right; the palace minister;
the counselors and grand counselors;
the consultants; the privy gentlemen
of the third, the fourth, the fifth ranks—
yes, everyone who was anyone,
every man who hoped for promotion,
every man of wealth and high office
came; not a single one stayed away.
At the En'yū lodge, an enormous crowd
filled every space within and without.
Those present took all this as a tribute
to the Mountain and to their abbot.

    On the twenty-eighth, the sovereign
made his way back to the city.
Kiso assigned to his protection
fifty thousand mounted warriors.
Yamamoto Yoshitaka,
a leader of the Ōmi Genji,
rode near him in the forward guard,
white banner flying. No such banner
had been seen to enter the capital
for a good twenty years and more.
These were astonishing events.

Meanwhile Yukiie crossed the Uji Bridge to enter the city.
Yata Yoshikiyo, Yoshiyasu's son, entered via Ōeyama.
The Genji from Settsu and Kawachi poured in like swirling mist or cloud.
Genji warriors filled the capital.

(speech)

Tsunefusa, the Kade-no-kōji counselor, and Saneie, the police chief and Left Gate Watch intendant, waited upon the cloistered emperor on the veranda of his lodging. From there they summoned Yoshinaka and Yukiie.

    Kiso no Yoshinaka wore Chinese damask-laced armor over a red brocade *hitatare* and, at his side, an imposing sword. The arrows in his quiver were fletched in mottled black and white, under his arm he clasped a lacquered bow closely rattan-wound, and his helmet hung over his shoulders on a cord. Yukiie, for his part, wore scarlet leather-laced armor over dark blue brocade. A sword with gold fittings hung

at his side, the arrows at his back were fletched in bold black and white
bands, and his bow was lacquered black over closely wound rattan. He,
too, had his helmet slung over his shoulders on a cord. Both men knelt
respectfully.
His Cloistered Eminence issued them the command
to crush former palace minister Munemori and all the Heike beneath him.
Below, on the ground, they received it with all humility.
They then submitted that neither had anywhere to stay.
Yoshinaka was granted a house at Rokujō and Nishi-no-tōin:
that of Naritada, the master of the cloistered emperor's table.
Yukiie received "Kaya House," the south pavilion of the Hōjūji residence.

> His Cloistered Eminence imagined
> only with great unhappiness
> the emperor spirited off, a captive,
> by his commoner relatives,
> roaming the waves of the western sea.
> He therefore issued a decree
> commanding that the emperor
> and the three regalia with him
> be returned forthwith to the city.
> However, the Heike ignored him.

Emperor Antoku's father, Takakura, had had three other sons.
The Heike had taken the second with them in their flight,
so as to make him heir apparent.
The third and fourth stayed behind.
On the fifth of the month, His Cloistered Eminence had those two visit him.
"Come! Come to me!" he called to the third, then in his fifth year.
The little boy looked up at him and shrank back.
"Off you go, then!" the sovereign dismissed him.
Next it was the turn of the fourth, then in his fourth year.
"Come!" he called, and with no hint of shyness
the fourth prince did so and clambered up onto his lap.
He seemed delighted to be there. Go-Shirakawa wept.

> "Truly," he said, "no little child
> but one so intimately related
> could set eyes on an old monk like me
> and still feel any affection.
> Yes, this boy is my true grandson,
> and just like his father at that age.
> To think I had not seen him before!"
> He simply could not stay his tears.

Present then in attendance on him
was the great lady of Jōdoji,
still known then as Lady Tango.
"Why, then," she said, "this is the prince
you should have succeed to the throne."
"Obviously," the sovereign replied.
Divination he had commissioned
yielded this solemn assurance:
"Should the Fourth Prince come to the throne,
his line will rule this land of Japan
for one hundred generations."

> The prince's mother was a daughter of Nobutaka, the director of up-
> keep. She had served Kenreimon-in while this lady was still empress,
> and the emperor had called her to his side so often that she gave him
> a succession of children.
>
> Nobutaka had several daughters, and he had aspired to see one be-
> come a consort or an empress. Believing that a house with a thousand
> white chickens is sure to produce an empress, he secured a thousand
> of his own,[198] and perhaps that is indeed why this one bore several
> princes. Privately, Nobutaka was delighted, but awe of the Heike and
> fear of the empress discouraged him from making much of them.
> However, Kiyomori's wife, Lady Nii, urged him to set his mind at rest.
>
> "I shall look after them myself," she said, "and make one heir appar-
> ent." She assigned several nurses to their care and saw to their up-
> bringing.

It was Lady Nii's elder brother Nōen, the head monk of Hosshōji,
who actually nurtured the Fourth Prince.
Nōen had fled westward with the Heike,
but in the turmoil and confusion he left his wife and the prince behind.
A messenger from the west then arrived with the command
that Nōen's wife should join her husband immediately, with the prince and his
    mother.
Hugely relieved, Nōen's wife set off with the prince, as required.
She had reached the western stretch of Shichijō when her elder brother,
Norimitsu, the governor of Kii, caught up with her.
"Are you out of your mind?" he demanded to know.
"Why, this prince has a golden future opening out before him!"
He stopped her right there,
and the next day the cloistered emperor sent a carriage to fetch the prince.

....

198. No explanation is known for this extravagant notion.

sent a volley of messengers
racing off to inform Eryō.
"It looks bad for Her Majesty's man,"
they said. "Something needs to be done."
Eryō was engaged at the time
in performing the rite of Daiitoku.
"Well, we simply can't have that!"
he declared. Smashing his *vajra*[200]
into his skull, he pounded his brains
to paste that he burned in the goma fire.[201]
Black smoke rose, and on he prayed,
rubbing his hands with frantic vigor,
until Yoshio claimed victory
and Prince Korehito the throne,
under the name of Emperor Seiwa [r. 858–76]
or, later, the Mizuno-o Emperor.
Ever since, the monks of Mount Hiei
have liked to say on every occasion,
"When Eryō smashed open his brains,
the younger prince gained the succession;
when Son'i wielded the sword of wisdom,
the spirit of Tenjin bowed to his will."[202]
But was dharma prowess all that did it?
They say that in every other case
the Sun Goddess made the final choice.
Off in the west, the outraged Heike learned what had happened
and rued not having fled with the Third and Fourth princes, too.
"But even if we had," Tokitada observed, "there is still Yoshinaka's patron,
that son of Prince Mochihito—the one that Shigehide, his guardian,
made a monk and took with him to the north.
His Cloistered Eminence would only have made *him* emperor instead."
Some objected that a prince who has left the world cannot succeed to the throne.
"That is not so," Tokitada replied.
"There have surely been in China, too,
sovereigns who once renounced the world.
Here, Emperor Tenmu comes first to mind. [r. 673–86]
During his time as heir apparent,

---

200. Japanese: *tokko*, a brass implement pointed at each end and essential in esoteric Buddhist ritual.
201. The sacred fire (Sanskrit: *homa*) burned on the altar during an esoteric ritual.
202. Son'i (866–940), then abbot of Mount Hiei, quelled the angry spirit of Tenjin (Sugawara no Michizane).

in deference to Prince Ōtomo
he shaved his head and disappeared
into the far depths of Yoshino,
but then he destroyed Prince Ōtomo
and became emperor after all.
Then, too, there is Empress Kōken, [r. 749–58]
who aspired to enlightenment,
put off every worldly adornment,
and came to be known as the nun Hōki
but who then rose to the throne again,
this time as Empress Shōtoku. [r. 764–70]
No, Yoshinaka's patron prince
could perfectly well have given up
religious life for the sovereign's."
On the second of the ninth month of that year, by the cloistered emperor's
    command,
a senior noble went as imperial envoy to Ise.
This envoy was the consultant Naganori.
        Earlier three retired emperors
        had sent just such an envoy to Ise:
        Suzaku, Shirakawa, and Toba.
        Each one of these did so, however,
        before giving up the profane world.
        None had ever done so *after*.

3. *The Reel of Thread*

Meanwhile the Heike in Kyushu had decided to build a new capital
but had not yet been able to decide where.
The emperor resided at Iwado, in the house of Tanenao.
        The houses of all the gentlemen
        stood scattered about in moor and paddy,
        and while no one there fulled hempen cloth,
        this could have been the village of Tōchi.²⁰³
        The palace itself was in the mountains,
        just like the log house in the old poem,
        and had an elegance all its own.

....

203. A *Shinkokinshū* poem by Princess Shokushi evokes Tōchi, a village not far from Nara, in connection with fulling (beating) hempen cloth. The name also sounds as though it means "remote place."

His Majesty went straight to the Usa Shrine,[204]
where he took as his residence
the house of the chief priest, Kinmichi.
Senior nobles and privy gentlemen
lodged in the shrine buildings themselves;
officials of the fifth and sixth ranks
had the surrounding gallery, and, in the court,
warriors from Shikoku and Kyushu,
in full armor, their weapons at hand,
ranged like gathering clouds and mists.
The red shrine fence, though venerable,
seemed in this way brilliantly renewed.
For seven days the retreat continued,
until on the last day, at dawn, Munemori
received an oracle in a dream.
The door of the sanctuary opened,
and an awesome voice spoke loud:

> Not even the gods
> command the vicissitudes
>   life inflicts on all.
> What, then, moves such fervent prayers
> at Usa in Tsukushi?

Munemori awoke, his heart pounding.

> Well, perhaps one day . . .
> Hope long harbored in the heart,
>   shrilling cricket song
> fade into mournful silence
> this nightfall, as autumn ends,

he said, sadly voicing an old poem.
The tenth of the ninth month came and went.
Evening winds swept the bending reeds
while the men slept alone, fully clothed,
weeping into desolate sleeves.
Deepening autumn melancholy
weighs on everyone equally,
but never more unbearably
than on those who are far from home.
On the thirteenth night of the month,
so famous for its brilliant moon,

....

204. Usa Hachimangū, a major shrine to Hachiman.

tears of longing for the city
helplessly clouded every eye.
For Tadanori, nights at the palace
making poetry under the moon
returned so vividly to mind
that he offered this:

> *Do only those friends*
> *who, this night a year ago,*
> > *watched the moon with me,*
> *far off in the capital,*
> *now preserve my memory?*

Then Tsunemori:

> *I miss her, I say!*
> *Just a year ago, it was,*
> > *she and I, all night,*
> *sealed our love for each other.*
> *How it all comes back to me!*

And Tsunemasa:

> *The way here was long,*
> *through broad wastes laden with dew,*
> > *yet I, no dewdrop,*

The Heike nobles making poetry in Kyushu.

live on still to watch the moon
from a place so alien.

The province of Bungo came under the sway of Fujiwara no Yorisuke, lord of
Justice,
and Yorisuke had installed his son, Yoritsune, there to act for him.
From the capital he sent Yoritsune a directive:
"The gods have abandoned the Heike, and so has His Cloistered Eminence.
They have fled the imperial city and as fugitives roam the waves.
The men of Kyushu accept them, however, and make them welcome.
This is intolerable. The men of Bungo are not to acknowledge them.
They are single-mindedly to drive the Heike away."
Such was the burden of his message.
Yoritsune transmitted his order to the Bungo warrior Okata Koreyoshi.
Now, this Koreyoshi had a fearsome forebear.

> In a far-off mountain hamlet of Bungo province, there once lived a
> young woman, her parents' only daughter. She had no husband, and
> her mother never knew that a man visited her every night. The months
> and years passed, and in time the young woman came to expect a
> child.
>
> Her mother was baffled. "Who has been visiting you?" she asked.
> "I see him come," her daughter answered, "but I do not see him go."
> "Very well," her mother told her. "When he leaves, attach a thread
> to him and follow it to where he goes."
>
> The daughter did so. The man had put on his light blue hunting
> cloak one morning, in preparation for leaving, when she stuck a needle
> into the collar. A thread ran back from the needle to a full reel. She
> followed it all the way to the Bungo border with Hyūga, the neighbor-
> ing province. It entered a huge cave under a peak named Uba-dake.

The young woman stood at the mouth of the cave and listened.
She heard loud groaning inside.
"Here I am!" she called. "I want to see you!"

> "My form is not human," a voice replied.
> "To look on me as I really am
> would terrify you out of your wits.
> Go home now, as fast as you can.
> The child you carry will be a son.
> With bow and arrow and all weapons
> he will be the mightiest warrior
> known in Kyushu and the islands."
> "Never mind: Whatever your form,"
> the woman answered, "you cannot dismiss

The great serpent.

the love you and I have shared so long.
Let us two look upon each other."
"As you wish," then came the reply,
and from the cave a serpent emerged,
five or six feet across when coiled
and some hundred and fifty feet long.
The needle she believed she had slipped
into her lover's hunting cloak
was caught in the serpent's gullet.

The young woman's wits indeed left her at the sight. The dozen or so
women with her collapsed with terror, screamed with fear, and fled. At
home again, she soon gave birth—and yes, it was a boy.

Her father, Daitayū, agreed to bring the boy up. Before even his
tenth year, he was broad of back, long of face, and tall. He came of age
in his seventh year, and they named him Daita, in keeping with his
grandfather's name. His arms and legs were so heavily chapped, sum-
mer and winter, that people knew him as "Chapped Daita."

The great serpent of the story
is actually the vehicle
of the god of Takachio,
whom all of Hyūga reveres,

and whom Okata Koreyoshi
claimed as his direct ancestor,
only five generations back.
And just because he descended
from a being so terrifying,
the provincial governor's letter—
sent as from the sovereign himself—
to all the warriors of Kyushu,
of Iki and of Tsushima,
secured obedience from each one
to Koreyoshi's orders.

4. The Flight from Dazaifu

The Heike had decided to establish their capital, with a new palace, in Kyushu,
when the news of Koreyoshi's rebellion threw them into confusion.
The grand counselor Tokitada suggested to Munemori,
"This Koreyoshi was Shigemori's retainer.
A son of Shigemori might go to him and try to talk him around."
Munemori approved. Sukemori therefore crossed over into Bungo
with five hundred horse, and he did his best to be persuasive,
but Koreyoshi would not listen. He even went so far as to declare,
"By rights I should detain you here at once, but, as they say,
'Grand design ignores petty detail.'
Releasing you could hardly make any difference.
So go straight back to Dazaifu
and with the others suffer whatever fate awaits you all."
He sent Sukemori packing.
Next he dispatched his second son, Nojiri Koremura, to Dazaifu to say,
"I owe the Heike a weighty burden of gratitude,
and properly I should therefore remove my helmet and unstring my bow.
By His Cloistered Eminence's command, however,
I am required to expel you at once from Kyushu.
You are to leave immediately." Such was Koreyoshi's message.
Tokitada came out to receive him wearing a *hitatare* with red sleeve cords,
a kudzu-cloth divided skirt, and a tall *eboshi* hat.

> "His Majesty, our sovereign lord,"
> he said, "descends in direct line
> forty-nine generations long
> from the great Goddess of the Sun.
> He is the eighty-first human emperor.

The Sun Goddess and Hachiman
keep him under their protection.
Consider that the late chancellor
twice during Hōgen and Heiji
suppressed revolts against the throne
and, furthermore, that he invited
men of Kyushu to join the court.

> Yoritomo and Yoshinaka have successfully convinced the ruffians of
> east and north that meritorious service will win them provinces and
> estates, and you believe them. But you would be making a great mis-
> take to follow the orders of Bungo the Nose."
>
> By "Bungo the Nose" he meant Yorisuke, the Bungo governor, whose
> nose was enormous.

Koremura returned to his father and reported all this.
"What nonsense!" Koreyoshi exclaimed. "The past is past; now is now.
If that is all he has to say, then drive them out of Kyushu at once!"
News reached the Heike that Koreyoshi was mustering his forces.
The Heike warriors Suesada and Morizumi declared,
"We cannot let this corruption spread. We must arrest him."
To do so they rode off with three thousand men to Takano-no-honjō, in
    Chikugo,
and attacked for a night and a day,
but Koreyoshi's men swarmed like clouds and mists.
They were too much for the Heike, who could only withdraw.

The next word to reach the Heike
warned that Okata Koreyoshi
was already bearing down on them
with thirty thousand mounted men.
They dropped everything and fled Dazaifu.
The deity present there, Tenman Tenjin,
had seemed to offer sure protection,
and now it was very painful indeed
to leave behind his most sacred shrine.
In the absence of any bearers,
the emperor's majestic conveyance
bore in no more than august name
the golden flowers, the shining phoenix;
actually, in sober truth
he boarded the sketchiest palanquin.
His mother and her noble ladies
tucked up their divided skirts,

ministers and the greatest nobles
likewise hitched up their baggy trousers,
and out they poured through the single gate
in the ancient Dazaifu moat,
as fast as they could possibly go,
toward the harbor of Hakozaki.
Alas, it was raining cats and dogs,
sand was blowing on a stiff wind,
and their tears mingled with the rain.
They worshipped at Sumiyoshi,
Hakozaki, Kashii, Munakata,
praying at each one of these shrines
that His Majesty swiftly return
to their home, the old capital.
Mount Tarumi, Uzura beach—
those craggy heights, those endless sands
they endured, and on they went.
Not one had done the like before.
Their bleeding feet reddened the strand,
the scarlet of their divided skirts
darkened in hue, and their trousers' white
turned at the ankles into red.
Xuanzang, crossing the Shifting Sands
or laboring across the Pamirs,
could hardly have suffered worse trials.[205]
He, though, had gone to seek the Law
for the benefit of all beings,
whereas the Heike, in full flight
from an implacable enemy,
learned from their present misery
what agony their next lives would bring.
Harada Tanenao went with them,
leading two thousand of his men,
while, with several thousand more,
Yamaga Hidetō received them.
Tanenao and Hidetō
so heartily detested each other

....

205. Xuanzang (602–64) traveled to India from Tang China in order to seek the true Buddhist teaching and translated many sutras into Chinese. The Pamirs are a mountain range in Central Asia. The "Shifting Sands" may have to do with the Gobi Desert.

that Tanenao, fearing trouble,
turned around before the two met.
Passing the harbor of Ashiya,
the Heike remembered having seen,
between the city and Fukuhara,
a village with exactly that name,
and they felt pangs of desperate yearning.
Very gladly they would have fled
to Paekche, Koguryŏ, or Khitan,
to where the clouds and the ocean end,
but wind and wave were dead against them.
Hidetō escorted them on
to refuge in the Yamaga fortress.
But then came news that the enemy was bearing down on Yamaga, too.
They boarded small boats and through the night
sailed to the province of Buzen, to Yanagi-ga-ura.
Here their plan was to build a palace, but the site was too small.
Next, word had it that the Genji were on their way over from Nagato.
The Heike boarded little fishing boats and started once more across the sea.
Kiyotsune, Shigemori's third son, had always been given to gloomy reflection.
"The Genji drove us from the capital," he said,
"and now Koreyoshi has forced us from Kyushu.
We are like fish caught in a net. What escape do we have?
　　　No, there is no future left us."
　　　Outside the cabin this moonlit night,
　　　he sought to compose his feelings,
　　　played his flute, sang *rōei* songs,
　　　quietly turned to chanting sutras
　　　and calling Amida's holy Name;
　　　then he sank into the ocean depths.
　　　The men and women mourned in tears,
　　　but they had lost him forever.
　　　　　The province of Nagato was Taira no Tomomori's, and his deputy
　　　　　there was a man named Michisuke. Upon learning that the Heike
　　　　　were at sea in small boats, Michisuke furnished them with over a hun-
　　　　　dred large ones. On these the Heike crossed to Shikoku.
There Shigeyoshi mobilized the population to build, at Yashima in Sanuki,
a poor, board-roofed semblance of an imperial palace.
　　　Meanwhile it was unthinkable
　　　that His Majesty should inhabit
　　　some wretched house of the local folk;

therefore his ship became his dwelling.
The ministers, nobles, and officials
spent their days in reed-thatched huts
that housed the village fishermen
and night after night lay where they lay.
The dragon barge rode out to sea,
and aboard this wave-borne palace
not an instant was ever still.
The moon shone up from an abyss
as bottomless as their despair,
and in reeds burdened with frost
they saw the fragility of their lives.
Plovers crying on the sandbars
added new poignancy to dawn;
the sound of oars below the cliff
stirred agony deep in the night.
White herons flocking in distant pines
seemed to their eyes Genji banners;
wild geese calling far out at sea
kept them wakeful, imagining
armed warriors rowing in by night.
The bitter winds weathered their skin;
their black eyebrows and rosy looks
with passing time lost their last glow.
Hollow-eyed before endless blue waves,
they wept helpless streams of homesick tears.
Green curtains hung in crimson chambers[206]
now were reed blinds in mud-daubed huts;
smoke wafting from incense burners,
rush fires smoldering in hovels.
Scarlet tears of endless sorrow
so smeared the women's eyebrows black
that one no longer knew them.

5. His Cloistered Eminence Appoints a Supreme Commander

In Kamakura, meanwhile, Yoritomo received from the cloistered emperor
a decree appointing him supreme commander of the imperial forces.
The documents clerk Nakahara no Yasusada, the envoy who brought it,

....

206. A stock Chinese-derived description of an elegant bedroom.

reached the Kanto on the fourteenth day of the tenth month. [1183]
Yoritomo said, "After years under imperial ban, success in battle has won me
His Cloistered Eminence's appointment to supreme command.
Would I have the effrontery to receive it simply at home?
No, I shall accept it at the new shrine of Hachiman."
He set forth there without delay.

>Hachiman's shrine stands at Tsuru-ga-oka.[207]
>The landscape setting there resembles
>the one familiar at Iwashimizu.
>There is an encircling gallery,
>an imposing gate, and an approach
>along a new, mile-long avenue.
>A discussion held to consider
>precisely who should take the decree
>from the hand of Yasusada
>settled on Miura Yoshizumi.
>Why? Because this great warrior,
>famed throughout the eight provinces,
>also counted among his forebears
>Miura no Heitarō Tametsugu.
>Besides, his father, Yoshiaki,
>had laid down his life for Yoritomo,
>and this gesture would light his way
>through the dark of the netherworld.
>That was how the reasoning ran.

Yasusada, the envoy bearing the decree, arrived with two retainers and ten
    attendants.
By his order a servant carried the decree in a bag around his neck.
Miura Yoshizumi came with retainers and attendants in equal numbers.
The two retainers were Wada no Saburō Munezane and Hiki no Tōshirō
    Yoshikazu.
As to the ten attendants, he had had ten major local lords provide in haste one
    each.
He wore that day, over a blue-black *hitatare*, black-silk-laced armor,
with, at his side, a mighty sword and, at his back,
twenty-four black-and-white-banded arrows.
Under his arm he carried a black-lacquered, rattan-wrapped bow,
and his helmet hung over his shoulders on a cord.
He accepted the decree with a deep bow.

....

207. The great Hachiman shrine in Kamakura, built by Yoritomo in 1180.

"You who take this decree in hand," Yasusada said, "who are you? Name
   yourself!"
      Miura proudly announced his full name:
      Miura no Arajirō Yoshizumi.
The decree was in a document case, which Miura presented to his lord.
Yasusada soon got the case back.
He opened it, because this time it was heavy:
It contained one hundred taels of gold dust.
Next he was treated to wine in the shrine's worship hall.
Chikayoshi, an official in the Kamo Priestess's household,
served him his meal, assisted by a man of the fifth rank.
Then three horses were led before him, one of them saddled.
Kudō Ichirō Suketsune led that one; he had served Her Grand Imperial
   Majesty.[208]
Finally the envoy was installed in an old, rush-thatched house, done up for the
   occasion.
            A chest containing two thickly padded bed jackets awaited him there,
            together with a thousand bolts of cloth, some white, some printed
            with indigo patterns, dark or light. Wine and food were served him in
            plenty, with superb elegance.
      The following day Yasusada
      called on Yoritomo at home.
      The guardhouse outside the compound
      and a second within the gate
      were, each of them, sixteen bays long.
      The outer guards, kinsmen and allies,
      sat formally, shoulder to shoulder.
      The inner guards, seated above,
      were Genji warriors, and below
      sat greater and lesser local lords.
      Yasusada was conducted
      to the Genji seat of honor.
      He paused there a little while,
      then went on to the main house.
      They seated him in the lower aisle,[209]
      on a mat with a purple border.
      Above him lay ready another mat,

....

208. The lady whose story is told in 1:7.

209. The aisle (*hisashi*) was the space in a house surrounding the central chamber, between the chamber
and the veranda. It was lower than the central chamber by the depth of the lintel (*nageshi*). This aisle
(*hirobisashi*) is a second one beyond the first, again a lintel's depth lower.

black-and-white-bordered, behind raised blinds.
Then in he came: Yoritomo,
wearing the plainest of hunting cloaks
and on his head an *eboshi*.
Broad of face and short in stature,
he had pleasing looks and spoke language
untainted by any uncouth accent.
He set forth the situation at length:

> "The Heike have fled the capital in fear of my might, but Kiso no Yo-
> shinaka and Jūrō Yukiie have come in behind them, and they have
> been collecting offices and promotions at will, as though the triumph
> were all their own. They have even been turning up their noses at the
> gift of this province or that. Their behavior is intolerable. In the north,
> Hidehira is now governor of Mutsu and Satake Takayoshi of Hitachi,
> and both ignore my orders. What I need is a decree from His Clois-
> tered Eminence commanding me to crush them at once."

> Yasusada spoke in turn: "I should properly present you now with
> my formally recorded name, but because I am His Cloistered Emi-
> nence's envoy, I will prepare it and send it to you as soon as I return to
> the capital. My younger brother, the clerk Shigeyoshi, wishes me to
> give you the same message."

> Yoritomo smiled. "Your formal identification is the last thing on my
> mind at present," he said. "However, I shall expect it from you, since
> you tell me to do so."

Yasusada then announced his return to the capital that day,
but Yoritomo insisted that he stay a day longer.

The next day Yasusada returned
to Yoritomo's residence.
Yoritomo had gifts for him:
a suit of green-laced armor,
a sword trimmed with silver,
and a rattan-wrapped bow accompanied by a set of arrows.
Thirteen horses were then led before him. Three were saddled.
Yasusada's twelve men received clothing and even saddles.
Thirty packhorses bore all this,
including fifty bushels of rice
for each post station on the way
from Kamakura to Kagami.
The quantity was so great, they say,
that a good deal of it went in alms.

6. Nekoma

Yasusada returned to the capital, called at the cloistered emperor's,
and there, in the inner court, described his journey to the Kanto.
His Cloistered Eminence was impressed,
and the senior nobles and privy gentlemen smiled with satisfaction.
Yoritomo was clearly a gentleman through and through.
Kiso, though—his comportment while he held the capital
was boorish in the extreme, and so, too, his manner of speaking.
Well, no wonder: Between infancy and the age of thirty,
he had lived in a mountain village in the Kiso region of Shinano.
How could he possibly have acquired any polish?

>Once a gentleman, the Nekoma counselor Mitsutaka, had something
to discuss with Kiso.

>Kiso's man announced, "Lord Nekoma is here, sir. He says he has
something to talk to you about."

>Kiso roared with laughter. "*Neko*ma, you say? A *cat's* here to see
me?"

>"Sir, the gentleman is a senior noble known as the Nekoma coun-
selor. I believe that Nekoma is the place where he lives."

>"All right, send him in." But even then Kiso could not bring himself
to call his visitor Lord Nekoma.

>"Lord Pussycat's turned up for once! Feed him something!" he or-
dered.

>"Dear me, no, not now!" the counselor protested.

>"But why? Here you are, it's time to eat, and I *must* treat you!"

>To him anything fresh was "unsalted," salt fish being all he had ever
known, so he went on, "We have some nice, unsalted oyster mush-
rooms. Serve them at once!"

>Nenoi no Koyata served the meal: a lidded bowl, vast, rustic, and all
but bottomless, heaped with rice; three side dishes; and oyster mush-
room soup. He set the same before Kiso.

Kiso grabbed his chopsticks and ate.
Lord Nekoma eyed the rustic rice bowl dubiously and just sat there.
"That's my bowl for when I'm fasting," Kiso remarked.
His visitor, who knew how rude it would be to eat nothing,
picked up his chopsticks and went through a few motions.
Kiso noticed. "You don't have much of an appetite, do you, Lord Pussycat!" he
   said.
"Well, they say kitties never finish their dinners. Come on, dig in!"

Lord Nekoma was so put out
that he never thought to say a word
about what he had to discuss.
No, he left as soon as he could.
Kiso had gathered that a newly promoted official
does not present himself for duty in a warrior's *hitatare*,
so for the first time in his life he donned a hunting cloak.
From the tip of his tall *eboshi* to his baggy trouser bottoms,
he looked utterly absurd.

Somehow he managed nonetheless
to squeeze himself into his carriage.
How enormously better he looked
on horseback, in armor, bow in hand,
at his back a quiver of arrows!
The carriage belonged to Munemori,
just now away at Yashima.
The oxherd, too, was Munemori's.
The boy had of course bent to the times.
Being a captive, he did his job,
but he so resented every minute
that he just left his master's ox—
a magnificent animal—
tied up all day long in its stall.
When it came to be time to start,
trouble was nearly guaranteed
at the very first touch of the whip.
The ox hurtled forward. In the carriage
Kiso tumbled head over heels.
Sleeves spread like butterfly wings,
he struggled manfully to get up,
but the effort ended in failure.
"Oxherd" not being a word he knew,
he shouted instead, "Hey! Hey, you!
You, the brat leading the ox!"
What the oxherd got from this was
"Hey, you brat, give him his head!"
He galloped the ox several hundred yards.
Whip and stirrup, Imai no Shirō Kanehira urged his horse to catch up.
"What do you mean by handling my lord's carriage this way?" he roared.
"This ox is very hard to control, sir," the oxherd explained,
and perhaps hoping to get back into Kiso's good graces, he added,

"Please, my lord, keep hold of that hand grip over there."
Kiso gripped it hard. "Very clever!" he exclaimed.
"Was this your bright idea, kid, or your old master's?"
Eventually the carriage reached the cloistered emperor's residence.
Kiso had the ox unhitched and was starting out the back of the carriage
when a servant of his, a man of the capital, made bold to remark,
"A gentleman boards a carriage from the rear and leaves by the front."
"Just because it's a carriage," Kiso protested,
"why do you have to go in one end and out the other?"
In the end he went out the back.

> Lots of other funny things happened,
> but people feared to talk about them.

7. The Battle at Mizushima

From Yashima the Heike seized control of the eight San'yōdō provinces
and the six of the Nankaidō: fourteen in all.
This news disturbed Kiso, who then and there sent a force against them,
commanded by Yata Yoshikiyo and, under him, Unno Yukihiro from Shinano.
Over seven thousand horse strong, they followed the San'yō road
to Mizushima in Bitchū, where they assembled a fleet of boats.
Soon they were ready to sail and attack Yashima.

> On the first of the intercalary tenth month, a small boat appeared off
> Mizushima. It looked like a fishing boat, but it was not. No, it bore a
> messenger from the Heike.

At the sight, the Genji with shouts and cries
dragged down to the water five hundred boats ready for them on the beach.
The Heike, in a thousand boats, stormed in to attack.

> At the head of the main Heike force,
> Tomomori; in the rear guard,
> Noritsune, who shouted out,
> "Men, what's the matter with you,
> waging such lukewarm battle?
> You'll be sorry, count on that,
> if those ruffians from the north
> ever manage to take you alive!
> Get our boats tied up together!"
> They roped the thousand boats,
> bow, stern, and amidships together;
> laid planks all the way across them;
> and so made of the fleet one deck.

Both sides uttered their war cries,
traded arrows, drove their boats
together in a ferocious clash.
Those more distant wielded bows,
those nearer slashed away with swords.
Some fell afoul of grappling hooks,[210]
others grappling-hooked their man.
Some pairs, struggling hand to hand,
plunged into the sea; some died
run through by each other's blades.
Every man fought as he pleased.
The Genji deputy commander,
Unno Yukihiro, was slain.
The sight moved Yata Yoshikiyo,
commander of the Genji force,
to run a boat, he and six men,
out into the thick of the fray,
but then some mishap occurred.
The boat sank, and they all died.
The Heike, who had brought on board
saddled horses, reached the shore,
disembarked the horses, mounted,
and with fearful war cries charged.
Undone by their commander's loss,
the Genji all fled for their lives.
Mizushima cleansed the Heike
of the shame from old defeats.

8. The Death of Seno-o

This news shocked Kiso. Ten thousand men set off down the San'yō road.
Now, the Heike retainer Seno-o no Tarō Kaneyasu, from the province of Bitchū,
had been captured during the wars in the north
by Kuramitsu no Jirō Narizumi, a man from the province of Kaga,
and given into the custody of Nariuji, Narizumi's younger brother.
Seno-o was a warrior so well known for strength and prowess
that Kiso dismissed any thought of executing him.
He was also so pleasant and considerate that Nariuji treated him well.

....

210. *Kumade,* a set of iron hooks mounted on a long handle.

Su Wu, captive among the Xiongnu,
Li Ling, who never returned to Han—
he was like them. For as they say,
confinement in an alien land
deeply distressed the men of old.
Leather elbow guards and felt tents
gave them shelter from wind and rain,
raw meat and kumiss, food and drink.
At night Seno-o did not sleep.
He spent his days serving his captor
by doing any work assigned him,
save only cutting wood and grass,
and meanwhile he kept sharp watch
for any possible opening
that might let him rejoin his lord.
He was a man of daunting spirit.
One day Seno-o met Nariuji and said,
"Having my unworthy life spared this fifth month past
has shaken my old convictions about loyalty to one lord or another.
In the future I shall charge ahead in battle and give my life for Lord Kiso.
An estate of mine, at Seno-o in Bitchū, offers rich pasture for horses.
By all means speak to Lord Kiso about it and have him award it to you."
Nariuji did so. Kiso replied, "How absolutely remarkable!
Then have Seno-o take you down there right away
and make sure that he has pasture enough for more horses."
Nariuji thanked his lord and rode off, very pleased, to Bitchū,
accompanied by thirty men. Seno-o rode before them.

> Seno-o's eldest son, Kotarō Muneyasu, was a Heike ally. At the news
> that Kiso had released his father, he called his established retainers
> together and, with fifty of them, set off to greet him. The two parties
> met at the Harima provincial seat and continued ahead together. On
> the way they stopped at the Mitsuishi post station in Bizen. Men close
> to Seno-o joined them there with wine, and the welcoming party went
> on far into the night. They got Nariuji and his thirty men dead drunk
> and then, one after another, killed them all. Now, Bizen was Yukiie's
> province, and Yukiie's deputy was in residence at the time. They at-
> tacked and killed him, too.

"I have been released," Seno-o announced, "and here I am.
Let every man loyal to the Heike follow me when Kiso arrives,
and greet him with an arrow."

The warriors of Bizen, Bitchū, and Bingo had offered the Heike
horses, arms, and every able follower. The old, retired ones
    in haste secured across their chests
    the cords of some persimmon-dyed
    hitatare that came to hand,
    tucked up the skirts of some common robe,
    mended some suit of clanking armor,
    stuck a few arrows in a quiver—
    bamboo, or the kind hunters use—
    clapped it on their backs, and raced,
    raced to gather around Seno-o.
    Over two thousand mounted men
    followed him all the way to Bizen,
    to Fukuryūji Nawate,
    and there, at Sasa-no-semari,
    they dug themselves in behind a moat
    twenty feet wide and twenty feet deep,
    laid abatis, built shooting towers,
    put up an unbroken wall of shields,
    and, bristling with ready arrows,
    awaited the enemy's assault.
After Seno-o killed Yukiie's deputy in Bizen,
the deputy's men fled up toward the capital.
At Funasaka, on the Bizen-Harima border,
they met Kiso and reported what had happened.
"I don't like this at all," Kiso said ruefully. "I should have executed him."
"I warned you!" Imai Kanehira replied. "I could tell he was no ordinary man.
I urged you a thousand times to do it, but no, you had to spare him."
"I can't see that it matters much, though. Go on after him and kill him."
"Then I shall go down there and see what I can do," Imai replied.
He galloped off with three thousand men.
    Fukuryūji Nawate:
    a strip of land a bow length wide
    and many hundreds of yards long.
    To right and left, rice paddies
    too deep for a horse's footing.
    The three thousand longed to charge,
    but they had to move slowly.
When they pressed in toward the fort,
Seno-o emerged up on a shooting tower and called in a great voice,
"From the fifth month past to this very day, I have owed my foe my life,

and just for him I have prepared this welcome."
He had assembled several hundred exceptionally powerful archers,
who now loosed a fierce volley of arrows that forestalled any advance.

Imai Kanehira, Tate, Nenoi,
Miyazaki no Saburō, Suwa,
Fujisawa—fiery warriors
such as these bent forward and down
to expose only their neck plates;
tugged and dragged the dead, men and horses,
into the moat; managed to fill it;
and with deafening howls attacked.
Some plunged into the paddy fields
up to their horses' chests and bellies,
with never a thought for the risk they ran,
to attack in swiftly formed bands;
some, oblivious to the deep trench,
pressed their assault in repeated waves.
The battle lasted all day. By dusk
Seno-o's hastily mustered force
had gone down to final defeat.
Very few of his men survived;
almost all had died in the fight.
His fortress now fallen, Seno-o
retreated over into Bitchū,
where, beside the Itakura River,
he put up a wall of shields and waited.
Imai all too soon approached.
Bamboo and other makeshift quivers
emptied in spirited defense,
and when the last arrow was gone,
the survivors fled with desperate haste.

Seno-o and just two others reached the bank of the Itakura River
and flew from there toward Midoroyama. Narizumi, who had taken
Seno-o alive in the north, meanwhile reflected angrily that his younger
brother was dead. He decided to capture Seno-o again and left his
band to pursue him on his own, some hundred yards behind him.

"Stop, Seno-o!" he shouted. "You are a disgrace, turning away from
the enemy! Come back, come back!"

Seno-o was crossing the river westward. He stopped in midstream
and waited.

Narizumi galloped up beside him. They grappled hard and fell.

The fight between Narizumi and Seno-o.

Equals in strength, they rolled over again and again, and into a deep pool.
Narizumi could not swim. Seno-o, an expert swimmer,
pinned him to the bottom, lifted the skirts of his armor,
stabbed him so fiercely three times that hilt and fist plunged into the wound,
and took his head.

Seno-o then mounted Narizumi's horse, his being winded, and con-
tinued his flight. His son, Kotarō Muneyasu, was fleeing, too, with one
of their men, on foot rather than on horseback. Although still a young
man in his early twenties, Muneyasu was too fat to run even a hun-
dred yards, and despite having discarded his equipment he made slow
progress.

His father left him behind and fled nearly another mile. Then he
and his man met. "Normally when I fight an enemy in the thousands,"
he said, "the world seems bright around me, but now everything ahead
seems dark. Perhaps that is because I abandoned Kotarō. Even if I were
to live and serve the Heike again, my fellows might well say, 'That
Kaneyasu, he's over sixty and doesn't have that many years left—can
those years really have meant so much to him that he abandoned his
only son, to flee?' I would be covered with shame."

"That is exactly why I urged you to meet your fate with him," his man replied.

"Sir, please turn back."

"Then I will," said Seno-o, and he did.

He found his son lying there with terribly swollen feet.
"I came back to die fighting with you, since you couldn't keep up. All right?"
Tears streamed down his son's cheeks.

> "I am so hopeless," he answered,
> "that I should have killed myself.
> And now you, too, because of me,
> at any moment will face death—
> which makes me guilty, it seems to me,
> of the foul crime of patricide.

Turn back! Flee! There is no time to lose!"
"No," said his father, "my mind is made up." As they waited,
Imai Kanehira bore down on them at the head of fifty howling riders.

> Seno-o shot his last arrows,
> seven or eight of them, rapidly—
> five or six riders fell, stricken,
> dead or not, there is no telling—
> drew his sword, beheaded his son,
> and charged into the enemy,
> slashing at every man around him.
> They answered with many blows,
> until at last they struck him down.
> While his man's valor rivaled his lord's,
> weakened by his grievous wounds,
> he failed to kill himself, as he wished,
> and instead was taken prisoner.
> Only a day later, he died.
> They hung the heads of all three men
> in Sagi-ga-mori of Bitchū.
> Lord Kiso inspected them.
> "Ah," he sighed, "these were true warriors,
> each worthy to face a thousand.
> What a shame I could not spare them!"

9. Muroyama

Lord Kiso meanwhile gathered his forces at the Manju estate in Bitchū,
so as to prepare an attack on Yashima.
Higuchi no Jirō Kanemitsu, left in charge in the capital,
sent a messenger to inform him,
"In your absence, Lord Yukiie is conveying slander about you
to the cloistered emperor, through the sovereign's trusted advisers.

Please put off your planned western campaign and return in haste."
Kiso accordingly raced day and night back to the city.
Yukiie apparently preferred to stay out of trouble,
because to avoid him he set off for Harima by the Tanba road.

> Kiso returned to the capital through the province of Settsu. The Taira,
> in turn, were planning an attack on Kiso. Their commanders were
> Lords Tomomori and Shigehira, assisted by Etchū no Jirōbyōe Mori-
> tsugi, Kazusa no Gorōbyōe Tadamitsu, and Akushichibyōe Kagekiyo.
> Twenty thousand mounted men and more crossed to Harima on a
> thousand ships. They established their camp at Muroyama.

Yukiie may have hoped to regain Kiso's goodwill by fighting the Heike.
With over five hundred men, he moved against Muroyama.

> The Heike camp had five sections.
> One, Moritsugi's two thousand men;
> Two, Iga no Ienaga's two thousand;
> Three, Tadamitsu and Kagekiyo
> at the head of three thousand men;
> Four, Shigehira with three thousand;
> Five, Tomomori with ten thousand.
> On came now with whoops and yells
> Yukiie and his five hundred.
> Camp One, under Moritsugi,
> went through the motions of responding,
> opened, and let them all through.
> Camp Two, under Ienaga,
> parted also and let them pass.
> Camp Three, under Tadamitsu
> and Kagekiyo, did the same.
> Camp Four, under Shigehira,
> let them come in and on through.
> Beforehand all five had agreed
> that they would surround the attacker
> and shout as one their war cry.
> Yukiie, with no escape,
> recognized that he had been trapped.
> He never flinched or feared for his life
> but fought, fully expecting to die.
> "Engage him! Engage their commander!"
> Every man among the Heike
> longed to do that, but none dared.
> Tomomori's most trusted men—

Ki Shichizaemon, Ki Hachiemon,
Ki Kurō, and others—fell before Yukiie.
So it was that the five hundred
dwindled down to a paltry thirty.
All around Yukiie the foe;
with him very few men indeed.
How he was now to get away,
he had not the slightest idea,
but with the courage of desperation
he cut through the mass around him
and got out, unscathed himself—
although his twenty followers
were, nearly all of them, wounded—
managed to get on board a boat
at Takasago in Harima,
and sailed from there to Izumi.
He crossed next into Kawachi,
where he found refuge at last
at the fortress of Nagano.
For the Heike two victories—
Muroyama and Mizushima—
mightily increased their strength.

10. *The Tsuzumi Lieutenant*

The whole capital teemed with Genji,
who burst in everywhere and committed a great many thefts.
On land belonging even to Kamo or Hachiman,
they cut green rice plants to feed to their horses.
They broke into storehouses and took what was in them;
they stole from travelers and stripped off their clothes.
"When the Heike held the city," people said,
"Lord Kiyomori was only a general sort of threat.
No one ever stole all your clothes.
Better the Heike than the Genji."

The cloistered emperor sent Kiso a message. "Put a stop to this lawlessness," it said.

The police lieutenant Tomoyasu, a son of Iki governor Tomochika, delivered it. He was so good on the *tsuzumi* hand drum that people then dubbed him the "Tsuzumi Lieutenant." Kiso summoned him. Without a word of reply to the message, he asked, "So they call you the

Tsuzumi Lieutenant, do they? Is that because you have everyone beat-
ing and thumping on you?"

Tomoyasu said nothing and returned to the cloistered emperor.
"Yoshinaka is a fool," he reported. "At any moment he will turn against
the court. I urge his suppression immediately."
His Cloistered Eminence should then have issued suitable orders, but he did not.
No, he had the abbots of Mount Hiei and Miidera mobilize their fighting monks.
The senior nobles and privy gentlemen raised a force
consisting of stone-throwing boys, wastrel youths, and beggar clerics.
At first the warriors of the five inner provinces had sided with Kiso,
but news of the sovereign's displeasure with him
turned them all into the cloistered emperor's allies.
Even Murakami no Saburō, the Shinano Genji warrior, shifted allegiance that
    way.
To Kiso, Imai Kanehira said, "This is extremely serious, you know.
I mean, how can you possibly fight a sovereign endowed with all virtue?
Take off your helmet, unstring your bow, and submit!"
Kiso was furious.

"When I came out of Shinano,"
    he said, "I attacked at Omi and Aida;
    then up in the north at Mount Tonami,
    at Kurozaka, Shiozaka,
    and Shinohara; then out in the east
    at Fukuryūji Nawate,
    at nearby Sasa-no-semari,
    and at the fort of Itakura;
    and not once, through any of that,
    did I show my back to the enemy.
    Cloistered emperor he may be,
    sovereign in name and in virtue,
    but no, I will not, even for him,
    doff my helmet, unstring my bow,
    and, at a word from him, submit.
Every man guarding the capital has a horse—so he's not supposed to ride it?
There are paddy fields everywhere.
What business does he have, this cloistered emperor,
censuring them for feeding their horses rice leaves from a few?
After all, my young men have no army granary to supply them.
What's so terribly wrong with their going off sometimes to help themselves?
It's not as though they were breaking into the houses of ministers and princes.
That Tsuzumi Lieutenant is out to get me, I just know it.

Go, beat his drum for him—beat it and smash it!
I expect this to be my last battle. Oh, yes, Yoritomo will hear about it!
Now, get out there, all of you, and *fight*!" And off he went.
The men from the northern provinces had gone home.
He divided the mere six or seven thousand horsemen he had left
into seven corps, this practice having favored him in the past.
The first, two thousand under Higuchi Kanemitsu,
headed for Imagumano, to attack from the rear.
The other six corps set off to the Kamo River, each from its own station.
At an agreed signal, they were to assemble on the Shichijō riverbank.
   It was the eleventh month, the nineteenth day, in the morning, when the
     battle began.
Word spread that twenty thousand troops were stationed
in the cloistered emperor's Hōjūji residence compound.
His men wore identifying badges of pine needles.
Surging forward to attack the west gate,
Kiso found the Tsuzumi Lieutenant directing operations,
wearing a red brocade *hitatare* but, purposely, no armor—
only a helmet bearing an emblem of the Four Celestial Kings.
Tomoyasu climbed up to stand on the wall beside the west gate,
a halberd in one hand and in the other a *vajra* bell that he shook furiously.
Sometimes he also leaped and danced about.
The young nobles laughed at the sight.
"Disgraceful!" they exclaimed. "He's got a *tengu* in him."
In a great voice Tomoyasu cried,

     "In days gone by, when a herald
     read out the sovereign's decree,
       dead plants and trees put forth flowers,
       fruit promptly ripened on the bough,
       and demon powers bowed in assent.
That we now live in the latter days makes no excuse
for turning upon the sovereign endowed with all virtue
and drawing the bow against him.
The arrows you shoot will turn back to strike you!
The swords you draw will cut *you*!"
"Silence him!" Kiso shouted, and his men roared their great war cry.

     The flanking force under Kanemitsu
     added their voices from Imagumano.
     Then they shot burning humming arrows
     into the Hōjūji residence compound.
     At the time a strong wind was blowing.

Fierce flames leaped up and filled the sky.
Tomoyasu, the man in command,
fled the first of anyone there,
but once he was gone, all the others—
His Cloistered Eminence's twenty thousand—
fled likewise, every man for himself.
Some in the helter-skelter panic
took their bows but forgot their arrows;
some took their arrows but not their bows.
Some bore their halberds upside down
and cut themselves about the legs;
some got a bow tip somehow stuck
and when they could not pry it loose,
simply had to abandon the bow.
The Settsu Genji, who had secured a position at the east end of Shichijō, fled
    westward.
The cloistered emperor had issued an order that anyone caught fleeing be killed,
so the inhabitants of the city, perched behind shields on rooftops
and ready with all the stones that weighted their roofing,
cried at the sight, "Fugitives! Here they come!"
They picked up their stones and rained them down.
"We fought for His Cloistered Eminence!" the Genji shouted.
"Beware of committing a grave offense!"
"Silence them!" the rooftops shouted. "Our sovereign has spoken! Kill them all!"
Some, as the stones came pelting down, abandoned their horses and crawled
    away;
some were hit and really did die.
The Hiei monks had held the east end of Hachijō.
Those of them who feared shame died fighting; the shameless fled.
Wearing green-laced armor under a light green hunting cloak,
Chikanari, the head of the Water Bureau, fled up the Kamo riverbank on a pale
    roan.
Imai Kanehira chased him and shot a deadly arrow straight through his neck.

> Chikanari's father was Kiyowara no Yorinari, a chief secretary. "A scholar of the classics has no business donning helmet and armor," people muttered.
>
> Murakami no Saburō of the Shinano Genji, who had turned from Kiso to the cloistered emperor, was cut down. Next the Ōmi captain Tamekiyo and Echizen governor Nobuyuki, also on the sovereign's side, were slain and their heads taken. Mitsunaga, the governor of

Hōki, and his son Masatsune were both killed. Lieutenant Masakata, a grandson of the Azechi grand counselor Sukekata, went into battle in armor and a tall court hat. Higuchi no Jirō Kanemitsu took him prisoner.

Meiun, abbot of Mount Hiei,
and Cloistered Prince Enkei of Miidera
had sought safety with the sovereign,
but the black smoke came down on them.
On horseback they rushed to the riverbank,
where volleys of arrows greeted them.
Both of them died, shot from their horses,
and Kiso's warriors took their heads.

Lord Yorisuke, too—the governor of Bungo and lord of Justice—
had confined himself in the residence,
but fire beset him and he raced to the bank of the river.
There the warriors' lackeys stripped off his clothes and left him naked.
It was the nineteenth of the eleventh month, in the morning,
and the wind blowing down the river was freezing cold.
Yorisuke had a brother-in-law, a ranking monk named Shōi,
whose acolyte had come out to the riverbank to watch the battle.
He noticed Yorisuke standing there, naked, and ran to him with a cry of horror.
He wore his cassock over two white *kosode* robes
and should properly have taken *those* off to clothe the poor man,
but no, he removed that short cassock of his and threw it over Yorisuke.
It remained draped over Yorisuke's head, not even secured with a sash,
and from behind, it must have looked ridiculous.
Yorisuke then set off with the acolyte monk in white,
but not at a pace that matched the circumstances.
No, he kept stopping here and there to ask,
"Whose house is that?" "Who lives there?" "Where are we?"
The onlookers clapped their hands with glee.

The sovereign boarded a palanquin
and started for somewhere else—anywhere.
The warriors showered him with arrows.
The Bungo lieutenant Munenaga,
in a tan *hitatare* and folded *eboshi*,
accompanied him. "Beware!" he cried.
"This is His Cloistered Eminence!
Take care not to violate his person!"
The warriors all dismounted and knelt.

"Who are you?" the sovereign inquired.
Yashima no Shirō Yukitsuna, from Shinano, announced his name
and lent his men's strength to the palanquin.
They broke into the Gojō Palace,
installed the cloistered emperor there, and mounted stern guard.
    The child emperor boarded a boat [Go-Toba]
    and sailed out onto his garden lake.
    When volleys of arrows followed him,
    the consultant Nobukiyo
    and Norimitsu, governor of Kii,
    out there on the water with him,
    called, "We have His Majesty with us!
    Avoid committing a grave offense!"
    The warriors dismounted and knelt.
    Then they escorted His Majesty
    as far as the Kan'in Mansion.
    The pathetic nature of this progress
    truly defies description.

The battle during which Yoshinaka kills Meiun and Enkei. Hōjūji burns, while the child emperor takes refuge on his garden lake.

11. *The Battle at Hōjūji*

The Ōmi governor Nakakane, one of the cloistered emperor's allies,
held the west gate of the Hōjūji residence with fifty horsemen
when Yamamoto Yoshitaka, of the Ōmi Genji, came galloping up.
"What are you all doing here?" he asked. "Whom are you fighting to protect?
It seems both their majesties, cloistered and reigning, are gone!"
"Fine!" Nakakane cried. With a great shout, he drove in among the enemy
and laid about him so fiercely that with seven remaining men he broke through.
Among them was a warrior-monk named Kagabō, of the Kusaka League in
    Kawachi.
He rode a pale roan with an extremely hard mouth.
"This horse is too dangerous," he complained. "I can't handle him."
"Take mine, then," said Nakakane.
Kagabō mounted Nakakane's chestnut with a white-tipped tail,
and with whoops and yells they charged into Nenoi no Koyata's two hundred
    men holding Kawarazaka.
Five were killed, cutting Nakakane down to just two.
Kagabō's move to his master's horse did not help. He, too, was killed.
Now, Nakakane had a houseman named Nakayori.
Separated from his lord by hostile forces,
Nakayori did not know what had happened to him.
Then he spotted a chestnut horse with a white-tipped tail, fleeing the battle.
He summoned his servant.
"That looks like Nakakane's horse," he said. "He must have been killed.
I promised that if we had to die, we would die together.
The thought of dying apart from him is too painful.
Did you see what body of men he charged into?"
"I believe he attacked the one on Kawarazaka.
That is the one his horse bolted from."
        "Then go back now, immediately,"
        Nakayori replied, to make sure
        that the man would loyally carry
        word of his end to those at home.
        Then, alone, he charged into the foe
        and in a great voice announced his name:
        "Behold Shinano no Jirō Nakayori,
        second son of Shinano governor
        Nakashige and descended
        nine generations from Prince Atsumi!
        This year is my twenty-seventh.

Come, if you think you can best me—
here I am, ever at your service!"
Slashing about him in all directions,
he raced through them, killing many,
until he himself at last was slain.

Nakakane knew nothing of this. Together with his elder brother, the governor of Kawachi, and just one of his men, he fled south. Meanwhile the regent, Motomichi, had left the city for Uji to escape the fighting. Nakakane caught up with him in the Kohata hills.

The regent stopped his carriage, suspecting that the three might be Kiso's men. "Who are you?" he demanded to know.

"Nakakane and Nakanobu," they answered.

"How extraordinary! I was afraid that you were rabble from the north. Your arrival is very welcome. Stay with me and guard me."

With respectful obedience they conducted him to the Fuke Mansion. From there they fled on toward Kawachi.

The next day, the twentieth, Kiso went out to the Kamo riverbank at Rokujō, where he had the heads taken the day before hung in rows and recorded. There were more than six hundred and thirty.

Among them were those of Meiun,
the Tendai abbot, and of Enkei,
the cloistered prince of Miidera.
Everyone who saw them shed tears.
Kiso then had his seven thousand
turn their horses toward the east
and three times utter such a shout
as to shake heaven and earth.

Alarm spread again through the city, but the shout was for victory rather than war.
The consultant Naganori, son of the late minor counselor Shinzei, called at the cloistered emperor's current residence, the Gojō Palace.
"I have a report to make to His Cloistered Eminence.
Let me through!" he demanded, but the warriors on duty refused.
There was only one thing to do. He entered a hut nearby, shaved his head, became a monk, and donned black robes.
"Surely you cannot object to me now!" he said. "Let me in!"
And they did. He went to His Cloistered Eminence
and reported in full the names of the chief figures killed.

The sovereign wept copiously.
"Never did I imagine," he said,
"that Meiun would die before his time.

It is I whose end was near,
and he gave his life in my place."
He could not stop his streaming tears.
On the twenty-first of the month,
Kiso gathered those closest to him
to discuss what course to take next.
"Yes," he declared, "I, Yoshinaka,
faced the sovereign in battle and won.
I might now become emperor,
or perhaps cloistered emperor.
Emperor *would* be good, but then,
wearing my hair like a little boy
in the end would not suit me at all.
Cloistered emperor would be fine,
but I could hardly become a monk.
No, I will be regent instead."
Kakumei, the secretary
he kept always beside him, observed,
"Ever since Kamatari, my lord,
the regent has been a Fujiwara,
and *you* are a Minamoto.
Unfortunately, you cannot do that."
"So be it, then. Those are not for me."
Forthwith he appointed himself
director of the sovereign's stables
and took over Tanba province.
Just imagine! He had not known
that an emperor, once retired,
is "cloistered" if he becomes a monk
and that an emperor not yet of age
wears his hair like the boy he is.
Kiso also took over the former regent Motofusa's daughter
and imposed himself on the gentleman as a son-in-law.
On the twenty-third of the eleventh month,
he cashiered the Sanjō counselor Tomokata and forty-eight other high officials,
whom he then placed under house arrest.
The Heike in their day had dismissed forty-three at once,
but not forty-nine. Kiso's outrage was worse.
    Meanwhile, in Kamakura, Yoritomo sent his younger brothers
Noriyori and Yoshitsune to end the havoc Kiso was causing.
News that he had burned the Hōjūji residence and taken the sovereign prisoner,

plunging the realm into darkness, gave them pause.

"No," they decided, "we cannot just go straight up to the capital and do battle.
We must inform Yoritomo."

They were lodging with the head priest of the Atsuta Shrine, in Owari,
when Kintomo and Tokinari, two members of the cloistered emperor's guard,
came racing down there to bring them the story.

Yoshitsune said, "Kintomo must go to the Kanto.
A messenger not fully informed could only give confusing answers when
    questioned."

Accordingly, Kintomo galloped on to Kamakura.

> Kintomo's underlings had fled, to escape the fighting, and he therefore
> took with him his eldest son, Kinmochi, then in his fifteenth year.
> They reached the Kanto, and Kintomo made his report.
>
> Thunderstruck, Yoritomo sent this message by courier to the capi-
> tal: "The Tsuzumi Lieutenant, Tomoyasu, fed the sovereign such
> strange advice that His Cloistered Eminence's residence burned and
> two monks of the highest distinction were killed. This is unacceptable.
> Tomoyasu, at least, already amounts to a rebel against the throne.
> There will only be further serious trouble if His Cloistered Eminence
> listens to one more word from him."

This brought Tomoyasu racing day and night down to Kamakura, to justify
    himself.

Despite an order that no one should see or speak to him,
he presented himself daily at Yoritomo's residence.

In the end he returned in shame to the capital.
Thereafter he apparently lived unknown, somewhere near Fushimi Inari.

> Kiso sent the Heike a message.
> "Come back to the capital," it said.
> "Let us unite and attack the east."
> Munemori welcomed the idea,
> but not Tokitada or Tomomori.
> "Whatever ruin the world may threaten,"
> they warned, "do not let Yoshinaka
> seduce you now into returning.
> That would be most unfortunate.
> Here we have with us His Majesty,
> complete in virtue, and his regalia.
> You would do far better to say,
> 'Doff your helmet, unstring your bow,
> come to us here, and submit.'"

That is the answer they gave, but Kiso ignored them.
Motofusa, the former regent, invited Kiso to come and see him.
"Lord Kiyomori behaved very badly," he said,
"but good karma such as his is very rare,
and he kept peace in the realm for twenty years.
Evil ways do not suffice for governing.
You should instead restore to their posts
all those from whom, for no reason, you took them."
Despite his thoroughly barbaric demeanor, Kiso complied.
He restored all the dismissed officials to their posts.
Motofusa's son, Moroie, was then still only a captain and counselor.
Kiso at his own initiative raised him to minister and regent.
Since no ministerial post was actually vacant at the time,
for the purpose he borrowed that of palace minister from Tokudaiji Sanesada.
People always have some remark to make about anything,
and they called this new regent the "Upstart Minister."

> On the tenth day of the twelfth month,
> His Cloistered Eminence left Gojō
> and moved to the house of Naritada,
> the master of the sovereign's table,
> at Rokujō and Nishi-no-tōin.

On the thirteenth came the year-end Seven-Day Rite.
Next the appointments list was announced.
In accordance with Kiso's wishes, every man got the post he desired.

> There the Heike were in the west,
> and there Yoritomo in the east,
> while Kiso lorded it in the city.
> It was just like those eighteen years,
> between the Early and Later Han,
> when Wang Mang wielded usurped power.
> The barriers everywhere were shut.
> No tax goods could be collected;
> no estate revenue came in.
> Everyone throughout the capital
> suffered like fish in dwindling water.
> Under these parlous circumstances,
> the year at last came to a close.
> The third year of Juei began. [1184]

BOOK NINE

1. Ikezuki

(recitative)

On the first day of Juei 3, there was the cloistered emperor,
installed in the home of Naritada, the master of the imperial table,
at Rokujō and Nishi-no-tōin.
The house so little resembled an imperial residence
that to observe the customary rites was out of the question.
The cloistered sovereign received no formal new-year greeting,
and the counterpart morning greeting to the emperor was omitted as well.

> (song)
> The Heike saw the old year out,
> the new year in at Yashima,
> where despite this fresh beginning,
> rites to mark the first three days
> fell sadly short of what they wished.
> No doubt His Majesty was present,
> but there was no new-year feast,
> nor did the emperor greet the gods.
> No festive trout arrived from Kyushu,
> no Kuzu men from Yoshino.
> "Yes, the times were troubled then,
> but this is not the way things were
> when the capital was ours."
> So they talked among themselves.
> Spring came, bringing every day
> balmier breezes down the shore
> and milder sunshine. But, alas,
> the Heike felt still caught in ice,
> like birds of the Himalayas.
> "'On either bank, to east and west,
> willows leaf out soon or late;
> on plum branches north and south,
> some flowers open, others fall.
> So do all have their own time.'[211]

....

211. From a *Wakan rōeishū* poem in Chinese by Yoshishige no Yasutane.

Ah, how lovely it was then,
on mornings beneath the blossoms,
on nights bright with a perfect moon,
to make music and poetry,
to sport at kickball, archery,
to vie for the prettiest fan,
for the most attractive painting,
the most amusing bug or plant!"
So they shared their memories
to relieve the melancholy
of the lengthening spring days.
On the eleventh of the first month,
Kiso no Yoshinaka called on Cloistered Emperor Go-Shirakawa
to announce his approaching departure for the provinces of the west
on a campaign to suppress the Heike.
On the thirteenth, even as word went out that he was leaving,
news came that Yoritomo was on his way from the east
with many tens of thousands of mounted men,
aiming to put a stop to Kiso's insubordination,
and that he had reached even now the provinces of Mino and Ise.
Kiso, thunderstruck, dismantled the Uji and Seta bridges
and divided what men he had to mount a defense.
At the time there were few enough of them.

> To meet the main attack, at the Seta Bridge,
> he dispatched there eight hundred men
> commanded by Imai no Shirō Kanehira.
> To the Uji Bridge went Nishina,
> Takanashi, and Yamada no Jirō,
> at the head of five hundred horse.
> To Shida no Saburō Yoshinori,
> his uncle, Kiso assigned Imoarai
> to hold with a band of three hundred.
> The main Genji force, coming from the east,
> followed the orders of Noriyori,
> the flanking force those of Yoshitsune.
> Thirty lesser commanders led,
> in all, sixty thousand warriors.

Lord Yoritomo had two superb horses in those days: Ikezuki and Surusumi.
Kajiwara Kagesue had often begged him for Ikezuki, only to be told,
"When the time comes, I will ride Ikezuki into battle.
Surusumi is just as good, though." He gave Kajiwara Surusumi.

When Sasaki Takatsuna came to say good-bye, Yoritomo replied for some
   reason,
"Many others have asked for him. I want you to know that."
And he gave Sasaki Ikezuki. Sasaki respectfully answered,
      "On this horse I shall be first
      of all men across the Uji River.

      (speech)

      If you hear that I died there, you will know that someone crossed be-
      fore me. If you hear that I am still alive, you will know that I crossed
      first." With this, Sasaki withdrew from his lord's presence.
Those present, great and small, whispered among themselves,
"He certainly talks big!"
      Each corps of men left Kamakura,
      some taking the route by Ashigara,
      some preferring to go by Hakone.
      On reaching Ukishima-ga-hara
      in Suruga province, Kajiwara
      rode up to a high place and there paused
      to consider all the horses below.
      Each one carried a different saddle,
      each a crupper in a new color.
      Some followed a single lead rope, some two.
      There were thousands and thousands of them,
      and among the endless procession
      Kajiwara noted with pleasure
      none to compare with the Surusumi
      he had received as a gift from his lord.
      But then all at once it seemed to him
      that he saw before him Ikezuki:
      gilt-edged saddle and tasseled crupper,
      foaming mouth and spirited prancing
      that defeated the constant efforts
      a crowd of grooms made to control him.
Kajiwara rode up to them and asked who owned the horse.
"He belongs to Lord Sasaki, sir," they replied.
"I don't like this at all," Kajiwara muttered to himself.
"Sasaki and I both give our lord equal service,
but somehow our lord has come to prefer *him.* This is very galling.
I might go up to the capital and die in battle
against Imai, Higuchi, Tate, and Nenoi, Kiso's famous Four Heavenly Kings,
or I might continue on toward the provinces of the west

and die fighting Heike warriors known each gladly to face a thousand,
but neither course would help if my lord feels that way about me.
No, better to fight Sasaki, to kill him and die by his hand,
and so at a stroke to deprive Lord Yoritomo of two good men."
So he reflected while awaiting Sasaki himself.

> And here he came, walking along,
> unsuspecting, thinking no harm.
> Move up beside him and grapple?
> Meet him head-on and topple him?
> One or the other;

> > but first Kajiwara confronted him in words. "Well now, Sasaki," he
> > said, "our lord seems to have made you a present of Ikezuki!"

> > Sasaki suddenly remembered hearing that Kajiwara, too, had
> > longed to get his hands on the horse. "This is what happened," he an-
> > swered. "There I was, setting off on this crucial campaign, certain that
> > they would have dismantled the bridges at Seta and Uji, and I had no
> > horse up to swimming a river. I thought of asking for Ikezuki, but I
> > gathered that even you had been refused him, and the idea seemed
> > hopeless. So I decided to risk whatever I might have coming to me
> > later on.

On the night we were to leave, I got one of the grooms to help me
steal our lord's treasured Ikezuki,
and here I am now, riding him to the capital!
What do you think of that?"
Kajiwara forgot his anger.
"Damn," he exclaimed, "I should have stolen him myself!"
And off he went, roaring with laughter.

2. First Across the Uji River

The mount granted Sasaki Shirō was a dark chestnut,
muscular and powerful in the extreme,
that bit any horse or man who came near him:
hence the name Ikezuki, "Pound of Flesh." He was unusually tall.
The horse given Kajiwara was equally powerful
and so black as to be named Surusumi, "Ground Ink."
Neither yielded anything in quality to the other.
From Owari on, the army advanced in two bodies, the main and flanking forces.

> Noriyori commanded the main force,
> and with him rode Takeda no Tarō,
> Kagami no Jirō, Ichijō no Jirō,

Itagaki no Saburō, Inage no Saburō,
Hangae no Shirō, Kumagai no Jirō,
and Inomata no Kobeiroku,
leading thirty-five thousand horse.
They came to Noji and Shinohara
in the province of Ōmi.
The flanking force rode under the orders of Kurō Yoshitsune,
accompanied by Yasuda no Saburō, Ōuchi no Tarō, Hatakeyama no Jirō,
Kajiwara Genda, Sasaki Shirō, Kasuya no Tōda, Shibatani Uma-no-jō,
and Hirayama Mushadokoro, leading twenty-five thousand.
They passed through the province of Iga and drove on to the Uji Bridge.

The planks were gone from both bridges,
Uji and Seta, and abatis
tied to stakes in the riverbed
strained against the rushing current.
It was the first month of the year,
and well past the twentieth day.
From the mighty peak of Hira,
from all the mountains of Shiga,
from Nagara the winter snows
had vanished; with the last of the ice
melting now from every valley,
the river was rising. Foaming waves
surged past on the mounting flood,
roaring rapids broke the current,
eddies spun at dizzying speed.
Night was giving way to dawn,
but thick mist along the river
turned both horses and armor gray.
The commander, Yoshitsune, strode to the bank and gazed across.
Perhaps he wished to try his men's mettle, for he remarked,
"This looks bad. Perhaps we should go around by Yodo or Imoarai.
Or perhaps we should wait for the river to drop."
Hatakeyama was then in only his twenty-first year,
but he stepped forward nonetheless. "In Kamakura," he declared,

"we heard all about this river.
It is not as though you saw before you
a river of which you know nothing.
This river drains the lake in Ōmi.[212]

....

212. Lake Biwa.

Wait? No, we could wait forever
before the water level drops.
And who, then, will build us a bridge?
Look at that battle during Jishō:[213]
Ashikaga Tadatsuna
crossed well enough—do you suppose
some god or devil carried him?
I, Shigetada, will test for you the depth and footing."
Five hundred riders, mostly of the Tan League,
pressed forward, bridle to bridle, to join him.
From the tip of a little promontory,
Tachibana-no-kojima,
just northeast of the Byōdō-in,
two warriors galloped at breakneck speed.
Kajiwara Kagesue was one,
the other Sasaki Takatsuna.
No one had guessed what they were planning,
but secretly each had sworn to be first.
Kajiwara was several lengths ahead
when Sasaki shouted, "Of all the rivers
here in the west, this is the biggest!
Your girth looks loose. Better tighten it!"
Kajiwara must have believed him:
He held the stirrups away from his mount,
tossed the reins over the mane,
undid the girth, and cinched it tighter.
Meanwhile Sasaki galloped past him
and plunged with a splash into the river.
No doubt knowing he had been tricked,
Kajiwara plunged in right behind him.
"Look out, Sasaki! Don't play the fool
out of a desperate thirst for fame!
There must be ropes stretched underwater!"
So he shouted, at which Sasaki
drew his sword and slashed through the ropes
that already threatened his horse's legs.
Riding none other than Ikezuki,
the most marvelous steed in the world,
he cut straight across the Uji River

....

213. The battle at the Uji Bridge (4:11).

and scrambled up on the opposite bank.

Kajiwara, on Surusumi,

found himself swept far down the river

before he, too, came up on dry land.

Sasaki rose in his stirrups and in a great voice declared his name:

"Descended from Emperor Uda

nine generations in the past,

fourth son of Sasaki Hideyoshi,

I am Sasaki Shirō Takatsuna,

the first man across the Uji River!"

Hatakeyama's five hundred men crossed then and there. An arrow from the far bank, from the bow of Yamada no Jirō, sank deep into the forehead of Hatakeyama's mount. In midstream Hatakeyama abandoned the stricken animal and continued on foot, bracing himself with his bow. Waves crashing over the rocks spattered his helmet to eye level, but he ignored them. He got across, treading the bottom, and was about to climb onto the bank when he felt a sharp tug from behind.

"Who's that?" he demanded to know.

"Shigechika!"

"What? Ōkushi Shigechika?"

"Yes." Hatakeyama had presided over Shigechika's coming-of-age.

"The current was so fast it swept my horse from under me," Shigechika explained. "I had to hang on to you."

"You youngsters, you're always getting grown men like me to save you!"

Hatakeyama hauled him up and tossed him onto the bank.

Instantly Shigechika righted himself.

"Ōkushi no Jirō Shigechika,

from Musashi: Yes, I am he,

the first across the Uji River!"

he announced, and, friend or foe,

all who heard him roared with laughter.

Hatakeyama had found a new mount

when one of the enemy came forward,

red-laced armor worn over olive green,

gilt-edged saddle on a dappled gray.

"Who are you, advancing on me?"

Hatakeyama asked. "Name yourself!"

"I am a kinsman of Lord Kiso,

Nagase no Hangandai Shigetsuna."

He was the day's offering to the god of war:

Hatakeyama moved beside him,
gripped him fiercely, threw him down,
twisted his head around, and cut it off.
One of his men, Honda no Jirō,
tied it onto the back of his saddle.
So for Lord Kiso's men it began:
Those sent to secure the Uji Bridge
managed to hold it a little while,
but the easterners, once all across,
cut them to pieces and sent them fleeing
for the Kohata hills and Fushimi.
As for Seta, Inage Shigenari
devised their success: At Tanagami,
they crossed over the Kugo shallows.

3. *The Battle Beside the River*

Kiso's forces were beaten.
A courier raced to Kamakura with an account of the battle.
"And Sasaki?" asked Yoritomo at once. "What about *him*?"
"He crossed the Uji River first," the courier replied.
Yoritomo opened the formal report and read,
"First across the Uji River: Sasaki Shirō Takatsuna.
Second across: Kajiwara Genda Kagesue."
There it was, in writing.
    On learning that Uji and Seta had fallen,
Kiso went to Rokujō, where Go-Shirakawa was staying, to bid him farewell.
The sovereign and the senior nobles and privy gentlemen around him
were wringing their hands, crying, "This is the end of the world!
Oh, what are we to do?" and making impassioned vows.
Kiso got as far as the main gate,
only to hear that the men from the east had driven on to the bank of the Kamo
    River.
Having nothing really to say to His Cloistered Eminence, he turned back.
A gentlewoman whose company he had begun frequenting
lived near the Rokujō-Takakura crossing.
He went to her for a last farewell and could not soon tear himself away.
There was a new man in his service, one Echigo no Chūda Iemitsu.
"How can you dawdle like this?" Iemitsu reproved him.
"The enemy is already at the Kamo River. You risk dying like a dog."
But still Kiso could not bring himself to leave.

"Very well," said Iemitsu, "then I will go on ahead and await you on the Mountain
    of Death."
He cut open his belly and died on the spot.
"That was a call to act," Kiso acknowledged. At last he left.

> His men numbered a mere one hundred—
> chief among them, from Kōzuke province,
> Naha no Tarō Hirozumi.
> They ventured onto the riverbank
> at Rokujō and saw before them
> thirty men, seemingly from the east.
> Two warriors rode forth from among them.
> Shionoya no Gorō Korehiro was one,
> the other, Teshigahara no Gosaburō Arinao.
> "Should we await reinforcements?"
> wondered Shionoya. Teshigahara:
> "A beaten force leaves stragglers weakened.
> After them!" And, with war howls, they charged.
> Kiso fought with all the fury
> of one who knew that this day was his last.
> The men from the east advanced on him,
> each of them eager to take his head.

Yoshitsune, their commander, left the fighting to his men
out of concern for the cloistered emperor, to assure whose protection
he took five or six men in full armor to Rokujō, where the sovereign was staying.
Shaking with fear and surveying the scene from up on his east wall,
Naritada saw half a dozen warriors riding his way, visibly fresh from battle—
their helmets having slipped back over their shoulders—and brandishing a white
    banner.
Their left sleeves in fluttering tatters, they galloped toward him, raising black
    dust.
"Oh, no, here comes Kiso!" Naritada cried.
"This is the end, then!" The sovereign and his entourage lapsed into panic.
"But no!" Naritada reported again. "Their badges are different!
They must be the eastern warriors who have just entered the city!"
He had no sooner spoken than Yoshitsune
raced up to the gate, dismounted, knocked, and announced in a great voice,

> "I am Kurō Yoshitsune,
> younger brother of Yoritomo,
> arrived from the east, at your service!
> Be kind enough to open the gate!"

> Naritada was so relieved that he jumped straight down off the wall and

hurt his back. Too happy to feel the pain, he dragged himself inside and reported Yoshitsune's arrival. His Cloistered Eminence, deeply stirred, had the gate opened at once.

Yoshitsune wore that day, over a red brocade *hitatare*, armor laced with purple cords shaded from light to dark, a helmet with spreading *kuwagata* horns, a gold-trimmed sword, and, in his quiver, arrows fletched with mottled feathers. An inch-wide strip of paper spiraled, right to left, down the upper part of his bow. It showed him plainly to be in command.

The cloistered emperor peered out through the slats of a window by the gate. "These look like sturdy fellows," he said. "Have them announce their names."
So they did: first their commander, Kurō Yoshitsune,
then Yasuda no Saburō Yoshisada, Hatakeyama no Jirō Shigetada,
Kajiwara Genda Kagesue, Sasaki Shirō Takatsuna, Shibuya no Uma-no-jō
  Shigesuke.

They were six including Yoshitsune, each in armor of a different color but equally resolute in demeanor. The sovereign had Naritada conduct Yoshitsune to the broad aisle before his chamber and questioned him at length on the day's conflict.

With great respect Yoshitsune replied, "Yoshinaka's rebellion so shocked Yoritomo that he dispatched Noriyori and myself, with thirty senior officers, at the head of an army exceeding sixty thousand horse. Noriyori marched via Seta and has not yet arrived. I took the river crossing at Uji and came straight here to protect Your Majesty. Yoshinaka fled up the river, and I sent men after him. They must have killed him by now." He spoke with perfect equanimity.

His Cloistered Eminence was impressed. "Excellent!" he said. "Stragglers from Kiso's men may easily turn up here and cause trouble. I want this house well guarded."

Yoshitsune respectfully assented. He had all four gates secured and waited. Warriors raced to join him, until soon they numbered ten thousand.

Kiso had meant, should things go awry,
to seize the sovereign, flee westward with him, and join the Heike.
He had kept twenty sturdy menials ready for just this purpose,
but news that Yoshitsune now had the sovereign under his protection
put an end to that plan. It was all over, and he knew it.
With a great cry, he charged into a force of several tens of thousands of men.
Time and again he seemed sure to be killed, but he always broke through.

"Had I known it would come to this,"
Kiso declared, shedding bitter tears,

"I would not have sent Imai to Seta.
As boys we played with bamboo horses.
We swore that should we ever face death,
the two of us would die together,
and now we are to be killed apart.
How I wish that this were not so!
I must know what has happened to him,"
he went on, and started off up the river.
On the bank between Sanjō and Rokujō,
an enemy force swept down on him.
Again and again he whirled to face them.
Half a dozen times, his tiny band
repulsed a foe as overwhelming
as clouds or mists. Abruptly he crossed
toward Awataguchi and Matsuzaka.
Only last year he had left Shinano
leading an army of fifty thousand;
now, passing the brook at Shinomiya,
he had only six riders with him,
and how many of these would he keep
beneath the skies of the bardo world?
The thought is exceedingly painful.

4. The Death of Kiso

Lord Kiso had brought with him from Shinano two beauties:
Tomoe and Yamabuki.
Yamabuki was unwell and stayed in the capital.
With her lovely white skin and long hair, Tomoe had enchanting looks.
An archer of rare strength, a powerful warrior,
and on foot or on horseback a swordsman to face any demon or god,
she was a fighter to stand alone against a thousand.
She could ride the wildest horse down the steepest slope.
In battle, Kiso clad her in the finest armor,
equipped her with a great sword and a mighty bow,
and charged her with the attack on the opposing commander.
She won such repeated glory that none could stand beside her.
And that is why, when so many had already been cut down in their flight,
Tomoe remained among the last seven.
Word spread that, via Nagasaka,
Kiso was now heading for Tanba,

or that he was crossing Ryūge Pass,
aiming at last to reach the north.
Actually, desperate to know
what had become of Kanehira,
he was in full flight toward Seta.
Meanwhile Imai Kanehira,
who with a force of eight hundred
had done his best to hold that crossing,
now was reduced to fifty men.
Banner furled, he was heading back
toward the city, anxious to know
what fate had overtaken his lord,
when the two men found each other
in Ōtsu, along the Uchide shore.
Each knew the other a hundred yards off.
They urged their mounts forward and met.
Kiso took Kanehira's hands.
"It seemed all over for me," he said,
"on the riverbank at Rokujō,
but I so longed to know about *you*
that I broke through swarms of enemies
and managed to reach you after all."
Imai replied, "You do me too much honor.
I had meant to die in battle at Seta, but concern for you led me here."
And Lord Kiso: "Then the bond between us still holds.
The enemy has scattered my men and driven them into the woods.
They must be somewhere nearby.
Raise that furled banner of yours!" Imai did so.

> Had these men fled the city or Seta? There was no knowing, but the
> sight of Imai's banner brought three hundred racing to join him.
> Lord Kiso was very pleased. "With this many," he said, "we can at
> least fight our last battle. Whose men are those, swarming over there?"
> "I gather that their commander is Ichijō no Jirō, from Kai."
> "And how many with him?"
> "Six thousand horse."
> "A fine opponent, then. If I must die anyway, I might as well get
> myself cut down by someone worthy, among a superior force." With
> these words he moved straight ahead.

Lord Kiso wore that day Chinese damask-laced armor over a red brocade
hitatare,

a helmet with *kuwagata* horns, and a dauntingly long sword.
At his back the few arrows left to him after the day's battles projected above his
    head,
fletched with eagle feathers. He carried a black, rattan-wrapped bow,
and his exceptionally powerful steed,
famous under the name Demon Roan, bore a gilt-edged saddle.
He rose in his stirrups and announced in a great voice,

      "You will have long heard tell of me:
      the man from Kiso. Now with your eyes
      behold the chief left equerry
      and also the governor of Iyo,
      famed as the Asahi Shogun,
      Minamoto no Yoshinaka!
They say you are Ichijō no Jirō, from Kai.
Then hear me! We are worthy opponents, you and I!
Take my head and show it off to Yoritomo!"
With that he charged.

      Ichijō cried, "The man who just now
      shouted his name is their great commander!
      See that he does not slip away! Get him,
      young men of mine, strike him down!"
      Surrounding Kiso with a mass of men,
      Ichijō went for his life and his head.
      Kiso's three hundred, amid six thousand,
      slashed left, right, up, down, everywhere,
      meanwhile retreating till they broke out,
      just fifty now, cutting through all comers
      until they met a force of two thousand
      under Doi no Jirō Sanehira.
      They broke through that, too, and, farther on,
      through four or five hundred, through two or three,
      through a hundred and forty or fifty,
      then a hundred, each time at a cost,
      until Kiso had only four left.
      This last remnant band of five
      still included Tomoe.

           Lord Kiso said to her, "Go, woman, go quickly, anywhere, far away. For
           myself, I shall die in battle or, if wounded, take my own life, and it must
           not be said that at the end I had a woman with me."
              She still did not go, but he kept pressing her until at last she replied,

"All I want is a worthy opponent, so that you can watch me fight my
last fight."

And while she waited,

Onda no Hachirō Moroshige, a man from Musashi famed for his strength,
rode up with thirty men. Tomoe charged, caught him in an iron grip,
forced his head down to her pommel, kept it pinned there, twisted it around,
cut it off, and tossed it away.

Then she abandoned her arms and armor and fled toward the east.

Tezuka no Tarō was killed.

Tezuka no Bettō fled.

Imai and Kiso were alone.

Kiso said, "This armor of mine—

I never gave it much thought before,

but it feels heavy today!"

Imai Kanehira replied, "There is still life in you, and your horse is not yet winded.
Why should mere armor weigh heavily on you?

Perhaps because losing all your men has made you a coward.

There is only one of me, I know, but think of me as a thousand.

I have seven or eight arrows left. I will cover you for a while.

Look: Over there is the pinewood of Awazu.

Go in among the pines and take your life."

They were urging their horses that way when a new band of fifty appeared.

"Go in among the pines, my lord," said Imai. "I will keep them off."

"I should have faced my fate in the capital itself," Kiso replied, "but
I fled all the way here to die with you. I want us to die together, not
apart." He brought his horse up beside Imai's and prepared to charge.

Imai dismounted in haste and took his lord's bridle.

"A man who wields the bow," he said,

"may have won great and lasting fame,

but a misjudgment at the end

may tarnish that fame forever.

Yes, you are exhausted, I know.

You have lost every one of your men.

It would be a very great shame

if the enemy were to cut you off

and some nobody's follower

drag you down and manage to kill you.

'Ah, Lord Kiso,' people would say—

'everyone in Japan knew of him,

but then some nobody did him in.'

Please, just go into those pines over there."

"Very well," Lord Kiso replied,
and at a gallop he set off
for the pinewood of Awazu.
Imai Kanehira, all on his own, charged in among the fifty men,
rose in his stirrups, and in a great voice announced his name:
"You will have heard of me long ago.
Now, see me. I am before you:
Imai no Shirō Kanehira,
foster brother of Lord Kiso,
in my thirty-third year.
Yoritomo, too, must know of me.
Kill Kanehira and show him my head!"
The eight arrows remaining to him
he shot in merciless succession,
and eight men fell, dead or alive.
Then he drew his sword and attacked,
slashing until not one dared face him.
Oh, he took his full share of trophies!
Crying, "Shoot him! Finish him off!"
they rained arrows from all around him,
but his armor was good—it stopped them,
and since none hit any chink or joint,
not one of them wounded him.
Lord Kiso galloped off, alone,
toward the pines of Awazu.
It was the first month, the twenty-first day.
The light was failing, and thin ice
spread across the surrounding paddies.
Never knowing the depth of the mud,
he rode his mount straight into one.
The horse sank in over its head.
No stirrup, no whip could move it.
Lord Kiso glanced back, worried about Imai,
so that his tilted helmet offered an opening.
Ishida no Jirō Tamehisa, close behind him, drew to the full, and his arrow sped
through.
The wound was mortal. Kiso slumped forward onto his horse's neck.
Two of Ishida's men fell on him and took his head.
Ishida impaled it on his sword, held it aloft, and shouted,
"Lord Kiso, so famous lately throughout Japan, has fallen to Ishida no Jirō
Tamehisa!"

The death of Kanehira (right). Small in background: Yoshinaka (left) and Ishida no Jirō Tamehisa (right), with drawn bow.

Imai Kanehira, still fighting, heard.
"Well then, I have no one left to protect!
Watch me now, gentlemen from the east!
Learn from the greatest brave in Japan
how a warrior ends his life!"
He took the point of his sword in his mouth,
hurled himself headlong from his horse,
and died transfixed. So it came to pass
that no battle took place at Awazu.

5. The Execution of Higuchi

Imai's older brother, Higuchi no Jirō Kanemitsu,
had crossed over into Kawachi province, to the fortress of Nagano,
meaning to dispose of Yukiie, but Yukiie was gone.
Word placed him instead at Nagusa in Kii.
Higuchi started straight off after him,
but news of fighting in the capital drew him there in haste.
At the bridge over the river at Yodo, he ran into one of Imai's servants.
"Oh, no!" the man cried. "Where are you going?

Lord Kiso is dead, and Lord Imai has killed himself."
Higuchi wept bitter tears.

"Hear me now, gentlemen!" he called.
"All of you loyal to Lord Kiso:
Go henceforth wherever you wish—
leave the world, enter religion—
live in mendicant poverty,
and pray for him in the life to come!
I myself shall go to the city,
die there in battle, and once more
in the afterlife see my lord
and my brother, Imai Kanehira!"

His five hundred men withdrew here and there as he went,
and only twenty still rode beside him
by the time he reached the south gate of the Toba Mansion.
News that Higuchi Kanemitsu would enter the capital that day
brought provincial warriors high and low
racing down Shichijō and Suzaku, toward Yotsuzuka, to face him.
Now, among his band there was one Chino no Tarō.
This Chino burst in among the host gathered at Yotsuzuka and shouted,

"Does anyone among you, tell me,
belong to the men commanded
by Ichijō no Jirō of Kai?"

"So you refuse to fight anyone else?" they replied with hoots of laughter.
"Come on, try any of us!" Chino therefore announced who he was:

"I am Chino no Tarō Mitsuhiro,
son of Chino no Tayū Mitsuie,
from Suwa no Kami-no-miya
in the province of Shinano!
No, I certainly do not insist
on fighting one of Lord Ichijō's men,
but, you see, Chino Shichirō,
my younger brother, is among them.
Back in Shinano I have two sons,
who in their grief will wish to know
how their father died, well or ill.
Were I now to die in combat
before my brother Shichirō's eyes,
he could bear witness to my children.
I am ready to fight any man."

This way and that he lunged, and three men

fell before him. He closed with a fourth,
and both men crashed to the ground,
where they stabbed each other to death.

Higuchi no Jirō had long been close to the Kodama League. The Ko-
dama men therefore gathered to discuss his plight. "A warrior mingles
widely with others in the hope of gaining a moment's relief under
threat, and so of living a little longer," they reflected. "No doubt that is
why Higuchi no Jirō allied himself with us. Let our merit now serve to
win us his life."

They sent him this message: "Once Imai and Higuchi were famed
beyond all of Lord Kiso's men, but now Lord Kiso is dead. So surrender
to us. Nothing prevents you from doing so. We will claim your life in
reward for our merit." Despite Higuchi's martial renown, his days of
glory were clearly over. He surrendered to the Kodama League.

The league put their request to Yoshitsune, who informed the cloistered
emperor.
Higuchi's life was spared, but not without protest
from those close to the sovereign, from the senior nobles, and from the
gentlewomen.
"Kiso attacked your Hōjūji residence," they complained,
"and his men's battle cries troubled His Majesty.
He set fire to the buildings, he killed a great many people,
and everywhere one heard the voices of Imai and Higuchi.
It would be quite wrong to spare the life of either."
Higuchi's death sentence was therefore reinstated.

The twenty-second of the month
brought the new regent's dismissal.[214]
The old one returned to his post
after a space of just sixty days,
thus breaking off the new one's dream.
Just so, once, the Awata Regent[215]
offered thanks for his appointment
and seven days later was gone.
Short though they were, those sixty days
still included the new-year banquet
and the appointments-list announcement,
thus leaving the dismissed gentleman

....

214. The "new regent" was Fujiwara no Moroie (1172–1238), the "old one" Fujiwara no Motomichi
(1160–1233).
215. Fujiwara no Michikane (961–95).

precious memories after all.
    On the twenty-fourth of the month,
the heads of Kiso and his last four
were paraded down the avenues.
Higuchi had surrendered, yes,
but he begged nonetheless to join them
and did so, in a tall *eboshi* hat
and an indigo-patterned *suikan* robe.
They killed him on the twenty-fifth.
Noriyori and Yoshitsune pleaded for him in every way,
but no: "Imai, Higuchi, Tate, Nenoi—
those were Kiso's Four Heavenly Kings, and this man was one of them.
To spare him would be to court grief, as does one who nurtures a tiger."
This, they say, was the sovereign's considered verdict.
It sealed Higuchi's execution.
    As history tells the tale,
when the Wolf-Tiger's[216] empire failed
and local warlords swarmed like wasps,
Liu Bang was the first among them
to enter the Xianyang Palace;
yet fearing that nevertheless
Xiang Yu might come after him,
he took to himself no man's wife,
though she be the greatest beauty,
nor seized, to enrich himself,
gold or silver, pearls or jewels
but, empty-handed, mounted guard
over the Han Valley barrier,
by slow degrees subdued each foe,
and took possession of the realm.
If only Kiso in this spirit,
and despite taking the city first,
had listened to Lord Yoritomo,
he might have done equally well.
The Heike had left Yashima, in Sanuki, the winter before;
crossed over to the Naniwa coast in the province of Settsu;
installed themselves at Fukuhara, their old capital;
established a fortress at Ichi-no-tani to the west;
and, to the east, placed the access gate for their main force in Ikuta Wood.

....

216. The First Emperor of Qin.

The men garrisoned at Fukuhara, Hyōgo, Itayado, and Suma
came from the eight San'yōdō provinces and the six of the Nankaidō;
thus fourteen provinces in all had answered the Heike call.
They numbered over one hundred thousand.

    Ichi-no-tani:
    mountains northward, sea to the south,
    narrow of access, spacious beyond,
    and cliffs sheer as folding screens.
    From the foot of the cliffs to the north
    and far out into the southern shallows,
    they had heaped a wall of boulders,
    felled mighty trees to lay abatis,
    and in the deeper water ranged ships
    side by side like a wall of shields.
    On the towers by the fortress entrance,
    Kyushu and Shikoku warriors,
    each battle-ready and far-famed
    for fierce courage to take on a thousand,
    clustered like dense clouds and mists.
    Below the towers saddled horses
    stood, keen for war, in ready ranks.
    Huge drums pounded a martial beat.
    Poised before every archer's breast,
    the drawn bow swelled like a half-moon.
    Like autumn frost a three-foot sword
    gleamed at each waist, and on the crests
    red banners streamed, leaping flames
    in the spring wind through high heaven.

6. Six Clashes

After the Heike move to Fukuhara,
the Shikoku warriors' allegiance to them waned.
The Awa and Sanuki provincial officials especially
rejected them and turned their sympathies toward the Genji.
"However," they acknowledged, "we have followed the Heike almost to this day,
and the Genji will hardly believe us if we suddenly now declare ourselves allies.
No, let us first loose an arrow or two against the Heike
and go over to the Genji on the strength of that gesture."
Having learned that Taira no Norimori was at Shimotsui in Bizen

with Michimori and Noritsune, his two sons,
they sailed there with ten boatloads of men to carry out their attack.
      Noritsune heard they were coming.
      "The scoundrels!" he cried. "Why, the other day
      they were cutting grass to feed our horses,
      and now, just like that, they turn against us!
      Very well, then! Go, men, kill them all!"
      Aboard a fleet of boats, they struck, howling,
      "Get them, get every single one!"
      The warriors from Shikoku had meant
      to shoot a few arrows merely for show
      and then withdraw, but this fierce assault
      convinced them, it seems, that they were lost.
      They were gone before the foe got near them
      and fled up toward the capital.
      On the way they came, in Awaji province,
      to the harbor of Fukura.
      In Awaji there were two Genji men,
      both descended from the great Tameyoshi:
      Kamo no Kanja Yoshitsugi
      and Awaji no Kanja Yoshihisa.
      Under the orders of these two,
      they built a fortress, and they waited.
      All too soon here came Noritsune,
      on the attack. The fight lasted out the day.
      Yoshitsugi was killed, Yoshihisa wounded
      so grievously that he took his own life.
      More than one hundred and thirty men
      had loosed arrows in the fort's defense.
      Noritsune beheaded them all,
      made a complete list of their names,
      and forwarded it to Fukuhara.
Lord Norimori then went to Fukuhara in person,
while his sons crossed to Shikoku to attack Kawano no Shirō, of Iyo,
who had failed to answer their rallying call.
Michimori, the elder, first reached the fort of Hanazono, in Awa.
The younger, Noritsune, went over to Yashima, in Sanuki.
The news prompted Kawano to cross over to Aki,
to join up with a man of that province: Nuta no Jirō, his maternal uncle.
Noritsune started from Yashima in pursuit as soon as he heard.

He landed at Minoshima, in the province of Bingo,
and the next day he closed in on Nuta's stronghold.

> Nuta and Kawano together
> were there to mount a sturdy defense.
> Noritsune attacked forthwith,
> and the fight went on a whole day and night,
> until Nuta must have felt all was lost,
> for he doffed his helmet and surrendered.
> Kawano, however, refused to yield.

>> He sallied forth with the mere fifty left from his initial five hundred men, only to be surrounded by two hundred under Heihachibyōe Tamekazu, a retainer of Noritsune's. These left him just six. Hoping nevertheless to escape, he fled shoreward down a narrow path, pursued by Tamekazu's son, Yoshinori, a powerful archer. Yoshinori closed within range of his quarry and felled five. Kawano alone remained, with one companion.

Yoshinori moved up beside this man, for whom Kawano was ready to die,
grappled with him until both fell, and was about to take his head
when Kawano turned back, cut off Yoshinori's,
and tossed it into the deep mud of a rice field.
He then cried in a great voice,

> "I am Kawano no Shirō,
> by birth Ochi no Michinobu,
> in the twenty-first year of my life,
> and behold! This is how I fight!

>> Let any man with the heart for it try to stop me!" He slung his companion over his shoulder, galloped off, boarded a boat, and sailed back to Iyo. Noritsune had failed to finish off Kawano, but he took Nuta, his prisoner, with him to Fukuhara.

There was yet another man, Ama no Rokurō Tadakage of Awaji,
who lent his support to the Genji.
In two large vessels laden with arms and commandeered rice,
he sailed up toward the capital.
At the news Noritsune set out after him in ten smaller boats.
Off Nishinomiya, Ama no Rokurō turned back to engage him.

> So fierce was Noritsune's attack
> that Ama must have foreseen disaster,
> for he retreated to Fukehi,
> a port in the province of Izumi.
> Sonobe no Hyōe Tadayasu,
> a man from Kii, was yet another

who dropped the Heike for the Genji.
Learning that Ama no Rokurō,
under attack from Noritsune,
had sought refuge at Fukehi,
he galloped there with a hundred men
to join forces with him. Noritsune
followed and attacked again.
The two men held out a day and a night,
but, confronted by catastrophe,
under cover of their men's arrows
they fled up toward the capital.
All two hundred of those archers
Noritsune ordered beheaded,
hung their heads in menacing view,
and returned at last to Fukuhara.

Next Kawano no Shirō from Iyo, in league with two Bungo warriors,
Usuki no Jirō Koretaka and Ogata no Saburō Koreyoshi,
led a force of two thousand men into the province of Bizen,
where they barricaded themselves in the fortress of Imagi.
Noritsune learned of this, too. From Fukuhara
he sent an attack force against them in haste, three thousand strong.

"These scoundrels will make no easy foe,"
Noritsune reported to Fukuhara.
"I need reinforcements!" Word then spread
that tens of thousands were on their way.
The men in Imagi gave it their best,
taking trophies and earning great honor,
but they knew that the Heike were many.
"And," they said, "there are so few of us!
We cannot possibly win this battle.
No, we had better escape from here
and give ourselves time to catch our breath."
Usuki and Ogata, by boat,
managed to get all the way to Kyushu,
while Kawano crossed over to Iyo.
There being no enemy left to fight,
Noritsune went back to Fukuhara.
There, Munemori and all the Heike—
senior nobles, privy gentlemen—
with one voice lauded the exploits
of Taira no Noritsune.

7. *The Roster of Forces at Mikusa*

On the twenty-ninth of the first month,
Noriyori and Yoshitsune called on the cloistered emperor
to report their departure for the west, to destroy the Heike.
His Cloistered Eminence replied,
"Three treasures have come down in our realm since the age of the gods.
They are the mirror, the jewel, and the sword.
See that you return them safe and sound to the capital."
The two men respectfully undertook to do so. Then they withdrew.
At Fukuhara the fourth of the second month was the anniversary of Lord
    Kiyomori's death,
and the memorial rites for him went forward as prescribed.

> Constant campaigning had left confused
> the passage of the months and days,
> but the old year had turned to the new,
> bringing a melancholy spring.
> Had the world only been theirs,
> what stupas[217] they might have erected,
> what offerings made to the Buddha,
> what generous gifts to the holy monks!
> But the surviving sons and daughters
> could only come together and weep.

The occasion called for the announcement of new appointments,
and clerics and laymen alike received promotions.
When Lord Munemori announced that the counselor Norimori
was to become a grand counselor with the senior second rank,
Norimori said,

> *Is this really I,*
> *this man, unaccountably*
> *still alive today?*
> *What he sees before him now*
> *is a dream within a dream.*

    In consideration of this reply,
    he was not made a grand counselor.
Morozumi, the son of chief secretary Nakahara Moronao,
was appointed a chief secretary.
Masaakira, an assistant deputy in the Bureau of War,
was appointed concurrently a fifth-rank chamberlain.

....

217. Here, funerary monuments.

People therefore called him the "Chamberlain-Assistant."

> Of old, Taira no Masakado
> conquered the eight eastern provinces
> and established his capital
> in Sōma county of Shimōsa.
> Claiming the title of "Taira Prince,"
> he appointed all his officials,
> save a doctor of the calendar.[218]
> This case, however, was different.
> The Heike had lost the old capital,
> but the emperor, who was with them,
> possessed the three regalia,
> hence full, sovereign authority.
> Nothing at all prevented them
> from announcing new appointments.

News that the Heike had fought their way up as far as Fukuhara
and soon would be back in the capital
greatly heartened and cheered those who had stayed behind at home.
The prelate Senshin, long resident at the temple of Prince-Abbot Jōnin,
corresponded with his old friend, who wrote in one of his replies,
"It is painful to imagine your life under such unfamiliar skies.
There is no peace in the capital either."
At the end he added this poem:

> *This fond heart of mine,*
> *where you live in memory*
> *shared by no other,*
> *I now send forth, to be yours,*
> *westward with the sinking moon.*

> Senshin pressed the letter to his face,
> overwhelmed by tears of sorrow.

> All this time Lord Koremori
> mourned more intensely, day by day,
> being torn from the wife and children
> he had left behind in the city.
> Merchants sometimes brought him letters,
> and he suffered so from knowing
> what her life in the city was like
> that he thought of having her join him,

....

218. The correct establishment of the calendar was a government function so vital that even Masakado did not seek to usurp it.

to have both of them share one fate,
but while bearing up himself,
he hated to inflict all this on her.
He therefore cultivated patience,
day after endlessly trying day,
in a manner that clearly showed
the depth of his feeling for her.

> The Genji had meant to attack on the fourth, but they desisted when
> they learned that it was the anniversary of Kiyomori's death, so as to
> let the proper rites take their course. On the fifth the westward di-
> rection was blocked, and on the sixth all travel was forbidden. They
> decided on an initial arrow exchange with the Heike on the seventh,
> at the hour of the hare, at the east and west access points to Ichi-
> no-tani.

Nonetheless the almanac had the fourth down as a lucky day,
so it was then that the commanders of the army's two divisions,
the main and the flanking force, set out from the city.
   Noriyori commanded the main force,
   supported by the following men:
      Takeda no Tarō Nobuyoshi,
      Kagami no Jirō Tōmitsu,
      Kagami no Kojirō Nagakiyo,
      Yamana no Jirō Noriyoshi,
      Yamana no Saburō Yoshiyuki.
   And these were his field commanders:
      Kajiwara Heizō Kagetoki;
            Genda Kagesue, his first son;
            his second, Heiji Kagetaka;
            his third, Saburō Kageie.
      Also Inage no Saburō Shigenari,
      Hangae no Shirō Shigetomo,
      Hangae no Gorō Yukishige,
      Koyama no Koshirō Tomomasa,
      Nakanuma no Gorō Munemasa,
      Yūki no Shichirō Tomomitsu,
      Sanuki no Shirō Hirotsuna,
      Onodera no Tarō Michitsuna,
      Soga no Tarō Sukenobu,
      Nakamura no Tarō Tokitsune,
      Edo no Shirō Shigeharu,
      Tamanoi no Shirō Sukekage,

Ōkawazu no Tarō Hiroyuki,
Shō no Saburō Tadaie,
Shō no Shirō Takaie,
Shōdai no Hachirō Yukihira,
Kuge no Jirō Shigemitsu,
Kawara no Tarō Takanao,
Kawara no Jirō Morinao,
Fujita no Saburō Yukiyasu.
Under these rode fifty thousand,
who, on the fourth of the second month,
early in the hour of the dragon, [ca. 8 A.M.]
made their way out of the capital
and that same day, during the hours
of the monkey and on to the bird, [ca. 4–6 P.M.]
established their camp at Koyano,
in the province of Settsu.
Yoshitsune commanded the flanking force,
supported by men of his own:
        Yasuda no Saburō Yoshisada,
        Ōuchi no Tarō Koreyoshi,
        Murakami Yasukuni,
        and Tashiro Nobutsuna.
And these were his field commanders:
        Doi no Jirō Sanehira;
            his son, Yatarō Tōhira;
        Miura-no-Suke Yoshizumi;
            his son, Heiroku Yoshimura.
        Also Hatakeyama no Jirō Shigetada,
        Nagano no Saburō Shigekiyo,
        Sahara no Jūrō Yoshitsura,
        Wada no Kotarō Yoshimori,
        Wada no Jirō Yoshimochi,
        Wada no Saburō Munezane,
        Sasaki Shirō Takatsuna,
        Sasaki no Gorō Yoshikiyo,
        Kumagai no Jirō Naozane,
            and his son, Kojirō Naoie.
Plus Hirayama Sueshige,
        Amano no Jirō Naotsune,
        Ogawa no Jirō Sukeyoshi,
        Hara no Saburō Kiyomasu,

Kaneko no Jūrō Ietada,
Kaneko no Yoichi Chikanori,
Watariyanagi no Yagorō Kiyotada,
Beppu no Kotarō Kiyoshige,
Tatara no Gorō Yoshiharu,
     and his son, Tarō Mitsuyoshi.
Lastly Kataoka no Tarō Tsuneharu,
Genpachi Hirotsuna,
Ise no Saburō Yoshimori,
Satō no Saburō Tsuginobu,
Satō no Shirō Tadanobu,
Eda no Genzō,
Kumai Tarō, and
Musashibō Benkei.
These led a force of ten thousand.
The men left the city that same day,
at the same hour, by the Tanba road
and in a day covered a distance
more commonly covered in two.
They came to the Harima-Tanba border,
and there they stopped at Onobara,
under the eastern slopes of Mount Mikusa.

8. The Battle of Mikusa

The Heike side had stationed over three thousand horse
seven or eight miles from Onobara, below the *western* slopes of Mikusa.
Taira no Sukemori, Arimori, Tadafusa, and Moromori led them,
with the help of field officers Heinaibyōe Kiyoie and Emi no Jirō Morikata.
That night, at the hour of the dog, Yoshitsune summoned Doi no Jirō
     Sanehira. [ca. 8 P.M.]
"I'm told that there is a large Heike force seven or eight miles from here,
under Mount Mikusa, to the west.
What do you say? Attack tonight or wait for tomorrow?"
Tashiro stepped forward to reply,
          "If we leave the battle until tomorrow, reinforcements will join the
          Heike.
     There are three thousand of them,
     but we ourselves have ten thousand.
     We are by far the stronger force.
          I advise attacking tonight."

"Well said, Tashiro!" Sanehira exclaimed. "Then, if you will, sir, let us move out!" And off they rode.

The warriors murmured among themselves, "But it's so dark! How will we find our way?"

"What about the usual torches—the great, big ones?" Yoshitsune asked.

"By all means!" Sanehira replied. He set fire to the houses of Onobara.

They went on to set fire to moor and mountain, grasses and trees,
so that they covered those seven or eight miles
over Mount Mikusa in light as bright as day.

This Tashiro was the last son
of the counselor Tametsuna,
the former governor of Izu—
born of his father's love affair
with a certain lady, the daughter
of Kano-no-suke Mochimitsu.
His mother's grandfather brought him up
and made a warrior of him.
Regarding his further ancestry:
He looked back five generations
to Prince Sukehito, the third son
born to Emperor Go-Sanjō.
His was a noble lineage,
and he was a fine warrior, too.

As for the Heike, they never imagined an attack that night.
"We'll fight tomorrow, no doubt about that," they told themselves.
"Feeling drowsy in battle is dangerous—better get some proper sleep first."
A few among the advance guard nonetheless stayed alert,
but those in the rear lay down, pillowed on helmets, armor sleeves, quivers,
and slept there the sleep of the just.

It was the middle of the night
when ten thousand Genji warriors
rode down on them with fearsome cries.
Such panic overwhelmed the Heike
that one took his bow but forgot arrows,
another arrows but forgot his bow.
Scrambling back to avoid charging hooves,
they left the enemy free passage.
The Genji pursued them as they fled
hither and yon, till five hundred Heike

lay dead, struck down by Genji archers.
Many more of them suffered wounds.
Sukemori, their senior commander,
Arimori, and Tadafusa
must have felt overcome by shame,
for they boarded a boat at Takasago
in Harima and sailed away
to Yashima, over in Sanuki.
Moromori gathered together
Heinaibyōe and Emi no Jirō
and took both to Ichi-no-tani.

9. *The Old Horse*

Lord Munemori had an official named Yoshiyuki take the Heike nobles this
     message:
"It appears that Kurō Yoshitsune has routed our men at Mikusa
and that he will burst into Ichi-no-tani at any moment."
The nobles all excused themselves at once.
To Noritsune, Munemori sent this:
"Please forgive these repeated requests,
but would you be good enough to go out to face them?"
"War is my life," Noritsune replied. "All will be well.
No one ever won victory by fighting only on his own ground,
like a fisherman or a hunter, and avoiding unfavorable terrain.
I will gladly face a powerful enemy as often as you like.
Victory will be mine this time. You may set your mind at rest."
Buoyed by Noritsune's confidence, Munemori assigned him
ten thousand mounted men under Moritoshi, the former governor of Etchū.
With his elder brother Michimori, Noritsune secured the side against the
     mountains—
in other words, the terrain below Hiyodori Ravine.
Michimori called his wife to Noritsune's command post
and there bade her a tender farewell.

> Lord Noritsune was furious. "This is the most dangerous side of the
> fort," he objected, "and that is exactly why I was sent here. Yes, it is
> critical. The Genji could fall on us from up there at any moment. We
> might never have time to snatch up our bows, and if we did, we might
> still not get an arrow to the string—or, worse, never even get a chance
> to shoot it! And there you are, mooning about—you are a waste of
> time!"

Apparently Michimori got the point, because he hastily took up
arms and sent his wife back where she came from.
On the fifth, toward sundown, the Genji started from Koyano
and little by little drove on to Ikuta Wood.

The view toward the Suzume Pines,
the Mikage Woods, and Koyano
revealed camp after Genji camp,
their fires plain to see from afar.
As darkness fell, they blazed so bright
the moon might have been coming up
over the nearby mountain ridge.
"Let us light some fires of our own!"
the Heike said, and managed a few
in Ikuta Wood. By the light of dawn,
those Genji fires shone like stars
glittering in a cloudless sky.
That old poem about fireflies
flitting around beside a river—
now they beheld that very scene.

As for the Genji, they camped here and rested their horses,
camped there and fed them. They were in no hurry.
The Heike meanwhile quivered with apprehension,
expecting attack at any moment.
On the sixth, at dawn, Yoshitsune divided his ten thousand into two.
Seven thousand, under Doi Sanehira, he sent to the west side of Ichi-no-tani.
Three thousand he took around by the Tanba road, in a flanking
    movement
behind Ichi-no-tani, with a view to charging down Hiyodori Ravine.
His men murmured among themselves,
"But everyone knows that Hiyodori is impassable!"
"If I'm going to die, I want at least to die fighting the enemy.
I don't want to get myself killed just falling off a rock!"
"There must be *someone* around who knows these mountains!"
Hirayama Sueshige, from Musashi, came forward to say, "I do. I know them."
"But you are from the east," Yoshitsune objected.
"You have never even seen these mountains of the west.
You cannot possibly know anything about them."
Hirayama insisted,

"And *you* cannot possibly mean that.
Poets know the cherry blossoms
of Yoshino and Hatsuse;

a true warrior knows all about the terrain behind the fortress where his enemy lurks." His words reeked of insolence.

The next to speak was another Musashi man, Beppu no Kotarō Kiyoshige, a young fellow still in his eighteenth year:

"My father always used to say that when you are lost in the mountains, never mind whether you have an enemy after you or are just out hunting,
the thing is to bridle an old horse and let it go ahead of you.
It will always find you a trail."

"Well spoken!" said Yoshitsune.

> Even when all is deep in snow,
> they say, an old horse still knows the way.
> On an old horse, a pale roan,
> he placed a saddle with steel trim,
> gave the creature a polished steel bit,
> let the reins lie loose over its neck,
> and sent it ambling on ahead.
> Off it went, among unknown mountains.
> This was early in the second month.
> High up, patches of snow lingered,
> looking for all the world like flowers.
> Down in the valleys, warblers sang,
> and at times they wandered through mist.
> They climbed toward brilliant, soaring clouds,
> descended green, thickly wooded cliffs.
> Snow lay unmelted on the pines;
> moss shrouded the narrow track.
> Snowflakes blew past them like plum petals.
> Eastward, westward they whipped their horses
> until dusk settled over their path
> and they dismounted to make camp.

Musashibō Benkei brought in an old man. Yoshitsune asked who he was. "A hunter in these mountains, sir," Benkei replied.

Yoshitsune addressed the hunter. "Then you must know these mountains well," he said. "I want straight answers."

"Of course I know them," the old man replied.

Yoshitsune explained, "My idea is to charge down from here into the Heike fort at Ichi-no-tani. What do you think of it?"

"You will never make it. No one could get all the way down a ravine like that, several hundred yards long and blocked by huge, rocky outcrops. And you want to do it on horseback? Impossible! Besides, they

seem to have dug pit traps inside the fort and planted sharpened
stakes. They are all ready for you."
    "All right, but do *deer* get down there?"
"The deer, yes, they get through.
When the season warms up a bit,
the Harima deer take that trail to Tanba
to enjoy the lush pasture there,
and when the cold comes back again,
the Tanba deer take it to Harima
to feed there on Inamino,
where there is never that much snow."
"Why then," Yoshitsune exclaimed, "it sounds like a veritable riding ground!
If deer can get through, so can horses.
I want you to show us the way, right now."
The man protested that he was too old.
"You must have a son, then."
"Yes, I do." He presented Kumaō, in his eighteenth year.
Yoshitsune had Kumaō come of age on the spot,
and since his father's name was Washino-o no Shōji Takehisa,
he gave him the name Washino-o no Saburō Yoshihisa.
He had Yoshihisa ride before them to show them the way.
    Later, after the Heike defeat,
    when, pursued by his brother's wrath,
    Yoshitsune was killed in the north,
    this Yoshihisa died with him.

10. *First or Second to Engage the Foe*

Until well into the night of the sixth, Kumagai and Hirayama lay low in the
    flanking force.
Kumagai then called over his son, Kojirō.
"When these men charge down that treacherous ravine," he said,
"none will be able to claim having made it before the others.
Come, let us take the Harima road to where Doi Sanehira is posted
and be the first of them all into Ichi-no-tani."
"By all means," Kojirō replied. "I had the same thought.
Let us be on our way, if I may join you."
His father replied, "As a matter of fact, Hirayama is here, too,
and he has no taste either for mass combat."
"Go, have a look at what Hirayama is up to," he added to a servant.
Sure enough, Hirayama was already preparing to leave.

"Others can please themselves," he was muttering,
"but I have no intention of letting anyone get a step ahead of me."
Hirayama's servant was feeding his master's horse.
"You brute!" the man cried. "Won't you *ever* finish?" He struck the beast.
"Stop that! This is his last night!" Hirayama rebuked the man. And off he rode.
Kumagai's servant raced back with the news.
"I knew it!" said Kumagai. He, too, started at once.

> Over a blue-black *hitatare*,
> Kumagai wore red-laced armor
> and a red neckpiece on his helmet.
> He rode the famous Gonda Chestnut.
> Kojirō wore a *hitatare*
> lightly dyed with arrowhead leaves
> and armor with zigzag-braid lacing.
> He rode Seirō, a pale red roan.
> Their standard-bearer, in olive green
> under armor laced with dark blue leather
> sprinkled with small, yellow-tinted flowers,
> rode behind them on a sorrel.
> The key ravine dropped off to their left.
> They followed, farther on to the right,
> the old, long-abandoned road that led
> past Tai-no-hata and, beyond,
> to where the waves broke at Ichi-no-tani.

Night still shrouded Shioya, a locality near Ichi-no-tani,
where Doi Sanehira lay in wait with his seven thousand.
Under cover of darkness, Kumagai stole past him, along the sea's edge,
to launch an assault against the west access gate to the fortress.
These were the small hours. From the enemy within, only silence.
Not one Genji rider followed.
Kumagai called his son to him and said,
"Many out there must be burning to break in first.
I am not so dull as to imagine that we are alone.
They are probably here already, prepared to move, only waiting for dawn.
Let us announce our names."
He went up to the wall of shields and called in a great voice,

> "Kumagai no Jirō Naozane
> and his son, Kojirō Naoie,
> both residents of Musashi:
> We declare ourselves first to challenge
> the fortress of Ichi-no-tani!"

The Heike, within, warned one another to keep quiet.

"Let them wear out their horses!" they said.

Kumagai got no reply.

Meanwhile a single warrior rode up behind them. "Who goes there?" asked Kumagai.

"Hirayama Sueshige. And you?"

"Kumagai Naozane."

"Really! When did you get here?"

"During the night."

"I should have been right behind you," Hirayama explained, "but Narida Gorō tripped me up and delayed me. He swore that he wanted to die with me, if it came to that, and I agreed. So we set out together. But then he began remonstrating with me. 'Do not be too eager to attack first, Hirayama,' he said. 'To be first you must have the others behind you, to witness your success or failure. To charge alone in among many and get yourself killed for your pains—what is the point of that?' I saw he was right, so I rode to the top of a little slope, let my horse drop his head, and awaited the others. Then Narida turned up again.

I assumed that he had in mind
to stop beside me and have a talk
about the battle and how it might go,
but not at all. He shot me a cold glance
and galloped straight past. 'Oh, no!' I thought.
'This fellow has been planning all along
to make sure *he* is the one to be first!'
He had sixty or seventy yards on me,
but I saw that I had the stronger horse,
and soon enough I caught up with him.
'So,' I called out, 'you have the gall
to play a low trick on a man like me!'
and on I went. He fell far behind.
I doubt that he ever saw me again."

Meanwhile dawn was spreading across the sky.

The five riders—Kumagai, Hirayama, and their men—waited.

Kumagai had already declared his name,
but perhaps he meant to announce it again for Hirayama to hear,
because he approached the shield wall and roared,

"Kumagai no Jirō Naozane
and his son, Kojirō Naoie,
both men of Musashi province,

first challenge Ichi-no-tani.
Come, any Heike warrior
brave enough to test my mettle,
come out and try me, Naozane!"

Some Heike warriors muttered in response, "All right, let's go and get them, this Kumagai, father and son who have been bellowing at us all night! Let's drag them in here!"

And the men who advanced to do that, who were they? Etchū no Jirōbyōe Moritsugi, Kazusa no Gorōbyōe Tadamitsu, Akushichibyōe Kagekiyo, and Gotōnai Sadatsune, followed by others, some twenty in all. They threw the gate open and charged.

Hirayama wore a *hitatare*
tie-dyed to leave a pattern of spots
under armor with scarlet lacing
and a double-barred-circle neckpiece.
He rode a steed named Mekasuge.
His standard-bearer, in black-laced armor,
sported a broad, sturdy neck plate
and sat mounted on a red roan.
"Behold Hirayama Sueshige,"
he cried, "a warrior from Musashi,
one of the vanguard in the battles
fought in both Hōgen and Heiji!"
Lord and standard-bearer, together,
galloped forward with fierce cries.
Where Kumagai charged, Hirayama followed,
where Hirayama, Kumagai.
Each determined to best the other,
they cut and slashed until the sparks flew.
The Heike, so grievously assaulted,
must have seen they could not prevail,
for they retreated within their fort,
battling to keep out the enemy.
Struck in the belly by an arrow, Kumagai's horse reared.
Kumagai got over its flailing legs and dismounted, to stand on firm ground.
His son, Kojirō, announced name and age—he was in his sixteenth year—
and fought his way so forcefully forward
that his horse touched the shield wall with its muzzle,
but Kojirō's bow arm, his left, took an arrow.
He leaped from his mount to stand by his father.

"What is it, Kojirō? Are you wounded?"

"Yes." "Make sure your armor is straight,
let no arrow work its way through,
and keep your neck plate tight against you.
See that nothing gets under your helmet."
So his father instructed him.
Kumagai ripped out the arrows stuck in his armor,
glared at the men within the fort, and roared,

"Last winter, leaving Kamakura,
I offered my life to Lord Yoritomo,
and came here to Ichi-no-tani
resolved that here my body should lie.
Look at me! I am Naozane!

Where is Etchū no Jirōbyōe, who claims great exploits at Murayama
and Mizushima? Where are Kazusa no Gorōbyōe and Akushichibyōe
Kagekiyo? And Lord Noritsune—where is *he*? The greater the foe, the
greater the glory. Fighting just anyone is a waste. So come out and
fight! Fight Naozane!"

Etchū no Jirōbyōe heard this.
He was wearing that day the outfit he favored: an indigo-dyed *hitatare*,
lighter blue above and darker below, under armor with red lacing.
His mount was a pale gray.
He fixed his gaze on Kumagai, father and son, and moved toward them.
Resolved not to be parted, the two stood fast side by side,
drawn swords pressed to their foreheads.
They yielded not an inch; no, they kept advancing.
Apparently daunted, Etchū no Jirōbyōe turned and retreated.
"Well?" Kumagai cried. "I know you! You are Jirōbyōe!
Is there something about us you dislike?
Come here, right here to me, and fight me!"
"I prefer not to," Jirōbyōe replied, and moved off.
Before this spectacle Kagekiyo exclaimed, "Talk about groveling!"
He nearly charged forward to answer the challenge himself, but Jirōbyōe caught
    his sleeve.
"Lord Noritsune has greater threats to contend with. Just drop it!"
His reproof convinced Kagekiyo to desist.

Next Kumagai got a fresh mount
and charged again, with fierce cries.
While he and his son pursued their war,
Hirayama first rested his horse,
then caught up with them and joined them.
Few among the Heike were mounted.

Archers on the towers shot volleys
that fell on the men below like rain,
but the Genji, a tiny number
lost amid the enemy swarms,
never took a single arrow.
Despite repeatedly issued orders
to take the fight up to each Genji man,
the overridden Heike horses,
fed only rarely and too long confined
on the ships that had brought them across,
were little more than skin and bone.
Kumagai's and Hirayama's,
well fed, glossy, and powerful,
could have knocked any Heike mount flat.
Not one warrior took their challenge.
When an arrow killed his standard-bearer,
a man he loved as he loved his own life,
Hirayama broke into the enemy,
took the head of the man who had shot it,
and got out again, safe and sound.
Kumagai, too, took many trophies.
He had been the first to attack,
but at the time the gate was closed
and he had not been able to enter.
Hirayama attacked only later,
but with the gate open, in he went.
That is how the two came to dispute
which of them had been first, which second.

11. *The Double Attack*

Eventually Narida Gorō turned up as well.
Doi no Jirō pressed the assault at the head of his seven thousand,
their many-colored standards lifted high, their voices raised in fierce cries.
Meanwhile the main Genji force of fifty thousand secured Ikuta Wood.
Among them were two from Musashi, Kawara no Tarō and Kawara no Jirō.
Kawara no Tarō summoned Jirō, his younger brother.
"A man of power may do little himself," he said, "yet gain glory through his
    retainers.
The likes of us must win glory on our own.
Here we are, with the enemy before us, yet we have not shot a single arrow.

I cannot stand it. I will steal into their fortress and shoot one,
and since I have next to no chance of coming back alive,
I want you to stay behind and bear witness to my deed."
In tears, Kawara no Jirō replied,

> "How I hate to hear that from you!
> All we have is the two of us.
> If you, my elder brother, are killed
> and I, the younger, am left alone,
> what glory have I then to hope for?
> No, rather than die apart,
> let us meet our fate together."
> Each of them called on his servant
> to tell his family how he died.

They went on foot, in straw sandals and leaning on their bows as upon staffs.
They clambered across the abatis surrounding Ikuta Wood and entered the fort.
By starlight alone they could not make out the colors of armor.
Kawara no Tarō cried in a great voice,

> "Men from Musashi, we are
> Kawara no Tarō Takanao
> and Jirō Morinao,
> first from among the main Genji force
> in Ikuta Wood to challenge you!"

>> The Heike men heard them. "These eastern warriors are as scary as
>> they come," they muttered. "Here we are, a whole army, and just two
>> of them invade us! But what harm can they do? Fine, let's humor them
>> a bit." Nobody moved to shoot them.

> Now, both brothers were mighty archers,
> and each loosed a stream of arrows.
> Up went a cry: "Enough of that! Kill them!"
> The western provinces, too, boasted
> powerful archers: two brothers from Bitchū,
> Manabe no Shirō and Gorō.
> Shirō was in Ichi-no-tani, Gorō in Ikuta Wood.
> Shirō drew his bow all the way back.
> The arrow flew from the string
> and straight through both breastplate and man.
> Kawara no Tarō, transfixed,
> propped himself upright with his bow
> until his brother raced to his aid,
> slung him rapidly over his shoulder,
> and was climbing over the abatis

when a second arrow from Manabe
struck between flaps of his armor skirts.
The two men went down together.
Manabe's servant fell upon them
and took both the brothers' heads.

    Lord Tomomori said when he saw them, "Ah, those were brave men—
men truly worthy to face a thousand! I am so sorry that I could not
save them."

    The Kawara brothers' servants cried, "The brothers were first inside
the fortress—first inside and first to die!"

    Kajiwara Kagetoki responded, "This is all their confederates' fault.
They are the ones who got them killed! And now, at last, the time has
come. Attack!" He uttered his battle cry, and fifty thousand men rode
out after him with one vast roar.

Kajiwara had foot soldiers clear the abatis
and charged with his band of five hundred yelling horsemen.
His second son, Heiji Kagetaka, got so far ahead that his father sent a man
    after him.
"No one in the lead shall have a reward until the others have caught up,"
the message ran. "Our commander in chief so orders."
Kagetaka paused for a moment, then said,

      "Once a warrior
   has drawn the catalpa bow
     his line bequeathed him
   and loosed his arrow, no man
     can require it to return.

Tell him that!" With a shout he charged on.
"Give them no chance to cut Heiji down!
After him, men! Save Kagetaka!"
His father and both of his brothers,
Genda and Saburō, followed behind.
Kajiwara's five hundred galloped
in among a great host of men
and fought with furious energy,
till by and by only fifty remained;
then, abruptly, they drew back and left.
Somehow or other it happened
that Genda Kagesue was not among them.
"And where is Genda, men?" Kagetoki asked.
"He went deep in among the enemy. He may well have been killed."
At this news Kagetoki declared,

"I desire to remain alive
only for the sake of my sons.
If now Genda has been cut down,
there is no point in my living on.
Turn back!" He returned to the fray.
In a mighty voice, he then announced his name:
"During the Later Three Years' War,[219]
when Hachimantarō Yoshiie
attacked the fortress of Senbuku
at Kanazawa, in Dewa,

> a young man in his sixteenth year led the assault. Shot through the left
> eye, right back to his neckpiece, he still managed an answering arrow,
> slew his foe, and left a great name: Kamakura no Gongorō Kagemasa.
> I am his descendant, Kajiwara Heizō Kagetoki, a warrior worthy to
> face a thousand!

Any man with the heart to fight me,
let him kill me and show his lord my head!"
With fierce cries he charged.
Lord Tomomori shouted in turn,
"Kajiwara is famous, you know,
through all the provinces of the east!
See that you get him! Kill this man!"
They surrounded him and attacked.
Without a single thought for himself,
Kajiwara searched only for Genda,
meanwhile racing, cutting, slashing
backward and forward, left and right,
until he found him: Genda, at last,
helmet slumped back over his shoulders,
horse shot from beneath him, fighting on foot
backed up against a twenty-foot cliff,
five attackers around him, on each side
one man of his own, eyes fixed ahead,
giving his all to fight his last fight.
Seeing him like that, still alive,
Kajiwara dismounted in haste.
"Here I am," he cried, "your father!
Listen, Genda! Die if you must,
but never show your back to the foe!"

....

219. A campaign (1083–87) during which Minamoto no Yoshiie put down a rebellion in the far north.

Father and son slew three attackers
and wounded two. "For a warrior,
advance and retreat each has its time.
Come, Genda!" said Kagetoki.
He took his son up onto his mount
and got away. This is what they mean
by "Kajiwara's double attack."

12. *The Charge Down Hiyodori Ravine*

Thereafter the warriors of Chichibu, Ashikaga, Miura, and Kamakura,
the men of the Inomata, Kodama, Noiyo, Yokoyama, Nishi, Tsuzuki, and Shi
    leagues
threw themselves into a free and furious battle, Genji against Heike—
endless sallies and sorties, endless fierce challenges as men roared out their names,
until the mountains quaked and charging hoofbeats rang out like thunder.
Arrows rained down in volleys and countervolleys.
Some carried the wounded off on their shoulders;
some, only lightly wounded, fought on;
some, mortally struck, lay dead or dying.
Pairs grappled side by side, fell, stabbed each other to death.
Here a man pinned another's head down and cut it off;
there a man's head rolled from his shoulders.
Neither side betrayed any sign of weakness,
and the Genji main force by itself seemed far from sure to prevail.
At this juncture Yoshitsune swept his flanking force around to the rear.

> At daybreak on the seventh, he climbed up behind Ichi-no-tani, to the
> top of Hiyodori Ravine. He was about to start the descent when two
> stags and a doe, presumably startled by his men, fled all the way down
> to the Heike fortress.

Their arrival caused consternation below.
"Perhaps those deer are used to being around humans," the men said,
"but even so they should have run from us farther into the mountains.
It makes no sense for them to be fleeing right into an army.
The Genji must have frightened them down from up there!"
Takechi Kiyonori, from the province of Iyo, stepped forward.
"Perhaps," he said, "but nothing from off toward the enemy must get by."
He shot both stags and let the doe pass.
Moritoshi protested,
    "Shooting those stags made no sense!
    With just one of those arrows,

you could have kept off ten enemies!
Now you have committed a sin[220]
and wasted your arrows, too."
Yoshitsune stood looking out over the fortress below.
"Let's send some horses down there," he said, "and see how they do."
They drove down a number of saddled horses.
Some broke their legs and fell, others got down safe and sound.
Three saddled steeds landed on top of Moritoshi's quarters and stood there,
    trembling.
Yoshitsune was convinced. "As long as the riders are careful," he declared,
"the horses can get down there perfectly well.

So down we go! Do as I do!"
And down he went, with thirty men.
The whole force poured after him.
The slope was so steep that those behind
found the front of their stirrups bumping
the helmets of the riders ahead.
Swiftly, over mixed sand and pebbles,
they slid for some two hundred yards,
until, on a flat spot, they halted.
From there they looked down.
Huge, mossy boulders dropped plumb before them
a good hundred and fifty feet.
"This is it, then," they muttered, frozen.
But Satō no Jūrō Yoshitsura stepped forward.

"In Miura, where I come from," he said,
"we gallop over places like this
anytime, just chasing a bird.
This is a Miura riding ground!"
And down he went. Everyone followed,
stifling whoops and shouts to the horses.
The drop was so steep they shut their eyes.
The feat seemed all but superhuman—
something for gods or demons, not men.
Short of the bottom, they roared their war cry:
three thousand voices, answered by echoes
swelling them to ten thousand strong.

Murakami Yasukuni loosed fire among the Heike camp buildings and
burned every one to the ground. The strong wind then rolled billows

....

220. A sin because the Buddhist commandments forbid taking the life of any sentient being.

The Genji pour down Hiyodori Ravine and set fire to the Heike camp.

of black smoke over the Heike men. They panicked, and most raced to
save themselves by plunging into the sea. Many ships lay ready there,
but with hundreds and hundreds of armed warriors clamoring all at
once to board them, disaster was sure to follow. Three sank in full
view before they got more than a few hundred yards offshore.
It was next decided to let men of rank board but not the lower orders,
who were to be fended off with swords and halberds.

> Knowing full well what awaited them,
> these held on for dear life nonetheless
> to ships they were forbidden to board.
> Some of them had their arms cut off,
> some their forearms, and there they lay
> at the water's edge, red with blood.
>   Never once throughout many battles
> had Lord Noritsune's courage faltered,
> but now, for reasons best known to himself,
> he mounted his horse, Usuguro,
> and fled west as fast as he could.
> At Akashi, over in Harima,
> he boarded a ship and set sail at once
> for Sanuki province and Yashima.

13. *The Death of Moritoshi*

In both the main force and the one now on the beach at Ichi-no-tani,
the Musashi and Sagami men fought without a thought for their lives.
Lord Tomomori battled on, facing the east,
when a man of the Kodama League approached him from toward the mountains.
"Sir," he said, "you were once the governor of Musashi,
and the men of the Kodama League therefore wish me to tell you:
Look behind you!" Tomomori did so, and his men with him.
Black smoke billowed overhead.
"Oh, no! The west flank has fallen!" They dropped everything to flee.
Now, Moritoshi was the field commander of the Heike force below the mountains.
No doubt he felt it too late for flight, for he turned back to await the enemy.
Inomata Noritsuna saw in him a worthy opponent.
Whip and stirrup, he raced to Moritoshi's side
and grappled fiercely with him. Both crashed to the ground.

> Inomata was a warrior famed
> through the eight provinces of the east.
> There was that time, so the rumor went,

when he had torn a deer's antlers apart
like nothing at all. Moritoshi,
for his own part, preferred to confess
to the strength of twenty or thirty men
but secretly could haul up or launch,
all by himself, a ship that required
sixty or seventy men to move it.
So it was he who seized Inomata,
crushed him to the ground, and held him.
Pressed down that way, his fingers splayed,
Inomata could not draw his dagger
or even get a grip on the hilt.
He tried to speak, but no voice came.
At any moment his head would be off.
Although not the stronger of the two, Inomata was brave.
Unfazed, he caught his breath and asked calmly,
"Did you hear me announce my name?
When a man slays an opponent, he may glory in the deed
only if, before taking the head, he speaks his name and has his foe do the same.
What will you gain from taking my head when you do not know who I am?"
Moritoshi must have seen he was right, for he replied,
"Although born a Heike lord, I was good only for war:
My name is Moritoshi, once governor of Etchū. Who are you?"
"Inomata no Kobeiroku Noritsuna, from Musashi,"
Inomata answered. "As far as I can see,
the Genji are now too strong and the Heike face defeat.
If your great lord still lived, then yes, taking an enemy's head
might win you glory and rich reward, but he is gone.
Spare me this once and you will have your reward:
I will save for you the lives of dozens of your men."
Moritoshi was furious.
    "I am not good for much," he said,
    "but I am a Heike after all.

        I have no intention of seeking help from any Genji, nor do I imagine
        any Genji wanting mine. You should have held your tongue!"

            He was about to strike when Inomata spoke again. "For shame!" he
        said, "to take the head of a man who has already surrendered!"

            "Very well," Moritoshi answered, "your life is yours." He drew Ino-
        mata to his feet. Before them the ground was dry and hard, like an
        upland field; behind them stretched a paddy filled with deep mud.
        They sat down on the path that bordered it and rested.

Soon a single warrior came galloping toward them, clad in black-laced armor and riding a pale roan. Moritoshi peered suspiciously at him.

"That is Hitomi no Shirō, a good friend of mine," Inomata said. "He is probably heading this way because he has seen me. There is no need to worry."

All the time, though, he was thinking, "If I grapple with Moritoshi when Shirō gets close, he is bound to join in."

By now the man was hardly more than a few yards away. Moritoshi at first kept an eye on both, but with Shirō so near now, he reserved his watchful gaze for this new foe. His eyes were off Inomata when, with a shout, Inomata jumped to his feet, shoved Moritoshi's breastplate with both hands, and knocked him backward into the paddy.

While Moritoshi struggled to rise,
Inomata leaped on top of him,
drew the dagger from his foe's waist,
pulled open the skirts of his armor,
plunged in the dagger thrice, hilt and fist,
and took the head. Then Shirō arrived.
To forestall any possible dispute,
he roared, "Inomata Noritsuna
has slain Taira no Moritoshi,
famed so long as a demon or god!"
His exploit earned him pride of place
on the roster of valorous deeds that day.

14. The Death of Tadanori

Tadanori, governor of Satsuma, commanded the west Heike force at Ichi-no-tani.
He wore black-laced armor over a dark blue brocade *hitatare*,
and his powerful black horse sported a lacquered saddle sprinkled with silver and gold.
Amid a hundred of his men, he coolly fought a series of skirmishes, meanwhile retreating,
until Okabe Tadazumi, of the Inomata League, spotted him as a commander.
Whip and stirrup, Okabe caught up with him.
"Who are you?" he demanded to know. "Declare your name!"
"One of yours," Tadanori replied. He glanced back at the man,
who glimpsed blackened teeth in the helmeted face.
"Heavens! No one on our side blackens his teeth!" Okabe reflected.

"He must be a Taira noble!"

Okabe rode up beside the man and seized him.

Tadanori's hundred, all forcibly drafted, came from an assortment of provinces, and none rushed to his aid. At the sight every man fled as fast as he could.

"You wretch!" said Tadanori.
"When I told you I was one of yours,
you should have let it go at that!"
Having been brought up at Kumano,
he was a strong man and very quick.
In a flash he drew his dagger.
He stabbed Okabe twice on horseback
and once more after he had fallen.
So it was that he struck three blows.

The first two of these glanced off the armor, failing to penetrate it.
The third went inside the helmet, but the wound was too light to kill.
He had Okabe's head pinned to the ground and was about to cut it off
when the man's page galloped up from behind, drew his sword,
and cut off Tadanori's dagger arm at the elbow.

Tadanori knew that this was the end. "Leave me a moment," he said.

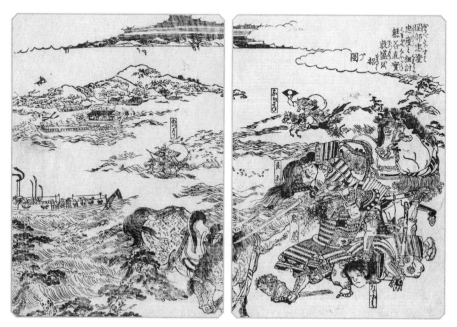

*Right panel: The death of Tadanori. In background: Atsumori in the water (left)
and Kumagai challenging him to come back (right).*

"I wish to call the Name ten times."
He gripped Okabe and shoved him a bow length away.

      Then he turned his face to the west,
      called ten times on Amida, and ended,
      "You who illumine the worlds,
      you gather to you without fail
      all sentient beings who call your Name!"
      That very instant Okabe,
      from behind him, struck off his head.
      He knew he had killed a commander,
      but not who that commander was.
      He then read a strip of paper
      attached to the slain man's quiver.
      It bore a poem on the topic
      "Blossoms at a Wayside Inn":

            Nightfall on the road,
          and should one then seek lodging
             beneath a cherry tree
          the blossoms themselves, that night,
          might prove a most gracious host.

      The signature read, "Tadanori."
      He knew then who was his prize.
He impaled the head on his sword, lifted it high, and announced in a great
    voice,
"I, Okabe Tadazumi, have slain the great Heike commander
Tadanori, governor of Satsuma!"

      Both sides, on hearing these words,
      were struck with pity. "Alas," they cried,
      "for a gentleman so accomplished
      both in poetry and in war!
      This great commander will be missed!"

15. Shigehira Taken Alive

Lord Taira no Shigehira, a Guards captain with the third rank,
was the deputy commander in Ikuta Wood,
but all his men had died or fled; with him he had only one left.
That day he wore a dark blue *hitatare* embroidered with bright yellow plovers
under armor with purple lacing darker toward the bottom
and rode a superb steed named Dōji Kage.
His foster brother, Gotōbyōe Morinaga, wore a dappled tie-dyed *hitatare*

under scarlet-laced armor,
and he rode Shigehira's treasured Yomenashi, a light gray.
Kajiwara Kagesue and Shō no Shirō Takaie spotted him as a commander
and, whip and stirrup, raced after him.

    Ships that promised salvation
    lay in great numbers along the shore,
    but the enemy, in hot pursuit,
    never gave him a chance to escape.
    Across the Minato River he fled,
    across the Karumo River,
    past Hasu Pond on his right
    and on his left Koma Wood,
    past Itayado and Suma,
    driving onward toward the west.

      Shigehira's was a very fine steed.
    The pursuers' horses, exhausted,
    seemed unlikely ever to catch him;
    in fact, he drew farther and farther ahead.
    Kajiwara Kagesue
    therefore stood tall in his stirrups
    and took a chance on a very long shot.
    The arrow sank deep into the rump
    behind Shigehira. His mount weakened.
    Gotōbyōe Morinaga
    must have feared that Shigehira
    would demand *his* horse, for he fled,
    whip high. "What is this, Morinaga?"
    Shigehira called. "What you swore to me
    all those years ago is something else.
    Where are you off to, abandoning me?"
    Morinaga pretended not to hear.
    He stripped the red badge from his armor,
    tossed it from him, and galloped away.
    The foe was near; his horse was failing.
    Shigehira rode into the sea,
    but the shallows ran out much too far
    to allow him to drown. He dismounted,
    cut the band that secured his armor,
    untied the shoulder cords, took it off,
    and made ready to slit his belly,
    but Shō no Shirō came charging up,

leaped down from the saddle, and cried,
"Oh, no you don't! You're coming with me!"
He got Shigehira onto his own horse,
tied him to the saddle pommel,
mounted a new steed, and off he went.
Morinaga, whose horse had unusual stamina, got away easily
and became in time a Kumano monk under a master named Onaka.
After this master's death, his widow, a nun,
went up to the capital to pursue a lawsuit, and Morinaga went with her.
Many there knew him as Lord Shigehira's foster brother.
"He's a wretch, this Morinaga," they said, snapping their fingers in anger.
"He wouldn't die with Shigehira, who was always so good to him,
and now he turns up as a monk, with some nun or other!
He should be ashamed of himself!"
Indeed Morinaga *was* ashamed.
They say he kept a fan over his face.

16. *The Death of Atsumori*

The enemy army was finished, and Kumagai Naozane remarked,
"The Heike lords will be falling back down to the water,
so as to get away on their ships.
I would gladly do battle with a worthy commander."
He rode toward the shore and found a warrior there,
wearing a silk *hitatare* embroidered with cranes under delicately tinted green
    armor,
a helmet with spreading horns, a sword with gold fittings,
and, on his back, arrows fletched with mottled feathers.
He carried a lacquered, rattan-wrapped bow
and rode a dappled gray with a gold-trimmed saddle.
Eyes fixed on a ship out at sea,
he plunged into the water and swam toward it some fifty yards.
Kumagai shouted a challenge to him:

> "My eyes tell me that you are a man of high rank. For shame, to turn
> your face from an enemy! Come back! Come back!"
>
> He beckoned urgently with his fan, and the other came. Kumagai
> halted beside him even as he rode up onto the shore and gripped him
> hard. The pair fell. Kumagai pinned the head to the ground and, to
> take it, tore off the helmet. He beheld a youth in his sixteenth or sev-
> enteenth year, his face lightly powdered, his teeth blackened, and
> about the same age as Kumagai's son, Kojirō. He was very pretty, too.

Kumagai could not bring himself to begin. He spoke instead: "Who
are you, if I may ask? Tell me your name. I will spare you."
    "And who are *you*?" the other answered.
"Nobody you can have heard of:
Kumagai no Jirō Naozane
from the province of Musashi,"
Kumagai replied.
"Well then, nothing about you requires me to give you my name.
I am a worthy opponent. Take my head anyway and ask around.
Others will know me."
    "Ah!" Kumagai said to himself.
"Then he *is* of very high rank!
And what if I do behead him?
His losing army cannot win.
If, on the other hand, I do not,
    our winning army still cannot lose.
Kojirō's wound, though slight, was still a terrible shock.
How this young lord's father, then, will suffer when he learns that his son has
    been killed!
No, I simply must spare his life."
But then he glanced behind him.
He saw Doi and Kajiwara galloping his way with fifty men.
Struggling to hold back his tears, he said,
    "What I want, you know, is to spare you,
    but the great host of men on my side
    will never allow you to get away.
    Rather than leave your fate to others,
    I prefer to see to it myself
    and to pray for you in the afterlife."
So he spoke; and the lordly youth:
"Just take my head now. Only be quick."
Kumagai, overcome by pity,
hardly knew how even to begin.
His sight darkened, his courage faltered,
he barely knew what he was doing,
but there was simply no escape:
In tears, he took the head after all.
"Alas," he murmured in bitter grief,
"the warrior's calling is harder than any.
Had I not been born to a warlike house,
never would I have known such sorrow!

What cruelty has been forced on me!"
He pressed his sleeves to his eyes and wept.
A moment went by. There was more to do.
He took off the young man's *hitatare,*
meaning to use it to wrap the head,
and found at his waist a brocade bag
containing a flute. "Oh, how awful!
At dawn today, within the fortress,
you could hear men making music,
and obviously he was one of them!
We boast in our army from the east
warriors by the tens of thousands,
but I am certain not one of them
brought a flute with him into battle!

These noble gentlemen are so refined!" Kumagai went to present him-
self before Yoshitsune, and the sight of the head drew tears from
every man present. Only later on did Kumagai learn that the youth
had been Atsumori, the son of Taira no Tsunemori, the director of
palace upkeep. He had been in his seventeenth year. It was then that
Kumagai felt rise compellingly within him the aspiration to enlight-
enment.

Now, as to Atsumori's flute,
his grandfather, Tadamori,
a most accomplished musician,
had once received it as a gift
from Retired Emperor Toba.
He then passed it down in his line,
and it had come, or so they say,
for his talent, to Atsumori.
The name of the flute was Saeda.
It is a touching thought indeed
that the giddy charms of music
served to turn a warrior's mind
to praise the way traced by the Buddha.

17. *The Death of Tomoakira*

Chamberlain Narimori, the last son of the counselor Norimori,
died in combat with Tsuchiya no Gorō Shigeyuki, from Hitachi.
Tsunemasa, of the grand empress's household and Tsunemori's eldest son,
fled to the water, to escape on one of the ships,

but the men of Kawagoe no Kotarō Shigefusa surrounded him and struck him
    down.
Tsunetoshi, Kiyofusa, and Kiyosada, the governors of Wakasa, Awaji, and Owari,
charged together into the enemy, fought fiercely, took many trophies, and died
    together.
The counselor Tomomori had commanded the Heike force at Ikuta Wood,
but after losing all his men he fled to the shore with just two others,
his son Tomoakira, the governor of Musashi, and a man of theirs, Kenmotsu
    Tarō Yorikata.
They, too, hoped that a ship would save them.
Alas, just then ten riders, apparently from the Kodama League,
flying a banner emblazoned with a battle fan,
came down on them with ferocious yells.

> Kenmotsu, who wielded a mighty bow,
> shot an arrow straight into the neck
> of their standard-bearer, who rode ahead.
> He toppled headlong. There was another,
> apparently their commander:
> He pulled up right beside Tomomori
> to seize him, but Tomoakira,
> his son, burst in between them, grappled,
> crashed down with him, and took his head.
> He was getting again to his feet
> when the man's page attacked and took *his*.
> Kenmotsu Tarō fell upon him there,
> gripped the page hard, and disposed of him.
> He then emptied his quiver, drew his sword,
> and killed many of the enemy men,
> until an arrow struck his left knee.
> He died where he sat, still fighting.

Amid the confusion Tomomori swam his superb steed
a mile or so out into the sea and caught up with Lord Munemori's ship.
The ship was too crowded, and they turned the horse back.
"That animal will fall into enemy hands," Shigeyoshi warned.
"I'll kill him with an arrow."
He put one to the string and moved forward to shoot, but Tomomori stopped him.
"Let anyone claim him who will," Tomomori said.
"He saved my life, after all. I will not have it."
Shigeyoshi was forced to desist.

> The horse, unwilling to leave his master,
> for some time remained near the ship,

still swimming toward the open sea,
but the ship drew ever farther ahead,
and at last the horse returned to shore.
As soon as he found footing again,
he looked back once more toward the ship,
and two or three times he neighed.
Then he came up on dry land and rested awhile.
Kawagoe no Kotarō Shigefusa took him in hand
and presented him to the cloistered emperor.
He went straight into the sovereign's stables, where he had lived
    before,
in the stalls reserved for the most valued steeds.
Lord Munemori had gone to thank the sovereign
for his elevation to palace minister, and had received him then as a gift.
Tomomori prized the horse when he gained possession of him
and on the first of each month prayed to Taizan Bukun that the steed should
    thrive.[221]

Perhaps that is why the horse lived long
and why he saved his master's life.
He had grown up in Shinano,
at a place there named Inoue,
and so his name was Inoue Black.
After Kawagoe got him
and presented him to the sovereign,
his name changed to Kawagoe Black.
Tomomori came before Lord Munemori and said,
"I have lost Tomoakira.
Kenmotsu Tarō, too, is dead.
Nothing is left me but despair.
What kind of man would see his son
challenge the foe to save his father
and then . . . ? What kind of man, I say,
seeing him stricken, would not save him
but rather, like me, run away?
Ah, what sharp words I would have had
for anyone who had done the same!
But now that that man is myself,
I have learned all too convincingly

---

221. Originally the deity of Taishan in China, Taizan Bukun was widely addressed in medieval Japan in prayers to obtain prosperity and avoid misfortune.

how desperately one clings to life.
What other people must think of me now,
I can only shudder to imagine."
He pressed his sleeves to his eyes and wept.
Munemori answered him in these words:
"It is a very fine thing indeed that your son should have died for you.
He was strong and he was brave—a thoroughly worthy commander.
He was just Kiyomune's age, I believe—this year was his sixteenth."

He glanced aside, toward his son,
the intendant of the Gate Watch,
and his eyes as he did so filled with tears.
All the Heike retainers present,
tender of feeling or hard of heart,
moistened their armor sleeves with tears.

18. *Flight*

Lord Shigemori's youngest son, Moromori, governor of Bitchū,
was boarding a boat to flee with six of his men
when Seiemon Kinnaga, one of Tomomori's, came galloping up.
"Aha, Lord Moromori's boat, I see!" he cried. "Please, let me board!"
They rowed the boat to the water's edge,
but there was bound to be trouble when so large a figure, in full armor,
tried to leap directly into the boat from his horse.
The boat was not big, and over it went.
There Moromori was, floundering in the sea,
when fourteen or fifteen of Hatakeyama's men, under Honda no Jirō,
raced up, hauled him out with a grappling hook, and cut off his head.
This year was his fourteenth.

Lord Michimori, who commanded the Heike force below the moun-
tains, wore that day a *hitatare* of red brocade and over it Chinese
damask-laced armor. His horse, a sorrel, bore a silver-trimmed saddle. He
had fallen behind, wounded by an arrow that had penetrated his helmet,
and the enemy had come between him and Noritsune, his brother. He
was fleeing eastward, seeking a quiet place to end his life, when
Sasaki no Kimura no Saburō Naritsuna, from the province of Ōmi,
and Tamanoi no Shirō Sukekage, from Musashi,
surrounded him with a half dozen men and soon cut him down.
One follower had stayed with him, but then he, too, fled.

Hour after hour the battle raged
at the fortress's east and west gates.

Countless Genji and Heike died.
There before each of the towers
and up against the abatis
rose heaps of dead men and horses.
Ichi-no-tani, once green, was red.
Apart from those slain by arrow or sword
in Ikuta Wood, below the mountains,
or on the shore, the Genji had taken
and put up on public display
the heads of over two thousand men.
The main Heike figures killed included Michimori;
Narimori, his younger brother; Tadanori; Tomoakira;
Moromori; Kiyosada; Kiyofusa; Tsunemori's eldest son, Tsunemasa;
his younger brother Tsunetoshi;
and *his* younger brother, Atsumori—no fewer than ten.
And now that their army had suffered defeat,
the grieving Heike boarded their ships, carrying their emperor with them.

 Wind and tide bore some ships toward Kii;
 others rowed out, to drift off Ashiya.
 Some coasted from Suma to Akashi.
 No harbor called, only boundless waves.
 They lay forlorn on tear-soaked sleeves
 under a moon veiled by spring mists,
 each prey to deep misery and despair.
 Some rowed through the Awaji Strait
 to drift down the rocky Eshima shore,
 hearing the far-off crash of pounding surf,
 and every plover strayed from its flock
 recalled to them the plight that they shared.
 Others, still at a loss where to go,
 just rode, motionless, off Ichi-no-tani.
 So at the whim of wind and wave they drifted,
 island to island, stretch to stretch of shore,
 each ignorant of the others' fate.
 Fourteen provinces they had conquered,
 marshaled one hundred thousand horse,
 and driven so close to the capital
 that it lay only one day's march away.
 This time, they believed, success was sure,
 but then their Ichi-no-tani fort fell,
 dashing every last shred of their hopes.

19. *Kozaishō Drowns*

There was a man of Michimori's named Kunda Takiguchi Tokikazu.
Kunda came to the ship that bore his lord's wife and told her,
"Seven men surrounded Lord Michimori near the mouth of the Minato
    River,
and in the end they killed him.
Chief among the assailants were two who announced their names
as Sasaki no Kimura no Saburō Naritsuna, from Ōmi,
and Tamanoi no Shirō Sukekage, from Musashi.
By rights I should have stayed and met with him the fate that awaited me,
but he had already given me this command:
'Should anything happen to me, do not for that give up your life,
but strive to live on and go to my wife, wherever she may be.'"
The lady had not the strength to reply; she only lay with a robe over her head.
This clear report of his death did not yet quite convince her,
and in case he should come back alive after all, she waited two or three days,
as she might have done for him to return after a brief absence,
but a day or two later hope faded and she sank into melancholy.
       Her nurse, her only gentlewoman,
       shared her pillow, crushed by sorrow.
Between twilight on the seventh, when the news reached her,
and the night of the thirteenth, she never rose at all.
They were to reach Yashima on the fourteenth, the next day.
The lady lay motionless through that final evening,
until silence fell over the ship in the last hours of the night.
She then said to her nurse, "During the days just past,
I simply could not believe the news that he was gone,
but I do now, ever since this night began.
One report after another has it that he was killed near the mouth of the Minato
    River,
and no one has mentioned seeing him alive after that.
       The night before he was to ride forth, we saw each other briefly, and he
       seemed very downcast. He said, 'I know that I will not survive the
       battle tomorrow. What will you do when I am gone?' He was always
       going off to fight, though, and I did not take him seriously. If only I
       had! If I had known that I would never see him again, I would have
       sworn to go with him into the next life. It hurts so, to think about it!
I had not yet told him that I was carrying his child,
but I did not want him to think I was hiding it, you see, so I told him then.
He was very happy. 'Here I am,' he said, 'already in my thirtieth year,

and childless still. I hope it is a boy!
At least, in this sad world of ours, he can preserve my memory.
How many months has it been? How are you feeling?
How can you hope for a peaceful birth, confined this way on a ship at sea?'
That is the sort of thing he said. Oh, the poor, foolish fancy!

> They do say, and perhaps it is true,
> that when at last the moment comes,
> nine out of ten women will die.
> I shrink from so shameful an end.
> Yes, I would like an easy birth
> and, afterward, to bring up the child
> in memory of the husband I lost,
> but every glance at the little one
> would only make me miss him more,
> and ever-growing melancholy
> would leave me not a moment's peace.
> No, for me there is no escape.
> If I should still, against the odds,
> manage to linger on in life,
> this world is always so contrary
> that I would only fear, you know,
> some new, unimagined trial,[222]
> and the thought is unbearable.
> Asleep, I see him in my dreams;
> awake, I find his face before me.
> Rather than let yearning consume me,
> I have simply made up my mind
> to sink to the floor of the sea.
> You, I ask to remain behind,
> despite what I know you will suffer,
> to gather together all my clothes
> and give them to any worthy monk,
> to pray for my husband's enlightenment,
> and for my birth in the life to come.

And please, take to the capital with you this letter that I have written."
Presented with these careful instructions, her nurse could only weep.

> "I abandoned my own small child,
> left my aged parents behind

....

222. A second marriage.

to follow you all the way here,"
she said. "Can you doubt my devotion?

> Besides, could *any* wife of a gentleman killed at Ichi-no-tani take her
> loss lightly? You must not imagine this misfortune to be yours alone.
> Once you have quietly given birth and brought up the child, then by all
> means find whatever remote retreat you please, become a nun, call the
> Name, and pray for the departed to reach enlightenment. You must
> long to share one lotus throne with him, but you cannot know where
> in the six realms and the Four Modes of Birth your own rebirth will
> take you. Drowning yourself would mean nothing, since you cannot
> count on reunion with him. And those left behind in the capital—who
> do you think will look after them, with this talk of yours? I refuse to
> hear any more!"

> The lady no doubt understood, after this tearful entreaty, that her
> words had been taken ill, for she answered, "Well, try putting yourself
> in my place. Grief often drives people to speak of drowning. If I decide
> really to do it, be sure that I will let you know. Now, it is late. Let us
> sleep." Such talk from a lady who for days had taken hardly a sip of water
> convinced her horrified nurse that she meant to go through with it.

"If your mind is really made up, my lady," the nurse replied,
"then please allow me to accompany you to the bottom of the sea.
I cannot imagine remaining alive one instant after you."
Lying there next to her mistress, she nonetheless dropped off for a moment.
Her mistress stole to the side of the ship.

> The vast ocean spread before her.
> Which way was west she did not know,
> but she must have guessed that the moon
> sank yonder behind the mountains,
> for she quietly called the Name.
> Plovers crying on the sandbars,
> oars creaking off across the strait
> lent the night a piercing sadness
> while, very low, one hundred times,
> she called the Name of Amida
> and, weeping, begged him from afar,
> "Hail, in your Western Paradise,
> World Savior, O Buddha Amida,
> O honor your Original Vow,
> lead me hence to your Pure Land,
> restore to me the love I lost,
> seat us both on one lotus throne!"

Then with a last cry of "Hail!"
she sank beneath the ocean waves.
It was the middle of the night, and the ship was on its way over
from Ichi-no-tani to Yashima. No one realized what had happened
except one helmsman, still awake, who saw.
"Oh, no!" he cried. "A lovely lady just threw herself from that ship into the sea!"
The nurse awoke and felt around beside her
but found no sign of her mistress. She cried out in horror.

    Many plunged in to bring her up,
    but spring nights are always hazy,
    and, alas, to make matters worse,
    clouds were drifting in from all sides.
    Time and again they dove for her,
    but dim moonlight revealed nothing.
    When at last they did bring her up,
    she was no longer of this world.
    She was wearing two layers of silk
    under a white divided skirt
    that streamed water, like her hair.
    They had found her too late to save her.
    The nurse took her poor lady's hands
    and pressed her tearful cheek to hers.
    "Oh, why, if you *had* to do it,
    did you refuse to take me with you,
    down to the bottom of the sea?
    Instead you just abandoned me!
    But even now, oh, please, one word,
    please let me hear one word from you!"
    For all the agony of her longing,
    no answer came, nor ever would.
Her mistress's faint breath had ceased.
Meanwhile the moon sank down the spring night
and dawn restored light to the misty sky.
Boundless grief had still to yield before the task at hand.
Lest the lady rise again, they wrapped her in full armor—
a set that her husband had left behind with her—
and lowered her once more into the sea.
Her nurse's only thought was now to follow,
but the others managed to restrain her.
Despair left her nothing else to do
but with her own hands to cut off her hair,

become a shaven nun under Michimori's younger brother,
the ranking monk Chūkai, to uphold the precepts
and, ever in tears, pray for her lady's rebirth in the life to come.

>Many wives have lost their husbands,
>since time out of mind, and nearly all
>have donned a nun's modest habit;
>rare are those who preferred drowning.
>"The loyal subject serves not two lords;
>the chaste woman knows no second man,"
>they say, no doubt with such things in mind.

Michimori had married the daughter of Lord Norikata,
a gentlewoman in the service of Princess Shōseimon-in.
She was the beauty of the palace, and her name was Kozaishō.
One spring in the Angen era, in her sixteenth year, [1175-77]
Shōseimon-in went to Hosshōji to view the blossoms.
Michimori, still an official of the empress's household, went with the party.
He fell in love with Kozaishō at first sight.
After that he felt her always beside him and thought of nothing but her.
He sent her constant poems and endless tender, sorrowful letters
in mounting numbers, but she accepted none.
Three years passed, and Michimori sent her what he meant as the last.
The gentlewoman who usually took them in happened to be away.
The messenger was returning, his mission a failure,
when he came across Kozaishō herself, on her way from home to the palace.
It was too bad not to deliver his master's letter at all,
so he managed to run up to her carriage and toss it in through the blind.

>She asked those with her who it was from.
>"No idea!" was the best they could say.
>So she opened the letter and read it—
>yes, it was from Lord Michimori.
>The carriage offered nowhere to hide it,
>and she could not quite bring herself
>merely to toss it into the street,
>so she thrust it into her waistband
>and went on her way to the palace.

She was busy with her usual duties when, as luck would have it,
the letter slipped out right in front of Her Highness,
who spotted it, picked it up, and hid it in her sleeve.
"I have found something curious," she announced. "I wonder whose it is."
The gentlewomen swore by the buddhas and gods that they knew nothing
  about it,

but there among them was Kozaishō, blushing and silent.
Her Highness already knew that Michimori had been courting her.
She opened the letter and read it.

> The fragrance it gave off was delicious;
> the brush moved with unusual skill.
> "That your heart remains hardened against me
> by now to me is a source of joy . . ."
> and so on. He had written at length
> and added, at the end, this poem:

> > *All my devotion*
> > *turns just as a simple log*
> > *laid across a brook*
> > *turns and re-turns underfoot,*
> > *yielding nothing but wet sleeves.*

> "He resents your ignoring him,"
> Her Highness said. "My dear, take care!
> Those excessively hard of heart
> only bring suffering on themselves."
> And indeed, not that far in the past
> there lived one Ono no Komachi,
> a dazzling and passionate beauty
> whose every look and every word
> ensnared and tormented men.
> Alas, her heart—so everyone said—
> remained forever unyielding,
> and perhaps that is why, in old age,
> the bitterness gathered against her
> stripped her of shelter from the wind,
> left her nothing to ward off rain.
> Moon and stars shining through her roof
> gleamed back, reflected in her tears.
> Green shoots rife in the meadows,
> *seri* parsley thick in the swales—
> she picked these to sustain her life.
> Her Highness said, "He *must* have an answer."
> Graciously she called for an inkstone
> and wrote Kozaishō's reply herself.

> > *Nonetheless, have faith,*
> > *for that simple log of yours,*
> > *laid across the brook,*

turns again and gives footing.
Step forth: It is time to cross.
In Michimori's breast the fire of love
rose as smoke soars above Mount Fuji;
tears drenched his sleeves as ocean waves
break on Kiyomi-ga-seki shore.
Beauty flowers from happy fortune:
Michimori made Kozaishō his wife,
and they loved each other deeply.
So it was that he took her with him,
even onto a wave-borne ship
westward bound toward distant skies.
Norimori had lost two sons,
Michimori and Narimori,
elder and younger; all he had left
were Noritsune and the monk Chūkai.
That is why Kozaishō, to him,
had meant the memory of his son.
Now that he had lost her as well,
he sank into bottomless despair.

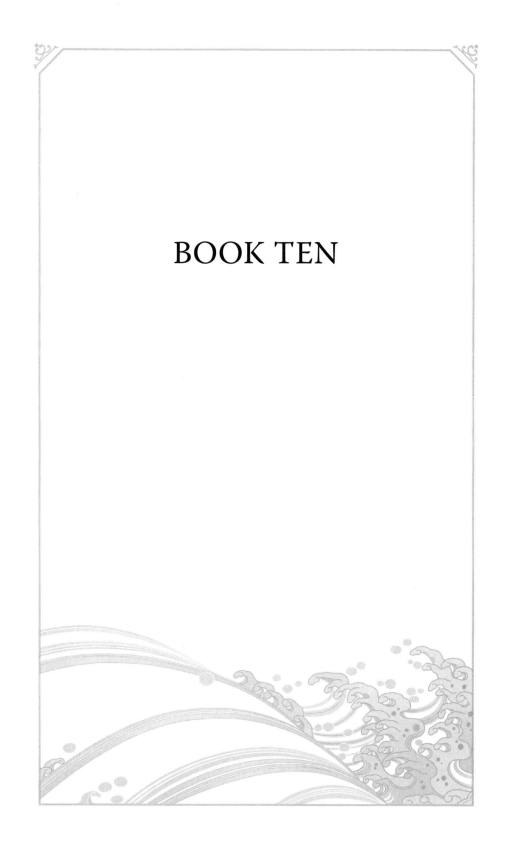

BOOK TEN

1. The Parade of Heads

(recitative)
Juei 3, the second month: [1184]

The heads of the Heike slain on the seventh at Ichi-no-tani reached the capital on
the twelfth.

Those with a tie to these men wondered in anguish what fate might await
them now,

and none more so than Lord Koremori's wife, in hiding at Daikakuji.

"Nearly all the Heike gentlemen were killed at Ichi-no-tani," she heard
someone say,

"but a senior noble, a third-rank Guards captain, was taken alive.

He is on his way up to the city."

"That must be my husband!" she cried, and collapsed with a robe over her head.

A gentlewoman of hers insisted, "No, my lady, it is Lord Shigehira."

"Then his head is among the others!" She remained desperately anxious.

> *(speech)*
> On the thirteenth, Nakayori of the police went to the Rokujō river-
> bank to receive the heads. Noriyori and Yoshitsune asked Cloistered
> Emperor Go-Shirakawa to have them paraded northward up Higashi-
> no-tōin Avenue and hung in the trees before the prison gate. Uncer-
> tain how to proceed, the sovereign discussed the matter with the
> chancellor, the left and right ministers, the palace minister, and a
> grand counselor, Tadachika.

These five senior nobles reached unanimous agreement:

"No precedent authorizes parading the head of a senior noble through the
streets.

Moreover, these gentlemen were the former emperor's[223] commoner relatives,

and they gave long service to the imperial house.

You cannot approve this request."

The decision therefore forbade a parade of heads.

However, Noriyori and Yoshitsune pressed their case further.

> *(song)*
> "In Hōgen, long ago, these men
> stood against our grandfather,

....

223. Antoku's.

Tameyoshi, and, in Heiji
against our father, Yoshitomo.
To placate our sovereign's anger
and to cleanse our forefathers' shame,
at the risk of our own lives
we have destroyed the emperor's foes.
If we may not parade these Heike heads through the streets,
what warning hereafter will serve to deter evildoers?"
The two put their case so forcefully that His Cloistered Eminence yielded.
The parade of heads went forward.
The onlookers could not even count them.

Past attendance at the palace
now caused many to quake with fear.
No witness to the spectacle
failed to taste pity and sorrow.
Saitōgo and Saitōroku,
servants assigned to Rokudai,
Lord Koremori's little son,
worried so about their master
that the two of them, in disguise,
went to see the heads parade past
and recognized many of them,
but neither saw Koremori's.
Nevertheless in shock and grief
they could not restrain floods of tears
that they feared others might notice.
They hastened back to Daikakuji.

"What? Tell me! What did you see?" their mistress asked.
"Moromori's head was the only one we saw from among Lord Shigemori's sons."
They went on to name the others.
"My family—all of them!" she cried in a storm of weeping.

> After a moment Saitōgo spoke, struggling against further tears. "I have been in hiding the past year or two," he said, "and few people know me. I would have stayed for a more thorough look, but I ran into someone who knew the whole story. 'In the recent clash, Lord Shigemori's sons were charged with securing Mount Mikusa, on the Harima-Tanba border,' he told me, 'but after Kurō Yoshitsune defeated them, they— Sukemori, Arimori, and Tadafusa—put to sea at Takasago in Harima and sailed from there to Yashima in Sanuki. For some reason Moromori is the only brother who stayed behind to be killed at Ichi-no-tani.' I then asked what had happened to Lord Koremori. He answered, 'He

fell gravely ill before the battle and crossed over to Yashima. He was
never at Ichi-no-tani.' He told me everything."
"He must have been sick with worry about *us*," the lady said.
"Every day when the wind blows,
I picture him at sea and tremble.
Talk of battle leaves me faint,
imagining him being killed.
And now he is so very ill,
who is there to look after him?
Oh, how I long to learn more!"
And her little son and daughter:
"But why did you never ask
what really is wrong with him?"
Their concern was sad and sweet.
They felt about Lord Koremori exactly as he felt about them.
"They must be so worried about me, in the city!" he said.
"No, my head is not on parade,
but I could just as well have drowned or died of an arrow wound.
They cannot possibly assume that I am still alive!
How I wish I could let them know that my dewdrop life still lingers!"
Such were his thoughts, and in this spirit he sent a man of his up to the capital.
He wrote three letters.
The first of these was to his wife.
"No doubt," he wrote, "the capital
so teems with countless enemies
that you hardly know where to hide,
and having the children with you
must make this all the more painful.
How I would love to bring you here,
so that we might share the same fate!
But whatever may become of me,
I simply could not subject you to that."
He wrote at length, and at the end
he added this single poem:
What reunion, when,
awaits us, I cannot say;
let these spindrift lines
gathered from my tide-borne brush
be your memory of me.
To each of the children, he wrote the same message: "How are you
managing to pass the time? I promise to bring you here very soon!" His

man took these letters on up to their destination. They renewed his wife's grief.

Four or five days later, he begged leave to return, and in tears she wrote her reply. The children, too, dipped the brush to write their own. "What answer should we write to Father?" they asked.

"Why, whatever you like" was all she could think of to say.

So they did, each the same: "Why have you *still* not had us join you? We love you! We want to be with you! Please, have us come to you *soon!*"

The messenger took their letters back to Yashima. Koremori read the children's first. He seemed more downcast than ever.

"I do not have it in me now,"
he said, "to spurn this sullied world;
the ties of love are just too strong.
I have no wish for the Pure Land.
Rather I will cross the mountains,
make my way up to the city,
visit my dear ones a last time,
then take my life. That will be best."
He spoke amid streaming tears.

2. *The Gentlewoman at the Palace*

On the fourteenth, Lord Shigehira, taken alive, was paraded eastward along
    Rokujō.
His carriage bore a small, eight-petal flower motif.
The blinds were raised, and the windows on both sides stood open.
Doi no Jirō Sanehira, in light armor over a tan *hitatare*,
commanded the thirty guards who rode before and behind the carriage.
People of every degree, from all over the capital, came to watch.
"Poor man!" they said. "What karma was his, to make him deserve this?
That this should happen to *him*, of all Kiyomori's many sons!
His father and mother both cherished him, and all the Heike esteemed him.
Whenever he called on the emperor, reigning or retired,
everyone, young or old, gave him courteous welcome.
He burned the temples of Nara, though—this must be retribution."
The carriage moved on to the riverbank, then turned back.
They put Shigehira in a chapel near the Hachijō-Horikawa crossing—
one formerly owned by the late counselor Fujiwara no Ienari.
Doi Sanehira mounted guard.
The cloistered emperor's envoy, the chamberlain Sadanaga, arrived.

In red, he carried sword and baton.
Shigehira wore a tall *eboshi* hat
and an indigo-dyed *hitatare*
dappled with spots of darker blue.
He had never given a thought
to Sadanaga in bygone days,
but the fellow struck him this time
as a very minion from hell,
come to deal harshly with the damned.
"His Cloistered Eminence has this to say to you," Sadanaga announced:
"'If you wish to return to Yashima, get in touch with all of the Heike.
They are to restore the three regalia to the capital.
If they do, then yes, you may go back there.'
That is the burden of his message."
Shigehira replied, "Not for the lives of a thousand or ten thousand Shigehiras
would Lord Munemori or any man of the Heike trade away the regalia—
although I suppose that my mother might, being a woman.
However, I shrink from rejecting His Cloistered Eminence's wish out of hand.
I shall pass his message on and see what response it receives."
Heizōzaemon Shigekuni went to represent him personally,
and it was Hanakata, one of the sovereign's servants, who bore the formal decree.
No private letters being allowed, all messages were to be delivered orally.
One of the messages went to his wife,
Lady Dainagon-no-suke:
"Together under distant skies,
I gave you comfort, and you me;
how miserable you must be now,
when life has torn us each from each!
The bond between us remains whole,
I assure you, and I promise
that in the lives that lie before us,
I will be born with you again."
He wept as he spoke his message.
Shigekuni swallowed tears and set out.
Shigehira had long retained in his service a man named Moku Uma-no-jō Tomotoki. Although currently serving the Hachijō Princess, Tomotoki went to Doi Sanehira and said, "I served Lord Shigehira for many years and should properly have accompanied him to the west, but I could not do so because by then I had already joined Her Highness's staff. Today, however, standing among the spectators on the avenue, I found the sight too painful to watch. I request leave to go

to him one last time, if I may, to talk over the old days with him and to console him a little. I am not much of a warrior and never followed him into battle, but I used to serve him day in and day out. If you nonetheless suspect my motives, please take charge of this dagger of mine and make this one exception for me."

Doi Sanehira was a kind man.

"You could hardly get up to much alone," he answered, "but even so . . ."

He asked for the dagger, and Tomotoki gave it into his care.

    Tomotoki, very pleased,
    hurried in to see Shigehira.
    He found him visibly downcast—
    in fact, so thoroughly wilted
    that Tomotoki could only weep.
    Shigehira, when he saw him,
    thought him a dream within a dream
    and remained speechless. He only wept.

Sometime later, after they had talked over past and present, Shigehira asked,

"Now, that gentlewoman you used to take letters to for me—
do you know whether she is still at the palace?"

"I gather that she is."

"She had no letter from me when we went down to the west,
not even a last word or two, and to my shame
she must believe that I was lying when I swore to love her forever.
I want very much to get a letter to her.
Will you take one and find her for me?"

"I will indeed, my lord," Tomotoki replied.

Hugely relieved, Shigehira wrote the letter at once and gave it to him.

"What letter is this?" the guards demanded to know. "We cannot let it go."

"Show them," said Shigehira. Tomotoki did so.

"No problem there," the guards declared, and returned it.

Tomotoki went off with it to the palace,
but it was daytime and there were too many people about.
He spent the day concealed in a shed nearby,
then went to stand by the back entrance to the gentlewomen's rooms.
There he overheard a voice that sounded like hers, saying,

    "Of all the people in this world,
    how awful that Shigehira
    should have been taken prisoner
    and put like that on public display!
    Everyone says this is what he gets
    for having burned Nara. So does he.

'It was not actually my idea,'
he told me. 'Those scoundrels around me—
they are the ones who set the fires
and burned down the temple buildings.
As beads of dew gather into drops
that drip down the trunk of the tree,
the blame will fall on me alone,
I know it will!' Those were his words,
and all too clearly he was right!"
She wept bitterly as she spoke.
Tomotoki, struck with pity, saw he had found a companion in grief.
"I beg your pardon!" he called, and she asked, "Where are you from?"
"I bring you a letter from Lord Shigehira."
In the past she had always kept out of sight,
but now, no doubt moved by passionate feeling,
she came running out, crying, "Where is it? Where?"
She took the letter with her own hands and read it on the spot.
Shigehira had written at length how he had been captured in the west
and how, as things now stood, he might never see the morrow.
At the end he had added this poem:

> *River of salt tears!*
> *As I am, I spread abroad*
> *a most dismal fame,*
> *yet for all that I still long*
> *for one last moment with you.*

The lady, at a loss for words,
slipped it into the fold at her breast
and went back in to weep her fill.
In time she collected herself to write the required answer.
She described her worry and pain during all the time he had been gone.

> *All because of you,*
> *I, too, spread abroad these days*
> *a most dismal fame,*
> *yet I would gladly, with you,*
> *sink into the ocean depths.*

Tomotoki took Lord Shigehira her reply. As before, the guards de-
manded to read it, and Shigehira allowed them to do so.

"Fine," they said, and returned it to him.

Now he read it himself. A wave of feeling swept through him. "I was
with this gentlewoman for years," he said to Doi Sanehira, "and there
is something I simply must tell her, one last time, in person."

In his kindness Sanehira replied, "If all you really want is to spend a moment with this lady, then I see no objection." He authorized the meeting.

Shigehira gladly borrowed a carriage and sent it for her.
She boarded it without delay and came straight to him.
The news that it had drawn up to the veranda brought him out to greet her.
"Do not get out," he warned her. "The guards will see you."
Instead he went in to her under the front blind.
They took each other's hands, pressed their foreheads together,
and for a moment said nothing. They only wept.
Then at last Shigehira spoke.

"When we went down to the west," he said,
"I wanted to see you one last time,
but, caught up in such vast confusion,
I could never get word to you
before we all fled the capital.
After that I still longed to write
and to have the pleasure of your reply,
but this endlessly painful travel
meant clashes and battles day and night,
and I let time slip by in silence.

No doubt I suffered this shocking fate so that we two might meet again."
He pressed his sleeves to his eyes and lowered his head.
The state of his feelings and hers is easily imagined.
The night was far advanced when he sent her home.
"The streets are very dangerous lately," he said. "You must go now."
They brought her carriage forward.
Fighting back tears of parting, he tugged at her sleeve.

> *Your presence with me*
> *and this dewdrop life of mine*
> *have this in common:*
> *that tonight, for all I know,*
> *the end is to come for both.*

Striving likewise not to cry, she replied,

> *If this is the end*
> *and the two of us must part,*
> *then this dewdrop, too,*
> *is certain to melt away,*
> *my love, even before you.*

She then returned to the palace.
That was the last meeting his guards allowed,

although letters still passed between them.
She was Taira no Chikanori's daughter,
a dazzling beauty, warm and kind.
When she learned that Nara had claimed him
and he had been executed there,
she at once entered religion,
put on robes of the darkest black,
and prayed for him in the afterlife.
Theirs is a very touching story.

3. Go-Shirakawa's Decree to Yashima

Meanwhile the two envoys, Shigekuni and Hanakata, reached Yashima,
and there they presented His Cloistered Eminence's decree.
Lord Munemori and every one of the Heike nobles gathered to examine it:

> *Years have passed since our hallowed monarch went forth from the
> imperial precincts on a progress to the provinces, and now, to the con-
> sternation of the court and the ruin of the realm, the three regalia
> molder on Shikoku in the southern ocean.*
>
> *With respect to Lord Shigehira, the rebellious subject who burned
> Tōdaiji: While he fully deserves the death penalty demanded by Lord
> Yoritomo, he is currently a prisoner and severed from the company of
> his fellows. As a caged bird longs for the clouds, he must long to soar a
> thousand leagues across the southern sea; surely he is as desperately
> lonely as a goose lost from the flock on its homeward journey in spring.
> Pardon shall be his, on the condition that you reverently return the
> three regalia.*
>
> *His Cloistered Eminence has spoken. These are his words.*[224]
> *Juei 3, second month, the fourteenth day* [1184]
>
> *Submitted on His Cloistered Eminence's behalf by Naritada, the
> master of the imperial table, to the grand counselor Taira no Tokitada*

So the document read.

4. The Heike Reply

Shigehira conveyed privately to Munemori and Tokitada the tenor of the decree,
and to his mother, Lady Nii, he addressed a long letter.
"If you hope for reunion with me," he wrote,
"you must persuade Lord Munemori to give up the regalia.

....

224. The oral delivery of such a text was primary and had greater authority than writing.

Otherwise I doubt that I will ever see you again in this life."
Speechless, Lady Nii slipped the letter into the fold at her breast and lay
    facedown.
Her thoughts are painful indeed to imagine.
Meanwhile Lord Tokitada and the Heike senior nobles and privy gentlemen
gathered in council to discuss their reply.
Lady Nii pressed her son's letter to her face,
slid open the door into where the gentlemen were assembled,
prostrated herself before Munemori, and cried, in tears,

> "It is too terrible, what Shigehira has written from the city! And how
> dreadful he must be feeling! Please, please, if only for my sake, return
> the regalia to the capital!"
>
> Munemori answered, "Your wish is my own, yet I shudder to imag-
> ine how the world at large would take our doing so. Such would be our
> humiliation, before Yoritomo, that that step is out of the question. In
> any case, only the regalia confer sovereignty on the emperor.

Whether or not to honor a mother's love depends on circumstance.
Are we to neglect, for Shigehira alone, his brothers and the rest of his family?"
So Munemori spoke, and Lady Nii resumed her entreaty.

> "After I lost my husband and lord,
> I never thought to survive him long,
> yet soon our emperor had to embark
> on a voyage that tore at my heart,
> and I so hoped to assure his reign
> that I remained, after all, alive.
> The news that at Ichi-no-tani
> Shigehira was taken captive
> almost destroyed me. My only wish
> in this life is to see him again,
> but even dreams bring him no nearer,
> and in the grip of mounting anguish
> my throat closes against even water.
> Now there has come this letter from him,
> to confuse the last of my wits.
> Were I to hear that Shigehira is gone,
> I would wish only to follow him.
> Lest I suffer that second blow,
> please, I beg you, let me die now!"
> So she pleaded with piteous cries,
> and every man present was moved.
> All wept and listened with downcast gaze.

Tomomori expressed his view.

"Even if we did return the regalia to the capital," he said,

"they would never, ever, really send Shigehira back.

Our only choice is to refuse."

Munemori responded, "You are undoubtedly right."

He wrote the Heike reply.

Weeping, Lady Nii began her answering letter to her son.

Tears blinded her to the movement of her own brush, yet love guided it at length.

She gave the letter to Shigekuni, for him to deliver.

His wife, Dainagon-no-suke, only wept.

To answer him was far beyond her.

The agony that she must have felt

is all too easily imagined.

Shigekuni withdrew in tears,

wringing the moisture from his sleeves.

Taira no Tokikata summoned Go-Shirakawa's representative, Hanakata.

"You are Hanakata?" he asked.

"Yes, my lord, I am."

"You have braved the ocean waves to bring us His Cloistered Eminence's decree, and you shall have a lifelong memento of your journey."

The branding of Hanakata.

He had the *namikata* brand, a wave pattern, burned into the man's cheek.

Hanakata returned to the city.

The sovereign remarked at the sight of him,

"Very well, I have no choice. I shall have to call you Namikata."

He laughed.

> *Your Cloistered Eminence's decree, dated the fourteenth of this month, reached us at Yashima in Sanuki province on the twenty-eighth. We have given its content full and respectful attention. Our considered opinion on the matter follows:*
>
> *Lord Michimori and many other gentlemen of our house met death at Ichi-no-tani in Settsu. Could your pardoning Shigehira alone then restore us to good cheer? The situation is this: Our emperor succeeded to the imperial dignity upon the abdication of the late Emperor Takakura, and he is already in the fourth year of his reign. While he sought to emulate the ancient ways of Yao and Shun, the barbarian hordes of east and north banded together and swept en masse into the capital, so profoundly distressing him and his mother, and so enraging his commoner relatives, that he withdrew for a time to Kyushu. How could the three regalia possibly be parted from his august person, until he himself returns?*
>
> *The sovereign is his subjects' heart; his subjects are their sovereign's body. When he is at peace, so, too, are his subjects, and when they are at peace, so is the realm. Should the sovereign grieve, his subjects have no joy. Should the heart within suffer, the body without knows no pleasure. Our ancestor Taira no Sadamori crushed the rebel Masakado, and ever since we have protected the imperial fortunes.*
>
> *So it came to pass that during the Hōgen and Heiji conflicts, the late chancellor, my father, repeatedly risked his life to honor an imperial command, and it was not for himself that he did so, no, but solely for His Majesty. Note especially that despite an imperial death sentence pronounced against Yoritomo, when his father, Yoshitomo, rebelled in the twelfth month of Heiji 1, [1159] the late chancellor in his compassion had the sentence reduced. Nonetheless, Yoritomo forgot old kindness and ignored goodwill to raise abruptly, as might a starving wolf, foul rebellion. Such indescribable folly begs divine chastisement and courts lasting destruction.*
>
> *The sun and moon do not quench their light for one single creature; the enlightened sovereign does not bend his rule for just one man. Do not for one bad deed discard much good; do not for one slight flaw disregard broad merit. If Your Cloistered Eminence has not forgotten the services rendered by my house over many reigns, as well as my late*

father's repeated acts of devotion, he might (if I may be forgiven an impertinent suggestion) consider undertaking the journey to Shikoku. Then we shall receive his favorable decree, return to the ancient capital, and cleanse ourselves of the shame of defeat. Should he not do so, we will continue on our way to Kikai-ga-shima, Korea, India, and China. Alas! In this, the reign of our eighty-first human sovereign, are we to waste the sacred treasures of our realm upon a foreign land?

Please convey these words, as appropriate, to His Cloistered Eminence.

I, Munemori, bow my head in reverence and awe.
Juei 3, the second month, the twenty-eighth day
Taira no Munemori, of the junior first rank

So the document read.

5. The Precepts

This news reached Shigehira. "I expected that," he said.
"How little the men of my house must think of me!"
Bitter regret surged through him, but in vain.
No, he had never believed himself so valuable to them
that for his sake they would surrender the regalia, our realm's priceless treasure.
He had steeled himself beforehand to hear the reply he expected.
As long as that reply had not yet actually been voiced,
his mood had remained one merely of gloomy apprehension,
but hope was lost now that it had come and he faced being sent down to
     Kamakura.
Comfortless, he could only miss desperately the capital that he would soon leave.
He therefore summoned Doi Sanehira.
"I wish to renounce the world," he said. "Would that be possible?"
Sanehira reported his request to Yoshitsune, who communicated it to the
     sovereign.
Go-Shirakawa replied, "I can say nothing until Yoritomo has seen him.
I could not by any means authorize it now."
"Very well then," Shigehira said when informed of his answer,
"I wish to see a holy man to whom I have long been devoted and to discuss the
     afterlife with him."
"What holy man do you mean?" Doi Sanehira asked.
"His name is Hōnen, and he lives in Kurodani."[225]

....

225. Hōnen (1133–1212), the founder of the "exclusive *nenbutsu*" (*senshū nenbutsu*) practice of Pure Land Buddhism, is one of the most famous figures in Japanese religious history.

"I see no objection." Sanehira allowed the meeting.
Greatly relieved, Shigehira summoned Hōnen and said, in tears,
"Being taken prisoner has allowed me to see you again.
What can I do to achieve salvation in the life to come?

> When I was the man I used to be,
> official duty blotted out all else;
> the business of government kept me tied.
> An abyss of conceit and arrogance
> yawned in me. I gave never a thought
> to future salvation or to perdition.
> Then the fortunes of my house sank low
> and the world lapsed into chaos.
> After that there was nothing for me
> but a battle here, a skirmish there.
> All I ever thought of was killing
> or evading death—preoccupations
> so evil as to stifle everything good.

>> Then came the great fire in Nara. One does not question an order
>> from the sovereign or from the highest military authority. The monks
>> were behaving outrageously, and I went down there to quell them.
>> The next thing I knew, the temples had burned, but certainly not be-
>> cause I ever meant them to. The truth is that I could do nothing to
>> stop it. I was in command, though, and, as they say, the man at the
>> top shoulders the blame. No doubt the crime will be laid solely at my
>> door. Presumably the inconceivable shame heaped upon me is al-
>> ready retribution for it. All I want by now is to shave my head, uphold
>> the precepts, and practice the Buddha's Way, but unfortunately I am
>> no longer in a position to please myself. The end could come for me
>> at any moment, today or tomorrow, and I bitterly regret that no prac-
>> tice I might undertake could possibly lighten a particle of my karma.

> Looking back over my whole life
> and all my deeds, I see bad karma
> soaring higher than Mount Sumeru
> and not a scrap of stored-up good.
> If my life is to end so wasted,
> there is no doubt: Fire, blood, and sword[226]
> loom before me in the hereafter.

>> Please, Your Reverence, I beg you,

----

226. The evil realms of hell, beasts, and hungry ghosts.

show this sinner, in your compassion,
some way still toward salvation!"
The saintly Hōnen dissolved in tears and remained for a moment speechless.
"No sorrow," he said, "could adequately mourn so sad a return
from possession of a human body, always exceedingly rare, to those three dire
    realms.
But if only you will now shun this polluted world and aspire to the Pure Land,
if only you will renounce evil and arouse longing for the good,
then the buddhas of past, present, and future will surely rejoice.

    Now, there are many paths to release,
    but in these latter days of the Law,
    when minds are polluted and confused,
    the best of all is calling the Name.
Only aspire to the nine levels of birth in paradise
and confine practice to the six sacred syllables,[227]
and absolutely anyone, however foolish and benighted,
can find a way to call the Name.

    Let your sins be ever so grave,
    never, never condemn yourself.
    The ten crimes, the five perverse deeds—
    those who commit them, even they,
    should they turn their thoughts to good,
    are born at last into paradise.
    Having amassed so little merit
    makes no reason for you to despair.
    Call the Name once, call it ten times
    in the fullness of heartfelt faith,
    and he will come to welcome you.
    Accept the words a great saint left us:[228]
    'By single-mindedly calling his Name,
    you will reach his Western Paradise.
    In each and every instant of thought,
    call the holy Name and repent.'
    So he taught. You need only believe.
    The salvific sword is the holy Name,

....

227. There are nine levels of rebirth into Amida's paradise. On the lowest the soul is born into a closed lotus bud that will open only after the passage of ages. On the highest the soul is reborn onto a fully open lotus throne. The "six syllables" are those of the invocation *Namu Amida Bu(tsu)*, the last syllable of which was not usually voiced.

228. The Chinese Pure Land patriarch Shandao (613–81).

and no demon will dare approach you.
Call once the Name, and sin is gone.
Keep that in mind, and it will be true—
that is what he wrote in his book.
The heart of the Pure Land teaching
has been described in many ways,
but all come down to this quintessence.
Yet whether at death you are really reborn
straight into the Western Paradise
depends on one thing: your depth of faith.
Believe, only believe and never doubt.
Take this teaching into your heart
and it will be all the same to you where you are and what the hour,
whether you go or whether you stay, whether you are sitting or lying—
no gesture of yours, no word, no thought will neglect invoking the Name,
and when your time comes, you will leave the world,
this world of pain, for birth into the land of eternity.
That is impossible to doubt."
Shigehira, thus instructed, felt a surge of joy.
"I would gladly now keep the precepts," he said,
"but I assume that I cannot do so unless I become a monk."
"No, no," Hōnen replied, "many a layman keeps them."

He touched a razor to Shigehira's forehead,
went through the motions of shaving his head,
and bestowed the ten precepts upon him.
Shigehira received them with tears of joy.
In his compassion for all beings,
Hōnen found his eyes misting over
and wept as he explained the precepts.

By way of an offering, Shigehira sent Tomotoki to fetch an inkstone that he had left with a man of his household, one whom for years he had visited often. He then presented the inkstone to Hōnen. "Please," he said, "never give this to anyone else, but place it instead where your gaze often falls upon it, and each time you remember that it came from me, consider me to be present in person and call the Name for me. I will be very grateful, too, if whenever you have a moment, you will read a scroll of the sutras and dedicate the merit to me." He wept as he spoke.

Hōnen accepted the offering in silence, put it in the fold of his robe,
and returned to Kurodani, wringing tears from his ink-black sleeves.

Left panel: Tomotoki brings Shigehira the inkstone, to present to Hōnen. At far right: Shigehira.

Shigehira's father, Lord Kiyomori, had received this inkstone
after presenting the emperor of Song China with a great weight of gold dust.
    It was a return gift, inscribed,
    "To the Great Taira Chancellor,
    of Wada in the land of Japan."²²⁹
    Kiyomori called it Matsukage.

6. Down the Tōkaidō

In Kamakura, meanwhile, Yoritomo was demanding Shigehira,
so his journey there was arranged.
Doi Sanehira first transferred him to Yoshitsune's residence.
On the tenth of the third month, Kajiwara Kagetoki started with him for
    Kamakura.
Taken alive in the west and distressed merely to be back in the capital,
he was now on his way down to the east through Ōsaka Pass.
His feelings are easily imagined.

....

229. Wada (now Hyōgo-ku in Kobe) was where Kiyomori had convened a great gathering of monks (6:9).

First came Shinomiya:[230]
There beside the babbling brook,
his thoughts wandered back in time
    to Semimaru,
Emperor Daigo's fourth prince,
who hearkened to rushing gales
    while plucking his biwa.
Blow or not the wind that day,
shine or not that night the moon,
    Hakuga no Sanmi
stood listening and learning,
for himself, the Three Pieces.
That hut of straw had stood there
    in days now long past,
but the memories lived on.
He rode across Ōsaka,
and his horse's hooves
thundered over Seta Bridge.
    Larks sang in the sky
down the Noji village road
    to the Shiga coast,
lapped by little springtime waves.
    Ahead, through the mist,
rose clouded Mirror Mountain
    and off to the north
the towering mass of Hira.
Mount Ibuki now drew near.
    Not all that striking,
yet eloquent in ruin,
the Fuwa barrier-guard hut
    spread its board eaves,
receded, to tidal flats
and worries (what awaits me?)
on the way past Narumi,
    sleeves wet with tears;
    then Yatsuhashi

....

230. This full-scale *michiyuki* ("travel song") is unique in the tale, and the translation follows its approximate five- or seven-syllable meter. The passage relies more on wordplay than on grammar to take Shigehira from the brook at Shinomiya (the Ōsaka barrier) to Ikeda in present Shizuoka-ken. It begins with the story of Semimaru (Introduction, "The Capital, the Provinces, and the Tōkaidō"), from whom Hakuga no Sanmi secretly learned the three essential biwa pieces.

in the land of Mikawa,
    where once Narihira
voiced teeming sorrows
in that poem he left us,
    "Robe from far Cathay
long and comfortably worn . . . "[231]
    —ah, who could but sigh?—
and across Hamana Bridge:
    chill wind in the pines,
inlet shore noisy with waves
    adding little more
to the gloom of traveling
    through failing light
and the dark thoughts of nightfall
    he came at long last
to the inn at Ikeda.

Yuya, the woman who kept the post-station inn, had a daughter named Jijū,
and Shigehira lodged at Jijū's house that night.

She said when she first saw him,

"I could never have given you a poem in the past, not even through someone else.
How extraordinary, then, to see you here today!"

And she presented him with this:

    Beneath unknown skies,
    this earthen-floor house of mine,
        doubtful as it is,
    must make you miss all the more
    the city so long your home.

Shigehira replied,

    My home, the city,
    no, I do not miss at all
        beneath unknown skies:
    Not even the capital
    can shelter me to the last.

"Her poem is so nicely done!"
he exclaimed. "Who on earth is she?"
Kajiwara politely replied,

    "My lord, do you not yet know her? When Lord Munemori, now at
    Yashima, governed this province, he called her into his personal ser-

---

231. Part of a poem from *Ise monogatari*, episode 9: "Robe from far Cathay, / long and comfortably
worn, / bound by love to stay, / I cover these distances / shrouded in melancholy." Translation from
Mostow and Tyler, *The Ise Stories*, p. 33.

vice and loved her beyond all others. Having left her old mother here,
she often asked for permission to go home, but he would never grant
it. One year, early in the third month, she gave him:

> *What am I to do?*
> *Springtime in the capital*
>   *I would sorely miss,*
> *yet in the east the blossom*
> *I love may now be falling.*

That did the trick: He let her go.
There is no other poet like her
anywhere along the Tōkaidō."

They had left the city days earlier.
More than half the third month was gone,
and spring would very soon be over.
Blossoms high on the distant mountains
resembled patches of lingering snow.
"What cruel karma brought me to this?"
he murmured, and his tears flowed on.

To the chagrin of Lady Nii,
his mother, and of his wife,
Lady Dainagon-no-suke,
he had no children. All their prayers
to gods and buddhas had gone unheard.
"And just as well!" he reflected.
"Imagine how miserable my son would be, if I had one!"
That thought, at least, yielded a grain of consolation.

Starting up Saya-no-nakayama,
he knew he would not return this way,
and such fresh sorrow burdened him
that floods of tears soaked his sleeves.
Mount Utsu loomed, its path dark with vines;
lost in gloom, he crossed those slopes, too.
Far to the north, after Tegoshi, he saw
a high mountain range white with snow:
Shirane, they said it was, in Kai,
and he left off weeping to reflect,

> *For this life of mine*
> *I really do not care that much,*
>   *and yet I am glad*
> *to have lived to see this sight:*
> *the Shirane peaks in Kai.*

After Kiyomi-ga-seki
came the plain below Mount Fuji.
To the north rose green mountains;
gentle breezes sighed through pines.
Southward stretched the sea's vast blue;
waves crashed on the rocky shore.
> "If you really missed me,
> you should be thinner:
> So you didn't miss me—
> I can tell!"
So once sang the mountain god
to his wife, when he came home
to Ashigara—which dropped behind,
and so, too, Koyurugi Wood,
Mariko River, and the shore
at Koiso and Ōiso,
Yatsumato,
Togami-ga-hara,
Mikoshi Point—
he passed them all, not in haste,
and yet day succeeded day
until he reached Kamakura.

7. Senju-no-mae

Yoritomo soon admitted him to his presence.
"My resolve to calm the sovereign's wrath and cleanse my father's shame,"
    he said,
"certainly included the goal of destroying the Heike,
but I never imagined actually meeting *you*.
At this rate I imagine that I will be seeing Munemori, now at Yashima,
    too.
Tell me, when you destroyed Nara, did you do so on your father's orders,
or was it an on-the-spot decision of your own?
They call it a particularly awful atrocity."
Shigehira replied, "Burning Nara was neither my father's idea nor mine.
I went there to put down the monks' lawlessness.
The destruction of the temples simply happened. I could do nothing about it.
I need hardly repeat that in the old days
the Genji and Heike vied with each other to support the imperial house
but that more recently the Genji fortunes declined.

Meanwhile my own house time and again,
in Hōgen and Heiji and ever since,
quelled all those who offended the court.
My father, honored beyond his station,
became the commoner grandfather
to the one lord who rules under heaven,
so lifting high sixty Taira and more.
The Heike for over twenty years
flourished more than words can describe,
but now those days are over for us,
and I myself have been captured alive,
at last to appear here before you.
He who strikes down his sovereign's foe
enjoys imperial favor to seven generations, or so they say,
but really, all this goes to reveal the saying as false.
It is a matter of common knowledge that my late father, Lord
   Kiyomori,
risked his life again and again for His Majesty.
Is his glory nonetheless to last no longer than his life,
and must his descendants then suffer my fate?
So it was that when our fortunes failed and we left the capital,
I accepted that my corpse would lie in the wilds
and my name vanish among the waves of the western sea.
I never imagined ending up here.
How bitterly I regret the karma from past lives that caused all this!
The book reads, 'King Tang of Yin
languished in the prison house of Xia;
King Wen was taken prisoner at Youli.'
So it was in the earliest times,
hence equally in this degenerate age.
To die at the hands of the enemy
may appear to shame a warrior,
yet truly it is no shame at all.
I ask of you only the courtesy
of beheading me without delay."
He said no more. Kagetoki cried,
"Spoken like a great commander!" He wept with emotion.
Every man present likewise moistened his sleeves.
Yoritomo himself declared,
"The Heike are no personal enemies of mine,
but I give weight to our sovereign's words."

Senju arrives to bathe Shigehira.

Nonetheless Shigehira had destroyed the temples of Nara,
and the Nara monks would certainly want him at their disposal.
So Yoritomo entrusted him to Kano-no-suke Munemochi, of Izu province.

> Such is the human sinner's plight
> when in the afterworld he passes
> hand to hand every seven days
> among the ten judges of the dead.

> > But Munemochi was kind. Far from treating Shigehira harshly, he
> > made him comfortable, prepared the bathhouse, and had a bath drawn
> > for him. Shigehira took it that he preferred to kill someone clean rather
> > than rank with the sweat of a long journey, but no, because a very
> > lovely, white-skinned young woman of twenty or so now opened the
> > bathhouse door and entered, wearing a blue-patterned bath apron over
> > an unlined, tie-dyed robe. Soon a girl of fourteen or so, in an unlined
> > blue robe dappled with spots of darker blue and with her hair hanging
> > the length of her jacket, brought in a basin and combs. With the young
> > woman's assistance, he enjoyed a leisurely soak and washed his hair.

She said when she left him,

> "Lord Yoritomo had me come
> because you might object to a man.
> He thought you would not mind a woman.

       'If the gentleman wants anything,'
       he said, 'make sure that you let me know.'"
       "As I am now," Shigehira replied,
       "what request could I possibly have?
       All I want is to leave the world."
       The young woman reported his words.
       "No," Yoritomo replied, "not that.
       I could not even consider it.
       A personal enemy might be different,
       but I am responsible for this man
       as an enemy of the court.
       His wish is out of the question."
Shigehira said to his warrior guard,
"That young woman just now was very nice. What is her name?"
"Her mother runs the inn at Tegoshi," the guard replied.
"She is so sweet and pretty that Lord Yoritomo took her to serve him two or
    three years ago.
Her name is Senju-no-mae."

       That evening a light rain was falling,
       and all the world looked very bleak
       when the young woman of before
       brought in a biwa and a koto,
       and Munemochi himself appeared,
       accompanied by a dozen housemen,
       with a gift of wine. Senju poured.
       Shigehira accepted a little,
       but with a very doleful air.
       Munemochi assured him,
"As you may have gathered already,
Lord Yoritomo wishes me to make you perfectly comfortable.
'Take good care of him,' he said,
'and do not complain if I find reason to reproach you.'
Being from Izu, I myself am only visiting Kamakura,
but I mean to do for you everything that I can."
And to Senju he added, "Sing him something—whatever you like."
Senju put the wine dipper down
       and sang once or twice this *rōei:*

           "So heavy the robe's crepe and damask,
           I hate the cruelty of the weaver."[232]

....

232. A *Wakan rōeishū* passage by Sugawara no Michizane, the "Kitano Tenjin deity" mentioned below.

Shigehira had this to say:
"The Kitano Tenjin deity
has promised to fly three times a day
to protect the singer of this song,
but he has in this life forsaken me.
There is no point in my joining in.
I will, though, if you sing something to lighten my sin."
Senju-no-mae at once sang the *rōei*

       "Though your crimes span the ten evils,
         Amida will yet draw you to him,"
then, four or five times the *imayō*
       "He who aspires to paradise,
         let him call Amida's Name."
Shigehira now tipped the cup
and drank. Senju took it, passed it on
to Munemochi, who drank in turn
while she beautifully played the koto.
"This piece," Shigehira remarked,
"is known to all as *Gojōraku,*
but tonight it will be, for me,
Goshōraku, Song of Paradise.[233]
Allow me to play the final movement,
the one entitled 'Rebirth in Bliss.'"
He tuned the biwa and played the piece.
The night grew late. Feeling at peace,
he said, "It never occurred to me
that I might find here in the east
anyone as lovely as you!
Sing me another—anything!"
Senju sang with exquisite feeling
a *shirabyōshi* dancer's song:
       "Seeking shelter beneath the same tree,
         drawing water from the same stream—
         these things prove a bond from past lives."
Shigehira then added the *rōei*
       "The lamp burns low;
         down the cheeks of Lady Yu
         trickle streams of tears."

....

233. Such becomes the phonetic meaning of the name of the *gagaku* piece *Gojōraku* when the *jō* is changed to *shō*. "Rebirth in Bliss" (*ōjō*), below, plays phonetically on the name of another *gagaku* piece, written with entirely different characters.

This song comes from a Chinese story.
Long ago, in the land of Tang,
Han Gaozu and Xiang Yu of Chu,
in rivalry to win the throne,
fought seventy-two battles,
and every time Xiang Yu won.
But in the end there came a loss
that destroyed Xiang Yu forever.
With his consort, Lady Yu,
he moved to flee, riding Zhui,
a steed that in a single day
could race a full thousand leagues,
but Zhui, unaccountably,
stood fast and refused to move.
Xiang Yu wept. "Yes, my power is gone,"
he said. "Now there is no escape.
Never mind the coming attack.
The only thing I cannot bear
is that my consort and I must part."
So he lamented through the hours,
and when at last the lamps burned low,
Lady Yu shed tears of sorrow.
The night advanced, and battle cries
closed in on them from all four sides. . . .
Tachibana no Hiromi
turned this story into the song
that sprang to Shigehira's mind
with such superlative elegance.

> Dawn broke at last, and the attendant warriors took their leave. Senju-no-mae withdrew as well. That morning Yoritomo was chanting the Lotus Sutra in his personal chapel when Senju presented herself before him. He smiled. "I enjoyed playing go-between for you, Senju," he said.
>
> "What are you talking about?" asked Chikayoshi, who happened to be there in his capacity as his lord's scribe.

"I always assumed that those Heike knew nothing but arms," Yoritomo replied,
"but I stood there all night listening to Shigehira play the biwa and sing,
and, I must say, he is an extremely accomplished gentleman."
"I wish I had been there, too," said Chikayoshi. "I stayed away because I felt
  unwell.
After this I must not miss any such occasion.

Over the generations the Heike have boasted many poets and men of talent.
In years past, people have compared them to flowers
and Lord Shigehira in particular to the peony."
"Well," said Yoritomo, "he certainly is cultivated.
We may never again hear such a touch on the biwa and such *rōei* singing."
As for Senju-no-mae, that night seems to have started her on the path toward
melancholy.

> So it came to pass that when she heard
> that they had turned him over to Nara
> and he had been executed there,
> she put off all her finery,
> clothed herself in the deepest black,
> gave her life to pious practice
> at Zenkōji, in Shinano,
> and prayed only that the next life
> bring him rebirth in paradise;
> and in the end she, too, they say,
> achieved birth in the Pure Land.

8. *Yokobue*

Although in the flesh at Yashima,
in spirit Lord Koremori wandered off time and again to the capital.
The wife and children he had left there were ever present to him.
Not for a single moment did he forget them.
"My life means nothing without them," he said to himself.
On the fifteenth of the third month of Juei 3, he stole away from his Yashima
quarters [1184]
in the company of three others: Yosōbyōe Shigekage, a page named
Ishidōmaru,
and a servant named Takesato, a fellow who knew all about boats.
Boarding a small craft at the village of Yūki in Awa,
they rowed via Naruto toward the province of Kii.

> Waka-no-ura, Fukiage,
> the Tamatsushima Myōjin Shrine
> where Princess Sotōri resides,
> present as a divinity—[234]
> these he passed and passed as well
> the noble sanctuaries

....

234. Princess Sotōri is one of the patron deities of Japanese poetry.

of Nichizen and Kokuken.
At last he reached the harbor of Ki.[235]
From there he longed to continue on
through the mountains up to the city,
to be again with the family
he loved so much, but he reflected,
"They took Shigehira prisoner,
they paraded him through the streets,
they subjected him to ghastly shame
in the city and in Kamakura,
and should I fall into their clutches,
my fate would bloody my father's grave.
No, that I could never bear to do."
A thousand times his heart said Go!
and a thousand times he fought it.
In this tormented state of mind,
he traveled to sacred Mount Kōya.

There lived on Mount Kōya a holy man whom he had long known:
Saitō Takiguchi Tokiyori, son of Saitō Mochiyori of the Left Gate Watch.
Tokiyori had once served in Koremori's household.
In his thirteenth year, he moved to the palace, to join the corps of Takiguchi
    guards,[236]
and there he met Yokobue, a girl in the service of Kenreimon-in.
He fell desperately in love.
"There I was," his father raged, "looking to make you some fine gentleman's
    son-in-law
and set you up well in life—but no, you have to fall for a girl who is nothing!"
This was his son's response:

"There lived, once upon a time,
a Queen Mother of the west,[237]
but no longer: She is gone.
So, too, the wizard Dongfang Shuo:
His name remains, but he does not.
In this world of ours, the young
too often die before the old,
extinguished like a flint-struck spark.
Common talk of a 'long life'

....

235. Now the port of Wakayama.
236. Warriors stationed at the Takiguchi guard post, northeast of the Seiryōden.
237. A Chinese goddess of immortality. The wizard Dongfang Shuo, below, served Emperor Wu of Han.

means seventy or eighty years,
no more, and of all these the best
number perhaps barely twenty.
Life is a dream, an illusion—
why then suffer while we live
any distasteful company?
For me to make my love my own
would be to disobey my father.
Very well then: I will spurn
the fleeting sorrows of the world
and follow the true path instead."
In his nineteenth year, he shaved his head
and, at Ōjō-in in Saga,
began a life of ardent devotion.
Yokobue said to herself when she heard what he had done,
"How awful of him to abandon me and make himself a monk!
All right, so he renounced the world—but he could at least have let me know!
Perhaps he believes he is above all that now,
but I will go and find him and let him know just what I think of him!"
At dusk one day, she left the city and wandered off toward Saga.
The tenth of the second month was past.
The spring breeze through Umezu village
wafted, from somewhere, plum-blossom scent.
The moon shed upon the Ōi River
a radiance dimmed by veils of mist.
Sorely troubled, she knew all too well
at whose door to lay bitter reproach.
She learned the way to Ōjō-in
but did not know which lodge was his
and so faltered in her search.
The poor thing just could not find it.

At last, from a tumbledown monk's lodge she heard a voice calling the
Name. It was Tokiyori's—no doubt about that. She had the girl with
her take him this message: "Here I am. I have found you. I have come
to see you a last time, in your new guise."

The heart of Tokiyori—now the Takiguchi Novice—beat fast. He
cracked open a sliding panel and peeped out: Yes, there she was, look-
ing all the more pitiful for having had such trouble finding him. The
sight was enough to sway any devout practitioner. He sent someone
out at once: "There is no one here by that name. You must have the
wrong place." So she had to leave after all without seeing him.

Yokobue visits her lover, now a monk (right panel).

Angry and hurt, Yokobue could only go home again, trying to swallow her tears.
To his fellow monks in the lodge, the Takiguchi Novice said,

"This is a very peaceful place
where nothing hinders calling the Name,
but a woman I regretted leaving
came and discovered where I live.
That first time, yes, I steeled myself,
but if she ever turns up again,
I know that my heart will go to her.
So good-bye now to all of you."
He left Saga, climbed Mount Kōya,
and settled at Shōjōshin-in.
Yokobue, too—so he soon heard—
took the step that he had taken.
He sent her this poem:

> Yes, I shaved my head,
> having much against the world,
>   but if truth be told,
> it is still a joy to me
> that you now tread the true path.

She answered,

> Shave your head you did,
> but why hold that against you?
>   For if truth be told,
> you could not have changed your mind,
> nor could I, who follow you.

For Yokobue, grief, it seems,
led her to Hokkeji in Nara,
where before long she was gone.
The Takiguchi Novice heard
and redoubled his devotions.
His father pardoned him at last,
and his family revered him.
The Holy Man of Mount Kōya—
that was what they called him then.
And there Koremori visited him.

In the old days, in the capital,
the Takiguchi Novice wore
the costume and *eboshi* hat
proper to his worthy station,
neat and clean, his sidelocks smooth.

He had been a striking youth.
But now that he had left the world,
this first glimpse revealed a monk
who looked old, emaciated,
although not yet even thirty,
his robe and stole as black as ink:
the picture of a saintly man.
Koremori must have envied him.
No Seven Sages of Jin in their bamboo grove,
no white-haired hermits of Han on Mount Shang
could ever have impressed him more.

9. Mount Kōya

The Takiguchi Novice recognized Koremori.
"I can hardly believe my eyes," he said.
"What brings you all this way from Yashima?"
Koremori replied, "You may well ask.
With the others I left the capital and went down to the provinces of the west,
but I missed my children too much ever to forget them.
I suppose it was all too obvious that I had dark worries on my mind,
because Lord Munemori and Lady Nii suspected me of divided loyalty, like
    Yorimori,
and they took care to keep me at a distance.
Life lost all meaning for me, and I could bear it no longer.
So I fled Yashima and made my way here.

> If only I could somehow follow the mountains back to the city and be
> together again with those I love! But the awful fate of Lord Shigehira
> makes that impossible. I might as well instead renounce the world here
> and extinguish my life in fire or water. I did once solemnly vow,
> though, a pilgrimage to Kumano."

"This dream, this illusion that is life
does not matter," Takiguchi replied.
"Endless birth and rebirth in darkness—
that is where true misery lies."
Under Takiguchi's guidance
Koremori set off straightaway
to salute every hall and pagoda.
Soon he came to the Oku-no-in.
    Between Mount Kōya and the city
lies a distance of two hundred leagues.

The nearest settlement is far off;
no human voices break the silence.
Only breezes rustle the green leaves;
the setting sun sheds a tranquil light.
Eight peaks rise, eight valleys drop away.
The heart there can be truly at peace.
Flowers bloom on the misty forest floor,
while bells ring from clouded heights.
Ferns grow from between the tiles;
mosses cloak the long compound walls
in this realm of timeless stars and frosts.
During the Engi Emperor's reign, a sacred dream moved His Majesty [Daigo, r. 897–930]
to present a dark brown robe to the Great Teacher, Kōbō Daishi.
His envoy for the purpose, the counselor Sukezumi,
took with him to Mount Kōya the Hannyaji abbot, Kangen.
They opened the portals of the Great Teacher's tomb,
meaning to lay the robe across his shoulders,
but a thick vapor veiled him from them,
and their reverent gaze distinguished nothing.
In profound affliction, Kangen wept.
 "Never," he said, "since I was first born
 and became my master's disciple[238]
 have I broken a single precept.
 Why, then, can my eyes not see him?"
 Prostrating himself on the ground,
 he shed bitter tears of repentance—
 whereupon the vapors melted away
 and, as though the full moon shone forth,
 the form of the Great Teacher appeared.
  Kangen clothed him in the robe, weeping with joy. The Teacher's hair
  had grown so long that Kangen enjoyed the blessing of shaving him.
  But while the envoy and Kangen both beheld the Teacher, Kangen's
  disciple Shun'yū, the palace chaplain from Ishiyama—still an acolyte
  at the time, accompanying his master—was deeply distressed to find
  that he could not. Kangen took his hand and touched it to the Great
  Teacher's knee. For the rest of Shun'yū's life, that hand gave forth a
  delicious fragrance.
The fragrance passed, so they say, to the scripture scrolls of Ishiyama.
To the emperor the Great Teacher replied,

....

238. His master was Shōbō (832–909), a fourth-generation disciple of Kōbō Daishi.

"Of old I came before the bodhisattva,[239]
who gave me all the mudra and *darani.*
I then declared a sacred, peerless vow
to be present in this distant, alien land,
where I bestow compassion on the people
and uphold the vow of merciful Fugen.
In my own body I entered samadhi[240]
and now wait for Miroku to come."
Such was his answer, and just so, it seems,
Mahā-Kāshyapa, the Buddha's great disciple,
waits in the depths of the cavern where he dwells
for spring winds announcing that glorious day.
The Great Teacher entered into samadhi
on the twenty-first day of the third month of Shōwa 2, [835]
in the first quarter of the hour of the tiger. [ca. 3 A.M.]
Three hundred years have passed since then,
and there lie ahead, until the King of Mercy[241]
addresses that morning his Three Assemblies,
five billion six hundred and seventy million years.
The patient waiting has a long time to run.

10. *Koremori Renounces the World*

"This is what is left of me,"
the unhappy Koremori said,
tears starting from his eyes:
"Like that Himalayan bird
(the one that only cries and cries)
I tell myself, I must! I must[242]
today, today or tomorrow!"
Darkened by the salt sea winds,
wasted by endless wretchedness,
he looked nothing like himself,
yet still surpassed other men.

....

239. Fugen (Sanskrit: Samantabhadra), understood as having received initiation directly from the cosmic buddha Dainichi.

240. The Sanskrit term for a stable state of deep meditation.

241. Miroku (note 135).

242. Renounce the world. On freezing nights the "Himalayan bird" utters endless, piteous cries expressing its realization that it *must* make a nest. Every day, though, it forgets and never does.

The two of them returned at dark
to Takiguchi's hermitage
and talked over through the night
old times and new, the past and now.
The holy man's every gesture
soon persuaded Koremori
that devotion beyond sounding
moved him toward enlightenment
and that the bell calling to prayer
in the last hours of the night,
and again at break of day,
must awaken him from sleep
to the truth of birth and death;
and he longed to be just like him,
could he but summon the resolve.

When day returned, Koremori called in the saintly Chikaku, of Tōzen-in,
and prepared himself to renounce the world.
He summoned Shigekage and Ishidōmaru.
"For myself I suffer from a secret grief," he said,
"and the narrow path ahead offers little escape.
Soon I may be no more.
Many others, though, are prospering even now.
Nothing need keep you two from doing equally well, one way or another.
So stay by me to the end; then hurry on up to the city.
Secure your livelihoods there, look after your wives and children,
and pray for me at the same time in the life to come."
The two men wept bitterly. For a time neither could speak.
At last, however, Shigekage swallowed his tears to say,

"My father, Yosōzaemon Kageyasu,
during the tumult of the Heiji years,
attended his lordship your late father
until, near the Nijō-Horikawa crossing,
he was obliged to fight Kamadabyōe
and died at the hands of Akugenda.

Shall I, Shigekage, show less devotion? I was not yet then into my second year, so I do not remember his death. In my seventh my mother died, and I had no close family to look after me. His late lordship, though, said, 'The boy's father gave his life for me, after all,' and he brought me up himself. In my ninth year, on the night when you, my lord, came of age, he kindly had my hair, too, put up into a topknot. And he did me the great honor of saying, 'The *mori* character belongs

to our house, so it goes to Godai.[243] Matsuō shall have the *shige*. And
so it was that he named me Shigekage. In fact, I got Matsuō, my child-
hood name, when my father took me in his arms and presented me to
his lordship on the fiftieth day after my birth.' Lord Shigemori said,
'Komatsu is the name of my house, so *matsu* should bring him good
luck.' And he called me Matsuō.

It was a blessing for me, I think, that my father died a noble death.
All the retainers were very good to me, too.
On his deathbed Lord Shigemori gave no thought to the world and never spoke,
but he called me nonetheless to his side.

　　'I am so sorry,' he said.
　　'To you I have been as your father;
　　to me you have been the presence
　　as of Kageyasu himself.
　　In the next round of appointments,
　　I was planning that you should have
　　an officer post in the Gate Watch
　　so I could call you by the title
　　I used then to address your father,
　　but, alas, it is too late now.
Never part ways with Lord Koremori.' That is what he said to me.
How could you for one moment imagine me, during these days,
unprepared to see you through whatever you must face?
I blush with shame that you should think such a thing of me.
'Many are prospering even now,' you said.
No doubt they are, but all at present are on the Genji side.
　　Whatever might be my success,
　　once you, my lord, have passed aloft
　　to the realm of gods and buddhas,
　　could I prosper a thousand years?
　　And should I last even ten thousand,
　　would my life really never end?
　　No, this moment proposes to me
　　a lesson in the highest truth."
　　With his own hand, he cut his topknot
　　and, weeping, had Takiguchi
　　shave his head. Ishidōmaru
　　severed his topknot at the sight.
　　He had been with Koremori

....

243. Presumably Koremori's childhood name.

since his eighth year and enjoyed
favor to equal Shigekage's.
He, too, had Takiguchi shave him.
Seeing these two take so momentous a step before him,
Koremori felt more downcast than ever.
There was only one thing to do.

"Transmigration among the Three Worlds
only perpetuates the bonds of love.
Who gives up love to enter the true way,
through him love yields its truest reward."
After chanting these lines three times,
he at last rid himself of his hair.

"Alas," he said, all too sinfully, "I would have no regrets now if only my
dear family could have seen me one last time as they used to know
me!" He and Shigekage were both in their twenty-seventh year,
Ishidōmaru in his eighteenth.

Koremori now called the servant Takesato to his side. "I want you
to go straight back from here to Yashima," he told him. "Do not go up
to the capital. Of course everyone will find out in the end what I have
done, but I know that my wife will become a nun at once if she has
clear confirmation. So go to Yashima. This is what you are to say there
for me: 'Life had become a burden to me, as you noticed yourselves.
Too many terrible things were happening. That is why I kept from you
what I have now done. Kiyotsune died in the west. Moromori was
killed at Ichi-no-tani. Now I know how it will pain you to learn that
even I have become what I am. That is the only thing that I deeply
regret.

The suit of armor called Karakawa and the sword named Kogarasu—
these heirlooms in my line came down to me across nine generations
from the great warrior Taira no Sadamori.
Should we by some miracle regain our standing in the world,
they must go to Rokudai.' Tell them that."

Takesato answered him,
"I shall start for Yashima, my lord,
when I have seen you to your end."

"Very well," Koremori replied, and he kept Takesato with him. He had
Takiguchi accompany him, too, to guide him on the path.

So it was that he set out from Mount Kōya toward Sandō,[244] in that
same province, in the guise of a mountain ascetic. He worshipped at

....

244. A locality on the road to Kumano. There are small "Ōji shrines" all along the way.

the Ōji Shrine in Fujishiro and at all the others along the way. He was
before the Iwashiro Ōji Shrine, north of Senri-no-hama, when seven
or eight horsemen came upon them. Assuming that the riders would
seize them, he and his party put their hands to their daggers, ready to
slit their bellies; but although the riders indeed approached, they
showed no sign of threatening violence. Instead they dismounted in
haste, bowed low, and passed on by. "They recognized me!" Koremori
exclaimed. "Who can they be?" He quickened his pace.

At their head rode Yuasa no Shichirōbyōe Munemitsu,
the son of a man of the province, Yuasa no Gon-no-kami Muneshige.
"Who was *that*?" his men asked.
"I can hardly bear to tell you," he replied through his tears.
"That was Koremori, Lord Taira no Shigemori's eldest son.
I wonder why he fled here all the way from Yashima.
He has renounced the world, and Shigekage and Ishidōmaru, his companions,
   with him.
I wanted to go up and greet him,
but I was afraid to embarrass him, so I just passed on by.
      What a pathetic sight he makes!"
      He pressed his sleeves to his eyes, sobbing,
      and every one of his men wept.

11. The Pilgrimage to Kumano

On Koremori went, and the passing days brought him to the Iwada River.
"For him who once crosses this river," so he assured himself with deep faith,
"all evil karma, all the passions, all sins from beginningless time melt away."
He came to the great shrine of Kumano Hongū, knelt there before the Shōjōden,
and for a time offered the divine presence there his chanting of the sutras.
He then gazed upon the inexpressibly majestic hills.
      The mists of nurturing compassion
      trailed about the Kumano mountains;
      beside the Otonashi River,
      the gods, workers of peerless wonders,
      revealed their presence here below.
      Upon these banks reigned devotion
      to practice of the One Vehicle,[245]
      while a spotless moon, aloft,
      shone down in sign of generous boons.

....

245. Practice of faith in the Lotus Sutra.

No dewdrops of deluded thoughts
gathered in these holy precincts
where prevailed only repentance
for the sins of the six sense roots.
All this inspired his deepest faith.
Late that night, while others slept,
he prayed and movingly recalled
how his father before this shrine
had begged the gods to take his life
and save him in the life to come.
"You who make manifest the Buddha Amida himself,
O honor your Original Vow to gather each believer to you and abandon none!
Guide me, I beg, to your Pure Land!"
And to this prayer he added, the poor man,
"Grant peace, I beg, to the wife and children I have left behind!"
Alas, these words made it all too plain
that after spurning this sorry world
and entering at last the true way,
he still indulged in deluded clinging.
At dawn he sailed down from the shrine to Shingū
and worshipped there the sacred Rock Seat.[246]
Through the pines towering on those heights
sighed breezes to dispel deluded dreams;
the pure waters of the flowing streams
washed him clean of all polluting dust.
Having paid homage at the Asuka Shrine,
he traveled past the pinewoods of Sano
and on into the mountains of Nachi.
Water pouring down the triple cascade[247]
rebounded from below, thousands of feet,
and there appeared on the falls' rocky lip
the mountain's sacred figure of Kannon,
as though this were Mount Fudaraku itself.
Through the mist came the sound of voices
so devoutly chanting the Lotus Sutra
that the place could have been Vulture Peak.
Ever since the deity first descended,

....

246. The rocky outcrop (*iwakura*), high on the hillside, inhabited by the Shingū deity. Such outcrops were often, and still are, associated with a divine presence. This one was especially revered.

247. Two lower falls precede the Nachi waterfall proper.

Left panel: Koremori on a bluff overlooking the Nachi waterfall.
Right panel: Takiguchi, followed by Ishidōmaru and the others. In the background
(center right): Yuasa Munemitsu and his men.

all in our realm, whether high or low,
have bent their steps thither, bowed their heads,
hands folded in prayer, and enjoyed blessings:
hence the rows of monks' lodges,
the press of pilgrims, clerical and lay.
That summer during the Kanna years, [985-87]
Cloistered Emperor Kazan fled the throne
to seek rebirth in highest paradise,
and here was the site of his hermitage.
Perhaps to honor so noble a past,
an old cherry tree stood there in full bloom.

> One monk on retreat at Nachi must have seen Koremori often in the
> past, for he said to his companion, "I was just wondering who that as-
> cetic over there could be when I recognized Lord Shigemori's eldest
> son, Koremori. Back in the Angen years, at Cloistered Emperor Go-
> Shirakawa's fiftieth jubilee, he was still a lieutenant at the fourth rank.
> His father was palace minister and left commander, and his uncle, Lord
> Munemori, sat below the steps as counselor and right commander.

Lord Tomomori and Lord Shigehira were there as well,
and likewise every Taira gentleman, in the full splendor of Heike glory.

When Lord Koremori stepped forth from their circle to dance *Blue Sea Waves*,
with a spray of blossoms in his hair,

>he could have been a dew-laden flower.
>The swaying of his wind-tossed sleeves
>lit up earth and illumined heaven.
>The cloistered emperor's greatest lady[248]
>sent him the regent, bearing a robe.
>His father rose from his seat to take it
>and laid it across his son's right shoulder;
>then he humbly bowed to the sovereign.
>This gift was so plainly a signal honor
>that the privy gentlemen looking on
>must have felt, ah, what pangs of envy!
>A palace gentlewoman even remarked,
>'No bayberry could stand out more
>from any thicket of nondescript trees!'
>He was so obviously destined then
>to serve as minister and commander,
>yet there he is now, a wreck of a man.
>I never thought to see such a thing.
>Talk about life's vicissitudes!
>Poor fellow! What an awful fate!"
>He pressed his sleeves to his eyes and wept,
>and all the monks on retreat at Nachi
>likewise moistened the sleeves of their robes.

12. *Koremori Drowns*

His Triple Kumano pilgrimage safely accomplished,
Koremori repaired to the Seashore Shrine[249]
and rowed a boat out over the vast blue sea.
Far in the offing lay Yamanari Island.
He brought the boat up to it, disembarked on the shore,
and into the trunk of a large pine tree there carved his rank and name.

>"Grandfather: Chancellor Taira no Kiyomori,
>   name in religion Jōkai.
>Father: Palace Minister & Left Commander Shigemori,
>   name in religion Jōren.

....

248. Kenshunmon-in (Taira no Shigeko), Go-Shirakawa's empress.
249. Hama-no-miya, on the shore at Nachi.

His son: Third Rank Captain Koremori,
   name in religion Jōen,
   in his 27th year, this day,
   Juei 3, 3rd month, the 28th,
   drowned himself in the sea off Nachi."
So he wrote, then reboarded his boat
and rowed toward the open ocean.
He had made up his mind to do this,
but now that the time had come to act,
he felt sorrow and apprehension.
Late as it was in the third month,
haze veiled the sea into the distance,
evoking a mood of melancholy.
Sadness pervades the sunset sky
any spring day, and this one, of course,
weighed upon him like no other.
Just when he thought a distant boat
had vanished for good into the waves,
up it came again, plain as could be,
and his thoughts turned to his fate.
A line of homing geese flew by,
calling, toward the northern marches,
and he longed to send a message home,
as had Su Wu from that barbarian land,
filled with all the trials he had suffered.
"But what is this?" he reproached himself.
"Profane attachment must rule me still."
He turned to the west, palms pressed together,
and called the Name, but these thoughts crept in:
"They could never suspect, in the city,
that this moment, for me, is my last.
No doubt they believe that news of me
is on its way to them even now.
But everyone will know in the end.
And when they learn that I am gone,
ah, how deeply they will despair!"
These thoughts besieged his calling the Name.
He stopped and dropped his hands. "Alas!"
he said, turning to Takiguchi.
"No man should have a wife and children.
In this life they are a constant worry,

and, even more unfortunately,
they hinder enlightenment in the next.
Just now, again, they troubled my thoughts.
That such things should still upset me
must be a grave sin, and I confess it."
His words saddened Takiguchi, who shrank from betraying similar weakness.
The holy man wiped his eyes and began with a show of composure,
"I do not wonder that you should feel as you do.
No man, high or low, can keep from treading the path of love.
For a husband and wife above all, a single night spent side by side
confirms, they say, a bond established over five hundred lives.
A tie founded so long in the past is very far from casual.
All those who are born must die, it is true. All who meet must part.
That is simply the way of this world.
As one dewdrop may fall in its time from the tip of a leaf
and another trickle straight down the stem to the root,
one will precede the other sooner or later.
Could the moment for that parting then never come?

> That autumn night in the Lishan Palace,
> those lovers sealed between them a bond
> that in the end only broke their hearts.
> Love shared in life, in the Ganquan hall,
> sure enough in the end came to naught.
> Songzi and Mei Fu met their last hour.[250]
> The loftiest among the bodhisattvas
> still follow the law of birth and death.

> > You would not escape that final sorrow, my lord, even if you came to pride yourself on the pleasures of a long life. The same grief would find you in the end, as it does now, even if you were to live a hundred years. That heretic Maō in his sixth heaven, who lords it over all six heavens in the realm of desire, resents that in our world sentient beings should free themselves from birth and death, and to keep them from doing so he assumes the guise now of a wife, now of a husband. In contrast the buddhas of the Three Ages love all sentient beings like their own child and urge them to enter the immutable Pure Land paradise. To this end, the Buddha emphatically discourages love for any wife or child, for through the aeons of beginningless time these have always bound one to the wheel of transmigration.

....

250. The first pair of lovers ("in the Lishan Palace") are Yang Guifei and Emperor Xuanzong, of Tang, in Bo Juyi's "Song of Everlasting Sorrow"; the second ("in the Ganquan Hall") are Lady Li and Emperor Wu of Han, also celebrated by Bo Juyi. The last two names are Han immortals.

So do not, I implore you, allow your resolve to falter.
The great Genji founder, the Iyo novice Yoriyoshi,
spent twelve years in the north, by imperial order,
warring against the barbarians Sadatō and Munetō.
In that time he beheaded sixteen thousand men and more,
quite apart from killing by the millions beasts of the field and fish of the rivers.

    And yet when the end came for him,
    they say he aroused a faith so pure
    that he attained his cherished goal:
    rebirth in Amida's paradise.

> Above all, to renounce the world and become a monk is to gain the
> very greatest merit. A man might build a pagoda of the seven precious
> substances as high as the heaven of the thirty-three gods, and still not
> earn the merit of one day as a monk. He might make offerings to the
> Hundred Arhats[251] for a hundred or a thousand years and still fail to
> earn the merit of that one day. So the Teaching tells us.

The profoundly sinful Yoriyoshi was also a man of ardent courage,
and that is why he achieved rebirth.
You, then, who have done nothing especially sinful—
why should you not go straight to the Pure Land?
Besides, the divinity of these mountains reveals the very presence of Amida.
Every single one of his vows,
from the first—to abolish the three evil realms—
to the last—to triply enlighten all bodhisattvas—
was conceived for the salvation of sentient beings.
Among these vows the eighteenth says,

    'Should I reach the brink of buddhahood
    and sentient beings everywhere,
    in faith and joy believe my vow,
    desiring birth in my Pure Land,
    and call on me by name ten times
    yet not have the birth they wish,
    I shall decline final enlightenment.'
    So the Buddha Amida taught.
    Therefore call the Name ten times
    or only once, and trust in him.
    Let no doubt invade your heart.
    Arouse ardent, peerless faith,

....

251. The Hundred Arhats (Japanese: Hyaku Rakan) are the vaguely conceived ideal followers of the
Buddha.

call on him ten times or once,
and the Buddha Amida
will draw down his infinite vastness
into a body sixteen feet tall
surrounded by Kannon and Seishi,
by a great host of holy beings,
by transformed buddhas and bodhisattvas
rank on rank into the distance,
and come forth, singing hymns of praise,
from the east gate of paradise
to welcome the newly departed soul.
You will believe that you are sinking
into the depths of the blue ocean
but really will mount the purple cloud.
Once enlightenment dawns for you
and you are free in buddhahood,
you will return to your home in this world
to guide your wife and your children,
as do all those from the Pure Land
who 'return to this sullied earth
to save both humans and devas.'
Of this there is no doubt at all."
The holy man now rang his bell
and urged Koremori to call the Name.
Trusting his true spiritual friend,
Koremori righted his error,
faced the west, palms pressed together,
one hundred times called out the Name,
and with a last "Hail!" plunged into the sea.
Shigekage and Ishidōmaru
called the Name as he had done,
then followed him into the depths.

13. *The Three-Day Heike*

The servant Takesato moved to follow, but the holy man stopped him.
"For shame!" he cried. "Why, you nearly disobeyed Lord Koremori's final
    command!
Servants! What a hopeless lot!
Just devote yourself to prayer for him in the life to come!"
So, in tears, he reproved the man,

but so distraught was Takesato at being left behind
that the idea of praying for his late master meant nothing to him.
He only writhed in the bottom of the boat, groaning and crying,
  his grief no less profound than Chandaka's
  when Prince Siddhartha long, long ago
  retreated to the Mount Dandaka wilds
  leaving him Kanthaka, his steed,
  to take back to the royal palace.
  The holy man rowed about for a while,
  peering down into the water, but the three
  had sunk too deep; there was no sign of them.
  In time he chanted scripture, called the Name,
  and prayed that they enter paradise.
  His tender concern was very moving.
  Meanwhile the sun sank toward the west
  and darkness spread across the ocean.
  With many a pang of lingering sorrow,
  he rowed the empty boat back to the shore.
  Drops from the oar, teardrops on his sleeves—
  which was which, there was no telling.
  Takiguchi again climbed Mount Kōya.
  Takesato returned, weeping, to Yashima.
There he gave Sukemori, Koremori's brother, a last letter from his master.
  "How awful!" Sukemori cried.
  "If only he had understood
  how much he meant to all of us!
  Lord Munemori and Lady Nii,
  suspecting him of being in league
  with Yoritomo—like Yorimori—
  assume that he went off to the city
  and so look askance at me, too.
But no! Apparently he has drowned himself in the sea off Nachi!
He could have taken me with him, so that we might drown together,
and I hate to think that our bodies must now lie apart.
Did he give you no spoken message?"
"This is what he asked me to say," Takesato replied.
"'First, Kiyotsune died in the west, then Moromori was killed at Ichi-no-tani,
and now I, too, have met my end.
For you this must be a terrible blow, and that is my only regret.'
He went on to say a good deal about Karakawa, Kogarasu, and so on."
  "I cannot imagine now living on,"

Sukemori said, sleeves to his eyes,
weeping piteously, and no wonder.
He made a very sad sight indeed.
He looked so eerily like his brother
that everyone present wept as well.
His retainers, gathered around him,
could only dissolve in helpless tears.
Lord Munemori and Lady Nii,
who thought that he, like Yorimori,
had cast his lot with Yoritomo,
now understood that this was not so,
and they, too, lamented and mourned.

    On the first of the fourth month, Yoritomo, in Kamakura, was awarded the senior fourth rank, lower grade. This represented a five-step leap, since his previous rank had been junior fifth, lower grade. The promotion rewarded his suppression of Kiso Yoshinaka.

    On the third, Retired Emperor Sutoku was transferred in spirit to a newly built shrine at the east end of Ōi-no-mikado, where the battle had been fought,[252] there to be honored as a god. The initiative came from Cloistered Emperor Go-Shirakawa. The reigning emperor and his court apparently knew nothing about it.

    On the fourth of the fifth month, Yorimori started down to the Kanto. He had received in the past, from Yoritomo, repeated letters conveying this assurance: "I continue to hold you in the highest regard. For me your mother lives on in you, and I mean to discharge to your benefit my obligation toward her." These letters had led him to part ways with his house and stay behind in the capital. "No doubt Yoritomo does feel that way about me," he reflected anxiously, "but I wonder about the other Genji." So when the pressing invitation to Kamakura arrived, he went.

There was a retainer of Yorimori's, a man named Yaheibyōe Munekiyo.
Although a key adviser, he did not go down to Kamakura with his lord.
"But why?" Yorimori asked.
"I simply prefer not to, my lord. You yourself are doing well,
but it pains me that the other gentlemen of your house should be roaming the
    waves of the western sea,
and I cannot yet fully reconcile myself to their plight.
I shall follow you when I have achieved a somewhat more settled frame of mind."
Shaken and embarrassed, Yorimori replied,

. . . .

252. The decisive battle that took place during the Hōgen Conflict.

"I am far from proud of myself for having abandoned my house and stayed
    behind in the city,
but I valued my standing and my life too much not to grasp at this straw.
As a result I am in no position not to go.
How can you decline to make this long journey with me?
Why, if you feel that strongly, did you not speak up when I made up my mind
    to stay?
After all, I discussed every aspect of the matter with you at the time."
Munekiyo sat up perfectly straight and answered with due respect,

> "Anyone, whether high or low,
> values his life above all things.
> Who gives up the world, they say,
> still cannot give up himself.
> I do not mean that you were wrong
> back then not to flee the city.
> The only reason Yoritomo
> now enjoys such great good fortune
> is that he had his own life saved.
> When he was sent into exile,
> her ladyship the nun, your mother,
> ordered me to escort him
> to the Shinohara post station.
> I gather he still remembers that,

and I do not doubt that if I were with you,
he would shower me with gifts and feasts. I would find that distressing.
The gentlemen now in the west, or men of theirs, might hear of it,
to my everlasting shame. Please, allow me this time to stay where I am.
You cannot possibly now not go to Kamakura, since you never left the capital,
and of course my concern will follow you down the long road.
If you meant to attack an enemy, I would gladly lead your men,
but this time you can easily do without me.
Please tell Yoritomo, if he asks about me, that I am ill."

> Every man of heart there that day
> shed tears upon hearing this speech.

Yorimori, thoroughly abashed, still knew that he had to go. He left immediately and reached Kamakura on the sixteenth. Yoritomo received him at once. "Is Munekiyo with you?" he asked.

"Unfortunately, he is currently unwell and so did not accompany me," Yorimori replied.

"Unwell? What is wrong with him? He must have his reasons. I will never forget his kindness in the old days, when I was with him, and I

counted on his coming down with you. I looked forward to seeing him. It is a great disappointment that he stayed away." Yoritomo had prepared many land-grant decrees, as well as horses, saddles, and other accoutrements, and the chief men around him had eagerly followed suit. All were disappointed that Munekiyo had failed to appear.
On the ninth of the sixth month, Yorimori hurried back up to the city.
Yoritomo urged him to stay longer,
but he protested that people there would worry about him.
A request to His Cloistered Eminence secured for Yorimori
possession of all estate rights and private land that he had owned before
and reinstatement also in his grand-counselor post.
He took home in addition thirty saddled and thirty unsaddled horses
and thirty long chests filled with feathers, gold, dyed cloth, silk rolls, and so on.
Yoritomo's consideration for him moved the others around him, great and small,
to commensurate generosity with their gifts.
The horses that he led away numbered in all three hundred.
Yorimori had not only managed to stay alive,
he had also returned to the capital rich.

On the eighteenth, Hirata Sadatsugu,
the Higo governor Sadayoshi's uncle,
led a force of men from Iga and Ise
out into the province of Ōmi,
where local Genji stalwarts engaged them
and killed or dispersed every one.
For these long-standing Heike retainers,
it was undoubtedly admirable
not to forget their old allegiance,
but the idea was rash presumption.
The "Three-Day Heike," people called them.

Meanwhile Lord Koremori's wife
had not had for a very long time
any breath of news from her husband.
"Oh, what can have become of him?"
she wondered, more and more worried.
"He always wrote to me once a month."
While she waited and waited in vain,
spring slipped by and high summer came.
Then she heard that someone had said,
"Lord Koremori? Oh, no,
he is no longer at Yashima."
Frantic now with apprehension,

she managed to send a man there.
He seemed in no hurry to return.
Summer faded into autumn.
The seventh month was nearly over
when her messenger came back at last.

"Tell me, tell me! What news do you bring?"

He answered, "Lord Koremori left Yashima on the fifteenth of this
third month past and went to Mount Kōya, where he shaved his head.
Then he went on to Kumano. He threw himself into the sea off Nachi,
praying ardently for paradise. I heard this from Takesato, the servant
who was with him."

She cried, "Oh, I knew there was something wrong!" and collapsed
with a robe drawn over her head. Her little son and daughter wept and
wailed.

Her son's nurse said, weeping, "My lady, this should not surprise you.
It is no more than what you expected.
Just think how awful it would have been if Lord Koremori had been taken alive,
like Lord Shigehira!
That he should have renounced the world on Mount Kōya,
prayed with fervor for that true rebirth, and died with nothing but right
thoughts—
these things call for gladness in the midst of sorrow.
So, my lady, set your mind at rest
and resolve that you will bring up your children in whatever wilderness may be
your lot."
With these words she did what she could to comfort a mistress
whose only thoughts now were memories of her husband
and who seemed in no condition to live out the day.

The lady became a nun at once
and gave herself, as best she could,
to pious rites and litanies
and prayers for her husband in the hereafter.

14. Fujito

Yoritomo in Kamakura learned of Koremori's death.
"If only he had come to see me in person," he said, "I could have saved his life.
I had the greatest respect for his father, Shigemori,
since it was he who, speaking for Yorimori's mother,
got my sentence commuted from death to exile.
For that I owe him a great debt of gratitude—

one so unforgettable that I hold his sons, too, in high regard.
Besides, Koremori had renounced the world.
It would have been perfectly easy to save him."
    The Heike heard this news once they were back at Yashima:
"Tens of thousands of fresh warriors have reached the capital from the east,
and they are on their way down here to attack."
And this: "The Usuki, the Betsugi, and the Matsura leagues
have joined forces against us and are coming over from Kyushu."
Both alarming reports stirred only terror.

> Few of the great Heike nobles
> had survived Ichi-no-tani.
> More than half their chief lieutenants were gone,
> and their house was gravely weakened.
> One Shigeyoshi and his brother,
> both powerful squires from Awa,
> sought to rally the men of Shikoku
> and assured them that all would be well.
> The Heike looked to them with hope,
> as though to high mountains and deep seas,
> while their huddled women only wept.
> The twenty-fifth of the seventh month came.
> "It was a year ago today,"
> they reminded one another,
> "that we fled the capital together."
> They reviewed with tears and laughter
> the frantic horror of it all.

The twenty-eighth brought the new emperor's enthronement.[253]
Never before, they say, in all the eighty-two reigns since Emperor Jinmu,
had the event taken place without the mirror, jewel, and sword.
On the sixth of the eighth month, the appointments list was announced.
Noriyori became the new governor of Mikawa
and Kurō Yoshitsune an aide in the Left Gate Watch.
An imperial order also made him an officer in the police.

> Now came chill winds to bend the reeds
> and dews gathering under the *hagi* fronds.
> To the plaintive song of crickets,
> rice plants rustled, leaves fluttered down—
> a sight to cloud the most carefree heart
> under strange skies, as autumn waned.

....

253. The formal enthronement of Go-Toba.

Imagine, then, what melancholy
weighed on the hearts of all the Heike!
Of old, in the ninefold cloud dwelling,[254]
they sported among the blossoms of spring;
now, on the shore at Yashima,
they gazed sadly on the autumn moon.
No verse of theirs evoked its brilliance
without thought of that night in the city,
and so they spent their nights and days
relieving their hearts and shedding tears.
Taira no Yukimori wrote, in this vein,

> *Since our lord is here,*
> *the moon in the sky above*
> *is the palace moon,*
> *yet the yearning heart still longs*
> *for the capital and home.*

On the twelfth day of the ninth month,
Noriyori set out for the west
on a mission to suppress the Heike.
These are the men who rode with him:
  Ashikaga no Kurando Yoshikane,
  Kagami no Kojirō Nagakiyo,
  Hōjō no Kojirō Yoshitoki,
  Saiin no Shikan Chikayoshi.
And these were his field commanders:
  Doi no Jirō Sanehira
    and his son, Yatarō Tōhira.
  Also Miura-no-suke Yoshizumi
    and his son, Heiroku Yoshimura.
  Hatakeyama no Jirō Shigetada,
  Hatakeyama Nagano no Saburō Shigekiyo,
  Inage no Saburō Shigenari,
  Hangai no Shirō Shigetomo,
  Hangai no Gorō Yukishige,
  Oyama no Koshirō Tomomasa,
  Oyama Naganuma no Gorō Munemasa,
  Tsuchi no Saburō Munetō,
  Sasaki no Saburō Moritsuna,
  Hatta no Shirō Musha Tomoie,

---

254. "Ninefold" is a noble epithet for the imperial palace (the "cloud dwelling").

Anzai no Saburō Akimasu,
Ōgo no Saburō Sanehide,
Amano no Tōnai Tōkage,
Hiki no Tōnai Tomomune,
Hiki no Tōshirō Yoshikazu,
Chūjō no Tōji Ienaga,
Ipponbō Shōgen,
Tosabō Shōshun,

leading thirty thousand mounted men.
Their march took them to Muro in Harima.
Command of the Heike army went to these men:

Captain Taira no Sukemori,
Lieutenant Taira no Arimori,
Adviser Taira no Tadafusa;

and these men were their field commanders:

Hida no Saburōzaemon Kagetsune,
Etchū no Jirōbyōe Moritsugi,
Kazusa no Gorōbyōe Tadamitsu,
Akushichibyōe Kagekiyo.

Aboard a fleet of five hundred vessels, they reached Kojima in Bizen.
The Genji left Muro at this news, to camp likewise in Bizen,
at Nishi-Kawajiri and beside a narrow stretch of sea known as Fujito.[255]

Five hundred yards of water separated them from the Heike, and the only way across was by boat. Their army spent day after wasted day on the slope across from the foe. Young Heike hotheads would row out, flourishing fans and shouting, "Here! Here's the place! Come right over!" The Genji were at their wits' end.

Then, on the night of the twenty-fifth, Sasaki Moritsuna fell to talking with a local fisherman. He won the man over with a white *kosode* robe, a pair of widemouthed trousers, and a dagger with a silver-wrapped hilt. Then he asked, "Isn't there anywhere along here where you can just ride across?"

"Yes, there are two places," the man replied. "Few of the shore people know about them, but I do. They are like river fords. The one to the east is good early in the month and the one to the west later. They are about two-thirds of a mile apart. You can easily ride straight across."

Sasaki, very pleased, kept this intelligence from his men. He stole off alone with the fisherman, took off his clothes, and tried it. Indeed the water was not very deep. In some places it came up to his knees,

255. Since Kojima is no longer an island, Fujito, which separated it from the mainland, no longer exists.

his hips, or his shoulders. Sometimes he even got his sidelocks wet.
Where it was deep, he swam to new footing.

The fisherman said, "It is much shallower south of here, but enemy
arrows await you and you have nothing on. You had better not go any
farther."

"Right you are," Sasaki answered, and turned back. This thought
occurred to him, though: "Who knows who this fellow really is or
where his loyalty lies? Someone else might get the same information
out of him just as easily as I did. No, nobody else must know." He ran
the fisherman through, cut off his head, and tossed it away.

On the twenty-sixth, at the hour of the dragon, [ca. 8 A.M.]
another Heike boat rowed out to taunt the Genji with raised fans
and invitations to "Come right on over!"
Sasaki knew just where to do that.
Wearing a dappled tie-dyed *hitatare* under black-laced armor and riding a pale
    gray,
he led seven of his men straight into the sea.
    "Stop him!" shouted their commander,
    Noriyori. "Stop that man!"
    Doi Sanehira, whip and stirrup,
    galloped off in hot pursuit.
    "What has got into you, Sasaki?"
    he cried. "Are you out of your mind?
    You are forbidden to go farther!
    This is insubordination!"
    Sasaki ignored him and went on.
    Having failed to turn him back,
    Sanehira simply joined him.
    The water touched the horses' bellies
    in places, or the chest ropes, or higher.
    Sometimes it washed across their saddles,
    and where it was deep, the men swam on
    until their mounts trod bottom again.
    Noriyori saw what this meant.
    "Sasaki has put one over on us!
    The water is shallow! Go on! Cross!"
    At his order the thirty thousand
    plunged straight in and headed out.
    "Oh, no!" the Heike cried on their side,
    and launched a great number of boats,
    from where they loosed a rain of arrows.

The undaunted Genji warriors,
heads well down, necks protected,
leaped straight into them from horseback
with fierce cries and fought hand to hand.
Some boats, overloaded in the melee,
sank, and with them many went down;
some overturned, to general panic.
The battle lasted the rest of the day.
That night the Heike put to sea.
The Genji came ashore on Kojima, to rest men and horses.
At dawn the Heike rowed back toward Yashima.
The Genji were eager to pursue them, but they had no boats.
They gave up any further attack.

"Many warriors past and present
have ridden their horses across rivers,
but to ride that way through the sea—
why, the like has never been known
in India, China, or our own realm!"
And so it is that Sasaki received
the island of Kojima in Bizen,
by Yoritomo's written command.

15. The Enthronement Festival

On the twenty-seventh, in the capital,
Kurō Yoshitsune received the fifth rank and appointment as a lieutenant in the
    police.
People then acknowledged these titles by calling him Kurō Tayū no Hōgan.

Meanwhile the tenth month came around.
At Yashima storm winds swept the shore
while high waves crashed on the rocks.
No warriors turned up to attack them,
and few merchants managed the crossing.
They yearned for news of the capital.
Then leaden skies pelted them with hail,
until they foundered in blank despair.
In the capital there was to be an Enthronement Festival.
His Majesty accordingly made a progress to undergo the required purification.
The palace minister, Tokudaiji Sanesada, oversaw the event.
Taira no Munemori, likewise palace minister at the time,
had overseen the previous emperor's purification two years earlier.

Seated within his curtained enclosure, the dragon banner raised before him,
Munemori had looked extremely imposing,
from the fit of his cap to the drape of his sleeves and the fall of his court trousers.
Other Heike gentlemen—Tomomori, Shigehira, and lesser Palace Guards
    officers—
had held the ropes of the imperial palanquin,
and it was plain to see that none could compare with them.
This time Yoshitsune led the procession.
Although used to the capital, quite unlike Kiso Yoshinaka,
he still fell short of the least of the Heike.
The Enthronement Festival was held on the eighteenth of the eleventh month.

> Ever since the Jishō and Yōwa years, [1177–82]
>
> the common people and the peasants
> throughout every province of the land
> had suffered Genji depredations
> and destruction at Heike hands.
> They had abandoned hearth and home
> to flee into mountains and forests.
> In spring they forgot to till their fields;
> in autumn they could harvest nothing.
> How, then, was this feast even possible?
> And yet it could not be omitted.
> Therefore it was followed at least in form.

Noriyori's attack, pursued without break, would have finished the Heike.
But no, he disported himself instead at Muro and Takasago,
day after day, month after month, among courtesans and singing girls.

> The many eastern leaders, great and small,
> could act only at their commander's order.
> The province's resources went to waste,
> and great misery afflicted the people.

BOOK ELEVEN

1. Bow Oars

(recitative)

Genryaku 2: On the tenth of the first month, [1185]
Kurō Yoshitsune called at the cloistered emperor's palace
and through Yasutsune, the lord of the Treasury, submitted this declaration:
"The gods and the sovereign alike have abandoned the Heike,
who have fled the capital and now wander the waves.
Nonetheless these three past years they have survived further attack
and have blocked passage to and from many provinces.
Now I, Yoshitsune, undertake never to return to His Majesty's seat
until I have pursued the Heike even to Kikai-ga-shima,
to Korea, India, or China if need be, and destroyed them forever."
This stalwart pronouncement greatly impressed the sovereign.
"By all means," Go-Shirakawa responded,
"pause neither by day nor by night until victory is yours."
Yoshitsune returned to his lodging and announced to the warriors from the east,
"Representing Lord Yoritomo in Kamakura, I have received this day
His Cloistered Eminence's decree ordering me to destroy the Heike.
I shall pursue them by land as far as a horse can go,
by sea to the farthest range of the oar.
Those whose hearts are not wholly with me, let them leave now."

> *(song)*
> At Yashima, meanwhile, time sped by.
> The first month soon became the second;
> spring green dulled into the waning year;
> the first breath of autumn on the wind
> came bearing its shiver of surprise;
> then the autumn wind was gone, for spring
> had come again, bursting with new green.

Three times they saw the old year out and the new year in.
"Tens of thousands of fresh warriors from the east are on their way down from
  the capital to attack us."
Such was the news that reached them, and this rumor, too:
"The Usuki, the Betsugi, and the Matsura leagues have joined forces
to cross over from Kyushu and mount a campaign against us."
Both disturbing reports aroused only terror.

Kenreimon-in, Lady Nii, and their women clustered together to share their
    lament:
"Oh, what miseries await us now? What ghastly news is to reach us next?"
Lord Tomomori declared,

        "The men of the east and the north
        enjoyed our favor time and again
        yet forgot everything they owed us
        and shifted their allegiance elsewhere,
        to follow instead Yoritomo,
        Yoshinaka, and more of that ilk.
        I had no doubt the men of the west
        would in their time do just the same,
        and that is why I myself favored
        meeting our fate in the capital,
        but that was not my decision to make.
        So we weakly gave ground and fled,
        only to suffer our present misfortune.
        How I wish that it were not so!"
        Sad to say, he was perfectly right.

On the third of the second month, Kurō Yoshitsune set out from the capital
and assembled a fleet of boats at Watanabe, in the province of Settsu,[256]
to mount an attack against Yashima.
Noriyori left the capital on the same day
and likewise assembled a fleet at Kanzaki, also in Settsu,
so as to sail down the coast of the Inland Sea.
On the thirteenth, imperial envoys from the Bureau of Shrines
were dispatched to the Grand Shrine of Ise, to Iwashimizu, Kamo, and Kasuga.
They and the chief priest at each were ordered to pray:
"O grant safe return to the emperor and the three regalia!"
On the sixteenth the Watanabe and Kanzaki fleets were ready to launch
when a north wind swept down on them, strong enough to fell trees.
Huge waves scattered the vessels and damaged them.
The fleets remained in harbor that day, to allow for repairs.

    (speech)
    At Watanabe local squires great and small gathered in council. "We
    are not trained for seaborne combat," they declared. "We do not know
    what to do." Kajiwara Kagetoki recommended installing bow oars for
    the coming battle.

....

256. Near the mouth of the Yodo River, on the south bank.

"Bow oars?" inquired Yoshitsune. "What are they?"

Kajiwara replied, "You can easily turn a galloping horse left or right,

but not a boat. That is much harder.

So you fit the bow, too, with oars and add side rudders as well.

Then you can move the boat readily in any direction."

To this, Yoshitsune:

"A warrior heading into battle

resolves not to take one backward step

but usually does so nonetheless

when faced by an overwhelming threat.

Why prepare in advance to flee? What a way to get started! Bow oars, get-out-fast oars, whatever you call them—by all means, gentlemen, give your boats bow oars by the hundreds and thousands, but for me the oars normal for any boat are good enough."

Kajiwara retorted, "To my mind a good commander defeats the enemy by advancing when he can, retreating when he must, and staying alive: That is what good command means to me. Charging blindly ahead, fighting like a maddened boar: That for me is no good at all."

"Boar, deer—who cares?" Yoshitsune retorted. "Making war means attack, attack, and victory is sweet."

The men feared Kajiwara too greatly to laugh aloud,

but they exchanged looks and nods, and a buzz ran through them:

The two seemed on the point of coming to blows.

By and by the sun set and night fell.

"The repairs are done," Yoshitsune announced. "The boats are as good as new.

Have something to eat, gentlemen, have a drink, celebrate!"

As though laying out a feast, he had the boats loaded with arms and
    provisions

and had horses, too, brought aboard. Then he issued the order "Go!"

The captains and helmsmen protested.

"Yes," they said, "the wind is behind us, but it is unusually strong,

and at sea this must be quite a blow. How can we possibly launch the boats?"

Yoshitsune was furious.

"Whether you die in the wilderness or drown in river or sea," he roared,

"that is up to the karma you bring from past lives!

So you get out to sea and find it's blowing a gale? Too bad!

You'd rather cross *against* the wind?

You'd be mad! But no, it's *behind* you!

Perhaps it's a little strong today,

but this chance is too good to miss!

How dare you suggest staying put?
If you refuse to launch the boats,
I'll have every last one of you shot!"
That was his command.
Satō Saburōbyōe Tsuginobu, from Mutsu, and Ise no Saburō Yoshimori
stepped forward, each with an arrow in hand.
"What is this nonsense?" they demanded to know. "You have your order.
Obey it now or we shoot you all!"
    The captains and helmsmen listened.
    "If we're to be shot, there's nothing to lose—
    might as well die running down the gale.
    Go for it, men!" Of two hundred boats,
    only five actually put to sea;
    all the rest, for fear of the wind,
    or perhaps in terror of Kajiwara,
    never budged. Yoshitsune said,
    "Merely that others refuse to go
    makes no excuse for doing the same.
    Good weather keeps an enemy watchful.
    When howling winds and foaming waves
    seem to guarantee perfect safety,
    that is when an attack hits hardest."
    The five boats in question belonged
    first to Yoshitsune himself,
    then to Tashiro no Kanja,
    to Gotōbyōe, father and son,
    to the two brothers Kaneko,
    and to Yodo no Gōnai Tadatoshi,
    who had brought the fleet together.
    Yoshitsune instructed them,
    "Light no flares aboard your boats.
    I will lead in mine. Keep an eye
    on those lit at my bow and stern.
    Too many fires and the enemy
    will be alarmed and stand on guard."
    They ran all night, and a crossing
    that should have taken them three days
    took them instead a mere six hours.
    It was the sixteenth of the second month
    when, at the hour of the ox, they left [ca. 2 A.M.]

Watanabe and Fukushima[257]
and daybreak, at the hour of the hare, [ca. 6 A.M.]
when, gale-borne, they reached the Awa coast.

2. Katsu-ura and Ōzaka Pass

Day dawned. A few red banners fluttered along the beach.
"Oh, no!" Yoshitsune cried. "They have a welcome for us!
We'll make easy targets if we tip the boats to disembark the horses.
No, get the horses off before we come to the beach,
tie them to the boats, and make them swim alongside.
Once they have footing to keep the lower edge of the saddle dry,
then, gentlemen, mount them and charge!"
    What with all the arms and provisions,
    those five boats carried just fifty horses.
    When they came within reach of the shore,
    the men threw themselves into the saddle
    and with fierce battle cries attacked.
    The hundred riders on the beach
    could not muster a moment's resistance
    and fell back a good two hundred yards.

Yoshitsune paused on the beach to let his mount catch its breath. Then he summoned Ise no Saburō Yoshimori and said, "Some of those men over there must be worth something. Get one over here. I have some questions for him."

Yoshimori respectfully complied. All alone he galloped in among the enemy and managed to persuade one, a man of about forty in black-laced armor, to doff his helmet, loosen his bowstring, and come with him back to the Genji commander.

"Who is this?" Yoshitsune asked.

"A local, sir, from Banzai," Yoshimori replied. "His name is Kondōroku Chikaie."

"Fine. Never mind his name. Don't disarm him. He's going to guide us to Yashima. And don't let him out of your sight. If he makes a run for it, gentlemen, shoot him!"

"What is the name of this place?" Yoshitsune asked.

"Katsu-ura," the man replied.

Yoshitsune laughed. The name sounded like "Victory Beach."

....

257. The harbor of Fukushima adjoined Watanabe.

"Why, I'm flattered!" he said.

"It really is Katsu-ura, sir. People here call it 'Katsura,' because that is easier to say, but it is written with the two characters *katsu* and *ura*."

"Listen to this, gentlemen!" Yoshitsune exclaimed.

"Here I am, on my way to fight, and I land at Victory Beach!
How is that for a good omen? By the way,
are there any Heike sympathizers around to shoot arrows after us?"

"Yes, sir, there is Sakuraba no Suke Yoshitō,
the younger brother of Awa no Minbu Shigeyoshi."

"Then let's get him out of the way first."

Yoshitsune chose thirty riders from Kondōroku's hundred and added them to
his men.

> Descending on Yoshitō's redoubt,
> they found a marsh bordering three sides
> and a fosse the fourth. Across the fosse
> they therefore attacked with ringing cries.
> The warriors within the redoubt
> loosed on them a shower of arrows,
> which the men of the Genji ignored.
> Heads low, protected by neck plates,
> they pressed their assault, howling for war.
> Yoshitō must have seen he was lost.
> Under cover of his men's arrows,
> he mounted a chosen sturdy steed
> and barely managed to escape.
> Yoshitsune decapitated
> twenty of the defending archers
> and offered their heads to the god of war.
> Then he uttered a shout of triumph.

"A good start, that!" he declared.

He summoned Kondōroku Chikaie.

"How many do the Heike have at Yashima?" he asked.

"Surely no more than a thousand horse."

"Why so few?"

"Because they have stationed small garrisons of fifty or a hundred, like ours,
all along the Shikoku coast and on the islands.
Besides which, Dennaizaemon Noriyoshi, Shigeyoshi's eldest son,
has led three thousand horse over into Iyo,
to attack Kawano no Shirō for failing to answer a rallying call."

"So the timing is perfect. And from here to Yashima, how far?"

"Two days' march, sir."

"Then attack before they find out we're here!"

Now at a gallop, now at a walk, now cantering, now resting,

they spent the night crossing Ōzaka Pass, between Awa and Sanuki.

During the night Yoshitsune found himself on the path beside a letter bearer and struck up a conversation with him. The man never guessed in the dark that he was talking to an enemy. He spoke freely, probably assuming that these warriors were on their way to join the Heike at Yashima.

"And that letter—who is it for?" Yoshitsune asked.

"Lord Munemori at Yashima," the man replied.

"Who's it from?"

"A gentlewoman in the capital."

"What does it say?"

"Nothing much, as far as I can see. She just mentions that the Genji have reached the mouth of the Yodo River and are now launching their boats."

"No doubt they are. We're on our way for Yashima, too, but we don't know exactly how to get there. You must show us."

"Oh, yes, I go there a lot. I know the way. I'll accompany you."

"Take that letter off him!" Yoshitsune commanded. It was done. "Tie him up! Don't take his head, though. That would be wrong."

So there in the mountain wilderness, they tied the man to a tree and went on their way. Yoshitsune opened the letter and read it. Yes, it did seem to be from a gentlewoman:

"Kurō Yoshitsune is crafty.

He will attack, I know he will,

however high the wind and the waves.

Take care not to disperse your forces!"

Yoshitsune said after he read this,

"Why, this is a blessing from heaven!

I want Yoritomo to see it too!"

He put it away in a safe place.

The next day, the eighteenth, at the hour of the tiger, [ca. 4 A.M.]

they came down to a spot called Hiketa in the province of Sanuki.

There they rested their horses before pressing on,

past Niū-no-ya and Shirotori, toward the fortress of Yashima.

Again Yoshitsune summoned Kondōroku.

"Tell me about the Heike quarters at Yashima," he said.

"Apparently, sir, you do not realize that the sea there is very shallow.

Left panel: Musashibō Benkei (upper left) guards Yoshitsune while the letter is read. Right panel: The messenger tied to a tree.

At low tide you can ride out to the island and not even wet your horse's belly."[258]
"Fine!" Yoshitsune exclaimed. "Then attack at once!"
He set fire to the houses of Takamatsu and bore down on the Yashima
    stronghold.
At Yashima, Dennaizaemon Noriyoshi was back from his foray into Iyo,
with his three thousand horse,
to punish Kawano no Shirō for failing to answer the call.
Having missed his man, he had beheaded instead over one hundred and fifty
    Kawano housemen
and brought the heads back to the emperor's Yashima palace.
"Rebel heads may not be inspected in the palace." Such was the decision,
and the inspection therefore took place at the residence of Lord Munemori.
The heads numbered one hundred and fifty-six.
During the inspection a clamor arose: "Takamatsu is burning!"
"This is no accident, not in daytime," Munemori stated.
"It must be an enemy attack. They fired the houses on purpose.
There must be a lot of them. We cannot allow ourselves to be surrounded.

....

258. Yashima was then an island separated from the mainland by a narrow passage of sea, most of which
is now filled in.

Hurry! Get out to sea as fast as you can!"
The boats stood moored along the beach before the main gate.
Everyone hastened to board them.

> Onto the imperial barge
> rushed Kenreimon-in, the regent's wife,
> Lady Nii, and their gentlewomen.
> Lord Munemori and his son[259]
> boarded one of the boats together.
> The others took whatever they could
> and rowed out a good hundred yards
> in some cases, in others less.
> Meanwhile the Genji warriors—
> seventy or eighty, fully armed—
> burst onto the beach before the main gate.
> The tide at the time was all the way out,
> down that gently shelving stretch of shore.
> In places the water rose no higher
> than a horse's hocks or belly,
> and here and there it was shallower still.
> The spray kicked up by the dashing hooves
> glittered through the prevailing mist,
> from which emerged streaming white banners
> that to the Heike meant a great host
> had come to finish them off forever.
> To make sure that the Heike never guessed
> how few men he really had with him,
> Yoshitsune had them advance
> in small groups: five or six, eight or ten.

3. *The Death of Tsuginobu*

Kurō Yoshitsune wore that day a *hitatare* of red brocade
under armor with purple lacing, lighter above and darker below.
Gold fittings adorned the sword at his side,
and arrows fletched with mottled feathers rose from the quiver at his back.
Gripping his rattan-wrapped bow, he announced in a great voice,

> "You see before you the messenger
> sent by His Cloistered Eminence,
> police lieutenant of the fifth rank,

....

259. Kiyomune.

Minamoto no Yoshitsune!"
Thus he declared his name.

    Those who did so after him included Tashiro no Kanja Nobutsuna,
    from Izu; Kaneko no Jūrō Ietada and Yoichi Chikanori, from Musashi;
    and Ise no Saburō Yoshimori.

These were the next to announce their names:

    Gotōbyōe Sanemoto;
    his son, Shinbyōe Motokiyo;
    Satō Saburōbyōe Tsuginobu
    and Satō Shirōbyōe Tadanobu,
    both from Mutsu;
    Eda no Genzō, Kumai Tarō;
    and Musashibō Benkei.

The cry went up from the Heike: "Shoot them!"
Some boats arced arrows in from afar;
some shot them straight from closer range.
The Genji warriors loosed them left
as they charged past or loosed them right,
rested their horses behind beached boats,
and with fierce cries pursued the fight.
Gotōbyōe Sanemoto, a seasoned old fighter, avoided the fray
to burst instead into the palace, where he lit many fires.
The smoke had hardly risen before the building burned to the ground.
Munemori mustered his men.
"How many Genji are there, really?" he asked.
"At present, my lord, only seventy or eighty."
"How awful! We have more than enough
to deal with this enemy even one hair at a time!
It is a painful thought that instead of surrounding and killing them all,
we fled in panic to our boats and let them burn the emperor's palace!
Lord Noritsune, are you present? Please take the fight to them on land."
"Certainly," Noritsune replied.
He and Etchū no Jirōbyōe Moritsugi boarded a small boat
and landed on the beach by the burned-out main gate.
Yoshitsune and his eighty men kept their distance a bowshot away.
Moritsugi stood in the boat's open bow and shouted,

    "I did hear you announce your names,
    but I was a long way out at sea,
    too far to catch them properly!

Who today commands this Genji force?"
Ise Yoshimori stepped forward to answer, "Who do you think?

Lord Kurō Yoshitsune, of course,
tenth-generation descendant of Emperor Seiwa,
younger brother to Yoritomo, Lord of Kamakura!"
"Oh, yes, I know him!" Moritsugi answered.
"The boy orphaned when his father got killed, back during the Heiji Conflict,
and kept as a temple pet at Kurama.
Then he served a gold peddler—
carried the man's food and gear for him all the way down to Mutsu.
That's the young fellow you mean?"

> Yoshimori retorted, "How dare you, with that slick tongue of yours,
> speak so of my lord? Oh, yes, I know who you people are: the ones who
> barely saved your skins in the battle at Mount Tonami, then fled north
> and begged your way, crying, back to the capital!"

> Moritsugi retorted, "Our lord's generous bounty could *never* have
> reduced us to beggary! Oh, no, *you're* the ones who lived off banditry—
> you, your wives, and your children—in the Suzuka mountains of Ise.
> That's what I've heard."

> "Gentlemen, this empty war of words leads nowhere," Kaneko
> Ietada broke in. "Anyone, on either side, could spout the same non-
> sense. You saw well enough, last spring at Ichi-no-tani, what the young
> warriors from Musashi and Sagami can do."

He was still speaking when his younger brother Yoichi, beside him,
drew an arrow twelve handbreadths and two fingers long,
and let fly with a mighty twang.
It pierced Moritsugi's breastplate and sank into the flesh beyond.
That put an end to the war of words.

> Noritsune wore no *hitatare*,
> preferring, for battle at sea,
> to wear a tie-dyed *kosode* robe
> under Chinese damask-laced armor,
> with at his side a long, daunting sword.
> The twenty-four arrows in his quiver
> boasted gray-mottled eagle feathers,
> and he bore a rattan-wrapped bow.
> He was the capital's mightiest archer:
> No man caught in range of his arrows
> escaped having one pierce him through.
> The target he aimed to hit this time
> was Yoshitsune, but the Genji
> knew very well what he was up to.
> Satō Tsuginobu and Tadanobu,

Ise Yoshimori, Eda no Genzō,
Genpachi Hirotsuna, Kumai Tarō,
Musashibō Benkei—every one
a man worthy to face a thousand—
raced to ride before their commander,
bridle to bridle, so as to block
any arrow sent flying toward him.
Yoshitsune was beyond reach.
"Out of the way!" Noritsune cried.
"You servant rabble, give me a clear shot!"
He loosed a furious volley of arrows
that unhorsed ten men in full armor—
one, the man stationed farthest forward:
Satō Tsuginobu, from Mutsu.
The arrow struck his left shoulder
and went through to his right side.
He crashed headlong from his mount.

Kikuō, Noritsune's outstandingly strong and brave page, wore
green-laced armor and a helmet with a three-plate neckpiece. He
unsheathed his halberd, one with a plain shaft, and rushed forward

Noritsune shoots Tsuginobu. (The text has Noritsune on a boat, not a rock.)

to take Tsuginobu's head. To save it, the fallen man's older brother,
Tadanobu, loosed a powerful shot that went straight through
Kikuō and came out where his armor joined in the back. Kikuō
collapsed.

The sight brought Noritsune at one bound from his boat, his bow in his left
hand.

With his right he lifted Kikuō and tossed him aboard,

so that even if Kikuō died of his wound, the enemy never got his head.

Kikuō had once been a page to Michimori,

but he came to serve Noritsune, the younger brother, after Michimori was killed.

He was in his eighteenth year.

Noritsune gave up the fight, deeply affected by this loss.

Yoshitsune had Tsuginobu carried to the rear of the Genji position.

There he dismounted and took Tsuginobu's hands.

"How are you feeling?" he asked.

Under his breath Tsuginobu replied, "It is all over for me, my lord."

"Tell me, have you any regrets?"

"None at all, my lord. Why should I?

But I am sorry that I must die

before you rise high in the world.

Otherwise I have always known,

as do we all who wield the bow,

that every arrow could bring death.

More than anything else, though, for a warrior such as I,

it is the crowning honor of my life that in generations to come,

people should be able to say of one Satō Tsuginobu, from Mutsu,

that he died to save his lord on the shore at Yashima."

With these words the last of his strength failed.

Yoshitsune shed bitter tears.

"Is there no holy priest nearby?" he asked. They managed to find one.

"A wounded man has just died," Yoshitsune told him.

"For the comfort of his soul, I want the full Lotus Sutra copied in a day."[260]

He gave him a powerful black horse with a gold-trimmed saddle.

When Yoshitsune got the fifth rank,

he had awarded this steed the same

and dubbed him Commissioner Black.

This was the horse he chose to ride

at Ichi-no-tani, in the descent

down the steep Hiyodori Ravine.

....

260. *Ichinichikyō*, a particular form of intense Lotus Sutra devotion.

The slain man's brother, Tadanobu,
and every other man present wept.
"Any man would be only too glad
to give up his life for such a lord."

4. *Nasu no Yoichi*

While all this was going on, men of Awa and Sanuki,
once Heike allies but now at Genji disposal—
fourteen or fifteen at a time, or as many as twenty—
came drifting in from scattered peaks and hollows
until soon Yoshitsune commanded over three hundred horse.
"The sun is low," he remarked.
"Too little day is left to decide victory or defeat."
He was just drawing his men back when, from farther out at sea,
a prettily decorated boat came rowing in toward land.
Some hundred yards out, it turned broadside to the shore.
All were wondering what it was up to when a stunning girl, not yet twenty,
wearing a fivefold "willow" layering[261] and a red *hakama* divided skirt,
came to the side and planted there, upright, a red fan bearing a sun disk.
She then beckoned toward the land.

> Yoshitsune summoned Gotōbyōe Sanemoto. "What does she want?"
> he asked.
>> "She seems to want us to shoot the fan. But I suspect that the idea
>> is really to tempt you, our commander, into range for a better look at
>> her and then have some sturdy fellow bring you down with an arrow.
>> Anyhow, you should probably have someone shoot the fan."
>> "And who among us is up to that?"
>> "We have many fine archers, but the best of them is probably Nasu
>> no Yoichi Munetaka from Shimōsa, a son of Nasu no Tarō Suketaka.
>> He is short but very good."

"How do you know?" Yoshitsune asked.
"Whenever they go shooting birds on the wing, he hits two out of three."
"Very well, bring him here." Sanemoto did so.

> Yoichi, then in his twentieth year,
> was wearing a dark blue *hitatare*
> trimmed, collar and sleeves, with red brocade
> under green-laced armor. His sword
> hung at his side from a silver ring,

261. A "willow" layering consisted of white over green, here repeated five times.

and the few arrows that the day's clashes
had left him lifted their eagle feathers,
black-and-white-banded, over his head,
in company with a humming arrow
fletched from both eagle and hawk,
and tipped with deer horn. Under his arm
he clasped a lacquered, rattan-wrapped bow,
and his helmet hung over his back.
With every mark of deep respect,
he knelt before Yoshitsune.
"Now, Yoichi, I want you to score a bull's-eye on that fan
and show the Heike a thing or two."
Yoichi made bold to reply, "But, sir, I am not sure that I *can* hit it,
and if I miss, the shame will be ours forever.
Please give someone else this task—someone more likely to succeed."
Yoshitsune retorted in fury,
        "No man come to the west with me,
    all the way from Kamakura,
    may decline when I give an order!
            Any backchat from anyone and I want the man gone!"
            Yoichi must have thought better of refusing a second time. "I may
    or may not miss, sir," he said, "but I will try, since you wish it."
            He withdrew from his commander's presence. Mounting a power-
    ful black horse with a tasseled crupper and a saddle inlaid with a sea-
    squirt motif in mother-of-pearl, he got a good grip on his bow, drew in
    the reins, and started toward the edge of the water.
            His fellows watched him from a distance. "He'll do it, I know he
    will!" they were saying, and Yoshitsune, too, seemed sure that he
    would.
The fan was so far away that Yoichi rode out thirty or forty feet,
but from there it still looked a good hundred yards off.
        It was the eighteenth of the second month,
    the hour of the cock—very late in the day— [ca. 6 P.M.]
    and a strong north wind was blowing.
    High waves were breaking on the beach.
    The drifting boat tossed up and down,
    the fan kept fluttering on its pole.
    The sea was dark with Heike boats
    gathered to watch, while on the shore
    the Genji gazed out, bridle to bridle.
    Both sides seemed in a festive mood.

With one hand Yoichi covered his eyes
and silently prayed the following prayer:
"Hail Hachiman, Great Bodhisattva,
and you, gods of my home province,
Nikkō Gongen of Utsunomiya,
Yuzen Daimyōjin of Nasu,
I beg of you, guide my arrow
to hit the center of that fan!
For should the arrow miss its mark,
I shall break my bow and die,
nor ever again face any man.
If you wish me to return,
let this arrow of mine strike home!"
Once more he opened his eyes.
The wind had dropped just a little;
the fan looked easier to hit.
He took out his humming arrow,
put it to the string, and let fly.
Small as he was, it was still long—
twelve full handbreadths and three fingers—

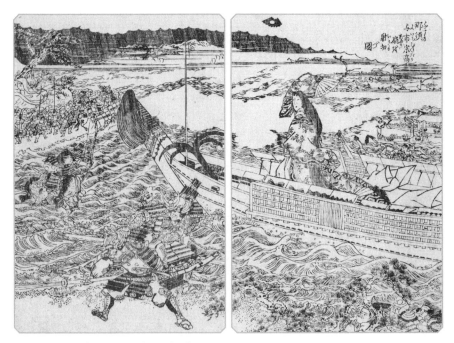

Nasu no Yoichi's arrow hits the fan.

and he drew a strong man's bow.
The arrow's song rang out afar.
Unerringly, it struck the fan
an inch above the pivot pin
and flew straight on into the sea.
The fan shot up into the air,
fluttered there a moment or two,
then, buffeted by the spring wind,
dropped to the water with a splash.
The waning sunset's slanting rays
lit the red fan, with its sun disk,
adrift on the white-foaming waves,
bobbing high and low. The Heike,
out at sea, in admiration
pounded the gunwales of their boats,
while on shore the delighted Genji
beat on their quivers a sharp tattoo.

5. *The Dropped Bow*

So spectacular was the hit that a man of fifty or so,
no doubt swept away by a wave of enthusiasm,
emerged from amidships in his black leather-laced armor, plain-wood halberd
    in hand,
to dance about where the fan had stood.
Ise no Saburō Yoshimori rode up behind Yoichi.
"An order from our commander," he announced. "Shoot him."
Yoichi took the next arrow from his quiver, put it to the string,
drew, and sent it thudding into the man's neck.
The fellow toppled headlong to the bottom of the boat.
Dead silence fell on the Heike side.
The Genji again beat their quivers.
        "Got him!" cried some, and others,
        "Just plain cruel, I'd call it!"
The Heike can hardly have been pleased,
for now three of their warriors emerged on the shore,
one wielding a shield, one bearing a bow, one brandishing a halberd.
The one with the shield planted it on the ground and shouted,
"All right, come and get us!"
"Fine!" said Yoshitsune. "Go, you young roughriders, clear them out!"
Five men—Mionoya no Shirō, Tōshichi, and Jūrō, from Musashi,

Niū no Shirō from Kōzuke, Kiso no Chūji from Shinano—
charged with fierce cries. From behind the shield,
a lacquered, black-fletched arrow buried itself to the nock
in the chest of Mionoya's charging horse, on the left side, near the breast collar.

> The horse fell like a flattened screen.
> The rider swung his right leg over,
> so as to alight to his left,
> and drew his sword. From behind the shield,
> a Heike halberd came at him—
> too dangerous, he must have felt,
> to try to counter with his short sword,
> for he made himself small and fled.
> The attacker raced in pursuit.

The halberd looked poised to fell him,
but no—the attacker instead clasped it under his left arm,
stretched out his right hand, and reached for Mionoya's helmet neckpiece.
Mionoya ran for all he was worth, to keep the hand off it.
Three times the attacker missed, but he got a good grip on the fourth.
The neckpiece held until Mionoya tore it loose from the helmet and got away.
To save their horses, the other four riders just watched.
Mionoya hid behind one to catch his breath.
The pursuer stopped, leaned on his halberd, raised his neckpiece, and shouted,

> "You will have heard of me by now,
> and here I am, before your eyes:
> the one I hear the youth of the city
> call Akushichibyōe Kagekiyo
> the hard man from Kazusa!"

> Heartened, the Heike cried, "Don't let them get Akushichibyōe! Forward, men! Stay with him!"

> Two hundred came up on the beach, their shields overlapping like chicken feathers. "All right, you Genji, try us!" they shouted.

> "I don't like this," Yoshitsune observed. He gave the lead to Gotōbyōe, father and son, and to the Kaneko brothers; posted Satō Shirōbyōe from Mutsu and Ise Yoshimori to his left and right; assigned Tashiro Nobutsuna to his rear; and charged with eighty fiercely yelling men. The enemy were not mounted, most being foot soldiers. They drew back for fear that the horses might trample them and reboarded their vessels.

Yoshitsune's men scattered the shields far and wide, like counting sticks.
Then, flushed with victory, they rode their horses belly-deep into the water, to
    fight on.

While Yoshitsune sallied forth deeper still,
men on the surrounding boats reached for his neckpiece with grappling hooks
and caught it several times, but with sword and halberd
his own warriors managed each time to knock the hook away.
Then, somehow, one snagged Yoshitsune's bow, and he dropped it into the sea.
He bent down and tried several times to retrieve it with his whip.
"Let it go, let it go!" his men cried,
but he got it back in the end and returned, laughing, to the beach.
The older warriors snapped their fingers in disapproval.
"You should not have done that, sir!" they protested.
"How could you possibly trade your life for a bow, whatever its value in coins?"
"It was not the bow I wanted," Yoshitsune replied.

>"If mine, like my uncle Tametomo's,
>took two or three men merely to string it,
>I might have dropped it for them on purpose.
>But with their hands on this weak little bow,
>they would have laughed: 'Why, just look at that!
>This is the bow he draws, Yoshitsune,
>the man who commands the Genji force!'
>No, I could not allow that to happen.
>That is why I risked my life for it."
>His words deeply impressed them all.

Meanwhile the sun had set.
The Heike rode in their boats, offshore,
while the Genji withdrew to camp for the night
on the heights between Mure and Takamatsu.
They had had no rest for the last three days.
Two days past, they had left Watanabe and Fukushima,
only to spend a sleepless night buffeted by rough seas.
The day before, they had fought a skirmish at Katsu-ura,
then spent the night crossing the mountains
toward another whole day of fighting.
Every one of them was exhausted.
Some pillowed their heads on their helmets, others on their armor or quiver,
and there they all lay, dead to the world.

>Only two men, Yoshitsune
>and Yoshimori, did not sleep.
>The first went up to a high place
>to keep a lookout for the enemy;
>the second went to lurk in a hollow,
>to shoot enemy mounts in the belly.

The Heike meanwhile gave Noritsune
a force of five hundred mounted men
to strike the Genji that very night,
but there arose between Moritsugi
and Emi no Jirō Morikata
a quarrel over which would lead.
The night went to waste, and dawn came.
Had they managed that night attack,
they would have finished the Genji.
That they did not made it all too clear
that the Heike had had their day.

6. The Clash at Shido

At dawn the Heike boarded their boats and rowed to Shido Bay, also in Sanuki.
From among his three hundred, Yoshitsune chose eighty men and horses to
    pursue them.
Noting how few they were, the Heike set out to surround and dispatch them.
A thousand men stormed up on the shore and attacked, uttering fierce cries.
Then they saw the two hundred left at Yashima galloping their way.
"Oh, no," they cried, "they have a whole Genji army right behind them!
There must be tens of thousands of them! We can't let ourselves be surrounded!"
They boarded their boats once more.

So it was that the Heike fled
at the whim of wind and tide.
They had no idea where to go.
Yoshitsune had driven them
from the whole island of Shikoku,
and Kyushu, too, was closed to them.
They were like souls caught in the bardo.
There, on the shore of Shido Bay,
Yoshitsune got down from his horse
to inspect the heads of the slain.
He summoned Ise Yoshimori.
"Dennaizaemon Noriyoshi,"
he said, "the son of Shigeyoshi,
went after Kawano no Shirō
because Kawano ignored his call.
He crossed with three thousand horse into Iyo,
missed Kawano himself, and instead
took one hundred and fifty heads

from his housemen and retainers.
All those heads arrived yesterday
at the palace at Yashima,
and today, or so I am told,
Noriyoshi is on his way here.
So go and meet him on the road,
make up whatever story you please,
and bring him back with you, straight to me."
Yoshimori promised to do so.
Flying the banner that his lord gave him,
he galloped off with just sixteen men,
every one of them dressed in white.
By and by he met Noriyoshi.
The red banners and the white
stopped some two hundred yards apart.

Yoshimori sent a man to Noriyoshi with this message: "I am Ise no Saburō Yoshimori, a close associate of the Genji commander, Kurō Yoshitsune. I have come to meet you because I bear a message. My presence here has nothing to do with battle, and my men and I are therefore unarmed. We have neither bows nor arrows. Please allow us passage though your men."

The three thousand warriors made way for him.

Yoshimori came up beside Noriyoshi. "As you probably know," he began, "Kurō Yoshitsune, the younger brother of Lord Yoritomo in Kamakura, has received from the cloistered emperor a decree charging him with destroying the Heike, and that mission has brought him to Shikoku. The day before yesterday, he landed at Katsu-ura in Awa, where your uncle, Sakuraba no Suke, was killed. Yesterday he attacked Yashima, burned the emperor's palace, and captured Lord Munemori and his son. Lord Noritsune killed himself. The other Heike nobles died on the field or drowned themselves in the sea. Your father surrendered and has been placed in my custody. 'Alas,' he keeps lamenting. 'Noriyoshi knows nothing about this, and tomorrow he is certain to die in battle. It is too hard!' I pitied him enough to come forward to warn you. Whether you now die in the fight or surrender and see your father again, that is entirely up to you."

Noriyoshi, a renowned warrior, must nonetheless have been out of luck, because he said, "That is just what I have heard." He removed his helmet, unstrung his bow, and gave them to one of his men to carry. Once their commander had done so, his three thousand riders did the same.

Yoshimori and his mere sixteen men returned with the meek captives.
"What a marvelous ploy!" Yoshitsune exclaimed, lost in admiration.

> Noriyoshi was made at once
> to give up his arms and armor:
> Yoshimori took charge of them.
> "But what about all the others?"
> Yoshitsune wanted to know.
> "Men from such remote provinces,"
> Yoshimori replied, "hardly care
> what leader's orders they follow,
> as long as he suppresses trouble
> and succeeds in imposing peace."
> That sounded so reasonable
> that Yoshitsune simply added
> the three thousand to his own men.

On the twenty-second of the month, at the hour of the dragon, [ca. 8 A.M.]
the two hundred or so boats that had remained behind at Watanabe
reached the Yashima coast, Kajiwara's in the lead.
"Kurō Yoshitsune has conquered all of Shikoku," the men already there
remarked, chuckling.
"Who needs Kajiwara? He's as useless as altar flowers picked too late for the rite,
a sweet-flag root the day after the festival, a stave once the quarrel is over."

> After Yoshitsune left the capital,
Nagamori, the chief priest of the Sumiyoshi Shrine,
went to the cloistered emperor's residence.
There, through Yasutsune, the lord of the Treasury, he reported as follows:
"On the sixteenth just past, at the hour of the boar, the sound of a humming
arrow [ca. 10 P.M.]
issued from the shrine's third sanctuary and sped off westward."
Deeply impressed, the sovereign offered Sumiyoshi, through Nagamori,
a sword and many other sacred treasures.

> When Empress Jingū attacked Silla,
> the rough spirits of two deities
> came from Ise to spearhead her progress.
> They posted themselves at bow and stern,
> and Silla fell without difficulty.
> On the journey back to Japan,
> one of these deities stayed behind
> at Sumiyoshi in Settsu province:
> This was Sumiyoshi no Daimyōjin.
> The other preferred to fix his seat

at Suwa in the province of Shinano:
This was Suwa no Daimyōjin.
The sovereign, who had not forgotten
the triumph of this punitive campaign,
felt sure that the deities, even now,
would crush the enemies of the court.
His officials shared his confidence.

7. The Cockfights and the Battle at Dan-no-ura

Kurō Yoshitsune pushed straight on from Shido Bay
across the sea to the province of Suō,
where he linked forces with Noriyori, his elder brother.
Meanwhile the Heike reached Hikushima in the province of Nagato.
Now, the Genji had landed at Katsu-ura in Awa
and then gone on to defeat the Heike forces at Yashima.
Strangely enough, the Heike had fled to a place with *hiku*, "retreat," in its name,
while the Genji stopped at Oitsu, "Chaseport," in the same province.
Tanzō, superintendent of Kumano, owed the Heike a great deal,
but now he forgot all that to dwell on this sudden dilemma:
"Should I join the Heike or would I do better to join the Genji?"
He offered *kagura* at the Imagumano Shrine in Tanabe and prayed to the god.
The oracle told him to follow the white banners.
Still in doubt, before the shrine he pitted seven white cocks against seven red.
Not a single red cock won. All seven lost.
That decided it: He went over to the Genji.

    Mustering all the men of his house,
    Tanzō gathered two thousand horse.
    They sailed aboard two hundred vessels.
    At his prow rode Nyakuōji,[262]
    present in his sacred substance;
    his banner bore the name Kongō Dōji.
    As his boat approached Dan-no-ura,
    Genji and Heike both bowed low,
    but the Heike could only despair
    when his fleet went to join the Genji.
    Then Kawano no Shirō Michinobu,
    the man from Iyo, came rowing up

....

262. One of the Kumano Hongū divinities. Tanzō's ship carries the divinity's *mishōtai*, or *shintai:* the object in which the divine presence inheres.

with one hundred and fifty war craft,
and he, too, swelled the might of the Genji.
Yoshitsune saw things going his way.
The Genji had three thousand vessels
and the Heike a mere one thousand,
a few of them large, in Chinese style.
So the Genji strength only grew,
while that of the Heike dwindled.

    Genryaku 2, [1185] third month and twenty-fourth day, the hour of the hare: [ca. 6 A.M.] The Genji and Heike exchanged opening arrows in the strait between Moji-no-seki in Buzen and Akama-no-seki in Nagato. Yoshitsune and Kajiwara Kagetoki had already nearly come to blows.

    Kajiwara said to Yoshitsune, "Let me go first into battle today."

    "If I were somewhere else, fine," Yoshitsune replied, "but I am here."

    Kajiwara retorted, "That is not right. You are our commander, sir, after all."

    "Absolutely not," Yoshitsune retorted. "Our commander is Lord Yoritomo in Kamakura. I am his agent and follow his orders, just like the rest of you."

His hope of going first dashed, Kajiwara muttered,
"This lord lacks what it takes to be a leader of men!"
Yoshitsune heard him. "You are the biggest fool in Japan!"
he snapped, and put his hand to his sword.
Kajiwara replied, "I take orders from Lord Yoritomo himself, no one else!"
He, too, reached for his sword.

    Kajiwara's three sons moved to him:
Kagesue, Kagetaka, and Kageie.
Seeing the threat to Yoshitsune,
Satō Tadanobu, Ise Yoshimori,
Genpachi Hirotsuna, Eda no Genzō,
Kumai Tarō, and Musashibō Benkei—
each man ready to face a thousand—
came at Kajiwara from all sides,
each eager to kill his lord's enemy.

    Miura no Suke, however,
rushed to Yoshitsune's side,
while Doi no Jirō clung to Kajiwara.
Both, rubbing their hands in supplication,
begged the two men to desist.
"With such a crucial battle before us," they protested,
"a fight between our commanders would only strengthen the Heike!

It would be a disaster for the news to reach Lord Yoritomo!"
Yoshitsune calmed down, and Kajiwara could not pursue the matter.
Thereafter Kajiwara so hated Yoshitsune that his slander destroyed him.
Meanwhile some two miles of sea separated Genji and Heike.
The tide was ebbing fast past Moji, Akama, and Dan-no-ura,
against the course of the Genji fleet, which it swept steadily backward.
The Heike fleet came down on the Genji with the tide.

> Out in the strait, the flow was so strong
> that Kajiwara hugged the shore,
> thus crossing paths with a Heike boat,
> which his men caught with a grappling hook.
> Old and young, they all boarded it
> and with their blades, bow and stern,
> laid about them mercilessly,
> so that they gathered many trophies.
> In the list of exploits that day,
> theirs figured first of all.

At last the contending sides clashed, with thunderous battle cries
that must have reached the Brahma Heaven above
and alarmed, below, the Dragon King of the sea.
Lord Tomomori stood on the cabin of his boat and announced in a great voice,

> "Today's battle will be our last!
> Men, banish all thought of retreat!
> Never have India or China,
> never has our land of Japan
> seen the like of our warriors,
> yet our days of glory are over,
> and nothing can remedy that.

>> But you still have honor to uphold. Show the men from the east no weakness. Saving your skins will gain you nothing. That is all you need remember."

>> "Heed your commander, gentlemen!" Hida no Saburōzaemon Kagetsune, from beside him, confirmed his order.

>> Akushichibyōe of Kazusa came forward. "Warriors from the Kanto talk fast on horseback," he declared, "but when did they ever learn naval combat? They might as well be fish and climb trees! So catch them now, every one, and throw them back in the sea!"

>> Etchū no Jirōbyōe Moritsugi remarked, "In fact, you might as well go after Kurō Yoshitsune himself. He's a pale, scrawny fellow with buckteeth. He may be hard to make out, though, because he keeps changing his *hitatare* and armor."

"He's a fighter," Akushichibyōe added, "but he's too small to bother
anyone. I'll just clap him under my arm and throw him in."
After issuing his command, Tomomori came before Lord Munemori.
He said, "The men seem to be in fine fettle today,
but that Shigeyoshi from Awa looks as though he may have betrayed us.
I would gladly cut off his head."
"How *could* you?" Munemori objected. "I see no reason to suspect him.
He has always given us loyal service."
He summoned Shigeyoshi, who appeared before him
in a tan *hitatare* under armor laced with white leather.
"Tell me, Shigeyoshi," Munemori asked, "have you turned against us?
You do not look that lively today.
Order the Shikoku men to fight well. Are you afraid?"
"Certainly not, my lord," Shigeyoshi replied, and withdrew.
"Oh, yes," Tomomori said to himself, "how I want that man's head!"
Gripping his sword hilt hard enough almost to crush it,
he glanced time after time at Lord Munemori,
but Munemori never allowed him to act. He had to give up.

    The Heike split their thousand vessels
    into three: The first group, under
    Yamaga no Hyōdōji Hidetō,
    rowed forward with five hundred boats;
    the second followed, a good three hundred
    manned by those of the Matsura League;
    and the third, behind with two hundred,
    carried the scions of the Heike.
    No warrior in all of Kyushu
    could match Hyōdōji Hidetō,
    who had picked to accompany him
    five hundred less elite warriors.
    These he stationed from prow to stern
    shoulder to shoulder, all in a line,
    to loose five hundred arrows at once.
    The Genji, with their three thousand boats,
    had the clear advantage of numbers,
    but with such a barrage of arrows
    coming at them from all directions,
    they could not see where the best archers were.
    Their commander, Kurō Yoshitsune,
    fought at the head of all his men,
    but it was too much: No shield or armor

could withstand so fierce an onslaught,
which took its toll—the Genji buckled.
The Heike, now sure of victory,
beat their war drums, shouting with joy.

8. Long-Distance Arrows

One of the Genji, Wada no Kotarō Yoshimori, never boarded a boat at all
but lurked instead on the beach. A groom carried his helmet.
Feet thrust hard into the stirrups, he loosed from his mightily drawn bow
arrows that missed no target in a range of some three hundred yards.
One flew especially far, and he waved to the enemy out there,
as much as to say, "I'll have that arrow back!"
Tomomori called for it and looked it over.
The plain shaft, fletched with goose and black-tipped crane feathers,
was thirteen handbreadths and two fingers long.
A handbreadth from the tip, it bore Yoshimori's name, written in lacquer.
Few among the many fine Heike archers seem to have been expert at a great
  distance,
and it took some time to find Nii no Kishirō Chikakiyo, from Iyo.
Tomomori summoned him and gave him the arrow to shoot back.
It flew the three hundred yards to the shore and hit Miura no Ishizakon no
  Tarō,
well beyond Yoshimori, squarely in the upper left arm.
"And Yoshimori thought nobody could shoot as far as he!" The Miura men laughed.
"He'll have to think again. Just look at him—he's so embarrassed!"
Yoshimori heard this and did not like it one bit.
He got into a boat, had it rowed out to sea,
and sent the Heike a volley of arrows that killed or wounded many.

> Another arrow with a plain shaft hit Yoshitsune's boat from out at sea,
> accompanied, like Wada's, with gestures signifying "Please return."
> Yoshitsune pulled it out for a look. Fletched with pheasant tail feath-
> ers, it was fourteen handbreadths and three fingers long and inscribed
> with the name "Nii no Kishirō Chikakiyo, of Iyo."
>
> Yoshitsune summoned Gotōbyōe Sanemoto. "Do we have a man
> able to shoot this arrow back?" he asked.
>
> "Asari no Yoichi of the Kai Genji, sir: He is your man."
>
> "Call him here, then," Yoshitsune replied.

Asari no Yoichi arrived.
"This arrow came from out at sea," Yoshitsune explained,
"and the archer is defying us to return it. Can you do that?"

"Allow me a look at it, sir."

He took one end in each hand and flexed the shaft to test strength and
    straightness.

"The arrow is a little weak and, I would say, a little short.

I might as well use one of my own."

The lacquered bow he carried, closely rattan-wound, was nine feet long.[263]

He took a black-fletched arrow fifteen of his huge handbreadths long,

fitted it to the string, drew far back, and sent it whizzing over four hundred yards.

It hit Chikakiyo where he stood in the bow of his ship, square in the torso,

and sent him crashing headlong to the ship's bottom,

whether dead or alive one could not tell.

Asari no Yoichi was a remarkable archer.

They say he could hit a running deer every time from two hundred yards away.

    Thereafter the Genji and Heike,
    with a fierce roar from either side,
    joined furious, merciless battle.
    Neither seemed stronger or weaker,
    but it was true: The Heike had with them
    the emperor and his regalia.
    The Genji were doubting their success
    when what seemed at first a white cloud
    floating above them in the sky
    turned out to be no cloud at all
    but a white banner, fluttering down
    free, from nowhere, until the cord
    meant to fasten it to a pole
    brushed the bow of a Genji boat.

"Great Bodhisattva Hachiman has appeared to us!" the delighted Yoshitsune
    cried.

He rinsed his mouth and bowed reverently. All with him did the same.

Also, thousands of dolphins surfaced and swam from the Genji toward the
    Heike.

Lord Munemori summoned the yin-yang diviner Harenobu.

"Dolphins are common enough," he said, "but I have never seen *this*.

Find out for me what it portends."

"My lord," the diviner replied,

"if these dolphins turn back, still taking in air at the surface, the Genji are lost.

If they dive under us, then we face grave danger."

. . . .

263. The normal length was seven and a half feet.

He had hardly spoken when the dolphins dove straight under the Heike ships. "This is it, then," said the diviner.

    Shigeyoshi had served the Heike loyally these past three years
and had often risked his life in battle to defend them,
but now that his son Noriyoshi had been taken alive,
he no doubt saw that further devotion to them was pointless:
He abruptly shifted his allegiance to the Genji.
The Heike plan had been to put their nobles in war boats and foot soldiers in the
    Chinese ships,
so that when the Genji went for those ships, the boats could surround and kill
    them,
but the Genji ignored the Chinese ships once they had Shigeyoshi.
Instead they attacked the boats bearing the Heike commanders in disguise.
"What a disaster!" Tomomori exclaimed. "That Shigeyoshi! I should have
    beheaded him!"
A thousand vain regrets assailed him.

> Now the men of Shikoku and Kyushu,
> as one, dropped the Heike for the Genji.
> The follower loyal until this day
> drew his bow now against his lord,
> wielded against him his naked blade.
> While the far shore seemed to beckon,
> high waves put it beyond Heike reach;
> the near shore, appealing at first glance,
> bristled with waiting Genji arrows.
> The struggle these two had waged so long,
> to achieve dominion over the realm,
> visibly ended on this day.

9. The Drowning of Emperor Antoku

> Now came the Genji warriors,
> pouring onto the Heike vessels,
> slaughtering with arrow and sword
> every crewman, every helmsman,
> leaving not one to row or steer.
> Their bodies lay littered underfoot.

> Tomomori rowed a small boat to the imperial barge. "As far as I can see," he said, "we are finished. Please throw anything unsightly into the sea." Racing about from prow to stern, he swept, wiped, collected rubbish, and with his own hands cleaned all he could reach.

"How is the battle going, Lord Tomomori?" the gentlewomen asked.

"Ladies," he answered, roaring with laughter, "you will soon meet some rare gallants from the east!"

They wailed, "How can you joke at a time like this?"

For some time Lady Nii had expected what she now saw.
She threw her two gray nun's robes over her head,
lifted high her beaten silk trouser-skirts,
clasped the sacred jewel to her side,
thrust the treasure sword into her sash,
and lifted the emperor in her arms.
"I may be a woman," she said, "but I will not let the enemy take me.
No, Your Majesty, I shall accompany you.
All those loyal to our sovereign, follow me!"
She stepped to the side of the boat.

> His Majesty, in his eighth year,
> was thoroughly grown up for his age,
> and his beauty shone around him.
> His rich black hair hung below his waist.
> "Where are you taking me, Grandmother?"
> he asked with wonder in his eyes.
> "You still do not know, Your Majesty?
> Your virtuous karma from past lives
> made you sovereign over the realm,
> but now the influence of some evil
> has brought your grandeur to an end.

First, Your Majesty, if you please,
face east and say good-bye to the Grand Shrine of Ise;
then, trusting Amida to welcome you into his Western Paradise,
face west and call his Name.
This land of ours, a few millet grains scattered in remote seas, is not a nice place.
I am taking you now to a much happier one, the Pure Land of Bliss."
So she addressed him, weeping.

> Robed in dove gray, his hair in side loops
> like any boy's, cheeks streaming with tears,
> he pressed his dear little hands together,
> prostrated himself toward the east,
> and bade farewell to the Ise Shrine,
> then turned to the west, calling the Name.
> Lady Nii said, her arms around him,
> "Down there, far beneath the waves,
> another capital awaits us"—

and plunged into the fathomless deep.
Alas! The spring winds of transience
in one brief instant swept away
the beauty of this lovely blossom;
the billows of a heartless fate
swallowed His Sovereign Majesty.
Everlasting Life, it was called,
the dwelling given him forever;
Eternal Youth, announced the name
upon its gate, locked against old age,[264]
and yet before even his tenth year
he lay at the bottom of the sea.
The happy destiny of the monarch
no longer meant anything at all.
The dragon, fallen from the clouds
to the ocean depths, was now a fish.
A Brahma in his lofty palace,
an Indra in his stern citadel,
he whose word had once been law
to ministers and senior nobles
first sought refuge aboard a ship,
then met his end beneath the waves:
as sad a tale as any ever told.

10. *The Death of Noritsune*

Before this spectacle the emperor's mother, Kenreimon-in,
slipped a warming stone[265] and an inkstone into the left and right folds of
    her robe,
and threw herself into the sea, but without knowing who she was,
a man of the Watanabe League, Gengo Uma-no-jō Mutsuru,
caught her hair with a grappling hook and retrieved her.
"How awful!" the gentlewomen cried. "Why, that is her ladyship!"
Yoshitsune, once informed, returned her at once to the imperial barge.
Lady Dainagon-no-suke tried to throw herself into the sea,
clutching the chest containing the sacred mirror,
but an arrow pinned her skirts to the vessel's side so that she tripped and fell,
and the warriors saw to it that she got no farther.

....

264. Everlasting Life and Eternal Youth are names associated with the Chinese imperial palace.
265. A fire-heated stone slipped into clothing for warmth.

A composite scene: Antoku and Lady Nii (upper left) are poised to leap into the waves. Below them: Munemori, in court dress, is retrieved alive. At far right: Noritsune prepares to leap into the sea with two enemy men; another has already fallen in. Above them: Warriors save Kenreimon-in from drowning.

Then they broke the chain that secured the chest and were starting to lift the lid
when suddenly their vision failed. Blood poured from their noses.
Taira no Tokitada, by then a prisoner, declared,
"That chest holds the sacred mirror. No common man may look upon it!"
At this the warriors drew back.
Thereafter Yoshitsune, in consultation with Tokitada,
saw to it that the chest was bound securely shut as before.
Meanwhile the brothers Norimori and Tsunemori, arm in arm,
leaped in their armor, bearing an anchor, into the sea.

> So, too, the young lords Sukemori,
> Arimori, and Yukimori,
> arm in arm, sank from sight together.

While others were thus engaged, Lord Munemori and his son Kiyomune
betrayed no sign of meaning to drown
but went instead to the side of their boat and looked around in horror.
Shocked Heike men shoved Munemori into the water, as though pushing past,
and Kiyomune leaped straight in after him.
All the other men had entered the sea in full armor,
carrying heavy objects to ensure that they sank at once,
but not so this father and son, both of them strong swimmers.
They did *not* sink.
"If Kiyomune goes down, I will, too," Munemori told himself. "If he survives, so
    will I."
Kiyomune likewise reflected, "I will sink or swim with him."
While they swam around, keeping an eye on each other,
Ise no Saburō Yoshimori rowed up in a small boat.
He caught Kiyomune at once with his grappling hook and hauled him aboard.
Munemori saw it happen but did nothing.
Yoshimori got him, too.

> Lord Munemori's foster brother,
> Hida no Saburōzaemon Kagetsune,
> boarded Yoshimori's boat from his own.
> "Who are you," he demanded to know,
> "who dare to lay your hands on my lord?"
> He drew his sword and swiftly attacked.
> Yoshimori seemed in grave danger
> when his page intervened to save him.
> Coming between them, he attacked back.
> The first stroke from Kagetsune's sword
> split the page's helmet in half,
> and the second cut off his head.

Yoshimori remained under threat
when Hori no Yatarō Chikatsune
shot full force from a boat alongside
an arrow that caught Kagetsune
under the helmet. His attack flagged.
Chikatsune then boarded the boat
and fought Kagetsune hand to hand.
A man of his came straight after him,
raised Kagetsune's armor skirts,
and stabbed him twice. For all the fame
Kagetsune enjoyed as a fighter,
his time had come: The wounds were deep,
the enemy many. They cut him down.
Dragged alive from the water, Munemori
before his own eyes saw his foster brother killed.
How can he have felt about that?
As for Noritsune, no one courted an arrow from him, and he had none left.
Perhaps he had known that this day was his last,
for over a *hitatare* of red brocade he wore Chinese damask-laced armor.
Wielding in one hand a dauntingly long sword and in the other
a plain-handled halberd with a naked blade,
he laid so fiercely about him, left and right,
that no man there dared face him, and many died.

      Tomomori sent a man to him.
      "Lord Noritsune," his message said,
      "spare yourself bearing too many sins.
      Was any man here a worthy opponent?"
      "I see," Noritsune said to himself.
      "He wants me to take on their commander."
      Gripping his sword and halberd short,
      he boarded one Genji boat, then another,
      with fierce cries, always on the attack.
      Not knowing which man before him
      was Yoshitsune, he raced about,
      suspecting anyone finely equipped.
      Yoshitsune saw what he was up to.
      He made a show of moving forward
      but managed never to join with him.
      Somehow or other, however,
      Noritsune succeeded after all
      in leaping with a shout of triumph

straight onto Yoshitsune's boat.
Yoshitsune must have thought himself lost,
because he in turn, halberd under his arm,
sprang twenty feet to another boat
filled with warriors of his own.
No doubt Noritsune knew all too well
that he was nowhere near that agile.
He made no attempt to follow.
Seeing now that this was the end, he threw sword and halberd into the sea,
doffed his helmet and tossed it away, tore off the lower skirts of his armor,
loosed his wild hair, spread his arms wide in a stance inexpressibly terrifying,
and cried in a great voice,

"Any man who feels up to it,
let him come forward, fight with me,
and take Noritsune alive!
I shall gladly go down to Kamakura
for a word or two with Yoritomo!
Come, gentlemen, come and get me!"
No one would even approach him.

Now, there was a man from Tosa province,
one Aki no Tarō Sanemitsu,
son of Aki no Dairyō Saneyasu,
the head man of the district of Aki.
Endowed with the strength of thirty men,
he had a retainer as strong as he,
and Jirō, his younger brother,
was also far sturdier than most.
The spectacle of Noritsune
inspired Sanemitsu to remark,
"A mighty man he may indeed be,
but once we three get hold of him,
no demon even a hundred feet tall
could resist submitting to us."
He and the other two took a small boat,
brought it up beside Noritsune's,
leaped aboard, their neck plates well down,
their swords drawn, and had at him.
Noritsune, perfectly calm,
moved up beside the strongman retainer
as the fellow was coming straight at him
and kicked him with a thunderous splash

into the sea. The next, Sanemitsu,
he clamped under his right arm,
caught brother Jirō under his left,
gave the two an almighty squeeze,
and said, "Fine, you're coming with me,
you two louts, on the road to death,"
and in that, his twenty-sixth year,
he plunged with them into the waves.

11. The Mirror's Return to the Capital

"I have seen enough," said Lord Tomomori. "It is time to die."
He summoned his foster brother, Iga no Heinaizaemon Ienaga.
"Does the old pact between us still stand?"
"Need you ask?" Ienaga replied.
He helped his lord into a second layer of armor and donned one himself.
Arm in arm, the two plunged into the sea.
Twenty or more of Tomomori's men refused to lag behind;
they, too, arm in arm, sank from sight together.
For one reason or another, however, some escaped—among them
Etchū no Jirōbyōe, Kazusa no Gorōbyōe, Akushichibyōe, and Hida no Shirōbyōe.
These got away and fled.

    Red flags and badges littered the sea
    like autumn leaves stripped by the wind
    and scattered on the Tatsuta River.[266]
    Once white, the waves on the shore broke pink.
    Boats drifted, empty and abandoned,
    at the will only of wind and tide,
    aimlessly rocking: a desolate scene.
    These Heike nobles were taken alive:
        Munemori, once palace minister;
        the grand counselor Tokitada;
        Kiyomune, Right Gate Watch intendant;
        Nobumoto, lord of the Treasury;
        the Sanuki captain Tokizane;
        Masaakira, deputy lord of War;
        Munemori's youngest son, in his eighth year.
    These monks were captured:

266. The hills and river of Tatsuta (south of present-day Osaka) were associated in poetry with brightly colored autumn leaves; Tatsuta-hime was the goddess of autumn.

the great prelate Senshin;
    Nōen, the superintendent of Hosshōji;
    Chūkai, a master of discipline;
    the Kyōjubō adept Yūen;
and these major retainers:
    Gendayū Suesada,
    the Settsu magistrate Morizumi,
    Kichinaizaemon Sueyasu,
    Tōnaizaemon Nobuyasu,
    Awa-no-minbu Shigeyoshi and his son—
    in all, thirty-eight men.
Kikuchi no Jirō Takanao,
Harada no Taifu Tanenao,
and with them every one of their men
had surrendered before the battle.
As for the ladies, they included Kenreimon-in herself;
the regent's wife, another daughter of Kiyomori;
a third daughter, the Mistress of the Gallery;
Lady Dainagon-no-suke, Shigehira's wife;
Lady Sotsu-no-suke, the wife of Tokitada;
Tomomori's wife, Jibukyō-no-tsubone;
and many more—forty-three in all.
    What kind of year can it have been,
    what kind of month, that in Genryaku 2,
    as spring was drawing to a close,
    the emperor himself should have drowned
    and his officials roamed the waves?
    The emperor's mother and her ladies
    fell into barbarian hands,
    while tens of thousands of warriors
    swept off ministers and great nobles.
    These regained their home in the end,
    but not, to their infinite chagrin,
    wearing brocade like Zhu Maichen,
    and the trials that the ladies suffered
    taught them the grief of Wang Zhaojun
    on her way to the land of the Xiongnu.[267]

....

267. Zhu Maichen, a man of the Han dynasty, returned home in triumph, wearing brocade. Wang Zhaojun (Japanese: Ōshōkun), a palace beauty, was sent by Emperor Wu of Han, much against her will, to the king of the barbarian Xiongnu people.

On the third of the fourth month, Yoshitsune reported to Cloistered
Emperor Go-Shirakawa, through Genpachi Hirotsuna, the Heike
defeat on the twenty-fourth of the third month past, in the strait
between Ta-no-ura in Buzen and Dan-no-ura in Nagato, and he an-
nounced the safe return of the three regalia. Throughout the residence
the news caused a great stir. The cloistered sovereign called Hirotsuna
into his private court, questioned him closely about the battle, and in
his joy appointed him a lieutenant in the Left Watch. On the fifth he
sent Tōhōgan Nobumori westward, to find out whether the return of
the regalia was really assured. Nobumori did not even go home but
galloped straight off, whip raised high, on one of the cloistered sover-
eign's own horses.

On the fourteenth, Yoshitsune,
on his way up to the capital
with the Heike captives, men and women,
reached Akashi in Harima.
Over this famous stretch of shore
there rose into the deepening night
a moon as brilliant as any in autumn.
The gentlewomen clustered together.
"Never did we imagine," they said,
"on passing this way two years ago,[268]
that we would ever see the like."
Each of them wept her secret tears.
Gazing aloft, toward the moon,
Lady Sotsu-no-suke reflected,

> *Gaze lifted skyward,*
> *from my tear-drenched sleeves I catch*
> *the gleam of the moon.*
> *Tell me, moon, all that you know*
> *of life there above the clouds!*

Jibukyō-no-tsubone:

> *The face of the moon*
> *I once knew above the clouds*
> *shines here, too, unchanged,*
> *but the brilliance of its light*
> *only darkens my sad heart.*

And Lady Dainagon-no-suke:

....

268. In Juei 2 (1183), on their return to Fukuhara.

I am the one
travel brings to spend a night
on Akashi shore,
yet in the waves beside me
lodges a companion moon!

"They must so desperately miss better days!"
Yoshitsune said to himself,
kind as he was even in battle.
He felt intense pity for them.
    On the twenty-fifth of the month,
the mirror and the jewel in its chest
reached Toba, and from the palace
the news brought these gentlemen to receive them:
    the Kade-no-kōji counselor Tsunefusa,
    the Takakura consultant-captain Yasumichi,
    the provisional right controller Kanetada,
    the Left Gate Watch officer Chikamasa,
    the Enami captain Kintoki,
    the Tajima lieutenant Noriyoshi,
accompanied by these warriors:
    the Izu chamberlain-commissioner Yorikane,
    the Ishikawa magistrate Yoshikane,
    the Left Gate Watch officer Aritsuna.
That night at the hour of the rat, [ca. midnight]
the mirror and the jewel in its chest
entered in solemn dignity
the precincts of the Council of State.
The imperial sword was lost.
As for the jewel, apparently
Kataoka no Tarō Tsuneharu
found its chest floating and rescued it.

12. The Sword[269]

The age of the gods bequeathed to us,
in this our realm, three spirit swords:
    Totsuka,
    Ama-no-hayakiri,

....

269. So sacred was the imperial sword that this chapter was treated as a "secret piece" by the guild of professional *Heike* performers.

Kusanagi.
They say that Totsuka is kept
in the Isonokami Shrine
at Furu, in Yamato province,
and Ama-no-hayakiri
at the Atsuta Shrine in Owari.
Kusanagi is kept in the palace;
it is now the priceless sword
among the three regalia.
        This is the story of Kusanagi.
Of old, Susano-o-no-mikoto
had a palace built for himself
at Soga in Izumo province.
Seeing the sky there forever covered
by eight-colored clouds, he made this song:

> Where rise eightfold clouds,
> Izumo, an eightfold fence
>   to keep my wife home
> I put up, an eightfold fence,
>   yes, a fence I build, eightfold!

This was the first poem, ever,
made in thirty-one syllables.
The cloud he noted explains why
he called the province Izumo:
"Land of Ever-Rising Cloud."

In that far-off time, Susano-o-no-mikoto descended to the headwaters of the river Hi in the province of Izumo, and there he met a pair of earthly deities named Ashinazuchi, the husband, and Tenazuchi, the wife. They had a beautiful daughter called Inada-hime. All three were weeping.

"Why do you weep?" Susano-o-no-mikoto asked.
To his question they replied,
    "Once we had eight daughters.
The serpent swallowed all of them
except the one that you see here,
and soon it is to have her, too.
This serpent's eight heads and tails
slither over eight peaks and valleys.
On its back grow queer plants and trees.
Its years number uncounted thousands,
and its eyes are like sun and moon.

Every year it devours humans.
Children mourn their parents, eaten;
parents mourn their eaten children.
Whether south or north of our village,
cries of mourning never cease."
Moved to pity, the god changed their daughter to a pristine comb
and concealed it in his hair.
He filled eight tubs with sake,
made a likeness of her, and stood it up on a high place.
The sake reflected her form.
The serpent, thinking she was real,
drained the tubs to the last drop and lay there drunk, dead to the world.
The god drew the Totsuka sword from the scabbard at his waist
and fiercely slashed the serpent to pieces.
One tail, though, he could not cut. This struck him as strange.
He slit the tail open lengthwise, peered inside,
and discovered there a spirit sword,
which he took and presented to the Sun Goddess.
"This," she said, "is the sword that I dropped long ago on the High Plain of
    Heaven.
While it was in the serpent's tail, thick cloud always covered the land,
so it bore the name Ama-no-murakumo no Tsurugi, 'Sword of Celestial
    Cloud.'"
        The Sun Goddess, once the sword was hers,
        made it a treasure of her heavenly palace.
        When, later, she sent the celestial grandchild
        down to earth, to rule as lord
        over the Central Land of Rich Reed Plains,
        she gave him, with the mirror, this sword.
        Until the reign of Kaika, ninth of the line,
        it remained with the emperor himself,
        but in the reign of the tenth, Sujin,
        in terror of the dire spirit might
        the Sun Goddess wields, her shrine was moved
        to hallowed Shiki in Kasanui,
        there in the province of Yamato,
        and the sword, too, remained in her shrine.
        His Majesty then had a copy made,
        to serve him as his constant protector,
        and its might matched that of the first.

The sword Ama-no-murakumo spent three reigns, Sujin to Keikō,
reverently honored within the Sun Goddess's shrine.
When in the reign of Emperor Keikō, the sixth month of his fortieth year,
the eastern barbarians raised rebellion,
his son, Yamatodake-no-mikoto, stout of heart and superb in strength,
received the imperial commission to go down to the east.
He went first before the Sun Goddess to bid her farewell.
Through his younger sister, the High Priestess,[270]
she enjoined care and diligence and gave him the sword.
When he reached the province of Suruga, the rebels there tricked him, saying,
"This province is rich in game. Enjoy the hunt!"
Then they set fire to the meadows and almost burned him to death,
but he drew his spirit sword and with it mowed the grass for miles around.
Next he set his own fire, which the wind at once blew over the rebels.
Every one of them died in the flames.
Thereafter the sword Ama-no-murakumo was called Kusanagi, "Grass Mower."

Yamatodake-no-mikoto pressed ahead with his campaign and for three years conquered rebels everywhere. Having subdued the evil-doers in province after province, he was on his way back up to the capital when illness struck. In the seventh month of his thirtieth year, at Atsuta in the province of Owari, he at last passed away. Wonder of wonders, his spirit became a white bird that flew up into the sky.

As for the captured barbarians,
by Yamatodake's command
his son, Takehiko-no-mikoto,
presented them to the emperor.
The sword Kusanagi, meanwhile,
went to the Atsuta Shrine.
In Emperor Tenchi's seventh year, [668]
Dōgyō, a monk from Silla,
made up his mind to steal this sword
as a treasure for his own land.
Out at sea, the sword hidden aboard,
he encountered so violent a storm
that his ship at once began sinking.
Recognizing the spirit sword's curse,
he begged forgiveness, went no farther,
and returned the sword to Atsuta.

....

270. Yamato-hime, the High Priestess of Ise. The Sun Goddess moved to Ise early in Keikō's reign.

Next Emperor Tenmu, in Shuchō 1, [686]
called it back, to remain in the palace.
This is the sword of the regalia.
It has overwhelming spirit power.
When Emperor Yōzei, in his madness, [r. 876–84]
unsheathed it, his sleeping chamber
exploded in sparks and flashes
exactly resembling bolts of lightning.
Terrified, he cast the sword from him.
It snapped by itself back into its sheath.
That is how impressive the sword was, in times gone by.
It could hardly have simply disappeared,
even after Lady Nii sank with it in her sash to the ocean floor.
The best women divers were summoned to dive for it;
holy monks went on retreat at the greatest temples and shrines,
there to make sacred offerings and pray that it be recovered—
but no, the sword was gone.
Those versed in usage and precedent declared,

> "In ancient times the Sun Goddess
> vowed that she would protect forever
> the emperors sovereign over the realm,
> and that vow stands, as firm as ever.
> The line born of Iwashimizu[271]
> runs as ever it did in the past;
> hence the shining disk of the sun
> does not yet lie fallen to earth.

These latter days, though degenerate, do not mean the end of the imperial
   sway."
So they pronounced themselves, and one learned doctor added,[272]
"The great serpent slain of old by Susano-o-no-mikoto,
at the headwaters of the river Hi in the province of Izumo,
so profoundly desired the spirit sword he had lost
that in token of his eight heads and tails
he took the form of the eightieth human sovereign
and, in the person of an emperor in his eighth year,
took it back and dove with it to the bottom of the sea."

> In the depths of the ocean abyss,
> the sword was now the Dragon God's prize.

....

271. The line of descent from Emperor Ōjin.
272. A doctor of yin-yang astrology and divination.

Naturally, no one could expect
to see it again in the human realm.

13. *The Parade of Heike Captives*

It was then that the Second Prince, Morisada,[273] returned to the capital.
Cloistered Emperor Go-Shirakawa sent a carriage to meet him.
Removed against his will by the Heike,
he had spent three years wandering the waves of the western seas.
His mother and his protector, the Jimyōin consultant, had long worried about him,
and his safe return brought the whole household together, weeping tears of joy.
On the twenty-sixth, the Heike prisoners entered the capital
in wickerwork carriages bearing small, eight-petal blossom motifs.
The front and rear blinds on each were raised, and the windows on either side
    stood open.
Lord Munemori wore a white hunting cloak.
Kiyomune, in a white *hitatare*, rode at the back of his father's carriage.

The carriages bearing Munemori and Tokitada.

....

273. A younger brother of Emperor Antoku and an older brother of the currently reigning emperor,
Go-Toba.

Tokitada's carriage followed.

Tokizane, his son, had been due to accompany him, but illness prevented that.

Nobumoto, having been wounded, traveled by quieter streets.

Lord Munemori, once so handsome and imposing,
looked in his now-reduced state quite unlike his former self.

Still, he gazed about him and showed no visible sign of despair.

Kiyomune lay facedown and never raised his eyes. He seemed despondent.

Doi no Jirō Sanehira, in light armor over a tan *hitatare*,
commanded the thirty mounted guards posted before and behind the carriages.

Spectators old and young crowded to watch,
not from the city alone but from provinces near and far as well, and from many
 temples.

The unbroken press of people ran from the Toba Mansion's south gate
all the way to Yotsuzuka. There seemed to be millions of them.

> No one could even turn around,
> nor could a single carriage move.
> The famine of Jishō and Yōwa, [1180–82]
> the long warfare in east and west
> had brought death to a great many,
> but quite plainly many had lived.
> It had been only two years
> since the Heike fled the city,
> and memories of their glory
> were still fresh in everyone's mind.
> The dismal spectacle today
> of men who had once inspired terror
> might almost have been a dream.
> Ignorant rustics, humble women
> wept, all of them, wringing their sleeves.
> Imagine, then, the emotions
> felt by those who had served the Heike!
> Debts owed for long-standing favor,
> loyalty over the generations
> made the past all too hard to dismiss,
> and yet these people had to live.
> Most of them had joined the Genji
> but even now could not forget
> that old, old association.
> Surely sorrow overwhelmed them,
> for many pressed sleeves to their eyes
> and stood there with downcast gaze.

The youth minding Munemori's ox was Saburōmaru.
Kiso Yoshinaka had killed Jirōmaru, his older brother,
for allowing the ox to bolt with the carriage
when he went to call on Cloistered Emperor Go-Shirakawa.
Off in the west, Saburōmaru had assumed the guise of a grown man,
but he still longed one last time to tend Lord Munemori's carriage.
At Toba he therefore approached Yoshitsune.
"An oxherd like me," he submitted urgently, "the lowest of the low,
cannot presume to claim finer feelings, but, such as I am,
I served Lord Munemori for many years and remain devoted to him.
With your permission, if it pleases you to grant it,
I should like to look after his carriage on his last journey."
"I see no objection," Yoshitsune replied. "By all means do so."
      Greatly relieved, Saburōmaru
      dressed himself in his very best,
      took the lead rope from his breast fold,
      attached it, and, blinded by tears,
      sleeves to his eyes, allowed the ox
      to move forward just as it pleased.
      The cloistered emperor stopped his carriage
      at Rokujō and Higashi-no-tōin
      to watch, as did both senior nobles
      and privy gentlemen, each from his own,
      drawn up there in row after row.
      So close had these men been to him
      that his heart softened after all,
      and he was moved to pity for them.
      Those with him must have thought this a dream.
      "One so longed somehow or other,"
      high and low remarked through their tears,
      "for recognition, for a word from them.
      Who would have thought it could end like this?"

        That other year, after receiving appointment as palace minister, Lord Munemori went to convey his formal thanks, followed by twelve senior nobles—the Kasan-no-in grand counselor foremost among them—each in his own carriage, and preceded on horseback by sixteen privy gentlemen under the head chamberlain Chikamune. Nobles of every degree, including four counselors and three captains with the third rank, glittered that day in their finery. Lord Tokitada, then the intendant of the Left Gate Watch, was summoned before the sovereign, there to receive gifts and otherwise to be magnificently entertained. On this day, however, not a single noble accompanied these Taira lords, only twenty of their followers, captured with them at Dan-no-ura, in white *hitatare* and roped to their saddles. The procession moved east along Rokujō as far as the bank of the Kamo River, then turned back. Munemori and his son went to Yoshitsune's residence at Rokujō-Horikawa.

Father and son were served refreshments, but neither touched any.
They merely sat in silence, exchanging glances and shedding endless tears.
Munemori did not loosen his clothing when night came
but just lay down on one of his sleeves and covered his son with the other.
Genpachibyōe, Eda no Genzō, and Kumai Tarō, his guards, noticed this.
"Alas," they observed, "for the greatest as for the least of us,
there is nothing more moving than the love between parent and child.

> How much good can it do, really,
> to cover him just with a sleeve?
> But, oh, what love the gesture shows!"
> Hardened warriors though they were,
> all of them wept.

14. *The Mirror*

On the twenty-eighth of the month,
Yoritomo in Kamakura received promotion to the junior second rank.
A rise of two grades already bespeaks signal imperial favor,
but this meant a rise of three.
The third rank would actually have been more correct for him,
but promotion to the second skirted the precedent set for Kiyomori.[274]
At the hour of the rat that night, the mirror moved from the Great Hall of
    State [midnight]
to the Unmeiden. His Majesty made a progress there,
and three nights of sacred *kagura* music and dancing followed.
Ō no Yoshikata, a junior officer in the Right Palace Guards,
by imperial command danced *Yudachi* and *Miyabito,*
two secret pieces handed down in his family line.
The reward he received brilliantly acknowledged a splendid performance.
Only his grandfather, the court musician Suketada, had known these pieces,
which were so secret that he withheld them even from his son, Chikakata.

....

274. Any analogy with Kiyomori's promotion would have been inauspicious, considering his ultimate fate.

Instead he transmitted them to the then-reigning emperor, Horikawa, [r. 1086–1107]
who taught them to Chikakata after Suketada's death.
Tears spring to one's eyes at the thought of His Majesty's zeal
to ensure that the art they required should never be lost.

> To speak now of the sacred mirror:
> Of old, when the Goddess of the Sun
> decided to shut herself away
> inside the celestial rock cave,
> she wished to leave her descendants
> a visible image of herself.
> She therefore had a mirror forged,
> one that did not satisfy her;
> so that she had a second made.
> The first is now enshrined in Kii,
> at the double sanctuary,
> Nichizen and Kokuken.
> The second she gave her son,
> Ama-no-oshihomimi-no-mikoto,
> saying to him as she did so,
> "Share your palace with this mirror."
> Thereupon the Sun Goddess
> confined herself in the rock cave,
> and darkness spread across the land.
> Then the swarming millions of gods
> gathered at the door of the cave,
> to dance and to sing *kagura.*
> The goddess's interest was piqued:
> She cracked open the cave door
> and peered out; then every face
> shone bright for all eyes to see.
> And that, they say, is how the word
> *omoshiro* entered people's speech.[275]
> Then the god of colossal strength,
> Tajikara-o, with a great heave
> threw the door wide open for all time.

Through the reign of Emperor Kaika, the ninth of the line,
the mirror remained in the palace of the sovereign,

....

275. In modern Japanese, *omoshiroi* ("white-faced," "bright-faced") still means "interesting," "curious,"
"fun."

but Emperor Sujin, the tenth, in fear of its spirit power,
moved it to a separate hall.
It has resided more recently in the Unmeiden.

> One hundred and sixty years had passed
> since the capital moved to Heian-kyō,
> when in Emperor Murakami's reign—
> it was the fourth year of Tentoku, [960]
> the ninth month and twenty-third day,
> at the hour of the rat—fire broke out
> for the first time in the palace grounds,
> at the Left Gate Watch headquarters,
> no distance from the Unmeiden,
> the hall where the mirror was kept.
> This was in the middle of the night.
> No woman from the palace staff
> was present on duty to save it.
> Fujiwara no Saneyori[276]
> hastened there, but the mirror had burned.
> "This is the end!" he said to himself,
> but while he wept, all on its own
> the mirror flew up out of the flames,
> to hang in the Nanden cherry tree[277]
> and shine there like the morning sun
> rising from behind the mountains.
> Then Saneyori understood
> that all remained well in the world,
> and tears of joy sprang to his eyes.

He went down on his right knee, spread his left sleeve wide,
and through his tears addressed the mirror. "Come," he said,
"if that vow the goddess made to protect the line of sovereigns
still lives, as it did of old, come now, lodge in my left sleeve!"
Before these last words were out, the mirror flew to him as bidden.

> He carried it, wrapped in his sleeve,
> straight to the Council of State office,
> whence in time it was restored
> once more to the Unmeiden.
> Who now, in this present age,
> could even conceive the like

....

276. The incumbent regent and left minister.
277. This cherry tree stood below the steps on the south side of the Nanden (Shishinden).

and welcome the mirror to his sleeve?
Those ancient times far outshone ours.

15. *The Letters*

Taira no Tokitada and his son were quartered close to Yoshitsune.
Tokitada might have resigned himself to his fate under the circumstances,
but no, he must still have thirsted to live,
because he called his son, Tokizane, to him and said,
"Yoshitsune seems to have obtained a box of letters strictly private in nature.
Many, no doubt including me, will die if Yoritomo in Kamakura ever sees them.
I do not know what to do."
Tokizane replied, "People credit Yoshitsune with being generally kind.
They say that when a gentlewoman approaches him with a heartfelt grievance,
he always listens, whatever the issue may be.
Now, you have several daughters.
What harm could come of presenting him with one?
You may well succeed if you raise the matter once you have that bond with him."
Tokitada shed bitter tears.
        "When I stood high in the world," he said,
        "consort or empress was the goal
        to which I aspired for my daughters.
        Never would I have considered
        giving one to some common fellow."
        His son answered, "As things stand,
        the time has come to forget all that.
        Your daughter by your present wife
        is now in her eighteenth year, after all."
That idea being more than Tokitada could stomach,
he gave Yoshitsune instead a daughter by his previous wife,
one now in her twenty-third year—a little old, perhaps,
but still lovely in face and figure and as sweet-tempered as she could be.
Yoshitsune was delighted to have her.
Since he already had a wife, the daughter of Kawagoe no Tarō Shigeyori,
he gave this new one a beautifully appointed house of her own.
When she mentioned the box of letters to him,
he promptly returned it to her father without even breaking the seal.
        Tokitada, hugely relieved,
        hastened to burn them, every one.
        What can possibly have been in them?
        Rumor suspected something bad.

The Heike were finished, the provinces were quiet at last,
and nothing impeded travel throughout the realm.
The capital was so peaceful that people began saying,
"There is simply nobody like Kurō Yoshitsune.
What did Yoritomo, in Kamakura, ever do for us?
If only Yoshitsune himself were in charge of everything!"
Their talk reached Yoritomo's ears.
"Why," he exclaimed, "that is outrageous!
I devised the strategy that sent our armies into battle
and gave us easy victory over the Heike.
Kurō Yoshitsune could never have imposed peace all on his own.
Talk like this must have gone to his head, so that he thinks his word is law.
And with all the people in the world he had to choose from,
he is now, I hear, the son-in-law of Taira no Tokitada
and goes out of his way to favor the man. That I cannot accept.
Moreover, he shows no respect in any of this for anyone else's opinion.
What does he mean by it?
When he gets down here, he will no doubt treat us to some fine strutting."

16. The Beheading of Fukushō

Word reached Munemori that on the seventh of the fifth month
Yoshitsune was to take the Heike prisoners down to the Kanto.
He sent Yoshitsune a messenger with this plea:
"I gather that you are to depart for the Kanto tomorrow.
A father's love is not to be broken.
I saw on the list of prisoners a boy in his eighth year.
May I ask whether he is still alive?
I would gladly see him a last time."
"What he said of a father's love is true for us all," observed Yoshitsune.
"He could hardly feel otherwise."
So he ordered Kawagoe no Kotarō Shigefusa, who had charge of the boy,
to take him to where Munemori was lodged.
Shigefusa borrowed a carriage and accompanied him with two gentlewomen.
The boy was very happy to see his father after so long.
"Come here!" Munemori took him on his lap and, in tears, stroked his hair.
Then he said to the guards,
    "Listen to me, every one of you!
    This little boy has no mother, you know.
    His mother gave birth easily enough,

       but she was very ill afterward,
       and in the end, you see, she died.
And this is what she said to me:
'Should you have in the future other children, by other women,
do not for that allow your feeling for this one to cool,
but bring him up in memory of me.
Do not just send him off for some nurse to look after.'
Her appeal so moved me that I replied,
'When I appoint Kiyomune over there commander
in some campaign to quell an enemy of the court,
I will ensure that this little boy goes as *fukushō*, his second-in-command.'
The way I called him 'Fukushō' pleased her so much
that it became her pet name for him to the end.
She died only seven days later.

       All of that comes back to me
       every time I see this boy,"
       he concluded, weeping tears
       that he could not keep from flowing.
       All the warriors guarding him
       likewise wrung tears from their sleeves.
       Kiyomune likewise wept
       and Fukushō's nurse, too.
"Very well, Fukushō, you may go now," Munemori said after a moment.
"It has been so lovely to see you!"
But Fukushō did not go.
Kiyomune, looking on, did his best not to shed further tears.
"Come, Fukushō," he said, "for today it's time to go.
A visitor is due at any moment. Hurry back tomorrow morning."
But Fukushō clung to his father's white sleeve.
"No, no! I don't want to!" he protested, crying.
This went on for quite a long time, until at last the sun went down,
but it could not go on forever.
The little boy's nurse picked him up and put him in the carriage.

       She and the other gentlewoman,
       pressing their sleeves to their weeping eyes,
       said good-bye, boarded their carriage,
       and started off. Munemori
       watched them fade into the distance,
       heart breaking as never before.
       No, he had never sent the boy off

for some nurse somewhere to look after.
Touched by the mother's deathbed plea,
he had brought his son up at home,
in his third year had him come of age,
and given him the name Yoshimune.
The boy grew up so bright and pretty
that his father, who loved him dearly,
never let him out of his sight,
not even aboard ship, under far skies,
sailing the waves of the western seas.
Then came defeat. The aftermath
had kept them apart until this day.

Kawagoe Shigefusa went before Yoshitsune. "Sir," he said, "may I ask you what you intend for this boy?"

Yoshitsune answered, "I cannot possibly take him all the way to Kamakura. Deal with him here as you see fit."

Shigefusa went to where the boy was staying. "Lord Munemori will go down to Kamakura," he told the two women, "but his son is to remain in the city. I, too, am going to Kamakura, so my orders are to pass him to Ogata no Saburō Koreyoshi. Have him board this carriage immediately."

The carriage was already drawn up, and the boy innocently got in. "Am I going to my father's, like yesterday?" the poor little fellow asked happily.

The carriage followed Rokujō eastward.
"Oh, dear, I don't like this at all!" the frightened women said to each other.
Fifty or sixty warriors rode up behind them as the carriage emerged onto the
  bank of the river.
They stopped the carriage and spread out a furry animal hide.
"Please alight," they said. The young lord obeyed.

He did so with grave misgivings.
"Where are they taking me?" he asked,
but the women had no answer.
One among Shigefusa's men,
keeping his drawn sword at his side,
circled around behind the young lord
and was just preparing to strike
when the boy saw him, dodged aside,
and fled into his nurse's embrace.
Not even this warrior had the heart
to tear him from her by main force.

She collapsed with her arms around him,
rent the air with full-throated screams,
and writhed in such obvious terror
that one could only feel pity for her.
But all this was taking much too long.
Shigefusa said, fighting back tears,
"Listen, please. You cannot save him.
It is time." He wrenched the child from her,
stretched him out at the point of his dagger,
and at last cut off his head.
Every man present wept, for the bravest warrior is neither stock nor stone.
Shigefusa went off with the head, to present it for inspection to Yoshitsune.
The boy's nurse followed him, barefoot.
"May I not at least have his head," she begged, "so that I can pray for him in the
hereafter?"
Yoshitsune, deeply moved, shed many tears.
"I understand completely," he said. "Of course you must have it. Here it is."
She took it from him, put it into the fold of her robe,
and, as far as anyone knew, returned, weeping, to the city.
Five or six days later, two women threw themselves into the Katsura River.
The one who drowned with a boy's head in her front fold was Fukushō's nurse;
the one who went down clasping a headless corpse was her companion.
That the nurse should have taken this drastic step was perhaps inevitable.
How admirable of her companion, though, to do so, too!

17. Koshigoe

Meanwhile Lord Munemori, accompanied by Kurō Yoshitsune,
passed Awataguchi at dawn on the seventh of the month,
thus leaving the world of city and palace behind.
The clear spring at Ōsaka barrier drew this from him, with tears:

> *That was my last sight,*
> *today, of the capital;*
>   *and the barrier spring—*
> *will I ever come again,*
>   *to see it reflect my form?*

He was so downcast on the way
that Yoshitsune, kind as he was,
did all he could to give him comfort.
Lord Munemori said to him,
"Please, I beg you, leave me my life."

"I expect that he will banish you to some far province or some distant island,"
Yoshitsune answered. "He will hardly have you executed, and even if he
     means to,
I will plead for your life in exchange for the reward due me for my victories.
By all means set your mind at rest."
This reassuring speech elicited the unfortunate reply,
"I will be grateful merely to keep this worthless life of mine,
even among the savages in the Chishima Islands."[278]
The days went by, and on the twenty-fourth they reached Kamakura.
Kajiwara Kagetoki got there ahead of them.
"You now control every corner of Japan," he said to Yoritomo.
"As far as I can see, your final enemy is your younger brother, Kurō Yoshitsune.
Why do I say that? This is what he said:
'Without my charge down from above Ichi-no-tani,
we would never have broken through the east and west gates.

> You are to present the prisoners and the dead to *me* and to no one else.
> The very idea of presenting them to Noriyori, who never lifted a finger!
> If he refuses to give me Shigehira, I will go and get him myself!' Yoshi-
> tsune and I almost came to blows, but I got Doi no Jirō to take charge
> of Shigehira, and your brother calmed down."
>
> Yoritomo announced, "I hear that Yoshitsune is due to reach
> Kamakura today. Men, I want you all on guard!"
>
> Warriors great and small raced to assemble. They soon numbered
> several thousand.
>
> Yoritomo put up a barrier at Kanearai-zawa, took charge there of
> Munemori and his elder son, and sent Yoshitsune back to Koshigoe.
> From within a many-layered circle of mounted guards, he declared,
> "Yoshitsune is crafty enough to pop out at any moment from under
> this mat, but no, he will not get past me."
>
> These were Yoshitsune's thoughts: "I crushed Yoshinaka in the first
> month of last year, then risked my life all the way from Ichi-no-tani to
> Dan-no-ura in the campaign to finish the Heike. I safely retrieved both
> the mirror and the chest containing the jewel, I took the Heike com-
> mander and his son prisoner, and now I have brought them here.
> Yoritomo cannot refuse at least to see me, whatever this strange busi-
> ness may be.

Not for a moment did I doubt
that he would offer me appointment
as commander over all Kyushu,

....

278. The Kurils.

or perhaps over the provinces
south of the city, to east or west
along one seacoast or the other;
or over all of Shikoku and Kii,
there to provide a bulwark for him—
but no, he now informs me that I am to have only Iyo,
and he will not even let me enter Kamakura!
I can hardly believe it! What does this mean?
Were not Yoshinaka and I
the ones who brought peace to Japan?
Yoritomo's father was mine, too.
Being born first makes him the elder,
second makes me the younger brother,
but that is all. Why, anyone
eager to rule the realm can do so.
And he will not even receive me,
but sends me back instead to the city?
I will never forgive him for this!
What apology does he want from me?"
So he muttered, but all in vain.
In solemnly sworn oath after written oath,
Yoshitsune assured his brother that he harbored no disloyal thoughts,
but Kagetoki's denunciation convinced Yoritomo to ignore them.
At last the weeping Yoshitsune sent Ōe no Hiromoto this letter:

> Minamoto no Yoshitsune with all due respect wishes to communicate
> the following:
>
> On behalf of Lord Yoritomo, at his express request and acting as an
> imperial envoy in accordance with the relevant decree, I overthrew the
> enemies of the court and cleansed the shame once incurred by our
> house. Precisely when reward was due me, however, foul slander sud-
> denly intervened to erase the great merit that I had accrued and to
> heap blame on my blameless self.
>
> Innocent and deserving, I nonetheless suffer Lord Yoritomo's wrath-
> ful ban, and for this I weep vain tears of blood. I cannot defend myself
> until the truth of the accusations is subjected to scrutiny and I am al-
> lowed into Kamakura. Meanwhile I endure wasted days. It is so long
> since I beheld my noble brother's countenance that my bond of flesh
> and blood with him seems almost to have lapsed and our fated tie to be
> null and void. Or could it be that evil karma from past lives is at work?
> Alas! Who but my august father, reborn, could now plead my unhappy
> case? Who will take pity on me?

At the risk of seeming to voice an unwelcome complaint, I cannot refrain from observing that my father passed away only a few days after my birth, leaving me an orphan. My mother then carried me in her arms to Uda county in Yamato, and since then I have never known peace. My unworthy life remained mine, but I could not frequent the capital; instead I hid far away, in remote provinces, under the care of local people and peasants. Then, however, my fortunes turned. I was called up to the city, to wage war against the Heike. I first crushed Kiso no Yoshinaka. Next, in pursuit of victory, I whipped my swift steed over precipitous crags, in utter disregard of my life, or braved wind and wave on the boundless sea, ever at risk of sinking to the depths and being devoured by great fish. I slept in the wilds, pillowed on helmet or armor, in steadfast pursuit of the calling of arms, solely to soothe the wrath of my ancestors and to attain the long-cherished goal of triumph. I also found myself appointed an officer of the police, with the fifth rank: a weighty post and, for our house, a signal honor. Nevertheless profound grief now burdens me. What can I do, failing the aid of the gods and buddhas, to convey my anguished plea?

Therefore I have sworn on the backs of protective talismans from countless temples and shrines that I have no ambition whatever, and I have presented prayers to that effect to divinities great and small throughout Japan. So far, however, he has not relaxed his suspicions. Now, this land of ours is the land of the gods, and the gods surely accept no offense against what is right.

I have no other recourse but you; to you alone I look for vast compassion. Should you successfully discern the moment to bring my appeal before Lord Yoritomo, should you devise a way to convince him so thoroughly of my innocence that he grants me his pardon, then the excellent karma accrued will win your house everlasting glory, even as smiles light up an anxious face now relieved of care and grateful for the prospect of a life lived in peace.

I might have said more, but I have kept my remarks purposely brief.
Your humble servant,
Yoshitsune
Genryaku 2, sixth month, fifth day

18. The Execution of Munemori

Meanwhile Yoritomo received Lord Munemori,
seating him in a room across an inner court from his own
and watching him through blinds.

Through Hiki no Tōshirō Yoshikazu, he addressed him as follows:
"I have no personal grievance against anyone of the Heike.
I would not have lived, despite Lady Ike's pleas,
if the late Lord Kiyomori had not permitted me to do so.
I owe the commuting of my sentence of exile entirely to his kindness,
and in exile I remained, for twenty years and more.
But then the Heike became enemies of the court,
and a decree from the cloistered emperor charged me with suppressing them.
Having been born and nurtured on imperial soil,
I could not for a moment ignore so august a command. I had no choice.
It is a pleasure for me to meet you."
When Yoshikazu came before Lord Munemori to convey these words,
Munemori straightened his posture and bowed, in a pitiful display of
    deference.
The local warrior chieftains, great and small,
gathered there from many provinces included men from the capital.
These snapped their fingers in dismay.
"Is sitting up respectfully straight going to save his life?" some muttered.
"He should have met his fate out there in the west.
No wonder he was taken alive and dragged all the way down here."
Others shed tears, and one among them said,
        "When the tiger haunts the mountains,
        every beast trembles with fear,
        but when caged he wags his tail,
        begging for food. What commander,
        however brave, reduced to this,
        would not find his courage failing?
        And so, too, Lord Munemori."
Kurō Yoshitsune meanwhile went on pleading with his brother,
but Kagetoki's slander persuaded Yoritomo to withhold any clear reply.
Then came this order: "You are to proceed without delay to the city."
So on the ninth of the sixth month, Yoshitsune started back up to the capital
in the company of Munemori and his son Kiyomune.
Munemori by this time was grateful for every added day of life.
Along the way he kept wondering, "Is this the place? Or this?"
But province after province, post station after post station went by.

> They came to Utsumi, in the province of Owari. Here Yoshitomo, the
> brothers' father, had been executed, and Munemori knew that he
> would be, too. But no: As before, they passed on by, and he felt some-
> what reassured. "Are they actually going to let us live?" he wondered
> pathetically to his son.

"Not a chance," Kiyomune wanted to answer. "They're just waiting
till we get close to the capital, to make sure our heads don't rot in this
heat." His father looked so miserable, though, that he kept his peace.
He just went on calling the Name.
Day followed day. The capital came closer.
They reached the post station at Shinohara in the province of Ōmi.
Yoshitsune, thoughtful as always, sent a man three days' march ahead
to summon from Ōhara the holy man known as Honjōbō Tangō.
Father and son had been together until the previous day,
but that morning they were separated.
"This, then, must be the day we die," they reflected in mounting distress.
Munemori shed bitter tears.
"Where is my son?" he cried. "Where is Kiyomune?
They will take our heads, I know,
but I thought that our bodies at least would lie together.
It is too hard, to be parted while we both still live!
He has never been away from me, not once in all these seventeen years.
It was for him that I did not drown myself in the western ocean
but lived on instead to spread abroad an invidious name!"
The holy man, moved to pity, shrank nonetheless from betraying similar weakness.
He dried his tears and said with affected detachment,
"You must not allow your thoughts to wander.
It would distress you both too much to witness each other's death.

> After receiving the gift of life,
> you enjoyed such wealth and pleasure
> as very few men have ever known.
> An emperor's commoner relative,
> you rose to the post of minister,
> and no shadow tarnished your glory.
> If for you it has now come to this,
> the cause is your karma from past lives.
> Blame neither the world nor any man.
> Samadhi in the Brahma Heaven,
> the highest pleasure, is soon gone.
> How swiftly, then, a life passes
> in this lower realm: like lightning,
> like the dews of early morning!
> A million times a million years
> spent in the lofty Tōri Heaven[279]

....

279. The heaven at the summit of Mount Sumeru, centered on the palace of Indra.

speed by like any fleeting dream.
The thirty-nine years you have lived
amount to no more than an hour.
Whose tongue has known the elixir
that sweeps away old age and death?
Whose length of days has ever matched
the Eastern Father's, the Western Mother's?[280]
The First Emperor of Qin, in his pride,
reached heights that no man could surpass
yet soon lay in his Lishan tomb;
Emperor Wu of Han craved endless life
yet fed in death the moss at Duling.
All born to live must also die.
Not even the Buddha Shakyamuni
escaped the clouds of sandalwood smoke
that rose above his funeral pyre.
Pleasure, they say, yields to sorrow.
For each celestial being, there comes
a day to know the five signs of decline.
So it is that the Buddha taught:
'The mind itself is emptiness.
Sin and success both lack substance.
See into the mind: There is none.
Dharmas do not inhere in Dharma.'[281]
Grasp therefore that good and evil
are both in their essence void
and you have the Buddha's meaning.
How, then, could the Buddha Amida,
after five aeons in deep thought,
conceive his most demanding Vow,
when we, hopeless beings that we are,
turn for aeons beyond counting
on the wheel of transmigration,
tread mountains of priceless treasure,
yet stagger on empty-handed?
Is this not the heart of black regret
and foolishness to dwarf any folly?
Never, never allow your thoughts to stray!" the holy man enjoined;

....

280. Dongfang Shuo and the Queen Mother of the West.
281. Discrete phenomena are not integral to all-pervading reality.

then he gave Munemori the precepts and urged him to call the Name.
Munemori recognized in him a true spiritual friend.
He renounced at once all deluded anxiety,
turned to the west, palms pressed together, and loudly called on Amida.

> Kitsu Kinnaga, drawn sword at his side,
> moved around behind him from the left
> and was already poised to strike
> when Munemori's voice fell silent.
> "And Kiyomune? Is it done?"
> he asked with affecting concern.
> Kinnaga was hardly in position
> when Munemori's head fell forward.
> The holy man burst into tears,
> and surely every man there was moved.

>> And Kinnaga, then, a hereditary Heike retainer who had served Lord
>> Tomomori from morning to night! Very well, people naturally change
>> with the times, but those present were disgusted by his obsequious
>> cruelty.
>>   The holy man gave Kiyomune the precepts in his turn and admon-
>> ished him to call the Name.
>>   "How was my father when he died?" Kiyomune pathetically in-
>> quired.
>>   "Magnificent," the holy man answered. "Have no fear on that score."
>>   Kiyomune wept with relief. "I ask nothing more," he said. "Now,
>> do it!"
>>   This time it was Hori no Yatarō who wielded the sword. Yoshitsune
>> took the heads into the city, while Kinnaga had the bodies buried in
>> one grave. This was because Lord Munemori had displayed so sinful
>> an attachment to his son.

On the twenty-third of the month, the two heads entered the capital.
The police contingent that came out to receive them, on the riverbank at Sanjō,
then paraded them along the avenue
and hung them in a chinaberry tree to the left of the prison gate.
Precedent in the Other Realm may authorize so displaying
the head of a gentleman of the third rank or higher
and hanging it at the prison gate,
but not in this realm of ours. It was unheard of.
No doubt in the Heiji years Nobuyori was beheaded for his evil deeds,
but his head was subjected to no such treatment.
The Heike suffered it first.

Munemori had come up from the west
only to be paraded, alive,
eastward the length of Rokujō;
then, when he came back up from the east,
off he went westward, in death, along Sanjō.
Paraded dead, paraded alive—
which meant the greater or lesser shame?

19. The Execution of Shigehira

Lord Shigehira had been in Izu province since the year before,
in the custody of Kano-no-suke Munemochi,
but the Nara monks kept clamoring for him.
"Very well, let them have him," came the order,
and Izu no Kurando Yorikane, a grandson of Minamoto no Yorimasa,
was sent to escort him down to Nara.
He took Shigehira not by the capital but through Ōtsu, Yamashina,
and on along the Daigo road to a spot not far from Hino.

> Lord Shigehira had taken to wife
> the Torikai counselor Korezane's daughter.
> The grand counselor Kunitsuna adopted her,
> and she became Emperor Antoku's nurse.
> Lady Dainagon-no-suke was her name,
> and she remained with His Majesty
> even after her husband was taken
> at Ichi-no-tani. At Dan-no-ura,
> where the emperor drowned in the sea,
> ferocious warriors captured her.
> She then returned to her home, the city,
> and lived with her elder sister at Hino.

When she learned that her husband's dewdrop life still hung on a leaf tip,
she imagined that she might see him a last time, not in a dream but real.
That was not to be, though, and tears alone consoled her night after night, day
    after day.
Shigehira said to his guards,
"Your recent kindness and consideration have given me great comfort.
Today there is one last favor that I would ask of you.
Having no children, I will leave no regrets behind me.
But my wife of all these years now lives, or so I hear, at Hino.
I would like to see her again and talk over her prayers for my next life."

So it is that he requested a short period of leave.
The warrior guards, being neither stock nor stone, wept to hear him.
They saw no objection and, to his great joy, allowed him to go.
He sent a man to her house to announce,
"Lady Dainagon-no-suke lives here, I believe?
Captain Shigehira is traveling past here toward Nara,
and he wonders whether he might have a word with her.
He would not actually enter the house."

> The instant the news reached her,
> she ran out, crying, "Where is he? Where?"
> There before her, beside the railing,
> stood in an indigo *hitatare*
> and a folded *eboshi* a man
> lean and deeply tanned: It was he.
> She approached the edge of the room,
> just within the blinds, and called out,
> "I must be dreaming! Come in! Come in!"
> Her voice started tears from his eyes.
> Tears blinded hers, too. She sat speechless.
> He leaned in toward her, under the blinds,
> weeping, and spoke to her: "Last spring,
> at Ichi-no-tani, I should have died,
> but in punishment for my crimes,
> I suppose, I was taken alive,
> paraded through the city streets,
> and shamed even in Kamakura.
> All this was terrible enough,
> but now I am going to Nara,
> to be handed over to the monks,
> who will behead me. My last wish
> was to see you one final time.
> I have done so now, and I ask nothing more.

>> I wanted to renounce the world and send you a lock of hair to remember me by, but they would not let me." With these words he separated a lock from his forehead, and, where he could reach it, bit it off. "Let this remind you of me," he said, and gave it to her.

>> She, who had worried so long about him, now showed signs of utter despair. "After you and I parted," she said, "I should have drowned myself, like Lord Michimori's wife, but no reliable report confirmed that you were gone, and I kept wondering whether by some miracle I might see you again as you had once been. That forlorn hope sustained me all

this time. Oh, it hurts so, to think that I will never see you again! I hoped that their letting you live this long meant that they would never . . ."

They talked on, amid endless tears, of things old and new.

"You look so shabby, though!" she said. "Do change into these!"

She brought out a matched short-sleeved robe and white hunting cloak.

He put them on and left with her the clothes that he had been wearing.

"Keep these to remember me by," he said.

"Of course I will," she replied, "but to remind me of you forever,

I would much rather have some little thing from your brush."

She gave him an inkstone, and in tears he wrote down this poem:

> These poor clothes of mine,
> wet with all the tears my eyes
> weep so helplessly,
> I give you now in this exchange,
> that you may remember me.

At once she replied,

> These clothes you give me
> in exchange for some from me—
> what good can they do,
> when the only memory
> they leave me is this last day?

"A couple pledged to each other are sure to be born together in the next life," he said.

"Pray that you and I be reborn on the same lotus throne.

Now the sun is low, and it is a long way to Nara.

It would be thoughtless of me to keep the warriors waiting."

He started away, but she clung to his sleeve.

"Oh, oh, do stay a little!" she pleaded, to detain him.

"I am sure you understand how I feel," he answered, "but there is no escape.

I shall be with you again in the life to come." And off he went.

> He would not see her again in this life,
> that he knew and longed to look back,
> but he steeled himself against such weakness.
> She collapsed at the foot of the blinds,
> writhed in anguish, and keened his loss.
> Her cries, which followed him out the gate,
> stayed him from urging his horse forward,
> for tears darkened the path ahead.
> Now he wished he had never seen her.
> *She* only yearned to run after him,

but that was more than she could do,
    so she lay still, a robe over her head.
In due course the Nara monks took custody of Shigehira, then met in
    council.
"So heinous is this Shigehira's crime," they concluded,
"that the three thousand crimes chastised by the five punishments do not even
    include it.
That such an act should call down commensurate retribution is entirely just.
This man is an enemy of the Buddha and of his Teaching.
We should probably drag him around the boundary walls of Tōdaiji and
    Kōfukuji,
and saw his head off, or bury him alive, upright, and *then* behead him."
However, the older monks objected.
"That is not the way monks behave," they said.
"We should just give him over to his warrior guards
and have them behead him beside the Kizu River."
They returned the prisoner to his guards,
who took him to the riverbank and prepared to do so.
Several thousand monks and countless other spectators watched.

A man long in Shigehira's employ, Moku Uma-no-jō Tomotoki by
name, now served the Hachijō Princess. He rode as fast as he could to
Nara, with liberal use of the whip, to witness the death of his former
lord, and he arrived just as Shigehira's head was about to fall. Cleaving
his way though the vast throng, he approached the condemned man
and said, weeping, "My lord, it is I, Tomotoki. I have come to be pres-
ent at your end."

"That is very good of you," Shigehira replied. "I should like my head
to fall while I worship the Buddha, but that seems impossible—my
crime is so very great."

"That presents no difficulty." Tomotoki discussed the matter with
the guards and brought Shigehira a buddha image from nearby. For-
tunately, it was an image of Amida.

He stood the Amida on the gravel riverbank,
undid the cord from a sleeve of his hunting cloak,
attached one end to Amida's hands, and gave Shigehira the other.
Shigehira, holding the cord, addressed Amida as follows:
    "I have heard that Devadatta,
    who committed the three offenses [282]
    and burned the eighty thousand scriptures,

....

282. Killing an arhat, spilling a buddha's blood, injuring a monk.

Tomotoki (right background) arrives just in time.

learned from the Buddha that in time
birth would be his as the buddha Ten'ō.
Despite the gravity of his crimes,
just having heard the holy Teaching
assured his enlightenment after all.
What foul crimes I myself committed sprang from no wish of mine,
but solely from natural obedience to orders from on high.
What man, intent on preserving his life, would make light of his sovereign's
    command?
What son would ignore his father's?
Sovereign or father, refusal is out of the question.
Only the Buddha can decide the right and wrong of the matter.
Now retribution is poised to strike, and my life is at an end.
The bitterest regret now comes too late.
However, the heart of all the buddhas is compassion,
and there are many, varied paths to salvation.
'The all-embracing doctrine teaches, in essence,
that wrong paths are the same as right'—
this saying is graven in my heart.

'Call once the Name of Amida and abolish countless sins.'
May this evil path of mine prove to lead only to good,
and may this last time I call the Name bring me to birth in paradise!"
He called the Name aloud ten times,
stretched forth his neck, and gave his head to the sword.

> Evil committed in the past
> requires due acknowledgment,
> yet what they now saw before them
> moved the monks in their thousands
> and the warrior guards to tears.

>> Shigehira's head was nailed up before the great torii of Hannyaji, for
>> this was where he had stood, that night during the Jishō wars, when he
>> burned the temples of Nara. His wife, Lady Dainagon-no-suke, sent a
>> palanquin to retrieve his headless body, so as to be able to give him the
>> last rites. The palanquin brought it back to Hino. Her feelings when it
>> arrived are easily imagined. The body had retained the full look of life
>> the day before, after the execution, but by now, in the summer heat, it
>> was sadly changed.

It was therefore imperative to proceed.
She roused the most worthy monks from nearby Hōkaiji to perform the services
  needed.
As for the head, she begged the Great Buddha holy man, Shunjōbō Chōgen,
  for it,[283]
and he had the monks send it to Hino. Head and body together turned to smoke.
She sent the bones to Mount Kōya and erected a funeral monument at Hino.

> The Lady Dainagon-no-suke
> changed to the habit of a nun
> and devoted herself to prayer
> that her husband in the life to come
> should attain enlightenment.
> Such is their deeply moving story.

....

283. The monk Shunjōbō Chōgen (1121–1206) led fund-raising to rebuild the Great Buddha Hall and recast the Great Buddha of Tōdaiji.

BOOK TWELVE

1. The Great Earthquake

(recitative)

The men of the Heike were no more, and all was quiet in the west.
Provinces obeyed their governors and estates their stewards.
People high and low were feeling secure
when, on the ninth of the seventh month, at midday, [1185]
the earth shook violently for quite a long time.
Within the confines of the imperial capital,
in the Shirakawa district of the city, the shock destroyed six great temples.[284]
Of the Hōshōji pagoda's nine stories, the upper six fell to the ground.
At Tokujōju-in seventeen bays of the thirty-three-bay hall collapsed.

> (song)
> Imperial palace buildings,
> the homes of the noblest gentlemen,
> shrines to the gods, imposing temples,
> houses of the least of the people
> came crashing down with a thunderous roar,
> while dust rose like smoke in billowing clouds.
> The sky turned black, blotting out the sun.
> Old and young grew faint with terror;
> fear struck courtiers and commoners.
>
> Provinces far and wide suffered equal disaster.
> The earth split open, and water gushed forth;
> great boulders cracked and rolled into ravines;
> mountains gave way and slid into rivers;
> the sea burst from its bed and swamped the shore.
> Waves flung coasting boats violently about;
> under the hooves of passing horses, the ground failed.
> When flood threatens, high ground offers safety,
> and crossing a river affords refuge from fire,
> but there is no escape from an earthquake.
> Only a bird could fly away through the sky;
> only a dragon could rise and mount the clouds.

....

284. More literally, the six temples with a character read *shō* in their names: Hōshōji, Sonshōji, Enshōji, Saishōji, Jōshōji, and Enshōji.

The number of people crushed beneath the ruins
around Shirakawa or Rokuhara
and throughout the city passed all counting.
Three among the four major elements—
water, fire, and air—cause harm often enough,
but not earth, surely. Moved by blind panic,
high and low shut themselves behind closed doors.
Each time the heavens roared or the ground shook,
a chorus of voices, certain of death,
rose in screams and loud appeals to the Name.
Seventy-, eighty-, or ninety-year-olds,
aghast that the world should end so very soon,
raised shrieks that set the children bawling.
Cloistered Emperor Go-Shirakawa happened then to be on a pilgrimage to
Imagumano.
So many deaths and the resulting pollution hastened his return to his Rokujō
residence.
What he and his entourage saw on the way must have torn at their hearts.
While the emperor rode in the imperial palanquin out to the shore of his lake,
the cloistered sovereign settled into a tent in the garden south of his mansion.
The greatest ladies fled their collapsed residences by palanquin or carriage.
Doctors learned in astrology rushed in, warning that that very night,
at the hours of the boar or the rat, the world would overturn. [ca. 10 P.M.–midnight]
To call this prediction terrifying would be a gross understatement.

They say that during the earthquake
in Saikō 3, third month and eighth day, [856]
under the reign of Emperor Montoku,
the head of the Buddha at Tōdaiji
fell to the ground. During another,
in Tengyō 2, fourth month, fifth day, [939]
the emperor fled his palace
for refuge in a fifty-foot tent
put up before the Jōneiden.
But all that happened too long ago
to merit that much attention now.
Surely the like of this disaster
will never in times to come recur.
The emperor had left his capital,
to drown far away in the ocean;
ministers and senior nobles
had been paraded through the streets

and their heads hung at the prison gate.
There has always been reason to fear
the vengeful rage of angry ghosts.
Everyone endowed with some sense
therefore looked with deep apprehension
to what the future might bring.

2. *The Indigo Dyer*

On the twenty-second of the eighth month, the holy monk Mongaku, of Takao,
hung around his neck the genuine and authentic skull of Minamoto no
    Yoshitomo,
Lord Minamoto no Yoritomo's father,
and around a disciple's neck the skull of Kamadabyōe Masakiyo.[285]
So equipped, he set off for Kamakura.
The Yoshitomo skull he had given Yoritomo in Jishō 4 was not the real one, [1180]
just some old skull that he had wrapped in white cloth
and presented to Yoritomo to goad him into rebelling.
And rebel Yoritomo did, seizing power over the land
in full faith that the skull really was his father's.
Now here came Mongaku again, down to Kamakura, with another he had
    turned up.
A certain indigo dyer long favored by Yoshitomo,
pained that his master's head should hang year after year at the prison gate
without anyone to pray for his happier rebirth in the hereafter,
approached the then-chief of the police, who allowed him to take it down.
"Yoritomo is in exile," he reflected, "but he will come into his own in the end.
When he does, he will start looking for his father's skull."
So the indigo dyer secreted it at Engakuji, in the Eastern Hills.
Apparently Mongaku heard about this and took him along to Kamakura.
On learning that Mongaku was to reach the town that day,
Yoritomo went out to meet him at the Katase River.
He then changed into mourning gray and returned to Kamakura in tears.
He seated Mongaku on the veranda and stood below him, on the ground, to
    receive his father's skull.
The warriors great and small present for this touching moment wept.
    Yoritomo cut away mighty rocks
    and erected a new temple,
    dedicated to his father,

....

285. A retainer of Yoshitomo's.

that he named Shōjōju-in.
The court, too, moved by his gesture,
announced at Yoshitomo's grave
his appointment to the second rank
and the post of palace minister.
The left grand controller Kanetada,
they say, spoke for the emperor.
Yoritomo's prowess in war
had lifted not only himself
and his house to impressive heights,
but also, for his father's spirit,
had obtained rank and position.
What a marvelous achievement!

3. *The Exile of Tokitada*

On the twenty-third of the ninth month, the court received from Yoritomo
an order banishing those Heike nobles left in the capital to one province or
  another:
Tokitada to Noto and his son Tokizane to Kazusa,
Nobumoto to Aki, Masaakira to Oki, the prelate Senshin to Awa,
the prelate Nōen to Bingo, and master of monastic discipline Chūkai to
  Musashi.

Some across the western ocean,
some far past the Kanto clouds,
their journey's end beyond surmise,
reunion only a fond hope,
swallowing vain tears of parting,
set out to take their separate ways
in misery anyone might share.
One among them, Tokitada,
called upon Kenreimon-in,
then resident at Yoshida.
"My offense is grave," he told her,
"and today I start into exile.
While I lived, like you, in the city,
I longed to know how you were getting on
and to place myself at your disposal,
but while the thought of what may lie before you is constantly with me,
I find the future impossible to imagine." So he addressed her, weeping.
"Yes," she replied, "you are the only one left me from the old days.

Who else now would feel sympathy for me or come to call?"
She could not keep her tears from flowing.

> *(speech)*
>
> Taira no Tokitada was a grandson of Tomonobu, the former governor
> of Dewa, and a son of the posthumous left minister Tokinobu. Being
> the late Kenshunmon-in's brother made him a close maternal relative
> of Emperor Takakura. The world thought very highly of him. Another
> sister of his, Lady Nii, had married Lord Kiyomori, which made avail-
> able to him any combination of appointments that he desired. For that
> reason he had risen quickly to the second rank and the post of grand
> counselor, and he had headed the police three times. When, in the lat-
> ter capacity, he arrested a thief or a robber, he cut off the man's right
> arm at the elbow without inquiring further and banished him from
> the city. This practice earned him the nickname "Police Chief from
> Hell."

When the cloistered emperor's decree demanded that the Heike,
then in the provinces of the west, return the emperor and the regalia,
and Hanakata, who delivered it, had the *namikata* brand burned into his cheek,
it was Tokitada who ordered the branding.
The cloistered emperor had looked forward to seeing him again,
his late empress having been Tokitada's sister,
but such foul behavior made him too angry to do so.
Yoshitsune, now equally close to Tokitada, hoped in vain to soothe his wrath.
Tokitada's son Tokiie, then in his sixteenth year, had escaped exile
and gone to live instead with Tokimitsu, his uncle.
With his mother, Lady Sotsu-no-suke, he clung to his father's sleeve
in despair that the moment of parting should be at hand.
"It was bound to come anyway, sooner or later," Tokitada bravely declared,
but no doubt he, too, was deeply affected.

> Now into his declining years,
> he had to leave the wife and son
> who long had meant so much to him;
> watch the city, his only home,
> vanish behind him into cloud;
> and set out for northern marches
> that once to him were only names:
> an endless and painful journey.
> "There are Shiga and Karasaki,
> look!" they told him. "And, before us,
> the Mano inlet and Katada coast."
> The weeping Tokitada made this poem:

> *I shall not return,*
> *that I know, at Katada,*
> *   watching nets drawn in—*
> *all the water streaming through,*
> *   as the tears stream through my eyes.*

He had roamed only yesterday
the waves of the western ocean,
until the fierce hatred of the foe
so overwhelmed his little craft
that today, buried under snows
heaped on him in the distant north,
he knew such miseries of loss
as weighed like sullen, brooding clouds
on all his memories of home.

4. The Execution of Tosabō

Meanwhile the ten warriors assigned by Yoritomo to attend Kurō Yoshitsune
learned privately of their lord's suspicions about his younger brother,
and in deference to their lord's feelings they withdrew to Kamakura.
These two men were not only brothers but also to each other as father and son.
Yoshitsune had crushed Kiso no Yoshinaka in the first month of the previous
    year,
then gone on to defeat the Heike in battle after battle,
until in the spring of the current year he destroyed them for good,
so bringing peace to the realm and calm to the four seas.
For this he deserved a reward, but somehow these rumors were spreading,
and no one, from the emperor down to the least of the commoners, knew why.
It had all begun that spring at Watanabe, in Settsu,
when Yoshitsune was gathering his fleet
and that argument had flared over whether or not to install bow oars.
At the time he had made a fool of Kajiwara Kagetoki,
who thereafter, in bitter resentment, let pass no chance to slander him.
That was how it had happened.
Yoritomo, who believed that Yoshitsune was plotting against him,
realized that dispatching a force up to the capital
would provoke stripping the planks from the Uji and Seta bridges,
chaos throughout the city, and other such dire consequences.
Instead he summoned a fighting monk named Tosabō Shōshun.
"Go on up to the capital," he said,
"pretend you are there for a pilgrimage, and kill him."

Tosabō respectfully assented.

He started straight up to the city without even returning to his lodge.

He arrived on the twenty-ninth of the ninth month, but by the next day he had still not reported to Yoshitsune. Yoshitsune sent Musashibō Benkei to summon him when he learned that Tosabō was in the city. Benkei quickly brought him in.

"Well? Have you no letter for me from Lord Yoritomo?" Yoshitsune demanded to know.

"No, sir," Tosabō replied, "he gave me nothing because he had no particular message. 'Just tell him,' he said, 'that I know the present calm in the capital is due to his presence there, and that he must continue to mount vigilant guard.' That was all."

"I do not for a moment believe that," Yoshitsune rejoined.

"You are here to assassinate me.

Dispatching a force up to the capital

would provoke stripping the planks from the Uji and Seta bridges,

chaos throughout the city, and other dire consequences;

so he obviously sent you instead, with orders to feign a pilgrimage

but really to kill me." Thunderstruck, Tosabō asked,

"What could possibly give you that idea, sir?

I have long been planning a pilgrimage to Kumano, and that is what I am
    here for."

Yoshitsune retorted,

"Because of Kagetoki's slander,
he barred me from Kamakura
and would not even talk to me.
Instead he had me turn around
and go straight back to the capital.
Just give me an answer to *that*!"

"I know nothing about that, sir," Tosabō protested.

"But as for myself, I have no dark intentions toward you,

and I will gladly sign an oath to that effect."

"Swear it or not, I still know that Lord Yoritomo has his mind set against me."

Yoshitsune was visibly angry.

To extricate himself from his peril, Tosabō wrote out seven oaths,

some of which he burned and swallowed and some of which he offered at
    shrines.

Once Yoshitsune had dismissed him, he informed the warriors guarding the
    palace

that the attack would take place that night.

The greatest of Yoshitsune's loves

was a young woman named Shizuka,
the daughter of Iso-no-zenji,
a *shirabyōshi* dancer.
She was never far from his side.

> Shizuka told herself, "I hear that the avenue outside is teeming with warriors. He never called them here, though. There's no reason for the men on palace guard duty to be carrying on this way. Oh, no! That monk today, with all his oaths—he must be the one behind it! I'll send someone out to see what's going on."

> Yoshitsune had in his service several of the "Rokuhara Boys" once at Taira no Kiyomori's beck and call, and she sent out two. They never returned. Next she sent out a servant girl, hoping that a woman at least would come to no harm.

> The girl soon came running back. "Two youths just like the two from here are lying dead in front of Tosabō's gate. His grounds are full of saddled horses, and behind the curtain there are fully armed and armored men all ready to attack. This has nothing to do with a pilgrimage."

> Yoshitsune leaped up, and in frantic haste Shizuka dressed him in his commander's armor. He tied just the shoulder cord, gripped his sword, and went out. A saddled horse stood waiting for him at the middle gate.

Yoshitsune mounted, ordered the gate thrown open, and awaited the onslaught.
Forty or fifty armored and helmeted riders soon swarmed toward him with
    fierce cries.
Yoshitsune rose in his stirrups and shouted in a great voice,
    "Attack by day or attack by night,
    there is not a man in Japan
    who can just dispatch Yoshitsune!"
    All alone, he charged straight at them,
    and those fifty warriors parted
    to let him through. Right behind him
    came Yoshimori from Ise,
    Satō Tadanobu from Mutsu,
    Eda no Genzō, Kumai Tarō,
    Musashibō Benkei, and others,
    each of them worth a thousand men.
    Next with cries of "A night attack!"
    a stream of Yoshitsune's men
    raced in from quarters everywhere,
    till sixty or seventy mounted warriors

Musashibō Benkei takes the captured Tosabō back to Yoshitsune's residence.

overwhelmed Tosabō's assault.
They so laid into the attackers
that few of the enemy survived;
the greater number died by the sword.
Tosabō, who only barely escaped, took refuge in the wilds of Mount Kurama—
wilds that Yoshitsune knew well, having once lived among them.
He had Tosabō seized and brought to his residence the next day.
Apparently the man had been hiding in the ravine called Sōjō-ga-tani.
They dragged him into the court before the middle gate,
and there he sat, in a blue-black *hitatare* and a black cowl.
Yoshitsune grinned. "This is what you get for swearing all those oaths," he said.
Unfazed, Tosabō sat up and laughed loudly.
"Yes," he said, "I swore falsely, and that did me in."
        "To honor the orders of your lord,"
        Yoshitsune then went on,
        "you gave no thought to your own life.
        That is extremely brave of you.
        If you prefer to stay alive,
        I could send you back to Kamakura.
        Is that what you wish me to do?"
        "The very idea is preposterous,"

Tosabō answered. "If I did,
do you imagine for one moment
that my lord would allow me to live?
'You are a monk, I know,' he told me, 'but you are the man to finish him.'
Once he had spoken his order, my life was his. Could I take it back?
No, just be good enough to behead me now."
"Very well," answered Yoshitsune.
"Cut off his head!" They took him out
to the riverbank at Rokujō,
and there they did what they had to do.
There was no one who did not praise him.

5. Yoshitsune's Flight

Now, there was one Adachi no Shinzaburō, a man-of-all-work.
Yoritomo had given him to Yoshitsune with the assurance,
"This fellow is a complete nobody, of course, but he is unusually sharp."
Yoritomo ordered Adachi to keep an eye on what Yoshitsune was up to
and to report to him whatever he noted.
After the execution of Tosabō, Adachi raced day and night down to Kamakura,
where he informed Yoritomo of what had happened.
Yoritomo commanded Noriyori, his younger brother,
to lead a punitive force straight up to the capital.
Noriyori declined repeatedly to do so,
but Yoritomo insisted so forcefully that in the end he gave in.
Noriyori appeared fully armed before Yoritomo to bid him farewell.
"Don't you go and follow Kurō's example," Yoritomo warned him.
Noriyori was so frightened that he put off arms and armor then and there
and gave up his expedition to the city.
He wrote out every day ten oaths
swearing undying loyalty
and every night read them aloud:
a hundred days, a thousand oaths
for his brother, Yoritomo.
But no, they still were not enough.
Yoritomo had him executed.
Yoshitsune learned next that a punitive force under Hōjō no Shirō
Tokimasa was on its way. He decided to flee toward Kyushu, and in
that connection he appealed for help to Ogata no Saburō Koreyoshi,
who was powerful enough to have driven the Heike from the nine
provinces of the island.

"All right," Koreyoshi answered, "one of your men, Kikuchi no Jirō
Takanao, is an old enemy of mine. Give him to me, and I will cut off
his head. Then you may count on me."

Yoshitsune complied at once. Takanao was taken out to the Rokujō
riverbank and beheaded. Koreyoshi then upheld his side of the bar-
gain.

On the second of the eleventh month, Yoshitsune called on the cloistered
emperor
and through Yasutsune, the lord of the Treasury, addressed him as follows:
"It is unnecessary at this juncture to rehearse
the loyal service that I have humbly rendered Your Cloistered Eminence in the
past.
In the present, however, slander issuing from among the men in Kamakura
has moved Yoritomo to order me killed.
I mean therefore to go down for a while to Kyushu.
For that reason I should be extremely grateful
if you were to have your office provide me with a letter of support."
The sovereign's response was to wonder what consequences might follow
if his having issued such a document came to Yoritomo's attention.
He therefore assembled the senior nobles in council.
All present agreed as follows:
"Should Yoshitsune remain in the capital and a large Kanto army then invade the
city,
endless violence and turmoil would ensue.
However, if Yoshitsune were to remove himself to some distant region,
that danger would for some time cease to exist."
Ogata Koreyoshi, the men of the Usuki, the Betsugi, and the Matsura leagues—
indeed every influential Kyushu warrior—therefore received a decree
requiring obedience to their commander, Minamoto no Yoshitsune.
The next day, the third, at the hour of the hare, [ca. 6 A.M.]
Yoshitsune left the capital with some five hundred mounted men.
His departure caused no disturbance whatever.

A warrior of the Settsu Genji,
Ōta no Tarō Yorimoto,
declared, "Must I allow this man
to pass my gate and never shoot
against him one single arrow?"
At a place named Kawarazu,
he caught up with Yoshitsune,
attacked, and joined battle with him.
Yoshitsune had five hundred men.

Yorimoto's small force of sixty
quickly ended up surrounded.
"Get them, men! Let no one escape!"
the cry went up. The fierce attack
left Yorimoto himself wounded
and most of his retainers killed.
Yorimoto beat a hasty retreat,
with an arrow in his mount's belly.
Yoshitsune took many heads
and hung them up for the god of war.
"A fine start, that!" he said, pleased.
He put to sea from Daimotsu-no-ura,
only to meet a westerly gale that drove him ashore at Sumiyoshi.
From there he sought refuge in the Yoshino wilds,
but the Yoshino monks attacked, so he fled to Nara.
When the Nara monks, too, attacked, he made his way back to the city
and set off from there toward the far north.
He had started out from the capital with a dozen women,
whom he abandoned at Sumiyoshi.
On the sand, under the pines, they stumbled about or lay weeping, forlorn,
until the Sumiyoshi priests
took pity on them in their plight
and sent them back to the city.
The boats carrying Yoshitsune's most trusted lieutenants—
his uncle Shida no Saburō Yoshinori, Jūrō Yukiie, Ogata no Saburō Koreyoshi—
were blown onto shores and islands hither and yon,
and none knew the fate of the others.
That sudden, violent wind from the west
seemed the work of the angry Heike dead.
On the seventh of the eleventh month, Hōjō no Shirō Tokimasa,
representing Lord Yoritomo in Kamakura,
reached the capital at the head of sixty thousand mounted men.
The next day, the eighth, he called on the cloistered emperor
to urge pursuit and suppression of Yoshitsune, Yukiie, and Yoshinori.
The sovereign granted the decree on the spot.
Just a few days earlier, on the second, at Yoshitsune's request,
his office had issued a call for rebellion against Yoritomo.
Now, on the eighth of the very same month,
a decree from him directed that Yoshitsune be crushed.
So it goes, alas, in this world where, morning and evening, everything
changes.

6. The Yoshida Grand Counselor

Meanwhile Yoritomo applied to the cloistered emperor, Go-Shirakawa,
for appointment as constable over all of Japan
and authority to levy military provisions from every quarter acre of land.
The sovereign remarked in response,
"According to a passage in the Sutra of Innumerable Meanings,
the reward for destroying the king's enemy has always been half of a state,
but Japan has never known such a case.
Yoritomo's demand exceeds his deserts."
However, the council of senior nobles conceded the merit of the request.
Yoritomo's application was approved.

> Yoritomo assigned a warden to each province and a steward to each
> and every estate. It was no longer possible to conceal a single blade of
> rice. In such matters it was through the Yoshida grand counselor
> Tsunefusa, among all the city's senior nobles, that Yoritomo commu-
> nicated with the court. This Tsunefusa was known for strict fairness.
> Once the Genji had seized power, Heike allies began appealing to him
> in letters and through messengers and flattering him this way or that,
> but he never budged.

So it was that when the Heike, in their heyday,
confined His Cloistered Eminence to the Toba Mansion
and assigned to the mansion two superintendents,
they chose the Kadenokōji counselor and this Tsunefusa.[286]
A son of the supernumerary controller Mitsufusa,
Tsunefusa lost his father in his twelfth year but rose swiftly nonetheless.

> He held at one and the same time
> three key posts and rose from there
> to head chamberlain, then consultant,
> grand controller, grand counselor
> at the senior second rank,
> and the post of Dazaifu deputy.
> He rose past many; none rose past him.
> Yes, a man's worth or worthlessness
> never leaves any doubt in the end,
> just as an awl pierces a bag.
> He was a most remarkable man.

....

286. Both are actually the same man. The Kade-no-kōji counselor Tsunefusa has already appeared twice
before (8:1 and 11:11).

7. Rokudai

Hōjō Tokimasa issued an announcement:
"Whoever brings forward a scion of the house of Taira,
he shall have the reward that he desires."
The people of the city, who knew their way about, coveted this reward.
They cruelly went looking for Heike children and found many.
They would present the pretty, pale-skinned son of any nobody,
describing him as Captain So-and-So's boy, or Lieutenant Whatnot's,
and claiming, despite the parents' tears and entreaties,
"His guardian identified him," or "His nurse says that's who he is."
Tokimasa's men drowned or buried the babies
    and smothered or stabbed older boys to death.
    No words can describe the mothers' grief,
    the desperate laments of the nurses.
    Tokimasa, a father himself
    and a grandfather many times over,
    hated to do it, but there it is:
    Such are the exigencies of duty.
Of special interest was Rokudai, Koremori's son and a grandson of Shigemori.
The scion of the senior Heike line, he was now growing up.
Tokimasa sent out search parties to capture him, but without success.
He was preparing to return to Kamakura
when a woman appeared at Rokuhara to report,
"West of here, beyond Henjōji and north of the mountain temple Daikakuji,
there is a place named Shōbudani.
Lord Koremori's wife is hiding there with her son and daughter."
Tokimasa sent a man straight there to reconnoiter.
He discovered, living in one of the lodges,
a group of women and children clearly anxious to keep out of sight.
Through a crack in the fence, he saw a white puppy come bounding out,
followed by a handsome boy eager to catch it.
A woman, apparently the boy's nurse, cried,
"Oh, no! Someone may see you!" and hastily drew him inside.
The man realized that this must be the boy he was after and raced back to
    report.
Tokimasa hurried there the next day,
surrounded the place, and sent a man in to announce,
"Hōjō Tokimasa, representing Lord Yoritomo,
has learned that Rokudai, the son of Taira no Koremori, is living here.
Produce him immediately!"

Rokudai's mother all but fainted.

> Saitōgo and Saitōroku
> went running about for a look
> and saw warriors on all sides—
> they could not possibly get him out.
> His nurse collapsed before her mistress,
> wailing in agonized distress.
> They had been keeping their talk low,
> hoping always to pass unnoticed,
> but now everyone in the lodge
> gave voice to loud lamentation.
> Tokimasa, moved to pity,
> simply waited, wiping his eyes.

Some time passed; then he spoke again.
"The world is not yet at peace, you see,
and I have come for this young man lest anyone start new trouble.
He will come to no harm. Please send him out at once."
Rokudai said to his mother,

> "There is no escape, you know.
> Let me go out there right away.
> If warriors come bursting in
> searching for me, they will find you
> in a most unfortunate state.

Even if I go with them now, I will request leave soon enough and be back. Please do not be so upset." He did his poor best to reassure her, but he had to comply.

In tears his mother smoothed his hair and dressed him. Just before sending him out, she gave him a beautiful little rosary made of black sandalwood beads. "Call the Name to the end," she said, "whenever the end may come, and go on to paradise."

Her son took it and gave her this touching reply: "Now that I must leave you, Mother, all I want is to go and join my father." At these words,

his young sister, now in her tenth year, spoke up in turn.
"I want to go and join Father, too!" she said, and started out at a run.
Her nurse stopped her from going farther.

> This year was only Rokudai's twelfth,
> though he seemed several years older,
> such were his looks and dignity.
> Lest the foe detect some weakness,
> he kept his sleeves pressed to his eyes,

but, alas, the tears overflowed.
He had to board a palanquin
wholly surrounded by warriors.
Saitōgo and Saitōroku
likewise went with the palanquin,
to left and right. Tokimasa
ordered his men off two fresh horses,
which he then offered the pair,
but both of them refused to ride.
All the way from Daikakuji
to Rokuhara, barefoot, they ran.
Mother and nurse appealed to heaven
or fell in agony to the ground.
The boy's mother could only weep and lament,
"I hear that lately they have been collecting Heike sons,
then drowning, burying, smothering, or stabbing them to death.
Oh, how, then, are they going to kill my darling boy?
They might behead him at least, if only he were a little older!
Some leave a son of theirs with a nurse
and see him only from time to time—
a common practice, though hard to bear
in defiance of parental love.
But, alas, since I bore my son,
I have not let him stray from my side!
Nobody else, so my heart told me,
ever possessed a treasure like him.
Day and night we two cherished him,
until his poor father was lost to me
and I looked for my only comfort
to my children, my constant company.
One is still here, but the other is gone.
What, after this, am I to do?
This has been my enduring fear
these three years past, yet day to day
I never thought to see it happen,
and I have prayed so long meanwhile
to Kannon at Hasedera!287
But no, they did come and take him.

....

287. A Kannon temple in the mountains east of Nara and a major pilgrimage center.

Oh, it is more than I can bear!
I suppose he must be dead by now."
The night advanced, but her heart was too full, and she could not sleep.
A little later, though, she said to the nurse,
"Just now I dropped off for a moment and dreamed
that he came to me on a white horse.
'I missed you so badly,' he said, 'that I got leave to come back for a while.'
Then he sat down beside me, weeping as though his heart would break.
At that point I awoke and felt about for him, but there was nobody there.
It was a dream, I know, and so short that I wish I had never woken up."
The nurse wept, too; the night dragged on, and they all but floated away on their
    tears.
At long last the crier of the hours announced dawn.
Saitōroku returned.

> "What news? What news do you bring?" the mother asked. They re-
> plied, "Nothing has happened yet. Here is his letter."
>
> She opened it. He had written, "You must be terribly worried.
> Everything is all right so far. I miss you so much!" It sounded very
> grown up. After reading it his mother said not a word but instead
> slipped it into the front fold of her robe and lay facedown. Her misery
> is all too pitifully easy to imagine.
>
> A good while later, Saitōroku said, "Time is passing, and I am wor-
> ried. I must go back."
>
> In tears she therefore wrote her answer and gave it to him. Saitōroku
> said good-bye and left.

The nurse, too distraught to sit still, went running out
and wandered in tears wherever her steps chanced to take her,
until she heard from someone on the way,
"In the hills beyond here is a temple known as Takao.
Mongaku, the holy man there, enjoys Lord Yoritomo's highest respect,
and they say he is seeking a noble youth to be his disciple."
The nurse kept this encouraging news to herself
and went alone to Takao, where she met the holy man.
"I have had a young lord in my care ever since he was born," she said,
"and this year is his twelfth. Yesterday a warrior came and took him.
In your goodness, reverend sir,
will you not beg for his life and accept him as your disciple?"
She prostrated herself before him, wailing in a paroxysm of grief.

> The holy man took pity on her
> and asked her to tell him more.

She rose and answered, in tears, "The wife of Captain Taira no Kore-mori has been bringing up the son of a close relative, and someone must have reported him as her own son, because yesterday a warrior came and took him away."

"What was the warrior's name?" Mongaku asked.

"He was called Hōjō Tokimasa."

"Then I shall go and inquire."

What he had said promised nothing,
but it restored her mood a little,
and she hurried back to Daikakuji.
There she reported what she had heard.
"I was afraid you would drown yourself,"
her mistress said, "and my own wish
was to drown in some river or pool."
She begged the nurse for the whole story.
She heard from the nurse a full account of all that the holy man had said.
"Oh, I so hope," she cried, weeping,
her palms pressed together in prayer,
"that my son's life will be granted him
and he will let me see him again!"

Mongaku went to Rokuhara to look into the matter.

Tokimasa replied, "Lord Yoritomo mentioned being informed that there were many Heike sons and grandsons hiding in the capital, especially Taira no Koremori's son by the daughter of the Naka-no-mikado grand counselor Narichika. He said that this boy, the scion of the senior Heike line, was now apparently growing up and he wanted him found at all costs and executed. Such was the order that he gave me. I captured a number of such children recently, but I could not find this one, and I was about to leave for Kamakura when the day before yesterday, to my astonishment, I learned where he was. Yesterday I went to fetch him. He is so attractive that I feel sorry for him, and so far I have done nothing further with him."

"I should like a look at him," Mongaku replied.

Tokimasa took him off to show him Rokudai.

There he was, in a *hitatare*
double-layered, brocade and damask,
with a rosary on his wrist
strung with black sandalwood beads.
The sweep of his hair, his comely figure
lent him such true nobility
that he hardly seemed of this world.

The night before, he must not have slept,
and his face, now a little drawn,
looked all the more touchingly sweet.
What the sight of the holy man
stirred in his mind is hard to say,
but tears filled his eyes. Mongaku, too,
moistened the sleeves of his black robe.

Mongaku did not see how anyone could possibly execute this child, whatever threat he might pose in the future. Therefore he addressed Tokimasa. "Perhaps I have some past tie to this young gentleman," he said, "because he strikes me as extraordinarily appealing. Please grant him another twenty days. I shall go to Kamakura and ask Lord Yoritomo to let me take charge of him. I was in exile at the time, but I nonetheless went up to the capital in the hope of giving Lord Yoritomo his proper place in the world, and on his behalf I requested a decree from the cloistered emperor. One night on the way there, I crossed the Fuji River, of which I knew nothing, and was nearly swept away. Then bandits attacked me in the Takashi mountains and only barely left me my life in response to my pleas. I reached Fukuhara and the residence to which the cloistered emperor was confined under house arrest, and Lord Mitsuyoshi obtained the decree for me. When I presented it to Lord Yoritomo, he promised that for as long as he lived, he would grant me whatever I wished; I had only to ask. After that I rendered him the further services to which you yourself can bear witness, so that I need not describe them. A man's word matters more than life. Lord Yoritomo will not have forgotten his, unless success has gone to his head." Mongaku set out at dawn the next day.

To Saitōgo and Saitōroku, the holy man now seemed a veritable living buddha.
They pressed their palms together in adoration and wept,
then hurried back to Daikakuji with their report.
How glad the boy's mother must have been to hear it!
The decision was still up to Yoritomo, and the outcome remained uncertain,
but Mongaku had set off with such obvious confidence
that this twenty-day reprieve brought mother and nurse alike a degree of relief.
They felt that they owed it entirely to the mercy of Kannon.

Dusk followed dusk, dawn followed dawn,
until twenty days passed like a dream,
but of Mongaku there was no sign.
Oh, what could have become of him?
In a state of mounting worry,
they felt their old agony return.

Tokimasa now observed, "The days promised Mongaku have passed.
I cannot stay in the city into the new year. I shall return to Kamakura now."
A hubbub of preparations arose.
Saitōgo and Saitōroku wrung their hands in despair,
but there was still no sign of Mongaku, nor even a messenger from him.
At their wits' end, the pair returned to Daikakuji.
"The holy man is not here yet," they said,
"and Lord Tokimasa goes down to Kamakura in the morning."
They pressed their sleeves to their eyes and shed a torrent of tears.
Imagine, then, the mother's anguish when she heard their news!
    "Oh, please, please," she implored them,
    "tell him to have someone mature,
    someone responsible, take Rokudai
    to meet that holy man on the way.
    It would be just too terrible
    if his request met with success
    yet they still executed my son
    before he could return to the city!
    Or are they, as far as you can tell,
    planning to execute him at once?"
    "I think it will be very soon, at dawn.
    I say that because the Hōjō housemen
    on duty now at Rokuhara
    are all looking very downcast.
    Some of them are calling the Name,
    while others are simply weeping."
    "And Rokudai himself—how is he?"
    "He seems calm in another's presence
    and fingers his beads, but when alone
    he presses his sleeves to his eyes and sobs."
    "That is too easy to believe.
    He is young, but grown up at heart.
    He must know this night is his last.
    Oh, how miserable he must feel!
    He said that he would not be gone long,
    since he would soon have leave to return,
    but now more than twenty days have passed.
    I have never once visited him,
    nor has he come to see me here.
    On what future day, at what hour
    will I ever see him again?

Tell me, you two, what are you going to do?"

    Saitōgo and Saitōroku replied, "We will stay with him to the end, and when he is gone, if that is to happen, we will take his bones to Mount Kōya, then renounce the world and pray for him in the hereafter."

    "I am so terribly worried!" she said. "Then go back to him. Go back now!"

    The two took their leave in tears and withdrew.

Meanwhile on the sixteenth of the twelfth month, in that same year,
Hōjō no Shirō Tokimasa set out from the city with Lord Koremori's son.
Saitōgo and Saitōroku, blind with weeping, went with him,
resolved as they were to stay by him to the end.
Tokimasa invited them to ride, but they refused.
"We are accompanying our master for the last time," they said,
"and walking is good enough for us."
They continued on their way, shedding tears of blood.

    Rokudai, who had left behind,
    in a parting most painful to him,
    his mother and nurse, now looked back
    from afar on the city, once his home,
    and set out, this first and last time
    down the highway toward the east,
    in a mood easily surmised.
    When a warrior urged his horse on,
    Rokudai blanched, imagining
    the man moving to behead him;
    when others talked among themselves,
    he trembled, sure that his time had come.
    The riverbank at Shinomiya:
    surely now! But before he knew it,
    the barrier had dropped behind them,
    and they reached the lakeshore at Ōtsu.
    At Awazu, then, he told himself;
    but no, that day, too, turned to night.
    On they went, province to province,
    one post station after another,
    until they came to Suruga.
    Now, he gathered, his dewdrop life
    was really and truly over.

At Senbon-no-matsubara the warriors dismounted, released the palanquin bearers,
spread an animal hide on the ground, and seated Rokudai on it.

Tokimasa approached him and said, "I have gladly brought you this far
in case we might meet that holy man on the way.
I have done all I could for you, but I cannot vouch for Lord Yoritomo's response
if I were to take you from here over Mount Ashigara.
For that reason I mean to announce that I executed you in Ōmi.
No matter who might appeal on your behalf to Lord Yoritomo,
you share the karma of all your house. No appeal could succeed."
He spoke in tears, and Rokudai said nothing in reply.
Instead he summoned Saitōgo and Saitōroku.
"Once I am gone," he said, "go back to the city
and breathe no word there about any execution on the way.
That story will come out in the end, of course,
but if my mother hears it now, she will mourn me too greatly,
and even after her passing, her grief will detain her on the path to higher rebirth.
Tell her that you saw me all the way to Kamakura."
Overwhelmed, the pair remained speechless a moment.
Then Saitōgo:

> "Once you are lost to us, my lord,
> I do not see how either of us
> could go on living as before
> and return to the capital!"

With downcast gaze he fought back tears.
The dreaded moment was now approaching.
Young Rokudai, with his own dear hands,
swept forward across his shoulders the beautiful hair that hung down his back.
"The poor boy!" murmured the warrior guards, wringing tears from their
   sleeves.
"Even now he shows such presence of mind!"
Rokudai turned to the west, palms pressed together, called the Name,
stretched out his neck, and waited.

> Kano no Kudōzō Chikatoshi,
> having been chosen to do the deed,
> came around from behind, sword at his side,
> and was getting ready to strike
> when his vision darkened, his courage failed.
> Blind to where the sword should fall,
> he hardly knew anymore where he was.
> "I simply cannot do it," he said.
> "You will have to choose somebody else."
> He dropped his sword and withdrew.
>   Tokimasa was assigning the task

to one of his men after another
when a black-robed monk on a russet roan
galloped toward them, whip raised high,
crying, "No, no, this is terrible!
Over there, in among those pines,
this man, Hōjō Tokimasa,
is arranging to execute
the loveliest boy in all the world!"
People flocked toward the place
while the monk—shouting "Murder! Murder!"—
urged them on with sweeping gestures;
then, lest waving his arms not suffice,
took off his broad, conical hat
and goaded them with it to greater haste.
Tokimasa thought he had better wait.
The monk raced up to him at top speed,
quickly dismounted, and caught his breath.
"I bring a stay of execution,"
he announced. "Lord Yoritomo
gave me the letter. I have it here."
Tokimasa read it. Sure enough:

> To: *Hōjō Tokimasa*
> From: *Yoritomo*
> *I understand that you now have in your custody the son of Taira no Koremori. Mongaku, the holy man of Takao, wishes to take him under his care. You may confidently give the boy into his charge.*

The note bore Yoritomo's seal.
Tokimasa read it several times,
put it down, and called it a miracle.
Saitōgo and Saitōroku
of course, and all Tokimasa's men
greeted the news with tears of joy.

8. *Rokudai at Hasedera*

Mongaku himself then arrived, clearly enchanted to receive Rokudai.
He said, "Lord Yoritomo objected that Koremori, the father,
commanded his side during the opening battle
and that no plea from anyone could excuse that.
In reply I warned him that he would lose divine protection if he crossed me
in this,

but he still refused. So when he went hunting at Nasuno,
I stayed with him and managed to change his mind.
You must have feared that I would never get here."
"The twenty days you and I agreed on were over," Tokimasa replied,
"and in the absence of authorization from Lord Yoritomo to extend them,
I very nearly made the mistake of executing him on the way."
He gave Saitōgo and Saitōroku each a saddled horse, sent them back up to
     the city
and accompanied them a good distance in person.
"I should like to see you off even farther," he assured them,
"but I have important affairs to discuss with Lord Yoritomo. Farewell."
So they parted, and he continued his journey.
He was truly a kind, generous man.

> Mongaku now took charge of Rokudai and hastened as fast as he could
> toward the capital. He saw the year out at Atsuta, in the province of
> Owari. On the fifth of the first month, in the new year, he reached the
> city and gave Rokudai a rest in a lodge of his at Nijō-Inokuma. They
> came to Daikakuji in the middle of the night. Mongaku knocked at the
> gate, but all was silence within. There was nobody there. Then Roku-
> dai's pet white puppy came scampering out through a gap in the com-
> pound wall, wagging its tail. "Where's Mother?" the despairing
> Rokudai asked it.

Saitōroku got over the wall and let them in through the gate.
There was no sign that anyone lived there.
Rokudai lamented,

> "I so wanted to stay alive,
> little though I deserved to do so,
> if only I might see once more
> the people I love so much!
> Oh, what can have happened to them?"

All night he wept, and, poor boy, no wonder.
When day came, they questioned a neighbor, who replied,
"I gather that they went off last month on a pilgrimage to the great Buddha of
     Tōdaiji
and that in the new year they were planning a retreat at Hasedera.
No one has been to their place since then."
Saitōgo rushed to Hase and told his mistress the story.
Neither she nor the nurse could believe that it was true.
"Is this real," she exclaimed, "or am I only dreaming?"
She hurried back to Daikakuji,

and such was her joy upon seeing her son that she just burst into tears.
"Quickly, have him renounce the world!" she urged,
but to Mongaku that seemed too great a shame. He did not do it.
They say that he took Rokudai straight to Takao
and from there assisted his mother in her reduced circumstances.

> Great in mercy and compassion,
> Kannon's salvation touches all,
> the guilty and the innocent.
> Many a tale from ancient times
> bears witness that that is so,
> but this was still a rare wonder.

[The eighteenth-century score that supplied voicing information lacks the text below, hence the translation into continuous prose.]

Hōjō Tokimasa was on his way to Kamakura with Rokudai when a messenger from Yoritomo met him at the Kagami post station.

"What brings you here?" Tokimasa asked.

"It appears that Jūrō Yukiie and Shida no Saburō Yoshinori have thrown in their lot with Yoshitsune. Lord Yoritomo wishes you to deal with them."

But Tokimasa had an important prisoner with him. At Oiso-no-mori he therefore told his nephew, Hōjō no Heiroku Tokisada, who had been with him on the road, "Hurry back, find those two, and kill them."

Tokisada obeyed and located a Miidera monk who claimed to know where Yukiie was. Under questioning, however, the monk said that he did not know personally but rather knew another monk who did.

Tokisada's men broke in on this second monk and arrested him.

"Why are you arresting me?" the monk asked.

"Because you're supposed to know the whereabouts of Jūrō Yukiie."

"Then you might just have asked me, instead of arresting me like this! He's supposed to be at Tennōji."

"So take us there!"

A force of thirty mounted men under Tokisada's son-in-law Kasahara no Jūrō Kunihisa, as well as Uehara no Kurō, Kuwabara no Jirō, and Hattori no Heiroku, set out for Tennōji. Yukiie was staying in two places: the home of the senior musician Kaneharu, in Tani, and that of two other musicians, named Shinroku and Shinshichi. The force split up and attacked both at once. Yukiie was at Kaneharu's house. He fled out the back when armed warriors burst in.

Kaneharu had two daughters, both Yukiie's mistresses. The men seized them and demanded to know where Yukiie was. "Ask my younger sister," the elder said, and the younger, "Ask my elder." Actually, Yukiie had left in such haste that he was unlikely to have told anyone where he was going, but they took the sisters up to the city anyway.

Yukiie fled toward Kumano. When the only man with him came down with a bad leg, he broke his journey at the village of Yagi, in Izumi. His host there recognized him and raced all night up to the city, where he reported Yukiie's arrival to Tokisada. Tokisada hardly knew whom to send, since his men were not back yet from Tennōji. He called in a retainer of his named Daigenji Muneharu.

"Is that Hiei monk of yours still around?" he asked.

"Yes, sir, he is."

"Then have him come here."

The monk arrived in response to the summons.

"Yukiie has been found," Tokisada informed him. "Kill him and claim your reward from Kamakura."

"Very well, sir," the monk replied, "but I will need some men."

"Then go with him, Daigenji," said Tokisada. "I have no one else." He sent just fourteen or fifteen underlings with him.

The monk in question, one Hitachibō Shōmei, went down to the province of Izumi and raced into the house mentioned. It was empty. He took up the floorboards and inspected the inner room, but no one was there. He then went out to the street, looked around, and spotted a woman of mature years—a farmer's wife, apparently—passing by. He seized her. "Have any suspicious-looking travelers been staying nearby lately? Tell me or you die."

"Yes," she said, "right there in that house you have been searching. Two splendid gentlemen were there till last night, but they seem to have left this morning. I believe they are now in that big house over there."

Hitachibō charged straight in, wearing black leather-laced armor with sleeves attached and girded with a long sword. A man of fifty or so in a dark blue *hitatare* and folded *eboshi* hat, seated beside a Chinese wine jug and a dish of refreshments, was just then offering another man a cup of wine. He fled on all fours when the armed monk barged in, but the monk caught up with him.

"Hey, you monk, you have the wrong man!" Yukiie cried. "Yukiie is *me*!"

Hitachibō rushed back. The speaker had on only a white, short-sleeved robe and widemouthed trousers. His left hand gripped a gold-fitted short sword and his right an impressively long one.

"Drop your swords," Hitachibō commanded. Yukiie laughed loudly. Hitachibō fell on him, and their swords clashed. He drew back and attacked Yukiie again. Another clash, another break. Clash and break, the fight went on and on until Yukiie moved to retreat into the walled inner room.

"Shame on you!" Hitachibō cried. "Don't you dare!"

"My very thought!" Yukiie retorted, and charged him.

Hitachibō dropped his sword and grappled with him hand to hand. They fell and were rolling over and over each other when Daigenji turned up. He was so flustered that instead of drawing his sword he picked up a rock and bashed it into Yukiie's forehead. Yukiie laughed again. "You crawling lackey!" he exclaimed. "A man strikes his enemy with a sword or halberd, not a rock!"

"Tie his legs!" Hitachibō ordered, but in the confusion Daigenji tied both men's legs together.

Next they tied a rope around Yukiie's neck and forced him to sit up.

"Give me some water," he said. They poured water over some dried rice and gave it to him, but he drank only the water and left the rice. Hitachibō took it and ate it himself.

"Are you a monk of the Mountain?" Yukiie asked.

"Yes, sir, I am."

"And your name?"

"Hitachibō Shōmei, from the North Ravine."

"So you're the monk who once wanted to serve me?"

"Yes, sir."

"Did Yoritomo send you? Or was it Tokisada?"

"I serve Lord Yoritomo in Kamakura. Have you really been planning to attack him?"

"What difference does it make whether I say yes or no? Did you like how I fight?"

"I have fought many a time on the Mountain, sir, but never against a man as strong as you. It felt like fighting three worthy opponents at once. But if I may ask, sir, what did you think of *me*?"

"What can I say? You got me, didn't you? Just give me a look at those swords." His showed not a single nick. In Hitachibō's there were forty-two.

They mounted Yukiie on a post-station horse and spent the night in the house of the madam of Eguchi.[288] From there they sent a messenger racing overnight up to the city. At midday the next day, at the Akai riverbank, they met Hōjō Tokisada coming toward them with one hundred riders, banners flying.

"His Cloistered Eminence has barred him from entering the capital," Tokisada announced, "and Lord Yoritomo concurs. Behead him immediately, take the trophy to Kamakura, and receive your reward." So there on the Akai riverbank they cut off Jūrō Yukiie's head.

Rumor had it that Shida no Saburō Yoshinori had gone into hiding in the Daigo hills. Tokisada swooped down on the area and hunted for him, but in vain. Then came news that Yoshinori had fled toward Iga. Tokisada sent Hattori Heiroku and others there. Further word placed him at the mountain temple at Sendo, and they

....

288. Eguchi, near the mouth of the Yodo River, was famous for its prostitutes and singing girls.

rushed there to take him. They found him lying sprawled in only a lined short-sleeved robe and widemouthed trousers. He had slit his belly with a gold-trimmed dagger.

Heiroku took his head and had it carried straight to the city, where he presented it to Tokisada. "Take it at once to Lord Yoritomo in Kamakura," Tokisada said, "and you will have your reward." Hitachibō and Heiroku each therefore took his trophy to Kamakura.

"Marvelous!" Yoritomo exclaimed, and forthwith banished Hitachibō to Kasai.

"I was sure a reward awaited me," Hitachibō said to himself. "But no! It was exile instead! I can hardly believe it. I would never have risked my life like that if I'd known." He bitterly regretted the whole thing, but it was too late now.

Two years later, though, Yoritomo called him back. "The gods withdraw their protection from the man who kills a senior commander," he explained. "I had no choice but to punish you awhile." Before Hitachibō left, he received the Tada estate in Tajima and the Hamuro estate in Settsu. Hattori Heiroku got back the property of Hattori, which had been confiscated from him because of his service to the Heike.

9. The Execution of Rokudai

Meanwhile Rokudai reached his fourteenth or fifteenth year,
and his beauty shone a brightening light on all around him.
"Alas," his mother said, perhaps more fondly than wisely,
"if the world were ours as it used to be,
he would be by now an officer in the Palace Guards!"
Lord Yoritomo found him a constant cause of concern.
In every letter to the holy man of Takao, he asked,
"And what news of Koremori's son?
Once upon a time you divined my quality and my future.
Tell me, then: Is he a man to destroy an enemy of the court
and cleanse the shame incurred by his forebears?"
Mongaku replied, "There is no depth to him. He lacks courage.
You may set your mind at rest."
Yoritomo remained anxious nevertheless.
"I know that monk will side with him," he remarked, "if he raises rebellion."
It was a frightening thing to say.

> Rokudai's mother heard about it. "Oh, what terrible, terrible news!" she cried. "You must become a monk at once!" And so it was that in his sixteenth year, in the spring of Bunji 5, [1189] Rokudai cut off his lovely hair at the shoulders, donned a persimmon-dyed robe, slung onto his back the religious wanderer's chest, took leave of Mongaku, and set out

on holy pilgrimage. Saitōgo and Saitōroku accompanied him in the
same guise.
He went first to Mount Kōya and called there on his father's spiritual guide,
the Takiguchi Novice, from whom he had the story
of how his father had renounced the world and how he had died.

There, before the Seashore Shrine,
he looked out to Yamanari Island,
where his father had gone that time,
and he longed to go there himself,
but wind and wave discouraged that.
All he could do was to gaze far off,
wanting to ask the white-crested waves
rolling in from the open sea
precisely where his father had drowned.
To him, the very sands of the shore
could have been his father's bones,
and his streaming tears drenched sleeves
undoubtedly not a salt maker's
but nonetheless constantly damp.
He spent one whole night on the shore,
calling the Name, reading sutras,
while his finger drew in the sand
likenesses of Amida Buddha.
At daybreak he called in a holy monk
to perform litanies for his father
and dedicated the merit of that
to the benefit of the departed.
Then he bade farewell to the dead
and set off in tears to the capital.

*[As before, the manuscript that supplied performance information lacks the text
below.]*

Taira no Tadafusa, a son of Lord Shigemori, vanished after fleeing the battle at
Yashima. News that he had sought help from Yuasa Muneshige, in Kii, and gone
to ground in Muneshige's fort moved such Heike loyalists as Etchū no Jirōbyōe,
Kazusa no Gorōbyōe, Akushichibyōe, and Hida no Shirōbyōe to join him, and the
men of Iga and Ise rushed there in turn when the word reached them.

Lord Yoritomo sent the Kumano superintendent Tanzō to attack this concen-
tration of hardened Heike sympathizers when he heard the news. Tanzō did so
eight times over a period of two or three months, only to be repulsed each time by

defenders to whom life meant nothing. The armed monks from Kumano were killed.

By courier, Tanzō reported to Kamakura, "I have attacked the Yuasa fort eight times in the past two or three months and have been repulsed each time by defenders prepared to fight to the death. I have therefore failed to reduce the enemy. Success will require additional resources from two or three neighboring provinces."

Yoritomo replied, "That would only achieve further loss of men and matériel. The outlaws in the fort are presumably bandits and pirates. Restrict them severely and keep them bottled up." Tanzō obeyed. Sure enough, soon not a man remained in the fort.

"One or two sons of Lord Shigemori must have survived," Yoritomo announced with an ulterior motive in mind. "Their lives are theirs to keep. After all, it is Shigemori who, through Lady Ike, had my own sentence reduced from death to exile." Tadafusa responded by going to identify himself at Rokuhara. He was sent straight to Kamakura, where Yoritomo received him.

"Go back up to the capital," Yoritomo said. "I have a discreet home for you in mind." But he sent men after Tadafusa, and they killed him at the Seta Bridge.

Apart from his six fully acknowledged sons, Lord Shigemori had another, Munezane. The left minister Fujiwara no Tsunemune had adopted Munezane in his third year and given him his own surname. Now in his eighteenth year, the young man had neglected the arts of war in favor of literary pursuits, and Lord Yoritomo made no attempt to hunt him down. In deference to the times, however, his adoptive father drove him out nonetheless.

Deprived of a future, Munezane went to Shunjōbō Chōgen of Tōdaiji, the holy man who had raised funds for recasting the Great Buddha. "I am Lord Shigemori's last son, Munezane," he said. "The left minister Tsunemune adopted me in my third year and gave me his surname. Now I am in my eighteenth year. I never cared for the arts of war and chose instead to cultivate letters. Lord Yoritomo has not come looking for me, but in deference to the times my adoptive father has nonetheless driven me away. Please, Your Reverence, accept me as a disciple." He cut off his topknot himself. "If the risk seems too great," he added, "then by all means inform Kamakura, and if my sins really weigh too heavily, then send me elsewhere."

Shunjōbō took pity on him and allowed him to renounce the world. For the time being, he lodged Munezane in the temple's lamp-oil storeroom and did indeed report his presence. "I shall decide what to do after seeing him," Yoritomo replied. "Send him down here at once."

Shunjōbō could not refuse. He sent Munezane to Kamakura. From the very day he left Nara, Munezane refused anything resembling food or drink. He would not swallow even water, warm or cold. He died at last at Sekimoto, just over Mount Ashigara. "There is no hope for me, you see," he explained, showing a terrifying strength of will.

On the seventh of the eleventh month of Kenkyū 1, [1190] Lord Yoritomo went up
to the capital. On the ninth he received the senior second rank and the post of
grand counselor, to which was added, on the eleventh, a concurrent appointment
to command the Right Palace Guards. He resigned both posts at once and re-
turned to the Kanto on the fourth of the twelfth month.

On the thirteenth of the third month of Kenkyū 3, [1192] Cloistered Emperor Go-
Shirakawa passed away in his sixty-sixth year. The bell for the esoteric litanies
ceased to ring that night, and the voice chanting the Lotus from memory fell silent
with the coming of dawn.

The Great Buddha of Tōdaiji was to be dedicated on the thirteenth of the third
month of Kenkyū 6. [1195] During the second month, Lord Yoritomo therefore went
again up to the city. On the twelfth of the third month, he went to the Great Bud-
dha Hall, where he summoned Kajiwara Kagetoki. "Over the heads of a crowd of
monks," he said, "I spotted a suspicious individual south of the Tengai Gate. Seize
him and bring him to me." Kagetoki did so forthwith. The man was clean-shaven,
with a full head of hair.

"Who are you?" Yoritomo demanded to know.

"I might as well tell you," the man replied, "since I am so thoroughly out of luck.
I am Satsuma no Nakazukasa Iesuke, a Heike retainer."

"And what are you doing here, looking like this?"

"Keeping an eye out for a chance to assassinate you."

"Good man!"

Yoritomo returned to the capital after the dedication ceremony. They beheaded
the fellow on the riverbed at Rokujō.

During the winter of Bunji 1, [1185] the Genji had hunted down every infant
Heike son or grandson, almost to the point of opening the mothers' bellies in
search of more, and they had killed them all. It seemed impossible that a single one
should have survived. Nonetheless Tomotada, Taira no Tomomori's last son, re-
mained alive. He was in his third year when the Heike fled the capital and aban-
doned him to the care of his guardian, Ki no Jirōbyōe Tamenori. Tamenori moved
about with him in order to remain in hiding, until he settled discreetly in the
province of Bingo, at the locality of Ōta.

As Tomotada grew older, he began to arouse the suspicions of the local steward
and warden. He therefore moved to the city and went into hiding at Ichi-no-hashi,
within the grounds of Hosshōji. Kiyomori, his grandfather, had dug there a double
moat surrounded by a stand of bamboo, so as to turn the place into an emergency
fort. Now a ring of abatis further defended it. During the day silence reigned, but
at night distinguished gentlemen gathered there to enjoy music and the pleasures
of poetry in Chinese or Japanese. Word of Tomotada's presence there somehow
leaked out.

The figure most widely feared then in the city was the novice monk Fujiwara no

Yoshiyasu,[289] and it came to the ears of Shinbyōe Mototsuna, a son of Yoshiyasu's retainer Gotōbyōe Motokiyo, that Ichi-no-hashi harbored an enemy of the court. On the seventh of the tenth month of Kenkyū 7, [1196] early in the hour of the dragon, [ca. 8 A.M.] some one hundred and fifty mounted warriors attacked Ichi-no-hashi, uttering battle cries. The thirty or so defenders bared both shoulders and from the shelter of the bamboo loosed a furious barrage of arrows that killed so many men and horses that the attackers had to desist.

However, the news of a court enemy at Ichi-no-hashi drew warriors there from all over the city. Soon there were one or two thousand of them. They tore down nearby houses to fill the moat and charged in, howling for war. The defenders raced out with drawn swords, only to be killed or suffer wounds so grievous that they killed themselves. Tomotada, then in his sixteenth year, suffered that fate. Tamenori cradled the body on his lap, sobbing and loudly calling the Name, before slitting his own belly. His sons Hyōe Tarō and Hyōe Jirō both died by the attackers' swords.

Nearly all the thirty-odd men from the fort were now dead, killed either by their own hand or in battle. The attackers set fire to the mansion, charged in, seized the heads of the slain, impaled them on swords and halberds, and rushed to Yoshiyasu's residence. Yoshiyasu rode his carriage to Ichijō to inspect the heads. Some people recognized Tamenori, but no one could have known what Tomotada looked like. To identify him they brought in his mother, Jibukyō-no-tsubone, then in the service of the Hachijō Princess. "He was in his third year when my late husband took me down to the west," she said, "and I have had no news of him since, but the look of this head reminds me of my late husband." She wept as she spoke. Yes, the head was Tomotada's.

The Heike retainer Etchū no Jirōbyōe Moritsugi had fled to the province of Tajima, where he now lived as the son-in-law of Kehi no Shirō Dōkō. Dōkō did not know who he was, but in the end the truth will out. By night Moritsugi would gallop about on one of his father-in-law's horses, shooting arrows, and then swim it a mile or two through the sea. This aroused the steward's and the warden's suspicions, and somehow they found out who he was.

Lord Yoritomo in Kamakura issued a directive.

To: Asakura no Tarō Takakiyo in the province of Tajima:

I understand that the Heike retainer Etchū no Jirōbyōe Moritsugi now inhabits your province. Summon him and deliver him to me.

Takakiyo called in Kehi no Shirō, his son-in-law. "How are we to capture him?" he asked.

"In the bath" was the decision reached. They let Moritsugi take his bath and sent in five or six sturdy men to seize him, but he flattened them when they went

....

289. Yoritomo's brother-in-law.

for him and again when they got back up. All were wet, and Takakiyo's men simply could not hold him down. In the end, though, one cannot prevail against many. Twenty or thirty men came at Moritsugi, beat him into submission with the flat of their swords and halberds, and sent him straight to Kamakura.

Yoritomo had him brought in and questioned him. "If you have such an old tie to the Heike," he said, "why did you not die with them?"

"Because they fell too easily. I have been looking for a chance to finish you. For that purpose I have been equipping myself with the best sword and with battle arrows of the finest steel. Now that my fate has caught up with me, I have nothing further to say."

"Good man!" Yoritomo exclaimed. "Come over to me and I will look after you. Will you do that?"

"A warrior does not serve two masters. Show a man like me leniency and you will regret it. I only ask that you cut off my head at once."

"So be it, then," Yoritomo replied. They took him out to Yui-no-hama and did so. No one failed to sing Moritsugi's praises.

The reigning emperor, Go-Toba, gave himself to music and poetry and left matters of government to Kyō-no-tsubone.[290] The result was a constant stream of grievances and complaints. A passion for swordsmen on the part of the king of Wu led to endless injuries throughout his realm; the king of Chu so loved willowy slenderness that many women in his palace starved to death. The sovereign's tastes influence those below him, and men of understanding all lamented the parlous weakness of this emperor's rule.

Now Mongaku, ever the scary monk, mixed himself up in things better left alone. He aspired to put the Second Prince[291] on the throne because this prince cultivated scholarship and valued high principles. While Yoritomo lived, he could do nothing, but on the thirteenth of the first month of Kenkyū 10, [1199] Yoritomo died. Mongaku at once prepared to rebel. News of his plan soon got out, and the police went to his lodging at Nijō-Inokuma. They arrested him, and he was exiled, in his eighties, to the province of Oki.

On his way out of the city, Mongaku declared, "Old as I am, a man whose every day may be his last, he could at least have vented his displeasure by consigning me to some odd corner near the capital—but no, he must banish me to Oki! The ball-playing brat—I can't stand him! Just wait till I have him join me there!" It was a terrifying speech.

This emperor was keen on the ball game of *gitchō*, hence Mongaku's gibe. Strangely enough, when he raised rebellion during the Jōkyū years, [1219-22] it was

290. Go-Toba's nurse Noriko, a daughter of Fujiwara no Norikane and the mother of his future empress, Shōmeimon-in.

291. Morisada, a son of Emperor Takakura and younger brother of Emperor Antoku.

to Oki, among all the possible provinces, that he was banished. They say that the late Mongaku's spirit went on ranting to him there.

All this while, Rokudai had been quietly pursuing his practice at Takao. "Look at whose son he is, and whose disciple!" the great lord in Kamakura[292] often remarked. "No doubt he has shaved his head, but not his heart." And so it was that Andō Sukekane was ordered to seize him and bring him down to the Kanto. At the Tagoshi River, Okabe Gonnokami Yasutsuna then executed the command to behead him. They say that Rokudai owed surviving from his twelfth to his thirtieth year entirely to the grace of the Kannon of Hasedera. So at last ended the Heike line.

Taken down by Yūa, a disciple of the Buddha

Ōan 3, eleventh month, twenty-ninth day [1370]

---

292. The shogun at the time would have been Minamoto no Yoriie (1182–1204) or Sanetomo (1203–19).

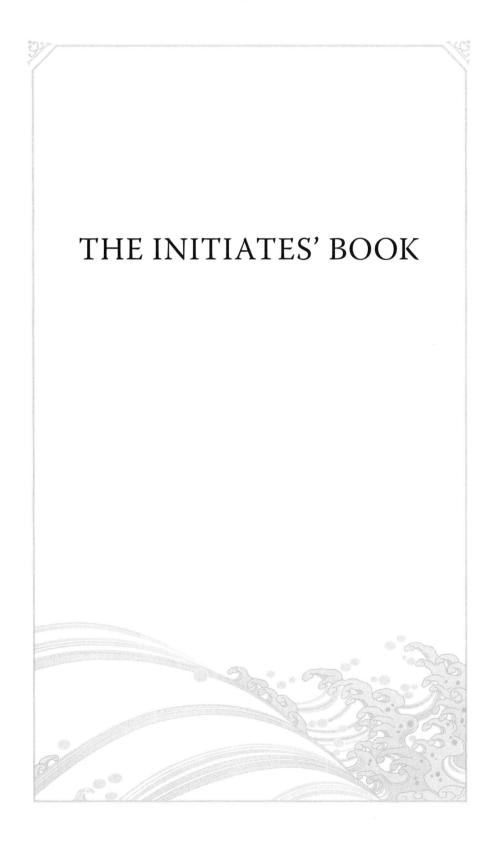

THE INITIATES' BOOK

1. Kenreimon-in Becomes a Nun

(recitative)

Kenreimon-in found lodging in the Yoshida neighborhood, below the Eastern
     Hills.
The place belonged to Kyōe, a senior monk in Nara.
Weeds grew tall in the garden after years of neglect,
and thick *shinobu* ferns fringed the eaves. The blinds were gone,
baring to view a sleeping chamber open to wind and rain.

> *(song)*
> Flowers blooming in many hues
> lacked any eye to appreciate them;
> the moon that shone in night by night
> met no admiring watcher's gaze.
> Of old, beauty and opulence
> illumined the only life she knew
> amid her hangings of brocade;
> now the loss of her whole house
> and refuge in a monkish hovel
> must have plunged her into despair.
> She was like a fish on dry land,
> a bird strayed too far from the nest.
> Faced with what lay before her,
> she missed the tossing of the waves,
> the miseries of life at sea.
> Far, far away blue billows rolled.
> Her thoughts flew to roam the clouds
> that wandered there a thousand leagues
> across the ocean in the west,
> while here, beneath the mossy thatch
> that roofed this poor hut of hers,
> she wept to see the moonlight fall
> on a small, neglected garden
> hidden in the Eastern Hills.
> No words could convey her sorrow.

So it was that in Bunji 1, on the first of the fifth month, [1185]
Kenreimon-in renounced the world.

Insei, a holy Chōrakuji monk, conferred the precepts on her.
She offered the Buddha in return Emperor Antoku's robe.
Her son had worn it to the last, and it retained his fragrance.
In his memory she had brought it from the west all the way to the city,
and she had meant to keep it with her as long as she lived,
but she had nothing else to give, and it might help him in the afterlife.
Weeping, she therefore brought it forth.
Rendered speechless by her gift, the monk withdrew in silence,
wringing the tears from his ink-black sleeves.

> Sewn into a sacred banner,
> the robe then hung, so they say,
> before the Chōrakuji altar.
> This lady in her fifteenth year
> had received the emperor's call
> and in her sixteenth become empress.
> Always at her sovereign's service,
> she loyally, every morning,
> sent him off to morning council
> and gave herself to him every night.

In her twenty-second year, she bore a prince
who rose to heir apparent, then to emperor in his turn,
so that she came to bear the noble title of Kenreimon-in.
She was even more than Kiyomori's daughter,
for the emperor was her son: She was the mother of the realm.
No one in the world enjoyed greater honor.
Now, this year was her twenty-ninth.

> Her peach and damson beauty still shone,
> so, too, her lotus-blossom looks,
> but, knowing that she no longer needed
> hair adorned with kingfisher glints,
> she cut it off and became a nun,
> setting aside every worldly sorrow
> to start out at last on the true path.
> Even so her mourning continued.
> Not while she lived could she forget
> how, when they saw that it was over,
> the men had all leaped into the sea
> or how those two had looked at the last:
> her emperor son and Lady Nii.
> To her it simply made no sense
> to linger on in this dewdrop life,

only to suffer new misery.
She could not stem the flow of her tears.
In this fifth month the nights were short,
but still, for her, very slow to pass,
and since all sleep eluded her,
no dream returned her to times gone by.
The lamp's dying glow, turned to the wall,
dark rain beating nightlong on the window
made her feel terribly alone.[293]
The grief of the Shangyang lady,
long confined in the Shangyang Palace,[294]
could hardly have surpassed her own.
Perhaps to renew old memories
the owner had planted near the eaves
a prettily flowering orange tree
that suffused the breeze with its scent.
Twice a cuckoo called, then again.
Memories returned. Kenreimon-in
wrote on the lid of her inkstone box,

> Cuckoo, when you come
> seeking from the orange tree
> that sweetest fragrance,
> do you call out of yearning
> for your loves of long ago?[295]

(speech)

Her gentlewomen had not bravely thrown themselves into the sea like
Lady Nii and Kozaishō. Carried off by rough warriors, they had all re-
turned to the city, their home; then young and old alike had renounced
the world. So changed in looks that no one could have known them,
they now inhabited improbable valley depths or craggy wilds.

The houses once theirs had gone up in smoke,
leaving behind only vacant wastes
now fast reverting to grassy moorland.
No one they had known ever came to see them.
Poor things, they must have felt like that man
who strayed long ago into the realm of the immortals

....

293. Lines inspired by a poem by Bo Juyi, as excerpted in *Wakan rōeishū*.

294. This lady retired into obscurity in the Shangyang Palace when Emperor Xuanzong became
infatuated with Yang Guifei.

295. An old poem also included in *Wakan rōeishū*, among other classic collections.

and met on his return only descendants
seven generations on from when he had left.
    Then, on the ninth of the seventh month, [1185]
    the great earthquake struck. Walls collapsed,
    the ruined palace pitched askew,
    and she lost all semblance of a home.
    No green-robed guard stood at her gate.
    Her garden fence, in desperate plight,
    gathered more dew than all the moors,
    while as though knowing their time had come,
    crickets began their plaintive song.
    Longer and longer grew the nights,
    while sleep fled ever further from her,
    until she feared day might never dawn.
    With autumn adding its own sadness
    to the boundless fund of her sorrows,
    life for her became hard to bear.
    All things in this world die away.
    Her old associations withered,
    and no one remained to comfort her.

2. Kenreimon-in Moves to Ōhara

Still, the wives of Lords Takafusa and Nobutaka, each in her own way,
managed secret visits to Kenreimon-in.[296]
"I never imagined," Kenreimon-in said, weeping,
"that I would ever need help from those two."
The gentlewomen attached to her wrung the tears from their sleeves.
    Her dwelling was not yet far from the city,
    and many people passed by on the road.
    While waiting for her own end to come,
    she longed to find some mountain fastness
    safely beyond the reach of bad news,
    but she had no idea where to look.
A lady then came to her and said,
"In the hills behind Ōhara, there is a quiet retreat named Jakkō-in."
Kenreimon-in reflected that a mountain village might indeed be very lonely
but that she would rather live there than here, among the miseries of the world,
and so she made up her mind to go.

....

296. Both were younger sisters of Kenreimon-in.

They say that Lord Takafusa's wife arranged a palanquin for her.
She moved to Jakkō-in late in the ninth month of Bunji 1. [1185]

    Her path wound through bright autumn woods
    that caught her gaze as she passed by,
    until the sun—were these hills *that* high?—
    began all too soon to drop from sight.
    Across the fields a temple bell
    boomed out the bleak end of the day.
    Gathering dews bent wayside grasses,
    fresh tears streamed to soak her sleeves,
    and fallen leaves raced by on the wind.
    The sky clouded over. Before long
    a cold winter rain began to fall.
    A stag belled somewhere in the distance,
    while failing cricket song swelled and died.
    Amid such concerted melancholy,
    no words could convey her wretchedness.
    "When we fled from shore to shore
    and wandered on from island to island,
    still, in those days things were better,"
    the poor lady kept assuring herself.
    Jakkō-in, amid mossy rocks
    and far removed from worldly cares,
    was the very spot she had hoped for.
    Perhaps she felt that the garden there,
    its dewy expanse of *hagi* fronds,
    frost-withered, and its chrysanthemums
    below the fence now turning brown,
    evoked all too well her own decline.
    She went before the altar and prayed,
    "May His Majesty's sacred spirit
    achieve unhindered awakening
    and swiftly reach enlightenment."
    She then felt him present beside her.
    Never, never would she forget him.

Next to Jakkō-in proper, she put together a ten-foot-square hut of her own,[297]
half given over to sleeping and half to her private chapel.
Day and night, morning and evening, she never neglected her litanies

----

297. "Ten-foot-square" (*hōjō*) has powerful associations that include the room occupied by the great layman Vimalakīrti (Japanese: Yuima), as described in the *Vimalakīrti sūtra* (Japanese: *Yuima-gyō*).

nor ever failed to honor her perpetual calling of the Name,
and so it was that she spent her months and days.
On the fifth of the tenth month, as dusk was falling,
there came a rustling among the fallen oak leaves in the garden.

"Oh, who can have come looking for me
in my retreat here, far from the world?
Go and see!" Kenreimon-in cried.
"If it is someone who must not find me,
then in all haste I will go and hide!"
It turned out to be a passing stag.
"Tell me," said Kenreimon-in, "what was it?"
Lady Dainagon-no-suke answered, doing all she could not to cry,

Who would tread his way,
seeking you here, through these rocks?
No, the fallen leaves
rustled only for a stag
that chanced to be passing by.

Moved by this news, Kenreimon-in
wrote the poem in her own hand

Kenreimon-in at Jakkō-in, among falling autumn leaves. At lower left: The stag.

on the door by her small window.
Amid the monotony of her life,
she noted happy similes
that comforted her in her sorrow.
The trees that stood before her eaves
were in her eyes the seven trees
of priceless jewels in the Pure Land;
pools glittering among the rocks
brimmed with the blessed waters
of the eight supernal virtues.
Transience? The flowers of spring,
so quickly scattered by the winds.
Life itself? The autumn moon
that slips so soon behind the clouds.
That morning in the Zhaoyang Palace,
the lady who had loved the blossoms
saw wind strip them of their beauty,
and she who in the Zhangqiu Palace[298]
one night in poems praised the moon
watched the clouds swallow its light.
Once jade towers and golden halls,
floors spread with cushions of brocade,
offered the empress wondrous lodging;
now her hut of bundled grasses
invited from all tears of pity.

3. The Cloistered Emperor's Visit to Ōhara

By and by, in the spring of Bunji 2, the cloistered emperor conceived the
 wish [1186]
to call upon Kenreimon-in at her quiet Ōhara retreat.
The wind in the second and third months was strong, the lingering winter cold
 severe.
The mountaintops were still white with snow, and ice choked the ravines.

> But once spring had passed, once summer had come and the Kamo Fes-
> tival was over,[299] he started out for Ōhara before dawn. Since this was a
> secret progress, he took only six senior nobles with him—Tokudaiji
> Sanesada, Kasan-no-in Kanemasa, Tsuchimikado Michichika, among

....

298. Both palace names refer to the palace of the Han empress.
299. The festival took place in the middle of the fourth month, circa modern May 15.

others—and eight privy gentlemen. A few of his guardsmen attended
him as well.

Traveling by the Kurama road,
he paused to contemplate on the way
what once had been Fudarakuji,
built by Kiyowara no Fukayabu;
and the spot where so long ago
the Ono Grand Empress had resided.[300]
He then boarded his palanquin.
Floating above distant mountains,
white clouds recalled fallen blossoms;
cherry boughs leafing out in green
stirred regret for the spring just past.
It was late in the fourth month.
Pushing on through the summer growth,
the sovereign, on his first such journey,
wondered anew at each passing scene
and noted with profound emotion
that signs of human presence were gone.

    To the west, up against the hills,
rose a single temple: Jakkō-in.
The rocks and waters of the garden,
the ancient grove eloquently
evoked imposing depths of time.
"Through broken tiles mists pour in,
keeping perpetual incense burning;
through gaping doorways moonlight shines,
sustaining eternal altar flames":[301]
These lines well describe the place.
In a garden thick with summer grasses,
green willow fronds swayed in the breeze,
and waterweeds drifted on the pond.
All seemed a wide brocade expanse.
Wisteria billows, twined around the pines
standing on the pond's central island,
blossomed in lovely purple shades,
while late cherries bloomed through green leaves,

....

300. Empress to Go-Reizei (reigned 1045–68).

301. The source of these lines is unknown. They liken mists and moonlight to the incense and flame kept perpetually burning on an active temple altar.

more wondrous still in their own way
than the first blossoms of the season,
and around the pond kerria roses
flowered in extravagant profusion.
Through a rent in the lofty clouds
came the call of a mountain cuckoo,
as though in welcome to the sovereign.
At the sight His Cloistered Eminence
was moved thus to express himself:

> *Fallen to the pond*
> *from boughs leaning overhead,*
> *cherry petals drift*
> *so richly on the water*
> *that the blossoms are the waves!*

The very sound of water trickling from among ancient rocks
lent the spot an absorbing charm.
The garden fence, entangled with vines,
the flowing ridgeline of wooded mountains
invited even as they defied the painter's brush.
There before his eyes it stood: Kenreimon-in's hermitage,
its eaves festooned with morning-glory vines,
fringed with *shinobu* ferns and forgetting lilies,[302]

in spirit evoking those old lines,
"The gourd and rice chest often empty,
thick weeds hem in Yan Yuan's hovel;
tall goosefoot chokes off the path
where rain beats on Yuan Xian's door."[303]
The cryptomeria-bark thatch
looked far too meager to exclude
cold rains, frost, dew, or probing moonlight.
Off behind it rose the mountains,
and before it spread the fields.
Thin bamboo grass rustled in the wind.
As often for the unworldly,
cares thronged about her flimsy door.
News came rarely from the city;
no one sought her tattered fence.

302. *Shinobu*, the name of a kind of fern, also means "remember." A "forgetting lily" is *wasuregusa*, a kind of tiger lily.

303. From a complaint about poor treatment by Tachibana no Naomoto (circa 950), included in *Wakan rōeishū*. Yan Yuan was a major disciple of Confucius.

The only sounds she ever heard
were monkeys calling on the hillside,
springing there from tree to tree,
or a woodman's ax, ringing
as he felled his firewood load.
Curling vine tendrils came her way,
but a caller, hardly ever.
"Is anyone at home?" His Cloistered Eminence called. There was no answer.
At last, from a great distance, an ancient nun appeared.
"Where can Kenreimon-in have gone to?" the sovereign inquired.
"To the hillside, Your Eminence, to gather flowers for the altar."
"Has she then no one to do that for her?
I know that she has renounced the world, but that seems too hard."
"Her excellent karma stored up from past lives," the nun replied,
"has run its course, hence her present misfortune.
Why should she mind, when she has renounced concern for the flesh?
As one reads in the Sutra of Cause and Effect,
        'Who seeks to know past cause
        must look to present effect;
        who seeks to know future effect
        must consider present cause.'
        Once one comes to understand
        past and future cause and effect,
        then one is free from sorrow.
        Prince Siddhārtha was nineteen
        when he left his Gayā palace
        and, under Mount Dandaka,
        hid his nakedness with leaves.
        Up he climbed to gather firewood;
        down he went to collect water.
        Thanks to these austerities,
        he came at last to achieve
        highest, perfect enlightenment."
            The sovereign could not make out whether her patched robe was silk
            or plain cloth, and he wondered that so shabby a nun should talk this
            way. He asked her who she was. For a time bitter tears kept her from
            answering him. At last she mastered them and replied,
"Painful as this is to confess,
my father was the late Shinzei,
minor counselor and novice:

For, you see, I was once known
as the Lady Awa-no-naishi.
My mother was the Ki-no-nii of whom Your Majesty was once so fond.[304]
That you do not know me only confirms the ruin I have become."
Overwhelmed, she pressed her sleeves to her eyes.
The sovereign could not bear to look at her.
"So you are Awa-no-naishi!" he exclaimed.
"Yes, it is true, I did not know you. But I am dreaming, surely!"
He could not keep himself from shedding tears.
The gentlemen with him murmured among themselves,
"I thought she was rather an unusual nun. Now I understand!"

    The cloistered emperor gazed about him.
    Dew-laden grasses in the garden
    leaned heavily against the fence
    while, beyond, overflowing paddies
    left nowhere dry for a snipe to land.
    He approached the hermitage,
    slid the door open, and looked around.
    There stood the three divinities
    who come forward to welcome the soul.
    The hands of the central Amida
    held a length of five-colored cord.
    To the left hung a painting of Fugen,
    to the right one of Abbot Shandao,
    and, beside it, one of her son.
    There lay the scrolls of the Lotus Sutra
    and likewise Shandao's great treatises.
    No fragrance here of orchid or musk,
    only the smoke of altar incense.
    Vimalakīrti's room, ten feet square,
    with seats for thirty-two thousand buddhas
    summoned there from the ten directions,
    must, he felt, have been just the same.
    Sacred texts on strips of colored paper
    hung here and there from sliding doors.
    One bore this poem by a monk,
    formerly Ōe no Sadamoto,[305]

....

304. She had been his nurse.

305. Ōe no Sadamoto renounced the world in 988, went to China in 1003, and died there in 1034.

composed while he was at Qingliang-shan:
"Harmonies of music and song
resound afar on that single cloud.
Now comes the heavenly host in welcome,
descending before the setting sun."
And a little apart hung this,
no doubt by Kenreimon-in herself:

> *Never did I think,*
> *then, that I should live one day*
> *among distant hills*
> *and behold the palace moon*
> *as a stranger, from afar!*

Glancing to one side, he noted
what could only be her sleeping room.
Draped over a long bamboo pole
hung a hempen robe and paper bedding.
All her damask, silk gauze, and brocade—
the very best from our land and China—
now amounted to only a dream.

> The senior nobles and privy gentlemen with him had seen her in her
> glory, and the memory was still vividly present to them all. Each
> wrung the tears from his sleeves.

Meanwhile, from up on the mountain,
two black-robed nuns picked their way down the rocky path.
"And who are *they*?" the sovereign asked.
The old nun answered, holding back more tears,

> "The one with the basket on her arm—
> the basket filled with azalea flowers—
> that lady is Kenreimon-in.
> The one with the firewood and bracken
> is Counselor Korezane's daughter,
> whom Lord Kunitsuna then adopted,
> the nurse of His Late Majesty:
> Lady Dainagon-no-suke."
> She was still speaking when fresh tears flowed.
> Deeply moved, the sovereign wept, too.

Despite having turned her back on the world,
Kenreimon-in felt too abashed to let him see her as she looked now.
She only wished she could vanish from sight, but, alas, it was too late.
Sleeves wet from drawing holy water every evening

and wet again with early-morning dew from the hillside,
she knew herself now helpless to dry them and so stood
>
> neither fleeing back up the slope
> nor hurrying into her hermitage,
> frozen by shame and misery.
> Awa-no-naishi went to her
> and took charge of the flower basket.

4. Passage Through the Six Realms

"You have rejected the world, after all," she said.
"What could be wrong with your seeing him?
Please do so at once, so that he can return to the city."
Kenreimon-in reflected, "When one calling of the Name
brings his kindly light shining in through the window,
and ten bring the heavenly host in welcome to the door,
this imperial visit is a strange surprise!"
She entered her hermitage and, weeping, received him.
The cloistered emperor considered her and said,

> "Eighty thousand kalpas spent
> in the most transcendent heaven
> are certain still to end in grief;
> the six heavens of the realm of desire
> offer no refuge from fivefold decline.
> All the delights of Indra's palace,
> the lofty bliss of Brahma's abode
> are karma rewarded in a dream,
> pleasures tasted in illusion.
> Transmigration turns on and on,
> exactly like the wheels of a carriage.
> The miseries of fivefold decline
> suffered above by celestial beings
> appear, too, in the human realm."

He continued, "Does anyone ever visit you?
Your thoughts must often linger on times gone by."
"No," she replied, "I hear nothing from anyone,
aside from a word or two, now and again,
from the wives of Takafusa and Nobutaka.
I never imagined those two in time looking after me."
She wept, and her attendant women with her.

At last she managed to swallow her tears.
"It is painful, of course," she then went on,
"to find myself reduced to what I am now,
but my present state is also a joy,
since it gives me hope for enlightenment in the hereafter.
I pray to join at once the ranks of Shakyamuni's disciples,
by the power of Amida's Original Vow to rise above the miseries
imposed by the five obstructions and the triple deference,[306]
to purify my six senses through the three periods of day and night,[307]
and to go straight to rebirth in the ninefold Pure Land.
I pray, too, for the happy rebirth of every member of my house,
and I yearn always for Amida, Kannon, and Seishi's welcome into paradise.
There is one thing that I will never forget, not in any life that may lie before me,
and that is how my son, the former emperor, looked then.
I do try to forget, but each time I fail;
I try to bear the pain, but no, I cannot.

> There is no surer path to grief
> than a mother's love for her child.
> And so for him, for his salvation,
> I miss no morning or evening prayer.
> He has become to me, you see,
> a proper spiritual friend."

"Our land is a few remote millet grains," the cloistered emperor rejoined,
"but upon me the tenfold blessings of superior karma
conferred sovereignty over all the powers of the realm,
so much so that nothing falls short of what I desire.
Born into a world devoted to the Buddha's Teaching,
I myself aspired to follow the Buddha's path.
Therefore I am sure of fortunate rebirth,
and the vanity of human life should not surprise me.
Nonetheless it pains me greatly to see you."

Kenreimon-in ventured to speak again:
"Born the daughter of the chief minister, Taira no Kiyomori,
I became in time an emperor's mother.
The realm and the four seas lay in my palm.
From the very first spring salutation
to the clothing color changes, season by season,

....

306. A woman may become neither a divinity like Brahma or Indra, nor a buddha, and she owes submission to her father as a child, her husband as a wife, and her son in old age.
307. *Sanji*, the three periods of the day (sunrise, daytime, sunset) and of the night (beginning, middle, late).

and to the buddha-names litany that closes the year,
I enjoyed such honor from regent, ministers, and senior nobles
that I rode, as it were, the clouds of the transcendent heavens,
surrounded by eighty thousand celestial admirers.
No official, however minor, held me in anything short of awe.

>As at home in the Seiryōden,
>as in the Shishinden,
>I was fêted within jeweled blinds.
>In spring I gave my heart all day
>to the cherry tree before the Nanden;
>amid the fiercest summer heat
>I scooped up, for casual pleasure,
>fresh water from a cooling spring;
>in autumn I was never allowed
>to watch alone the moon on high;
>and on freezing, snowy winter nights,
>many-layered covers warmed me.
>I desired everlasting youth
>and coveted the Penglai elixir
>that confers immortality.
>Yes, I wished only to live forever.

Dawn and dusk ushered in such renewed delights
that (so I felt) the beings whose reward is heaven
could hardly enjoy pleasure greater than mine.
But then, early one autumn in the Juei years,
for fear of a man named, I believe, Kiso no Yoshinaka,
the whole house of Taira fled the city that had long been our home,
left our own capital a burned-out ruin,
and from place to place that to us were once only names—
Suma to Akashi, along the shore—
we wandered, absorbed in our misery.

>All day we cleaved the waves with dripping sleeves;
>all night we cried like plovers on a sand spit.
>Shore by stretch of shore, island by island,
>we saw places famed in song and story
>but could never forget our home.

>>Thus denied refuge anywhere, we seemed clearly to be suffering that
>>ineluctable fivefold decline. All of us in the human realm taste the sor-
>>row of parting from someone we love and the distress of keeping com-
>>pany with someone we detest. The four pains and the eight agonies
>>touch us.

At any rate, we were somewhere called Dazaifu, in the province of Chikuzen, when this fellow—his name was Koreyoshi, I think—drove us all the way out of Kyushu. The mountains and plains seemed spacious enough, but we could not stop to rest anywhere. Late that same autumn,
the moon we had watched high above the palace
now floated over vast reaches of sea.
So days and nights passed. The tenth month had come
when Lord Kiyotsune said to himself,
    'The Genji drove us from the city,
    Koreyoshi hounded us from Kyushu.
    Like netted fish, we have no escape.
    I have no life left before me.'
    And he drowned himself in the sea.
    That was the first of our afflictions.
We spent the days riding the waves
and the nights confined to our ships.
Because tax goods no longer reached us,
nobody could prepare me meals,
and when there *was* anything to eat,
there was no water to wash it down.
There we were, on the vast ocean,
but salt water is not fit to drink.
Such are the sufferings, I felt then,
    that plague the realm of the hungry ghosts.
When we won at Muroyama and Mizushima,
we all managed to take heart a little,
but then, at that place they call Ichi-no-tani,
most of the men of our house came to grief.
No more court dress after that, or ceremonial wear.
No, everyone left went about clad in steel,
and battle cries rang out day and night;
just so, I felt sure, do the ashuras howl
in their endless battles to overthrow Indra.
And once Ichi-no-tani had fallen,
fathers found that they had outlived their sons,
wives their husbands. The least fishing boat
stirred fear that it might be the enemy,
and white herons clustered in some far grove of pines
looked terrifyingly like Genji banners.
        The battle between Moji and Akama-no-seki seemed certain to be our last, and Lady Nii, my mother, left me her final instructions. 'Our men

have next to no chance of lasting out this day,' she said, 'and no distant relative who might survive could be expected to devote himself to praying for the rest of us. But it has always been the custom to avoid killing a woman in battle, so see that you stay alive, to pray for His Majesty and to assure all of us a happier rebirth.' Those were her words. It all seemed a dream. But then a wind blew up, thick cloud covered us, our warriors panicked, and our fate was sealed. No one could do anything to save us. It was all over. Lady Nii took the emperor in her arms and advanced to the side of the vessel.

Looking very frightened, he asked,
'Grandmother, where are you taking me?'
To her little sovereign, she said, near tears,
'Why, does Your Majesty not understand?
Tenfold good karma from past lives
gave you birth as lord over the realm,
but evil influence intervened
to bring your good fortune to an end.
First, Your Majesty, if you please,
face east and say good-bye to the Grand Shrine of Ise;
then, trusting that Amida will welcome you into his Western Paradise,
face west and call his Name.
Our land, a scattering of remote millet grains, is not a nice place.
I am taking you now to a much happier one, the Pure Land of Bliss.'
In these words she addressed him, weeping.

Robed in dove gray,[308] his hair in side loops
like any boy's, cheeks streaming with tears,
he pressed his dear little hands together,
prostrated himself toward the east,
and bade farewell to the Ise Shrine,
then turned to the west, calling the Name.
Lady Nii then took him in her arms
and sank with him into the deep.
At the sight, tears blinded my eyes
and I felt the heart within me fail.
I would gladly forget but cannot;
nor can I bear the memory.
The shrieks and screams of those who remained

---

308. The color named (*yamabato-iro* ["mountain-dove color"], also *kikujin*) is a gray-green reserved exclusively for imperial use. This is noted here rather than in 11:9 so as not to interrupt reading at that dramatic point.

sounded to me as deafening
as the cries of sinners burning in hell.

> Then warriors seized me, and I went with them up to the city. At
> Akashi, in Harima, I dropped off briefly to sleep and dreamed that I
> was somewhere even more beautiful than the palace of old. My son,
> the former emperor, was there, and with him all the noble gentlemen
> of our house, in magnificently solemn array. I had not seen the like
> since we fled the capital, and I asked where I was. A figure I took to be
> Lady Nii replied, 'This is the Dragon Palace.' 'Everything is so beauti-
> ful!' I said. 'Is there then no suffering here?' 'The Sutra of Dragons and
> Other Beasts describes it,'[309] she answered. 'Pray for us devotedly in
> the life to come.' Then I woke up.

I gave myself more and more after that to reading the sutras and calling the
    Name,
praying for their enlightenment in the hereafter.
What I have been through corresponds, so it seems to me,
to experiencing the agonies of the six realms of reincarnation."
To this His Cloistered Eminence replied,

> "In China the Tripitaka Master
> Xuanzang, entering enlightenment,
> saw those six realms, and in our land,
> by the power of Zaō Gongen,
> the saintly Nichizō saw them, too—[310]
> so I have heard. But now, I gather,
> you have seen them with living eyes.
> That, truly, is a rare wonder!"
> Weeping robbed the sovereign of speech.
> All his gentlemen wrung their sleeves.
> Kenreimon-in, too, burst into tears
> and, with her, her gentlewomen.

5. Kenreimon-in Enters Paradise

> Meanwhile the bell of Jakkō-in
> sounded the end of another day.
> The late sun sank toward the west.

....

309. No such sutra exists.

310. Zaō Gongen is the divinity of the Ōmine mountains, between Yoshino and Kumano. In 941 the ascetic Nichizō recorded a vision in which Zaō Gongen showed him the afterworld. In this vision Nichizō met the triumphantly vengeful spirit of Sugawara no Michizane.

Deeply regretting the need to go,
the sovereign nonetheless, near tears,
started out once more for the city.
Her memories fresh again in her mind,
Kenreimon-in wept helplessly.
From afar she watched while his train
dwindled slowly into the distance,
then addressed the Buddha on her altar.
"May the former emperor's sacred spirit,"
she prayed, "may all the spirits of my house
attain perfect awakening
and swiftly achieve enlightenment."
So she spoke through a flood of tears.
Once she had faced east to invoke
the Ise Shrine, the Great Buddha Hachiman,
imploring them to prolong the emperor's years
and to grant him ten thousand autumns;
now it was westward, with joined palms,
that she prayed for the holy departed
to find his way straight to paradise.
Such was the sad burden of her plea.
She wrote on the door of her sleeping room,

> When was it my heart
> learned to entertain these thoughts
> so troubling lately:
> longing for all those I knew
> in service at the palace?

> Those times I once knew
> have faded now into the past
> and become a dream,
> and so, too, my wattled door
> can hardly last much longer.

And Lord Tokudaiji Sanesada,
who had accompanied the sovereign,
pasted this, so they say, on a pillar:

> Once you were to all,
> in those days of long ago,
> the moon in the sky,
> who in this mountain village
> dispel the darkness no more.

Amida comes with his heavenly host to welcome Kenreimon-in (behind the screen) into paradise. On the left: Awa-no-naishi and Dainagon-no-suke.

708 • THE TALE OF THE HEIKE

Kenreimon-in was reflecting on past and future, dissolved in tears,
when a cuckoo called, at which she:

> *So be it, cuckoo!*
> *Let us, you and I, compare*
> *the flow of our tears,*
> *for I, too, in this sad world*
> *do little but lift my cry.*

The men captured at Dan-no-ura had been paraded through the streets and beheaded or banished far from their wives and children. Not one remained alive or present in the capital, apart from the grand counselor Yorimori. However, no action had been taken against the forty or so women, who were still there with relatives of one kind or another.

Even within their jeweled blinds,
the lofty felt chilly blasts of wind;
even behind their brushwood doors,
the lowly watched dust shift in the drafts.
Couples once pillowed side by side
now were torn far from each other;
parents and lovingly raised sons
no longer knew where the other was.
Affection remained as ever fresh,
yet life offered nothing but sorrow.
And all of this had come to pass
because the chief minister, Kiyomori,
had held the realm and the four seas
before him in the palm of his hand,
without fear of the One Man above,[311]
without kindness for the people below,
passing, exactly as he pleased,
sentence of death, sentence of exile,
in utter contempt of all the world.
It was now clear beyond a doubt:
The fathers' sins fall upon the sons.

So the months and years went by, until Kenreimon-in became unwell.
The five-colored cord in the hand of Amida, in that central place on her altar,
she now took in her own and prayed, calling the Name,
"All hail, Amida Buddha, savior and lord of the Western Paradise,
O come, come and take me into your Pure Land!"

....

311. The emperor.

To her left and right, Dainagon-no-suke and Awa-no-naishi
wailed in bitter grief that her life should end.
>Her voice calling the Name died away.
In the west a purple cloud appeared,
a perfume not of this world filled the room,
and sweet music sounded in the sky.
Her time had come. In Kenkyū 2,[312] [1191]
midway through the second month,
she breathed her last. Her companions,
with her since she rose to empress,
were lost and helpless once she was gone.
Their old ties had died out long since,
and now they had nowhere to turn.
It is so touching that nevertheless
they managed each holy service due her.
At last they followed the Dragon Princess[313]
in attaining complete awakening
and fulfilled, like Queen Vaidehī,[314]
their hope for rebirth in paradise.

312. Other versions and sources give the year of her death as 1213, 1223, or 1224.

313. The dragon girl in the Lotus Sutra, who attained enlightenment (through a flash of reincarnation as a man) despite the teaching that no woman can do so.

314. An imprisoned Indian queen who was enlightened after hearing the Buddha's teaching.

ŌAN 4, THIRD MONTH, FIFTEENTH DAY: [1371]

Jōichi Kengyō finished taking down from my dictation my complete, secret text of the twelve books of Heike monogatari, with the addition of Kanjō-no-maki. Unworthy as I am, I am now over seventy years old and cannot expect to live much longer. After my death, a disciple of mine might forget this phrase or that and provoke a dispute on the subject. I have therefore had this reference text written down in order to forestall any disagreement. Under no circumstances may it be given or even shown to anyone outside my line. Let no one but my direct disciples copy it, not even my associate teachers and their disciples. May whoever violates these injunctions suffer divine chastisement.

Kakuichi, a follower of the Buddha [315]

....

315. The relationship between this colophon and the one at the end of Book Twelve is unclear. Kakuichi died in the sixth month of 1371.

GENEALOGIES

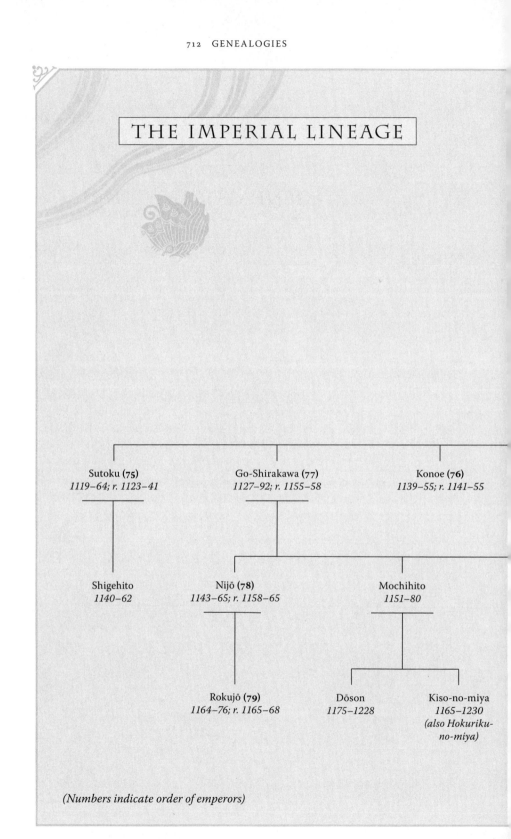

THE IMPERIAL LINEAGE

Sutoku (75)
1119–64; r. 1123–41

Go-Shirakawa (77)
1127–92; r. 1155–58

Konoe (76)
1139–55; r. 1141–55

Shigehito
1140–62

Nijō (78)
1143–65; r. 1158–65

Mochihito
1151–80

Rokujō (79)
1164–76; r. 1165–68

Dōson
1175–1228

Kiso-no-miya
1165–1230
*(also Hokuriku-
no-miya)*

(Numbers indicate order of emperors)

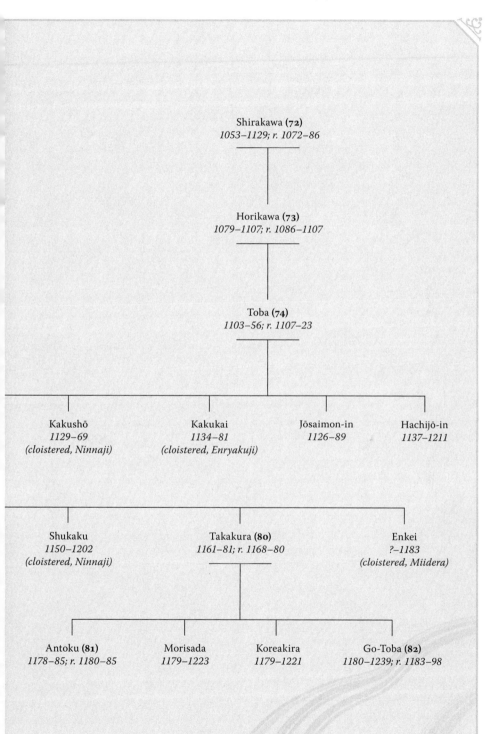

Shirakawa (72)
1053–1129; r. 1072–86

Horikawa (73)
1079–1107; r. 1086–1107

Toba (74)
1103–56; r. 1107–23

Kakushō
1129–69
(cloistered, Ninnaji)

Kakukai
1134–81
(cloistered, Enryakuji)

Jōsaimon-in
1126–89

Hachijō-in
1137–1211

Shukaku
1150–1202
(cloistered, Ninnaji)

Takakura (80)
1161–81; r. 1168–80

Enkei
?–1183
(cloistered, Miidera)

Antoku (81)
1178–85; r. 1180–85

Morisada
1179–1223

Koreakira
1179–1221

Go-Toba (82)
1180–1239; r. 1183–98

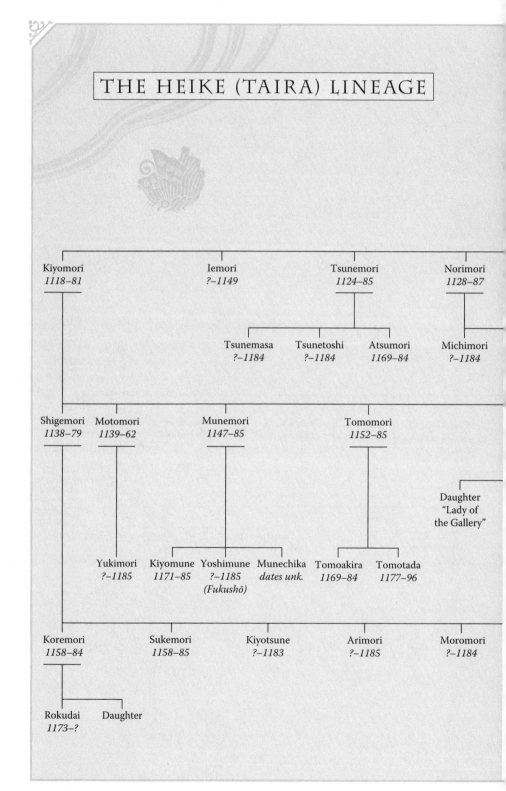

THE HEIKE (TAIRA) LINEAGE

Kiyomori
1118–81

Iemori
?–1149

Tsunemori
1124–85

Norimori
1128–87

Tsunemasa
?–1184

Tsunetoshi
?–1184

Atsumori
1169–84

Michimori
?–1184

Shigemori
1138–79

Motomori
1139–62

Munemori
1147–85

Tomomori
1152–85

Daughter
"Lady of
the Gallery"

Yukimori
?–1185

Kiyomune
1171–85

Yoshimune
?–1185
(Fukushō)

Munechika
dates unk.

Tomoakira
1169–84

Tomotada
1177–96

Koremori
1158–84

Sukemori
1158–85

Kiyotsune
?–1183

Arimori
?–1185

Moromori
?–1184

Rokudai
1173–?

Daughter

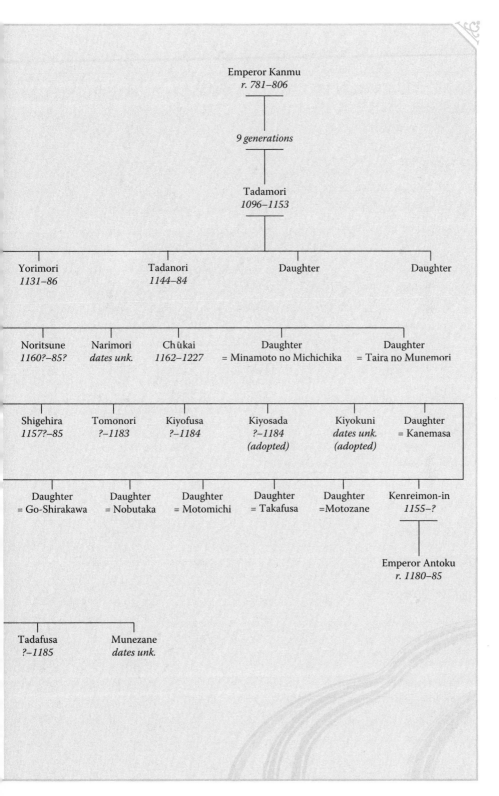

THE GENJI (MINAMOTO) LINEAGE

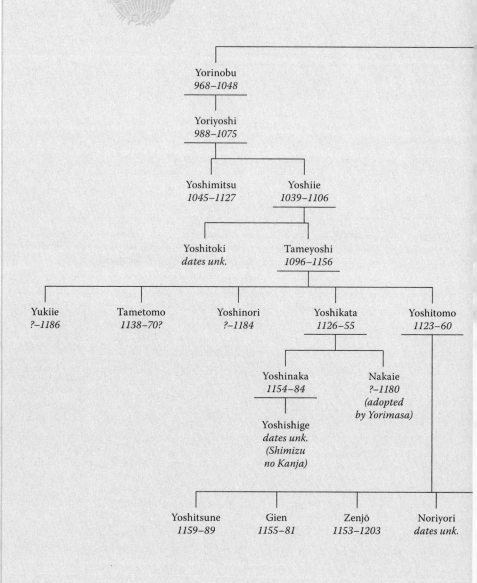

Yorinobu
968–1048

Yoriyoshi
988–1075

Yoshimitsu
1045–1127

Yoshiie
1039–1106

Yoshitoki
dates unk.

Tameyoshi
1096–1156

Yukiie
?–1186

Tametomo
1138–70?

Yoshinori
?–1184

Yoshikata
1126–55

Yoshitomo
1123–60

Yoshinaka
1154–84

Nakaie
?–1180
(adopted
by Yorimasa)

Yoshishige
dates unk.
(Shimizu
no Kanja)

Yoshitsune
1159–89

Gien
1155–81

Zenjō
1153–1203

Noriyori
dates unk.

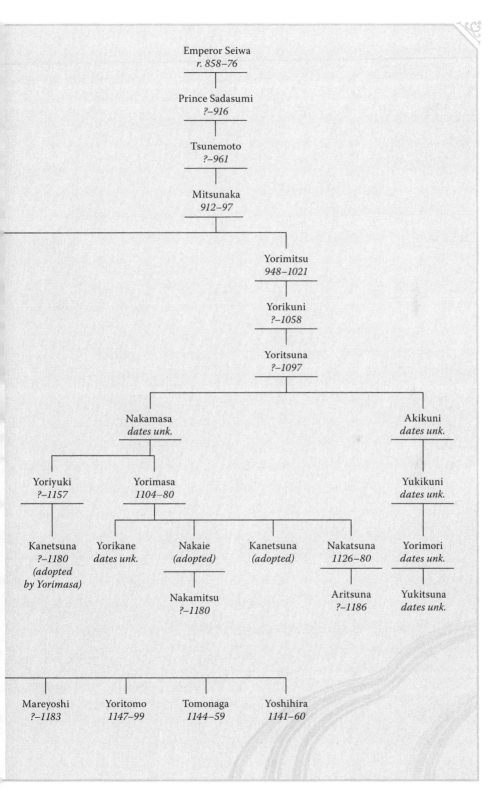

Emperor Seiwa
r. 858–76

Prince Sadasumi
?–916

Tsunemoto
?–961

Mitsunaka
912–97

Yorimitsu
948–1021

Yorikuni
?–1058

Yoritsuna
?–1097

Nakamasa
dates unk.

Akikuni
dates unk.

Yoriyuki
?–1157

Yorimasa
1104–80

Yukikuni
dates unk.

Kanetsuna
?–1180
(adopted
by Yorimasa)

Yorikane
dates unk.

Nakaie
(adopted)

Kanetsuna
(adopted)

Nakatsuna
1126–80

Yorimori
dates unk.

Nakamitsu
?–1180

Aritsuna
?–1186

Yukitsuna
dates unk.

Mareyoshi
?–1183

Yoritomo
1147–99

Tomonaga
1144–59

Yoshihira
1141–60

THE FUJIWARA LINEAGE

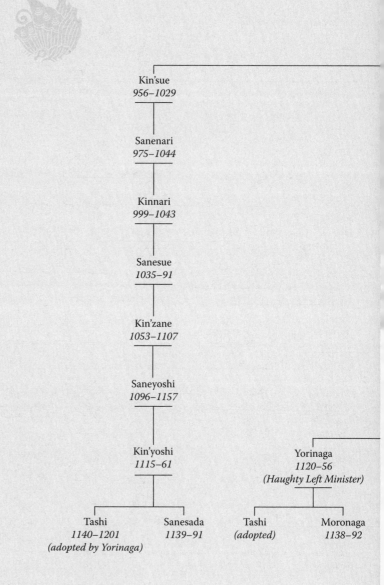

Kin'sue
956–1029

Sanenari
975–1044

Kinnari
999–1043

Sanesue
1035–91

Kin'zane
1053–1107

Saneyoshi
1096–1157

Kin'yoshi
1115–61

Yorinaga
1120–56
(Haughty Left Minister)

Tashi
1140–1201
(adopted by Yorinaga)

Sanesada
1139–91

Tashi
(adopted)

Moronaga
1138–92

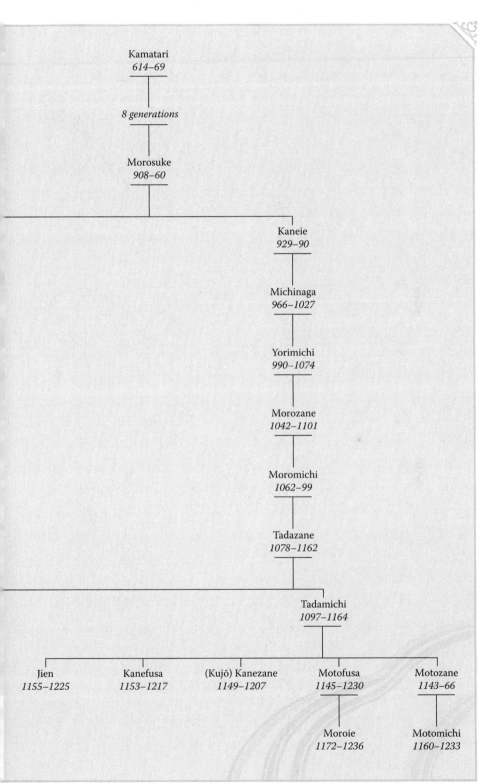

Kamatari
614–69

8 generations

Morosuke
908–60

Kaneie
929–90

Michinaga
966–1027

Yorimichi
990–1074

Morozane
1042–1101

Moromichi
1062–99

Tadazane
1078–1162

Tadamichi
1097–1164

Jien
1155–1225

Kanefusa
1153–1217

(Kujō) Kanezane
1149–1207

Motofusa
1145–1230

Motozane
1143–66

Moroie
1172–1236

Motomichi
1160–1233

MAPS

THE PROVINCES

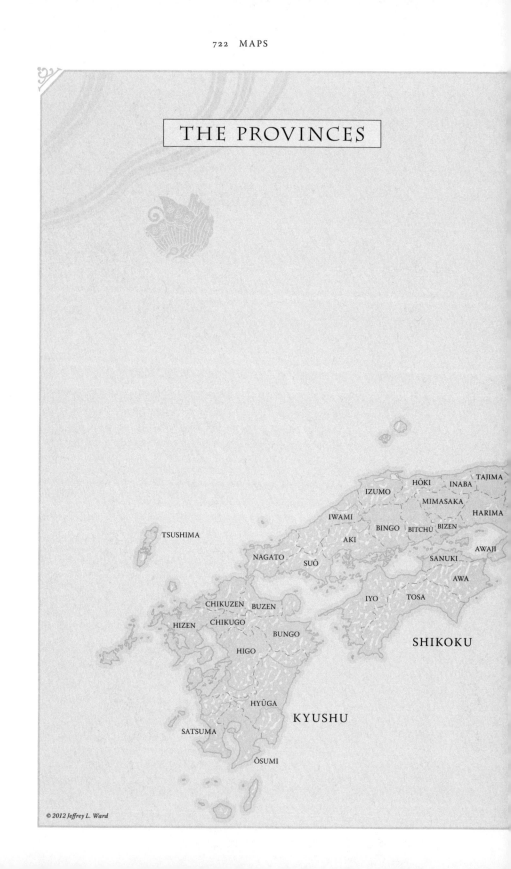

TAJIMA

HŌKI   INABA

IZUMO   MIMASAKA

HARIMA

IWAMI   BINGO   BITCHŪ   BIZEN

TSUSHIMA

AKI   AWAJI

NAGATO   SANUKI

SUŌ   AWA

IYO   TOSA

CHIKUZEN   BUZEN

HIZEN   CHIKUGO

BUNGO   SHIKOKU

HIGO

HYŪGA

KYUSHU

SATSUMA

ŌSUMI

© 2012 Jeffrey L. Ward

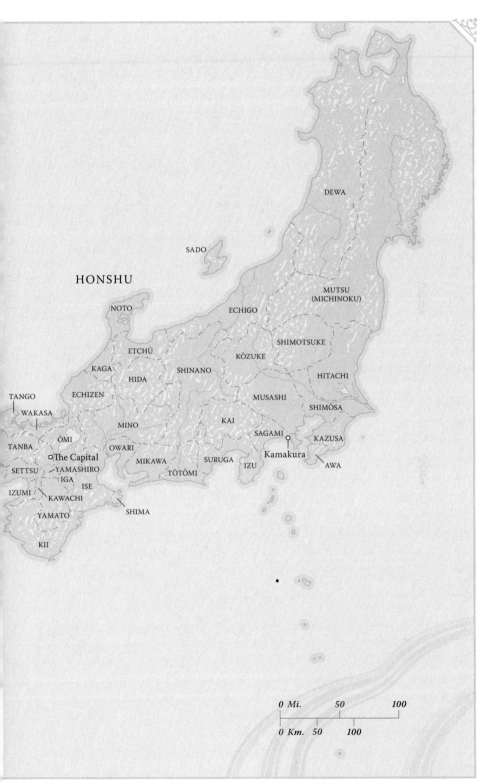

HONSHU

DEWA

SADO

MUTSU
(MICHINOKU)

NOTO

ECHIGO

ETCHŪ

SHIMOTSUKE

KÔZUKE

KAGA

SHINANO

HIDA

HITACHI

TANGO

ECHIZEN

MUSASHI

WAKASA

SHIMÔSA

MINO

KAI

TANBA

ÔMI

SAGAMI

KAZUSA

OWARI

The Capital

Kamakura

SETTSU

YAMASHIRO

MIKAWA

SURUGA

IZU

AWA

IGA

TÔTÔMI

ISE

IZUMI

KAWACHI

YAMATO

SHIMA

KII

0 Mi.   50   100

0 Km. 50   100

THE CAPITAL

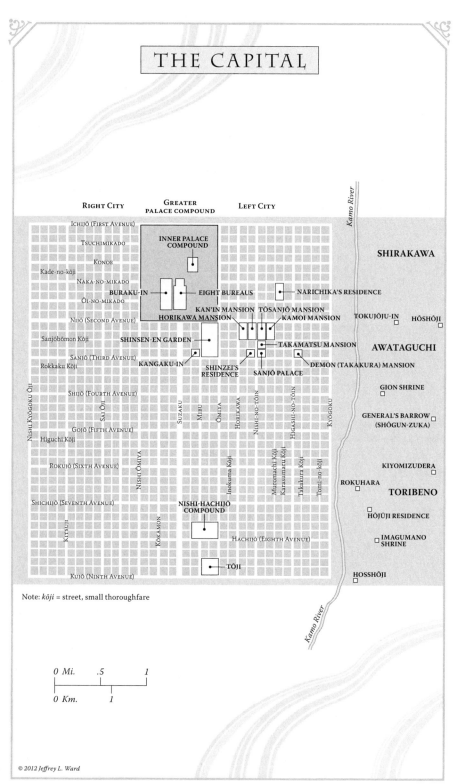

RIGHT CITY   GREATER PALACE COMPOUND   LEFT CITY

Kamo River

ICHIJŌ (FIRST AVENUE)

TSUCHIMIKADO

KONOE

Kade-no-kōji

NAKA-NO-MIKADO

ŌI-NO-MIKADO

NIJŌ (SECOND AVENUE)

Sanjōbōmon Kōji

SANJŌ (THIRD AVENUE)

Rokkaku Kōji

SHIJŌ (FOURTH AVENUE)

GOJŌ (FIFTH AVENUE)

Higuchi Kōji

ROKUJŌ (SIXTH AVENUE)

SHICHIJŌ (SEVENTH AVENUE)

HACHIJŌ (EIGHTH AVENUE)

KUJŌ (NINTH AVENUE)

INNER PALACE COMPOUND

BURAKU-IN

EIGHT BUREAUS

NARICHIKA'S RESIDENCE

KAN'IN MANSION

TŌSANJŌ MANSION

HORIKAWA MANSION

KAMOI MANSION

TOKUJŌJU-IN

HŌSHŌJI

SHINSEN-EN GARDEN

TAKAMATSU MANSION

AWATAGUCHI

KANGAKU-IN

SHINZEI'S RESIDENCE

SANJŌ PALACE

DEMON (TAKAKURA) MANSION

GION SHRINE

GENERAL'S BARROW (SHŌGUN-ZUKA)

KIYOMIZUDERA

ROKUHARA

TORIBENO

NISHI-HACHIJŌ COMPOUND

HŌJŪJI RESIDENCE

IMAGUMANO SHRINE

TŌJI

HOSSHŌJI

SHIRAKAWA

NISHI KYŌGOKU ŌJI

SAI ŌJI

Kitsuji

NISHI ŌMIYA

KŌKAMON

SUZAKU

MIBU

ŌMIYA

HORIKAWA

NISHI-NO-TŌIN

HIGASHI-NO-TŌIN

Inokuma Kōji

Muromachi Kōji

Karasumaru Kōji

Takakura Kōji

Tomi-no-kōji

KYŌGOKU

Kamo River

Note: *kōji* = street, small thoroughfare

0 Mi.   .5   1

0 Km.   1

© 2012 Jeffrey L. Ward

THE GREATER PALACE COMPOUND

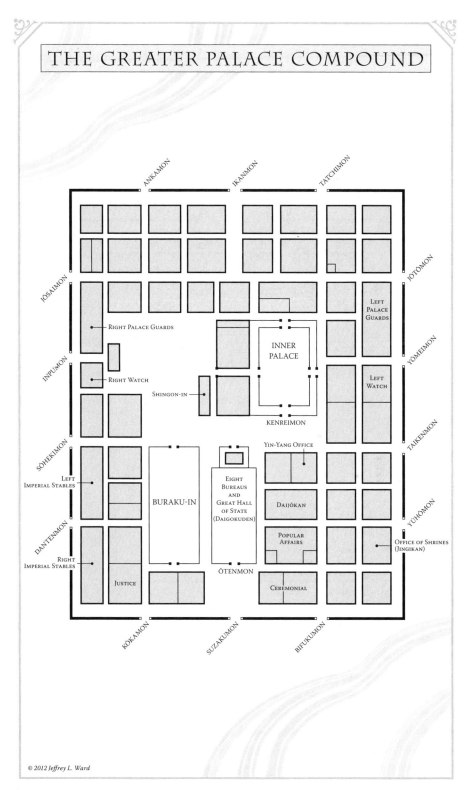

ANKAMON

IKANMON

TATCHIMON

JŌSAIMON

IOTOMON

Right Palace Guards

LEFT PALACE GUARDS

INNER PALACE

INPUMON

YŌMEIMON

Right Watch

LEFT WATCH

Shingon-in

KENREIMON

Yin-Yang Office

SŌHEKIMON

TAIKENMON

Left IMPERIAL STABLES

EIGHT BUREAUS AND GREAT HALL OF STATE (DAIGOKUDEN)

BURAKU-IN

DAIJŌKAN

DANTENMON

YŪHŌMON

POPULAR AFFAIRS

Right IMPERIAL STABLES

ŌTENMON

Office of Shrines (Jingikan)

JUSTICE

CEREMONIAL

KŌKAMON

SUZAKUMON

BIFUKUMON

© 2012 Jeffrey L. Ward

THE INNER PALACE COMPOUND

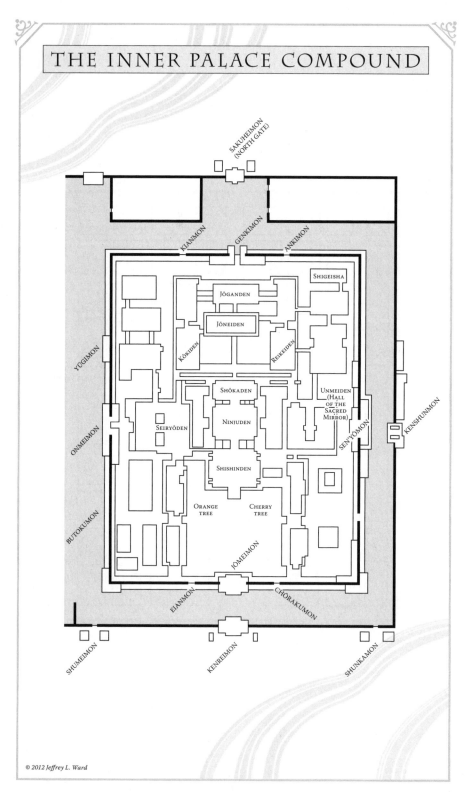

SAKUHEIMON
(NORTH GATE)

KIANMON
GENKIMON
ANKIMON

SHIGEISHA

JŌGANDEN

JŌNEIDEN

YŪGIMON

KŌKIDEN
REIKEIDEN

SHŌKADEN

UNMEIDEN
(HALL
OF THE
SACRED
MIRROR)

ONMEIMON

SEIRYŌDEN
NINJUDEN

SEN'YŌMON
KENSHUNMON

SHISHINDEN

BUTOKUMON

ORANGE
TREE
CHERRY
TREE

JŌMEIMON
CHŌRAKUMON

EIANMON

SHUMEIMON
KENREIMON
SHUNKAMON

© 2012 Jeffrey L. Ward

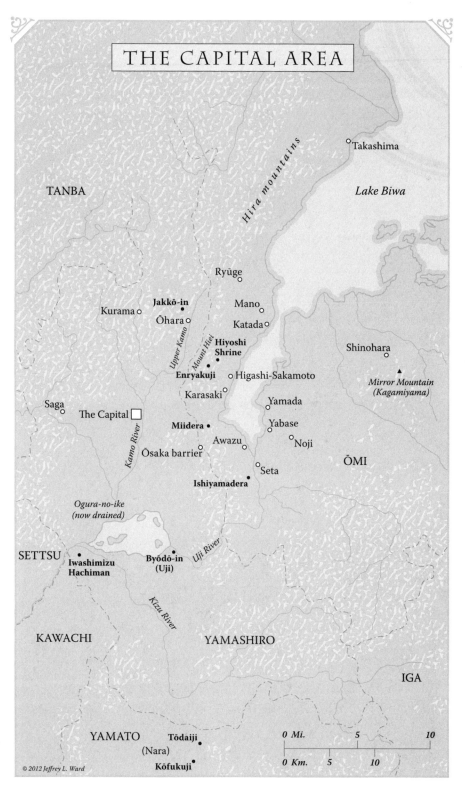

THE CAPITAL AREA

Takashima

TANBA

Hira mountains

Lake Biwa

Ryūge

Kurama

Jakkō-in

Ōhara

Mano

Katada

Upper Kamo

Mount Hiei

Hiyoshi
Shrine

Shinohara

Enryakuji

Higashi-Sakamoto

▲

Karasaki

*Mirror Mountain
(Kagamiyama)*

Saga

The Capital

Yamada

Yabase

Miidera

Awazu

Noji

ŌMI

Kamo River

Ōsaka barrier

Seta

Ishiyamadera

*Ogura-no-ike
(now drained)*

Uji River

SETTSU

Iwashimizu
Hachiman

Byōdō-in
(Uji)

Kizu River

KAWACHI

YAMASHIRO

IGA

YAMATO

Tōdaiji

(Nara)

Kōfukuji

0 Mi.   5   10

0 Km.   5   10

© 2012 Jeffrey L. Ward

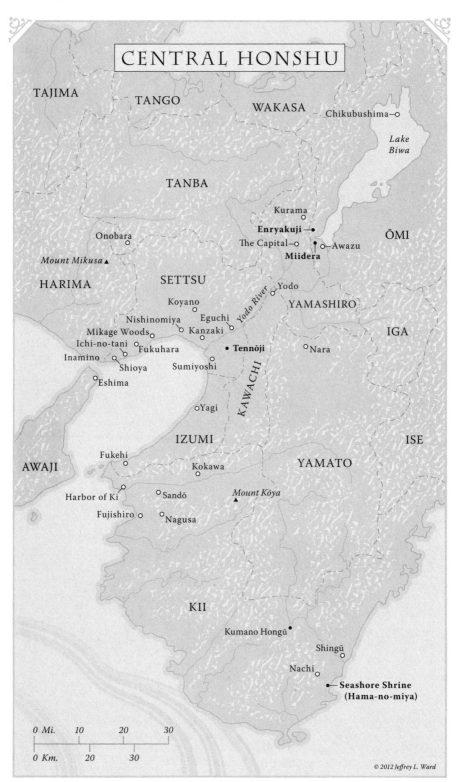

CENTRAL HONSHU

TAJIMA

TANGO

WAKASA

Chikubushima—○

Lake Biwa

TANBA

Kurama ○

Enryakuji — ●

The Capital—○　● ○—Awazu

Miidera

ŌMI

Onobara ○

Mount Mikusa ▲

HARIMA

SETTSU

Koyano ○

Nishinomiya ○　Eguchi ○

Mikage Woods ○　○ Kanzaki

Ichi-no-tani ○

Inamino ○　○ Fukuhara

Shioya

Sumiyoshi

Eshima ○

Yodo River

○ Yodo

YAMASHIRO

IGA

● **Tennōji**

○ Nara

KAWACHI

Yagi ○

IZUMI

ISE

Fukehi ○

AWAJI

Kokawa ○

YAMATO

Harbor of Ki ○

Sandō ○

Mount Kōya ▲

Fujishiro ○　○ Nagusa

KII

Kumano Hongū ●

Shingū ○

Nachi ○

● **Seashore Shrine (Hama-no-miya)**

| 0 Mi. | 10 | 20 | 30 |

| 0 Km. | 20 | 30 |

© 2012 Jeffrey L. Ward

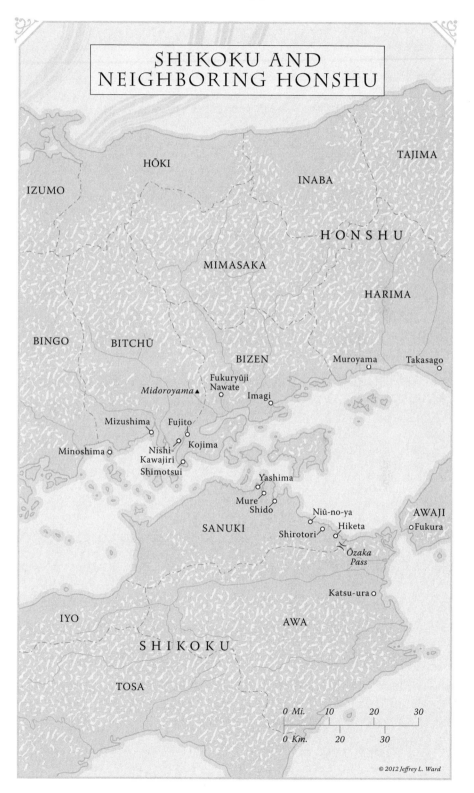

SHIKOKU AND NEIGHBORING HONSHU

TAJIMA

HŌKI

INABA

IZUMO

HONSHU

MIMASAKA

HARIMA

BINGO

BITCHŪ

BIZEN

Muroyama

Takasago

Fukuryūji
Midoroyama ▲ Nawate

Imagi

Mizushima   Fujito

Kojima

Minoshima

Nishi-
Kawajiri

Shimotsui

Yashima

Mure
Shido

Niū-no-ya

AWAJI

Hiketa

Fukura

SANUKI

Shirotori

*Ōzaka
Pass*

Katsu-ura

IYO

AWA

SHIKOKU

TOSA

0 Mi.   10   20   30

0 Km.   20   30

© 2012 Jeffrey L. Ward

NORTHERN KYUSHU

IWAMI

NAGATO

SUŌ

Uzura beach

Akama-no-seki   Dan-no-ura

Yamaga

Mount Tarumi

Ashiya

Moji-no-seki

Yanagi-ga-ura

Munakata

Kashii

Hakozaki

Sumiyoshi

CHIKUZEN

BUZEN

• Usa Hachiman Shrine

Iwado   Dazaifu

HIZEN

CHIKUGO

BUNGO

HIGO

Mount Takachio

HYŪGA

0 Mi. 10   20   30

0 Km.   20   30

© 2012 Jeffrey L. Ward

HOURS, ERAS, AND EMPERORS

THE TWELVE HOURS OF THE DAY

The day was divided into twelve "hours" (six for daytime and six for night), each named for one of the twelve beasts of the zodiac. These "hours" shortened or lengthened as the relative length of day and night changed from season to season. At the equinox, an "hour" therefore corresponded to two clock hours. The clock times indicated in the text correspond to the midpoint of the "hour" named.

Rat	11 P.M.–1 A.M.
Ox	1–3 A.M.
Tiger	3–5 A.M.
Hare	5–7 A.M.
Dragon	7–9 A.M.
Serpent	9–11 A.M.
Horse	11 A.M.–1 P.M.
Sheep	1–3 P.M.
Monkey	3–5 P.M.
Cock	5–7 P.M.
Dog	7–9 P.M.
Boar	9–11 P.M.

ERAS, OR YEAR PERIODS, NAMED IN THE TALE

Japan counts years not from a point of origin like the birth of Christ but within an "era" or "year period" (*nengō*) that belongs in a succession of similar eras. In modern times these eras coincide precisely with an imperial reign (Meiji, Taishō,

Shōwa, Heisei), but earlier they did not. A new era could be proclaimed at any time during the course of any year. Thus Kiyomori moved the capital to Fukuhara in Jishō 4 (1180) and died in Yōwa 1 (1181). These Japanese years correspond only approximately to 1180 and 1181, because the calendar then was lunar, not solar. A lunar month (like a lunar year) began roughly six weeks later than its numbered solar counterpart. For this reason the burning of Nara (5:14), conventionally dated to the end of 1180, properly occurred in the first days of 1181.

Angen	1175–77		Kanpyō	889–98
Bunji	1185–90		Kaō	1169–71
Chōkan	1163–65		Kashō	848–51
Daidō	806–10		Kenkyū	1190–99
Daiji	1126–31		Kōhō	964–68
Eichō	1096–97		Kōwa	1099–1104
Eikyū	1113–18		Kyūju	1154–56
Eiman	1165–66		Nin'an	1166–69
Eiryaku	1160–61		Ninpei	1151–54
Engi	901–23		Ōhō	1161–63
Enkyū	1069–74		Ōwa	961–64
Enryaku	782–806		Saikō	854–57
Gangyō	877–85		Shōan	1171–75
Genryaku	1184–85		Shōhei	931–38
Heiji	1159–60		Shōryaku	1077–81
Hōan	1120–24		Shōtai	898–901
Hōen	1135–41		Shōwa	834–48
Hōgen	1156–59		Shuchō	686
Jinki	724–29		Taika	645–50
Jiryaku	1065–69		Ten'an	857–59
Jishō	1177–81		Tengyō	938–47
Jōgan	859–77		Tenki	1053–58
Jōhō	1074–77		Tenpyō	729–49
Jōkyū	1219–22		Tenroku	970–73
Juei	1182–85		Tenryaku	947–57
Kahō	1094–96		Tenshō	1131–32
Kanji	1087–95		Tentoku	957–61
Kankō	1004–13		Yōwa	1181–82
Kanna	985–87			

EMPERORS NAMED IN THE TALE

Emperors earlier than the mid-sixth century are listed in italics. The dates attributed to their lives and reigns are not considered reliable.

EMPEROR	NUMBER	LIVED	REIGNED
Antoku	81	1178–85	1180–85
Chūai	*14*	*?–200*	*192–200*
Daigo	60	885–930	897–930
En'yū	64	959–91	969–84
Genmei (empress)	43	661–721	707–15
Go-Reizei	70	1025–68	1045–68
Go-Sanjō	71	1034–73	1068–72
Go-Shirakawa	77	1127–92	1155–58
Go-Toba	82	1180–1239	1183–98
Hanzei	*18*	*?–410*	*406–10*
Heizei	51	774–824	806–9
Horikawa	73	1079–1107	1086–1107
Ichijō	66	980–1011	986–1011
Ingyō	*19*	*?–453*	*412–53*
Jinmu	*1*	*711–585 B.C.*	*660–585 B.C.*
Jitō (empress)	41	645–702	690–97
Kaika	*9*	*208–98 B.C.*	*158–98 B.C.*
Kanmu	50	737–806	781–806
Kazan	65	968–1008	984–86
Keikō	*12*	*13 B.C.–A.D. 130*	*71–130*
Keitai	*26*	*450–531*	*507–31*
Kinmei	29	509–71	539–71
Kōken (empress)	46	718–70	749–58
Kōnin	49	709–81	770–81
Konoe	76	1139–55	1141–55
Kōtoku	36	596–654	645–54
Monmu	42	683–707	697–707
Montoku	55	827–58	850–58
Murakami	62	926–67	946–67
Nijō	78	1143–65	1158–65